MELISSA ADDEY

THE
COLOSSEUM
SERIES

Table of Contents

FROM THE ASHES

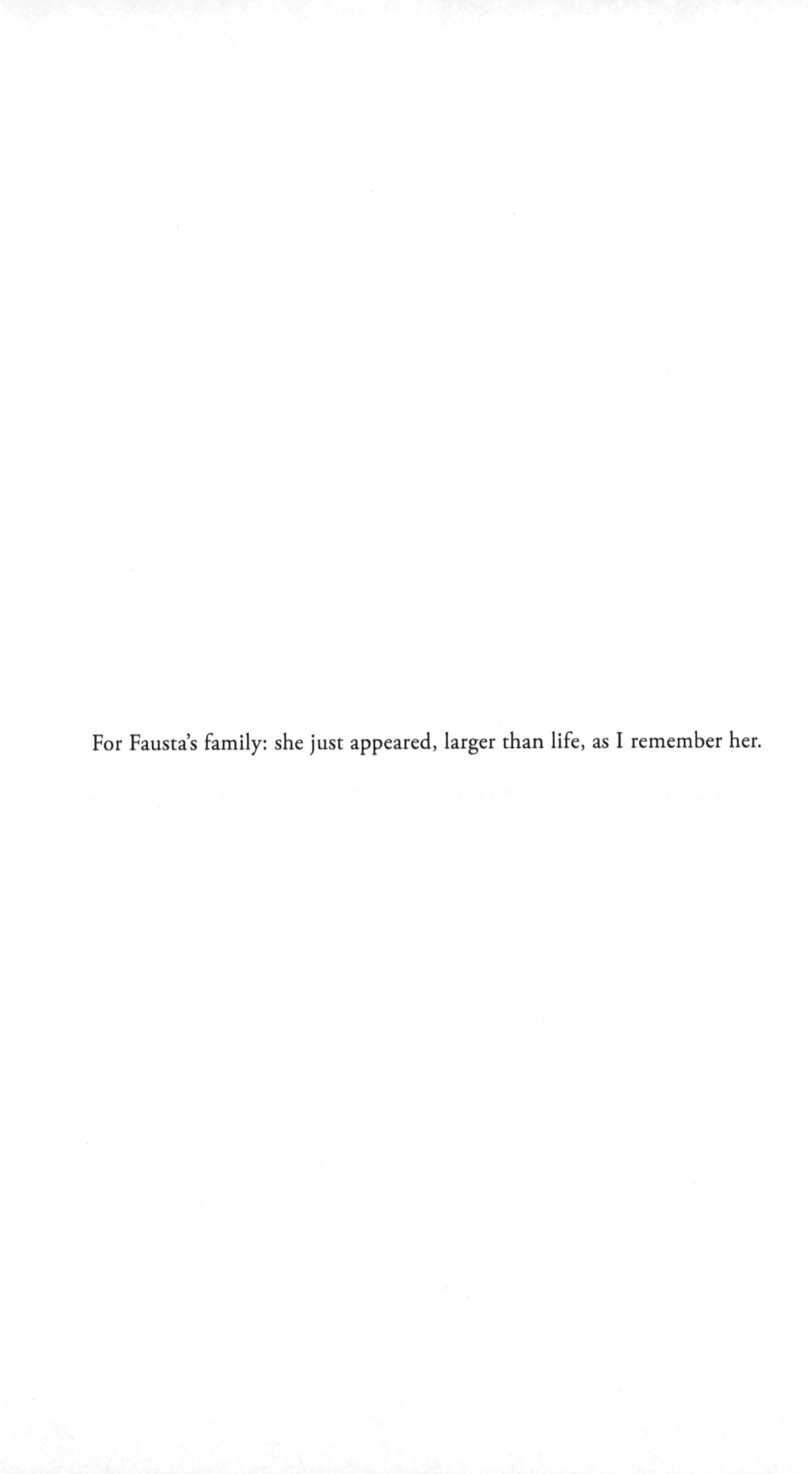

For Fausta's family: she just appeared, larger than life, as I remember her.

The eruption of Vesuvius, October 79AD

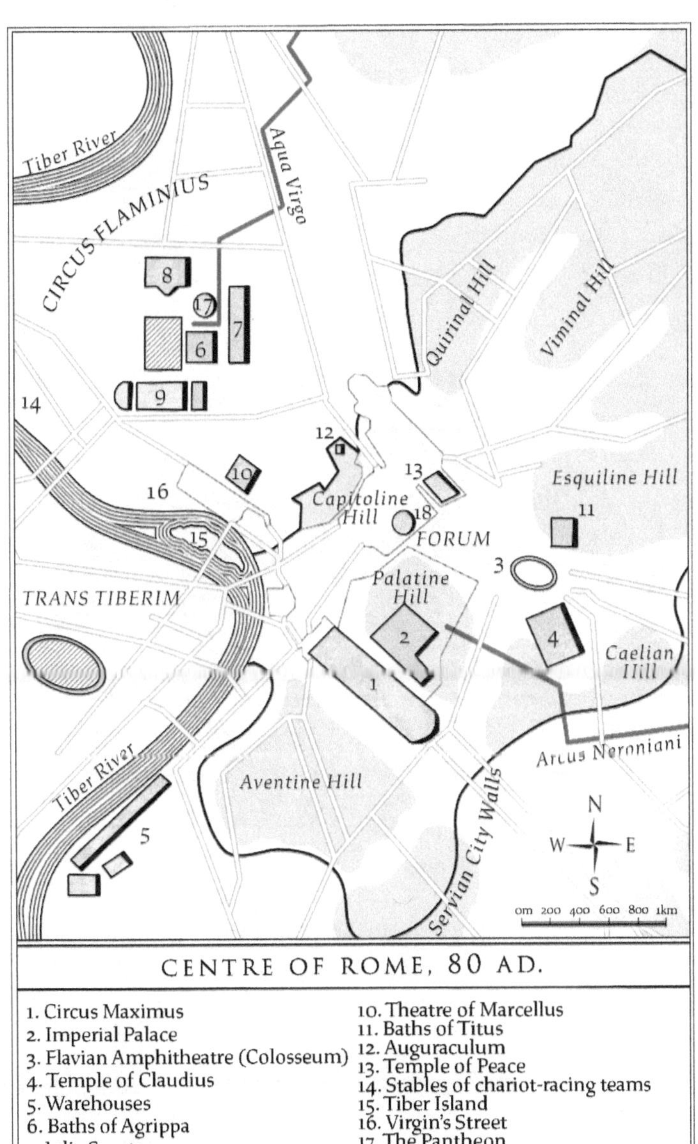

CENTRE OF ROME, 80 AD.

1. Circus Maximus
2. Imperial Palace
3. Flavian Amphitheatre (Colosseum)
4. Temple of Claudius
5. Warehouses
6. Baths of Agrippa
7. Julia Saepta
8. Baths of Nero
9. Theatre of Pompey
10. Theatre of Marcellus
11. Baths of Titus
12. Auguraculum
13. Temple of Peace
14. Stables of chariot-racing teams
15. Tiber Island
16. Virgin's Street
17. The Pantheon
18. Temple of Vesta

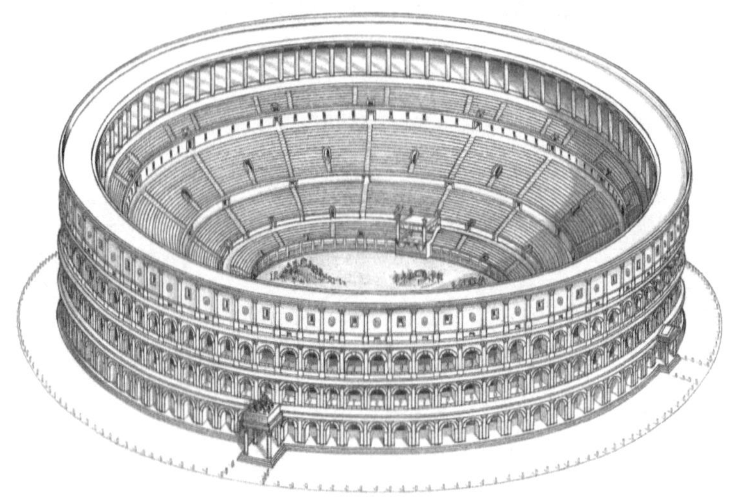

The Flavian Amphitheatre
'Roma Resurgens'
(Rome rises again)

Motto of the Emperor Vespasian, who commissioned the Colosseum.

BRIEF HISTORICAL BACKGROUND TO 79AD

IN 66AD THE ROMAN PROVINCE of Judea rebelled against Roman rule and drove the Romans out. Fearful that this might spark further rebellions in other provinces of the Empire, Emperor Nero recalled General Vespasian from exile (he had fallen asleep during a poetry reading by Nero) and sent Vespasian and his son Titus to quell the rebellion. This took four years, one quarter of the entire Roman army and ended in Titus' troops looting and burning the Temple of Jerusalem in 70AD. Hundreds of thousands of Jews were killed or enslaved during this period.

Emperor Nero died in 68AD, the last emperor of the Julio-Claudian dynasty. His reign was mostly associated with extravagance and cruelty, although he enjoyed some popularity among the lower classes. He had a large area of central Rome cleared to create his Golden House, a vast palace complex with a lake. Rumours said the Great Fire of 64 AD had been deliberately started by him to enable this, although he was also keen on building many cultural and public buildings.

Following Nero's death came the Year of the Four Emperors, which culminated in Vespasian taking power in 69AD and founding the Flavian dynasty, which lasted twenty-seven years. He was the first emperor to come from the Equestrian rather than Senatorial rank and he set in motion a large number of building works, including the Flavian Amphitheatre, known to us as the Colosseum, which was located on Nero's now drained lake and largely paid for with loot from the Temple and the sale of Jewish slaves. Vespasian died in June of 79AD and was succeeded by his son Titus.

Pompeii, late October 79AD

THE GOLDEN CUFF

"WHAT WERE YOU THINKING?"

THE TRICLINIUM OF MY MASTER'S house looks as though it has been turned into a brothel. The wall panels, which usually depict classical scenes befitting a grand holiday villa, have been repainted entirely since this morning with images more befitting… well, a brothel. The tables are opulently laid for tonight's gathering and the couches for the guests are draped with elegant throws and plumped-up cushions, but my mistress is staring at the household slaves, who have all been stripped naked. Their newly plucked private parts have been painted in gold, the better to highlight them. They stand huddled together, faces drained with shock.

"Lucius! What were you thinking?"

My mistress is appalled. She comes from one of the best patrician families, albeit a rather impoverished and distant branch. In marrying my master, a handily wealthy import-exporter from the equestrian class, she has had to put up with many failings of etiquette over the past few years, most of which she is adept at smoothing over, but this time he has gone too far. She stands in the doorway, trying to look away from the images on the walls, which leave nothing to the imagination. Men with men, women with women, men with women, women with beasts… all in fresh, bold paint, some of it significantly larger than life. Her young daughter is coming, and she puts out an unseeing hand behind her back, seeking to push the girl away.

"To your room, Lucilla."

"But mother –"

"To your room!"

Lucilla reluctantly departs. I'd like to follow her, but my mistress is blocking the doorway and I don't want to draw attention to myself. Although I am the only slave fully clothed, I fear that my apparel might offend her even more than if I were naked. I stay still, pressed against the wall in the corner.

"Splendid, isn't it," says my master, casting a lingering glance over one of the slave boys. "It'll be a memorable evening."

"Memorable?" My mistress' eyes are bulging out of her head, her already pale skin drained white. "It looks like something organised by –" her voice drops to a hiss "– *Nero!*"

"Fit for an emperor?" he asks. Deliberately misunderstanding.

"Fit for a madman," she spits back. "I cannot be seen at such a gathering!"

"Just as well I've arranged a substitute for you then, isn't it?" he says.

My heart sinks as he gestures towards me. A look of humiliated rage grows on her face as she takes in the expensive gauzes and finely woven fabrics draped around me, my elaborately dressed hair, the gold jewellery dangling from my hair, ears, neck. A slave, dressed as though I were the rich lady of the house, about to play her part as hostess for the evening, as though it were Saturnalia when slaves become masters and masters play the fools. But this is not Saturnalia. This is an important banquet, a dinner hosted by her husband for their rich and powerful neighbours before the autumnal return to Rome, leaving their Pompeiian holiday homes behind for another year. An ingratiating attempt to be part of a class he knows secretly look down on him, and on her for marrying him, wealthy or not. And now this evening is to be staged as a debauched orgy, something from the bad old days of Nero, when anything went?

She hovers, uncertain whether she should insist on being hostess and suffer the humiliation of knowing she is being laughed at for arranging such a vulgar event, or disappear into her rooms and pretend she knew nothing about it, dismissing it with an airy laugh if anyone mentions it, "Oh *men*, they can be so crude you know, but one has to indulge their needs sometimes. Best not to enquire what goes on at their 'little dinners'!" Her face colours as she contemplates the two options and I can't help but feel sorry for her, although I know that, ultimately, she will take this humiliation out on me, since she cannot take it out on her husband. There is a final hesitation, a welling-up of tears in her eyes and then she turns her back and leaves the room, trying to keep her head high in front of the servants, although they are humiliated enough themselves at this moment. They have never been treated like this. The women and some of the younger and more attractive men have put up with occasional wandering hands from the master, as well as some of his less refined guests, but they have never been presented like this, as though they were fruits to pluck from serving platters.

"I hope you're pleased with my gift?" asks my master.

I glance down at the heavy gold cuff on my wrist. It is worth a fortune, I could live humbly for years on what it cost him. I bow my head, force the words out of my mouth. "Thank you, Dominus."

"Excellent. I must go and wash before I change, I'm sweating like a hog." He slaps the nearest girl on the behind and leaves the room.

"At least you get a gold bracelet," mutters Myrtis to me. She's the cook and my best friend. She's seething with rage. I can smell the sour reek of it coming off her in waves. Her pendulous breasts and slack belly are past their prime, she feels the gold paint as only a mockery.

I look down again at the bracelet, feel its weight.

"What in Hades was Master thinking, employing that man, anyway?" asks Myrtis.

"What man?"

"The man organising all of this. Whatever his name is…"

"Marcus," supplies Felix.

"I don't know who you mean," I say.

"The man who runs the amphitheatre."

"Runs it?"

Myrtis is losing her temper. "What are you, stupid? You think the Games happen by themselves once an editor has said what he wants? You think no-one tells the gladiators when to step out? Who to fight? Who do you think orders in the animals and advertises the shows?"

I've never really given it much thought. I rarely go to the Games. When I do, I am there under sufferance and I try to leave before midday when the criminals are executed, or at least arrive after that, if our master is intent on watching the gladiatorial shows in the afternoons. My only thought when I am at the amphitheatre is how quickly I can leave. But yes, of course, there must be a team who make the Games happen, just like at the theatre: there must be costume-makers, rehearsals for re-enacting bloody legends, that sort of thing.

"Master said he wanted a 'real show' putting on for his guests," says Felix. "He said this man Marcus arranged Games with female gladiators and dwarfs last time he was at the amphitheatre."

Myrtis and I exchange glances. How vulgar. Not even proper battles, not even professional fighters fighting, and sometimes dying, like men, just speciality acts, titillation for a bored crowd who've seen it all before.

"But I was only out with the Master a few hours," I object. "How has all of this happened in one afternoon? He's repainted the *walls*."

"The *walls*? That's what's grabbing your attention in this room? Not twenty naked men and women with their tits and bits painted in gold?"

"Well, how did any of it get done?"

"The minute you and the Master went out a man arrived, with a massive team in tow. Ten painters came into this room and got to work. We were all dragged into the small baths down the road, which were empty except for us, they must have hired them out especially. There was a whole team of pluckers, and they gave us no choice about it. You should have heard Felix yell. For a big man, he's got an awfully high-pitched squeal. And an awfully tiny –"

"Shut your mouth, Myrtis," grunts Felix.

"After we'd all been plucked and washed, we were brought back to this room. And there were people waiting for us. I thought we'd be given clean robes or wear something fancier than usual, some theme, perhaps. But, oh no. Gold paint. And they had already finished the wall paintings. Though they're still wet. I've half a mind to smudge them all so the guests can't use them as instructions. Goddess Libertas, watch over us tonight, we're to be used as nothing better than whores."

There's not much I can say. It's clear that the household slaves can expect groping at the very best, or a great deal worse, tonight. I grimace. Our master, so far, has been more of a half-hearted groper than much else, and we've been grateful for it: we all know slaves who work in other houses and get a worse time of it. Looks like our time has come. "Where has this man gone who's organising all of this?"

"Oh, he dismissed the painters when they'd finished their tasks and went off to the kitchen with his own cooks. Apparently, I'm not fit to make tonight's meal, I'm just a bit of fun on the side."

"What are they serving?"

"How would I know? I told you, I'm not fit to cook a meal for his guests. After serving Domina's family for years, before she married this buffoon. I was expensive, you know. Price of three horses, they paid for me." Myrtis is clearly smarting in more ways than one.

"Should I go and see what's happening?"

"If you're allowed free rein of the house, why not? *We* were told to stay right here until the 'honoured guests' arrive."

But I am stopped by the closed door of the kitchen, guarded by a little weasel of a man, who nevertheless proves quite firm. No, I may not enter. Yes, he does know who I am. No, I may not enquire what is on the menu. Yes, his master is called Marcus. No, I may not speak with him.

"Look," he says at last, smiling as though he has been in this same situation more than once. "If I were you, I would just go back to the triclinium and wait. Everything will be taken care of. You need not worry about anything. Marcus is very experienced at this kind of thing. He will not disappoint your master."

"I'm not worried about my master," I hiss, beginning to lose my temper. "Half the slaves of this household are gathered in the triclinium, about to be groped and – and worse. I don't see *you* stripped naked and painted with gold."

He grins, showing missing teeth. "Sounds like I'm missing out." He touches my arm. "Seriously, don't worry. And tell the other slaves not to worry either. Marcus knows what he is doing, I swear on Sancus. You'll see."

AND SO, I HAVE NO choice but to wait with the others. It may be autumn, but it's warm for the time of year and there's not much of a breeze. Most of us are sweating, though whether because of the temperature or out of nerves, who knows.

There's noise from outside, the ripple of a lyre being strummed, a quick burst of chatter and then laughter. The others tense up and I find myself holding my breath. These must be the guests arriving, although they are earlier than I expected.

But when the door opens, I let out my breath in a gasp as twenty or more people stream into the room. Most are wearing light tunics, which they take off, throwing them to one of their number, who is catching them one-handed. Underneath they are naked and painted with the same gold paint our household has endured, but these newcomers seem entirely at ease in their lack of clothing. Some hold instruments: two lyres, a few flutes, various cymbals and rattles. They chatter amongst themselves and spread out across the room, arranging themselves, for the most part, closer to the dining tables. A tall, large-breasted woman, with tumbling black curly hair and olive skin bronzed from the summer, seems to be in charge, for she claps her hands together. The chatter and laughter stop, the newcomers turn to face her.

"Alright, spread yourselves out and take a partner from the household. Remember the rules, look out for them, no funny business. Adria and Galen, hand out some rattles and castanets to anyone who doesn't get passed a serving tray. We have a little time before the guests arrive, so explain things to them, would you?" She looks around the room and her eyes narrow at the sight of me. She strides over. "Why are you dressed differently to the rest of them?"

"I'm the master's scribe," I say. "Who are you?"

"Fausta," she says, as though this explains everything. "Is it his idea of a joke to dress his slave as though she were the mistress of the house and have her host his dinner party?"

"Yes," I say.

"Seen worse," she says cheerfully. "At least you have your clothes on. That bracelet is in very poor taste, though."

This, coming from a naked woman whose vast breasts are daubed with gold, should sound absurd, but I find myself warming to her for echoing my feelings about my master's gift. "I don't really understand what is going on here," I say.

"Oh, right," she says. "Well, your master hired Marcus, so he's getting the 'Marcus treatment'."

"I don't know your master," I say.

"He runs the amphitheatre," she says. "And stages events for rich men. Like tonight. For a price."

"I gathered that," I say. "But we... this household... we have never..."

"Oh, don't worry," she says, looking around the room at her fellows, who have paired up with our household slaves, as she instructed. I notice the faces of our own staff seem to have lost their tightness. "They don't have to do much. Stand in the background mostly, making up numbers. Possibly hand out some food, shake a few rattles, that sort of thing. If they all stay well back, no harm will come to them. Any music, dancing, especially the funny business, that's all on us." She looks me over again. "Not sure about you, though," she says, doubt creeping into her voice. "I've never had a master set a slave up like you at one of these events. We'll do our best. Does he usually use you for sex? Let his friends use you?"

I shake my head vigorously.

My look of horror seems to reassure her. "Oh well," she says more confidently. "Then with any luck it won't happen tonight, either." She frowns. "Never used you at all? Unusual."

"He likes to boast that I'm Greek and can read and write better than his wife," I explain. "He likes having an educated slave, most of his household aren't, you see. So, he makes a fuss as though I'm some sort of expensive trinket. It annoys the mistress. And anyway, he prefers men, on the whole."

"She's from a family that wouldn't have thought you anything special," she says bluntly. "You get all sorts nowadays. I mean, even the Emperor isn't from a patrician family. Your master may be rich, but he must be pretty thick if he thinks he's going to impress senators just by having a Greek slave who can read and write. They're more likely to want to feel you up. But see how you go. If you get in a tight spot, look my way and I'll try to help you out."

"Thank you," I say, though I'm getting more nervous rather than less. Our household slaves position themselves behind what I'm beginning to think of as Fausta's troops, and the guests arrive.

THE EVENING IS EVERYTHING MY mistress was wary of. Nine men, no wives attending. The meal is exactly the sort of overly lavish shopping list of luxuries that only serve to give you indigestion. The fatty sweetness of roast udders, the inevitable honeyed dormice, live birds released from inside a roasted pig which create nothing but chaos as they seek to escape into the garden, fluttering madly about and shitting on the floor. Apparently, they are not enough, for the guests are also served ostrich, sea urchins and heavy wines that have not been sufficiently watered down. The guests know better than this, they will make fun of my master behind his back for his showing-off, but still they stuff their faces and belch their way through the rich cheesecake and fruit platters in ornamental designs so elaborate it must have taken the cooks all day just to lay them out. Myrtis couldn't have presented such dishes in the time, even with her assistants. The mistress is more concerned with her waistline than the master appreciates, he being something of a glutton. I wonder how many staff have been in our kitchen.

There's only one moment when my eyes dart towards Fausta. My master has me wait on him throughout the evening, expecting me to hand-feed him morsels of each dish as though he were a child. He makes a show of it, and after too much wine has been drunk, one of his guests, reclining close to where I am kneeling, puts out a hand and squeezes my breast.

"Fine girl," he slurs. "Hope you make the most of her, Lucius."

"Not as fine as me, though," comes Fausta's voice at once. She appears by the senator's side, bending over him, her gilded breasts barely a handspan from his face. "Why, she has nothing but two flatbreads under all that frippery. Not like my well-risen loaves, eh?"

The guest is distracted at once. He is allowed some caressing before Fausta adroitly moves on to fill his cup with more wine and performs a dance for him at a safe distance. I catch her eye and she grins at my grateful nod. I've already noticed more of the same going on around the room, the quickness of Fausta's troops managing to direct any unwanted attention onto themselves, then, quick as eels, extracting themselves from the worst of it, although one of the girls does disappear off with one of the distinguished guests as the evening grows late, but only after a discreet nod from Fausta.

After the dancing there's a dwarf who can juggle and then the highlight of the evening's entertainment: two well-known local gladiators who come in, oiled up and dressed in armour that looks like it's never been used in battle, all fancy details and polished to a high shine, not a scratch or dent in it. They circle the room while the men jeer or cheer, their blades fast and sharp. Blood is drawn on both sides, enough to satisfy the audience, but not, I notice, enough to cause serious injury. There's a lot of drunken arguing over who won but eventually a jokey laurel wreath and a few coins are tossed towards the victor and the two men bow out of the room, leaving the guests to be gently nudged on their way by Fausta and her team.

"Thank you," I manage to say before she leaves. She nods, adjusting the heavy folds of a toga over her tunic. The male clothing will mark her out as a prostitute on the dark streets as she makes her way home and I am worried for her, it is very late. But I see the weasel man gesture in front of him, an indication he may be about to accompany her and her troop back to wherever they live, probably in, or close to, one of the many taverns that make a profitable living selling sexual favours as a side-line.

"I told you Marcus would manage everything," says the weasel.

I look about me. "If he could manage the mistress' displeasure tomorrow when these walls remind her of this evening…" I say, grimacing.

He winks. "I think you'll find your master paid for the complete service," he says and turns away. I suppose he means that everything else has been taken care of. It is for the master to manage his own wife's response to what he ordered done. It is not the weasel or his master Marcus who will suffer for all this, so they can hardly be expected to care. At least none of our own household has suffered anything but a loss of what little pride they had. The master is happy, his guests are well fed and entertained, even if they do look down on him. Let us hope there will be no more of this kind of thing.

I'm so exhausted I all but crawl onto my sleeping mat in the small room Myrtis and I share, as more senior members of the staff. Soon the birds will be singing and, not long after that, Myrtis will wake me. She has to rise early and likes someone to talk to while she prepares breakfast for the family. She's already snoring. My arm is uncomfortable, but I may not unfasten the bracelet. It has amused my master to give me an item of jewellery made in heavy gold but formed in the shape of an elaborate slave cuff, something I would be forced to wear if I were a troublemaker and standing on the slave block to be sold off. Its fastening is completed with a tiny chain and pin, which I have been warned against removing at any time, for any reason. The final detail prevents me from ever selling it to buy my freedom. On it is engraved, 'The Greek slave Althea, belonging to Lucius the garum merchant. Send her home if she has run away from me.'

Jupiter and Juno

THE TREMOR WAKES ME BEFORE Myrtis does. I think she is shaking me awake before I realise there is no-one there, that it is the half-dark room itself trembling. I brace in case it gets bad and I have to run, but it quickly fades away. Autumn is earthquake season in this part of the world, it's commonplace enough, although it always sparks a tiny fear that this will be the bad one, like the one that brought houses tumbling down here seventeen years ago. I was only a child in Kefalonia then but there are still plenty of buildings in Pompeii that have not yet been repaired, daily reminders of what the shaking earth can do to us, if the gods are displeased. There are cracks in the plasterwork in the servants' rooms, although those in the more important parts of the house get repaired regularly. The tremor gone, I think I should rise, but I'm so tired my eyes close again without my knowledge and when I wake the sunlight is streaming in the window. It's late.

I can barely keep my eyes open, yawning throughout dressing. My comb breaks two teeth on the tangles in my hair. I brace myself to greet my mistress, certain that she will still be offended by what has gone on in her house, readying myself to be treated spitefully in revenge. However, I cannot find her in her rooms, although her makeup is all laid out, white chalk powder for a delicate complexion dusted over her dressing table, her eyeliner and lip colour pots now closed, used applicators left out for her body slave to clean. I catch a quick glance of myself in the polished metal of her mirror, although my rippled reflection only shows how dark the shadows under my eyes are.

"Garden," says Felix when he sees me in the hallway looking for her.

I make my way back downstairs and head towards the garden, but the smell of wet plaster and paint seems even stronger this morning, which can't be right. I poke my head into the triclinium and then push the door open, amazed.

The wall panels of the room are a fresh blank white with a new coat of thin, wet plaster. There is no sign of the images that titillated our guests last night, they have vanished like a bad dream. Instead, there are two men touching up the red and gold trim that frame them, while six more and their respective assistants are busy filling the white spaces with new scenes. Two are already complete, elaborate garden scenes in the very latest intricate style, showing a variety of woodland animals and delicate flowers and plants, while the largest panel, which just a few hours ago framed a scene in which a woman was being serviced by an extremely well-endowed centaur, now features a larger-than-life image of Jupiter and Juno, gazing lovingly at one another, the very image of respectably clothed marital bliss. There is more than a hint of the mistress' lineaments to Juno's face, a suggestion of the master to Jupiter's curled locks and broad forehead. The image is everything it should be, proclaiming this household to be blessed with both high class wealth and marital wellbeing. It is almost complete. There are only another four small panels to fill up. The room will be entirely repainted by midday at the latest. The plasterers must have come the moment the guests left the room and the painters must have begun work while we were all asleep. More than that, these designs have been pre-planned to fit the space available, while Jupiter and Juno have required some prior study of our master and mistress' physiognomy. I stand gaping at the work and the painters, blinking several times in case I haven't woken up and am just dreaming.

"Help you?" asks one assistant over his shoulder.

"Who ordered this room repainted?" I ask, thinking I already know the answer.

"Marcus."

I nod and leave the room, half-tripping over Myrtis, who is all smiles. "I think I could bear to be plucked and painted from time to time, if that's the reward I get for it," she says.

"Reward?"

She fumbles in her tunic and pulls out a denarius, holding the silver coin out for my inspection. Two days' wages for a labourer, a precious sum for a slave.

"Where did you get that?"

"That little man popped in this morning, gave one to each of us. Said it was payment for our 'additional services', which luckily none of us had to provide, apart from the shame of it."

Marcus again. I know it. This invisible man has put on an extraordinary evening of spectacle and now is making all traces of it disappear, whether wall panels or the household slaves' resentment, as though it had never been.

I make my way to the garden and find my mistress sitting in the early sunshine wearing a new outfit, a long delicate woollen tunic in a pale blue. She is also sporting a new palla draped over her hair, with a trim in Tyrian purple stitched over with pearls, a level of finery I've more than once heard the master refusing to pay out for, despite his growing wealth. She's absurdly overdressed for a day at home, but she's evidently too thrilled with her new clothes not to wear them at once.

She beams when she sees me, which is not what I was expecting at all. "Althea, this is my new slave. I have named him Catulus. He is my little kitten, aren't you?" she croons to him.

"Yes, Domina," comes the obedient answer.

I look at the vast bulk of the handsome golden-haired man holding a parasol over my mistress' head. The name she has given him is ridiculous. "I did not know you had bought a new slave, Domina."

She looks up at him, still delighted. "He is a gift from your master, Lucius sent him to my rooms this morning to present me with these clothes… and himself. A little apology for his treatment of me yesterday. But that is all quite forgotten now. Have you seen the triclinium? I have been begging him for years to have it redecorated in the new style and it will be ready in time for dinner tonight. We will be able to dine elegantly at last."

I look Catulus over, wondering in what way exactly he 'presented' himself to my mistress that has left her in such a good mood. I think about the erasure of the night before and suspect that the man Marcus has had a hand in this soothing of my mistress, that he had already thought ahead and had these gifts ready to placate her: the finery and home decorations she has nagged her husband for, a handsome slave to accompany her wherever she goes, perhaps even to her bedchamber. As the weasel promised, his master has provided a complete service.

"When you're done with the master, I have letters to be written," says the mistress.

"Yes, Domina."

"I want to invite some of my friends to visit as soon as we return home," she says. No doubt she wants to show off her new clothes as well as her new slave.

"Yes, Domina."

I make a note that I must send messages home to Rome, advising the larger household there that we will be returning in the next few days, that they should prepare the villa for our arrival. I will also let them know that we have acquired the new slave, Catulus, so that they will prepare somewhere for him to sleep.

"It will be wonderful to return to Rome," she says. "Pompeii is really quite dull at this time of year, I don't know why we have to stay till the very dregs of summer are gone, there is hardly anyone interesting left here." By interesting, of course, she means the holidaymakers, the rich senators who come here for the summer months only and leave their villas empty the rest of the year. She does not have local friends. She ignores any merchants with whom her husband does business when we are here, preferring to give little thought as to where the wealth of this household comes from, trade not being quite elegant enough for her. "I wish your master could be persuaded to have a villa in Oplontis instead," she adds petulantly. "It is so much more elegant, only the best people have villas there. Pompeii has never been the same since the earthquake. It's getting quite shabby."

"It is only a few days now, Domina," I say. She knows perfectly well why we come to Pompeii and not Oplontis; Pompeii is a trading city and one of its biggest industries is the manufacture of garum, in which my master trades. But she would like to put a greater distance between the stink of fish sauce and herself.

For myself, I will miss Pompeii a little. I like to smell the sea and live in the smaller holiday household. In Rome the household is far larger and the city, although exciting, is also exhausting, the noise and smells endlessly intruding on any peace one might hope for. And the mistress' friends are boring, rich women with nothing better to do than gossip about those less fortunate than themselves – unless they are gossiping about the new Emperor and his choice of mistress. Still, we will return here next year, as we do every summer, escaping the unbearable heat of Rome for the sea breezes and larger gardens of Pompeii, the lighter clothes and lighter way of life a relief after the constant busyness of the capital.

MY MASTER, WHEN HE EVENTUALLY rises, is greeted by a loving wife and a refurbished triclinium, as well as a household of beaming slaves. I follow him to his study after he has eaten, where I look over the bill for the evening's entertainment. It's a ridiculous sum but he seems happy enough to pay it. I know he is rising in the world, but I did not expect him to pay such a sum without blinking.

"Not every day you have a dinner like that, eh?"

"No, Dominus," I say.

"Good man that," he says, wandering off to the window, from where he can see the garden. He's silent for a while, thinking. "Send for him, will you?"

"Marcus?"

"Yes."

I send one of the slave boys to find Marcus and ask him to visit the master as part of this morning's salutatio.

"What do you want him for?" I ask.

"A thought I had." He does not say anything else, which is odd. As his scribe, I am used to hearing most of his thoughts on one subject or another, but now he is acting as though he is keeping a secret from me.

IT'S A SUNNY DAY, THOUGH the morning air holds the approaching chill of autumn. We take up our places in the receiving hall off the main atrium, the master in his chair, ensuring his toga is draped correctly, while I sit to one side on my stool, my wax tablet in hand, ready to take notes for the daily salutatio. To be honest, I rarely need to write much for these morning salutations. They are mostly only a courtesy, a respectful morning visit by the clients of my master to their patron. They enter the villa, greet him with a show of deference, perhaps ask for help or advice on a matter of business or even personal affairs. Occasionally my master will mention what favour he, in turn, might require. Then they go about their business and another client will arrive. We have fewer clients in Pompeii. In Rome the whole boring business often takes up most of the morning, not to mention the poorer clients who go from door to door with no loyalty at all, hoping for handouts. This morning I am relieved to see only three men seated in the atrium, awaiting an audience. I open my tablet and wait.

The first two men are quickly dealt with, one only offers his respects and good wishes for our safe journey home. The other asks if his son, newly sent to Rome to serve in the Praetorian Guard, might also consider my master his patron and call on him, on our return there? Lucius is all smiles, of course, of course, that would be most agreeable. I know he considers it useful to have clients in all stations of life and any who serve the Emperor are, naturally, of particular interest, for who knows what they might see or hear that might be of use? Not that a client is a spy, of course not. Yet still, a client might mention something of interest to his patron… I make a note of the young man's name. We will expect him to call on us when we arrive in Rome. I search through the pot of scrolls at my feet. There is one which lists all of my master's clients, one for here and one in Rome. I will add the name to the list in Rome when today's salutatio is done.

"Marcus!"

I let go of the scroll and look up. The man walking into the room is taller and more handsome than I had expected. I had thought he would be more like the weasel, but he looks like an army officer. Dark brown hair, olive skin burnt brown by the sun. His blue tunic is clean, but he is not wearing a toga, as though his work does not allow for such impractical clothing, and I notice that his plain leather shoes are worn at the heel. A man who walks a lot, I think, although with a noticeable limp.

"Take a seat," says Lucius. "Will you join me in a little refreshment?"

Myrtis has sent up fresh grape juice, from the very last pressing of the harvest, now completing all across the slopes of Mount Vesuvius, its rich black soil the most fertile in the area. She has also provided a platter of her own just-baked honey cakes, the recipe for which she guards with her life. Every cook makes honey cakes, but Myrtis adds some combination of spices to hers, which are often remarked on for their delicate flavour. Marcus takes the offered seat and refreshments. As he sits, I see the horizontal scar on his upper calf, a faded white with a purple tinge that speaks of a deep wound, even if a long time back. I imagine a sword slashing at him while his back was turned.

"I trust everything was to your satisfaction last night," he begins.

"It most certainly was," says Lucius, beaming at Marcus. "Most certainly. Everything you promised, and more."

Marcus smiles. "I am glad to hear it," he says. "And I remain at your service for any future occasions."

"I appreciated your attention to details," says Lucius. "In particular the way you ensured a harmonious conclusion to the festivities."

Thank you for placating my wife with pretty clothes, a redecorated dining room and a muscled personal slave, I think. Thank you for ensuring I do not get nagged to death over the next few months, nor have surly-faced slaves smarting from their treatment, dragging their feet over household chores.

Marcus makes a small gesture of dismissal. "Anyone can bring in a cook and a few entertainers. But a man such as yourself requires more forethought than that. You should not be troubled by anything; you should only enjoy yourself."

"I most certainly did," says Lucius, still beaming. "As did my guests."

There is a brief pause, in which they both sip their juice.

"The wine should be a good vintage this year," says Marcus. "The rain fell at the right time in the summer for the grapes to swell and there have been no late rains to water down the sweetness."

Lucius nods, but he seems to be mulling something over. "I have a possible job for you," he says.

"I am all ears," says Marcus.

"It is not an evening's entertainment," says Lucius. "It is perhaps the greatest job of your life, if you agree to it."

I frown. Lucius does not usually exaggerate. Even when he buys and sells, he is not as given to hyperbole as most of his competitors, leading to him having a reputation as a fairly honest man, which is perhaps why the mistress' family overlooked his lack of glorious ancestry in their search for someone to shore up their fading fortunes.

"You will have heard of the Flavian Amphitheatre," says Lucius.

"Commissioned by Vespasian," says Marcus, nodding. "Shame he did not live to see it completed."

"Yes," says Lucius. "It is nearing completion now, though. They say it will be ready next year and Emperor Titus wishes to inaugurate it with one hundred days of Games to honour his father and entertain the people of Rome. It is supposed to seat more than fifty thousand spectators. I have seen it myself; it will be the greatest amphitheatre in the empire. There is nothing like it."

I think of the vast building site in the centre of Rome that has been a nuisance to all for the past seven years. There isn't a person in Rome who doesn't know someone working on it in some capacity or other, from officials dealing with its commission to architects, traders, stonemasons and slaves. The noise and dust and the endless, endless cartloads of wood, stone and concrete being delivered have been a distinctly unwelcome addition to the Forum for years, although the muttering critics held their tongues as the building soared above them, imposing its gleaming presence above the working ants scurrying below. Now that it is close to completion there is more praise for it, a discreet jostling over how one might attend the inaugural day of Games. To be able to boast that one was there will no doubt carry some social clout for many years to come.

Marcus' eyes have narrowed slightly. "How may I be of service?" he asks.

There are many things Lucius might be about to suggest: from an inaugural dinner, perhaps even with the Emperor Titus as a guest of honour, or possibly the use of Marcus' team in creating an element of the spectacle.

My master turns up his lips in a smug smile. "I happen to know the Aedile tasked with selecting a manager for the Flavian Amphitheatre," he says and, even as he speaks, I see a slight flush on Marcus' neck, his eyes widening. "He has been racking his brains as to the choice that would best please the Emperor. It is a vast task. There is less than a year left until the opening and think of what must be put in place just for the inaugural ceremony, let alone one hundred consecutive days of Games to follow. And after those one hundred days, why, my friend tells me the Emperor will expect perhaps two hundred days of Games each year. Think of the animals, the gladiators, not to mention all the other –" he waves his hands vaguely, "– scenery and tickets and musicians and whatnot. My friend will be delighted that I have found him a suitable man for the job. It is your attention to detail they will most appreciate. We had heard that you might be the right man for the task. The dinner last night was a small test."

I know who Lucius' contact is, of course: his own patron, a senator vaguely related to the mistress. He spotted Lucius as a promising young man and has guided him through various stages of his life, not least of which was arranging a suitable match whereby Lucius would step a little closer to a patrician family, while shoring up that very family with his considerable trading prowess and growing wealth. Recently, the senator nudged Lucius in the direction of even more high-placed contacts, the guests at the dinner party. In return, as a loyal client, Lucius is about to fix the senator's problem of finding a man who can manage the monstrosity of a job that will fall to the manager of the Flavian Amphitheatre. There is a real chance of securing imperial favour if this goes well, and my master has just seen Marcus prove himself as a man with an eye for detail and a flair for spectacle. Now I know why Lucius did not blench at the bill. The money came from the imperial purse.

Marcus is very still for a moment and then he gives a half-smile. "You are more than kind to offer me the opportunity," he says. "But I had intended to retire from my work soon and move to the countryside near Puteoli. There is a farm I wish to purchase, I have been saving towards it. Another few years in my role here and I will be ready to move. My wife and I want a quieter life."

"If you can successfully deliver the inauguration and the hundred days of Games you will be richly rewarded in less than two years," says Lucius. "You will be able to purchase whatever farm you wish and live out your days in comfort."

Again, there is that slight hesitation but also a flicker of interest. "It would be a great honour," says Marcus. "But it is also a vast enterprise."

"Come now," says Lucius. He has found the right man to please his patron and he is not about to let him go easily. "I know you could handle it. Why, they gave you the amphitheatre of Pompeii to manage ten years ago when it re-opened after the ban. You must have been a mere stripling then and yet there has been no more trouble at all."

Marcus gives a rueful smile. "I was already thirty," he says. "I am past my prime. Time for me to take on a gentler life, not out all hours of the day and night, nor trying to manage gladiators and actors."

And whores, criminals and weasel-like assistants, I think. A disreputable class.

"Nonsense," says Lucius. "You're a man who has proven himself, both under command and commanding, and now you can reap the rewards of your efforts. A couple of years creating the very greatest spectacles for the Flavian Amphitheatre and you can retire to your farm. Think on it."

Marcus rises as though he's been dismissed. "I shall do so and call on you tomorrow, if I may," he says courteously.

"Of course, of course." Lucius beams as though Marcus has already agreed. "Let me walk you to the door."

I watch them go. Lucius never walks anybody to the door unless there is something he wishes me not to hear, which is very rarely. I can't imagine what he would have to say to Marcus that I shouldn't hear, unless of course he's arranging some sort of dubious tryst with Fausta, or one of the women in her team. I shrug. Not my business. I'm just grateful he doesn't use me in that way, which I'm well aware would be more likely in some other household. Instead, I make a few notes in my tablet, then store it away along with the scrolls for later.

"What did you mean, after the ban?" I ask Lucius when he returns from waving off Marcus.

"Oh, it was a while back now," says Lucius. "Must be twenty years ago. There was a gladiatorial show in Pompeii's amphitheatre and there were taunts in the crowd between the locals and the people of Nuceria, you know how they despise one another. Taunts led to stone throwing and then one sharp stone too many led to knives being drawn and things got out of hand. The locals dished out rather too much of a beating and next thing was Rome had cartloads of wounded Nucerians arriving, not to mention hearing about bereavements. Emperor Nero had an inquiry held by the consuls and when the report came back the Senate barred Pompeii from holding any games for ten years. Of course, there was the odd show here and there, but nothing substantial. When the amphitheatre re-opened, Marcus was chosen to manage it. He should have been in the army still, but he was released early after a wound to the leg. But he was used to commanding and they didn't want any funny business happening again so they thought an army man would be a good choice. Anyway, it's been ten years since then and the crowds have been perfectly behaved."

I think of the raucous nature of gladiatorial audiences, the yelling and betting and odd fistfights that go on. Hardly what I'd call perfectly behaved, but I suppose if there's been no serious breakouts of trouble Marcus can be said to have done a good job. "I can't imagine the amount of organisation that would go into running the Flavian Amphitheatre," I say. "Just to get a slave to run from one end to the other with an instruction would take longer than your meeting with Marcus this morning."

Lucius laughs. "He'll need good organisation, that's for sure. Tomorrow morning, have your writing materials to hand. There'll be a contract to write."

"You're awfully sure of him saying yes," I say.

Lucius is already walking away from me. "Who could refuse what I am offering?" he calls back.

I nod slowly to myself. Certainly, such an offer comes only once in a lifetime. The question is, whether this Marcus seeks further adventure after a dangerous life in the army, followed by managing an already-busy amphitheatre, rather than the peaceful life he claims to desire. Anyway, I have been dismissed for now, so I make myself scarce. Out of sight means out of mind, as all slaves know. Lucius doesn't really need me much. He has another scribe back in Rome for his day-to-day business. I am mostly used as an adornment and for social matters.

I AM EARLY FOR THE next morning's salutatio, curious to know what Marcus' decision will be. I lay out papyrus, ink and reed pens as well as my wax tablet and stylus. If Marcus agrees right away, there will need to be some sort of contract, or at the very least a letter of introduction, depending on whether he travels to Rome with us in eight days' time or goes ahead of us. It sounds like the role has an element of haste to it. If there is no manager already in place for a vast arena due to be inaugurated next summer, time must be running out for all the organising that will need to be done if imperial wrath is not to fall on the heads of several people. I wonder whether the weasel assistant will accompany Marcus if he takes up the role.

My master is late; four men are already waiting to see him, none of them Marcus. I tap my foot against the floor in boredom and wonder whether perhaps he has taken against the idea, whether he will come in person to turn down the role.

Eventually Lucius arrives, yawning and somewhat more ruffled than usual. Maybe the mistress welcomed him into her bedroom last night, an uncommon occurrence. He disposes of the clients in quick succession, leaving me with little to do but watch the faint autumnal drizzle in the garden. The mistress is right, it's time we were headed back to Rome. Pompeii is hardly a fashionable place to stay late into the autumn. There's a chill to the mornings, a heavy mist over Mount Vesuvius which doesn't clear till the sun is high in the sky, the frequent tremors.

"Marcus! I thought you were not coming!"

"That would be gross ingratitude," he replies, running a hand through his hair to remove the wet from it. "I was delayed by the late arrival of some new animals. I had to ensure they were safely locked up. Can't have a lion on the loose." He smiles, nods at me and sits himself down in the chair opposite Lucius. "I see Althea is ready with her papyrus."

I don't recall him being told my name.

"So is the answer yes?" asks Lucius.

Marcus hesitates, as though conscious of what he is agreeing to. "Yes," he says, and then more formally, "I will take on the role of Manager of the Flavian Amphitheatre, as you have asked of me. I am grateful for your patronage in this matter and offer you my loyal friendship."

I make a note. Marcus will now be a client of my master; I will be seeing him regularly at the daily salutatio when we return to Rome. Lucius has given him the opportunity of a lifetime; he will expect considerable gratitude in return. The term 'friendship' means a great deal more than that in this context. I hide a smile. I can tell Lucius is already envisioning front-row seats at the inauguration of the Amphitheatre, regardless of his lack of senatorial rank. And quite possibly more dinners in his own home arranged by Marcus, no detail left to chance.

"Althea?"

I look up. My master and Marcus are looking at me. "Sorry, Dominus," I say. "Just making a note."

"Draft a letter to the Aedile," says Lucius grandly. "Explain that Marcus Aquillius Scaurus will be taking on the role he asked me to fill. Ask him to have his scribes draw up a binding contract. Get it ratified by the imperial household and delivered to the Amphitheatre where Marcus can sign it. We will send the letter ahead by the Imperial Post since it is a matter that concerns the Emperor." I can tell that he is proud to be able to say such things, that his missives will use the Imperial Post, restricted to matters of importance. "Marcus will leave tomorrow," he adds. "By the time he has reached Rome, and made some preliminary plans, the contract will be ready. His family can join him later on."

I nod and set to work. It does not take me long. Most of it is taken up with elegant forms of address and literary flourishes to make Lucius sound more important than he is, his securing Marcus a stroke of genius. I note Marcus' nickname, Scaurus, *Lame*, no doubt a reference to his past wound, and the limp it has left him with.

Lucius looks it over, affixes his seal and signs.

"I have two fine horses you can use," he says to Marcus. "They will make the journey more pleasant. You are sure you do not wish to travel with my own family? We will set off in eight days. I only have a few last trading meetings here."

"Thank you," says Marcus. "There will be so much to do, and I would prefer to travel at a faster pace than will be comfortable for your household, especially your lady wife."

He has a point. My mistress likes to travel in vast luxury, visit everyone she can think of along the way, and complain about the journey regardless. It often takes us as many as ten days to travel to Rome, although most people do it comfortably in six and it can be done in three at speed. I'm not sure why Marcus would need two horses though. Perhaps the weasel assistant will accompany him.

Lucius nods. "As you wish," he says affably. "And now about Althea."

"If you are sure," says Marcus.

I frown. What have I to do with this?

"Absolutely," says Lucius. "She is all yours."

I stare at my master in shock.

"Althea, you will need to draw up one last contract for me," says Lucius. "Write this down. 'The Greek slave Althea, scribe, formerly belonging to Lucius Hirtuleius Dives, is now bestowed upon Marcus Aquillius Scaurus and henceforth will be known as his slave. She will perform whatever services shall be required of her by her new master. She is given by Lucius Hirtuleius Dives in recognition of Marcus Aquillius Scaurus becoming the manager of the Flavian Amphitheatre and to mark the new friendship and loyalty between them.' Add whatever else is needed. Three copies."

I do not move. I stare at Lucius and then at Marcus.

"I am not sure Althea was aware of our agreement," says Marcus, his eyes steady on mine. "Are you willing, Althea? Lucius has told me he does not need two scribes, and I will most certainly need a scribe I can rely on if I am to run the Flavian Amphitheatre."

"Of course she's willing," says Lucius, waving for refreshments and moving to a less formal seating area. "Bored rigid working for me. Why, there's hardly anything to do. She'll be kept busy working for you. She's a good girl," he adds as an afterthought. "Doesn't have to be told things twice. Bought her from a very good household. Classy. Untouched, too, I can vouch for that. By the way, no offence but I will ask her to write in a *ne serva* clause. Given, you know, your line of work. Althea, add that in."

Marcus ignores him. "Are you willing?" he asks me again.

I look at Lucius, who is eating a honey cake while the wine is poured. He is oblivious to me, for I have been gifted to Marcus. I am no longer his slave, therefore I am of no further interest. I try to think what it will be like to approach my master's house in Rome as a visitor, to attend with Marcus as he pays his respects in the morning *salutatio*, since my master will have become his patron. I cannot imagine it at all. Will I see Myrtis again, or only watch her honey cakes being served, without being able to taste them? And as for my new master: what do I know of him? Nothing, except he is a man who will arrange for a houseful of slaves to be stripped naked and painted in gold if it pleases his clients, a man who works with beasts and gladiators and whores for a living.

I look into Marcus' eyes and all I can think is, at least he asked. At least he asked if I was willing, even though whether I am willing or not is irrelevant. I swallow.

"I am willing," I say so quietly that Marcus has to read my lips. But he nods.

"She agrees," he tells Lucius, moving over to sit beside him, accepting a glass of wine.

"Of course she does," says Lucius. "Draw up the contract, there's a good girl," he says over his shoulder. "She knows Rome like the back of her hand," he adds. "Her father was a scribe too, passed it on to her."

I start writing out the document, my startled mind wandering so that I nearly write the wrong words. I focus again, reflecting on Lucius' casual 'passed it on' as though my father's careful hours of tuition of me, his only child, were a mere trinket rather than the only legacy he could offer me, a skill he knew would elevate me above most slaves. My own diligent practise of calligraphy, shorthand, reading such books as I had access to in order that I might hold my own with an educated master… The document is complete. It includes the *ne serva* clause, so that Marcus cannot pimp me out as a whore, although it does not stop him using me for his own desires, should he so wish, of course. I make two additional copies. "I am finished, Dominus," I say, holding the first papyrus out, uncertain of which man I am addressing.

Marcus stands, takes the documents and my pen and inkpot from me, adds his own name and imprints his seal in the wax I have prepared, then passes each copy to Lucius, who does the same.

"You may go and pack," Marcus says to me. "I live in the insula by the gladiator barracks. When you have your things come and find me there, anyone will know my name."

I wait for Lucius to dismiss me before I realise that he is not going to speak to me, is not going to bid me farewell. I have been given a command by my new master, and I must obey him.

"Yes, Dominus," I say, backing away from them both.

"Sold? What do you mean, sold? Who is there to sell you to?"

"Marcus."

"Who?"

"The man who arranged the dinner."

Myrtis stares at me.

"You're burning the bread," I tell her. Acrid smoke is filling the room.

Myrtis snaps back to the flatbreads she was cooking on a griddle and flips the burning one off and onto the floor, half-charred, half-raw. "Sold? To him? What for? What have you done?"

"I need to pack," I tell her. "Can you come to our room?"

"Oy! You!" Myrtis calls to one of the slave girls podding beans. "Get through this lot." She indicates the floured board with balls of dough waiting to be shaped into flat circles and cooked. "Don't you burn any," she adds.

I fill her in as we make our way to the sleeping quarters. Once there, I look about me helplessly.

"Spare tunic," says Myrtis.

"Am I allowed to take extra clothes?" I ask her.

Myrtis shrugs. "Domina won't notice, what does she care about some old tunic?"

The chest we share for our belongings is hardly full. I pull out my leather satchel in which I keep my writing implements when we travel, and shake it out, dislodging a small scorpion which scurries away to hide in a crack in the wall. I pull out my spare tunic, identical to the one I'm wearing, a pale blue down to my ankles. I'm already wearing my shoes, my only leather belt is round my waist and a pink headwrap holds up part of my hair. I have another headwrap in brown, which I pass to Myrtis, who is folding my tunic. In Rome I had a thick brown cloak for winters, but we only have our summer clothing here.

"Don't forget your essentials," says Myrtis.

I take out a small linen bag containing a few pairs of underwear as well as the felt pads I use when I bleed and push it to the bottom of my satchel. It's not something I'd care to have fall out by accident in front of a man. Myrtis passes me my tunic and headwrap and I add my tablet, stylus and inkpot, making sure the lid is tightly closed so there are no leaks. I cannot take fresh scrolls of papyrus with me, so Marcus will need to purchase some. At the bottom of the chest is a small bundle, wrapped in a red cloth. I unroll it and look down at the reed pen. I never use it; it was a gift from my father on the day he told me he would make a scribe of me. The red cloth was my mother's headwrap. I run my fingers over them for a moment, while Myrtis watches me, then wrap them back up and put them in the satchel.

"Take this, too, yours is all broken," says Myrtis, handing me her own wooden comb. Some past suitor has carved her name into it.

"I can't take that."

"I can get another," says Myrtis grandly. "You don't want your new owners thinking you're a slattern because you don't comb your hair properly, do you?"

"Thank you," I say, and she shrugs as though it is nothing, although a gift from a slave who has barely any possessions is a precious thing. I tuck it away. Everything I have fits into this tiny bag, as wide as my forearm and hand.

"At least it's light," says Myrtis, her voice too cheerful and loud. "Don't want to be dragging stuff about, do you?"

I blink.

"I suppose you can't keep a new master waiting, can you? Best be off."

I swallow and nod.

"Although I should feed you up first," she says, pulling me down the stairs and back to her kitchen. "I mean, you never know how a master will treat you, do you? Half of them practically starve their slaves, we all know that. It might be your last good meal for a while."

She forces two freshly cooked flatbreads and almost a quarter of a cheese down me, followed by her honey cakes and then dates and figs, a handful of new walnuts she gets one of the girls to shell.

"I really can't eat anymore," I say, although I want to, even though my stomach's painful with too much food. I want to stay here, in Myrtis' domain, in the too-small smoky kitchen, eating her good food.

Myrtis turns her back on me, her shoulders heaving.

I hug her from behind, my own tears falling, in sadness at leaving her and fear at the unknown future. "You'll have to come and see me at the amphitheatre," I say into her back. "When it opens."

"Oh absolutely," she says, turning to face me, wiping the tears and snot off her face with the back of her hand and trying to smile. "I like a good show in the arena. Handy with a sword, are you?"

I snort and wipe my eyes. "More of a beast-hunter, if I'm honest," I say. "Lion-killing and such."

"Oh, that will be worth a look," says Myrtis. "I hear lions like a good meal."

"Where's Felix?"

Myrtis' shoulders drop. "Got sent on an errand."

I nod. "You'll tell him I said goodbye," I manage.

"Nah, he'll only think you fancy him if I tell him that," she says and we both try to laugh.

I stand a moment too long, then nod to the kitchen slave girls, who have been watching. "Goodbye."

"Goodbye," they chorus.

"May Libertas watch over you and lead you to freedom one day," says Myrtis to me.

"And you," I say. I look about me but there is no other way to delay, no other excuse to make.

"Do I have to say goodbye to the mistress?" I ask.

"I doubt it," says Myrtis, unwilling to follow any niceties. "She never really liked you anyway. You're too pretty. Made her look old."

I shake my head at her. "I'll go out the back, then," I say.

There's a small doorway out the back of the house, rather than the grand gateway into the front. This is the route we slaves take when we nip out on errands, our lazy guard dog doing little to keep it safe. Good thing it has a bolt on it at night. I scratch Theridamas behind his ears and he rolls over, showing me his belly.

"Useless mutt," says Myrtis.

I step out onto the pavement, looking up at Myrtis.

"Now, just because you're working for that Marcus, don't let me see you with your bits painted gold," she says.

"Thought that was your line of work."

"Be off with you, you cheeky girl."

I step backwards. "Goodbye then."

"Goodbye," she says. "Go with Libertas."

I HAVE TO WIPE AWAY more tears when I get around the corner and onto the main street. I try to cheer myself thinking I will see her again. The amphitheatre is only a short walk away from Lucius' house in Rome. If Marcus will give me a little free time now and then I can easily go to see her, and I know she won't be able to resist checking up on me.

I'm so busy thinking, I almost get run over by an oxcart as I cross the street and its owner yells at me. After that I try to keep my mind on where I'm going. It feels strange to have left Lucius' house and know I will no longer live there. To be heading to a new house, one I can't yet imagine but which will surely not be as grand. Lucius' house, near the northern wall of Pompeii, may not be as grand as the villas in Oplontis are rumoured to be, but it's certainly a cut above any normal merchant, a sign he is on his way up in the world. Marcus' home is near the gladiators' barracks, down by the Stabian Gate, on the opposite side of town, just before the southern walls.

I walk past the brothel SheWolves, though not quickly enough to avoid a few lecherous comments from men nearby, and to notice some of the larger lewd graffiti scrawled on the walls, including, 'Gaius recommends Cincinnata, she's hairy but you won't be disappointed.' Further down the street are the still-decrepit Stabian Baths, as yet unrestored after the earthquake, only the women's section still in use. By now I can see the main theatre with its smaller sister next to it. Gladiators often train there; their most ardent fans watch even the training of their favourites, checking their progress, studying their form for later gambling success.

The two-storey insula opposite the barracks has seen better days and looks highly disreputable. Once a rich man's house, it was bought up by an enterprising property speculator and converted into smaller flats with partition walls so thin a man could punch a hole in them, the landlord now coining in the rent. I hesitate before entering the small courtyard, the building's former atrium when it was a single family's home. Inside is chaos. Chickens and dogs are everywhere, as are numerous poorly clad children and rough looking men. The two women I see look harassed, grabbing at a passing child to give them chores or a clip round the ear, dragging large baskets of wet laundry which they're trying to hang up without it getting dirtier than it was before they washed it.

"Help you, pretty one?"

I step back from a man who's towering over me, his arm reaching out to clasp my bum. "I'm looking for Marcus Aquillius Scaurus."

The man pulls back his hand as if I've burnt him. "Scaurus? You know him?"

"I'm his scribe."

The man takes a step back. "Oh well, no offence meant. Didn't know you was Scaurus'. No offence taken, I hope."

I shake my head. Marcus clearly has a reputation round here if a man like this is afraid of offending him. "I was trying to find him."

"Down by the barracks, love. Most likely, this time of day. You want me to take you there?"

"No thank you," I say. "I can find my own way."

"Right you are."

We both back away with relief. I had hoped to avoid the barracks for fear of meeting just such a man, but it looks as though I have little choice. I don't know which apartment might be Marcus', so I'm better off finding him first.

I can hear the loud crack of practice swords even from outside the barracks. When I mention Marcus' name to the porter sitting inside a small room watching over the entrance, he waves me through. Inside the noise is deafening. The vast courtyard is full of men and fighting equipment. Most are fighting with wooden weapons, so as to avoid unnecessary injuries or any sudden uprisings, but a few have real blades. There's a lot of cursing and shouting and I creep round the edge of the colonnade, hoping to spot Marcus somewhere. In one corner I come across a billboard painter, working on two large boards. One is an old one, the paint flaking off it after months being displayed in all weathers, which reads, 'Twenty pairs of gladiators provided by Quintus Monnius Rufus are to fight at Nola, May First, Second, and Third. There will be a hunt.' The sign is completed with a dramatic close-up painting of a gladiator lying on the ground, covered in blood, begging for mercy, while the victor leans menacingly over him with his sword, waiting to dispatch him. The new board is almost complete and proudly proclaims, 'Thirty pairs of gladiators provided by Gnaeus Alleius Nigidius Maius quinquennial duumvir, together with their substitutes, will fight at Pompeii on November 24, 25, 26. There will be a hunt. Hurrah for Maius the Quinquennial! Bravo, Paris! There will be awnings.' I'm aware that there's a local actor called Paris who's a bit of a celebrity and I assume it's his likeness that the painter is currently portraying: a handsome man being depicted with very little armour on. If he's an actor, he'll be part of some pre-fight show rather than the main event.

"The ladies like them painted with a bit less on, if you catch my drift," winks the painter, catching me watching him. "Are you looking for someone?"

"Marcus Aquillius Scaurus."

"Scaurus? Over there."

"Hello, Althea." Fausta has found me. She's in her toga, hands on her hips, looking as if she owns the place.

"Hello," I say, a little awkwardly. I don't know what status I should be giving her. As far as I know she's a prostitute, but Marcus seemed to have put her in charge at the dinner party and here she looks fully in command.

"Heard Marcus was given you as some sort of sweetener to seal the amphitheatre deal," she says.

"Yes," I say.

"You pleased about that, or pissed off?"

"I don't know," I manage.

"Not sure about the rough crowd he hangs out with?"

"I suppose."

"Including me," she grins, watching the men.

"You helped me out," I say.

"Don't worry, he isn't going to use you at events like that. He really will need a scribe, if he's going to manage that place." Her face twists. "Be sorry to lose him, though. Best manager this dump's ever had. They'll replace him with some cut-throat bribe-taker who's just in it for as much money and women as he can get."

"Is he a good master?"

"Yes," says Fausta without hesitation. "He knows what he wants and if you can do what he asks and do it well, he'll treat you with honour. Mind you," she adds, "You screw him around and he'll have you out of here so fast you won't know what happened and you'll only have scars to help you work it out."

I nod.

"Met Livia?"

"Who's Livia?"

"His wife."

"No."

"Good woman," says Fausta. "Her family were appalled she married him, think he isn't respectable. But she knows what he's really like and she knows he's headed for better things."

"Like the Flavian Amphitheatre?"

"Nah, that'll be more of the same but worse, won't it?" she says. "He wants to leave it all behind and get his family farm back."

"He mentioned that," I say.

"He mentions it all the time," says Fausta. "I think he dreams about it at night. He won't rest until he – WATCH YOURSELF, YOU IDIOT!" she suddenly bellows, startling both me and the painter, who curses under his breath at the slip of the paintbrush that's just given his handsome gladiator an extra thumb. Fausta's already picked up the spear that landed too close to comfort and hurls it back at one of the men, making him duck to avoid it.

"Throws like a man," comments the painter, now painting over his mistake. "Like to see her in an arena."

"Bet you would," says Fausta. "You wouldn't last one round against me."

The painter shrugs, unoffended. "I'm a good painter, I'd make a poor gladiator," he says.

"You're not bad, I suppose," Fausta allows, looking down at his work. "Right, Althea, let's go get Marcus."

MARCUS IS STANDING WITH HIS arms folded, watching two men fighting. Their trainer is next to him.

"Bit more flair," Marcus is saying. "He's got to learn what fighting looks like in the top tier seats. You need bigger movements. It's not about getting a quick dagger under the ribs, it's a sword heading for the throat in the biggest arc you can manage."

"Was army-trained before he got in trouble," says the trainer. "He's fighting to kill."

Marcus shakes his head. "He'd better unlearn that fast," he says. "This is about spectacle and showing off technique. I need blood here and there but neither you nor I want 'to the death' fights unless we've advertised it. Waste of good men. Still, he's got army style and height, strong arms. Might make a good myrmillo gladiator."

The trainer nods. "I'll put him with one of the more experienced ones," he says. "He'll get the hang of it."

"Better do," says Marcus. "Tell him he wants a long life in the arena, not a short one. That's for the criminals." He catches sight of Fausta and me coming towards them. "I'll leave you to it," he finishes.

"Your girl found you," says Fausta, gesturing to me.

"Well done," he says. "Did you find my house?"

"No," I say. "A man said you would be here."

"I must be too predictable in my movements," he says, then turns to Fausta. "Still here? Thought you were taking a boat to Misenum?"

"Off shortly," she says.

"And you'll be back when?"

"Only going for a few days, keep the old man happy."

"We'll be leaving tomorrow morning, so I won't see you for a while," he says.

"I'll be sure and mess things up," she says, grinning.

He claps her on the shoulder as though she were a man. "Couldn't if you tried. I've left it in too good order."

"I'll give it a try," she says.

He laughs. "I'll miss you, Fausta," he says. "Fortuna bring you luck. And may your journey be blessed by Neptune."

"I will pray to Janus that your new beginning is successful," she says. "And I will make sure Livia has everything she needs when she sets out to join you."

"Thank you," he says. "Have fun with the old codger. Show him a good time."

"He gets what he pays for," she grins back. She walks away, exchanging the odd jest with the men as she passes them.

Marcus watches her go, then turns to me. "I'll take you home to Livia," he says. "Your new mistress should at least see you before we set off for Rome."

"Yes, Dominus," I say.

"Call me Marcus," he says. "I don't stand on ceremony."

I nod, though I am not quite sure I can bring myself to call him a name normally reserved for his family and close friends. I assume his nickname annoys him as it refers to his damaged leg, though most nicknames are hardly complimentary. "Who will run the amphitheatre here when you're gone?" I ask.

"Only the gods know that. Fausta ought to, she's been my right hand all these years, but they won't let a woman run it, so whoever takes over better make a friend of her, and fast."

"Where is she going?"

"Misenum. There's a rich old general who holidays there, he's had a soft spot for her ever since he was a young officer in the army. Couldn't marry her of course, she was a slave working in a brothel and he came from a well-off family, but he set her free so she could manage her own clients and he turns a blind eye to what she does when she's not at his side. She visits him for a few days now and then, comes back with pink cheeks and a new gift of jewellery. He'd have her as a mistress, I don't doubt he does love her and she him, in her own way, but Fausta's not suited to a soft life. She really is a she-wolf."

THIS TIME IT'S EASY TO enter the courtyard, I simply follow in Marcus' wake; the crowd parts easily for him, nods and greetings on all sides. We make our way up a sturdy outer staircase to the first floor, where a small wiry mutt meets us, first with wild barks, then with bouncing enthusiasm as it recognises its master. Marcus gives it a quick pat and then pushes open the door to an apartment.

"Livia!"

A woman appears from another room. "Marcus." She is small in stature, shorter than I am and delicately built, with hazel-coloured hair, surprisingly light for a local woman. There are a few late flowers tucked into her plaited bun. Behind her follows a little boy, who waddles keenly towards Marcus, before stopping short at the sight of me and grabbing hold of his mother's tunic. Livia laughs. "Oh, not so bold after all?"

Marcus kneels to coax the child forward. "Come, boy."

The boy plucks up his courage and flings himself into Marcus' arms, narrowly avoiding falling. Marcus lifts him and turns him to look at me. "Althea," he pronounces carefully. The baby stares at me. I offer a smile and he hides his face in his father's tunic, clasping his protective bulla for courage.

"You are welcome to our home," says Livia to me, smiling.

I bow my head to her. "Domina," I say.

"Come and help Anna make supper," she says. "She will explain anything you need to know about the household."

I follow her. The apartment is not a bad size, four rooms in all, and it even has a small cooking area, which is rare in humbler apartments. The household shrine has fresh flowers on it, the same ones that are in Livia's hair, as well as the usual candles and offerings of food. There is not a lot of luxury, the furniture is plain wood with little in the way of decoration. I have grown used to houses draped everywhere with rich fabrics and bright colours, mosaics on all the floors, but there is none of that here. There is a wooden crib in one corner and a loom, which stands waiting for its mistress to return to it.

At Livia's direction I put my satchel in a corner and take up a stool next to the slave girl Anna. She passes me a knife and I start chopping carrots to add to a savoury porridge, the evening meal. Anna eyes me up curiously.

"Is it really true we're all going to go to Rome?" she asks me in an overawed whisper.

"Yes," I say. "I'm to travel there tomorrow with the master." I still can't quite bring myself to call him Marcus, especially not to another slave. "I think the rest of the household is to follow us soon. Are there other slaves?"

"Just me."

A one slave household seems unusual for someone in my new master's position, I would have expected Marcus to earn more, as manager of the amphitheatre. I've never had to cook or clean in the households I was part of, where there were plenty of slaves. Each has their own tasks to do, and a scribe wasn't expected to chop vegetables. In a smaller household a slave must do everything. I look over my shoulder, but Marcus and Livia are in the furthest room, Marcus squatting down talking to his son. I lower my voice. "Are they good masters?" It's the question every slave asks, as soon as they get a chance in a new household. You have to judge by the tone of the response how accurate it is.

But Anna's face lights up in what looks like a real smile. "They are," she says, keeping her own voice low. "The mistress is very kind; she treats me like family. Master is hardly here but when he is there's no beatings or, you know, the other. And he said that if we all go to Rome there might be other slaves and I will be set over them, might even be the mistress' body slave."

I nod. To be a body slave to a kind mistress is one of the best positions a slave woman can hope for, for they will be more of a companion than a worker. They will hear their Domina's private thoughts and care for their feelings, be treated as a confidante and occupy a position of great power over the other slaves in the household.

"You're a scribe?" asks Anna.

I nod.

"And Greek?"

I nod.

She looks impressed. She is probably a local girl, a Greek slave who can read and write is not the sort of slave she might have expected to share a bed mat with. "Did you come from a *very* grand house?"

"Lucius Hirtuleius Dives."

"The garum merchant from Rome? In the holiday villa?"

"Yes."

"So you lived in Rome mostly?"

"Yes."

"What's it like?" she asks, eyes wide.

I throw the chopped carrots into the pot. "Big. Noisy. Stinky."

She looks disappointed. "But grand? With ladies with their hair all elegant and all the men in togas and a really huge Forum, all big statues and temples?"

I smile at her vision of Rome. "Some of that," I agree. "In the rich houses. But when you go out it's just like here: traffic and slaves, horse dung and ordinary men and women wearing ordinary clothes."

She nods, stirring the porridge. "I'd like to see it," she says. "But I'm a bit scared, too. I've never been anywhere but Pompeii. My parents are slaves here too, they live a few streets down and work at the fullery of Stephanus. They thought it was better to work for just one household. You don't get worked so hard, if you have kind masters who treat you well."

I wash my hands and lay out cups, a jug of water, spoons and bread on the table. Livia comes back into the room and watches me for a few moments. "I hope you will be happy serving Marcus," she says. "I know you have come from far grander homes. Ours is a bit shabby," she says, although she is smiling rather than apologetic. "We save everything Marcus makes."

I'm surprised she would comment like this on her home and their plans. I'm a new slave and yet she is treating me as though she has known me for years. "What for?" I ask tentatively, uncertain whether I am allowed such curiosity.

"There's an old farm further up the coast, in the countryside near Puteoli," she says, her eyes dreamy. "It's shabby too, no-one lives there anymore, but we could buy it for a good sum and then work on it. It has a lovely vineyard, fertile land, a stream running nearby. We mean to buy it soon and move there. It belonged to Marcus' family once, but his grandfather was an inveterate gambler and one night he gambled the farm and lost. The family had to scrabble for a living, the grandfather died of shame. Marcus used to play there as a boy, and it broke his heart that the new owners didn't care enough to look after it. They just sold all the goods, slaves and livestock and abandoned it."

The farm again. Her sharing of future dreams makes me a little bolder. "Doesn't he enjoy what he does?"

She laughs and takes a piece of bread, crumbles it at the household shrine, bows her head for a moment, then continues. "He's good at what he does, he can make a spectacle out of just about anything. But he says it is no life, he is tired of the violence. He wants to live quietly and enjoy the sun on his face. He spent happy times on the farm as a boy, so he has it in his mind as a golden time. I tell him it will be harder work than he thinks, but he says nothing can be as hard as befriending men and women before watching them be mistreated and often die."

I'm still shocked at how honest Livia is with me, sharing comments her husband must have made in their own home, disparaging the work he does. But there is an openness to her, she speaks as though we are friends or cousins, trustworthy and understanding. I have never had such a mistress, but I am grateful for her, already like her more than I expected to.

THE PORRIDGE IS TASTY, AND we're given generous helpings. Anna and I sit on the stairwell eating, watching the to-ing and fro-ing in the courtyard below while Livia sings Amantius to sleep and then Marcus joins her in the bedroom. I can hear the sound of their lovemaking amidst the noise from the courtyard. Anna chatters on to me, perhaps grateful of company, pointing out various locals and regaling me with the latest gossip regarding them. Slowly the courtyard empties as night falls and we make our way indoors, use sand and water to clean the dishes, then lay out sleeping mats in the main living area by the table. I try to think over the events of the day but too much has gone on, my thoughts are blurred and confused. At last I whisper a prayer to Libertas to watch over me in this new place and sleep.

I'M WOKEN AGAIN BY A tremor. "Get off, Myrtis," I mutter, before realising that this time I'm being shaken by both the ground and Anna, who has grabbed my shoulder. I can hear shouts of alarm from the apartments surrounding us. I sit up but the tremor stops and, although Anna and I sit waiting tensely for a few moments in case another one comes, there is nothing.

"Stronger than the other day," says Anna, yawning and rolling up her sleeping mat. "A bird flew into the window in the night, did you hear it? Animals act funny when there's tremors. Does Rome get tremors all the time like we have?"

"Not really," I say. "Occasionally, but years apart, not every autumn like you do here."

"Spring too," says Anna. She picks up an amphora in each hand and gestures with her chin towards another two in the kitchen. "Grab those," she says. "We need to get water."

This is the sort of task I have never been called on to do and I shiver in the half-light. At this time of morning I am used to being awake, but usually I'd be sitting in Myrtis' kitchen, petting the lazy dog and eating the first of the pancakes she cooks for the masters, cracking a few nuts and maybe drinking some of the grape juice that's so plentiful around harvest time, its rich sweetness a treat I associate with the last days of the holidays here. I'm already missing Myrtis and Felix, they've been my only friends for the past few years and I will only see them briefly from now on. I wait patiently behind Anna and other women at the nearest public fountain, then struggle back to the apartment with the load. I never realised how heavy two full amphorae were.

When we get back a dishevelled Livia is feeding Amantius but Marcus is nowhere to be seen. Anna lays out bread, wine and cheese, along with nuts and olives. Livia yawns, nods and eats while coaxing Amantius to pay more attention to his food and less to playing with the dog.

"Marcus will be back soon, he is fetching the horses," she tells me. "Are you ready to leave?"

I nod, fastening the strap of my satchel a little tighter.

Livia gives up on Amantius and stands. She takes a basin Anna has filled into her bedroom, where I can hear her washing.

Amantius stares at me. I hide my face behind my hands and then pop out and he giggles.

"Again," he says, and I do it again, to more giggles. He tries it himself, one eye unable to resist peeping out even while he should be hiding his face, then throwing his arms wide for the big reveal. I can't help giggling myself.

Livia is back, her hair now combed and twisted into a bun, her palla wrapped around her to keep her warm. "It's chilly," she says. "Take this, Althea." She is holding out a woollen cloak in a dark blue. "When we get to Rome, I will see to everyone's clothing, but you will need something for travelling. It needs mending but it will do for now."

"Thank you, Domina," I say gratefully, putting it on. The cloak is thick and very warm, I feel the morning chill leave me. She's right, it has a worn-out patch with a hole in it but it's nothing a little darning won't take care of.

"The horses are ready." Marcus stands in the doorway. He, too, has a cloak on.

"I will ask a blessing on your journey," Livia says.

Marcus nods and follows her to the household shrine, bowing his head. Anna and I stand behind them, while Amantius watches with interest, holding onto the dog for extra balance, as Livia lights a candle.

Livia raises her hands, palms upturned, and bows her head. "Gods of this household and of the world beyond our doors, it is I, Livia, mistress of this home, who asks for your blessing," she begins. "Look after my husband, Marcus Aquillius Scaurus, father of our son Amantius, on his journey to Rome. May his journey be worthwhile, and may this new endeavour be blessed by Janus, bear fruit and take our family closer to the day when we will return to the countryside and the ancestral farm, where we can restore the Aquillius family's honour and legacy." She looks briefly up at Marcus and then over her shoulder at me. "And may our new slave Althea be watched over also, now that she is part of our household. May her skills as a scribe be useful to Marcus. May he protect her body and honour as a good man should."

Perhaps this is a warning to Marcus not to try any funny business with me while we travel alone together, but there is something heartfelt in her words, an almost-innocent trust in Marcus and genuine care for me as a fellow woman that is touching. I have never worked in such a small household with so few slaves. Perhaps it is this that makes Livia treat me as though I were part of the family rather than an unimportant object to be bought and sold, commanded and punished on a whim.

Livia has finished her requests to the family gods and now she lifts Amantius up for Marcus to kiss. He stoops over the two of them, holding them both in a tight embrace.

"I won't be long," he says. "I'll send for you in a matter of days, once I have seen the amphitheatre for myself and found somewhere for us all to live. Then we will all be together again. It will be a great new adventure."

"All the hubbub of the capital," she murmurs.

"Only for two years," he reminds her. "Then we will be done with all of this and go to the farm. You will be as brown as a country girl in no time."

She laughs, although her eyes have filled up a little. "Stay safe," she says. "Don't go down dark streets at night. You don't know Rome like you do Pompeii."

"I will be the most cautious man in Rome," he assures her. "Now we must leave. Juno watch over you both." A last tightening of his embrace, then he kisses her upturned lips and ruffles Amantius' golden curls, before striding out of the house so quickly I turn in a fluster to follow him, but Livia has caught my hand in hers.

"Keep Marcus safe, Althea," she says, her large eyes still anxious. "Look after him for me." She jiggles Amantius on her hip as he starts to cry.

I nod and pull away, half-running towards the door. "Don't worry," I call back to her, trying not to trip over the threshold as I step out into the street. "I will keep him safe. I promise!"

STRAWBERRY GRAPES

Marcus is waiting at the end of the still-dark street with the two horses, a boy holding the reins of the first while Marcus attaches the reins of the second to the harness so that it will follow his lead. The horses are both tall, the second seems skittish and I stand well back from them.

"Have you ridden before?"

I shake my head.

"Not much to it," he says. "You'll ride pillion with me, we'll swap the horses over from time to time to give them a rest."

I am clumsy at climbing up from the mounting block. I try to pull myself up in one move, but I slip twice, and Marcus has to half drag me up the third time, his hand gripping my arm so hard that I have to rub the pain away once I am seated. The horse shifts beneath our combined weight and I am unsure of where to hold onto Marcus, trying to hold my body rigidly away from him. It seems too intimate a position, but if I do not hold onto him I will most certainly fall off the horse, since I am riding pillion, both legs to the left rather than astride, which would not be seemly.

"Hold on," he advises me.

I put both hands lightly on his waist, trying to touch him as little as possible.

"Can barely feel you," he says. "Don't fall off just for modesty's sake."

I don't reply, but I'm not about to encourage a new master to consider what he might do with a new female slave, far away from his wife.

After a few hours' travel boredom overtakes my anxiety and I simply keep one arm or the other around his waist, allowing my body to lean against his back. He seems entirely comfortable, the reins held in one hand, his body swaying with the movement of the horse.

We swap horses twice, each time taking the opportunity to drink some water. On one of these breaks, we eat bread and cheese Livia has sent with us, sitting in the shade of a tree. Marcus wanders away behind some bushes to relieve himself and I do the same. By the third time we mount I have grown better at the fast, hard push off required from the milestone mounting blocks.

"Were you born a slave?" he asks.

"No," I say.

"Want to tell me your story?"

"I was born in Kefalonia."

"I don't know it."

"A Greek island," I say. "My father was a labourer, but he could read and write. I was his only child. He had family in Athens. My mother and I were to accompany him there. But pirates took the ship we boarded."

He nods without speaking.

"We were taken as slaves and sold in Rome," I say.

"All three of you?"

I swallow. *Screams and blood, her hand losing its grasp on me.* "My mother was killed."

"I'm sorry," he says.

We are quiet for a little while.

"How old were you?"

"Ten," I say.

"And your father could not prove his freeborn status?"

"He had no connections," I say. "The slave trader was crooked."

My father sought ways to regain his freeborn status, year after year, the bitterness of failure eating away at him.

"Were you and your father sold to the same household?"

"Yes." *Crying on the slave block, my father on his knees, begging his new master to buy me too so that we would not be separated. Literate Greeks are desirable slaves. Classy.* "My father swore to the man who bought him that he would serve him with great loyalty if he would only keep us together. I could read and write a little already and speak Latin, so I could be useful. My father managed our new master's accounts. I became a body slave to his daughter Cornelia, as we were the same age. I kept her company and studied with her."

"Do you remember much of Kefalonia?"

"No." *The waves on the beach, the chickens in our yard, my mother humming as she hung out washing.*

"How did you end up with Lucius?"

"Cornelia married and her new husband had plenty of slaves. Lucius knew my master and was in need of a scribe."

"And your father?"

The bitterness claiming him, his hand, too, loosening its grip. No-one left to hold my hand. "He died a year before."

"And now you're to help me inaugurate the greatest amphitheatre there's ever been, and little enough time to do it. A different kind of business altogether."

"Can it be done in the time?"

"I doubt we have much choice," he says. "The contract I'm about to undertake will have me in the arena instead of under it, if I don't deliver what Titus wants."

"You don't sound very worried," I say.

"You can't worry," he says. "You can only work hard and think fast."

"I'll try and remember that," I say.

As NIGHT FALLS, HE STOPS outside an inn, and asks for stabling, a room and a meal.

"Can I offer you the use of a girl?" asks the innkeeper.

"No, thanks," says Marcus, patting the horses as he hands over the reins to a stable hand.

"You have your own slave, of course," says the innkeeper. "Very pretty too," he adds, leering.

"She is," agrees Marcus without smiling and my stomach drops. I should have known I was too lucky with Lucius. Marcus will use me tonight and there is precious little I can do about it. I offer a quick prayer to Libertas, that he will be gentle, it is all I can hope for.

But once in our room Marcus only takes a rough blanket from the bed and indicates that I should use it to sleep on the floor.

"Thank you," I say, surprised and unsure whether I am thanking him or Libertas, whether this is a one-off kindness or what I can expect always.

HE WAKES ME VERY EARLY. We have eaten some stale bread and a handful of olives and mounted before the sun has risen. It is cold and I am glad of his warm back. I press against him a little, emboldened by his courteous treatment of me last night.

"So was Lucius a good master?"

"Yes," I say.

"You didn't look like you had much to do," he observes.

"No," I say. "I mostly did the social engagements and salutatios; he had another scribe for the business side. His wife said a man of means should have a Greek scribe for his social life, someone who looked elegant. She said his usual scribe was too coarse for the sort of society he was moving into."

"Like her family?"

"Yes."

"I don't know what you'll think of the kind of people I do business with, then," he says. I can't see his face, but he sounds amused. "Gladiators, actors, prostitutes. The disreputable class."

I'm not sure what to say, so I say nothing. It is not my place as a slave to comment on my master's business.

"Still," he says, "I do know some of the better classes. When we arrive in Rome we'll stay with a Vestal Virgin."

"A Vestal Virgin?"

He laughs at my tone. "I should say she *was* a Vestal Virgin. Chosen when she was six years old. Served her time and then got married after the thirty years were over."

"Really?"

"I know, not many do. But she fell in love with a carpenter and married him. A nobody. Her family had nothing to do with her after that. But she's a good woman and he was a good man."

"Was?"

"He died after only a few years of marriage. Left her a crumbling insula. She filled it with all the down and outs who couldn't afford rent elsewhere. I had a room there for a while when I left the army, before I made my way to Pompeii."

"Is that where your family is from?"

"No. We're originally from the countryside near Puteoli, we'll pass it this morning. But after my grandfather lost the family farm we moved away, down the coast to Pompeii, so no-one would know us, not that it matters now. Plenty of work in Pompeii for my father. I joined the army and was stationed in Alexandria in Egypt, until Vespasian was declared Emperor. Got wounded in a skirmish and was discharged. Came back to Pompeii just as they were about to reopen the amphitheatre and they liked the idea of an ex-centurion keeping the plebs in order."

WE PASS PUTEOLI WITHOUT ENTERING the city, but only a little further down the northern road towards Rome, Marcus turns off the main road and onto a country track.

"Where are we going?" I ask.

"I want to see something," he says.

We pass a couple of farms, one close, one further away in the fields, before turning off again, this time down a track that looks like it barely gets any use, with tall grasses brushing against our legs. We pass through a little scrub of young trees, forcing us to duck our heads, and then emerge into a wider clearing.

"There it is," Marcus says.

Nearby is an abandoned farm and its buildings, set in an overgrown meadow, above olive groves and a stream that winds its way through the shallow valley. Marcus jumps down from the horse and I follow him, the horses left behind to munch on bushes while we wade through the long grass.

The outer gateway, set into a surrounding wall the height of Marcus' head, is open to anyone who wishes to enter, its wooden gate long gone. We pass through and find ourselves in the main courtyard, an olive mill to one side of us with cracked amphorae buried to one side of it, fallen beehives in a far corner, a dovecote beyond it, still standing. A sudden fluttering greets our arrival. One wall is a stable block, the stalls standing empty. I look back at the horses, but they are happy enough. In front of us is the main house, two storeys high, its shutters and door closed up. Low outbuildings complete the square of the outer wall, pigsties and chicken sheds now bereft of their former occupants. A pergola runs the length of the house, heavy with an unpruned vine and the remnants of its fruits. Marcus is walking the perimeter of the courtyard. I make my way to the pergola and find a few last bunches of grapes, the rest, no doubt, eaten by the doves. The grapes are a dark purple and very sweet with a fresh fragrance to them.

"Strawberry grapes," says Marcus from behind me.

He is right, the fragrance is of fresh berries rather than grapes. "I've never had this variety before," I say.

"I loved them as a child," he says, reaching up to pluck a bunch of his own and dropping a few grapes on the ground for the gods. "You never find them in the markets. Make a good wine, too. Might not be the best Falernian but it's very drinkable and doesn't give you the headaches you get from the local Vesuvinum and Pompeianum wines. There's a small vineyard on the other side," he adds, pointing beyond the back of the house.

We stand eating for a few moments, spitting the pips to the ground. "Is this the family farm Domina mentioned?" I ask.

He nods. "Did she tell you the story?"

"Your grandfather gambled it."

"Foolish old bastard. Yes. He couldn't help himself, he gambled everything he had and then he went too far. He ruined our family."

"Can you buy it back?"

"That was my plan when I came back from the army but at the time the man who won it was still alive and he set the price too high. Now he's dead and his heirs would sell, but I need more money, they're a greedy bunch. It doesn't look like much, but it has a lot of good land. If I can get the amphitheatre inaugurated successfully, I'll be able to buy it outright and my family will be able to hold their heads high again." He spits more seeds. "Besides, it's not just that. I liked this place, I grew up here. I enjoyed the life. I'd be a happy farmer."

"You wouldn't miss what you do now?"

He laughs out loud. "Oh, it has its fun moments. I have the best team a man could wish for, all of them mad, all of them fiercely loyal to me. We put on the best shows Pompeii has ever seen. But..." He puts more grapes in his mouth.

"But?"

He sighs before answering. "The gladiators are my friends and it hurts when one of them dies. The women we use for the shows are prostitutes and they get badly treated by clients from time to time and there's little that can be done about it. The animals are mostly terrified, we have to goad them to fight. The criminals we put to death: I have no quarrel with their sentence, but it would be kinder to cut their throats than make them re-enact some bloody myth."

"Why did you choose it then?"

"I didn't have much choice at the time." He spits some more seeds and half-laughs. "It turned out I was good at it. I kept the peace in the audience, I put on shows everyone remembered. I find ways to manage things that I think are right. Mostly."

I think back to the dinner at Lucius'. "Like keeping household slaves out of the way of being groped at your events?"

He grins. "Spotted that, did you? Fausta is my best woman. She should have my job. No-one lays hands on her without her permission, whether they know it or not." He looks around the courtyard. "We'd better go. I couldn't resist seeing it, since we were passing."

I follow him towards the gateway.

"So now you know my dream," he says over his shoulder. "What I work for. What's yours?"

"I'm a slave," I remind him.

"Everyone has a dream," he says, pulling the lead horse away from its meal. "What's yours?"

I don't answer.

He pulls himself up, reaches out a hand to me. There's no mounting block here, I'm going to struggle. I do my best and after a failed attempt he pulls hard enough that I only just avoid falling, grabbing hold of his waist for balance. Once we're settled, he turns the horse's head back into the thicket. "Your freedom, I suppose?" he says, ducking his head.

I duck my own head just in time to avoid getting a branch in my face. "I am loyal to you, Dominus," I say awkwardly. The friendliness I had felt between us evaporates. It is unthinkable for a slave to tell their master to their face that they want to be set free, it makes them sound like a troublemaker.

He snorts. "Every slave wants to be free," he says, as we emerge back onto the track that will bring us back to the main road. "Besides, I think you have already tried and failed for your freedom."

My stomach turns over and a hot flush rises to my cheeks. I'm glad he can't see my face. "Dominus?"

"Not all slaves wear a slave collar," he says calmly. "Mostly just the ones who have tried to run away. And yours may not be a cheap metal collar, but a fancy gold cuff that tells people to whom you should be returned if you're caught is as good as a slave collar."

I say nothing.

"We will make a deal," he says, after a pause. "You will be utterly loyal to me. You will work hard and think fast. And when the hundred days of the inaugural Games are over and I have been rewarded, I will leave with my family to buy the farm and I will set you free with a purse of money, to live as you wish, a freedwoman. We will both achieve our dreams in the arena."

I swallow. "As you say, Dominus." I fight not to feel a thrill of excitement. I still don't know if I can trust him to keep his word, but if there is a chance to be set free…

"Call me Marcus," he says. "But you must be more than my slave. You will work harder than you have ever worked before, but you are working for your freedom, so it is worth it. You will be my right-hand woman, as Fausta has been in Pompeii. Is it a deal?"

I think of tall, bare-breasted Fausta and her quick eyes, her broad shoulders, her loud voice. I am not sure being compared to a prostitute would be a compliment from anyone but Marcus, but there is something about the way he speaks of her, a real respect as though he were speaking of a man, that makes me feel differently about the comparison. "I will do my best, Domin-Marcus."

"Good," he says with satisfaction. "Then we will do well together. And if you're still wondering, I am not about to bed you, this evening or any other night. I have Livia and she is enough for me."

My shoulders slump in relief.

He laughs at the movement of my body. "I'm glad you are so relieved," he says. "I will tell my wife I am far uglier than she seems to think I am."

I give a small gasp of a laugh, unsure of whether I have just offended my strange new master.

"You'll get used to my ways and the work," he says. "But it will be a different kind of life for a dainty scribe slave from the fancy villas of the Caelian Hill. Prepare to rough it."

We have rejoined the main road. Soon we will join the Appian Way, which will lead us to the very gates of Rome. An ox cart rumbles past us, its noisy wheels all but obscuring my reply. "I am ready."

ON THE FOURTH DAY I sit a little straighter. We have made excellent time, even though my behind is aching from days of riding. The tall umbrella pines of the last stretch of the Appian Way make me feel at home. I forget how vast the city is every time I leave Rome and return to her. This last part of the journey is a mess of noise and traffic, the rumble of wheels, shouting and curses all around us. The evening will bring the carters and traders, only permitted to enter the city at night to drop off their wares, in an effort to leave the streets passable in the daytime, and so we find ourselves swept up in a rush towards the city gates.

There are shouts behind us and the sound of a horse at full gallop. I twist in my seat in time to see an imperial messenger on a sweating horse, who thunders past and on to the city gate, other traffic scattering before them.

"Feathers," says Marcus.

"What?"

"He was carrying feathers. Bad news."

"From where?"

"Who knows," says Marcus with a shrug, caught up in trying to guide our two horses through the city gate, fighting for a place in the throng. "May Roma bless and protect us in her city," he adds as we enter. I murmur an echo, anxious. Coming back to Rome should mean heading towards the Forum and then east to the wealthy region of the Caelian Hill and Lucius' home, which in turn is close to my first master's home. But Marcus turns the horse's head towards the river, and we make our way along it until we come to the bridge by the island.

"We are going to cross the Tiber?" I ask. The Trans Tiberim is a rough district, known for the stench of its tanneries and its overcrowded backstreets filled with the lower classes and Jews. No one of high class would willingly head there. I cannot imagine a Vestal Virgin residing there and I'm not sure I am brave enough to live there myself. Lucius may have said I knew Rome like the back of my hand but in truth a female slave to two rich households knows little more of Rome than the Forum and the shops and houses of her masters' own district.

Marcus chuckles. "Not quite. We're in the Ninth Region, the Circus Flaminius. Just off Sand Street."

"Sand Street?"

"Sand builds up in that area when the Tiber floods. It's a nuisance in winter. The locals call the side street we're on Virgin's Street because of Julia."

I'm relieved we aren't actually going to cross the Tiber, a step too far away from the areas I've known all my life. But I know nothing of the Ninth Region except it has a Circus barely worthy of the name, just a big oval of land without a proper racetrack, nor any seating. It's spoken of disparagingly by the higher classes, as a place less for entertainment and more of a vegetable market for plebs. Still, if Marcus knows the area, I can only hope I will be in safe hands. My days on the Caelian Hill feel like a long time ago.

Sand Street is broad and full of traffic, the first carters of the evening arriving with their slow ox-pulled carts, ponderously making their way with little heed for those trying to adopt a brisker pace. Many of the deliveries are of tanned skins, to be dropped off at leather workers and cobblers around the city. I catch an acrid whiff of the tanneries from the other side of the river. There's grumpy shouting up ahead and I'm glad when we turn off to the left, into a small street. A large four-storey insula towers above us. There's a broad green wooden gate that's barely hanging on to its hinges. On the ground floor of the insula, further up the street to our left, is a bakery, although it's closed for now, its shutters pulled to. To the right of the door, taking advantage of the corner of the building to give it two possible streams of customers, is a popina. There's a girl inside lighting lanterns while an older man is laying out big covered dishes of food to keep warm, but no evening customers as yet.

"It looks like a breath of wind would knock it down," I say, looking up at the insula. "It wouldn't last one morning in Pompeii with all the tremors we've been having lately."

Marcus laughs and slips down from the horse in one smooth moment, leaving me to drop less graciously to the ground. "You'd think so, but it's still standing ten years since I thought the very same. Vesta must continue to bless her handmaiden." He ties the horses up to a metal ring set into the wall and whistles loudly, attracting the attention of two little boys playing on the kerb. "If these two get stolen I'll give you a thrashing," he says, pointing at the horses with a cheerful grin.

"If they don't get stolen, do we get a coin?" asks the older boy.

Marcus winks. "You never know."

The boys jump up and stand by the horses, adopting fierce poses for nobody's benefit. Marcus pulls down the saddlebags and gives me one to carry. I follow him to the green gate, which he shoulders open, ignoring the rusty creaking.

The courtyard paving inside is as run-down as the building around it, cracked and uneven, weeds growing through the mortar. But all around the edges and dangling from every balcony all the way up to the third floor are tubs of flowers and plants, tumbling down or creeping upwards, spilling colour and greenery all over the faded and cracked walls, which must once have been painted the usual white with a dark red band on the ground floor. The white is now more of a memory, the red a blotched orange.

"Julia! JULIA! Visitors!"

The deafening bellow echoes round the courtyard. I'm surprised to match it to a large woman on the second floor who is sitting on her balcony, arms settled around a cushion balanced on the railing, there to support ample breasts. She is clad in a bold blue tunic, her palla tightly wrapped about her against the cool of twilight.

Marcus is laughing out loud. "Maria! You're still here! And better than any guard dog, as ever."

The woman peers over the balcony edge at us and then smiles broadly. "Marcus? Has Roma brought you back to us? And still just as handsome."

Marcus laughs. "How could I stay away from you? My wife is sick of hearing your name."

"Married? About time! Is that her?"

"This is my slave, Althea. Livia is at home in Pompeii, she will join me soon."

"And children?"

"One, a boy."

"May the Great Mother Cybele bless him."

Marcus nods his head in thanks.

"Marcus!"

Marcus turns and smiles, opens up his arms. "Julia!"

A woman is walking down the rickety wooden stairwell leading to the upper floors. She is perhaps fifty, of average height and beauty, nothing that anyone would remark on. But she carries herself in a way that only the Vestal Virgins do, I would know her for one at once, even without the white robes and red-bound hair. There is a practised grace to her, a certainty that people will step back and bow their heads, the knowing one is always, always observed. Even in a plain violet tunic and an unadorned green palla, she makes me want to take a step backwards from her presence. I can feel my head bowing without having thought about it. Marcus, however, steps forward and greets her at the foot of the staircase, the two of them relaxed with one another, a warm embrace between old friends. Marcus turns back towards me, waving an arm in my direction.

"This is Althea," he says.

"His slave girl," supplies Maria from above, keen to pass on the new gossip. "He has a wife now, though, and a son."

Julia looks in my direction. Her expression is solemn, but her eyes stay very steady on me for far longer than a slave would merit. I blink under her gaze.

"Welcome, Althea," she says at last. "May Roma welcome you to her city and protect you while you are here."

She speaks the words like a priestess, a formal prayer, not a casual blessing like most people throw into conversations. I feel I ought to be kneeling. I can't think of how to reply but she has turned back to Marcus.

"Still so brown," she says, patting him on the arm. "You look as though you never left the army. The amphitheatre is not a place for a soft life, I see."

"It is not," says Marcus. "And my life is not about to get easier. I have been tasked with something beyond my expectations. Hence my return to Rome after all this time."

"Come and tell me all about it," she says. "I will make a meal. Althea, you can take the bags to the roof. There is a little building there where you can both sleep. It is the larger of the two up there. I am sorry, Marcus," she adds to him. "If I had known you were coming, I would have offered you better sleeping quarters, but the insula is full at present. There are some soldiers staying who will be leaving soon, you will have a better lodging as soon as they depart."

"We are happy to lay down our heads wherever there is space," says Marcus. "I came in haste, there was no time to let you know we were on our way."

"Return to us afterwards," says Julia to me. "We will be in my apartment, it is just through there." She indicates a doorway on the first floor, at the far end of the courtyard. "Take the lamp with you," she adds, nodding up at a lamp burning on the first-floor balcony.

I take the two sets of saddlebags and make my way up the stairway, then add the lamp to my burden, staggering slightly to get my balance, my satchel bumping awkwardly against the arm carrying the lamp. I am being watched intently by Maria; I can feel her gaze on me. I'm glad to reach the rooftop and feel less scrutinised.

The rooftop is large, encircling the courtyard below, edged only with a thin wooden railing that I would not care to trust with my safety, old amphorae stacked here and there, some of them broken. In the corner nearby is a ramshackle little wooden hut, opposite, on the far side of the building is another, even smaller, with three beehives next to it. I edge my way into the closest hut, disturbing a flock of doves that take off from the rooftop with a wild fluttering of startled wings. Inside the hut the flickering lamp shows me an empty space, dusty with neglect. There is a man's chamber pot in the corner, but it has such a deep crack down one side that I am not sure it will survive even one night's service, and there is nothing for a woman. There are no beds, I can only hope Julia has some sleeping mats or we'll be on the bare floor. I gladly drop the saddlebags before removing my own satchel and placing it in the corner furthest from the chamber pot, hoping to avoid any unwary night-time accidents. There's a rough wooden ledge on one wall, which will be handy for placing a lamp.

Bags dropped, there's nothing to keep me here and I need the toilet, I hope the insula has one somewhere. Julia will be able to direct me, although it will feel strange to ask a Vestal Virgin where I can relieve myself. I pull the decrepit door open again and step outside, almost shoving my lamp into a face. I step back with a yelp.

"Who are you, girl?" In front of me is an old woman, shoulders hunched, neck twisted forward. Her dark clothes are faded, ragged here and there. Her face is deeply wrinkled. She is wearing a sort of cap over her head.

I try and gather myself. "Althea."

"Greek," she says.

"Yes."

"What are you doing here, a young woman alone? You're not a prostitute, are you? I won't live near a whore."

I blink, still confused by her sudden appearance. "I'm a scribe," I say. "A slave. My master is a friend of Julia's. We have come to Rome to work."

"Work as what?"

"Managing the Amphitheatre."

"What amphitheatre?"

"The Flavian Amphitheatre being built near the Forum. Emperor Titus is to inaugurate it next year —"

But at the name, the old woman draws back from me, her face crumples into a grimace of anger. "Titus? *Yimakh shemo!*" she says, and spits.

"What?"

"May his name be erased."

"I don't understand."

"He defiled and plundered the Holy Temple of Jerusalem, then burnt it to the ground. That place you mentioned, I will not speak its name, neither now nor ever. It is built from the blood and the gold of my people. And their sweat too," she adds as an afterthought. "Half the prisoners of war brought back to Rome are being used as slaves to work on it."

"You are a Jewess?" I ask.

She nods, peering up at me from her twisted shoulders. I think of the triumphal procession Titus received on his return, the endless treasures and prisoners of war from Jerusalem, paraded through the streets. In the vast crowd Cornelia and I waved palms and branches of laurels and shouted till we grew hoarse, excited by the floats and falling flower petals, the endless heavy marching feet of victorious soldiers bearing their standards thudding in our stomachs, giddy with twirling dancers and trumpets. Later we danced until Cornelia's mother said it wasn't proper for a girl from a good family to be dancing in the streets, making a spectacle of herself. It was a day of fun and celebrations, of Rome's triumph over some distant nation; I hadn't thought till now that it was a temple that was plundered.

"I am sorry," I say. "It was wrong of them to dishonour the god of your country."

She shakes her head. "What would you know? You are nothing but a child," she says. Her rage seems to have left her, she shrinks in height to a weary huddle, wrapping her shawl more tightly about her from the cold. "Go back to your master."

"Where do you live?" I ask.

She points into the growing gloom, over at the other hut. "There."

"Alone?"

"Who else is there?"

"Are you warm enough?"

She blinks at me. "What would you care?"

"I wouldn't want anyone to be cold."

Her face softens a little. "Good child," she mutters as though to herself. "A good child. I do well enough."

"I'll bid you goodnight, then," I say awkwardly, but she is already shuffling away from me, back to her hut. I make a mental note to warn Marcus of her existence, in case she startles him, too.

I make my way back down the staircase. It sways alarmingly and I wonder how firmly it is secured to the wall. I grip the bannister tightly and hope for the best.

"Met Adah, did you?"

I've reached the second floor and Maria has been watching me. Now that I'm level with her I can see she's shorter than she seems from the courtyard, although her breadth makes up for her lack of height.

"Is that the Jewess?"

"Yes."

"She didn't like me mentioning Titus."

"She says he will be punished for what he did to her people, now that he's Emperor."

"Do you believe her?"

"She's a mad old woman," says Maria. "Although," she adds, thinking it over, "they did defile a temple and that's not a thing to do, is it, whoever your gods are? What if their god is still able to punish Titus for desecrating their holy place? Look at what happened to Nero after he looted half the temples in Rome and the Empire to pay for his grandiose building plans."

I shake my head. "How does she live?"

"She sells the honey from her bees, it keeps her going. Heading back down? Can you find your way?"

"I think so," I say. "But I need the toilet. Is there one?"

"There is. Ground floor, just off the courtyard that way," she says, leaning perilously over the edge of the balcony to indicate a small door.

"Thank you," I say.

THE TOILETS ARE SHABBY, FIVE seats, not many for an insula this size and there's a smell that indicates the drains here are less than adequate. I think of my previous masters' houses, where there were ten seats just for the slaves and servants and running water was something we took for granted. There's no fountain in the courtyard here, I notice, so I can see it'll be me on daily trips to the nearest public fountain for water to drink and wash with. At least there are old amphorae all over the rooftop, I'll be able to find one or two that aren't cracked.

WHEN I FIND JULIA AND Marcus they are sat at a table, eating a thick bean stew with bread and olives. Julia passes me a generous plateful and I nod in thanks without interrupting their conversation, then take a seat on a stool to one side in the room. I'm tired, but the food is good and I'm grateful to be somewhere peaceful after the long journey.

"And Livia is happy to move here?" asks Julia, continuing their conversation.

"She will miss her family," says Marcus, ripping a piece of bread. "But it is only for a couple of years and then we will be able to go to the farm. She will like that, and it will be good for the boy."

"She will be welcome. I'm sure an apartment will be available soon."

"Thank you," says Marcus. "Livia will need a friend here, she's never even been to Rome. She will find it a little overwhelming."

"She will have Althea?"

"No, Althea will be too busy working with me. But we have a good girl at home, Anna. She's cheerful and works hard, we'll bring her along."

I think of Myrtis. Perhaps I'll be able to see her one day when we are settled. Lucius' house is not far from the amphitheatre. She will feed me her honey cakes and I'll tell her all about the new work and what Marcus has promised me. She'll probably be disbelieving, Myrtis always was a pessimist, but Felix will grunt and say that freedom is worth trying for, that perhaps the gods are smiling on me.

"Althea?"

"Sorry," I say. "I was thinking."

"Your eyes are tired," says Julia. "Time to sleep. As I recall, Marcus wakes horribly early. By the time the sun rose he was always gone. And tomorrow is the big day?"

He nods. "I'll be signing the contract and seeing the amphitheatre for the first time."

"Then take the sleeping mats from the corner and get some sleep. Althea, there are two blankets on the chair."

Sleeping mats are heavy, but Marcus lifts them as though they were nothing. "Carry up the lamp," he tells me and so I walk ahead of him up the dark internal staircase. On the whole, I prefer the rickety wooden contraption outside.

We don't speak. Marcus throws down the two mats in the hut, I lay out the blankets and we both lie down. Marcus is snoring by the time I have even thought through everything that has happened today. I relax. We have made it this far. We are back in Rome, if not quite in the sort of house I have been used to. Tomorrow we will visit the amphitheatre, I think sleepily. It must have changed since I last saw it, several months ago.

THE ASHEN SKY

I WAKE EARLY, THE SKY STILL dim. Pompeii's morning noise is nothing to Rome. Endless carts trundling by, hurrying to get out of the city early, for they are only permitted to make deliveries until a certain hour. Curses involving just about every deity float up to the rooftops. I creep out of the hut and make my way over to the outer edge of the roof, peering cautiously over the wall. I wonder if there will be space for us to walk safely, so narrow and busy is Virgin's Street. Sand Street may be wider, but it will be even busier. At the opposite corner of the rooftop the bees are already coming and going from their hives. There is the smell of woodsmoke as thousands of fires are lit across the capital, in homes and businesses.

I tiptoe back to the hut to get my shoes. If I can find an uncracked amphora, I can fetch washing water from the nearest public fountain.

"Take my purse."

I startle.

Marcus has woken. He has one arm over his eyes but gestures vaguely with the other hand. "I'll be downstairs in a moment."

"I was going to fetch washing water."

"We'll go to the baths later. Right now, we need food and then we'll go straight to the amphitheatre, I want to get there early. Go to the popina downstairs and order breakfast. I'll be there shortly."

I pack our clothes and pick up his purse, worn old leather, but heavy enough. He is taking a risk, letting a new slave walk out of a lodging house with a purse of money in a city the size of Rome. But where would I go? With a gold cuff on my arm that on closer inspection marks me as a slave? I make my way downstairs, use the toilet, then step cautiously out onto the street, glancing left and right and keeping well back against the wall out of the way of too-fast carts. To my right is the bakery, from where the good smell of fresh bread is coming. I turn left to the popina. The shutters are up and there's a wide counter against which bleary-eyed customers are half-leaning, munching bread and cheese. Two men who look the worse for wear are dipping their bread in wine as though to continue last night's fun.

The insula above us may look as if a good puff of wind would bring it tumbling down, but the bread smells good, no doubt from the bakery next door, and the girl at the counter has a cheerful smile under tumbling black curls, escaping her attempts to tie them back.

"Morning, love, what'll it be?"

I find a space that will fit two of us at the counter and lean an elbow on it for comfort. "Bread and cheese for one and…" I look behind her and see a jug of what I was hoping for. "Pancake with date syrup?"

She nods and pours batter out of the jug onto a hot griddle, then flips it over expertly while laying out bread and cheese. Scribbled on the wall at the edge of the popina is graffiti which declares, 'Hands off Cassia, she's mine,' next to which someone else has retorted 'Use your hands on yourself, Cassia is too good for you.' I wonder if the serving girl is Cassia and whether she manages to fend off her admirers if they get a bit too amorous of an evening.

"Marry me, Cassia!" calls a trader from the street as his cart rumbles by.

"Don't let my father hear you!" she calls back with a grin. "You don't want to feel the end of his stick!"

"You really don't," mutters one of the men eating wine-dipped bread. "Made me see stars."

Cassia brings the two dishes just as Marcus joins me. "Ah, I thought you were going to eat double helpings," she laughs at me.

Marcus nods to her and grimaces as I bite into the pancake. "Oh, a sweet tooth?" he comments. "Never really took to sweet foods first thing in the morning." He bites hungrily into the bread and cheese. "Good bread. Hate the stale stuff."

"That's the advantage of being next door to a bakery," Cassia says with a smile.

"I really don't know how this building is still standing," says Marcus. He leans back to look upwards at the crumbling insula.

"Perhaps Vesta looks out for it, since it belongs to her handmaiden," says Cassia over her shoulder, now frying another pancake for an elderly man who has taken the place of the two hungover customers.

"Bad luck to marry a Vestal Virgin," mumbles the old man. "Vesta does not share her handmaidens."

Cassia shrugs. "Julia is a kind woman," she says. "She was devastated when her husband died. I heard her crying like a child for months afterwards."

"And now?" I ask.

"She hasn't got a lot, but she keeps the rents low and looks out for others. The insula may be crumbling, but everyone gets by."

"We need to go," says Marcus.

"See you later," I say to Cassia. "We're staying for a few days."

She nods and smiles as we leave.

It takes all our concentration to cross Sand Street safely.

"I've never met a retired Vestal Virgin before," I start to say, but get distracted by Marcus leading us down a street so tiny I could touch the walls on either side with my arms outstretched. It stinks of piss and I fear, given the early hour, that someone will empty a chamber pot over our heads from above, rather than bothering to empty it in their building's toilets. I keep my clothes and satchel pulled close to me in case they touch anything and try not to breathe through my nose. "How do you know the way?" I ask.

"We need to head south-east," he says, which I know, although in this mess of tiny back streets I can't understand how he's keeping track of what direction we are headed in. I'm hopelessly lost. I don't have much choice but to follow him, so I offer a quick prayer to Mercury. The messenger of the gods must at least know how to find his way about Rome. No doubt, having been in the army, Marcus can look out for us if there's any trouble, but I still think I'd have preferred the main roads, however busy they are. A few people give us odd glances, knowing we aren't locals, and I catch one or two men leering at me. I keep close to Marcus.

When we emerge from the tangle of backstreets though, I glimpse the Forum in the distance and my shoulders relax. From here I know my way and at least we've left the worst of the stink behind. Plus, there's more room to walk here and less chance of chamber pots.

The Forum is already busy. Smoke drifts from the domed roof of Vesta's temple, assuring everyone that her fire still burns, tended by the Vestal Virgins within, ensuring that Rome will not fall. Street vendors are setting up little stands here and there, soothsayers and astrologers prepare for their day's work. The streetcleaners rest on their brooms, chatting rather than finishing their work. Beneath the basilica's colonnade the lawyers gather, ready to do business or take on new clients.

"Tell your fortune, Dominus, Domina?" calls out a woman as I pass. Her wrinkled eyes are thickly rimmed with soot, her hair is an unlikely jet-black and adorned with little gold beads in the Egyptian fashion. A mangy leopard skin has been spread out before her, on which are laid out her talismans and other tools of her trade. My half-decent tunic, leather satchel and especially the gold cuff I am wearing must make her think I am Marcus' wife rather than his slave. "I see great things for you both!" she adds as Marcus strides by with me trotting to keep up with his longer legs. "But warnings also, oh yes, you would do well to heed my warnings," she delivers to my back. My past mistress used to spend a fortune on these people, having her chart or palm read, listening with bated breath to their revelations, while Lucius scoffed and forbade her from inviting them to peddle their wares in the house.

Now that we are out in an open space, I can look about me. The morning is crisp and clear, one of those beautiful autumn days where one would swear it was the end of summer rather than close to the start of winter. The sky is a sharp blue, the rising sun still has some warmth to it. Ahead, and far above us, the Colossus glitters, the golden body of Nero now topped with the sun god's head so as not to waste such a fine statue. And next to it is the Flavian Amphitheatre, hundreds of workers already gathered around it, coming in and out of the great arches with tools, materials and carts. I can't help but feel a thrill. It is a vast undertaking and the spectacles that will be put on here will be the greatest in the Empire, that much I can be sure of. The closer we get, the further back my head has to tilt to take in its full height.

I nearly bump into the back of Marcus, who has stopped abruptly in front of me.

"Something wrong?" I ask, coming round to his side and seeing a frown on his face.

"No velarium?" he says, shading his eyes.

I follow his glance. At the top of any theatre or amphitheatre there should be a set of high wooden poles, forming the anchoring points of the awning which will stretch out across rigging, bringing shade to most of the seats on the blisteringly hot summer days. No audience can sit for long on the hottest days without an awning.

"Doesn't look like it's been built yet," I say.

"Make a note," he says. "Velarium."

I fumble in my satchel, pull out my tablet and stylus and jot down the word. Marcus is still standing, head turning from one side to the other, taking in the surrounding area. He nods to himself and straightens his shoulders, lifting his chin as though going into battle. I follow him through the largest entrance and onto a half-built wooden arena floor in the centre of the amphitheatre.

I can't help staring around me. I've been in a few amphitheatres, but this is on a different scale. It's still being built, but the main structure is in place and it is truly vast. Even the arena floor is double the size of any I've ever seen. I look upwards, at the rows upon rows of seating, mostly complete. The very top section is still being constructed, white stone slabs being fitted into place by sweating stonemasons and their teams who have had to carry them to the highest areas.

A distinguished looking man in an immaculate toga is standing a little way off. He is surrounded by five assistants, two of whom at least are scribes, I can see their own tablets at the ready. We make our way over to him.

"I am Marcus Aquillius Scaurus, I have been appointed as Manager for the Games. Are you the head architect?"

"I am," says the man, preening a little.

"Excellent," says Marcus. "I have a number of points to cover with you this morning."

The architect looks down his long nose. "I am sure you will find that everything has been designed on a more than magnificent scale and with every attention to detail," he says.

Marcus doesn't look impressed by this statement. "Why don't you tell me about it, and I'll ask questions as you go along," he suggests.

The architect nods as though he is doing Marcus a favour and takes up a pose, opening with a broad sweep of his arm as though he is acting a part in a play. "It is the largest amphitheatre in the Empire. It will seat fifty thousand people at the very least, although you know how slaves and the rougher sort cram themselves in," he adds with distaste. He waits for a nod, but Marcus only raises his eyebrows, and the architect continues. "There will be four seating areas. The first is the podium, that's for the patricians, senators and their guests, our most distinguished patrons. Best view in the amphitheatre, close to all the action. There are four terraces, but they are very broad, so you will be able to provide chairs for each performance. They'll have their own cloakrooms and latrines on this level. The podium level includes the Emperor's box and the box for the Vestal Virgins, facing him on the other side of the arena, a similar design but a little smaller. The next tier has a larger capacity, that's nine marble terraces for the equestrian class, but sitting on the terrace itself. They can bring cushions, as one does at the theatre. Then two more tiers, which hold thirty terraces between them, they seat everyone else. Slaves and women in the very top tiers at the back." He points at the work currently underway. "We're doing those in white travertine stone. You can't tell the difference too much from a distance, but the equestrian class will appreciate knowing their tier is more refined. It's these sorts of details that matter." He looks upwards, shielding his eyes against the sun's glare. "There's the possibility of adding wooden seating into the very top tier in due course, behind those columns, if it proves popular, but right now we have our work cut out getting this lot done in time, so it'll be standing space only. Toilets on every tier, over one hundred drinking fountains across the building. We haven't even finished the main building works and there's still all the decorative touches: a specially commissioned sculpture of Emperor Vespasian driving a chariot at the imperial entrance leading to the Emperor's box, statues in the second and third tiers of arches outside. On the inside, stone carvings up all the balustrades and, of course, family names will be carved into the podium terraces. Not to mention the paintings: fighting and hunting scenes in all the corridors on the way to each terrace." He pauses for Marcus' appreciation of the vast task before them.

Marcus doesn't seem to be paying much attention. He is looking into the darkness below the half-built wooden arena floor. It's just wooden scaffolding, set into a plain brick floor below. "Can we flood it?"

"What?"

Marcus gestures downwards. "If the Emperor wants a naval battle, we'd have to flood the arena floor, to a depth of at least a man's head to allow for large enough vessels. So, it'll need waterproofing."

"To the depth of a man? It'll flood the service corridors!"

Marcus shrugs. "Watertight doors."

The architect looks flustered. "How would you fill it fast enough? And drain it?"

"I thought you'd already installed drainage in the plan."

"For rain, yes. Not for deliberately filling up the arena floor with water!"

"Isn't this built over what used to be Nero's lake?"

"Yes?"

"I should imagine it's marshy underfoot, it'll probably half-flood itself."

"We've gone to a great deal of trouble *not* to let it flood," protests the architect weakly.

"I suggest you build in the capacity for naval battles," says Marcus, as though the suggestion is only a minor alteration to the plans. "I will not be the one to tell the Emperor he can't have naval battles put on, if it turns out he wants them. Will you?"

The architect's shoulders slump. His scribe is already making notes, having quickly understood that this is not an argument his master will win. I can see '*waterproofing/ flooding/drainage*' appear on the tablet, in a very poorly formed shorthand. I'm surprised he can read it all back later on.

"It needs to both flood and drain in less than half an hour either way," Marcus adds.

"That's hardly any time at all!"

"It's not impressive if takes any longer."

"It might not be possible!"

Marcus looks around him at the hundreds of slaves, the dozens of surveyors, draughtsmen, engineers, masons, everyone already sweating in the warming sun. "It's your job to make it possible. Mine to make it impressive."

"Anything else?" asks the architect sullenly.

"I need lifts installed around the edges of the arena with trapdoors above, to release animals and gladiators."

"Oh yes," says the architect, relieved to be back in control. "We've planned all of that in."

"How many?"

"Thirty-six trap doors, twenty-eight lifts will be placed underneath."

"Pens for the animals?"

"Space for thirty-two, around the edges. Can't fit elephants though," he adds defiantly. "If you want those, they'll have to come in via one of the main entrances and you must stable them elsewhere."

"How many entrances?"

"There are seventy-six public entrances. Your ticket will tell you where you're seated and which entrance to use. They'll look something like this." He hands Marcus a small clay tablet, with numbers marked on it. It's very plain.

Marcus turns it over in his hands. "That'll be easy to copy then, won't it?"

"Copy?"

"Forgers," says Marcus, handing it back. "You'll have ticket touts all around the building, claiming to offer better tickets: in the shade, closer to the Emperor, closer to the action…"

"But they use these at all the theatres!"

"None of them seat fifty thousand people. By the time everyone's in and discovered there's sixty thousand tickets, it'll be too late, you won't see the touts for dust."

The architect looks as though he is about to cry, I almost feel sorry for him.

Marcus evidently doesn't. "What are the other four entrances for?"

"Four entrances have their own special uses. The Emperor has his own entrance leading to the imperial box. That's on the south side. Opposite is the magistrates' entrance and the Vestal Virgins' box. To the east is the Gate of Triumph, where the gladiatorial processions will enter. The west gate is the Gate of Death. That's the exit for the dead bodies and so on."

Marcus gestures to me. "Make a note: the criminals must arrive at least the day before they're to be executed, we'll keep them under the arena floor in a pen."

"Why?"

"I'm not having a cartload of criminals bump into the Vestal Virgins as they arrive."

I make a note. He's right. Any criminal who crosses the path of a Vestal Virgin can be pardoned and set free. It's a very rare occurrence and tolerated, but if cartloads of them are going to arrive for execution just as the Virgins arrive to see a show, I can see the authorities eventually getting annoyed.

Marcus has wandered away, back through one passageway and out into the connecting corridors. He leans out of one exterior arch, looking down at the area outside the amphitheatre, at the endless labourers and materials moving like ants through the dust. We follow him. Peering down makes my stomach turn over.

"There will be a wide pavement surrounding the amphitheatre," says the architect reassuringly. "We will complete it at the end of the building programme, and it will give a very smart impression as one approaches the arena."

"How are we supposed to manage the crowds into the right entrances?"

"I told you, they have their tickets, which have the right entrance number."

"So they'll all just mill around outside trying to find their entrance numbers? Fifty thousand people?"

"What would you suggest?"

Marcus looks back down. "Stone columns surrounding the building, about chest height, with holes so we can pass ropes through them."

"Ropes?"

"The ropes will create pathways leading to each entrance, so that people begin to move into the right entranceway as soon as they arrive near the building."

"Nowhere else –" begins the architect.

"This building has no equal," Marcus cuts him off. "So, it must have features that no other theatre or amphitheatre has. Now: how high is the wall surrounding the arena? Before the first row of seating?"

"Almost twice the height of a man."

"Are you fitting it with rollers?"

"What?"

"Rollers. You make them out of ivory from elephant tusks, it works very well. Marble's too heavy. Wood gets damaged too easily."

"I meant what for?"

Marcus looks weary. "Do you not attend Games, yourself?"

"Occasionally."

"Have you never noticed the rollers? Set around the arena walls just below the spectator walls? Columns about this high set against the wall, with the ability to roll on an axle, like a wheel but staying in one place?"

"I thought they were decorative."

"They're to stop animals leaping the wall into the spectators' seating."

The architect looks at the wall. He looks back at Marcus.

"Trust me, they can jump that," says Marcus. "And a senator does not want a lion in his lap."

"Marcus Aquillius Scaurus?"

We all turn. There's a senator standing behind us, with an entourage of bodyguards, scribes and various hangers-on.

"Aedile." The architect practically disappears into a deep bow. "We are honoured with your presence."

A lot of flourishing and bowing and elaborate introductions go on. We scribes step behind our masters and take notes for future reference. The senator does not, of course, recognise me, even though it was he who suggested Lucius employ me. The senator is in good humour, pleased that someone has been appointed to the role the Emperor has asked him to fill and which he promptly entrusted Lucius with sourcing.

The contract they go through, and which Marcus signs and adds his seal to, is binding in the extreme. He may not leave Rome without permission. He may not resign until at least the inauguration and one hundred days of Games have been completed to the Emperor's satisfaction. If the Emperor should in any way be displeased with his work, it will go very badly with him. Throughout it all, Marcus remains smiling and relaxed, although perhaps it's just for show. At last the senator is satisfied and leaves.

"I've seen enough for today," Marcus tells the architect. "I'll be back tomorrow."

"Surely we've covered everything?" protests the architect.

"Barely even started," says Marcus with a grin. "But I'm in urgent need of a good bath. Till tomorrow."

We make our way back to the Circus Flaminius. Marcus points upstream as we pass near the river. "One day we'll go and visit the stables."

"The racing stables?"

"The very ones. Might borrow charioteers for some of the Games, it adds to the spectacle. We can re-enact some exciting battles with them."

"Do you know people there?"

"Where do you think our horses are staying?"

"Your horses are in the racing stables?"

Marcus winks. "I know some people there. Have you met Celer?"

"No, who is he?"

"Lives at Julia's, in one of the little rooms on the top floor. Retired charioteer. Did well in his day, drove for the Blues. Spent it all on women and wine," he adds. "But he can tell you some wild stories of the stables."

Close to the Pantheon are the Baths of Agrippa, which are free to all. I make my way to the women's section. It's been a good while since I was given leave to go to the baths, before the dinner party even. I put my belongings in one of the cubbyholes in the changing rooms, making a show of how grubby my tunic is and wrapping it round my satchel, to make it less likely anyone will steal it. The hot water is bliss and afterwards I approach another slave girl and offer to help her wash if she will do the same for me. Having been rubbed down with, and then stripped of oil, my skin feels better than it has in days. I rub my hair with oil, then give it a vinegar rinse. At least now it will be easier to comb. I pull on my clean tunic and wrap up my hair to be combed out later.

Marcus looks refreshed too, in clean clothes, his beard trimmed short and his hair cut. "Food," he says as a greeting. "We'll buy what's needed so Julia does not have to cook for us every day."

We return to Julia's with late grapes and melons, olives and cheese as well as still-warm breads picked up at the bakery. Marcus has added pickles and roasted spiced chickpeas to the bounty. I lay the table and pass them both plates of food, then take my own dish to the balcony, where I eat while watching the inhabitants come and go. Maria keeps up a running commentary for my benefit, mostly focused on the shops, complete with workshops, on the ground floor of the building.

"That's the baker's family: the parents are looking after the children while their son and daughter-in-law work, though on busy days it's all hands needed, even the little ones. That's Balbus the toymaker and his wife Floriana. He stutters, you know. Can't get five words out together. But they make beautiful toys, even sell them up on the Palantine Hill, the best households call them in for their spoiled brats. Rest of the workshop space on the ground floor is the cobbler's shop. He does a lot of work for the army. Good work that, never run out of business. Even supplies the Praetorian Guard. Could have a fancier place, but he says Julia brings him luck. Whole of this insula pays a lot of respect to Vesta."

Given that Maria seems to know everything about everyone, I venture the question I've been asking myself.

"I thought Vestal Virgins were rich when they retired. How did Julia end up with a crumbling insula and not much else?"

"The Vestal Virgins end up rich because some people leave them money in their wills. Julia gave away almost everything she had when she got married. She told me once she'd rather offer a real hearth and home to the people of Rome than stand guard for thirty years over a make-believe hearth." Maria frowns slightly, evidently viewing this statement as borderline heresy, but unable to argue with the charitable intention behind it. "That's why this insula is full of waifs and strays as well as respectable people," she adds, straightening her shoulders to indicate her own position as firmly in the respectable camp.

ON OUR SECOND DAY I at least recognise a couple of the streets on our way to the amphitheatre. When we arrive, Marcus announces his intention to walk all the way round it.

"Meet me inside," he says.

I walk through the arches, skirting round cartloads of gleaming white stone and already-sweating men. Inside, standing on the half-built arena floor, I am struck again by the size. I look upwards to the most complete side, and decide to climb up to the highest seats, to see what the view is like. My thigh muscles are aching within a few steps. By the time I get to the top seats I'm panting. I turn, thrilled at the height, the perilous swoop down to the arena floor. The view is still excellent, although not quite what the Emperor and his cronies will see: their seats are such that they will hear the gasps of dying men and smell their blood. From up here, it will be more like a play, a pretence of death rather than the reality of it. This is where the women sit, and they are less likely to desire the intimacy of death. The Games are mostly a man's world, although one hears whispers about wealthy women who pay good money to be taken to a gladiator's bedchamber the night before he must fight to the death, the tragic romance of it titillating them, not to mention the simple fact that a dead man is a lot more discreet than a live lover. I shade my eyes from the bright sun and wonder when Marcus will arrive.

"Enjoying the view?"

I twist to look up at Marcus. "How did you get behind me? I never saw you climb up."

He jerks his thumb over his shoulder to a treadmill at the very top of the building site. "Got myself hoisted over the wall like a block of marble," he says, as though this is an everyday way to arrive in an amphitheatre. He sits beside me and looks down at the arena floor, then takes out a pocket sundial. He looks at it, then puts it away again. "It's going to be dark down there," he says.

"Down where?"

"Under the arena. It's where you and I are going to be spending a good deal of our time. Make a note: we need to buy several water clocks for timekeeping. Sundials aren't going to be of much use in the dark."

"Is timekeeping very important?"

He grins at my ignorance. "If I release a lion at the wrong moment it'll be very important for the man who has to fight it. Timekeeping is everything in this line of work. Part of your job will be making plans of what has to happen and when during a given performance. We'll hold rehearsals for every part of the show. Then we give signals according to that plan. We spend shows above the arena, sending signals to those below as agreed. Before and after shows, we'll be down there in the dark. We use the water clocks, as well as sundials and our own eyes, although of course we may have to adjust events according to how it's going in the arena. If there's a really good battle happening, you can't interrupt it with some other distraction. But if the battle's getting dull you have to move quickly. No one wants a boring show. The audience gets restless and then you're in trouble."

I nod and make a note. "What do we need to discuss today?"

But Marcus is not listening to me. He is frowning at the southern sky, which is turning grey, vast clouds rolling in from that direction.

"I thought it would be sunny today," I say.

"So did I," he says. "Right, let's find the architect again before it starts to rain."

"I don't think he likes you," I say.

Marcus laughs out loud. "No, he doesn't," he agrees. "But he has to put up with me. He only has to build the place, then he can walk away. I have to run it. I'm not having stupid mistakes made. I barely covered anything yesterday."

I CAN ALMOST SEE THE architect sigh at the sight of Marcus and me. His toga is immaculately clean and pressed again, I wonder whether he wears a fresh one every day, a very expensive habit. He frowns down at an imaginary speck on his tunic sleeve, picking it away with disdain.

"So: a velarium," begins Marcus, with barely any niceties.

"It simply can't be done in time," huffs the architect. "We have to progress to the decorative stage as soon as possible."

"The audience will faint if they have to sit in the sun," says Marcus.

"Oh, they'll be fine," says the architect.

"The rich will," agrees Marcus. "They'll have slaves to carry a shade for them and fan them."

"Look, the Emperor and Vestal Virgins will have awnings," says the architect. "Then you can rig up smaller awnings for the senators and any extremely fussy or rich equestrians. That will have to suffice. There isn't time to have a full velarium erected and you'd need a lot of slaves to rig it each time."

"Sailors," says Marcus. "Two hundred, by my calculation. No-one else will have the knowledge and teamwork for it."

"There you are then. That's not happening in time for the inaugural Games."

Marcus sighs. "You may be right," he admits. It's the first time I've seen him not insist on having things his way. "It will have to be for after the inauguration. Althea: make a note, we will need awnings within the amphitheatre for the senators at least, or we'll never hear the end of it."

I jot down 'awnings, senators.'

The dark clouds keep coming. At least we will be able to shelter within the arches and continue our conversation. Drops of grey rain are beginning to fall, the storm coming closer. There are specks of dirt on the sleeve of my clean tunic. I brush them away but they only smudge, leaving marks. I look back at Marcus and the architect. Strange. The architect was so particular about his pristine toga, and yet it is now speckled all over with dirt. How has that happened? Marcus is not listening to the architect anymore. His face is tilted upwards, eyes narrowed. I follow his gaze.

The sky is raining grey. Tiny fragments float downwards from the dark clouds, slower than rain, silently landing all around us, on us. I hold out a hand and at once my skin is dotted all over, the grey landing so softly I barely feel it. I rub my fingers together, smell my hand. It must be ash; I can think of nothing else that looks and feels like this. I have had ashes fall on me when I was close to a funeral pyre, but where would a sky full of ash be coming from? The Temple of Vesta is nearby, but no temple fire is big enough to darken the sky. I look at Marcus and he glances at me. I shrug and he shrugs back, shakes his head.

All around us, silence falls. I look over my shoulder and see that the treadmill wheel is no longer turning, the men have stopped working. A few make discreet gestures against evil spirits.

"What is it?" I ask Marcus.

"Ash," he says.

I nod, wait for more, wait for his theory on what it can be from.

He says nothing, looks down at his hand again, rubs his fingers together.

The architect looks around. "Keep working," he says loudly. "It is nothing."

The men do not move. I hear one of them mutter something about the Great Fire. It's fifteen years' back, but most of these men would remember it. There would have been ash floating across the city for many days.

Marcus calls up to the men working on the highest points of the amphitheatre. "Is there a fire? What can you see?"

The workers lean over the edges, scanning the city. They should be able to see a long way from their vantage points, but one after another calls back, "Nothing," from all around the great oval.

"Work will stop for today," calls Marcus.

"You can't stop the work!" protests the architect, horrified. "We can't afford to lose a day's work."

"They're not going to do anything while this goes on," says Marcus.

"It is not your place to…" trails off the architect, but he can see for himself that there is nothing to be done about it. The men are already moving swiftly away from their places, heading downwards towards the exits, no doubt hurrying to find news about what is happening.

"Come on," says Marcus to me, turning to the nearest exit.

I follow him.

"What do I…" begins the architect, waiting for someone to tell him what to do.

"Whatever you think best," says Marcus over his shoulder.

We leave him hovering, alone in the vast space.

T̲h̲e̲ ̲F̲o̲r̲u̲m̲ ̲i̲s̲ ̲a̲l̲r̲e̲a̲d̲y̲ ̲b̲u̲s̲y̲, stalls everywhere, priests on their way to their respective temples. Someone is adjusting the public calendar, marking the day and which gods should be honoured, what activities avoided or undertaken, depending on their auspiciousness. But more and more people are stopping in the street, looking upwards and around, holding their palms out, as I did, inspecting the ashes as though expecting an answer. Marcus is looking for a herald and spots one further down the Forum, close to the Temple of Vesta, a crowd beginning to gather round him. We walk briskly that way, Marcus striding so fast that I am trotting by the time we reach the crowd.

"... we can presume the god Vulcan has been in some way displeased and shown his wrath, further messengers expected today with details of what has occurred. The great Admiral Pliny feared dead..."

Admiral Pliny is based in Misenum. "What's happened?" I ask, tugging at a woman's sleeve.

"A mountain has poured out fire and killed everyone in the region of Campania," says the woman, her eyes wide at the horror and the vast potential for gossip.

"What mountain?"

The woman shrugs. "I didn't catch it," she says vaguely, already extracting herself from the crowd so she can go and spread the news.

Marcus has pushed his way to the front of the throng and grabs hold of the herald's arm. The two bodyguards shove him back. "I need to know what has happened!" Marcus says.

The herald looks affronted at the loss of dignity. "You cannot assault an imperial herald," he says, adjusting his clothing.

"I beg your forgiveness," says Marcus quickly, raising his hands in the air. "I am from the region of Campania, what has happened?"

The crowd murmurs. This is making the news even more interesting.

The herald, enjoying their renewed interest, nods graciously and the two assistants retreat back to his sides. "*As* I was saying," he says and then lifts his voice to the right volume for a public announcement, "The mountain Vesuvius has opened up and poured out fire and ash across most of Campania. We have reports from Misenum, Puteoli and Neapolis, where it seems there was much fear and earth tremors as well as a falling of ash." He gestures grandly at the still-falling ash around us and gets a few frightened cries from women and many signs against evil spirits from the men. "We believe, from first reports, that the great Admiral Pliny may have died. Also reports, as yet unverified, that Herculaneum, Oplontis, Pompeii and Stabiae have disappeared."

"Disappeared?" says Marcus. "What do you mean, disappeared? A city cannot disappear."

"Sir," says the herald, drawing himself up, "I am announcing what I have been told to announce. Messengers have been arriving at the imperial palace both day and night since the occurrence, but we do not yet have all the details."

Marcus turns and walks away, his stride now so fast I have to run to keep up.

"What do you think has happened?" I ask, panting.

"I don't know," he says. "But we have to return. At once."

I try to nod while running and almost trip. "Will it be safe?"

"I don't know," he says. "Shall I leave you with Julia?"

"No," I say. "Take me with you." There is something about the silent falling ash that frightens me, that makes me want to be close to Marcus, who seems so commanding, as though he will keep me safe and know what to do, whatever strange and terrible thing has happened. I think of Mount Vesuvius, so green and peaceful, its slopes thick with vines and orchards and I cannot imagine what the herald means when he says that it opened up and poured out fire. I have heard of such mountains, but surely such a thing would be known about a mountain, it would give off smoke and tremble... "The tremors," I gasp. "Were they an omen? A warning?"

"I don't know," he says, his face tight. "Run back to Julia's, pack our bags. Tell her what we know. I will fetch the horses."

JULIA DOES NOT GASP, SHE does not repeat back what I have said and question me. She picks up a cloth bag and puts a loaf and half a cheese from her cupboard in it, fills two metal water bottles, the kind they use in the army.

"Where is Marcus?"

"Gone to get the horses."

"You can't travel at that speed," she says. "It'll take at least four days, like it did when you came here. You can't have the horses gallop continuously without changing them."

"Wouldn't a ship be faster?"

She's already out the door, making her way along the walkway and up the stairs to one of the small rooms on the top floor. I stand in the doorway clutching our supplies and when she emerges it is with a slight-framed man.

"It's the only way," Julia is saying and he nods and hurries past me.

"What is?" I ask.

"Chariot," she says.

"Racing chariot? We can't travel in those!"

"Whatever has happened," says Julia, her face very pale, "it is something serious. You need to get there fast. The horses cannot gallop endlessly with both of you. A chariot will be faster. Marcus can change the horses as you go."

"But a ship –"

"Marcus is afraid Livia will be headed on the roads towards Rome to find him if something bad has happened. He cannot risk missing her. And arranging passage on a boat may take time. He will not wait."

"They said Pompeii disappeared," I say, following her down the stairs. "What does that mean? Is it a thick fog, do you think? Or smoke from the fire? So they could not see it well?"

"I don't know," she says, but her tone makes me more afraid rather than less. "Would you rather stay here with me?"

"No," I say again. "I promised his wife I would look after him," I add, as though I had made a binding oath instead of uttered a hurried platitude. A sudden thought occurs to me. "Marcus is not allowed to leave Rome," I say. "The contract he signed forbids it."

Julia nods. "Pray you get there and back fast," she says. "I will send a message to say he is busy in other parts of Rome, making plans for his family. If all is well, make him return quickly. Livia and the boy can follow, as was planned before."

"Do you think all will be well?" I ask her, wanting reassurance.

She looks away. "I have heard of mountains with fire in them," she says slowly. "They can be dangerous. It is possible Pompeii has been badly damaged, but that does not mean Livia could not have found a way to escape. Marcus' friends would have looked out for her, for certain."

Marcus has to be restrained by Julia, but when she convinces him it is worth waiting for the chariot he reluctantly agrees. When it arrives, pulled through the streets by two stable hands, Celer oversees the harnessing.

"I picked a training chariot, sturdier than we use for the city races, but you will have to change horses as often as possible if you want a fast speed," he warns Marcus, who only nods, his mouth set in a tight line.

I hover, nervous. The chariot is tiny, it is made for one man to stand in, for maximum lightness and speed. It barely reaches our waists. I think of the rough roads more suited to lumbering wagons and slow walking horses. The only chariots that go really fast on the main roads are the imperial mail. I know they could reach Pompeii in under two days if it was a matter of urgency and that Marcus will want to do the same.

Half the building's inhabitants have gathered in the street to wave us off. Julia stops Marcus before he climbs into the chariot. "May Jupiter bless you," she says, one hand on his chest, invoking the greatest of the gods, her voice serious. "May you return safely to us, with your wife and son."

Marcus stares back into Julia's face as though he can't hear her, then turns to me. "Up," he says, as though to a dog, and I climb quickly into the chariot. We are pressed together, hip to hip, my satchel at our feet by his own small bag. I feel Julia's hand on mine and then we are moving.

We struggle to get out of Rome; the chariot with two people in it draws stares and the roads are not made for speed, full of traffic and pedestrians. I wonder whether the chariot is the best choice. They are made for smooth racetracks and quick laps to glory, not for a three-day journey on a main road. At last we reach the Appian Way where there is a little more space.

"Ha! Ha!" Marcus urges the horses into a fast gallop. His hands are tight on the reins, his face is set, his eyes darting across the road ahead, judging the best place to guide the horses to avoid other traffic and deep ruts in the road that would have us flung out of the chariot if the wheels were to unbalance. The speed is terrifying, I have never gone so fast before. I clutch the edge of the chariot below my waist, certain I will be thrown out at any moment, whimpering to myself when the chariot hits bumps in the road and jerks one way or another. I want to talk to Marcus because I want to hear him speak, want the reassurance I never got from Julia, but I can't think what to say and I am afraid of distracting him, am afraid of what he might reply. So we ride on and on, no words between us, the world rushing past, the endless hoofbeats and wheels against stone creating such a din in my head that after a while I can barely even think. I have never spent this long in abject terror. *Once, on a ship, the waves rocking, my mother gone, my father beside me in silent agony.* I am still afraid of our speed and the likelihood of an accident, but also afraid of what we are heading towards. Is it something very bad, but from which those we know have escaped? Or is it something so bad, something I cannot even imagine, is there news to come which will break the grim, silent man next to me? I try not to think of Myrtis. Try to imagine a horror not too great. I imagine fire emerging, somehow, from Vesuvius, perhaps setting fire to houses, people running and screaming, but, and this is what I spend my time imagining, running and screaming to safety, making their way to a safe place while many brave people fight the fires. The crowds will be bewailing possessions lost and perhaps even houses but nothing worse. Nothing worse. My imagination hones to perfection an image of Livia, carrying Amantius. Smudged with ashes, weeping at the sight of Marcus. But safe. And Myrtis. Somehow the two of them together, Anna trailing behind. All safe. I add Fausta, I add Felix. I even add the weasel as well as Lucius, his wife and their daughter Lucilla, because I need as many people as possible to be safe.

And yet the sky above me is still dark and ashes continue to fall on us. It coats my hands and I brush it away as though it were eating me alive.

We change horses twice that first day, each time I step shaking from the jolting chariot and run to relieve myself, then step back in because we must ride on, the fresh horses picking up pace as my fingers tighten on the chariot rim again. Marcus speaks only briefly to the innkeepers and it is his money that does the talking, the clink of coins bringing fresh horses, nervous at their new owners and new harness, no time to accustom them to us or to this mode of transport before they must gallop onwards as fast as Marcus can make them.

The dark sky above us makes nightfall come faster than it should do. Marcus slows the horses as we approach another inn and when the stable hand comes out, he steps out of the chariot.

"Change of horses," he says.

"We can't ride at night," I say, clutching at his arm, my legs unsteady. "We can't see anything, there'll be an accident. We can't ride for three days with no sleep."

"I can't sleep," says Marcus.

"You have to," I say. "Please. We'll ride on as soon as there is light. Please."

"We have to ride on," he says.

"If we have an accident in the dark, we won't get there at all," I say.

The stable hand waits for a decision.

"We will stay the night," says Marcus. "A room and care for the horses. We will keep them for tomorrow morning."

"Yes, Dominus," says the man.

"We need to eat," I say.

"I can't eat."

"We have to," I say. "You have to be strong for when we arrive, it may be that we have to…" I'm not sure what we may have to do. "Perhaps there have been more tremors," I say, alighting on the only thing I can think of that is likely. "Perhaps we will have to carry all your family possessions somewhere, or help others. You cannot be tired and hungry; you have to be strong."

He eats because I make him, and he lies down on the bed in our cramped room because I make him. But I am not sure he sleeps. I sleep at last, when my legs have stopped trembling and the exhaustion of hours of fear suddenly washes over me. I wake over and over in the night, startled from the poor sleep by dreams of fires, of ashes raining down on me, the shaking of the chariot reverberating through me even though I am lying on the floor. When dawn comes, we are on the road again, my face no doubt as pale as Marcus'. The first burst of speed frightens me again but after a while the exhaustion takes over from the fear as I cling tightly to the rim of the chariot and keep my eyes on the road ahead. I try to stop thinking, repeating to myself over and over prayers to various gods. I am not really sure to whom I should be praying. Perhaps to motherly Juno, to keep Livia and Amantius safe? Or Vulcan, god of fire, who has somehow been angered and opened up a mountain of fire, which I still cannot imagine? Or Jupiter, greatest of the gods, since this is clearly an event of vast proportions? Twice in the morning we see imperial messengers heading for Rome, their horses sweating, and I dread seeing any more, for each additional one suggests worse news and when Marcus sees them, he urges the horses on ever faster.

The silence between us is louder than the noise of the horses galloping and our wheels, it hovers over the two of us. Marcus' voice is hoarse when he speaks to the stable hands at the two inns where we stop briefly. I offer him food, but he waves it away and I have to press the bread into his hands. He eats a few bites but then shakes his head. Come nightfall I have to insist, again, that we must stop.

"We will reach Puteoli tomorrow, we are making good progress," I say. "They will have more news there. But we must be rested."

Marcus looks at me as if he does not understand what I am saying. He must be dizzy with tiredness, as I am. He looks down at his bare arm and the ashes that have fallen on it, his skin turned grey. "It is still falling," he says, and it comes out as a guttural whisper. "How can it still be falling?"

I look down as though I am unaware of being covered in ashes myself, as though it is a surprise to me rather than the growing dread I have been holding in me, a question I have not dared to ask. "We are closer to the source," I say. "By now it will no longer be falling in Rome."

"But it is still falling," he says, one hand loosening its grip on the reins so that the stable hand can take the horses away. "What kind of fire is it, that is still burning after so many days?"

I think of the Great Fire, which lasted six days and destroyed half of Rome and swallow. "I don't know," I say, and my voice starts too high, I have to lower it before tears start to fall. "I don't know, but we must eat and sleep now, come."

He allows himself to be led, as though a child, the grim determination from when he was driving gone. He sits, I order food, insisting on a thick vegetable porridge to warm us, pushing bread towards him as he eats in silence. I pour him more than one glass of wine and refill his plate against his refusal. He spoons food into his mouth as though it has no taste. Halfway through the second plate he pushes the bowl away and walks up the stairs to the small room we will stay the night in.

He does sleep, but fitfully, as do I. We are too tired not to sleep at all, but I wake regularly and when I do Marcus is often awake too. By dawn we are both lying, eyes wide open, waiting for enough light to depart.

At first the day begins like yesterday. Soft ash still blows through the cold air and the grey-yellow sky does not fully lighten, despite the sun rising. The road is fairly empty, as one would expect first thing in the morning. But soon we see a family come towards us, in a donkey cart. Behind them, only a few moments later, another family, this time on foot, with one pack mule between them, laden with possessions. When a third family come into sight I pull at Marcus' arm and he slows the chariot. When we are almost abreast, he stops. This family have two horses, pulling a large cart. On the cart are a man and woman, three children and various possessions: a few pieces of furniture, a chest that might hold clothes. The children are asleep, the man and woman look drained. Everything is coated with the fine ash that will not stop falling.

"Where are you from?" I ask.

"Herculaneum," says the man.

I feel my shoulders relax. The cities have not 'disappeared' then, as those gossips in Rome would have it. Clearly what I imagined was true: there has been a bad fire and some people, like these, may have lost their homes but here they are, a family together at least, still with some possessions. "How bad is the damage to the city?" I ask.

The couple stare at me. At last the woman speaks. "It is gone," she says.

"Gone?"

"Gone," says the man. "Vesuvius opened up, there was a vast black cloud, so vast, it…" He looks about him, as though to find something to compare it with, to explain it to me.

I nod, pointing up at the ashen sky. "It is very bad, it came as far as Rome."

The man shakes his head. "This is nothing," he says. "This would not harm anyone."

"Have many people been harmed?" I ask.

They look at me as though I am a fool. They shake their heads a little, open their mouths to explain and then close them again, unsure of how to begin. It is the man who finally manages to speak. "The cloud was black and filled with fire," he says. "It rose up and up and then burning stones and ash began to fall. My brother is a fisherman, he said we could sail to Misenum. We left with him and his own family, sailed away. There was a wave of heat that came across the bay…"

"Like opening an oven door," says his wife as he trails off. "Then the ash fell and fell. We barely made it to Misenum. There were tremors and a great darkness in the daytime as if it were night. A great wave rose up and then the sea withdrew, pulled back from the shore, further than it has ever been. By then we had reached the town but, when the sky grew light again, my brother-in-law went back. The shoreline was full of animals from the depths of the sea, some he had never seen before, thrown onto the land, dying. Many of the boats were gone but he found his. We slept there one night. In the morning he said he would go back to Herculaneum to see what had happened and if he might help others, or if it were safe to return."

"And?" Marcus has spoken at last; he is leaning forward.

The man shakes his head. "He said it was gone. That there was no trace that a city had ever stood there."

"How can that be?"

"He said all of the land was grey with ashes and that he could not make out any part of the port nor the city or land beyond, that everything had disappeared. He has fished from that port for his whole life and he no longer knew its shape. He –"

I yelp. Marcus has suddenly used the whip and the horses leap forward. I clutch at the chariot as we race away down the road.

WE DRIVE SO FAST THAT the ever-falling ashes are driven into our faces. I have to keep my eyes narrowed so that I will not be blinded, wiping and wiping again, the other hand clutching at the side of the chariot.

We are very close to Puteoli when Marcus veers left, away from the main road and down a smaller one. The chariot rocks at the sudden change of direction and I can feel the right wheel lift entirely off the ground. I cry out, certain that we are about to be thrown to our deaths. But the wheel slams back down onto the road and we are safe. I want to ask Marcus what he is doing, but when I wipe my eyes again, I see what he has seen.

Ahead of us is an encampment. To the left, a mess of ramshackle shelters, tiny and misshapen. To the right, a detachment of marines is working to create a far more organised area. There are men digging latrines and trenches, others putting up brown army tents, which range in size, some of them truly vast, the full floor span of Lucius' holiday villa. These are arranged immaculately, row by row, bringing order to the scene of chaos before us. An entranceway has been created, a wall of posts with a gate, to which Marcus drives without hesitation.

At the gate stands a centurion accompanied by a scribe.

"We are not yet ready to house refugees," says the centurion as soon as he sees us. "You have to make your way over to the other encampment and wait. We should have the first tents ready by tonight for those with children."

"We're not refugees," says Marcus. "We've just arrived from Rome."

The centurion looks us over with a frown. Clearly, we are not messengers from the Emperor, or from anyone else. "What are you doing here?" he asks.

"I've come back to look for my wife and son in Pompeii."

Something passes over the centurion's face, but he doesn't answer right away. He glances at the scribe, then back at Marcus. "Pompeii got hit pretty bad," he says at last. "You'll need to search the refugee camps here and below Stabiae."

"How bad?" Marcus asks. "What happened, exactly?"

The centurion shakes his head. "Can't go into that," he says. "You need to go into the other encampment," he repeats. "Some of my men are there, taking names of everyone who is missing and the people who are looking for them. Tell them your name and who you are searching for. The tents here will mostly be ready tonight, everyone should be housed by tomorrow evening. Orders direct from the Emperor. Detachments of the Praetorian Guard will be arriving tomorrow. We've been promised whatever is needed, he's even going to send two senators to manage the region in person."

For a moment I think Marcus is going to argue, perhaps tell the centurion that he, too, was once an army man, try to claim some kind of bond between them so that he can have more information, but he only nods and pulls at the reins, directing the horses back towards the makeshift shelters that stretch out across the fields, into the distance.

THERE ARE NO WOODEN POSTS here to form a barricade, only individual soldiers, spaced out along the edge of the field where shelters begin. This must be some farmer's land, I think, perhaps willingly given over to this crisis, perhaps simply commandeered. This camp is like nothing I have ever seen before, worse than the rougher backstreets of Rome, where at least there are insulae, however dirty and crumbling. These are fields full of people, covered by the ever-falling grey ash, kneeling to crawl into tiny shelters made of whatever came to hand, sticks, cloaks, upturned carts, even branches from nearby trees, still thick with red and yellow leaves from the changing days of autumn.

I stand in the chariot, gazing out over the fields, almost unaware that Marcus has now jumped down and is fastening the reins of the horses to a tree. He nods to the nearest soldier.

"Keep an eye on them, will you?"

The marine nods, and Marcus strides out into the camp.

It takes me a moment to gather my thoughts, my satchel and his bag, and hurry after him, almost falling into a rainwater ditch before finding my footing and joining him in the field.

For a moment Marcus hesitates, looking to one side and then the other, before turning around and addressing the soldier again. "Who's in charge?"

"Marinus. Over by the red tent."

He's right, there is indeed an army tent set up in the middle of the camp, and Marcus is already heading towards it. I stumble after him, the already harvested field's last remaining stalks of barley scratching at my ankles.

Inside the tent is an older man with dark brown skin and short tightly curled hair, who looks exhausted. He has two scribes sitting with him, each with many rolls of papyrus at their feet in large containers. Clearly they have been doing this work for many hours.

"Name?"

"Marcus Aquillius Scaurus."

"And the woman?"

"My slave, Althea."

They don't note down my name. A slave who is looking for someone is hardly worth registering in this situation unless someone is looking for them. I can imagine there are plenty of slaves who will use the disaster to escape.

"Looking for?"

"My wife Livia and son Amantius."

"Age of child?"

"Not yet two."

There is a pause, while the two scribes check through their current lists, hesitating here and there when they find another woman named Livia, only to shake their heads when there is no mention of a child. I daren't look at Marcus' face. At last there is a final shake of the head and Marcus lets out the breath he has been holding.

"If we come across them, where are they to find you? We're crosschecking the refugees from all the camps we find, copying lists of names and sending them to the other camps."

"They should stay here in the military camp until I come for them. I will seek them myself in Pompeii first of all."

The scribes continue making notes, but the man in charge looks up at Marcus and the same look crosses over his face that I saw on the centurion. "Pompeii is gone," he says. He says it with a measure of gentleness, but also with absolute certainty.

"What do you mean, gone?" asks Marcus and there is nothing gentle in his tone. "A city cannot disappear."

"It has been covered in ashes," says the man.

"Of course," agrees Marcus. He holds out his own arm, still lightly covered in ash from our journey. "It's still falling. Of course it is covered in ashes."

The man stands up. He is tall, his gaze is level with Marcus. "Most of the roofs of the houses have caved in under the weight of ashes and stones," he says slowly. "When seen from the sea, in a ship we took to carry out a reconnaissance, there is nothing left. Only ashes."

Marcus says nothing. His face shows no emotion. My own face must have gone very pale, because the man glances at me and indicates a stool I may sit on if I wish. I shake my head but have to swallow more than once to calm the desire to vomit. If what this man is saying is true, then how can anyone have escaped? I cannot imagine what he's saying, I cannot imagine a city disappearing under ashes, as though it were a child's toy house made of little blocks of wood rather than a city of brick and stone. And people. The man has not mentioned the people. It is not my place to speak, as a slave, but I can't help myself.

"How many survived?"

The man's eyes flicker towards Marcus but then come to rest on me. "We don't know," he says honestly, and I see again the exhaustion in his eyes and the slump of his shoulders. "There are hundreds arriving in makeshift camps every day since it happened, but…" He pauses. "There should be more," he says at last. "There should be far, far more people arriving. We now know Stabiae is still standing, although it is severely damaged, there is a huge refugee camp nearby. But the camps on this side, we've had hardly anyone from Pompeii, Herculaneum and Oplontis. There should be a lot more."

"Perhaps the people from Pompeii went to Stabiae," I say.

"Perhaps," says the man, but he drops his gaze from me as he says it. I think of what he said before, that Pompeii has gone.

I'm about to ask for more details, I want to know more from this man, I want him to describe Pompeii in more detail, I want to know exactly what he saw, and from what distance, whether perhaps he was mistaken, if there was mist or fog even, mixed with the ashes, making it hard to see from the ship. I want to challenge him, to suggest that, if he was on a ship, he cannot have been that close to the shore and perhaps he was mistaken.

"Your master has gone," points out one of the scribes and I turn to see Marcus ducking out of the tent flaps, striding away. I have no choice but to hurry after him.

OUTSIDE THE TENT ARE THREE more people, two women and one man, waiting to register their names and the names of their loved ones. The women are weeping, the man looks like Marcus, his face set in grim disbelief. One of the women has a child, who is clinging to her knees, grey face streaked with tears.

I catch up with Marcus, who turns to me when he becomes aware of my presence and takes his bag from me, slinging it over one shoulder.

"We will work the field together," he says. "Line by line. Do not miss a single shelter. Start on this line and make your way to the end of the field. Then work your way back along the next line and so on. I will work from the bottom up and meet you when we have both finished."

"We have registered our names and theirs," I start. "They said they weren't here. Yet," I add hastily.

"They've only just started registering people, they could easily have missed some," says Marcus. "Start."

THE SEARCH IS EXHAUSTING, AND not just because it stretches over more than three fields over the scratching, scraping barley stalks. My ankles are bleeding by the time I have covered three rows. At each tiny shelter I must call out, ask to see the inhabitants, all of them shaken, ashen, afraid. Children cry, women too. The men do not know what to do, everything has been taken away from them, even the ability to provide for their families. They have been told to wait. They have been told they will be fed by the army this evening and housed in military tents as soon as possible. There is nowhere else to go. Most of the people I meet have already travelled further from their homes than they have ever done before, and they are lost, bewildered. They believe they have incurred the wrath of the gods and yet escaped with their lives and they do not know whether to be grateful or guilt-ridden. They ask me questions to which I do not have answers. Is Rome sending more soldiers to help? Will there be money to rebuild their houses, replace livestock, fishing boats? How long will they be able to live in tents, with winter coming? They are afraid and their fear builds in me, as I make my way from shelter to shelter and person to person. I ask for Livia and Amantius, but also for Fausta, Myrtis and Felix. I even ask for Lucius and his wife, certain that a wealthy man like my past master must surely have had the means to escape this disaster. I want to ask these people for more details of what happened, but I know that Marcus will want me to complete my checks as quickly as possible.

I finish my allotted part and find Marcus already waiting, shifting from foot to foot, nervous and fretful.

"Nothing?"

I shake my head. "I'm sorry."

"And you asked for them by name? In case they had been seen elsewhere?"

"Yes."

He takes a deep breath, looks one way and another, then stiffens, narrows his eyes. "Fausta?" He raises his voice. "Fausta!"

A woman, hesitating at the entrance to the military encampment, turns, then makes her way at speed across the uneven field.

"Marcus!" Her black curls are in disarray, her tunic and toga filthy. "I give thanks you are already here, and I have found you," she says, clasping her hands and looking upwards as she covers the last few steps between us, then embracing Marcus. "I will sacrifice as I vowed," she adds. "Althea! The two of you must have travelled at such speed! I am glad to see you."

"Where are Livia and Amantius?" asks Marcus.

"You haven't found them?"

He shakes his head.

Tears start from her eyes and she claps a hand over her mouth. "I have looked everywhere."

"Where?"

"Puteoli and the camps here both yesterday and today, I have combed them."

"She may have gone south," he says. "Perhaps to her family in Stabiae, she would have known I would seek her there if she had not already headed to Rome."

"Yes, of course," says Fausta quickly, although there is doubt in her eyes. I know she is thinking what I am thinking: how could a woman and small child have made their way to Stabiae so fast after such a disaster? They would have had to ride on horseback at speed and no-one is travelling at speed. The families we have seen have been on foot or with slow carts. And besides, the rumours said Stabiae had disappeared too, would she have headed there?

"I will search this camp once more, the far field where the new people are arriving, then we will head to Pompeii," says Marcus. He is already striding away.

I sink to the ground, exhausted. Fausta squats near me. "I have already searched," she says, and tears trickle down her face. "They are lost, all of them."

"Have you found no-one you knew?" I ask.

"No," she says. "Most of the people in this camp come from the villages or farms at a greater distance from Pompeii, not from the city itself."

"Were you still in Misenum when it happened?"

She nods, wiping her eyes.

"What did you see?"

She shakes her head. "Nothing on the first day, the morning was clear, a blue sky. I was with the old man in his bedchamber till late morning. The sun was just past its highest point, he was dozing, but I heard shouts down by the bay. I looked out from the balcony and there was a strange dark cloud over the mountains. I know now it was Vesuvius, but I couldn't tell from that distance. The cloud was vast, like nothing I've ever seen before. It went straight up, like a tree trunk or a mast and then it started fanning out, it looked like an umbrella pine. It was black at first and then it started flaring out, first dark, then bright with fire, red and yellow flashes, then it would go black again and then the fire would show again, over and over."

I stare at her, trying to imagine what she is describing.

"The old man sent a slave running to a friend of his and so we heard that word had come. They said it was Mount Vesuvius and they were afraid Pompeii was in grave danger."

"They said Admiral Pliny died trying to rescue people?"

"That's what I've heard. Certainly, he set out, we saw the galleys setting sail. But later we heard they couldn't land at Pompeii. There were burning rocks falling into their boats and giant boulders which rolled down and blocked the shoreline. I spoke to one of the surviving sailors yesterday, not all the galleys returned. They tried further down the coast and made land at Stabiae. The sailor said there were noxious fumes, tremors, one after another, burning stones and ashes falling everywhere, people running in the streets with pillows held over their heads to protect themselves from being struck."

Myrtis and Felix, did they run with pillows or were they forced to obey Lucius' orders, maybe told to go to their rooms?

Fausta runs a hand through her hair, her fingers shaking. "He said even though it was still daytime, you couldn't see anything. Pitch black. The waves were so strong it was hard to make a landing and almost impossible to bring anyone to safety."

"And in Misenum?"

"Constant tremors. We realised by then they weren't just the usual tremors you get at this time of year. They were a warning, an ill omen, but none of us knew that." She tries and fails to pin her hair back, eventually giving up. "We stood on the balcony all day, watching the cloud spreading. We tried to sleep that night, but the tremors grew worse and worse, we were almost flung out of our bed. We didn't dare stay indoors after that, we went to the garden and waited for the dawn, the old man, me, all his slaves, even his daughters were there. Everyone praying and sobbing for Misenum to be spared and me thinking, what's happening in Pompeii? I knew it had to be worse than where we were. We waited for the dawn and there was only a yellowish half-light. The sea suddenly rolled back on itself, as if it was being pulled back from the shoreline against its will. That's when the old man said we should get out of the city, the countryside would be safer. He called for carts and horses but none of the stable hands could manage the horses, five of them bolted, none of them would be harnessed. In the end we managed to get a couple of carts lined up and let the rest of the horses go, they were unrideable, rearing up and trying to run, kicking out, they'd have broken someone's leg if they'd caught them. The old man's stupid daughters were trying to grab all the valuables, running in and out of the house with armfuls of clothes and boxes of jewels. The old man shouted at them in the end saying they'd be dead if they didn't hurry up. I kept watching Pompeii and the cloud was growing all the time, flames still flashing inside it, like sheet lightning in August when the summer heat breaks. Then it started lowering, losing the pine shape, moving low down and across the whole coastline. The Island of Capri disappeared first, then the cloud was creeping across the sea towards us like some beast out of a nightmare, everyone screaming at the sight of it, great crowds trying to follow anyone who looked like they knew what they were doing. We had more than four hundred trying to follow us. In the end we couldn't even see the promontory of Misenum, the cloud had reached it." Her voice cracks, hoarse with the telling and the fear.

I offer water and Fausta gulps it loudly, wipes her chin. She takes a deep breath and puffs the air out, as though trying to get rid of something inside her.

"Then what?" I ask.

"We set out on the high road, although we couldn't go fast, there were too many people and everyone shouting at those ahead to walk faster. When we looked back the cloud was low over the ground, following us like a dark mist. We tried to run, but the old man couldn't go that fast and I was afraid we'd be trampled, people were pushing and shoving from behind to go faster. There were ashes falling everywhere, clouds of them, it made it hard to breathe. We were holding up our clothes over our mouths, but it hardly helped. In the end I told the old man we had to step away from the main road, we'd die underfoot if he fell. He ordered the daughters and his slaves off the road, though some of the servants refused and carried on ahead. We'd barely got off the main road, found ourselves a little area we could stand in a field and then the mist caught up with us."

She breathes again, a shuddering breath. It's making me uncomfortable seeing Fausta so shaken.

"It was like being shut up in a dark room, no moon or stars, no lamp, just black night and screaming all around, children crying, women shrieking, men shouting, angry in their fear, cursing the gods while the women prayed to them. Then there was a sudden burst of heat and flames, I thought we would die for sure if more came, but there were only ashes after that. They fell so thickly we had to shake them off every few moments or we would have been buried under them." She stops again, then speaks quickly. "The old man died," she says. "Maybe he couldn't breathe, I don't know, he clutched at his chest, he was gasping and then he was gone, even in the dark and with all the screaming, I felt him go limp, I knew he was gone. I held him till the light came back," she adds, her chin held too high, tears trembling in her eyes as she fights not to let them fall.

"I'm sorry," I say. I remember Marcus talking about Fausta's lover, how he would have made her his mistress and given her a soft life, how they had been lovers since she was a young woman. I touch her hand and she gives a quick nod that makes a couple of tears fall.

"The light came back eventually," she says. "But it was strange, a half-light like an eclipse. When his daughters saw their father was dead, they started screaming and wailing, then they turned on me. They've always wanted to," she adds. "He wouldn't let them speak ill of me or be rude to my face, but they hated me, didn't like that he favoured me over their mother even when she was alive. The moment they saw he was dead they were screaming insults at me."

"What did you do?"

"Got up and walked away," she says and I see her lips tighten in an effort not to cry at the thought of walking away from the old man she had loved and been loved by for years, the pain of being chased away from his side. "Walked back to Misenum, found a fisherman the next day who'd take me to Puteoli at least. No-one would sail to Pompeii. I kept checking the city and then the camps as the refugees started arriving. I knew Marcus would arrive eventually, but I was afraid I'd miss him. I've done nothing but search for our team, but I've found none of them. They would have sheltered in the amphitheatre or the gladiator's barracks until it was too late."

"And his wife and child?"

Fausta puts her face down on her knees, her voice comes out muffled. "They would have gone to the amphitheatre, they would have known our team would protect them from anything, anything at all. But how were they to protect them from what happened? Who can stand against the wrath of the gods?"

"They might have escaped," I try.

Fausta looks up and rubs at her already-red eyes. "He won't find them," she says, and it is only now I see how much she has held back, what a brave face she has put on for Marcus' benefit. "Vulcan has taken them. There are so few who have survived and most of them only through luck: living a little way out of town so they had a head start, or fishermen who took to their boats and made it further down the coast, the people who were out of the city on business, as we were. A woman with a small child would have sought shelter, not struck out on her own. Livia was no adventurer." She gulps back a sob. "They are all gone," she repeats. "All of them. I know it."

"But Pompeii…"

She shakes her head. "The ashes were falling so thickly," she says. "And that was in Misenum, we were far away. Puteoli's ankle deep in ashes as it is, Pompeii…" her voice trails away.

"They said it had disappeared," I say, hoping she will disagree, but she nods.

"I can believe it."

"Believe what?" Marcus is back.

Fausta shakes her head, stands up. "Nothing," she says. "Now what?"

"Now we sail to Pompeii."

I gape at Marcus. "Sail to Pompeii? Who will take us?"

Marcus is already walking towards the chariot. The horses look downcast, the grass and leaves they might have nibbled on are layered over with ashes. "With enough money, anyone will take you anywhere, you must know that. Fausta, you stay here and watch over the camp in case Livia or any of our team arrive." He holds out a hand with a few coins. "Eat. Sleep. Rest. We will be back soon."

Fausta follows us to the chariot. "Surely by now all the survivors will have left?"

Marcus backs the horses round to rejoin the road, then gestures to me to climb into the chariot. "There may be many survivors. They may be searching for loved ones themselves and if so, they would not leave the area. And if the soldiers have seen the city only from the deck of a ship…" He steps into the chariot beside me, our bodies once again pressed together. I have stopped noticing it by now, there is no intimacy in it, only desperation.

Fausta steps away from the horses. "Neptune grant you safe passage," she says and then steps forward again, one hand on the closest horse's neck. "Come back safe, Marcus," she says, and her loud voice is very small.

Marcus doesn't reply, he only whips up the horses to the fast gallop that I am almost used to. "Where are we going?" I ask, gripping onto the front of the chariot, not daring to look back at Fausta for fear of growing dizzy.

"The docks of Puteoli," he says.

THE DOCKS OF PUTEOLI STINK. Not the normal stink of any docks, of fresh or frying fish and sweating men, smoking braziers for warming hands, garum sauce and whatever has spilled on the quayside that morning whilst being loaded and unloaded. This stink is everywhere and overwhelms everything. It is the stink of vast quantities of rotting dead fish.

"Never seen so many dead fish washed up on the shore," says a man when I ask. "We couldn't clear them away fast enough, they just kept coming. There's still loads of them floating on the sea. Most of the fishermen's boats have been wrecked and those that haven't won't go out again, they're too scared. They say Vulcan hasn't finished with us yet. They're afraid Neptune might have been angered too, there was a giant wave that came up. The men are saying sea monsters might rise from the deep at his command. They won't risk it."

I look at Marcus, but he doesn't seem bothered by this information, by the idea that there might be nobody to sail us to Pompeii. He settles himself down on the quayside, as though he has all the time in the world and looks up at the man. "Spread the word," he says. "My name is Marcus and I will pay a month's wages to whoever will sail me to Pompeii tonight."

"No one will sail to Pompeii tonight," says the man. "It's already growing dark. I doubt they'll even sail tomorrow."

"A month's wages," Marcus says again. "But I must be there before dawn."

"What's the rush? Want to feel the wrath of Vulcan for yourself?"

"I'm looking for my wife and son," says Marcus. "A month's wages," he repeats.

THE MAN WATCHES US FOR a while, but Marcus doesn't move and eventually I settle down beside him to wait. I cannot imagine that anybody will set sail tonight, in the dark, to a place that may or may not have been cursed by Vulcan, that may or may not still exist. I look up at the sky, which is still grey. A sailor would need the stars to help him navigate, surely, they would not risk going out without them at a time like this. The man wanders away.

"Are you hungry?" I ask Marcus but he shakes his head, as I expected. I ignore him and boldly hold out my hand. "Money," I say, as firmly as I dare.

He doesn't argue and hands me his purse. I take it, make my way along the quayside until I find a popina. It looks deeply disreputable, with lewd graffiti everywhere suggesting that the barmaid and several of her sisters are for hire, at cut rate prices. I pull my cloak around me and quickly place an order for bean soup and bread, along with two cups of wine. I take them back to Marcus and all but force him to eat, returning our cups, spoons and bowls to the popina when we are done.

"What if no one will take us, what will we do?" I ask.

"Someone will come," he says.

Hours pass, although it's hard to tell the time with no stars. It grows dark and the only light comes from two windows of a house nearby and from the popina, where I can hear raucous laughter and the gurgle of cups being refilled. Occasionally I take a deep breath to try and steady my constant nerves, and when I do, I retch at the smell of rotting fish, which I thought I'd got used to. Every so often, a man will wander out of the popina and stare down the quayside at us, our huddled shapes barely visible. Clearly the word is being spread, but there are no takers as yet.

I MUST HAVE FALLEN ASLEEP, though I don't know when. I wake when Marcus digs me in the side and I find that I have been sleeping slumped against him, my head on his shoulder, although he has not moved away from me. Standing over us is the shape of a man.

"A month's wages?"

"Yes." Marcus' voice is not eager, only flat. Perhaps it convinces the man he is telling the truth, that the offer is genuine.

"And it can't wait till tomorrow?"

"No."

"Why not?"

"I'm looking for my wife and child."

"You can't search for them in the dark."

"No, but I don't want to waste more time. You can get me there by dawn?"

There is a pause. "Have you heard what happened?"

"Yes."

"I've seen it," says the man. His voice changes, I can't see his face in the dark but he sounds as though he is about to cry. "It's like nothing you've ever seen before. It's like the opening to the underworld."

Marcus stands up and I follow, although one of my legs has gone completely numb so I almost fall over again. "Let's go."

THE BOAT IS SMALL. I stand on the quayside looking down into it, while the man holds a flaming torch up so we can see to get in. Marcus climbs in and then turns to me, holding up a hand.

I want to refuse.

I want to say I will wait here.

I am afraid we will never make it, that the fishermen are right and sea monsters will rise from the deep. I want to tell Marcus that the last time I was on a boat I saw my mother die and my father become a slave. Perhaps ordinarily I might tell him I am afraid, but I look at his face, white even in the flickering yellow light, and I cannot let him go alone to search for his wife and child. I take his hand, wondering if he can feel my fingers shaking and find myself aboard the boat, the rocking under my trembling legs bringing tears to my eyes. I lower my head and sit down as quickly as I can, huddle into my cloak and murmur a prayer to Libertas under my breath.

"Watch over me, Libertas, as I enter the realm of Neptune, intercede with him for me, for us. Beg him to let us pass, we need to know the truth of what we must grieve for."

HADES

I SLEEP, BUT ONLY BECAUSE MY eyes close against my will. I cough often and sometimes so hard that I wake myself up in a panic, clutching at the side of the boat, forgetting why I am rising and falling. When I remember I stare blearily about me and can vaguely make out the shapes of the fisherman and Marcus by the still-flickering torch, but I cannot see any details, and my eyes close again even as I search for a glimpse of light on the horizon.

A fit of coughing wakes me again, shaking me to life. A pale hint of light is growing in the sky, and when I turn to spit over the side of the boat, I see my spit is dark. Marcus is still in the same position. The fisherman has his back to me, standing in the prow of the boat. I try to make out something, anything, but I cannot, perhaps it is still too dark. The fisherman looks over his shoulder at me and when he sees me peering to the left, he shakes his head.

"There it is," he says and his voice cracks. He gestures ahead to the left as though we are unaware of where the shoreline is and indeed, he is right, for the water is grey and the land is grey, there is no difference. It is like seeing by night, when even a full moon cannot show the colours of the day, only a strange shadow copy of it.

He must have made a mistake. What is in front of me cannot be Pompeii. He has erred in his calculations; this is some other place. The shape of Vesuvius is wrong, the mountain is a third less tall, its outline different. Where its summit was once a tall cone, now it is a broken flattened ridge. The port is changed too, vast black rocks jut out of what used to be a clear stretch of blue water, an easy mooring for ships to come home to. And beyond the water there is nothing. No city walls, no houses. There is only a dense and endless grey. I look back at the man and shake my head.

"This is not Pompeii," I say with certainty. "It must be further down the coast."

"Pompeii is gone."

"The people…" I begin, but he shakes his head before I have finished.

"Gone," he repeats. "All gone."

"They didn't run?" I ask.

"Some ran," he says. "The heat reached out and touched them and they died there and then."

"From heat?" I say, uncomprehending.

"The anger of the gods is hotter than any fire you have ever known," he says. "Hotter than the white heat of a blacksmith's iron."

"No-one escaped?"

"Some," he says. He swallows and when he speaks again his voice is croaked. "A few," he manages. "There are refugee camps further down the coast."

I clutch at Marcus' arm. "They will have escaped," I say, my voice too high and too joyous. "For sure, they will have run and..." I trail away, unsure of what I am saying. I look again at the grey world spread out before me and shake my head. "A fisherman," I start again, "Livia will have asked for help and one of the fishermen will have taken pity on her, since she had a child, he will have rowed with her and his own family to safety, to Stabiae, or..." I look to my right, down the coast as though I might spot fresh green trees and a sandy beach where all the inhabitants, save perhaps a very few unlucky ones, will be gathered. But there is nothing to see, only the smoking mountain to my left, the ashen nothingness before us and to my right, the sea leading onwards into still more devastation.

Marcus says nothing, does not move. Suddenly I am afraid to touch him again. I pull my hand back. He stays still and silent while the fisherman sails closer to the shore, using a pole to guide his way around the larger rocks.

"Can't get much closer," he says at last. "You'll have to wade."

Marcus stands, unsteady in the boat, then slips over the side. The water reaches his chest and I am afraid, for I stand shorter than him by at least a head's height and I cannot swim. Once in the water he holds out his arms to me and I dare not refuse. I clutch at my satchel, but Marcus shakes his head.

"You will wait for us," he tells the fisherman. I have not heard his voice for many hours, it comes out as a croak. The fisherman nods. Reluctantly, I leave my satchel in the boat and slip over the side into Marcus' arms. The water is cold and my feet scrabble to gain purchase, but he holds me until I have found my footing, his face blank. The water is up to my chin, but I can feel the bottom, and Marcus keeps one hand on me as we wade towards the shore. I go under once, tripping over a rock beneath the surface, but he yanks me upwards and I find my balance again. We have to crawl to get out of the water, for the shore is littered with rocks. I touch something soft and yelp, then see a dead sheep floating, its wool trailing in the water, eyes white and body bloated. I pull back in disgust, scramble more quickly, scraping my knee. I still don't really know where I am. The harbour was always a bustling place, there were jetties and walls with heavy iron rings where the boats were tied up. I cannot see the walls. There are no jetties, only the odd floating plank of wood, another dead sheep's body drifting past, rocks everywhere.

At last we are both standing on solid ground, if it can be called that. The ashes here are so thick they have mixed with the sea and formed an oozing mud. My feet sink in and soon my shoes have all but disappeared, the paste clinging to my calves. We trudge through it, heads down to take care over each step we take. When we are further from the water, the ashes become dry. They are too soft, though, each step we take sinks us down until a rock finds us. One patch comes up to my knees before I hit rock. I panic, thinking I will sink down into endless ashes and suffocate, try to take a deep breath to steady my thoughts and then realise that this is the fate that befell the people of Pompeii, the soft soft ashes filling their houses and mouths. I have to take a few more quick breaths, panic rising in me at the thought. I put my hand on a large rock, try to calm myself and look around me, the invisible sun behind the yellow-grey sky lending me some light with which to see.

This is Hades.

This is the land of the dead.

Everywhere is grey and black. There is no other colour. I shake my head, blink my eyes, for they seem to have lost the ability to see colour. But there is no colour. The sky is grey. The broken mountain is grey and black. The whole of the land beneath the sky, no matter where I turn, is grey, with black chunks of rock here and there. What used to be trees are now black charred arms stretching out of the devastation, reaching out to the gods to beg for their forgiveness, to placate their anger. Behind me is the sea and that, too, is grey, a silver-grey that shifts while before me is a soft grey that also shifts with the wind, clouds of it billowing. The air smells of rotting eggs and occasionally another smell drifts past, the harder sweeter stench of rotting flesh, from the fallen. I try to think only of the bloated sheep I saw bobbing in the bay and not of the people who stumbled while trying to escape, who ran but were felled by raging heat or trampling feet in the darkness that followed, who did not rise again. Now only the smell rises.

I should not have thought of it. My body is forced over as though by a blow to the back and bitter yellow bile spews from my mouth onto the ground, mixing with the soft grey. I straighten up, spitting the taste from my mouth, sweat trickling under my eyes. Ahead of me Marcus does not turn at the sound of me retching. Has he just walked over the top of the city walls? Is he walking up one of the main streets of the city? Or is he trampling over the rooftops as though he were a cat? I keep trying to find an anchor, an understanding of where I am, of where Pompeii is, but it has vanished so completely I am adrift. I stumble after him. If the mountain is there, if the sea is behind me, then is this the Marina Gate? If I walk after Marcus and we head that way, will we come to the gladiatorial barracks again, will we find his house nearby? And how will we judge how far we have walked when there are few landmarks and we stumble at every step, slowing us so that we lose track of how far we have come? If we used to say walk fifty paces, how many paces through the thick slow ash is that?

Marcus is still walking, now a long way off, stride by long stride, sometimes stumbling a little, once falling. He walks as though he is certain of a destination, as though he is in a hurry to reach it and all these ashes are merely in his way. Because I do not know what else to do, I follow him. I cannot hope to keep up with him, he has too great a head start and his legs are far longer than mine. I walk as fast as I can, falling often until I slow my gait. I cannot catch up with him, so I had better save myself from further scrapes and bruises.

"I AM SO SORRY," I keep saying, as though it were a chant, as though if I say it enough times there will be nothing to be sorry about; the ashes will rise back into the sky and uncover Pompeii just as it was before, its inhabitants crouched safely under its weight, scared of course, but relieved beyond measure to see us. Marcus will embrace his wife and child; he will smile and nod permission for me to run to Lucius' villa and find Myrtis and Felix, and all the others in the household. Myrtis will grumble about the state of the house, with all this damage and ashes everywhere, and want to know who is going to clean it all up, and Felix will hug me without words, glad I have been spared their experience. Marcus has finally stopped. I've only just caught up with him. He walks so much faster than I, even in this landscape.

"I am so sorry," I say again to his back.

He turns towards me, his face full of such rage that I step back, afraid that my words have offended him, that my helplessness is a burden to him. He reaches me in a few quick steps and for a moment I think he is going to beat me, or rape me, or something else terrible and I do not know why, nor how I can escape. I stumble, lose my footing, and fall into the ashes, their softness pulling at me. Marcus grasps my wrist, but he is not pulling me to my feet. Instead he jerks at my arm, impatient, while I struggle to stand but he pulls me off balance again. There's cold air on my wrist and a soft thud and then he lets go of me and walks away again, each footstep sinking, a grey cloud following him. I look down at my arm. He has undone my gold cuff, which is now half-buried in the ashes, the tiny pin on a chain beside it. My arm feels cold and light without it. I claw the cuff back out of the ashes and rock from all fours onto my knees and then stand, precariously.

"What have you done?" I call out to him. "Why have you taken it off?" I don't understand what he means by it. I don't know what I am to do. Is he taking it away as a punishment? But he left it lying in the grey softness as though it were of no importance. Clasping the cuff in my left hand, my other arm outstretched for balance, I follow him to where he stands looking out over the endless grey. When I am only a few steps away I stop. "Why?" I ask.

He turns to me, stares at my puzzled face and then reaches out a hand. I hold out the cuff, but he shakes his head and gestures that I should give him my right hand. I hold it out. He takes it roughly, pulling me closer to him.

"I, Marcus Aquillius Scaurus, do give you, Althea, your freedom. This is your manumission. You are a freedwoman from this day forward. Now go." He drops my hand, strides away to the right, his head still turning this way and that, as though he will suddenly see something he recognises.

I drop the gold cuff and it lands in a soft puff of ashes. My hand is shaking so hard I can barely lift it. I stand in the hellscape, looking down at my wrist, the cuff now gone. I am free. I have been set free by my master. I am a freedwoman. *My father on his knees. I beg you, I beg you will buy my daughter also, I will serve you loyally if you will only buy her, if you will only take her as a slave. I beg you.* My tears fall into the ashes at my feet and stain them, tiny black blotches of happiness and wonder amidst the devastation. I scoop up the cuff. Its weight will assure me of money for a long time to come, I need only find a jeweller who will buy it from me for a fair price. After that... I am not sure what I will do. I can offer myself as a paid scribe to a rich household or live a simple life and write letters for those who cannot write for themselves. But I am free and nothing else matters.

Except those who have been lost.

The wild thrill dies as I look about me again. The landscape shocks me, over and over. I have seen some form of it for days now and the worst of it for many hours, and still it is so shocking, so horrible, that I cannot comprehend it. I think of the layers upon layers of stones and ashes beneath my feet and below them crushed invisible bodies. I step to one side as though to lift my weight away from them, yet for all I know I am now standing on another person, unknown to me or worse, known to me, their body crushed still further under my unknowing weight, their lungs unable to breathe because of my ignorance of their whereabouts. I begin to walk, unsure of where I am going, only that I cannot keep standing in one place in case I am causing further torment, even though I know that the suffering is gone now for the dead and is felt only by the living.

Marcus.

He has made his way to a place a little way off and is on his knees, scooping up ashes and throwing them to one side. I wade towards him, the soft ashes fooling me so that I step on hard rocks more than once, fall over twice.

"Marcus?"

"The apartments were here, I have worked it out." He coughs. The ashes he is scooping up are filling the air. I pull my head wrap across my mouth.

"How can you be sure?"

He sits back on his knees, suddenly eager to tell me, eager to be certain. "That must be the barracks because there is the very top of the roof of the theatre and I took fifty paces this way and then I would have turned left and entered the courtyard there, you see?" His arm flings out in a wide arc, points to the endless grey, to a place that in his mind is the entryway to his home. "And so, the roof must be below here, I think it must have fallen in, because it should be higher than the ashes, but perhaps the weight of the rocks and ashes caused it to give way. But we were only on the first floor, so it's possible that the second floor protected our apartment..."

I kneel next to him. My tears start to fall. The sight of this man, alone in this devastation, who has chosen a spot which might, or might not, be the right place, who has started digging without any possibility of finding his loved ones, is too much to bear. "Marcus," I say, as gently as I can, "Marcus, they are gone."

"No," he says and digs again, the air around us growing ever thicker with clouds of ash so that I cough and cough again.

"Yes," I say. "Marcus, please. They are gone." I touch his arm.

The shove he gives me is so hard I find myself rolling with the force of it. My mouth fills with ashes. I crawl onto my knees, spitting and coughing, desperate to get the ashes out of my mouth. When I have wiped down my face I see Marcus is still on his knees, trying to scoop away the ashes.

He digs for hours. But the ashes shift with the slightest breeze and he makes slow progress. He finds what seems to be a rooftop, but it is broken and crushed and even though he lifts away tiles and beams, grunting and sweating with the work, it is only a tiny part of what would have to be excavated. He will not let me come near him. In the end I sit watching him, as though by witnessing his efforts I am somehow helping him.

I pray. At first, I am not sure to whom I should be praying, other than Vulcan, god of fire, who must have been angered. The sun moves across the sky and I have to sit and watch a man I barely know search for his wife and child, even though I am already certain they are dead, like all the rest of the people who used to live in this city that has disappeared, buried beneath the grey. Myrtis and Felix.

I start at the beginning. I pray to Jupiter to strengthen this man and to Juno to care for his dead wife. I pray to the Great Mother Cybele for the tiny child I only saw for a few hours. I pray to Vulcan, apologising for whatever has angered him. I pray to Mercury, messenger of the gods, to bring us mortals a message to tell us what to do, to take back to the gods a plea from us begging for forgiveness. I pray and pray, I think of every god I can, beg each for forgiveness, I beg for their influence in taking away some of this horror, in whatever realm of life they control. I pray to Mars, who watches over soldiers, for Marcus was once one of his men. I pray to Venus for the love this man has lost. I pray to Libertas, at first thanking her that she protected me, an insignificant slave, from certain death, but I also pray to her for Myrtis and Felix and other slaves I have known, now lost in the choking ashes and then it is hard not to berate Libertas, not to ask in anger why they had to die.

"We need to return."

The fisherman's voice startles me from my prayers. Marcus pays no attention; he is still digging. I twist round to look up at the fisherman, his arms and legs coated with ashes where he has stumbled and fallen on his way to find us.

"There is still digging to be done," says Marcus, without stopping.

"We need to return now, there is not long until twilight. I will not sail in the darkness again."

Marcus ignores him. The man looks at me and I stare back at him, as though what he is asking is impossible, though I know he is right. Livia and Amantius have not escaped. Now that I have seen the horror that was once Pompeii, I can no longer believe in happy endings. Myrtis and Felix are dead, Lucius, his wife and daughter also. This desolate landscape is why so few refugees have arrived. If everyone had escaped, there would have been fifteen thousand or more from Pompeii alone, and there have only been a few hundred, perhaps one or two thousand at best so far. The truth is that Marcus' wife and son are dead, buried far beneath the ashes that he is helplessly digging through. He will not reach their bodies alone, and, even if he were to, what joy would that give him? And yet his desperation is so strong that if he were to believe them dead, I fear he would take his own life here and now, with the fisherman and I as his only witnesses. My only choice, if I wish to keep him alive, if I wish to keep him safe as I promised his wife, is to lie. The promise I made her, so fleeting and casual, has in the past few hours taken on the strength of an oath in my mind, unbreakable. I swore to a woman who is now dead that I would look after her husband, 'keep him safe', and now I feel the burden of the promise I made so lightly.

"Marcus," I say.

He does not stop digging. Perhaps he knows what is coming, what I'm about to say.

"Marcus," I say again. "We need to sail back to Puteoli while we still can."

"No," he says.

I take a deep breath. I have to lie; I have no other choice. "They cannot possibly still be here," I say. "They must have fled at once; they will have seen what was happening and asked for help. Perhaps from your assistant, perhaps from someone at the amphitheatre. They would have thought to reach Fausta in Misenum. You said yourself she was your right-hand woman. Livia would have thought of her in your absence. She would have known Fausta would look after her until you sent word or came back. She must have found a boat to take her to Misenum or, even better, Puteoli. She knew that would be on your route back from Rome when you came to look for them. You need to be at one of the refugee camps, ready to receive them when they arrive from wherever they sought shelter. And besides," I add, "now that the soldiers have arrived, they will be registering more and more people, and crosschecking them. We need to be there. You need to be there."

Marcus sits back on his heels and turns to look at me. His face and arms are covered in ashes. He looks like something unearthly and I want to draw away from him. Instead I lean forward and touch his arm, as though to draw him back to the realm of the living from this dead place. "We have to go," I repeat. I lie again, more forcefully. "They will be in one of the refugee camps," I say. "You must go to them there."

I see my lie in his eyes. I see that he knows the truth already, that he has been digging for their bodies, not to save their lives. But I also see that he wants so desperately to believe me, to still cling to hope that they are alive, that he will do anything, go anywhere, if I might only be proven right.

I look back, once we are in the boat. Twilight is beginning to fall, and this will be the last time I ever see Pompeii. I stare at the unending flat grey, trying to remember the city that lies beneath it, trying to lay that image over the grey, and failing.

Pompeii has gone.

In the brief time we have been away, the military camp has expanded. As Pompeii has disappeared, so a new city of tents has risen. The regimented rows and uniformity of the tents promises order, promises safety from the chaotic wrath that has gone before. The tiny mismatched shelters are beginning to disappear, as family after family are transferred into the military encampment. A cohort of Praetorians has arrived and is busy creating a second camp, to accommodate any leftover from the first and any further refugees who may arrive. Vast outdoor kitchens have been set up, with vats of savoury porridge, flatbreads, hot soups and bean stews. But back in the administrative tent first one scribe and then another shakes their head, checking their lists of names both here and at the other main refugee camp in Stabiae.

"We can't guarantee we have everyone," they admit. "But we've tried to consolidate all the refugees into these two camps, so that we can more easily look after them and help them find their missing families."

"But it might take a while for people to get here?" I ask.

There is a shrugged nod, but by now the explosion from Vesuvius was six days ago. Even on foot, most of the refugees should have reached one camp or the other, depending where they started from. Arrivals of new refugees have slowed to a trickle, many of them were staying with family or friends until they heard about the camps. The scribes do not say so, but there is little chance of many more survivors. There are messengers on the roads between here and Stabiae twice a day, every day, making their way through whichever routes are still passable, reports are returning the information that most survivors have now joined one or the other of the two camps. Even those with other places to go to have made themselves known, if they wish to trace relatives or friends. The scrolls at the scribes' feet are growing longer and more numerous, but Livia's name is not among them.

We find Fausta.

"You're back." She embraces Marcus, who stares over her shoulder at the lines of tents, then embraces me. "Did you reach Pompeii?"

"Yes," I say, when it appears clear that Marcus will not reply.

"How was it?" she asks, her voice low.

"She can tell you," says Marcus. "I need to search the tents." And he is gone, striding towards the first tent in line, ready to check each one again in the hopes of finding what he is searching for.

Fausta turns to me. "Tell me about it," she says, pulling me by the hand to sit under a tree.

I sit and look into her expectant face. And my shoulders heave, the tears pour out of me that I held back for too many hours whilst Marcus dug. Fausta leans towards me and takes me in her arms. I bury my face in the folds of her toga and weep as I have not wept since my father died.

When I have told her everything, Fausta sits for a long time, staring out across the fields. "I didn't know such a thing could happen," she says at last. "I can't really imagine that I will never see Pompeii again." She takes a deep breath and exhales, her shoulders dropping. "And the people…"

"I lied to him," I confess. "I didn't know how else to make him come back. But they can't have escaped. The only people who can have escaped were those who were out of the cities for some reason, like you and me and Marcus, or traders, fishermen who saw the danger and left quickly. All the others…"

"What else could you do?"

"I was afraid he would…"

Fausta turns her head towards the military encampment, watches as Marcus makes his way from one tent to another. "He would," she says. "What else is he to live for now? Better an honourable death than a miserable life when you've lost everything you hold dear."

"I promised his wife I'd keep him safe," I say. "I can't let him do that."

We sit in silence for a little while.

"Why aren't you wearing the gold cuff?" asks Fausta suddenly.

I search in my satchel and hold it out. "He – he set me free."

Fausta stares at me. "When?"

"In Pompeii, in the ashes."

"Why?"

"I don't know," I say. "He just took it off and said the words. I think he wanted me gone, he didn't want to have to look after me, he wanted to be alone to search."

"Was there a witness?"

My stomach dips. "No," I say reluctantly. "Does that mean it's not valid?" The thought of it, of having my freedom taken away from me just when I thought it had been granted, is almost too much to bear on top of everything else that has happened.

Fausta shakes her head. "No," she says firmly. "It doesn't matter, there doesn't have to be a witness. So long as he stands by his word, which Marcus would." She thinks for a moment. "But then why are you worrying about him? That bracelet would be enough to live on for a couple of years if you're careful, you can just travel back to Rome and become a scribe to some rich man, you'd be paid well."

"I can't do that," I say. "I watched him digging through the ashes to find his wife and child and I knew all the time they were dead. I can't leave him to discover that for himself, all alone."

"You've a good heart," she says. "There's plenty wouldn't stand by him."

I look down at the cuff, heavy in my hand, knowing what she says is true. There is no reason for me to be loyal to a man who's been my master barely a week. I am free now, I could do as I wish, I could simply leave, return to Rome, and take up life as a freedwoman. But I can't find it in myself to leave a man whose whole life has been shattered in one instant, and besides, the idea of being utterly alone, without friends or family, is frightening. A slave who has been set free is normally regarded as part of their past master's circle. At the very least, he would be their patron, they would take his name, and his family and friends would become part of their own extended social connections. If I left now, I would have nothing but a piece of gold and it does not seem enough, with all that has happened. I want to know that someone would search for me if I were lost among the ashes, that someone would mourn for me if I died. I shake my head, tucking the cuff back in my satchel. "I can't leave him," I repeat again. "I promised his wife I would keep him safe."

"That's going to be a hard promise to keep," says Fausta, not unkindly.

"I have to try," I say.

She nods.

"And the others?" I ask, not having dared to before now.

"What others?"

"The people you and Marcus used to work with," I manage. I don't know how else to describe them. Gladiators, whores, dancers, slaves.

Fausta shakes her head, her face set as though she has already accepted this new grief. "Gone," she says and even though her tone is harsh two tears fall from her eyes which she quickly dashes away, as though, if she starts to cry, she will not stop. She takes a deep breath. "This contract he signed to manage the amphitheatre," she says, "what happens if he breaks it?"

"He wasn't even allowed to leave Rome," I say, lowering my voice in case someone can hear us. "There will be punishments just for that if they find out. If he abandons the job, he'll be a wanted man."

Fausta watches as Marcus begins checking the last line of tents. "So," she says at last, "it comes down to this. You, Marcus and I have nothing and nobody left except that gold cuff and the management of the amphitheatre. If they think he's abandoned that job, he'll find himself in the arena and you and I will have no man to protect us. You may find a job as a scribe, but I'll be back in a brothel, on my knees to earn a living. We have to stop Marcus from taking his own life and we must get him back into the amphitheatre to continue his work. If we don't manage that, he will die, and you and I will struggle to live."

I know what she is saying is true, but I have not allowed myself to state it so baldly until now. I think over her words, trying to find another way, but there isn't one. Marcus has secured a job which carries with it both money and, if he succeeds, a certain level of respect, if not status, given the nature of the job and the people he will be associating with. Fausta and I will be a great deal safer if we have a man who will protect us. If he is working, Marcus can pay me to be his scribe, so I will have a job ready made for me.

"What do we do?" I ask.

"How much money does Marcus have left?"

"I'm not sure," I say. "He can't have very much left. We had to change horses all the way down here, he'd have to pay to get back the ones we left after the first change. And he paid a month's wages to the fishermen to take us to Pompeii."

Fausta grimaces. "Then we have no choice," she says. "Marcus must return to Rome and continue the job. We have to make that happen or all three of us will suffer for it."

"But he won't want to leave," I say. "He will want to stay here until he finds Livia."

Fausta nods. "I know. He won't leave until he believes he's done enough to find them, and if he believes they're dead…"

"So how – what do we do?" I repeat.

Fausta takes a deep breath. "You must return to Rome," she says. "When you get there, you stall them, make them believe Marcus is still in Rome and that he is still doing the job." She holds up a hand to stop my interruption. "I'll stay here with him until he has searched this camp and perhaps the one at Stabiae to his satisfaction. Then I'll suggest that there's still a slim chance Livia is alive and that if she were, she would head to Rome to find him, she knows where Julia's insula is, she would go there. I'll tell him we must return to Rome, continue the work and Livia will find us there."

"But she won't," I say and feel tears welling up again at the thought of it.

"No," says Fausta, and her firm tone wavers for a moment. "But if we can keep him alive long enough, he'll see that he must go on, for our sake as well as his. Marcus is loyal to those with whom he works," she adds. "He'll come to see that his death would only cause more misery. For you, for me, for other people who depend on him. But we must keep him alive until then. Even if it means lying."

I open my satchel and pull out the gold cuff again, pass it to Fausta. "Can you get money for this?" I ask.

"Yes," she says. "If you're sure?"

"I've got no one else," I say. "I'm too afraid to be alone."

Fausta lays her rough hand against my cheek for a moment. "I know," she says. "It's a hard choice, but it's the only one I can think of right now. Let's hope it's the right one." She stands as Marcus comes towards us, squaring her shoulders and lifting her chin, ready to do what must be done.

HE TRIES TO ARGUE WITH us of course, he says he will not return to Rome, that he does not care about the job, that Livia is all that matters. But Fausta keeps calm and works on him. She reminds him of the binding terms of his contract, but only briefly, preferring to remind him that he must still provide for Livia and Amantius when he finds them, and how will he do that with no job, given that his savings are now lost beneath the ashes of Pompeii? In Rome at least he has a job and a place to live, Julia will welcome Livia with open arms when she arrives. He has a scribe in me and Fausta, as she was before, will be his right-hand woman to help run the amphitheatre, if she is needed. She appeals to his sense of loyalty, to his protection of us as two women who will otherwise be alone in the world. She emphasises the importance of keeping the job at the amphitheatre, before suggesting that I return to Rome and stall for time, freeing the two of them to search for Livia. She holds up the cuff and tells him that even though he has freed me I have proven loyal and thrown in my lot with them, that the money they get for it will allow them time to search, as well as feed us until he is next paid.

There's a moment where I think he will refuse, that he will tell her what we already know, that Livia and Amantius are dead and therefore there is nothing left for him to live for, that he will walk away from us and take his own life, somewhere out here in the field, an honourable death allowing him to follow his wife and child into the underworld. But somehow, I find Fausta pressing a few coins into my hand, enough to keep me in food for a couple of weeks. She finds a trader heading north back to Rome with a wagon of goods which he reluctantly agrees I may ride on. I don't like the way he looks at me, running his eyes up and down my body before agreeing to take me. I want to refuse, but Fausta leans close to him and whispers in his ear. I watch his face drain pale and he nods hurriedly, backing away from her, gesturing to me to take my place on the wagon without any more glances at my body.

"What did you say to him?" I ask Fausta.

"I said if he so much as laid one finger on you, I'd put a curse on his dick and it would fall off the next time he tried to use it. Sleep in the wagon when he stops at an inn, don't relieve yourself anywhere near him. When you get back to Rome, go straight to Julia and tell her what happened, she'll help you for Marcus' sake. I'll bring him back as soon as I can. Until then, hold your nerve and stall for time. I know you're scared, but you have to do this."

"What will I say to stall them?"

"You'll think of something. You've got four days of travel to come up with something clever. Work hard and think quickly."

Marcus' words, I think, he must have used them to her too. I clutch at her hands a little too tightly, afraid of letting go. "May Feronia keep you safe until I see you again," she says and turns away.

I look at Marcus, somehow hoping that he will intervene, that he will decree that he will come back to Rome with us now, take charge so that I do not have to be sent on this mission alone, but he is standing looking over the hundreds of tents now being erected by the Praetorian cohort.

"Goodbye," I say. "I pray you find Livia quickly," I add and Fausta nods at me.

He tries to focus on me. "Stay safe," he says. "I will be back as soon as I have found them. Julia will care for you." He turns away again, lost in his own desperate need.

FREEDWOMAN

Wary of Fausta's abilities to curse his genitals, the trader keeps his hands to himself, but he also refuses to talk to me or be pleasant in any way. I spend four lonely days travelling back to Rome and, by the time I reach Julia's, my very bones feel cold as well as thoroughly shaken by the endless trundling of the cart. The courtyard feels like a homecoming.

"You're back. Where's Marcus?"

I look up at Maria. Sat in her usual place, she has spotted me at once. "He's still in Puteoli."

Julia appears in her doorway. She takes one look at me and waves me indoors without a word. I nod to Maria, then follow, grateful to be taken in.

"What happened?"

I cry, telling her. I try to describe Pompeii and fail; it cannot be described to someone who has not seen it. I can only tell her that it has gone, there is no hope of recovering it. I repeat Fausta's descriptions of the events from the viewpoint of Misenum and I falter when I have to describe Marcus searching through the ashes. I sob and Julia does not pat or hug me, she does not tell me not to cry. She sits apart, watching me solemnly; she knows that not to cry for such an unthinkable horror would be a horror in itself. She lets me cry as though it were my sacred duty to do so, like a ritual at a ceremony in a temple and, having held back as many tears as possible for Marcus' sake and then been all alone for the journey home, the relief in crying without restraint is comforting in itself. By the time I have finished, darkness has fallen, and I sit, exhausted, silent.

Julia stands and lights candles at her household shrine. She lifts her palms and prays silently for a while. Then she puts a thick vegetable porridge in front of me and I eat. The heat in my belly is soporific, I find myself almost falling asleep while I eat.

"I have to make them believe he is here in Rome," I say, and I almost sob again at the thought of it, it seems like such an impossible task. "I have to convince them he is working on the amphitheatre when I don't even know when he'll be back."

I want Julia to give me a ready-made plan, to tell me exactly what to do, but she only clears away my bowl and spoon. "You need to sleep," she says. "You cannot think when you are so tired."

"But how will I convince them?" I ask.

"Sleep," she says. "The roof hut is yours until Marcus returns and tells me what he wants to do. He would not have freed you if he did not believe in you, Fausta would not have sent you back here alone if she did not think you could do what must be done."

I stare at her, my eyes sore with crying and tiredness. "How do you know he freed me?"

She looks down at my wrist. "Your cuff has been taken off. You would not have removed it without permission. Now go and sleep."

THE SKY IS NOT EVEN light when I fetch cold water and, shivering, wash myself. I put on a clean tunic and wrap up my hair, pull my cloak around me before packing my satchel with my tablet and stylus. I walk down the rickety stairway shivering more with nerves than the cold.

"You look like a slave girl," comes Maria's voice.

I startle, having not seen her, already at her place on the balcony despite the early morning hour. She is munching on a hot fruit roll and looking me over, none too satisfied.

"I'm clean and neat," I say, slightly offended.

"That's all that a mistress expects from a slave girl," agrees Maria. "It's not what a freedwoman aspires to."

I hesitate. "What would you change?" I ask in the end.

Maria puts her head on one side. "Brighter colours," she starts. "You need different clothes; those look like the slave livery of a well-to-do household."

"They are," I say. "And they're all I have."

She tuts and then lifts herself heavily from her seat and disappears into her apartment. I stand waiting, unsure of whether she is about to return or not but, after a brief pause, she reappears holding something in her hand. "Wear these."

I approach her and look at what she is offering. A delicate pink tunic, a head wrap in dark blue, with tiny shells attached to the edge. "I can't take those."

"Consider them a loan," she says, pushing them into my hands. "You'll never fool them if you look like a slave girl. You need to look like you have some authority."

"Thank you," I say and hurry back upstairs, where I change as quickly as possible and then come back downstairs feeling absurdly overdressed.

But Maria is still displeased. "You *move* like a slave girl," she says, frowning. She crosses her arms under her ample bosom and stands her ground, blocking my way.

"What do you mean?"

"Head down, shoulders hunched, quick little steps like you're worried you're going to bother someone," she says brutally. "Get your head up, shoulders back, *stride*."

"I'm not a man," I object.

"Oh, you don't think the great ladies of Rome stride? Think about how Julia moves."

"She's – was a Vestal Virgin," I say.

"And nobody messes with her," says Maria triumphantly. "Try to walk like her."

I think about Julia, how she moves. I lift my head so that my neck feels like it has doubled in length, stick my breasts out so my shoulders go back and then walk down the stairs as if I'm approaching a temple altar, slow and solemn, my very person sacred. I can hear Maria laughing from above me.

"That's more like it, my girl. Bona Dea watch over you and Minerva give you quick thinking."

"Thank you," I call. I look up, but her features are hidden in the morning gloom. I can only see the solid comforting bulk of her, seated at her favourite spot, waiting for her watchdog duties of the day to begin.

IT TAKES ME OVER AN hour to walk into the amphitheatre. It is just too big, I think helplessly, pacing back and forth along the Forum, trying to summon up my courage while the sun rises ever higher. How can I hope to hold my own against the architect, the various heads of the guilds, even the Aedile, should he take it upon himself to conduct an inspection? How will I convince them Marcus is still in Rome and working on the project? They will know I am lying for sure. And if I fail, then Marcus will be a wanted man, Fausta will be forced to work in a brothel, and me? I will be some rich man's scribe, and I can't guarantee I'll be lucky a third time. I'll find myself a plaything against my will, possibly even enslaved again, for I have no paperwork to prove I am not a slave. And a rich man does not much care for a freedwoman's protests, if she has no man to protect her. I have no family, no friends, no-one to protect my honour except myself.

I try to think how it would be if Marcus were here. He would be asking one awkward question after another; I think to myself. He would be enraging the architect, who doesn't get a moment to think when Marcus is here. At last I stand outside the shadowy arches of the imperial entrance and take a deep breath. One day at a time. I need only fool them for one day at a time. Work hard and think fast.

"Ah, the scribe girl."

The architect is standing behind me, scowling. His scribes stare at me with undisguised dislike.

"Good morning," I say with a bright smile. "I am delighted to see you. Marcus has given me a list of items I should check with you."

"A list? Is he not here himself? Where is he?"

"Did you not receive our message? I sent a messenger boy. Marcus has been ill for over a week," I say. I lean a little closer. "A bad oyster at a dinner party."

The architect isn't quite sure how to respond. Oysters suggests Marcus has been dining with a well-off patron. He hesitates.

"So, my list for today," I say, forcing my smile a bit wider. "Shall we go through it now?"

"When will he be back at work?"

"Oh, he is back already," I say. "Didn't you see him? He walked the whole amphitheatre at dawn this morning, gave me the list and went off to Ostia to see some contact. A beast-hunter, I believe. It'll probably take a few days, what with setting up exactly what will be needed, as well as the journey."

The architect looks disgruntled. The port of Ostia is most of a day's journey from Rome and all the best beast-hunters operate out of there, so that they can coordinate shipping of animals from Africa. He can't really argue with my story and I have just bought myself three or four days. My smile becomes brighter all by itself.

I ASK ENOUGH QUESTIONS AND make myself irritating enough to the architect over the next three days that he starts actively avoiding me, arriving very late on the fourth day and leaving for the baths extremely early.

"I assume I can at least expect to see Marcus tomorrow?" he asks before he departs.

"Of course," I say. "He may wish to try out the flooding soon," I add cheerfully, knowing this is one of his pet horrors, and watch him blench at the very idea.

ON THE FIFTH DAY I arrive at first light and hurry up to the architect as soon as he arrives. I can see his eyes roll at the sight of me as I approach.

"Marcus has gone to seek housing for his family today," I say. "He may be a little late. Meanwhile, he says that the pens under the arena are not suited to purpose."

"In what way?"

"Not strong enough," I say. "He says they must be remade entirely. Also, he thinks they should be spaced out better or the animals will fight, even through the bars."

The architect splutters with rage. "Those pens are the finest – strongest – he cannot –"

I shrug, looking down at my tablet, which is full of meaningless scribbles. "I don't know what to tell you. That's what he asked me to raise with you. He said it was very concerning. He can't have expensive wild animals getting damaged before a show, especially if the Emperor will be in attendance, which of course for the inaugural Games he will be most days, I should imagine. I mean, it would look bad, wouldn't it? And they'll want to know who built them, won't they? Which won't be Marcus, will it? I'll leave it with you, shall I?"

FOR ALL MY SMILING BLUSTER at the amphitheatre, when I return to the rooftop hut each day I sit and cry. I am so afraid that Marcus will not come back at all. I am afraid that at any moment the Aedile might visit, or the architect will absolutely demand to see Marcus and I will be unable to produce him. I try to keep myself busy at the end of each working day, washing myself and my clothes, buying stuffed bread and olives or nuts, eating, sitting on the rooftop to catch the last light and writing notes to myself of other awkward requests I can make at the amphitheatre. I'm not sure how long my money will last, either, I have enough for perhaps a week more of food. If Marcus and Fausta do not arrive by then I will have to ask Julia for money, and she is already housing me without asking for rent. How long should I stick with this plan before I have to give up and go and seek work elsewhere, revealing the fraud I have helped to perpetrate? And can I manage to pass as a freedwoman with no paperwork proclaiming me so? I wonder whether I can fake some paperwork, falsify Marcus' signature. The thought of becoming a slave again makes my stomach turn over.

"Not back yet?"

I look up to see the old Jewess, Adah, standing over me. I've not seen her since my return. "No," I say. "I don't know when he will be back," I confess.

"Is it like they say? The mountain of fire?"

I nod.

"The cities gone?"

I nod.

She lowers herself to sit next to me, her knees making a loud clicking noise as she does so. "Did you lose people?"

Myrtis, Felix. I nod. I can't say their names. I'll cry, and I am afraid to cry, I have to stay strong.

She pats my arm, her hand a mass of wrinkles. "I'm sorry, child," she says. "It's a hard thing to lose those we care for."

I swallow. The tears are already welling up in my eyes.

"No shame in crying."

A sob escapes me and now it is too late, the tears are falling.

Adah does not keep her distance as Julia did, she puts her bony arms round me. I put my face into the cloth of her dress and cry. It is a different kind of crying, it is not a sacred grief for Pompeii or any of the other cities, not for Marcus and the frightened refugees. Instead I cry for Myrtis and Felix, for my own terror and loss over the past days, for my constant fear that I will not be able to do what is asked of me and will end up enslaved again, just when freedom was so close.

Adah rocks me and murmurs something in a language I do not understand, but I recognise the words a mother murmurs to a child who is hurt, the same sounds in all tongues. When I end up hiccupping and pull away, sniffing, she uses the edge of her shawl to wipe my face.

"He'll be back. How many days have you kept them at bay?"

"Five."

She chuckles. "Cunning girl."

"I can't think of anything else," I say, hiccupping again. "I worry they'll find me out."

"Make them worry," says Adah. "Then they won't have time to think about you." She gets up, using my shoulder as a support, letting out a little groan as she straightens up. "Goodnight, child."

"Goodnight, Adah," I say. "Thank you," I add, though I am not sure she heard me, already halfway across the rooftop and back to her own little hut.

"You want to do *what*?"

"Test the toilets," I say, as though this is obvious.

"They've *been* tested. They work perfectly. The plumbing of this amphitheatre is second to none. It's better than some of the finest villas in Rome."

"Not with a high volume of people."

"What?"

"They've not been tested with lots of people," I say, peering into one of the toilets in the third tier. "Sponges for wiping," I add out loud, making a note on my tablet.

"How many people would you like to test them with?" he asks.

"Three hundred?"

"*What?*"

I spread my hands, stating the obvious. "We can seat fifty thousand people. There's what, fifty toilets on each tier. The full day goes on for several hours. How many people do you think will be using them at any one time? Especially during the breaks, or the less popular parts of the show?"

"And just how are you going to test them?"

"Gather up three hundred people and get them all to use one of the toilet rooms as quickly as possible. We can see how long the queues are. Whether we get any blockages. How quickly an attendant can clean the room again with people coming and going. How fast we run out of sponges if they fall off the sticks and go down the drains."

He stares at me in horror.

"Tomorrow, then?" I ask. "The foremen can get all the men to use the third-floor toilets tomorrow morning, as a test. We must have more than three hundred men on site at the moment?"

He wants to refuse; I can see it. "Where is Marcus? I want a word with him."

"Racing stables," I say.

"What's he doing there?"

"We need chariots and some racing teams for the opening Games," I say, making it up as I go along. "Re-enacting a battle."

"Is he going to oversee this ridiculous test tomorrow?"

I make an appalled face. "I shouldn't think so," I say. "Why would the manager oversee a toilets test? He has much more important things to organise. By the way, the imperial box looks awfully plain. Is it going to be decorated at all?"

The architect looks harassed. "The mosaic-makers are late delivering," he says. "I've commissioned a magnificent floor for the imperial box but most of the best makers are working on the imperial palace at the moment, Titus is having works done."

I raise my eyebrows. "Well, as long as it gets done in time…" I say doubtfully. "It would be awkward if the Emperor came to see the works and thought his own box wasn't being included in the decorations. I mean, you're already decorating the arena wall, which is hardly the main priority, and his box isn't even carved or painted yet?"

The architect swallows and I depart, head held high.

The toilet test buys me a full two days, as the first round is a disaster, queues blocking the corridors, the attendant barely able to keep up, so that we now know we will need two slaves per toilet room. I insist on a second day of tests which fortunately go better, although the architect doesn't even turn up on the second day, having developed a severe headache after watching the first day's shambles. Eight days. I have managed eight days. I feel oddly proud at the antics I have managed to force on the poor man, although I still worry about how much longer I can keep going.

On the ninth day I ask rather pointedly how the statues to decorate the outer arches are coming along, given that there are over one hundred and fifty to be made and painted, featuring various past emperors, august personages and divinities. The architect launches into a spirited defence of the time they are taking, to which I respond by grimacing and taking notes on my tablet in my most unreadable shorthand, before shaking my head and saying that surely we are due an inspection very soon by, at the very least, the Aedile and quite possibly the Emperor himself. After all, he can see the building from his palace windows, he must be curious about our progress? The architect looks as if he's going to be sick.

"Althea! ALTHEA!"

I'm washing, the cold water nothing like the warm baths I'd like to be in, but I can hear Maria's bellow even from inside my little hut. Opening the door, I peer over the edge.

"He's back!"

I stare down. In the courtyard below me are two figures, recognisable even in the evening gloom. Marcus and Fausta. I run down the stairs and nearly hug Marcus, then settle for embracing Fausta instead.

"You're back! The gods be praised!"

Fausta smiles broadly. "The gods be praised indeed. The horses are almost dead, but we made it back."

"I'll take care of them." Celer has appeared on the walkway above and now he makes his way down the stairs and out of the courtyard gate, with a quick pat on the shoulder for Marcus.

"Come inside." Julia is beckoning.

"I'll be with you in a moment," says Marcus. His voice is quiet and so hoarse I barely recognise it. He walks to the toilets and I turn to Fausta, lowering my voice as Julia joins us.

"Livia?"

Fausta shakes her head. "We searched everywhere, even went to the family farm in case she'd hidden herself there." She shakes her head again. "They're dead, they can't have survived what happened. You can tell just by looking at the refugee camps. If a lot of people had escaped there should have been many thousands. There weren't many more when we left than when you did," she says to me.

Julia keeps her voice low too. "How is he?"

Fausta sighs. "He still maintains she's alive. He won't accept the truth. In the end the only way I could get him back here was to agree with him and say that he'd better come back here and hold down the only means he has for making money at the moment. That she would know where to find him. I thought I wouldn't be able to convince him but, in the end, he gave in. Maybe he was just too tired to fight me anymore. Neither of us has slept properly since it happened."

I FETCH WATER FROM THE public fountain so they can both wash, offer Fausta my spare tunic so she has something clean to wear. Julia gives Marcus a faded green tunic that used to belong to her husband. While they wash and dress, I run to the bakery for bread, then sit in Julia's kitchen chopping up cabbage, carrots, garlic and onions to add to soaked beans and sprouted barley. By the time they join us the stew is bubbling fiercely. Without her toga Fausta looks smaller somehow; the usual bulk of cloth stripped from her frame makes her appear more delicate.

"Smells good," says Fausta. "I haven't had a hot meal since – in weeks. It's been snatched mouthfuls of bread and a bite of cheese, if we were lucky."

They sit and I serve everyone. Marcus stays silent, but he eats as if he's eaten nothing since I saw him. The food is good, the hot stew filling and heating us all at once. When we've eaten our fill, Julia sets a bowl of nuts on the table and some sweet wine cakes.

"Here," I say, passing Marcus a scroll of papyrus.

"What's this?"

"A list of lies I've told as well as questions and issues you've raised in your absence," I say.

He looks down the list and a small smile reaches his lips, the first time I've seen him smile since we saw the ashes begin to fall in Rome. "You're very inventive," he comments. "I'm dissatisfied with the hinges on the Gate of Triumph?"

"And the Gate of Death," I confirm. "Both of them are prone to squeaking despite being re-oiled three times. The squeaking noise will detract from the sense of occasion."

He shakes his head, still smiling. "I don't like the green arena sand sent in for my approval?"

"It was the wrong shade of green," I say firmly. "So was the blue. They're sending new samples tomorrow."

"And I've requested two women go onto the payroll as my assistants? Is that you and Fausta?"

"Yes," I say.

Fausta laughs out loud. "She's a better negotiator than you," she says. "I think from now on she should be the one to talk money when there's money to be talked. You better learn that list off by heart."

"Agreed," says Marcus. His smile fades, he looks as though maintaining a conversation is about to finish him off.

"You should sleep," I say hurriedly.

He stands, nods to the three of us and then leaves. I can hear the rickety stairs creaking as he walks up them.

"I should get some sleep too," I say.

Julia and Fausta nod.

"Is he all right?" I ask Fausta, pausing in the doorway to look back at her.

She looks away, then shrugs and meets my gaze. "No," she says bluntly. "He must know they're dead, but he won't admit it and I didn't dare say it out loud in case he took his own life. So I kept my mouth shut and he keeps talking about her possibly still being alive. Maybe he has to do it to survive each day, but I'm still afraid for him. I'd feel better if I knew he'd accepted the truth."

"The truth can take a long time to accept," says Julia.

Fausta nods.

I stand in silence for a few moments. "Goodnight," I say at last.

"Goodnight," they chorus.

WHEN I REACH THE ROOFTOP hut, Marcus is already lying down. I blow out the lamp I've carried up, casting the room into instant blackness, lie down and pull the blanket over myself. I try to stay very quiet, thinking him already asleep, but he speaks.

"I'm sorry," he says in the darkness.

"For what?"

"Setting you free."

I lie still, hardly breathing at what I am hearing, my heart thudding. There was no witness to my manumission, just the two of us in the landscape of horror that used to be Pompeii. If Marcus wishes, he could claim he never set me free and it would be the word of a woman against her master, a slave against a citizen of Rome. I would stand no chance. I think of the gold cuff closing around my wrist, of a life ahead of me bound back to slavery after a confused taste of freedom.

"I do not mean to enslave you again," he says, when I don't speak. "I did not mean that."

I take a deep breath, feel my muscles relax.

"I meant to free you with honour," he says. "It should have been done before a lawyer, with witnesses, you would have been given a scroll with the details. I would have given you my name and a freedwoman's cap, a purse of money. I thought it would happen some years from now and that Livia..." He stops. There is silence for a few moments before he starts again. "Livia would have held a feast and given you new clothes."

"I don't need –" I begin but he cuts me off.

"I wanted to do it with honour, not in anger and despair. But when I did it, I just wanted to get rid of you, to have no burdens, no responsibilities, so that I could hunt for Livia without any hindrance. It was not right, nor auspicious for your new life as a freedwoman. And I am sorry for it, especially as you have shown me such loyalty."

"I have only done what anyone would do," I say.

"No," he says. "You could have fled, you could have gone anywhere and done anything with that gold cuff."

I stay silent.

"I will do right by you," he says at last. "If you will stay by my side as we planned, I will do right by you. I do not have much for now, but I made you a promise. And…" He pauses again. "I told Livia I would look after you." Another silence. "I did not mean it as an oath," he says at last. "I meant it only as a reassurance to her. But I said the words to her, I promised to look after you until she should arrive." He takes a deep breath. "Perhaps she is still alive," he says, and tears fall down my cheek at the hope in his voice. "And if she is, I must stand by my promises to her."

"I promised too," I say.

"What?"

"You left the house so quickly and I was running after you, but she took my hand and said I should look after you. And I promised I would." I swallow. "I did it as you did, I said it quickly, I said it without thinking, only out of politeness to my new mistress. But they were my last words to her. I will not break my word to her, wherever she is."

The dark is very dark. I turn my head and can barely see any shape at all, even though I can hear Marcus' ragged breathing and I know tears are falling. He takes a deep breath. "We are sworn to each other then, is that it?"

I do not know if he is making fun of me, but his tears tell me otherwise. "Yes," I say.

In the dark I feel his hand seeking me out and I tense, unsure of what he is doing. He finds my arm and follows it to my hand, then takes it in his. "I swear to care for you, Althea, and do right by you, by Libertas who cared for you as a slave and Feronia to whom you passed as a freedwoman. I do it in the name of my wife Livia, who asked it of me and to whom I made my promise. When I see her again, I will be able to tell her I did as she asked."

He makes to pull away, but I hold onto his hand and speak into the night. "I swear to stand by your side, Marcus, and keep you safe as I promised your wife Livia, my last mistress before I became a freedwoman. May Feronia help me in this, my new life and undertaking."

Our hands unclasp and we lie in silence. When I sleep, it is the first deep sleep I have had in weeks.

KARBO

Late November dawns are bleak things, cold and misty. But they begin to take on a shape, a regularity, which, after all that has happened, I find comforting.

I rise first and fetch water, carrying the heavy amphorae back up the rickety wooden staircase. By the time I reach the rooftop Marcus has awoken. He washes and dresses quickly, then heads to the popina, while I do the same. By the time I reach him, my still-damp skin shivering from the early morning cold, there will be a hot pancake waiting for me, or sometimes a fruit-stuffed bun, a speciality of the bakery. Fausta prefers the bread and cheese that Marcus favours and she makes short work of it, knocking back a glass of wine and then striding along with us as we make our way to the amphitheatre. She has gone back to wearing her toga, though she could have disguised her origins on moving here, to a new city. I suppose by now it is part of how she thinks of herself, a she-wolf through and through. She has taken a tiny room on the top floor of the insula, just below the rooftop. I wonder what Adah would make of her if she knew she was indeed now sharing a dwelling with a prostitute, but perhaps she hasn't found out yet, I don't see her often. Maria, meanwhile, seems to treat Fausta with a kind of formal respect, not warm enough to be friendly, not cold enough to be disparaging. Maybe she can tell she is not a person to argue with.

Every day that passes is a day taking us closer to the by now almost-legendary hundred days of Games that we must deliver. The inauguration will be on the sixth of July. Every year between the sixth and thirteenth of July it is customary to hold the Games of Apollo, an annual week of theatrical shows, feasting, races and gladiatorial combats, so it makes sense for the inauguration to tie into these festivities. If we begin the hundred days of consecutive Games then, it will take us through the two weeks of Roman Games honouring Jupiter in September and we will finish by mid October. After that the weather will not be on our side anyway.

"Things have to be done right," says Fausta.

She has Marcus and me leave work early one day and, instead of heading to the baths, she takes us to the Forum, to the colonnade where the lawyers wait for clients. There she has Marcus repeat his manumission of me and, in just a few moments, I hold in my hand a witnessed scroll proclaiming me a free woman. I look down at the papyrus, see my name Althea, now accompanied for the first time by Aquillius. It is customary for a slave to take her master's name when she is freed and, although Marcus shrugs and says I may choose whatever name I wish, he looks a little pleased when I choose his.

"Well, give her the gift," prompts Fausta.

Marcus hands me a small parcel. "It's nothing," he grunts.

"It is everything," retorts Fausta. "Open it," she adds to me.

Inside a small piece of linen is a pretty woollen cap in a fresh green. I run my hand over it, unsure of whether I should wear it at once. "Thank you," I say to Marcus, though my eyes take in Fausta as well, for organising it.

"You're a freedwoman, you should have a freedwoman's cap," says Fausta. "The colour suits you. Pop it on."

I pull it shyly over my head.

"There you are," says Fausta with satisfaction. "Don't you look grand?"

"Thanks be to Feronia," I say.

"Thanks be," Fausta echoes and Marcus nods.

MARCUS WANTS OUR OWN IN-HOUSE group of musicians. He picks them from here and there to form a group that suits his purposes, then has them rehearse, endlessly, for all kinds of different situations, from the Emperor arriving in the imperial box to beast hunts, gladiatorial bouts, dancing girls and even the execution of criminals.

"Creates atmosphere," he says.

"I can't make myself heard," I complain. "How are you supposed to hear me, or I you, when you're under the arena and I'm up here in the seating? They never stop playing."

"She needs a whistle," says Fausta from several seats above me.

I twist in my seat to look up at her and she pulls a leather thong out from under her tunic, to which is attached a bronze whistle like the ones centurions use in battle to signal different formations. I look back at Marcus, thinking he'll laugh, but he pulls out a matching one from around his own neck and nods.

"I'll get you one," he says. "Useful things. You can hear them even above the roar of the crowd when they get overexcited."

"Yes, but can you hear them over the sound of your musicians?" I retort.

A few days later he presents me with my own whistle. At first, I'm hesitant to use it. It seems very loud, even compared with the musicians, and I feel silly blowing it but, after a few times when I've tried and failed to catch Marcus' attention by any other means, I get used to it. One long blast to call for him, two short puffs to tell everyone else to shut up. I'm tempted to use the two short puffs regularly with the musicians as well as the carpenters who are constantly hammering. But the work must go on, our ears sacrificed on the altar of this amphitheatre's future success.

WINTER EVENINGS COME ON EARLY. We stop work soon after lunch, then go to the baths to warm our bodies in the hot water. After that, Fausta and I head back to Julia's, the courtyard a safe haven on the early dark nights when no-one respectable likes to roam Rome's pitch-black streets. In the courtyard at least we all know each other, a stranger would be spotted at once. Flickering lamps and torches keep daylight lingering longer than the sun and often we share meals together, with Julia or Maria. Sometimes we eat at Cassia's popina, elbows on the counter, chatting to each other, and Cassia when she's not too busy. Sometimes we discuss work, other times just gossip about the locals.

But Marcus does not return to the courtyard in the evenings. Each night full darkness falls and still there is no sign of him. When I have yawned once too often, I take up a lamp and make my way up to the rooftop. Every evening I look over the edge, down into the narrow street below, hoping to catch a shadow that moves like him, but I never do. I lie on my mat, huddled under our rough blankets, my cloak added for extra warmth, and I wait. Sometimes I fall asleep waiting and only wake again when Marcus trips over me, cursing under his breath. He snores when he sleeps and sometimes lets out a cry. He works without stopping every day, even smiles and jests, but his pale face and the dark rings under his eyes in the mornings, as well as his wine-soaked breath, tell Fausta and me all we need to know about his nights. I want to stop his night-time wanderings and drinking, but I don't know how. The streets of Rome at night are a dangerous place to be, dark and full of people one would rather not meet, even by daylight.

We seem to spend our days collecting waifs and strays. Then there are those craftsmen who realise that an amphitheatre of this size, holding regular Games on this scale, will bring in a good income, and that they should therefore not turn their noses up at the kind of people they would normally avoid associating with. There are a few sly looks and comments at Fausta's presence but, after a carpenter gets his nose punched for putting his hands on her without her permission, they stop abruptly. After that, for the most part they seem to treat her as a man, exchanging bawdy banter and heavy-handed slaps on the shoulder as greetings or farewells. This suits Fausta. She relishes the wider opportunities of this role, using it here and there to help her own kind.

It takes her only a few weeks to seek out and identify the most suitable women to join our team. We need a group of dancing girls who will provide entertainment between the main Games. The girls must be pretty, good movers and not easily offended by lewd comments from the crowd. Those best suited are prostitutes and Fausta makes it her mission to find those who fit the bill. We will pay for their costumes, prostitution licence fees, and a small stipend. In return they will learn the steps, perform as and when required and enjoy the added bonus of being called up into the stands after the shows if a spectator happens to take a fancy to them. It suits them, for their days are mostly quieter than their nights and they view it as easy work. Fausta commissions the costumes in bold bright linen with decorated ribbons, leaving precious little to the imagination. They use the arena to practise, occasionally moving to one side when the carpenters come too close with their scenery or scaffolding, exchanging banter and rude gestures, laughing boisterously.

"Fausta here?"

"Who's asking?" I ask, looking up from my tablet and abacus, where I am currently calculating the wages of the scenery painters.

The woman standing in front of me is a prostitute without any doubt. There is something of Fausta about her, a fierce stance that speaks of a woman who has had to stand her ground more than once and won more often than not. "They call me Acca," she says.

The name of the she-wolf or prostitute who suckled Romulus and Remus. A professional name. "What do you need?"

"Want to know if I can have my girls outside after shows without any trouble from the management."

"You need to speak to Marcus, not Fausta."

She gives me a look that tells me Fausta is already known to the she-wolves of Rome, that she is seen as the right person to talk to, if it concerns prostitutes.

"Over there," I say, giving up and waving a hand towards Fausta, who is sitting on the topmost tier, wrapped in her toga, surveying the arena floor. She says you have to sit where the plebs sit to truly see the arena. Acca lifts her chin to me and strides up the steps, swiftly reaching Fausta and sitting beside her

"What did Acca want?" I ask Fausta later.

"Wants us to know her girls will hang around dressed as gladiatrix when the Games are over, waiting on customers coming out. Doesn't want any trouble about it."

"Dressed as gladiatrix? Why?"

Fausta shrugs. "Says the men like it after they've seen armed combat, think it's sexy."

I shake my head.

"Oh, it goes on all the time," says Fausta. "Men and women. Plenty of pretty boys dressed as gladiators get called into carrying litters by the rich women of Rome, and the men, come to that. They know they're not the real thing, haven't got the scars, but it's wonderful what a bit of shiny armour does for a man's looks."

She looks thoughtfully out over the arena and then changes the subject. "Where was Marcus last night?"

"I don't know."

"Not with you?"

"It's not like that between us," I say, blushing slightly.

"Not ever?"

I shake my head.

"Where was he, then?" she asks. "I didn't see him come home, after the baths, did you?"

"He didn't come home until very late," I say reluctantly.

Fausta's eyes narrow. "Is he coming home late every night?"

I nod.

"Cack," says Fausta.

"Do you think he's gambling?"

She snorts. "Not with their family history. His father took him out and flogged him once for gambling. He barely tolerates it in the amphitheatre. He wouldn't get caught up in it after what happened to their farm."

"Women?" I ask awkwardly.

She thinks. "I'd have said he'd come to you for that, the way he looks after you. But maybe I'm wrong." She considers. "He knows he's always welcome at my door, I'd not turn him down after what he's been through, but I'm not sure he thinks of me in that way."

It's the first time I've heard Fausta speak of sleeping with men for money, and I feel awkward, but she speaks of it as if it were nothing, a simple fact of life, which it is, I suppose.

Fausta sighs. "Well let's keep an eye on it," she ends. "He can do what he likes, I just don't want him getting into trouble, that's all."

Marcus gets paid and this, at least, removes some money worries from all of us for the time being, since Fausta and I, as his assistants, also get paid. I take a coin to Feronia's shrine, in gratitude for my first payment as a freedwoman. Then, mindful of Maria's kindness to me, I buy bright woollen cloth and make myself new clothes, so that I can return those she lent me, along with some honeyed walnuts as a thank you.

"Keep them," she says, when I try to return the clothes, washed and neatly folded. "They don't fit me anymore, haven't worn them since I was a girl and had a waist like yours. Get off," she adds as I hug her, but she looks pleased. Sometimes I sit with her on her balcony in the evening and we watch the comings and goings of the courtyard, so that she can impart the latest gossip to a fresh ear. There is nothing she does not observe, nothing she does not know about everyone who lives here.

"There's a street brat I keep seeing," she says one day. "Fast as a rat he is, scampering in and out of here, trying to steal things."

"What does he look like?" I ask. There are plenty of children who come in and out of our courtyard, some who belong here and others who are their playmates and treat the place like their own home.

"Black as soot," says Maria. "Brought over from Africa, I should think."

"Does he have a family?"

"Doubt it. Probably a runaway slave."

"I'll look out for him," I say.

"You'll never catch him, much too fast," she says.

I think for a minute. "If you can catch him, I might have a job for him," I say.

Saturnalia is being celebrated across Rome but none of us much feel like celebrating. Fausta and I give each other little cakes and the amphitheatre is quiet for a few days while the workmen have time off. But Marcus does not speak of the festivities, nor show any sign of wanting to take part in them.

I wait up for Marcus one night, hoping to find out where he's been. The moon is halfway across the sky by the time he returns, I can hear the wooden stairway creaking as he makes his way up it. The door opens and he stands in the doorway, blinking at the light of the lamp.

"What are you doing up?"

"Where have you been?"

"Out," he says.

"Have you been gambling?" I ask.

He snorts as though I've said something funny. "My father took me out and flogged me when he found me gambling once."

"I know," I say, pulling at his arm. "Then come home earlier."

"Home?" he asks. He's swaying on his feet. "Pompeii?" he adds.

I stare at him. There are tears trickling down his face. "No," I say more gently. "Just back here."

"I can't go home," he says. "It disappeared. Livia disappeared. Amantius…"

I know," I say softly. "I know. But you need to rest. We have so much work to do, you can't do it if you're drunk every night and don't get enough sleep. Please come home earlier."

"Home," he says. "Home."

"Yes," I say. "Please. If street robbers see you like that, you'll have a knife at your throat for sure."

He shrugs as though this doesn't worry him, then kneels and looks about the room. "Lararium," he says.

"What?"

"Household shrine."

"I know what a Lararium is."

"We don't have one."

I nod. "I know."

"Why not?"

I want to say we are not a household, but then I suppose we are. Fausta installed a shrine in her room as soon as she arrived here. "Do you want me to set one up?" I ask.

"No, don't worry," he says. "I have one in Pompeii. We can use that, Livia will have found it, I suppose."

I sigh. "You need to sleep," I say again. "Lie down."

He doesn't even bother to remove his shoes, just slumps down on the bed and closes his eyes. I unfasten his shoes and place them to one side, then cover him with a blanket.

"Livia," he says, eyes still closed.

"Goodnight, Marcus," I say.

For a couple of nights, he comes home earlier, one night he eats with us, even talks a little and I think perhaps he has heeded my words, but the following night he does not come home until almost dawn, sleeping an hour or two at most, then rising again. I do not know how long he can keep it up before he makes himself ill with exhaustion.

"Been waiting for you. Got him!"

I've only just walked back into the courtyard after the day's work. I look up at Maria, who is holding a struggling boy by the earlobe. "Is that the child?"

"It is," she says with smug satisfaction.

"You must be faster on your toes than I realised," I say, laughing.

"Don't you be cheeky to me. I caught him by my wits, not by running around like a dithering hen."

I make my way up the stairs to her. The child looks to be less than ten years old, scrawny. His skin is truly almost black, as she said, though dull with lack of care and right now he looks furious.

"What's your name?" I ask.

He shakes his head.

"I'll shake your ears off if you don't tell her," threatens Maria.

"Karbo," mutters the child.

"Karbo?" I check.

I get a sullen nod in response.

"Maria said you're fast. Just how fast are you?"

"Let me go and I'll show you."

"He thinks I'm an idiot," Maria says.

I squat down, so that I can look the boy in the eye. "Have you seen the Flavian Amphitheatre?"

"Everyone's seen it, stupid," he says.

"Less of your cheek, you street rat," says Maria, shaking him by the ear again.

"I work there," I say. "And I need a messenger. There is work going on all the time, and once we get spectators, we won't be able to call to one another. We will need a quick boy who can run and find people in our team and pass on messages, or tell us if we are wanted for something. But the boy I choose must be fast. The amphitheatre is huge, it takes a long time just to walk from one end to the other. So how fast are you?"

"What makes you think I want a job?" he asks.

"I think you're a runaway slave," I say and his eyes widen in fear. "I don't think you have a family of your own, or a job in any household, or you wouldn't be running in and out of our courtyard all the time, trying to steal food. If you can show me how fast you are, I would pay you board and lodging to be our messenger boy."

"For how long?" he asks.

"At least a year, maybe two," I say. "Perhaps longer than that, if you're good at your job. You can live here with us. Fausta has space in her room. You can sleep there, and we will feed you."

He stares at me and I wait for an answer. Maria doesn't loosen her hold on his ear.

"Fine," he says at last. "Now let me go."

The minute her fingers leave his ear he streaks past me and down the stairs, bolting for our courtyard gate exit.

"I thought he'd stay," I say, disappointed.

"He'll be back," says Maria, settling back into her usual position, vast bosom leaning on her crossed arms.

"Will he?"

"You offered him food," she says simply.

THE NEXT MORNING I'M BLEARILY tucking into my pancake at Cassia's when I feel a tug on my arm and turn to see Karbo standing beside me.

"You promised me board and lodging," he says.

"You ran off."

"I'm here now," he objects.

"Bread and cheese for this boy, Cassia," I say.

"I'd rather have a pancake."

"Pancake it is."

"Two pancakes."

"What he said."

Cassia lifts her eyebrows, but swiftly cooks two pancakes, douses them in date syrup and hands them to Karbo. He demolishes them both before I've even finished my single one.

"Now you owe me a day's work," I say.

He trails behind me all the way to the amphitheatre.

"Huge, isn't it," I say to him, expecting him to be overawed by the size of it inside.

"It's a cold place to sleep," he says. "Nothing soft, just stone."

"Sleep?"

"Lots of people sleep here at night," he says as though this were obvious.

"Why?"

He shrugs. "Easy to get in. Lots of room in the corridors, can't rain on you. Some people sleep under the arena floor, say it's warmer there, but you get all sorts down there at night, can't trust them."

Marcus has been watching us, head on one side. "Right, boy, let's see what you're made of. Show me how fast you can run around the amphitheatre through the corridors. Quick as you can."

He manages it in an impressively short space of time.

"You might have hit on something," says Marcus to me. "That is, if he doesn't eat his weight in pancakes every morning."

Karbo turns out to be what we were looking for. He carries messages from one end of the amphitheatre to the other, with no need for whistles or yelling. He keeps an eye on strangers entering the building and finds out what they want and who they wish to speak to. At first, he is jumpy, not letting any of us touch him for any reason, but as the weeks go by and he is fed a hearty breakfast and dinner every day, as well as a good portion of bread and cheese for lunch, he seems to relax in our presence. He does not sleep in Fausta's room at first, only taking up a spot under the wooden stairs in the courtyard and accepting a sleeping mat, but one night it rains heavily and Fausta simply picks him up under one arm and dumps him in her room despite his protests. After that he seems to find her presence acceptable, curling up in a corner of the room. I can't persuade him to join us at the baths each day after work. He seems to find washing himself in the public fountains more acceptable, occasionally returning dripping wet but approximately clean. I think his skin could do with oiling but since he won't allow that I make him a new tunic, since his is both falling apart and woefully short. Maria watches over him, combining an odd mix of feeding him honeyed walnuts and boxing his ears, according to what she thinks he most needs.

"So, the basic structure of each day is the same. Beast hunts in the morning, gladiatorial procession before or after, depending. Then a bit of light stuff, dancing girls, actors, that sort of thing. Then the execution of criminals. Some of the audience will leave during that part. Haven't the stomach for it. Gladiator bouts in the afternoon. All of the audience will come back for that. In fact some people only attend the combats, not so interested in the animals. So the audience changes a bit over the course of a full day. Now the mornings, that's for showing off some of the rarer animals and hunting them, so we have beast-fighters in the morning and sometimes add them to the gladiator sessions in the afternoon if we want something different. Most of the gladiatorial bouts, we don't want anyone dying. Blood, yes, death, not so much. If we do a fight to the death, the trainers would rather we put up criminals against the real gladiators, or occasionally they've got gladiators who are troublemakers or on their way out, whatever. Point is, you don't want to lose your best fighters. But the audience gets bored if it's the same people all the time, so you need to spice it up. We use the speciality acts for that, also the re-enactments of past battles, myths and legends, that sort of thing, makes it more interesting, allows us to get away with fewer actual deaths, because you can pop some criminals in there to be killed off and, also, you can have a bit of fakery, acting dead rather than being dead. So we'll visit the two gladiator trainers we'll be using the most. No doubt there'll be others, but these two will be important for us." He thinks for a minute. "We'll get regular deliveries of criminals, but it would help if we knew how many we have before they arrive, it allows us to plan. We could ask them to save up a larger group for the first day, I suppose. Titus will want a good show, we can't just have a handful, which is all you get some days."

I'm supposed to be making notes, but I'm distracted. Marcus has come into work with a black eye, which he refuses to answer any questions about. His night-time excursions, whatever they are, have to stop or he'll end up with worse than a few bruises. I consider asking one more time, but I know he won't answer.

The first gladiator trainer we meet is a grizzly older man, standing in his training ground, much like the barracks of Pompeii. "Well, if it isn't Scaurus!"

"Paternus."

The two men embrace.

"This is my assistant and scribe, Althea," says Marcus.

The man gives me a look from under bushy eyebrows. "Always a female assistant, eh? What happened to the other?"

"Fausta is still with me. The Flavian Amphitheatre needs all hands on deck."

"Always liked the look of her," muses Paternus. "May have to pay you a visit one day and renew our acquaintance. Anyway, you're here for my men, is that right?"

"Can't run the greatest amphitheatre in the Empire without you," says Marcus.

"Flatterer."

Marcus shrugs. "Truth," he says. "I'm going to be your best client."

"Glad to hear it," says Paternus. "Hundred days of consecutive Games, that's what I'm hearing. Is that right?"

"Yes."

"That'll keep us all busy. I might have to get some new talent in."

"You do that. I'll take everyone you've got. And I want to discuss the first day's Games with you. I need something no-one's ever seen before."

"I don't do speciality."

"I know," agrees Marcus. I'll go to Labeo for that."

Paternus shakes his head. "Labeo would wet himself if he met a real gladiator."

Marcus shrugs. "He knows his side of the business, just like you know yours. There's room for everyone. But I don't want speciality on day one. I want legends. Can you get me Verus and Priscus?"

"Both of them?"

"Yes."

"Who do you want them to fight?"

"Each other."

Paternus stares, as do I. Verus and Priscus are legendary gladiators, undefeated, now close to retirement. They've never fought one another. Seeing them fight together would be a spectacle the whole of Rome would want to see. Paternus shakes his head. "And what kind of money's available for that? For one of them to lose their undefeated status, you're talking serious gold."

"Plenty of money in the purse if you can get them. And their freedom."

"For which one?"

"Both."

"That's unheard of."

Marcus grins. "I know."

A MAN NAMED STRABO JOINS us. He will be in charge of the dark under-arena area, supervising deliveries of animals and criminals, as well as keeping the space tidy and ready to receive the performers. He is cross-eyed, a large man with a deep voice, taller even than Marcus, pale-skinned with thick black curls.

"He used to manage the slaughter of livestock," says Marcus. "He can kill a bull with one blow of a hammer. We can probably use him for Charon, he's got the height for it."

I shudder. The role of the hooded Charon is to finish off any gladiator who is not fully dead, by a hammer blow that will see him to Hades in an instant. Strabo, a kindly enough man, seems ill-fitted for the role, but someone has to do it.

"Time to meet the other trainer," says Marcus.

"You don't sound keen," I say.

"A different sort entirely," says Marcus. "You'll see."

Labeo is a young man, his hair excessively curled and primped, even his eyebrows plucked, wearing a tunic in a bold blue and red stripe. He's wearing more jewellery than most women. We visit his training ground and are shown into a large room with doors at each end. The walls are painted with scenes of gladiator fights.

"I have heard so much about you," he says to Marcus. "A great appointment. I hope we can work closely together. My gladiators are guaranteed to create a real spectacle in any arena. In yours... it will be unforgettable. His eyes flicker over me, there's a hesitation before he flashes a dazzling smile. "And this is your... assistant," he says. "Delighted."

"Althea Aquillius," says Marcus, giving my full name so that Labeo is aware I am not a slave, although he will work out that I must have once been Marcus' slave, given that our names match.

"Delighted," repeats Labeo, waving us to a seating area. "Let me offer you some refreshment. Some hot wine on this cold day."

Marcus accepts wine for both of us and I take a small sip. It's not very good, a cheap wine overly sweetened and spiced.

"Now then," says Labeo enthusiastically. "Can I show you some of my fighters?"

"If you wish," says Marcus.

"I have *everything*," says Labeo. "And anything I don't have, you need only say the word and I will have it sourced for you specially, within a week at the very most."

"Glad to hear it," says Marcus. He looks tired.

Labeo gives a quick gesture and the room before us begins to fill up while he provides a running commentary. The men and women are wearing processional armour, highly elaborate and polished, not the battered items real gladiators wear during bouts. It almost looks like a play.

"So, first of all, my women. I have the greatest selection of female fighters in Rome. Fierce, they are, you wouldn't credit it from women, but they really can fight! I have some excellent trainers who work for me."

"They look like they've come from a brothel," mutters Marcus to me. He has a point. Their armour is deliberately skimpy in parts, showing off their bodies in a way that would make them extremely vulnerable to an opponent, their long hair left to hang down loose rather than tied up in what would surely be a more practical hairstyle for fighting.

"I also have dwarfs, always popular as you know," says Labeo, when over fifty women have paraded past. More than a dozen dwarfs make an appearance. "I swear there isn't a dwarf in Rome who can handle a sword I haven't managed to recruit. Then I have those of the opposite persuasion, shall we say?"

Four men shamble into the courtyard. They're tall, taller than any man I've ever laid eyes on, they make Marcus, who is tall, look like a dwarf himself. Their armour is designed to emphasise their size, with vast padded shoulders in leather broadening their already considerable chests.

"Impressive, aren't they?" smiles Labeo. "Crowds *love* them. We did an Odyssey re-enactment with one of them playing Polyphemus. Made a fantastic giant, well, I mean, he *is* one, isn't he?"

Marcus nods. "I can see you have what we need," he says. "I'll send a list of requirements, day by day as we draw up the schedule. You'll have plenty of advance warning, a couple of weeks at a time." He seems keen to leave, as though he finds the parade wearying.

"Oh goodness, you've hardly seen anything!" cries Labeo. "They're just the regular specials. I've got some really *particular* items to show you." He gestures and two men enter the courtyard.

I have to narrow my eyes to be sure of what I am seeing. They seem to be joined together, where each man's chest should end, it is instead joined to the other. They have four legs between them, but only two arms, one on each man, as well as a strange protuberance, like a hand without an arm, which pokes out from the shoulder of the man on the left. The fingers move. I lean back, making a gesture against evil spirits.

Marcus grimaces. "So I gather," he says. "I think we have seen all we need to."

"When they fight, they look extraordinary, but *imagine* when you slice the two of them apart! No one will ever have seen anything like it. It would be expensive, of course, because I'm not going to find another one like that in a hurry, am I?"

"We'll send you the list of what we need," says Marcus.

There is still a good part of the day left, but Marcus points me back towards the amphitheatre as we leave. "Make my excuses," he says. "I'm going to the baths."

I want to ask him to come back to the insula, to eat with us tonight, but I know he won't listen to me. I make my way back to the site, my stomach turned by Labeo's enthusiastic demonstration of his wares.

THE BEAST-HUNTER WE ENGAGE TO keep us supplied with animals is less well presented. Bestia is a hunched, lumbering hulk of a man with little interest in the welfare of the animals he sources.

"Shitting giraffes? Really? What in Hades do you want them for?"

"Giraffes are impressive, hardly anyone's seen them," says Marcus calmly.

"Bollocks are they impressive. They die if you look at them. Sodding scared of ships, if you ask me. How about rhinos instead? Solid buggers, reliable."

"As well as," says Marcus.

"You bastard."

"You want the job or not?"

"Got enough shitting work on."

"Fine," says Marcus. "I'll find someone who can get me what I need."

"Jupiter's dick. I'm the best and you know it."

Marcus shrugs. "I wouldn't call you that. I'd call you adequate. I'm going to need over three thousand animals a month. You show me the amphitheatre that's using that many animals and I'll show you a liar."

"You going to use Carpophorus in the beast hunts?"

Marcus nods. "Not on the first day, I've got something else planned. But yes, of course. He's the best beast-fighter there is."

Bestia sighs. "He'll be the ruin of me. That cackhead has no consideration for how difficult some of those animals are to get over here. Just kills them like they're no trouble at all."

"The crowds love him."

Bestia rolls his eyes. "Cackhead."

Julia takes me aside. "Marcus is not paying the rent he owes," she says. "It's not like him. Why doesn't he have any money?"

I stare at her. "He gets paid a good wage," I say. "He hasn't paid the rent?"

She shakes her head.

"Leave it with me," I say. "How many days is he behind?"

"Almost thirty," she says.

I tell Fausta and she looks troubled. Between us, we put together enough money to pay Julia what she is owed, but it leaves us with very little.

"But what's he doing with his money?" I ask her. "He can't spend that much on wine. And women…"

Fausta shakes her head. "Don't think it's women," she says. "But it's a lot. He's doing something with it."

It's February and the days of the dead are being celebrated. Tonight my cloak isn't thick enough for the protection I want it to give me. I hesitate before leaving the safety of our courtyard and the flickering torches that light it in the evenings. The street outside looks very dark. There is no lighting, only the odd small gleam coming from household windows, not enough to give me any sense of safety. The streets of Rome at night are known for being dangerous, people make truthful jokes about going for a stroll at night if you wish to end your life.

But I have to move quickly, or Marcus will disappear. Already I can only just make him out, striding northwards up Virgin's Street, about to disappear into a network of small streets where I will lose him for sure. I feel cold, colder than the night air warrants. I have to keep up with him or I'll be lost and if I get lost out in the nighttime on my own, I'm in a lot of trouble. But I need to know what's going on.

The street is horribly empty. The bakery is shut up for the day, its wooden shutters pulled to. Cassia's popina, further behind me, is open, but the light from it quickly fades as I make my way to the end of the street and see Marcus turn left.

I keep my footsteps quiet, afraid he will notice me following him, but I needn't worry, he never looks behind him.

Three streets in, he turns into what looks like a popina, lewd graffiti all over its frontage. Clearly there is no father here to threaten customers with a stick for touching the barmaids. I hold back, then edge forward, closer to the street counter when I see that he has gone all the way inside. There's a largish drinking room in the back, from which I can hear the rattling of dice. Perhaps Marcus is gambling after all, I think. Perhaps there is something in his blood that draws him to the betting tables, something dark left over from his grandfather's disastrous loss of the family farm.

"Help you?" The barmaid, wearing a tunic that has slipped down over one shoulder to give a, perhaps deliberate, better view of her cleavage, is staring at me.

I hold out a coin. "Cup of wine."

She obliges but can tell I don't belong here. "You looking for someone?"

I point discreetly to Marcus. He's sitting at a table with two men. I can't see any dice but perhaps it's only a matter of time.

"Oh, the Pompeiian man."

I frown.

"Isn't he from Pompeii?"

"Yes," I say. "How do you know that?"

"Half of Rome knows him, love."

"Why?"

"If you go around paying good money for nothing, people get to know you pretty quick."

"What's he paying for?"

The girl tips her head to one side. "Do you actually know him?" she asks. "Or has someone sent you looking for him? Though you're a funny person to send," she adds. "Is he in trouble with someone I should know about? The authorities? I don't need trouble in here, not with, you know," she winks, "my customers liking the sound of rolling dice."

"He's gambling?"

Again, the girl looks at me as though she finds my questions odd.

"Look," I say, desperately, afraid Marcus will spot me. "Just tell me what he does here, will you?"

"He pays for information," she says.

"What sort of information?"

"Anything related to Pompeii," she says.

"Like what?"

"Names of any new refugees from the area who've recently arrived in Rome. He'll meet anyone claiming to be from there, pays them money to sit with him and tell him exactly where they've been, who they've seen. Looking for a woman and a child, that's what I hear."

I drop my head onto my hands. I'm relieved but also saddened that Marcus is engaged in this endless, fruitless search, that all his money is being used up on useless information.

"You alright?"

I lift my head and sigh. "Yes."

"You know him, do you?"

"I work for him."

She pauses in wiping down the counter. "Seems like a decent man. Doesn't gamble though he gets plenty of offers. Never seen him with any of the women that hang around here."

"He is. But…"

"But?"

"He's searching for his wife and child," I say. "And…"

The girl grimaces. "No chance?"

I shake my head.

"Sounded like a bad business."

"It was."

"He put the word out he'll pay for information. And there's a few who might be able to really help, but…" She leans forward. "There's a lot of others who are just fooling him. They put on the Pompeiian accent, they say oh, they knew so-and-so, some common name that could be anyone. They say my brother's cousin's sister-in-law knew someone who said something… and he pays for their nonsense. Can't you stop him coming?"

I shake my head. "I've tried. He won't listen. Does he know they're fooling him?"

She shrugs. "Maybe. Maybe not. He's pretty drunk when he leaves here each night. Probably believes all sorts."

"He had a black eye the other day."

"Someone said Pompeiian women were all whores, didn't know he was here. He went for them, but he was too drunk to handle himself properly, got a wallop."

I sigh. "Can I try and take him home?"

"Be my guest."

I make my way into the back room, aware that the prostitutes are sizing me up, a possible competitor intruding on their turf. The men, fortunately, are mostly focused on their gambling. I reach Marcus and touch him on the shoulder.

He looks up and frowns. "What are you doing here?"

"I could ask the same question."

"Not your business."

"You can't go around giving your money to liars who claim to know anything about Pompeii."

"Who says they're liars?"

"I do. Come home."

One of the men at the table raises his eyebrows. "Oh, a woman come to take you home, is it? Worried about walking through the streets by yourself, Scaurus?"

Marcus ignores the taunt, keeps his eyes on me. "I don't have a home. It's buried under ashes and rocks, remember? You were there."

"Julia's is our home now."

He shakes his head and knocks back his cup of wine. "It won't be a home until Livia is with me again."

My eyes fill with tears and I blink them away. "Let's leave this place."

"There was a man who said he knew something, he left a message for me, said he'd be in tonight."

"But he's not here now, is he? Let's go."

He shakes his head, stubborn. "I need to hear from him."

I squat down by his bench, look up at him. "Please, Marcus," I say. "This is a bad idea. People will take advantage of a man who will give out good money for rumours, for half-lies and hearsay. Fausta and I had to pay your rent and we'll run out of money if we have to do it again. We can't go hungry or end up on the street because you're giving away your wages to every hustler in Rome."

He looks away from me.

"Oh, tell her to get lost," says another man at the table. "Why do women always have to ruin a good game with their whining?"

"Please," I repeat, touching Marcus again, this time on his hand.

He stands. "Fine. If you'll stop nagging me."

I stand up and walk swiftly out of the popina, looking back once to make sure he's following me.

"Thank you," I say in a low voice to the girl at the counter as I pass, and she gives me a quick nod.

OUT IN THE STREET MARCUS overtakes me and walks ahead, his strides fast and angry, shoulders hunched. I follow, grateful he has made so little fuss, and also glad to know what has been going on all this time. Perhaps, now I know what he has been doing, I stand some hope of stopping him in the future.

"You the Pompeiian?" A dark figure steps out in front of Marcus.

"I am."

"Heard you might be interested in what we do."

"And what is that?"

"Business in Pompeii."

"Business?"

"That's right."

I stand still in the shadows, heart beating fast, listening. I don't know if the man realises I'm here, it's very dark, I can barely make him out.

"Tell me about it."

"I heard you pay for information."

"I haven't heard any yet."

"I don't share without seeing what's on the table."

Leave, I think. Don't pull your purse out, this is the kind of man who will slit your throat and take everything you have.

But Marcus is pulling out his purse, I hear the coins clink together. "I want information on anything that's happening in Pompeii," he says and my hands ball into fists with fear of what is about to happen. "If you can tell me something that will help me find what I'm looking for, you'll find me more than generous."

I'm waiting for the man to attack, but he stays still.

"There's some interesting activity in Pompeii right now," he says. "Worth anyone's money to know about."

"Which is?"

"There are… goods available."

I frown. What's he talking about?

Marcus sounds confused too. "Goods? Speak more clearly. We're alone here."

The man lowers his voice a little, I struggle to hear him clearly. "There are tunnels."

"Tunnels?"

"That's right. Got a good crew. Discreet, quick, hardworking. You wouldn't believe the stuff coming out of there."

"Such as?"

"Jewellery, gold, money. Art. We tunnel into the big villas mostly, easier pickings. But we've found valuables in all sorts of places. People must have collected everything they had when they were thinking of escaping. There's good money to be made, if you want in on it. I could put a lot of work your way, easing the goods out, you know."

There's silence in the dark street. The man must gather something is wrong from Marcus' silence, because his tone changes. "So? Are you the man I took you for? Or am I talking to the wrong person?"

It's so fast I scream. Marcus shoves the man up against a wall, a blade to his throat. He's trying to struggle free, but Marcus has him in too tight a hold.

"You are tunnelling into the houses of the dead, stealing their goods?" he says, and I cringe, I've never heard his voice so full of rage.

The man tries to reply but Marcus must have his throat so tightly pressed against the knife it comes out as a guttural sound rather than real words.

"Marcus," I say, my voice shaking. "Let him go, Marcus." I'm afraid he is going to kill the man. I don't doubt he's capable of it, the rage I heard was that of a man on the edge of sanity and he's no doubt killed men while in the army, but right now, if he kills a man in peacetime, he'll be a murderer and end up in the very arena we're building.

"He's scum," Marcus says. "He deserves to die."

"Yes," I say, because I agree with him. "But you don't deserve to face the punishment for murder. Please. Please."

He hesitates, still holding the man against the wall. I wait for a cry, for the man to slump to the ground lifeless, but Marcus suddenly lets go of him. "If I ever see your face again, I will kill you," he says. "And no woman will stop me."

The man is already running, away down the street from us, his footsteps fading into the distance.

"Thank you," I say. My teeth are chattering against each other, I have to grit them together to make them stop.

"Don't follow me again," he says and walks away.

I trail him in the darkness until we reach Virgin's Street and Julia's insula. In the darkness, we enter the rooftop hut and lie down to sleep, though I stay awake long into the night, even after he is asleep.

A Visit from Titus

I F I THOUGHT MARCUS WOULD stop his night-time wanderings after the encounter with the grave robber of Pompeii, I was mistaken. I tell Fausta what he is doing, and she nods, grim-faced.

"I don't know how to stop him," I say. "He's so desperate to find Livia, but she can't still be alive, she would have come here by now for sure."

Fausta shakes her head. "He can't admit she's dead because then he'd have to grieve properly. And he can't do that because he has all of this," she sweeps her arm across the site, "to make happen. So it's easier to keep doing what he's doing."

"For him, perhaps," I say. "But not for us when he's arriving at work hungover and half asleep and sometimes not at all. And what if he gets his throat cut in a dark street one night? We won't even know about it; they'll throw his body in the Tiber and that will be the end of him. And of us."

"The Aedile is coming to inspect progress next week," says Fausta. "Let's just keep him going till then, shall we? After that we can think about what to do next."

THE AEDILE'S VISIT IS A tense one for all of us. Marcus is on time to work but his breath smells of wine and he looks white-faced.

"Jupiter strike you for the idiot you are," mutters Fausta when she sees him. "Chew on this." She stuffs mint in his mouth. He turns away and spits it out, but at least he's eaten some of it. "Now get your head up and be polite to the Aedile," she adds, as the senator and his entourage come into view, stomping through the Gate of Triumph as though they think they're part of a procession.

We huddle together, watching as Marcus greets the Aedile, manages to turn on something approaching charm, walks around the arena with him, answering questions and pointing to various items: the lifts under the trapdoors, the pens below, the names being carved into the seating, and so on.

"It looks like it's going well," I say to Fausta.

"Perhaps," she says, still frowning from her exchange with Marcus. "He better not bugger this up."

The Aedile departs, apparently satisfied and for that brief morning I think that perhaps this signals a change in Marcus, that he has turned a corner. But I'm wrong. After the visit, he barely comes to the site at all. I wake in the mornings to find him asleep and snoring. He will not rouse even if I shake him and he does not appear at the amphitheatre most mornings. The work of the manager falls more and more to Fausta and me.

"THERE'S A MAN WANTING TO see you," says Karbo.

I look up. Fausta and I are checking over the merchandise that twelve different stallholders have brought in for us to approve. These will be the official stalls, I've no doubt there will be many dozens of unofficial sellers of every possible kind of product, but these at least need to be good quality. We have examined a range of pottery items, including tableware and lamps, all featuring gladiatorial scenes and animal hunts, followed by painters who specialise in fast portraits of gladiatorial heroes and their fans.

"So we have a pre-prepared portrait of the gladiator Verus, for example," says the painter, explaining how they do their work. "And then if you want, we can do your portrait, right alongside him, see, we leave an empty space there."

I think of the speed at which Lucius' triclinium was painted and then repainted, at Marcus' instruction. "Very nice," I say. "Do people buy a lot of these?"

"Oh yes, very popular. People like having pictures of their favourite gladiators."

"There's a man wanting to see you," repeats Karbo.

"I'll leave you to it," I say to Fausta. "There's still the leatherworkers and then we have to approve the food and drink providers, who will be allowed to roam between the seats. I'll try and get back to you soon."

The man Karbo leads me to is tall and wiry, with light-coloured hair. At his side stands a tiny woman, who barely reaches his waist, but who looks just like him, the same light floppy hair and long nose, same light brown eyes and skin that only turns pale gold in the sun.

"Fabius," the man introduces himself, "and my daughter, Fabia."

I nod, waiting for an explanation.

"Marcus sent for me."

I tilt my head. "Did he?"

The man frowns. "I'm to be the physician for the amphitheatre. My daughter will be my assistant."

"Oh," I say, "I'm sorry, I didn't know to expect you."

"Marcus didn't tell you?"

"No," I say. "I'm sorry, he's not here today."

The man looks disappointed. "Ah, well never mind, never mind, we will find lodging somewhere nearby and return tomorrow. We served together; I was an army physician. I retired from the army when I married but my wife is no longer with us and so, when Marcus sent word, well, it was too good an opportunity to miss."

"My father finds ordinary ailments boring," says Fabia. "He misses sword wounds."

"I apologise for Marcus not being here to greet you himself since he sent for you," I say. "He is... not quite himself these days."

"We heard, of course,' says Fabius. "Terrible thing. It must have left a mark on him."

"Yes," I say. "But perhaps seeing an old friend will help. Will you come for dinner?"

I SEND KARBO TO FIND Marcus and tell him he must stay at the insula tonight, that we will eat with Fabius and Fabia, but when we return from work, he has already gone out and he does not arrive. Fabius arrives with gifts of delicious food: a large platter of freshly cut fruits as well as pickles and sliced hogshead. Julia steps in as hostess and looks after us well, but the meal feels awkward. Fabius and his daughter seem kind and make pleasant dinner companions, but Marcus, who should be here, is nowhere to be seen.

"So do you work at the amphitheatre too?" Fabia asks Karbo.

"Yes," he says proudly. "I'm the fastest boy in Rome."

I hide a smile.

"I'm sure you are," says Fabia. "Perhaps you will show me round the amphitheatre one day? You must know it better than anyone and if my father and are to work there, I will need a good guide."

Karbo's chest inflates. "I'll look after you, show you what's what," he assures her.

"If you need an apartment, let me know. If one comes free, I can keep it for you," says Julia at the end of the evening.

"I would be most grateful," says Fabius. "Perhaps I can keep Marcus company, bring him out of himself a little by talking of the old days in the army?"

I nod, grateful for his understanding.

THE NEXT MORNING, I TAKE Fabius on a tour of the under-arena space.

"I will need an area to lay out my tools," he says. "Stitching and amputations must be done as quickly as possible."

We identify a suitable space for him, far enough away from most of the cages for safety.

"Althea!" Fausta is kneeling on the arena floor above us, her head poking down through one of the trapdoors.

"What?"

"The Emperor is here."

"Now's not the time for pranks," I say, rolling my eyes.

"Not joking," she says, her face serious, voice flat. "Get up here, quick."

I climb up a ladder set into one of the trapdoors. The bright morning sunlight hurts my eyes after the gloomy space below but there's no mistaking a crowd of Praetorian Guards and lictors, deferentially surrounding a man in a toga trimmed in purple. "What do we do?" I ask Fausta.

"Go and talk to him, of course," she says. "Show him around. Reassure him that everything is going very, *very* well."

"With Marcus not even here?"

"Say he's beast collecting."

"Why can't you go and talk to him?" I ask.

She raises her eyebrows. As usual, she is wearing her toga. "The Emperor will not be impressed at being shown round the site by a prostitute," she says. "Go!"

TITUS IS A PLUMP MAN, his toga adding to his bulk, two chins wobbling when he laughs, which he does often.

"I hope the acoustics are good in here," he begins, as soon as introductions have been made. "Can't bear it when you can't hear properly at the theatre. You want to tell them to SPEAK LOUDER!" he adds, finishing on a bellow. "There, see, perfect sound," he says, pleased with his test.

I try to keep my eyes on him, but find myself flickering a quick look towards Fausta, sheltered in the centre of the huddled team, everyone watching us. She nods and smiles encouragingly.

"And where is this manager I've heard so much about? Scaurus something?"

"He will be devastated to have missed your visit," I say. "He is at – in – Ostia, there is a new animal they have found that may be suitable for a beast hunt. Some sort of water-creature," I finish weakly.

"Can you flood the arena?" he asks over his shoulder, turning on the spot to look around the whole space.

"Of course," I say, thanking the gods for all the conversations I have overheard between Marcus and the architect. "We can have a naval battle whenever you command it."

"Marvellous," says Titus. "I shall think when would be best."

"Of course," I say brightly, making a note. Marcus will curse me for agreeing to such a thing when we've not yet tested the plumbing to see if it could cope.

"Ah, shorthand, very good," says Titus, coming close and peering over my shoulder. "Pass me a tablet and let's have a race. I'm told my shorthand is as good as any scribe's."

I stare at him, but an aide, evidently used to this sort of thing, has already passed Titus a fresh wax tablet and a stylus while another has pulled out a choice of scrolls, which Titus inspects, then selects one.

"Good choice," he says. "The Iliad. Ready, Althea?"

The aide begins to read out a battle scene from the Iliad and I try not to think what an absurd situation I find myself in, focusing on the words and getting them down as fast as possible. When the man stops reading Titus holds out his hand and I put my tablet into it. He compares the two, then holds them up so the gathering can see them. "Well, well, Althea has beaten me!" he declares. "Why, I shall have to hire you for imperial service!"

My stomach rolls over. What if Titus decides to take me as a scribe and removes me from Marcus and my work here? I can hardly refuse the Emperor, even if I am a freedwoman. "I am already in imperial service," I say, trying to put a smile on my face and opening my arms to indicate the amphitheatre all around us.

"Quite right, quite right!" bellows Titus. "You are indeed. And I am glad to see it looking so well advanced. Although I shall expect more decoration, eh? Looking a little plain at the moment."

"It will be magnificent," I say. "There are hunting scenes planned in all the corridors, I can show you the designs –"

"I really think I should take you as my own scribe," he interrupts, beaming. "So efficient, not to mention very pretty."

I keep my smile fixed on my face. "Perhaps you should see the first day's Games before you make that decision," I say.

He laughs. "I am sure everything will be wonderful. Oh yes, before I forget, I saw two excellent executions of criminals, years ago, now. One was a criminal playing the part of Icarus, they made these extraordinary wings from real feathers and had him dropped from a great height, with scenery above him showing the sun. The other one was based on the legend of Prometheus stealing fire from the gods and being punished for it, they actually trained an eagle to eat his entrails until he died. It was very clever. Perhaps they could be incorporated into one of the days."

"I will see to it myself," I say, slightly appalled that he would want such grim spectacles repeated.

"I'm going to inspect the baths today as well," says Titus. "Building a whole new complex, just over the road from here, you must have seen it."

"It looks magnificent," I say, although the baths site looks like it is running behind to me. It has been built using some of the plumbing and heating systems left over from Nero's palace, the Golden House. Apparently, it was supposed to coincide with our inauguration, but I don't see that happening. They're still building the main pool, none of the mosaics have been put in yet and the gardens surrounding it are just bare earth. They'll have to do some serious transplanting of ready-grown trees and bushes if it's to look at all impressive. Still, if they're behind schedule they'll make us look better.

"I hope you will enjoy using the facilities when it opens," says Titus, allowing his gaze to travel over me.

"I'm sure our whole team will be very grateful for it every day after work," I say.

Titus finally departs, happy and with many promises to visit regularly, which I try to look enthusiastic about. When the last marching feet of the Praetorian Guard fade into the distance, I sit down on the steps, my legs weak.

"Good job," says Strabo, his large hand on my shoulder.

"Thank you," I mutter.

A few more people touch my shoulder and there are murmurs of congratulation as the team disperse, moving back to their jobs, chattering about the visit.

Fausta sits down next to me. "Bastard."

"Titus?"

"Marcus."

I want to disagree but she's right. My shaking turns into anger, my fright turning to rage at being put into a situation so fraught with danger with no warning, no support from the man who should have been in my place.

"Althea."

"What is it, Karbo?" I ask wearily.

"I found Marcus and brought him here."

I look to where he's pointing. Marcus is standing in one of the arches, looking over at me. I'm on my feet and striding towards him before I realise it.

"Where were you?" I ask, and my voice comes out low, shaking with anger.

He looks away. "Asleep."

"I know that!" I say. "You are out every night, chasing shadows, and then leaving me in the shit the next day. I have had enough!"

"I have to find Livia…" he begins and something in me snaps.

"Livia is dead!" I say too loudly, and the site falls silent around me.

The team forms into little huddles, pretending not to be there, but listening to every word. I want to stop but I have to say what must be said or Marcus will sink ever deeper into his hunt through the halls of Hades.

"She is dead, Marcus, and so is your son. And I am sorry for it, truly I am. If I could bring them back I would do so, no matter what it took. But I cannot, no one can. And you will get yourself killed wandering the backstreets of Rome at night, drunk and with a purse of money on you for some cutthroat to lay hands on. And then all of us will be screwed, because a man with less heart than you will be appointed, and we will be nothing to him. He will not care what becomes of us. Not that you seem to!" I'm almost running out of breath.

"I –" he begins but I cut him off.

"You put me in danger! You put this whole project in danger! If Titus had been displeased, it would be all of us in the arena, being mauled to death!" My voice has risen to a shout, echoing around the amphitheatre.

"Althea –"

"No! You can't fob me off with half-baked promises. You owe all of us an apology, you owe all of us your time and your presence here, doing the job you were hired for. Your wife and son are gone, there is nothing you can do for them. But we need you, Marcus. *We* need you." I let my tablet, full of the absurd shorthand rendition of the Iliad, fall to the ground. The wood splits in two, held together only by the wax inside it. I open my mouth, then control myself. What I am saying is true, but it is also cruel, and I am exhausted. I walk past Marcus and out of the amphitheatre, through the Forum, heading back to Virgin's Street.

I ARRIVE IN OUR COURTYARD with tears rolling down my face.

Maria peers down at me. "Back already?"

"Don't ask," I say.

"Did someone hurt you?"

I shake my head. "The Emperor visited the site."

She nods, serious. "And Marcus didn't make it in time? Karbo was trying to get him washed and over to you."

I shake my head. "Shame on him for making a child come and fetch him to his own workplace."

On the rooftop I find a half-full amphora of water and wash my face. I feel too hot, as though the sun has burnt me, although I know the heat is from the rage and fear of the past hour, as well as the fast walk home.

"Althea."

"Oh, leave me be!" I cry out. "Can you not stay on the site, where you're supposed to be, for once? Just once?"

Marcus shakes his head. "You're more important. What you said was more important."

"He could have had us thrown to the lions," I spit.

"He loved you," says Marcus with a grimace. "Fausta said you charmed him; he was delighted with the visit. You rose to the occasion better than anyone else could have done."

"Except you."

He nods. "It should have been me. And I am sorry, Althea. I have mistreated you, have poorly repaid your loyalty."

I look down. "I'm sorry for what I said," I say. "About Livia –"

"But you were right," he cuts me off.

I raise my eyes. His are swimming with unshed tears.

"She is dead," he says. "And my boy. They are both gone. I know it."

"Marcus," I start, moving towards him, but he holds up a hand to stop me.

"I will stop searching," he says. "I am done with that now."

"I am so sorry," I say, and the relief of finally being able to offer him sympathy for his loss, so long denied, makes my own tears fall. "She was a kind woman, Anna said so, she said Livia was the best mistress, she was glad to serve her. I am sorry I never knew her better. And Amantius was so much like you, he was a little copy. I know it must be unbearable. I do not know how to make it bearable for you." I'm talking too quickly, trying to say everything all at once.

He walks to the side of the rooftop and for a moment I feel a sudden lurch of terror that he will jump, that now that he has acknowledged his loss, he will want to end his misery. But he places his hands on the wall and looks down, then across the rooftops. "I have you and Fausta and Julia," he says. "I could not ask for better women to surround me."

I move to his side, rest my own hands on the wall. "I will do anything to help you," I say. "And Fabius is here now, he said he would spend time with you."

He nods. "He's a good man. We're lucky to have him."

We stand in silence for a while, side by side. "Will you eat something?" I ask at last.

He nods, a weary movement. "I am so tired," he says, his voice low.

"Food and sleep," I say.

"And work," he says.

"And work," I agree. "But better those three and nothing else than wandering Rome at night."

He nods again. "I am done with that," he repeats. "I swear it."

FEVER

T HE FIRST WARM MONTHS COME, bringing longer days but also interrupted nights.

"EXPLAIN TO ME WHY I am covered in bites and you haven't even one?" says Marcus, irritably scratching at his leg.

"I don't know," I say, a little smugly. "They don't bite Julia, either."

"Oh, so they only bite men, is that it?"

"They bite *me*," says Fausta. "I just don't moan about it."

"I haven't been bitten," I say, "but the whining noise they make keeps you up all night. You keep waiting for it to stop, waiting for a bite so you know where they are and can slap them."

"When the noise stops, you can take comfort in the fact that they've landed on me," says Marcus.

Fausta shakes her head, exaggerating the gesture so that the man standing on the other side of the arena can see her. "Can't see anything written on that board," she complains. "The writing needs to be a lot bigger, else you can't see the gladiator scores from this distance."

"They looked fine to me this morning," says Marcus.

"Yes, that's because you're always in the Emperor's box. I've told you before, you have to sit where the plebs sit. They need to see those scores clearly if they're going to place bets."

"I thought there were more than three scene painters due in today," I say, looking down at my list and frowning. "We've got over two hundred pieces of scenery to get ready, and only two months left. Someone explain to me how that's going to get done?"

Marcus grins at Fausta. "Getting good at this, isn't she? Hardly needs us at all. Got it all in hand."

Fausta nods encouragingly at me. "Once you've told the boss off in public it gives you a bit of confidence, doesn't it?"

I frown at her. I still worry that Marcus may do something stupid, should a black mood descend on him.

But Marcus takes it well enough, he shrugs and smiles, then walks away to find out why we only have three scene painters today. We watch him speaking to the foreman for a while.

"At least he's not drinking any more, nor seeking out trouble. He comes home at a reasonable time now, doesn't he?" asks Fausta, her eyes on Marcus' distant figure.

"Yes," I say. "He comes home and eats, but then he just sits on the rooftop, all alone. He doesn't want to talk. Sometimes I'm afraid I'll come up to the roof and find…"

"I don't think he'd jump," says Fausta in her usual blunt way. "More likely do it with a sword, soldier-like."

"Let's not talk about it," I say, keeping my voice low.

"He's just sad," says Fausta. "I think he's got past the stage of taking his own life. But he's grieving. He puts on too much of a front at work, it has to come out sometime. Better alone on the rooftop than the back room of a dirty popina on a dark street."

Marcus is climbing back up the steps towards us. "Five men off sick," he says, frowning. "Three scene painters and two more from the decoration team in the corridors. Some sort of fever. Have to hope it's not catching."

We all make a gesture to ward off bad luck, Fausta muttering under her breath to whatever god she feels is most likely to protect her.

"Are we supposed to wait for them to get better?" I ask. "Or do I need to find new painters?"

"They'll get better," says Marcus. "Don't worry about it."

BUT THE NEXT DAY THERE are ten men missing from the site, and the day after that thirty. Meanwhile, in Julia's insula, five of her tenants on the top floor, in the smallest rooms, go down with a fever, as does the elderly mother of the baker.

"She burns up and then she has shaking chills," says the baker's wife, her face worried as she returns early from work to spend time with her mother-in-law.

"Some sort of pestilence," says Julia and disappears for most of the day, praying at Vesta's Temple, perhaps speaking with her old colleagues.

The architect is beginning to look stressed again, just when he thought he had everything in hand. The stonemason sends word that over thirty of the statues destined for the arches around the amphitheatre will be delayed thanks to the pestilence.

"Put them at the back," says Marcus, unruffled, when he hears about it.

"The back's already full!"

"That is unfortunate," Marcus agrees. "Can't you shift them round?"

"That will take even longer!"

"You'll just have to wait then," says Marcus. "Presumably the men will be better soon."

"You don't seem very worried," spits the architect.

"Not my building," says Marcus with a smile.

"It is!"

"No, it's *your* building, they're *my* Games. Your statues are none of my business, they don't affect the spectacle."

"You are so mean to him," I say, as the architect stalks away. "Don't you feel sorry for him?"

"He has the easy job," says Marcus. "The building is mostly finished. It's our lives in the arena if the Games aren't up to scratch."

"I doubt they'll finish the decorations in time," I say, looking around me.

"They'll be decorating this place for years to come. They haven't even done the velarium, and that's not decoration, it's essential in the summers. Not to mention the under-arena space, which has just been thrown together, no proper building there at all, just a basic floor with some scaffolding over the top, lifts and pens around the edge. He hasn't even finished the waterproofing layer, tested the plumbing for flooding the space or ordered waterproof doors to seal off the entrances. Much he cares about us and our promise to deliver a naumachia."

"He might care more if you didn't antagonise him."

Marcus only laughs.

BUT NONE OF US LAUGHS over the next few days as the amphitheatre falls quiet and even the streets of Rome, so noisy, begin to empty. The pestilence spreads rapidly, and it does not respect anything, nor anyone. Senators and bricklayers, whores and priestesses, all of them fall ill. The patrician families hurry away to their countryside villas, certain that it is Rome's dirty air and streets that are the problem. Traders and farmers from the surrounding countryside, usually so keen to supply Rome and its hungry citizens, stay away and the market stalls grow empty.

Fabia and her father have begun their work earlier than expected, seeing to the many gladiators who have fallen ill.

"It starts with a fever, then the chills and shaking take over. But there are so many symptoms. Coughing, headaches, vomiting, diarrhoea, pain in the chest and limbs. I've seen all of them," Fabia reports to us.

"But most people are getting better, aren't they? Especially the gladiators? They must be stronger than most people."

"Doesn't matter how strong you are," says Fabia. "It comes in cycles. Fever, then chills, then sweats. Some people get better after the sweats, some die during the fever. Children and old people get it worst, but that doesn't stop strong men getting it. And pregnant women. I've seen eight die in two days now, couldn't save the child except in one case and that was touch and go." She sighs, rubbing her hands together against the morning chill. "And now I'm starting to see people who get through the sweats, they seem cured and then, the cycle starts again. Worst one I've seen had three attacks and then he died."

"Where is it coming from?" I ask.

She shakes her head. "I don't know. I can't tell. Sometimes it seems like it must spread in households, one person to the next, because a whole family goes down with it. But then you'll get a family and only one person falls ill, the rest go untouched. Some say it's the water in the public fountains, the old people say it comes from the marshlands outside of Rome, but they can't explain how it gets here. The air? The water? People who are already carrying the illness without knowing it? I just don't know. I've been working day and night, trying to help, but there isn't much we can do."

She rubs her hands over face. "I better go," she says. "Too much to do." She makes her way down the steps, which are too steep for someone of her size; she has to keep one hand on the wall to steady herself.

A FEW DAYS LATER THE architect goes missing and word comes that he, too, has fallen ill. Work on the amphitheatre has slowed to a trickle. No more statues are arriving from the stonemason's, the mosaic makers have left half of the imperial box unfinished. In the architect's absence, Marcus takes over, directing the few remaining craftsmen to to those parts of the arena most visible to those who matter most. The upper tiers, at this rate, will get no decorative flourishes whatsoever before the opening; all such works will be concentrated where the Emperor and the richest families of Rome can see them.

"So, we're carving family names into the marble seating, but the upper corridors won't even be painted? It's the plebs who take the Games seriously, attending day after day," Fausta points out.

"The Emperor is paying, and he wants his cronies impressed," says Marcus. "Stop whining and find out who the second-best mosaic makers in Rome are, because right now, they're the people I need. If nothing else gets done, the imperial box has to look magnificent."

Fausta grumbles, but she knows he's right and within two days a new team of mosaic makers are working on the floor. "It's the section behind his throne, so he won't be looking at it much," she comforts Marcus, who is still fretting.

"Fabius says more than a third of the gladiators might not be fit to fight during the inaugural Games," he says, appalled at a note he has just received. "I've been trying to get more gladiators from the south, promising them it's a big chance for their careers, but most of them are refusing. They're too scared of getting the pestilence themselves." He snorts. "So much for bravery. Bunch of cowards, under all those muscles."

"No FAUSTA THIS MORNING?" CASSIA asks, expertly flipping pancakes to feed Karbo and me.

"Lazy lie-abed," I say. "When you see her, tell her to come straight to work. We don't have time to wait for her, there's hardly anyone on site as it is. At this rate it'll be Karbo and me doing the painting and carving. We should have made and stored most of the scenery by now, we're falling behind. So much for telling Titus everything was going well, the gods must've heard us and decided we were too full of ourselves."

Much to my surprise, the architect has returned, although he looks as pale as his toga.

"I'm not sure you should be here yet," I say, keeping my distance in case he is contagious. "Are you sure you're better? You don't look it. Marcus can look after everything, you know."

"That's what I'm afraid of," he says sourly. "Jupiter be praised, I am well. I recovered quickly."

"As you wish," I say. "I'll leave you to it."

"Please do," he says.

But by early afternoon the architect is staggering and has to return home. Karbo comes to tell me in the nearby warehouse, where I'm making an inventory of the scenery that is complete and what still needs to be done, a depressing task given how much is missing and how fast time is running out.

"He shouldn't have come back to work so soon," I say. "He clearly wasn't well enough."

"And Fausta?" asks Karbo.

"What about her?" I snap, trying to hold two scrolls under my arm while making notes on a third.

"She never arrived," says Karbo.

I drop everything I am holding, leave scrolls and tablets fallen on the floor and run through the streets back to the insula, Karbo at my side. When I reach the courtyard, Maria is not in her usual place, instead she has moved up two floors and is keeping watch outside Fausta's door. I run up the wooden stairs, clutching at the bannister.

"It's the pestilence," says Maria. "I've left water for her just inside the door, but I won't go in."

"Thank you," I gasp. "Karbo, you stay outside."

"He sleeps by her bed every night," points out Maria.

Inside, the room is dark. I open the tiny window trying to get fresh air in. Fausta is lying on her bed, blanket crumpled at her side, naked. I touch her skin.

"She's burning up," I say to Karbo, who is hovering in the doorway.

I SPEND ALL OF THAT afternoon attending to her by the flickering light of a lamp. Karbo brings cold water more than once from the public fountains, I dip rags in it and lay them over her forehead, her breasts, her belly, her feet. I wipe her hands over and over again. Maria moves back to her normal spot and warns the others to stay away when they come home. Julia ignores her and comes to stand in the doorway.

"There are more than twenty people ill now, just in our insula," she sighs. "I'm doing what I can."

"Take Karbo to help you," I offer.

Fausta alternates between burning up and then shaking with cold, her hands like claws reaching out for the blanket and clutching it to her desperately. I add my cloak and tell Karbo that he must sleep, he has been helping Julia for hours. I send him to sleep in the rooftop hut with Marcus.

"Let me help," says Marcus.

"Someone has to go to work tomorrow," I say. "Go and get some sleep."

"Hot," croaks Fausta, and she throws my cloak and the blanket aside again.

THE NIGHT IS ENDLESS. SOMETIMES I sleep, but I am woken by Fausta's moans when she is too hot and by her teeth chattering when she is too cold, her whole jaw shaking so hard that I am afraid she will bite her tongue. Julia brings me slices of early cucumbers, still tiny, but I cannot make her eat. Instead I put the slices in her water cup and make her drink. Julia brings a tea made of marigolds and fennel, Fabia sends one of honeysuckle. They should reduce fever, but nothing makes any difference. By the morning I am exhausted and Karbo tells me that Marcus told him to stay with us while he goes to work.

"He said you are not to come," he says solemnly. "You must sleep. Cassia has sent you food."

I sip some water, try to eat a fruit roll and only get halfway through before I feel my eyelids droop. "Watch over her," I tell him. "Any change, wake me."

HE SHAKES ME AWAKE AND I blink at the sunlight streaming in through the window. Sweat is pouring off Fausta, as though a river were washing over her. I pull away the blanket and mop her with my rag, washing away the sweat as it seeps out of her. I trickle water into her mouth again and she opens her eyes, focuses on me, then Karbo.

"Bona Dea," she mutters, "Get the boy out of here."

I gesture to Karbo to leave us, though I think Maria is right, surely he would be ill by now if it were contagious. "Drink," I urge her.

She swallows more vigorously, and I get more than three cups of water down her, though she will not eat. When she falls asleep again, the sweating having eased, I pray to Juno to look down on her and bring her back to health, promising to sacrifice at her altar if she will do so.

My prayers are not so easily granted. Fausta becomes feverish again, then cold, the chills shaking her whole body.

"He found me," she mutters, her face turning from one side to the other, seeking a cool side of the pillow to rest her cheek on.

"What?" I say, unsure if I have heard her correctly.

"Vulcan," she mutters.

I make a sign against evil spirits. "What about Vulcan?"

"He found me in the end," she says. "I escaped his wrath, but he found me, even in Rome he found me."

A chill runs through me. "It is a fever," I say. "The pestilence is not from Vulcan." I say it more firmly than I believe. I have heard the same from others, that Vulcan is still displeased, that not content with obliterating city after city, he has come here to Rome to exact a greater punishment.

"Where is it from then?" she asks, her breath too fast.

"The bad air," I try. "The marshlands have bad air and everyone knows they sit too close to Rome, the air drifts here and…"

But her eyes have closed, she turns her face away and I do not think she is listening to me anymore.

By the morning of the third day I begin to have some hope. Once again, sweat has streamed from her body, but after a few hours it stops, and she gulps water as though her life depended on it. She sleeps, and when she wakes, she manages to eat a little soup made of spring greens, which I spoon into her, mouthful by mouthful. She gives a small smile at the sight of Karbo and when Marcus visits in the afternoon, she even props herself up on one elbow to talk to him.

"Amphitheatre falling apart yet without me?" she croaks.

"Getting on better than ever," he says promptly. "Should have got rid of you years ago. You've been holding me back."

She manages a small laugh and then sinks back onto the bed. I am cheered by the exchange, but Marcus appears at nightfall on the same day, and gestures to me to come outside.

"The architect died last night."

I stare at him. "But he came to work. I know he came back too early but…"

"The fever came back and he couldn't breathe."

I can't think what to say. "What will we do?"

Marcus shakes his head. "We can manage. So long as one of us instructs the craftsmen, it can be done."

"In the time we have left?"

"The parts that matter."

We attend the architect's funeral, ashes from the pyre fluttering through the hot air. Marcus looks grim and I wonder whether the ashes remind him of Livia, of the day when the sky turned ashen above the amphitheatre, when the architect's immaculate white toga grew speckled all over. Outside the city, where the burials take place, I look around in horror at the number of burials under way, not just dozens but hundreds. The road we are on is as busy as one of Rome's main streets.

"How many people have died?" I ask.

Marcus shakes his head. "They say almost a thousand just yesterday and more every day," he says. "Let's go. This is no place to linger."

To my vast relief, Fausta seems to be recovering. I insist she should have sunlight and fresh air, so I wrap her up in my cloak and seat her on the balcony, two floors up from Maria. They don't talk to each other but there is some sort of companionship as the two of them watch the comings and goings of the courtyard. The baker's family get well again, but five families within our insula lose one or more family members.

THE CITY FEELS STRANGELY QUIET, people keep to their homes if they can and everywhere there is the smell of burning incense, many people believing that the perfume may drive away the unseen pestilence. We must all get water from the public fountains but there is fear of coming too close to others, as well as the worry that perhaps the water itself is tainted. Candles burn constantly at all the street corner shrines, lit hurriedly in thanks for recovery or as desperate requests to avoid the illness.

Rumours are everywhere. Besides the water and the air, the older people blame the marshlands for carrying illness into the city, but they are waved off by other more frightening rumours.

"It's the ashes from Vesuvius, they are cursed with the spirits of those who died and now they have created a pestilence." Those who believe it wrap cloth round their faces, only their fearful eyes showing, hoping not to breathe in the spirits of the dead. They make sacrifices and offerings to Hades, asking that he collect up those who belong to him, asking that he prevent them from wandering the streets of Rome. "They were never properly buried or cremated," they say, and some even ask the priests to hold empty funerals for the dead of Pompeii, of Herculaneum, of Oplontis, and all the other towns and villages smothered under the unending grey ashes. They say that if there were funerals to guide the spirits of the dead they would not reside in the poisoned ashes; they would not seek out bodies and set them to burning them internally.

"It is Vulcan, trying to reach those who escaped his wrath and fled here." And those who believe it shun the refugees who escaped, will not speak with them or serve them and make gestures behind their backs and even to their faces to ward off evil spirits and curses.

Some say the refugees had a pestilence in their own region and now they have brought it here, that is why the pestilence descended not long after they came to Rome. And those who say it go one step further than shunning the refugees, they seek them out and let out their fear through anger, meting out violence, from spitting to beatings and worse.

The Jews whisper amongst themselves that this is their Almighty's revenge on Emperor Titus. He burnt their Holy Temple. Now he is being punished through the fire spewing from Vesuvius and the fever in his subjects who are burning up. When the whispers are heard by others their retribution is swift. "The Jews are to blame. They prayed for retribution on us for burning their holy places and now their vengeance has brought down a pestilence on us." And Jews are sought out and beaten or killed, in the dark nights when more and more bodies have been taken to the outskirts of the city and burned or buried, sometimes so many there is not even time to carve their names, and so they will be forgotten.

Some believe those who died deserved it. They say the fearful and the ill have brought it upon themselves, that they are being punished for something they have done. They claim that good people have nothing to fear, that the illness is a sign of impurity, or impiety, or improper respect for the gods. They make a show of their lack of fear, laughing at those who cover their faces and seeking out the refugees or the Jews to drink with, boasting of their own fearlessness, their certainty that they will not be touched. They celebrate the warmer days with picnics and sailing along the Tiber in barges with much wine-drinking and defiant merriment, while the more careful tut and suggest that meeting in large groups can only aid in spreading the pestilence.

And it does not matter that the fearless and the refugees sicken, and the Jews also sicken, nor that the ashes of Vesuvius have not been seen for many months now. It does not matter because everyone in the city has lost someone and everyone who is not ill is grieving and angry. When those who were already grieving and angry fall ill they cannot even summon the strength to fight the illness and so die even quicker.

I WAKE IN THE NIGHT, too hot. Summer is bringing warm nights. I shrug off the blanket that covers Marcus and me, leaving my half of it between us. But now I feel too cold. I pull the blanket back towards me and as I do so, a wave of heat comes towards me from Marcus' side. Despite sleeping side-by-side for all these months, we never touch while we sleep. Now, tentatively, I reach out a hand and touch his shoulder where it emerges from the blanket.

He is hot. So hot.

I get onto my knees, feel around me in the dark until I find the lamp, then strike the fire steel against the flint, the sparks falling to the floor more than once, my hands trembling. At last, the kindling catches fire and I use a taper to light the oil-soaked wick, which eventually flickers into life. Jupiter make me wrong, I pray. Let it be nothing, just the blanket too heavy for June. I pull away the blanket. Marcus mutters. I touch him again and there is no doubt. Fever. He has the fever.

Outside the hut is a full amphora of water, cooled by the night. I hurry outside, stub my toe against it, the pain shooting up my leg. I bite my lip to keep from crying out. I drag the amphora inside and look for something to use as a rag. There is nothing, I have left them in Fausta's room. I reach for my spare head wrap, dip it into the cold water and begin to wipe him with it. He lifts a hand to push me away.

"You're burning up," I say to him. "You have to let me cool you."

"Burning," he murmurs.

For the next few hours, until the dawn comes, I talk to him and continue to use the damp head wrap to cool him. He does not speak again. Sometimes he moans, turning from side to side, sometimes towards the coolness, sometimes seeking to escape it. The lamp flickers and goes out, but I do not refill it, only continue wiping him. When the first light comes through the window, I take a deep breath, the sunlight rescuing me from the lonely darkness. Now I can see Marcus better. His skin is flushed, his breathing shallow.

The door swings open and Julia stands in the doorway. Her eyes flicker across the pair of us, her face serious. "How long has he been like this?"

I shake my head. "Several hours."

"The chills?"

"Not yet."

"What can I bring you?"

I try to think. "More water, more rags. The teas. They didn't work for Fausta but they might help him. Send Karbo for Fabia."

Julia comes and goes all morning, bringing everything I ask for. When Fabia arrives, she shakes her head and prescribes everything we have already tried. I follow her outside the hut as she leaves.

"What else can I do?"

"Nothing," she says. "Keep him cool when he is hot, keep him warm when he is cold. Pray for the sweats, they may herald the end of this."

I want to ask her to stay with me, I am afraid of her leaving, but I know that she must see many others and that there is nothing that will magically cure this illness.

I make my way down the stairs to Fausta. She is pale, but has managed to get up by herself and take up a position on the balcony. Karbo has brought her food and water.

"You look better," I say.

"I feel dreadful."

"At least you are up. I promised a sacrifice to Juno for you if you recovered, I will do it as soon as Marcus can be left alone."

She gives a snorting laugh. "You asked Juno to heal a prostitute? Isn't her job to look after respectable Roman matrons and their households?"

"She can watch over anyone she cares to," I say. "I need to get back to Marcus. Will you be all right?"

"You can't kill a she-wolf that easily," she says.

I smile at her fierceness and turn away.

"Althea."

I look back at her.

"Take good care of him. You know what men are like, all bravado, then when they get sick, they turn into babies who need a nursemaid."

"I'll tell him you said so," I say.

"You do that. Tell him he's a lazy bastard that needs to get out of bed and do some work or find himself face-to-face with a lion in the arena. One month left, tell him, pestilence or no pestilence."

I'M RELIEVED AT FAUSTA'S CONTINUING recovery. If she can recover, so can Marcus. I make my way back to the hut and find him shaking with the chills. I cover him in blankets, in both our cloaks and still he shakes. There's nothing else to cover him with, so I lie next to him, pressing my body against his to give him my own heat. Eventually, I fall asleep, exhausted from a night spent awake. I wake up when he pushes me away. The fever is back.

"Livia," he mutters.

I pull away the blanket, our cloaks, reach for the water and the rags. "Drink," I say, filling up a cup and holding it to his lips.

His eyes suddenly open. "I'm burning up," he says.

"I know," I say. "Drink the water, it will make you feel better."

"Was it like this?" he says.

"What?"

"Was it like this?" he asks again.

I don't know what he's talking about. Perhaps he is delirious. "I don't understand," I say, wiping the damp rag across his face, dipping it in the cold water again and wringing it out. "Was what like this?"

His eyes are open but he's not looking at me, he is looking at something else, something not in the room. "Vesuvius," he says, and a chill runs through me. "Was it like this, Livia? Did you burn up inside? Did you die like this, is this how it felt before you died, before they all died?"

I fumble, wiping the rag across his dry lips as though to stop the words coming out.

"My boy," he says.

"Don't talk." I wipe his lips again. He's frightening me, he is making me think of everybody who died in Pompeii and all around, it is like hearing a spirit speak. "Don't talk," I say again. "Try to rest," I add, hopelessly.

"They burned up," he says. "All of them. Livia, my boy, my baby boy Amantius. This is what it felt like for them, isn't it? A heat ripping through them that got hotter and hotter – until they died."

"I don't know," I say, my voice cracking. I take a deep breath, trying to stay calm. He is delirious, only delirious. He doesn't know what he's saying. But he does, of course, I know he does. This burning fever is exactly what it must have been like, but worse. I think again of the woman who described it, even from a distance, as opening an oven, the heat rushing across your skin and nowhere to jump back to, no way to escape it.

"It would be the right way to die," he murmurs.

"What?" I ask.

"I could join them," he says. His eyes close. "I would know how they died, I could join them."

I shake him, my hands reaching out and grabbing him by the shoulders before I can think what I am doing. "You're not to join them!" I say, my voice too loud for the tiny room. "Stay here! You have to stay here!"

"How is he doing?"

It's Julia. I snatch my hands away from him, my breathing too fast. Marcus has kept his eyes shut, giving no response to either my words or actions. I stand up, make my way outside, closing the door behind me. I'm glad to leave him, his words are frightening me. I tell Julia what he said.

Her usually serene countenance creases in a grimace. "He needs to fight," she says. "To be ill when you are grieving for your wife and child…" She pauses. "He must not long to join them, or the fever will take him for sure."

"What am I supposed to do? How can I keep him here?"

"Give him something to live for," she says.

"He has nothing to live for!" Tears start falling and I wipe them away too hard. "Everyone he loves has died and he is doing a job he hates."

"He may hate his job, but he is good at it. And there is still the farm."

"The farm he can't afford to buy, now he's lost all his savings?" I say. "The farm he was supposed to make a home of with his wife and child?" I shake my head. "I have nothing I can say to him. Nothing!"

Julia takes me by the shoulders, looks into my face. "If there's one thing Marcus is," she says, her voice certain and calm, "it's loyal to those to whom he has made a commitment. You have to remind him of those people. Fausta, you, Karbo."

"What if we are not enough?"

"You have to make it be enough," she says.

"They say two thousand have died in one day. How is that possible?" I think of the amphitheatre, slowly filling with the bodies of the dead.

Julia shakes her head. She spends her days going from room to room, offering cold water and cold wet cloths on the faces and bodies of those who are ill, offering her coolness and calmness to those who are afraid. "It must abate soon," she says. She looks out over the city, hands on the wall, face turned towards the south east and the temple where she once served, though she cannot see it from here.

"Have you ever seen a time like this?"

"No," she says.

"What if everyone dies?"

"They won't."

"How do you know?" I ask, begging her, as though she were a speaker of oracles, a seer, as though she might look into the future and see Rome and her citizens healthy and well again.

She turns back to me. "We should visit the island."

I follow her along Sand Street and down to the river, over the bridge that takes us to the boat-shaped island in the middle of the Tiber river, home to the temple of Aesculapius. I've never had to pray at his shrine before, but now it is swarming with people come to ask the god of healing and medicine to help their loved ones. The snakes that usually live here, symbols of his powers, have slithered away to quieter parts of the site. We catch sight of one in the grasses near the entrance and another hiding beneath an altar. People are queuing to fill cups with the healing waters of the temple and some carry children in their arms so that they can be licked by the dogs of the temple.

Julia and I carry back two small pots of sacred water, giving the sick inhabitants of our insula a few drops each, in the hopes that it will help them.

"How is Marcus?" Maria asks as I pass.

I shrug. "He sleeps and I think he might wake up better but then he talks and sweats and he is back in the fever."

"What does he say?"

I don't answer.

"Livia?"

I nod. "I think he actually wants to feel the fever," I say miserably. "I think he feels closer to her and Amantius. He believes he knows what they suffered, he wants to feel it too."

"None of us know what they suffered," says Maria. "None of us can even imagine such a death."

I have made a mistake. For a moment when Maria spoke, I allowed myself to imagine Myrtis, the heat and the ashes choking her. Tears roll down my face. I try not to think of her, only of the moments when she scolded me or fed me, teasing me by calling me by the dog's name, saying neither of us knew the meaning of hard work. I think only of things she did that made me laugh. Nothing more. I wipe my face with a corner of my tunic and Maria catches my movement.

"You can only do what you can," she says. "Take the water to him, it will help."

THE DAY WINDS WEARILY ON. Marcus does not speak again, but I do. I talk about Fausta, passing on her insulting comments and inventing more, trying to recreate their ribald banter. I talk about Karbo, how well he has come on, how his face has filled out from one too many pancakes, how eager he is to learn from all of us, how he follows Marcus around like a lost puppy.

"If you die," I say, "I'll have to work for some dreadful rich man, who will forever be pinching my bum and worse. I'll have to live in some fancy villa and I certainly won't see any of the team again, a scribe working for a patrician family can't be hanging out with the likes of whores and gladiators, nor street waifs and strays. Think how lonely I will be." I say all of it only to provoke him, but there is a truth in what I'm saying. I have to pause to wipe away tears and collect myself. "See what you're doing to me?" I add. "You should be ashamed of yourself, making a woman cry over you. How am I supposed to work hard and think quickly with you lying around in bed like some softie? I thought army men were tougher than that."

He doesn't answer. I leave the room only briefly, to fetch more water and accept some soup from Julia. While I'm out, I look in on Fausta but she's already asleep, which is good, she needs the rest. I tell Karbo to stay with Maria tonight. I do not want Fausta disturbed.

I WAKE EARLY. THE SUN has already risen, for the mornings are at their lightest now that we are in June. Twice I sit up, then lie back down, uncertain. The third time I look down at Marcus, his breathing is still laboured. I reach out, touch his forehead, the skin still hot to the touch. I stand up, leave my shoes where they are, my headwrap on the bed mat, my hair uncombed. I feel inside my satchel, pull out a couple of coins, then run down the wooden stairs.

Vesta's Temple is already surrounded by women, all of them barefoot with dishevelled hair. Some hold fruit or cloth, bread or cakes. A few richer women hold jewellery in their hands. Their elaborate hairstyles abandoned, they can only be identified by the quality of their dresses, though it looks as though most have dressed in their simpler clothes, linen and wool rather than their accustomed silks and gauzes.

I hang back in the crowd, heart beating too fast. I am not sure if what I am doing is wrong. Vestalia is the one day when the shrine is opened to view and mothers may approach to beg favours of Vesta. I am not a mother. I hope no-one will ask any questions. In my hands I hold flowers, bought in the market as I made my way here, my feet tender on the dirty streets. But the crowd begins to move forward and I am in the queue now, there is no going back.

The six Vestal Virgins stand before Vesta's own fire, each one upright in her bearing, even their youngest recruit, a little girl barely eight years old, only two years served out of her thirty years of duty. The women in the crowd bow their heads, lay down their little offerings, whisper something, then move away, their faces lightened by the chance to beg the goddess herself for help.

Only five women in front of me, then three, then one, and suddenly the flowers have left my hands as I whisper the words I have prepared.

"Goddess Vesta, I come here not as myself but as a woman now gone from us, her name was Livia, mother to Amantius, wife to Marcus Aquillius Scaurus. He lies sick, Lady Vesta, he burns with fever and he will not fight it because he wishes only to join his wife and son. But I made a promise to Livia, Lady Vesta. I said I would look after her husband and now I ask for your help in doing so, for I can no longer do it alone. I bring you flowers, for Livia wore flowers in her hair. I beg for your help, Lady Vesta. Bring Marcus out of the darkness that surrounds him."

Behind me another woman is waiting, my time is over. I stumble away from the temple, narrowly avoiding stepping in mule droppings and almost end up being trampled by a donkey cart. I stop to gather myself, still uncertain whether I have done the right thing. Lady Vesta knows all, will she be angry that I came to her when I am not a mother? Is it wrong to come on behalf of another woman? Is it bad luck to come in the guise of a dead woman? I am not sure. I look down the Forum, seeing the amphitheatre standing at the end of it, vast and gleaming in the early light. I made a promise, I think, and I am not sure whether I mean the promise to Livia to protect her husband or to Marcus to help him see through the inauguration of this vast building, this all-consuming monument. Either way, I have work to do. On the way back I collect breakfast rolls and wine, as well as a treat of fresh plums from one of the only market stalls that still has fresh fruit from the countryside. The owner stands well back from me, keeping a cloth wrapped around his face.

"Can't be too careful," he says apologetically, gesturing to the covering, but I smile, grateful for the promise of fresh fruit. It will cheer Fausta and Karbo. And perhaps I can persuade Marcus to drink more water if I lace it with wine, or I could boil some of the plums to make him a juice. Perhaps Adah will even accept some. She has barricaded herself away during the pestilence, continually burning incense. Once or twice, I've worried, thinking her hut is on fire because there's so much smoke coming out of the window, but she seems well enough when I see her although she won't have anyone come near her. She allows the bakery to bring her loaves and she must collect water before dawn when there's no-one about, for I never catch her at it. I will lay some plums by her doorway; perhaps she will eat them when they have been smoked for long enough in her clouds of perfumed incense. The fresh air and sunshine, the short walk and the plums, all make me smile. There is hope yet. Perhaps Lady Vesta will intercede for Marcus and all will be well.

I hear Karbo wailing before I even enter the courtyard and I run, scattering plums from my basket. Karbo. Karbo, standing on the balcony, tears pouring down his face, a wordless wail coming from his open mouth. One door after another opens, there are heads, shouts, half-dressed men and women asking questions and I see only one thing behind Karbo. Fausta's open door, darkness within.

Julia takes over, caring for Marcus while I wash Fausta's body, still warm, one hand lifted up over her face in the convulsions that must have come in the night, the fever returning when she was all alone. I strip away her clothes, soaked in sweat, not even telling Karbo to stay away. He crouches in a corner, clutching her toga to him, his face pressed into it, the white cloth collecting his tears. Occasionally I hear him sob and I turn to touch him, to stroke his head and murmur words, but most of my actions are done in a daze.

Maria sends for an undertaker and, when they arrive, I let them carry Fausta away, one last glimpse of her black curls before she will be burnt up, before Vulcan claims her for his own. When they are gone, I want to run after them, to tell them to bring her back. I did not kiss her. I forgot to say anything to her. I was so tired and confused and shocked that I only washed her and dressed her in my own clothes and let Karbo touch her face.

He is asleep now, exhausted in his grief. I sit on her bed and take up a little corner of her toga, which he has wrapped himself in. I put it to my face as he did and smell the smell of her, a warm earthy aroma of sweat and herbs from where she used to trail her hands down over the leaves of Julia's many pots of herbs every morning, holding her fingers to her face to inhale their scents, before brushing her hands over her toga. I think of her raucous laugh and her coarse banter with Marcus, her confidence each morning, striding out in the toga that marked her out as a prostitute, her refusal to hide what she was. I think that I saw her cry only once, when everyone she knew and loved in the world except Marcus had died. She rose from the ashes to protect not just herself but Marcus and me. Still racked with fever, he does not even know that his best friend has died.

I hold her toga to my face and weep.

THE MINT

IT'S BEEN TWO WEEKS SINCE Fausta died. A lifetime ago and yesterday.

"TAKE YOUR PLACE."

I hover, one hand on the balustrade. "Shouldn't one of us be below the arena?"

"Jupiter and Juno! Sit *down*. The whole point is to see if it can run smoothly without us interfering all the time. It has to run on minimal signals. Sit."

I sit in the exquisitely carved chair next to Marcus, who is currently lounging on Emperor Titus' throne. The imperial box is otherwise empty. The arena below is also empty. Only Marcus and I know that eyes are watching our every moment from the metal grilles set into the walls surrounding the arena floor.

Marcus raises a hand and the vast Gate of Triumph slowly opens. A single woman walks solemnly across the arena, coming to a halt at its centre. She stands still for a moment, then turns her head up to us.

"Like that?" she calls up.

Marcus stands and leans over the side of the box. "Perfect, Julia, thank you."

"Again?"

"No, it was fine."

She nods and walks away. A hidden door in the arena wall opens and she disappears into the darkness.

"You're sure it won't seem too empty? Shouldn't there be a big procession or something?"

"There will be," says Marcus. "But first there must be a sacred moment."

"And they'll agree to it?"

"Why wouldn't they? The Vestal Virgins, at the very centre of the inauguration? It's perfect."

WE LEAVE THE IMPERIAL BOX and make our way through the corridors. By the closest exit a sullen looking man is standing waiting to speak to Marcus.

"These five hundred doves you want dyed?"

"What about them?"

"What colours do you want?"

"As many colours as you can manage. Not blue though."

"We've already done a few blue ones as a test."

"Well, don't do any more."

"What's wrong with blue?"

Marcus sighs and points out of an arch at the sky. "You won't see them if they're blue, will you?"

"You could just keep them white."

Marcus shakes his head.

"Why?"

"Boring. Everyone's seen white doves."

The man walks off, shaking his head.

"Lazy," comments Marcus. "Right. So that's the birds taken care of. These giraffes, how tame are they? Can someone walk them to the Gate of Triumph on a leash? Because the height they are, I can't keep them under the arena. Also, I want them to stay down the far end of the arena. I'd rather they didn't die in the beast hunting scene, they're ridiculously expensive and they're always dying on sea voyages. So let's try and use them several times, make the most of them, shall we, now we've got three all the way here and they're still standing."

I nod, make a note, then slump back in the chair.

"Tired?"

I nod.

"Go home and sleep," says Marcus. "I can manage."

"You're as white as a freshly-washed toga," I tell him. "It's you that needs to rest longer, you shouldn't be back at work yet."

"With the days running out? I had to come back."

I nod. None of us had a choice, all of us have come back to work too soon, pale and quiet, counting the hours each day till we can stop work, lying in the baths like stranded seals, before shuffling home and barely managing to eat before we fall asleep. Karbo's skin looks grey, he crouches in the shadows where he used to play in the sun and says nothing unless he's asked a question. Mostly he follows Marcus or me about and does what he's told. My heart hurts for him, but I'm so tired I can barely get through the days as it is, I cannot care for him properly. I make sure he's fed, and I have him sleep in the rooftop hut with Marcus and me, leaving Fausta's room empty. Julia could rent it out, of course, but there's a lot of empty rooms in Rome just now. The pestilence has faded away leaving ten thousand dead, with no need for rooms. Sometimes Marcus wakes late, or I see sweat on his brow and I panic, thinking the fever has come back, that it has not released him from its grip after all, but he remains well, only weakened by the illness and saddened by another loss. We waited until he was definitely on the mend before telling him and his grief for Fausta was so raw I feared a relapse. He still does not mention her name much. I see him trip over it several times a day when we are at work, see him about to turn to her and crack some joke that will make her laugh. And then there's the pain when he remembers she is not sitting above us where the plebs will sit, watching over everything. She is gone.

The trumpets have been practising for more than an hour by now, the same fanfare over and over again, to herald the arrival of the Emperor. I'm beginning to get a headache.

"Can they not practise something else?" I snap at Marcus after I've written the same word three times. The list of things that must be done is unending and we have only a week left until the inauguration. I'm beginning to panic that it will not all get done in time. Even Marcus, usually so unflappable at work, is snapping at people and has developed a deep worry line between his eyebrows.

He shrugs. "If you like." He leans over the balustrade, twisting so he is looking up at the musicians, who are sitting nearby. "Hey! HEY! Switch to the hunting scene. Practise that for a bit."

I deeply regret my request after it turns out that this involves contrasting drumming with flutes pitched incredibly high, almost a screaming wail. It's a sound designed to instil a mixture of suspense and fear and it is doing nothing for my head, which is pounding. As the date of the inauguration creeps closer, more and more people want something from either Marcus or me. Stallholders of food, wine, merchandise and toys want to know exactly where they can pitch their stands and then argue about the spots we give them. The bookies are always slipping in to ask Marcus 'just a few questions' hoping to find out what animals will be used on the first day, the first week, the first month, which gladiators will be showing so they can check up on their track records. Marcus tends to give them short thrift. We have recruited cleaners, ushers, toilet attendants, armoured guards who will surround the arena when we use wild beasts, ready to catch, incapacitate or kill any animal that presents a danger to the spectators. We've made arrangements with undertakers who will attend all the Games, ready to remove bodies at speed. The dead gladiators will be taken back to their barracks, for some have families, criminals will be dumped in the Tiber. We will have the carcasses of animals to dispose of too, some of which may be sold for meat, some we may use ourselves to feed the meat-eaters in their pens, although they can't be overfed, or they won't fight or kill on demand. My days seem full of death and my spirit feels so heavy, it's hard to think straight.

Karbo appears at my side. "There's a Praetorian Guard wanting to speak with you."

"Me?"

"He wants you and Marcus to go with him somewhere."

I feel a flutter of panic. Have we done something wrong? Perhaps they have found out Marcus left Rome against the strict conditions of his contract, though surely, we would be able to argue he did so for his wife and child, so they might show mercy? Or perhaps they found out about Marcus' night-time drunken brawling and have decided he should be sacked? I make my way out to one of the corridors and see a man waiting for me, standing at attention.

He towers over me. "Althea Aquillius?"

"Can I help you?" I ask, trying to keep my voice light.

"Emperor Titus wishes you and Marcus Aquillius Scaurus to attend him at the mint."

"Mint?" In my confusion I think of the pots of mint in Julia's courtyard, the herb's bright strong smell in the perfumed waters of private baths.

"He's having a new coin struck. He wants you there to see it. It's to be thrown into the crowd on the inauguration day."

I gather my thoughts. "Of course, at once, a moment while I find Marcus." I pull out my centurion's whistle, dart back through the arch into the arena and blow it as hard as I can. There's a pause and then one of the trapdoors is thrown open and Marcus emerges.

"What is it?" he calls up.

"We're wanted by the Emperor," I call back. I walk down a few tiers so I can speak to him without the guard hearing me. "Titus wants us to attend the production of a coin showing the amphitheatre."

Marcus rolls his eyes. "We don't have time for cack like that, we're up to our eyes in this."

"We don't have a choice," I point out.

Marcus utters some choice words under his breath, mostly referring to the various genitalia of the gods and where Titus can go about putting them. Fausta would have sworn so the whole amphitheatre could hear. Tears spring instantly to my eyes. Every time she comes into my mind, I cry, and it upsets Marcus and Karbo, so I try not to think about her. Sometimes at night I dream of her and wake weeping, hold a blanket to my face and try to sob quietly before I fall back asleep and wake in the morning with aching eyes and swollen eyelids.

"So we cut small pieces of the bars of metal and then each is hammered into shape, creating 'flans', blank coins. They're placed into the oven to soften them up, then put into two-sided dies. When the men use a hammer on the dies, they imprint onto the coins, you see?"

Marcus is looking bored. I try to make a show of being interested. "How many do you produce a day?"

"A good team can produce twenty thousand strikes a day."

"Strikes?"

"Coins."

"All of them are made like that?"

"Yes, we make all the denominations."

Marcus looks around at the large numbers of people working. "No stealing?"

The man laughs. "Not a chance. There's a supervisor on every team watching the men work and all the men are strip-searched when they go home. If you're found hiding coins… let's just say you'll be finding yourself *in* the arena, not just making pretty pictures of it."

One of the men hands over a denarius to Marcus, who looks it over and then passes it to me. On one side, Titus' head, on the other a Jewish captive kneels below a trophy of arms. I think of Adah, what she would do were such a coin to come into her hands. Marcus passes me another coin, this time a sestertius. A seated Titus on one side, on the other, the Flavian Amphitheatre, each tiny arch perfectly portrayed. Inside, it clearly shows the steps between tiers of seating and includes tiny raised dots for the spectators. It is a work of art, but the endless metallic hammering is making me tired and fearful. These hundreds of coins being created show the amphitheatre in all its glory, they promise something that has not yet happened. It is not the building that will be glorified, it is what goes on inside it and that is down to Marcus and me. The pressure on us mounts through the constant blows ringing in my ears, the endless shining depictions being created. I hold one of the coins, trying to steady my breathing. I think of Pompeii and all its inhabitants, of the fever that took not just Fausta but thousands of lives, so much death and destruction in just one year and yet we are creating a place that glorifies and amplifies death and destruction.

I stagger. Marcus grabs my elbow. "What is wrong?"

"I feel sick," I whisper.

He looks appalled. "The fever?" He touches my forehead, then shakes his head, I am not hot. "Shall I take you home?"

"No," I say. "He will notice your absence. He won't notice me leaving."

He hesitates, glances towards where Titus is still beaming at the hammering men, turning one of the coins over in his hands, then nods.

The noise follows me almost to the gates, where it finally dims. I vomit in a nearby bush, the hot bile in my mouth choking my nose and throat, coughing and spitting to rid myself of the taste. When it is done, I squat down for a few moments, feeling weak. I touch my forehead again, but it feels cool. After a while I get to my feet and begin the walk home, slow and occasionally wavering.

When I reach our insula my head still aches, but I feel the urge to stop by Balbus' toy workshop on the ground floor before I climb the stairs to sleep. He is still there, although the shutters are half-closed. His wife Floriana is sweeping the floor and re-winding scraps of yarn while Balbus is sharpening some of his whittling knives, ready for the next day's work. I tell them what I want and they both nod solemnly.

"I know it is not your usual line of work," I say, "but I would like it done by someone who knows Marcus. The little figures…" I swallow. "He was not yet able to run," I say at last. "And her hair was very light, like the shells of hazelnuts."

They nod, silent in the face of the tears that have filled up my eyes. I am too tired to be making this commission, I should be sleeping. "I will leave it with you," I say.

It takes me a long time to make my way up all the stairs to the rooftop, each step slow and tentative. When I reach the hut, I lie down on the sleeping mat and fall asleep almost at once. There is a moment when I think I hear Adah muttering, "Good child," and feel the blanket being tucked around me, but perhaps I am only dreaming.

FIRE

THE AREA BELOW THE ARENA is as dark as ever, the flaming torches along the outer walls only making it seem gloomier. The animals have been arriving all day yesterday and this morning, the pens are full to bursting. Some animals can be kept together for they find comfort in one another's company, but many must be kept apart in case they fight. Six lions, we have been assured, are all from one pride, five females and one male, but they've been kept near-starving. They could well turn on one another, so each must be kept in a different pen and none of them can be next to another animal, there must be spaces between each cage.

I fumble through the leather scroll holder at my feet, trying to find the right one to consult. "I have to personally check on over one thousand animals today. Karbo, you can accompany me. I'm going to have to teach you to read and write so you can take on this sort of task."

"I can read the date. The inauguration is in only two days after today."

"Don't remind me," I beg. "How can it be July already?"

"Is that all of the animals?"

I shake my head, find the right scroll. "Nothing like it, but we can't even hold all of them. We've just got most of the ones for the inauguration."

"But we've got lots of pens down here."

"For ordinary days, yes, especially in a regular schedule, perhaps one or even two hundred Games a year. Not for one hundred consecutive days. Nothing like enough. They're being stored down at the docks in a warehouse we've borrowed."

"Althea! Will you check the scenery?"

"Yes!" I call back to Marcus. "Last rehearsals tomorrow."

He lifts a hand in acknowledgment and disappears through one of the trapdoors.

"Come on, let's get this over with," I say. We make our way over to the towering man currently engaged in directing criminals into cages of their own.

"Strabo," I greet him.

"Althea."

"Have all the criminals arrived?"

"Most of them. There's a few women in this batch. They promised us one more woman and ten more men tomorrow, that'll take us up to the right number."

I swallow. There's a scroll detailing everything that will happen during the inauguration and I've had to make several copies so that different people can refer to it. The fate reserved for the female criminals is stomach churning. "Feed them properly, will you? They're in here for three days, don't starve them as well."

"Just as you say."

I pull out the scroll listing the animals and begin walking past each pen, counting and then annotating the list. "Antelope, seventy-five. Zebras, sixteen. Deer, fifty-nine."

I'm about to finish for the day, the site is almost empty. I'm sitting in the stands where the senators will sit, sorting through a bundle of scrolls, trying to ensure everything has been correctly labelled and sorted into the right leather cases so that we know where to find everything. I unfurl one scroll, read off the details of which items of scenery need to be brought out of storage and into the under-arena tomorrow. They'll take up a lot of space, but we need to test that they all work smoothly, so we'll just have to put up with the inconvenience.

But the scroll is speckled with something, some sort of dust or... I brush it away, then stop.

Ash.

There is ash, floating through the air.

I look up but I cannot see the thick black clouds that came rolling in from the south when Vesuvius erupted. But there are still floating bits of ash, not as heavy as that cursed day but still...

I pack away the scrolls, dropping more than one, hands grown suddenly clumsy. Then I start climbing the steps between tiers of seats, legs aching, panting. Higher and higher till I reach the topmost corridor and outer arches, peer out of them. I think I see a faint grey cloud to the north west, but I'm not sure.

My legs ache as I clamber down the steep steps to the ground floor. But as soon as I get out of the building, I can see something is wrong. The Forum is not full of the usual crowds strolling about. Instead it is half empty and the remaining people are hurrying. I grab a passer-by.

"What's happening?"

"Fire in the Ninth," says the man, hurrying away.

I run.

The courtyard is full. Julia is standing on the steps, her hands raised for quiet.

"The fire has spread rapidly since it started last night," she says, "It's all around the Pantheon and the Baths of Agrippa and it's spreading both south and west. The Vigiles from our own region have been there since the early hours, others have been coming from every region all morning."

"At least our Vigiles were close at hand," Maria says. The Vigiles' station house in our region is just opposite the Julia Saepta.

"Yes, and there's a pool of water right near the Baths of Agrippa, they're trying to keep filling that so that the siphon pumps on the fire wagons can keep going and supply the main hoses. But they need a lot more people. Men should go and help, there is already a double chain from the river with buckets, but they need more. Take buckets and any other receptacle from each household. We need to contain the fire as soon as possible, or we will be in danger of a Great Fire happening again. Women, gather your children and valuables in case we need to vacate the building, but meanwhile we are all safest staying out of the way unless we can help."

The crowd quickly disperses, men rushing out of our gate carrying buckets and amphorae, whatever they can find. The women bustle about the balconies, in and out of doors.

"I brought your belongings down to my rooms," says Julia.

"Thank you," I say. "Where's Marcus?"

"Already gone to help," she says. "He led the first group of men."

"How bad is it?" I ask.

"Bad," she says, her voice low. "It's gone beyond some of the usual ways of fighting it, the soaked quilts and vinegar are already useless. They're pulling down buildings, trying to form a firebreak. They've been calling for cushions and mattresses to break the fall of anyone trapped in upper stories of the buildings that are ablaze. The streets are so narrow..."

I nod. The Ninth was spared the worst of the Great Fire sixteen years ago, which was to its benefit then, but after the fire was over, two-thirds of Rome had to be rebuilt, and that meant wider streets, stronger buildings and less wood. The Ninth is still a jumble of narrow streets and old buildings, many made of wood rather than brick and so more vulnerable to fire. Every building contains many lamps filled with oil, so any building that catches fire will find multiple sources of vicious fuel waiting to contribute to the blaze. The top tiers of most buildings are wooden, as is almost all the interior furniture. Many buildings already have a fire burning inside: popinas, temples, glassblowers, private homes, baths, bakeries, all of them with ample stores of dry wood, perfect for burning.

"Will this insula be safe?" I ask.

Julia grimaces. "If the fire is put out soon, yes. If not, we lie directly in its path to the south."

I hear shouts outside and run to the courtyard gate, just in time to see two fire wagons rush past, the horses whipped to a fast gallop. Behind it run a group of Vigiles, two of whom stop to commandeer a cart from a trader who happens to be passing; they ignore his refusal and turn the mules' heads down Virgin's Street and onwards.

"I can go and join the men," I say. "I can pass buckets."

She nods. "Be careful. Vulcan protect you."

I don't say that I don't much trust Vulcan after all that happened in Pompeii. I hurry out, only stopping to fully tie up my hair and cover it with a wrap, afraid that loose hair might be too tempting for stray sparks.

I RUN DOWN TOWARDS THE river and join the human chain, passing rope-and-pitch buckets hand to hand. The daylight hours pass in a haze of smoke and water. We can smell smoke and slowly the cloud of it begins to drift our way, a demoralising sight, telling us the fire is still raging. As we pass the full buckets, they slop water onto us, so that we soon have wet legs and feet which is almost welcome, given the heat of the day. The first days of July are not a time to be standing in the direct sun. With the return of the empty buckets comes news back down the line, passed mouth to mouth, some good news, mostly bad.

"Nero's Baths are saved, they used the aqueduct to protect it."

"They've used ballista to knock down twelve insulae and a bakery."

"The Horologium is saved."

But the news becomes more grim, even as water from the Tiber continues to head north, bucket by bucket and now the sun is sinking, making the Vigiles' work harder as they struggle to see what they are doing, blinded by the raging flames in one direction, by darkness in any other. We keep sending the buckets, arms aching, drained more by the news coming back than the physical effort.

"The Julia Saepta is on fire."

"The Diribitorium too."

"The Baths of Agrippa are burning."

And on and on through the night, the clouds of smoke only growing stronger, so that we cough and choke even as we pass buckets to unseen hands. People change places, new hands take the place of old. As dawn breaks I stagger back to Virgin's Street, unable to keep going without sleep. The courtyard is full of people sleeping on the ground, curled into corners. The bakery and all the shops are closed for the first time I can remember. Only Cassia is still cooking, feeding anyone who needs it, passing out bowl after bowl of greens and barley. I take a bowl, squat down to eat, then drag myself up the stairs. Looking out to the north makes me afraid, I can smell the smoke ever more strongly, the ashes continue to blow through the air. I can hear the distant crackling of the fire even from here. I want to help more, but I can barely stand. I stagger into the rooftop hut and lie down without taking off my wet shoes.

WHEN I WAKE THE SMOKE is stronger, I am already coughing.

I head back to the buckets again, not knowing how else to help. Past the courtyard of huddled women and children, the women trying to feed soot-faced men and find them a place to sleep. Maria has taken over the popina, Cassia presumably needed to sleep. She passes me a flatbread and a cup of wine and I try to speak through a mouthful.

"Have you seen Marcus? Is Karbo safe?"

"Karbo is asleep. I gave him strict orders not to leave the courtyard when he wakes, he's to help us feed people, not go running off to be a hero. He brought a message from Strabo last night, all is well at the amphitheatre, he will take care of the animals and the criminals."

"The rehearsals," I gasp. "We were supposed to hold the final rehearsals... what day is it?"

"The inauguration is tomorrow. If it happens."

"If? We've spent months…"

"If the fire comes further south it could reach the top of the Forum," says Maria. "And the amphitheatre's at the other end of it."

I shake my head. "The gods preserve us. And Marcus?"

"Marcus was at the Pantheon last I heard, but it wasn't looking good, the buildings are all too close together round there, all the craftsmen and traders have tiny little shops made of this and that, they're going up like tinder."

"I don't know what to do," I say miserably.

"Get back in the chain. It may not feel like it's helping, but it has to be. They need constant water."

I go back to the chain and the handles of the buckets rub against my already sore hands. My damp shoes grow wet as the sun's rays beat down on us. A couple of people in the line faint by mid-afternoon and a third and then fourth chain develop, although the receptacles grow less and less suitable, people using anything they have, even absurd things like water bottles. As twilight falls the news begins to frighten all of us.

"The racing stables are being evacuated, the horses are going wild, trying to stampede."

"The Theatre of Pompey's stage is burnt out."

"The fire's spreading east, towards the Auguraculum."

Nobody says anything, but if it passes that point, it will not be far from the Forum itself.

And then the news I've been dreading. "It's headed south, towards the Circus Flaminius."

Virgin's Street sits on the edge of the Circus. I run.

"Where is Marcus? Where is he?"

"I don't know. Celer went to the stables. He said the horses were all panicking, and they needed every man they could lay their hands on to lead the horses away one by one or they would have fled. I saw him just now with one of the horses. Maybe Marcus was helping him?"

I run outside the courtyard but there is no sign of Marcus in the crowd. I can see six different racing horses, all of them nervous, one rearing up which prompts screams from the women and children. The men holding the horses are struggling to calm them. I make sure to keep my distance and head through the streets to the main area of the fire. It feels like running towards Vesuvius, the streets getting progressively more blackened and ruined. Families wander the streets, confused and frightened, clutching their valuables.

The Pantheon is a blackened hulk. My hand shapes into the gesture against evil spirts almost without my knowing. To see a temple of the gods reduced to a smoking black heap is frightening. Who knows whether their wrath at being thus disgraced might fall on onlookers? I lower my eyes just in case. I think of Adah, her rage and bitterness at the Temple of her people in Jerusalem being burnt. Perhaps she is right. Perhaps her god has decided to punish Titus, and in so doing, punish Rome. I try and shake off the shiver that runs through me at the thought. Marcus. I must find Marcus.

In the half-light the ruins of the Baths of Agrippa look as though they are still smoking. I look around me, uncertain of whether I should call for help, for more water.

"Steam," says Marcus. He's sitting on the side of the road, face smeared in soot, tunic ripped at one corner and filthy. His hands are shaking and I wonder whether this blackened landscape reminds him of our hours in Pompeii, of the fruitless lonely search for his dead family.

"You're alive," I say.

"Barely," he says. "I think if I try to walk, I will fall asleep on my feet."

"We need you back at Julia's," I say. "The fire's spreading that way."

He's on his feet at once, though he staggers. We hurry back through the streets together and now I can feel heat coming through the alleyways, somewhere to the left of us, but coming closer, the shouts growing louder.

"Run," says Marcus and we run, reaching Virgin's Street just as the screams begin, the courtyard gate impassable as people run out, pushing into us as we try to force our way in. Finally, we enter, and Marcus pushes me aside. "Watch out!"

A burning section of the wooden rooftop railing crashes at my feet and I step back, clasping my tunic in case of sparks. Looking up, I see to my horror that our rooftop hut is already aflame, as is the topmost balcony, just below the roof.

"The building next door went up like a torch, it's all wood," says Julia, appearing at my side. "The fire leapt the street and the whole of the upper storey of this insula is wood. Get out Althea, now!"

I turn to follow her and then realise Marcus is not next to me. "Where is Marcus?"

"Outside?"

"He was here a moment ago!"

Julia's face is very pale. "There."

Marcus has reached the rooftop through the interior stairs and is pushing at the rooftop hut with all his strength. "What is he doing?"

"Trying to flatten it so the fire won't spread as fast."

I start running up the wooden stairs, every step shaking, unable to see above me because of the walkways.

"Althea! Don't! It's not safe!"

I hear crunching above me and come up the last few stairs to see the rooftop hut collapsing under Marcus' efforts. It's burning, but now that it's collapsed, the flames slow and a cloud of smoke emerges.

"And the other one!" he shouts, seeing me.

I turn and see Adah's hut, a flickering already beginning in one corner as more chunks of the burning wooden railing give way around the edge of the rooftop nearest to it. I run and open the door, to see Adah huddled in a corner.

"What are you doing here?" I cry, entering and grabbing at her arm. "We have to get downstairs right now!"

"This is the only home I've got, I won't leave it," she screeches, fighting me off, her hands clawed, her nails scratching my skin. "I won't!"

I grab again and this time I don't let go. She may be old and hunched over, but she's stronger than I expect. But I'm frightened and desperate and I force her out, just as Marcus starts shoving at the little hut, its wooden structure already rocking before we've made our way to the stairs.

"Not the inside stairs," calls Marcus, coughing as he rocks the little hut, the wood creaking. "Too much smoke!"

I turn to the wooden stairway and push Adah onto it. "Go down!" I shout into her face and she cowers from me and makes her shuffling way down the first set of stairs. I turn back to Marcus and hurry to his side, pushing against the hut with him. It gives way suddenly, so that both of us fall onto it and I feel a scorching pain in my calf. I yelp and then am yanked so abruptly to my feet by Marcus that I slam into him.

"They have hoses next door," he says and already I can hear the hiss from somewhere nearby and clouds of steam rise above us. "We have to break the stairway," he adds.

I gape at him. "What?" He points and I step back, horrified. The wooden staircase is on fire. "How will we get down? If the other stairs are full of smoke?"

"We'll think about that later. If we don't take down the staircase the whole building will burn. If we can get the stairway off, there's a chance of saving the rest." He moves cautiously to the edge and peers down into the courtyard. "Julia! Get the men to pull down the staircase!"

There's a pause and then I hear crunching noises from below, hammering and see the top of the staircase, now in flames, beginning to sway precariously.

"Help me," says Marcus and the two of us kick at the base of the staircase where it is joined to the roof. At first it seems as though the rickety wooden structure, that has always felt as though it was about to collapse at any moment, is actually going to resist our best attempts, but then it gives way, so suddenly that I almost fall with it but Marcus pulls me back. We hear it crash into the courtyard below and then shouts and the gurgling of water as people put out the burning parts.

"Now the other side," says Marcus. "Quick."

He has spotted what I missed, that there are Vigiles with ladders trying to climb up onto our roof from the outer walls. We help them steady two ladders, then a fast-moving chain of buckets of water pours out across the rooftop, the two huts hissing. One part of the roof has collapsed into the floor below, having burnt through the wooden ceiling, but the brick floors are intact. The fire has passed us, we are alive, most of the insula is still standing.

WHEN IT'S ALL OVER AND almost dawn, an odd quiet descends. The smoking wreck of the staircase fills the centre of the courtyard, and a chain forms without speaking to take it all outside the main gate. The inhabitants of the building cluster round the edges of the courtyard and talk to one another. Some sleep, too tired to care about where, or in what position, they find themselves. Julia, Cassia and Maria are trying to feed those who need it. I find Maria, who as usual already knows everything there is to know and follow her lead, pouring water and wine into cups, offering them to everyone.

"The fire's under control at last. It got as far as the Temple of Jupiter Optimus Maximus on the Capitol. The Circus and all the houses around it are a mess, but most people are safe, praise the gods. Praise Vesta for sparing her handmaiden."

"It'll take years to put right."

"Titus has already made a statement. He says he'll put his own funds towards rebuilding, that it will be done as quickly as possible."

"Our insula too?"

Maria shakes her head. "Julia didn't have insurance. Looks like we'll have to find new homes. She doesn't have the money to rebuild it and most of it's not fit for living in now. There'll be public money for public buildings, but not for private insulae. Still, you and Marcus saved it from being burnt to the ground, it would have done for sure if you hadn't cut off the wooden parts."

"Have you seen Karbo?"

"He was here a moment ago. He's safe. So is Adah."

I wander away from her, dazed with the news and exhaustion. There's nowhere I can go to sleep. The ground floor and first floor rooms are already packed with the insula's families and local neighbours, the second and third floors are soot-thick and uninhabitable. I look about me and spot a man sitting in one of the corners of the courtyard, knees bent, arms resting on them, shoulders slumped.

Marcus.

I lower myself to sit next to him. We stare at each other, our faces soot-stained, hair dishevelled, eyes rimmed red. I let my breath out in a rush. "Is that what you had in mind when you said we would have to think quickly and work hard? It's not quite what I imagined."

He shakes his head. "I don't know who could have imagined this past year."

"Well, I'm grateful to you. The whole insula is. And now you need to sleep."

"You're welcome. And no, we can't sleep. We have the small matter of an inauguration to take care of," he says, resting his head on his folded arms, voice muffled.

"How can we? We never even finished rehearsals!"

He lifts his head up. "Because no matter what else happens in Rome today, the amphitheatre will be inaugurated. And if it's not done to the satisfaction of the Aedile and the Emperor, you and I will not just be sleepy, we will be dead."

I gesture at him. "We're covered in ashes, our clothes are half-burnt, we have no possessions. We're going to inaugurate the greatest amphitheatre in the Empire? Stand in the imperial box when Titus sends for us, looking like this?"

Marcus stands up shakily. I put out a hand to help him, but he shakes his head and steadies himself. "May the gods watch over us today, Althea, we're going to need them. Come on."

"But –"

"We will manage somehow," he says. "Come on."

THE AMPHITHEATRE LOOMS OVER US, vast, shining white stone climbing into a bright blue sky, as though nothing had happened, as though there had not been a fire for these past three days. Already in the colonnades nearby the ticket touts, prostitutes and bookies are gathering, ready to ply their wares. Closer to the building, more certain of their respectability, are the stallholders we approved, setting out their goods. I see the lamps and cups decorated with gladiators, the painters setting out their paints and brushes, boards on display already painted with local favourites from the past as well as current heroes.

Each entrance, as previously arranged, is guarded by a man under strict instructions to let no-one in unless they work here, no exceptions. Those who do have to show a special clay token painted red. Marcus handed them out as though they were gold coins.

"I don't have mine!" I suddenly panic. "It's back at Julia's."

Marcus shakes his head. "I'll have to leave you outside, then, won't I?" he says and pulls out two tokens he had tucked in his belt. The man nods and we enter.

The corridors are silent. I look through to the arena and am struck by the silence and calm. No-one would know today was the inaugural Games.

"Althea."

It's Karbo. He's standing holding a pile of cloth, with two buckets of water and a covered basket by his side.

"Karbo?"

"You need to be clean. Here."

The pile of cloth turns out to be a clean white tunic and a toga for Marcus. Under that is a woman's tunic in yellow and orange, a headwrap in red with tiny yellow flowers embroidered all over it, which I recognise as one of Cassia's very best outfits. "Where did you get a toga at such short notice?"

"It's Fausta's," he says, his voice small.

"Bona Dea bless you," says Marcus, giving the boy a swift embrace. He grabs one of the buckets and the bulky toga cloth and disappears around a corner.

"Thank you," I say gently.

I take the bucket and clothes and find a quiet archway. When I'm sure no-one can see me, I wash myself and then dress in the fresh clothes. I carry the bucket and my smoked clothes back to where Karbo is helping Marcus adjust Fausta's toga correctly over his shoulder.

"Maybe I should just wear the tunic," he says doubtfully. "There's a lot to do."

"The Emperor is likely to call you to his box," I remind him.

"Just before he throws me into the arena?"

I start to laugh, then find it hard to stop and soon Marcus and I are doubled over laughing. Karbo watches us uncertainly.

Marcus straightens up, still laughing. "Ah, Karbo. You've saved us. Thank you."

"Breakfast," says Karbo. He uncovers the basket which is filled with still-warm bread from a bakery and a double handful of dates. Marcus and I grab them gratefully and chew as quickly as we can. Karbo eats too, then hurries away with the buckets. "I'll be back before the crowds arrive," he says.

I look at Marcus. His face is pale with lack of sleep but at least he's now dressed respectably, indeed far more smartly than he usually is. "How did he manage it all?" I ask.

He grins, shaking his head. "Thank the gods for good neighbours."

I nod.

Marcus takes a deep breath. "You ready?"

I nod.

"Let me hear you say it," he says, smiling.

"Ready," I say.

THE SACRED FLAME

THE CROWDS HAVE ALREADY BEGUN to gather even though the Games will not begin for almost two hours. Excited to be attending the inauguration, the plebians take their seats quickly enough, unencumbered by attendants.

The women on show today, however, are the very greatest of Rome, and each is accompanied by her personal body slave and one or two extra, carrying parasols, perfumes, cushions and goodness knows what else to ensure their mistress' comfort. They are appalled at how far they will have to climb to reach their seats at the top of the steep stairs. The richest insist on their manslaves carrying them all the way up, then send them back downstairs to wait till the show is over. It makes for mayhem as people flow in both directions rather than just one, as planned. Outside, the litters take up even more room as they deposit their mistresses before waiting nearby to be summoned at any time. Marcus has to send out three men just to manage the litter bearers and show them an area where they can dawdle.

We have been summoned by a disturbance in the top tier, which we had hoped to seat quickly and without incident before more senior attendees make an appearance.

Marcus is being berated by a woman who is insistent that she should be able to have more than four slaves with her, despite her ticket showing she can only have three. "He can crouch at my feet," she points out, indicating the smallest man in her retinue.

"I'm sorry, he cannot."

"Do you know who I am?" she asks, drawing herself up.

"No," says Marcus pleasantly. "But I am due to attend the Emperor's arrival. Would you give me your name so that I may explain to him why I am late?"

The woman looks this way and that, but gathers no support from all of whom are pleased her over-large entourage is being limited. "Very well, you may go," she says, shoving the unfortunate slave in the back and making him trip over. "But I won't forget your insufferable rudeness," she adds to Marcus.

Marcus bows. "Nor will I," he promises, smiling as though offering a compliment.

"Is this going to happen every time?" I ask.

"Hopefully not every time." He sighs as we make our way back down to the next tier, where the plebian men are taking their places. "They are our real customers," he says, indicating them. "They follow all the gladiators; they know their stuff and they come every chance they get. They won't make trouble for now, they're just happy to be here today, especially with all that's gone on."

The next tier is beginning to arrive, the equestrians, proud of their status, dressed in their finest. They beckon the refreshment sellers, settle down with snacks and drinks, talk business with one another.

We reach the ground floor and I peer out. The crowd-control ropes are in place, the queues seem mostly orderly. "It's working," I say.

Marcus nods, but he's looking out the other way, into the empty arena. "Let's get the senators and patricians seated, then we'll know we've got it under control," he says. "Once they're all in place there's only the ceremonial entrances and they're much easier. Fewer numbers."

We somehow manage the arrivals of the equestrians, the senators, even the Vestal Virgins, five of them accompanied to their seats with much bowing and scraping on everyone's part. I wonder how they picked lots to be here, since one has been left behind in the Temple of Vesta, so that the sacred fire does not go out. Is the sixth Virgin cursing under her breath at being left out, or does she consider it a lucky escape?

Finally, the stands are full. Marcus disappears, gone to give a signal to the Emperor's entourage that they may now enter. It would hardly do to keep the Emperor waiting in public; once he takes his place in the imperial box the show must commence.

Titus is a showman, he knows how to make an entrance. The trumpets ring out as he enters the imperial box alone to a standing ovation, waving and smiling to all sides, bowing his head to the Vestal Virgins. He takes his seat and only once the crowd has settled down does the rest of his entourage also arrive in the box, his younger brother Domitian with his wife, a few other people, the guards. They are not to take away from the attention on him, they must wait their turn to be seated.

I look down at my tablet, noticing that my hands are shaking. We have spent the best part of a year planning for this day through one disaster after another, we have persevered. Planning, preparation, rehearsals. But it all comes down to now, to these next few hours. Perhaps a small error will be forgiven tomorrow or on one of the other ninety-nine days still to come. But not today. Today everything must go without a hitch, it must be perfection.

I press the tablet against my knees to stop the shaking. We have planned and rehearsed everything, but today, we can do nothing but watch.

Marcus is on the opposite side of the arena to me. I give a nod and he nods back, then turns his head towards the musicians, who are playing. The music is loud, bold, cheerful. It promises spectacle and grandeur, a day of entertainment.

Marcus raises his hand and the music stops, mid trumpet. The crowd murmurs, confused. The floor of the arena begins to move. What seemed to be thick sand, awaiting the blood of the battles to come, is revealed to be sand-coloured linen scatted over with a tiny amount of sand. The cloth is being pulled away by unseen hands, to reveal…

Black. A silent arena of black. And lying in the very centre, having appeared from nowhere, a golden egg in a nest of golden twigs. A vast egg the size of a laden ox cart. It lies, motionless. The Gate of Triumph opens, and a woman enters, all alone, robed in white, dwarfed by the arena. A Vestal Virgin. A murmur again from the fascinated crowd and all eyes turn to the box where the Vestal Virgins sit, to count them. Four are seated, one is absent, guarding the flame of Vesta in the temple close by. This is no actor. This is a true Vestal Virgin, the most senior of them all, and she is making her way towards the giant nest. In her hands is a brazier and on it are heaped burning coals. The crowd murmurs again. Surely these are coals from the temple of Vesta itself, from the sacred flame that ensures Rome's unending glory and safety.

She reaches the nest and kneels, tips the contents of the brazier onto the golden twigs and at once a flame licks the air. The Vestal Virgin stands, steps away from the nest and moves back through the gate she came from, her bearing always upright, her face solemn.

As the flames lick the golden twigs, Marcus raises a hand again. A slow, strange vibration begins, before the drums grow louder and faster and suddenly the egg breaks open and from the now-raging flames rises, higher and higher, atop a golden pole, a bird. Its head and wings are tucked close to its body but then its head rises and turns to one side, the wings unfold to a mighty span and this golden phoenix that has arisen from a fire set by a Vestal Virgin is revealed as the Eagle of Rome, the Emperor's own standard. The awestruck crowd breaks into rapturous applause, quietening only when a herald makes an announcement.

"Today we are blessed to witness the inauguration of the greatest amphitheatre the world has ever seen, the Flavian Amphitheatre, commissioned by Emperor Vespasian and dedicated today in his name by his son, Emperor Titus. Roma Resurgens!"

Titus rises in his seat and the trumpets sound. The crowd waits in anticipation. "My father commissioned this glorious amphitheatre as part of his commitment to rebuild Rome from the ashes of the fire and civil war," he begins. "It stands on the ground once claimed as the lake and gardens of a tyrant, used for his pleasure alone. Now it is given as a gift to the people of Rome. My father's motto, Rome Rises Again, is exemplified today in its inauguration. There will be one hundred consecutive days of Games held, such as have never been seen before. May Jupiter and all the gods look upon my father's gift and be pleased with it."

The crowd breaks into applause again and then all watch, enthralled, as the Praetorian Guard march into the arena, lift down the standard and present it to the Emperor, who accepts it, two aides arranged by Marcus taking it and fixing it onto the front of the imperial box, completing its decoration. As soon as the arena is clear once again the black floor is revealed as cloth, again pulled away, the still-burning nest disappearing below. Now the true arena floor can be seen, layered thickly with green sand. Trap door after trap door opens as a forest grows before our eyes, trees and even a hill rising from the green, some complete with birds who flutter into the air and fly away or resettle. Antelope, zebras, camels and deer, scatter across the arena, some taking shelter amongst the grove of trees. Most are drawn by piles of fresh-cut grass and buckets of grain. They have been kept hungry for days and rush to eat, giving the impression of a peaceful scene of foraging animals, grazing throughout the arena, accompanied by gentle music from the lyres and singers softly crooning shepherding songs. The audience are delighted, exclaiming over the zebras, a rarity most have not seen. The Gate of Triumph opens again and the crowd gasps as giraffes enter the arena, their height meaning they can look down on the first ranks of seating. The trees that have grown from nothing are indeed edible and they begin to eat, taking hungry mouthfuls of leaves. There is another round of applause.

Marcus is not looking at the arena at all but is watching the crowd. They lean forward, murmur at the animals, chattering to one another. The gentle lyres continue their melodies. But now people begin to sit back in their seats. The scene is delightful, it is unique, but it is not a hunt. They expected a hunt. They turn their heads from side to side, expecting one of the gates or trapdoors to disburse men in armour, the beast hunters who will put on a show.

Marcus senses the time has come and his hand moves again. Six trapdoors slide open, more quietly, more subtly than the others. At first nothing happens and then…

The crowd sees movement and everyone leans forward. They expect men but it is lions that emerge from the trapdoors, one from each of the six. The lyres stop strumming, there is silence and the crowd keeps quiet, watching the lions to see what they will do.

Unlike the previous animals who rushed to eat, the lions group together first. They nuzzle one another briefly. We have kept them apart for days; they reacquaint themselves with one another, re-establish their pride. But their timing is even better than Marcus'. The crowd has no time to grow restless. The lions fan out, crouching low and now Marcus moves his hand and the music begins, a slow drumbeat, the flutes over the beat building suspense.

The lions take their time, even though they must be hungry. They don't rush for the closest animal, but stalk the arena, their bodies low, using our scenery as camouflage, creeping from tree to tree. The herd animals shuffle, turn their heads, move a little further away. They smell something they should fear but they are so hungry they must take one more mouthful of the fresh grass we have cut for them, just one more…

The lions leap. They have identified a zebra and the beast lets out a whinny of terror, fleeing as best it can, but there is no vast grassland here to outrun its predators. It comes up against the walls of the arena and turns desperately to one side, running as fast as it can along the wall as the drums speed up the beat and the flutes rise higher, giving the illusion of cries. The other animals, panicked by the hunt going on around them, fearful of being caught up in it, also begin to run, causing confusion as they career about the arena floor, the vast giraffes with their long legs unable to build speed in the confined space, turning and turning on themselves as smaller animals dart past. But the lions are not distracted. They have identified their victim and it does not matter what else goes on around them, their eyes never leave the zebra. The other animals are only in their way. At last the closest lion leaps forward and the zebra screams as its throat is bitten, blood spurting, its legs still trying to run even as it falls to the arena floor. The other lions join the victor, ripping and tearing at the still-living animal, its last sight the hungry jaws of the six lions surrounding it.

The crowd are on their feet screaming, the trumpets sound again, and an armed troop enters. They stay well clear of the lions who are still feasting on their warm meal as the men round up the other animals. Some make a half-hearted attempt at escape, but most, well aware of the fate of the zebra, try to avoid the lions and are swiftly caged and taken below, the trapdoors closing one by one until only the two closest to the lions remain open.

Three of the men approach the lions with long hooked poles. They catch at the zebra's neck and torn-open flanks and slowly pull the body towards the trapdoor, the giant cats snarling and following their loose-limbed prey back down the lift shafts, into their pens. One swipes at a man but is pushed back by two others using their pronged poles. Having been fed, the lion decides that the men and their weapons are to be avoided after all; it follows the bleeding carcass it finds more interesting back to a sudden re-imprisonment. It roars but it is too late now, and the danger is over, each lion is locked in with a piece of meat to tear apart. The crowd sees none of this, only the lions disappearing into the arena floor. The hill opens upwards to reveal, hidden within and now streaming outwards, more than two hundred dancing girls in costumes which leave little to the imagination, swathes of coloured ribbons trailing behind them and rippling with every movement. Music fills the arena, the girls sway and glide in bare feet across the bloodied sand. Each of our normal dancing troupe leads ten girls of her own, having learnt the steps so that the others can copy her movements.

Titus stands in his box and begins to throw little wooden balls into the crowd, swiftly assisted and augmented by his strategically placed attendants located around the amphitheatre, who can throw a great deal further than he can. Shouts go up from the crowd as they catch and examine the balls, finding them marked with the names of gifts.

"A female slave!"

"A gold ring!"

"Fish!"

"A pack horse!"

"Bread!"

People leap into the air to catch the falling balls, there are scuffles and even one or two fistfights, swiftly broken up.

"An ox!"

"A silver cup!"

Besides the wooden balls there's the glint of bronze coins falling through the air. The bronze sestertius we saw being minted bearing the image of the Flavian

Amphitheatre. Those lucky and well-off enough to be here today may well keep them as a memento of the day.

Titus waves and smiles at the growing applause and now people begin to chant his name, "Ti-tus, Ti-tus, Ti-tus."

Officials stand waiting as the balls are brought to them and they dispense items or hand over scrolls which confirm the more handsome or large gifts. The dancing girls twirl and whirl while the gift-balls continue to be thrown out, until a final blast of trumpets signals the end and the girls make their way out of the arena as Titus acknowledges once more the ongoing chanting of his name and settles back down in benevolent comfort.

THE CROWD ARE HAPPY NOW. They have seen great things and we have barely started the day's events. When the Gate of Triumph opens again and the procession they expected arrives they jump to their feet at once, cheering and calling out the names of local favourite gladiators. The procession is thoroughly impressive. Every gladiator in Rome has been collected together today, whether they are fighting or not. All are dressed in the very finest ceremonial armour, nothing like the dull dented pieces they use for practise or wore in previous fights. There are hundreds of them in gleaming armour, helmets with mask-like features of men or animals, weapons glinting in the sunlight, the music at full volume. The procession makes its way round the whole arena before assembling in front of the imperial box. Within the crowd of fighters, a trapdoor opens and the men part to show two gladiators all recognise. The audience goes wild. The two men are Priscus and Verus, famous gladiators, of equal standing. They will be the last fight of the day, the headline battle. I can already see bets being laid in the crowd, both between friends and larger bets being placed with professional bookies. By the time the gladiators have bowed to Titus and the procession has left the arena, there are smiles on all the faces I can see.

NOW IS THE TIME FOR a little rest from the excitement we have had had so far. Vendors of food and drink begin to walk the tiers, peddling their wares. Meanwhile the arena must be kept busy at all times.

There's a comedy show by the actors, lots of bawdy romping and cheeky references to rumoured affairs and liaisons, some of which may be true. None of them dare reference Titus' own romance with the Jewish Queen Berenice, of course; that would be a step too far right in front of him and besides the senators were too relieved that he took their advice and sent her home rather than flaunt her round Rome like some minor Cleopatra, as they'd feared. Titus is in everyone's good graces today; he has been generous in the aftermath of Vesuvius and no doubt will be similarly so after the fire. He sent Berenice away without fuss and today he is inaugurating the greatest amphitheatre of the empire. It would be ungracious to make fun of him, so the actors stick to low-level nudges and winks. Their appearance is the signal that we are drawing close to lunchtime, and the execution of criminals. Those with weaker stomachs and little inclination to watch brutal slaughter can remove themselves now, if they wish. They can go and eat, chat with their friends with no hurry and still return in time for the main event of the day, the gladiators.

There's a shifting in the upper seats as most of the women leave. They don't much care for the executions as a whole, although the Vestal Virgins remain in their seats. Clearly, they have strong stomachs. Their slaves arrive with trays of food, the five Virgins picking through delicacies. The same thing is happening in the imperial box, where Titus is receiving one guest after another from the patrician classes. Men arrive, sometimes accompanied by their wives. There is a lot of bowing and perhaps the offer of a glass of wine or some dainty morsel before they are excused and another guest is received into the imperial presence. Little or no attention is paid to the actors except by the few plebians allowed in today. They are buying food from the many sellers wandering the tiers. There is wine, bread, cheese, fruits, olives, nuts and small cakes. One can even buy little cups of garum sauce in which to dip bread. Some of the dancing girls also offer refreshments. The water fountains and toilets get crowded but settle down again. Now that the grand women of Rome have made themselves scarce and will not return until the gladiatorial combats of the afternoon, the execution of the criminals can begin.

I SHUFFLE IN MY SEAT, wishing that I could sit far enough away from the action to believe it only a play, a pretence. But I have no choice. For these inaugural Games, Marcus has chosen to make a real show of the public executions, drawing on the mythology of the founding of Rome, beginning with the Trojan war. And so we see Agamemnon sacrifice his own daughter Iphigenia to bring luck to the Greeks as they set sail for Troy. This, at least, is a quick execution for the hapless female criminal. Her throat is cut on an altar, splashing the characters around her with blood. Most of the other actors in this scene are trained gladiators, wearing shining armour and clothing befitting the Greek kings for the occasion. Sacrifice made, a fleet of over 100 wooden toy boats skim across the arena, before the entry of a shining, glorious Achilles in a magnificent chariot borrowed from the racing stables. Behind him should be the corpse of Hector, dragged around the city of Troy by Achilles in retribution, but this is no corpse, it is a criminal who will lose their life by being dragged to death. His screams have me gritting my teeth and digging my hands into my thighs. I keep my eyes fixed on Marcus, who will give the signal to stop, but of course he does not give the signal until the man has died; to do so would be to risk the Emperor and the crowd's displeasure. The man's screaming can be heard even above the roar of the crowd and I shut my eyes, rocking in place, willing it to stop. The crowd cheers on each death, revelling in what? In justice being served? In relief at not finding themselves in the arena? In the lavish spectacle we have created, with costumes, chariots and music accompanying each execution? I do not know. I would prefer not to be here and yet I must stay, and not only for the executions today, but for the ninety-nine days to follow and who knows beyond then? I brace myself for what is still to come.

Achilles stands alone in the arena, but this is not the same man who drove the chariot, but another criminal, dressed in shining armour and pushed through the gates to meet his end. The armour reveals his leg and ankle, the weak spot of the demigod Achilles. He knows what will happen to him and tries to turn about on himself so that he cannot be easily shot. But there is not one archer but several, so that wherever he turns he is still a target. Marcus nods and the marksman's arrow flies across the arena striking the man in his calf. It is a flesh wound, nothing more, but just as in the myth, the arrowhead has been dipped in poison and the crowd leans forward, interested to watch someone die of poisoning. The man staggers before blood pours from his mouth and he falls to his knees. His body convulses in silence while the arena holds its breath and then lets it out in a cheer when the convulsions end.

Now comes the showpiece. It's elaborate for executions, but today is a special day. The Gate of Triumph opens yet again, and a vast wooden horse is rolled into the arena. The crowd whoops and stamps their feet, ready for a re-enactment on a greater scale than they had expected. Out of the horse come hundreds of Greek men, ready to do battle with the Trojans who have mistakenly let them into their city, believing the horse a gift from the defeated and disheartened Greeks rather than the trick it really is. The arena fills with fighting men, swords clashing, armour glinting. From here, it appears to be a magnificent battle, with high quality swordplay and real deaths, blood spouting across the sand and dismembered limbs accompanied by dying screams. It seems unrehearsed, just like a real battle. It is only if you look closely, if you know, that what you are really seeing is more than two hundred trained gladiators, working both sides of the story, shedding a little blood here and there but nothing dangerous. The deaths and dismemberments are coming from the hundred criminals who have been saved up for today. They look the same as the gladiators, wearing good quality armour, helmets, shields, but their swords are blunt. They have no chance against trained fighters. One after another goes down, the gladiators identifying them by the dot of red paint touched to each criminal's forehead before they spilled into the arena. Troy falls, the Greeks are victorious, the applause is deafening.

I stand up. I will not watch this next part. A wailing woman is pushed into the arena, dressed as a Trojan princess. This criminal has been given the part of Cassandra, warning against the trickery of Greeks. I step into the cool of the arches, making my way down the corridor as quickly as I can, hoping that from this distance I will not hear her screams as she is raped on scenery designed as Athena's altar before being mercifully stabbed to death offstage. Cassandra lived beyond her dishonour but a criminal cannot be permitted to survive. One more woman makes her entry, some other poor wretch dressed in cheap jewels and lavishly decorated clothes, another Trojan princess, Polyxena, sacrificed on the grave of Achilles. I hear their screams from a distance, but the roar of the crowd makes it clear that the re-enactment of this founding myth has been well received, combining mythology with justice towards the enemies of Rome.

Leaning against the cool stone in the shadowy corridor, I listen to the final touch Marcus has put on this vicious scene. I close my eyes and remember the rehearsals, a man representing Aeneas, brave survivor of Troy, leading a little group including an elderly man, Aeneas' father, carried on his pious son's back. Having reached the imperial box, Aeneas will be lifted into it by a prearranged signal; the actor portraying him will drop to his knees and crawl out of sight, leaving Titus to stand, replacing him. I hear applause break out and step back through the arch to see the response. Titus is all smiles, the crowd is delighted. Aeneas, founder of Rome, is now embodied in our latest Emperor, emphasising the continued glory and permanence of Rome. Marcus, as ever a true showman, has put a final flourish on proceedings. The executions are over. The women will return soon and then the gladiators will begin their bouts. I drink from one of the fountains and try not to think about what I have heard and seen.

THERE ARE A FEW BOUTS leading up to the main event, seasoned, high-quality gladiators who would normally be headliners, but for once only the hardened gamblers care about them, feverishly placing bets on each outcome, but they are not the main spectacle. What the crowd is waiting for is the big showdown between Priscus and Verus. These two gladiators have fought for years, each claiming life after life of less experienced gladiators, always victorious, wounded but never defeated. Their names and faces are known throughout the Empire, they are heroes in Rome. They have never faced one another though; this is a showdown years in the making, both of them now close to retirement, one last chance to see them at their best. The bets being placed have reached epic proportions for the two are closely matched and it's hard to know where to place one's money. Keen followers of Games in the audience swap notes on the many years they have been watching these two fighters. They comment on everything in their lives, from the women in their beds and how many children they've sired, to whether the heat favours or harms the chances of either. It's all speculation, nobody knows for sure, but that only makes the gambling more interesting.

Nothing has been left to chance. The men enter the arena in spectacular armour, ceremonial helmets depicting mythological creatures, armour which has never seen a fight in its life, polished to perfection. Each comes with his own entourage, his own music, while the crowd shouts a strange combination of encouragement and disparagement. Marcus lets the tension build. There's a lot of swaggering as the two men face up to one another, swapping ceremonial armour for something more battered and believable, leather soaked in blood and sweat, metal dented and scratched.

I don't generally find fights that interesting, but when watching two fighters who know their trade, it's hard not to be drawn in. The moves they make are large, exaggerated for the benefit of the upper tiers, but they are not without aggression or cunning tactics. The blades whip through the air and the sounds they make when they touch on metal leave your skin cold. A slicing sound as one sword comes round in an arc and a patch of red appears on an upper arm, the crowd screaming bloodlust and grief over gambling choices already made. But a cut to an upper arm is nothing to a gladiator. The battle continues despite drops of blood sputtering through the air, each man receiving more than one wound.

There is a referee to keep order and, knowing how to put on a good show, he calls for breaks here and there, allowing the entourages of the gladiators to rush forward and attend to their wounds, set cups to their lips and whisper tactics in their ears. The fight continues longer than one would have thought possible, neither man giving way. Titus, meanwhile, is gaining the crowd's approval by sending lavish gifts to both men, yet neither seem swayed by this, continuing to fight with vigour in their arms and bloodlust in their eyes.

I make my way to where Marcus is seated, leaning forward on his thighs, watching the fight intently.

"It's lasted twice as long as all the other bouts," I say. "Won't the crowd get bored?"

He glances at me with amusement. "Do you see them getting bored?"

He's right, the crowd is watching intently, still swapping bets which will cause those who have to pay out severe difficulties. "How will it end?"

"We will have to see, won't we?"

"You look like you know something."

"Shhh. Trying to make history."

"How?"

"You'll see."

"Are you hoping they'll kill each other?"

"Better than that."

"Which is?"

"Watch the Emperor."

"What do you expect him to do?"

Marcus sits back in his seat as though he hasn't a care in the world. "Free them."

"What, both of them?"

"Yes."

"But the Emperor always rewards the victor! Titus can't reward both. No emperor has ever done that."

"But if he did," says Marcus with a grin, "you'd remember it forever, wouldn't you?"

"How do you persuade the Emperor to do what you want?"

"Carefully," says Marcus, his eyes back on the fighters. "And part of it is down to the fighters," he adds.

"Are they trying for a draw?"

"No, it would be too obvious."

"So?"

"They both know it's in their interests to keep fighting and not get wounded too badly. They've already accumulated a nice set of gifts. Neither of them wants to die now."

"And Titus?"

"I sent a message up after the fourth round, reminding him that no emperor has ever set both fighters free."

"Did you say he should?"

"Of course not. You can't tell the Emperor what to do. But I think our Titus is not without astuteness when it comes to pleasing the plebs. He makes sure to be generous when it counts and when it's most visible."

I think of Titus' response to the disaster of Vesuvius, how visibly and generously he responded, including his own funds towards rebuilding damaged cities or those where refugees had moved to. And his most recent pronouncement about the fire. "I hope you're right."

"We'll see."

"I wish Fausta was here," I say. "She'd have loved it."

He is silent for a moment and I'm not sure he's heard me over the cheering and stamping of the crowd, who are sensing a finale as both men, bleeding and gasping, attack one another again on the referee's nod. "She'd have finished the pair of them off single-handed," he says and I should laugh at his joke, but instead two tears slip down my face and Marcus takes my hand in his briefly, a quick warm squeeze before he looks away. "She'd be proud of you. She'd say there was no need for her anymore, you're as good a right-hand woman as she was."

My hand is cool now his touch has gone but my cheeks are hot at his words, a sudden welling up of pride mixed with the grief of losing Fausta. I look round the arena again, trying to believe that I have had a hand in all of this, that it is my work that has helped Marcus create a spectacle the like of which has never been seen before.

THE FIGHT EXCEEDS ALL RECORDS for duration, when suddenly Titus stands and declares a draw. The crowd, most with money on the line, groans, Titus declares both men victors, and sets them both free, sending down two wooden swords and laurel wreaths, symbols of their freedom. The two bleeding men wrap their arms around each other, before kneeling in front of the imperial box, holding their wooden swords to their chests in a display of loyalty and gratitude. The crowd is delighted, they have never seen anything like it. It is an unheard-of event, one which they will tell their grandchildren. Today has been everything it should have been and more, it has exceeded everyone's expectations. Marcus watches the rapturous applause with me, leaning against a column in one of the corridors, nodding to himself, a small smile on his face.

Karbo's face peers round the column. "You're sent for."

"By whom?"

"Titus."

Marcus nods to me. "Come on."

"He didn't ask for me," I say.

"He'll remember you," he says.

We make our way out of the darkness and up through the staircase, along the corridors to the imperial box. The Praetorian Guards are blocking the corridor, standing guard. They seem to know who we are though; they nod.

"No weapons allowed in the imperial box."

Marcus spreads his hands wide. "No weapons."

They nod again and pull back the heavy silk curtain over the doorway.

The box feels crowded. I think of all the times Marcus and I have sat in here, looking out over the arena, leaning over the edge to give orders or pass on comments about how something works. Guards surround Titus and his brother Domitian, who is sitting to his side but a little further back. A woman with a preposterously elaborate hairstyle dressed in flowing silks must be Domitia, Domitian's wife. There are a few other grandly dressed people, presumably family or friends of the Emperor, although I can't identify them.

Marcus focuses on Titus. "You sent for me, Imperator."

"A most elegant show," says Titus.

Marcus bows.

"And you have many more delights planned, I am sure?"

"More than I could name, Imperator. Many designed specifically for your presence, should you continue to grace us with it."

"You can count on it. I understand the arena can be flooded for naval battles?"

I try not to laugh, thinking of the architect's outrage when Marcus asked the same thing.

Marcus keeps an entirely straight face. "Of course, Imperator."

"I would like to see a naval battle. Augustus used to hold them, I believe."

"He did, Imperator. We will outdo whatever has gone before. Perhaps for the closing ceremony at the end of the inaugural Games?"

"That is an excellent idea," says Titus. "Finish in style, something memorable."

I can't help but admire Marcus' swift thinking. Titus could have asked for a naval battle in a few days' time and we would have had no choice but to obey. Marcus' offer has given us three months' time to prepare.

Titus' gaze swivels to me. "Ah," he says. "The scribe who beat the Emperor at shorthand. Still as fast?"

I bow my head. "I hope so, Imperator."

"Very good," says Titus. He looks at Marcus again. "You have been well remunerated, I hope?"

"Generously, Imperator."

"Then take this as a small token of my appreciation." A gesture has an aide hurrying forward with a large leather pouch, which Titus takes and passes to Marcus. "Your opening scene was very appropriate, in the light of all that has gone on this year. Rome shall indeed rise again from the ashes."

"Your father's name shall live eternally," says Marcus.

Titus nods and Marcus withdraws, I follow him from the shadows as we make our way back down the corridors. Marcus pulls open the pouch and nods at what is inside. I catch a quick glimpse of large gold coins, before he puts the pouch away. "Not long to go now," he says. "Final procession and music, release the birds, then we're done. Let's get it over with."

THE FIVE HUNDRED WHITE DOVES have had their feathers stained every possible colour. As the procession of gladiators, dancing girls, actors and the tamer animals wind their way round the arena, the trapdoors open one more time and the birds take to the sky, drawing final chatter and applause from the audience, who take their flight as a good omen, no matter how stage-managed. The few blue-painted ones almost disappear once in the sky, proving Marcus right, but those of scarlet, green, yellow, pink and violet look magnificent. As they disappear, the crowds begin to disperse. Titus and all the other members of the imperial box were escorted outside while the procession drew everyone's attention elsewhere. He will already be safely on his way back to the imperial palace.

THE CROWDS ARE ALL GONE, their seats empty. I stand in the imperial box. The silk awning has been carefully rolled up and packed away, the Praetorian Guards have disappeared with the Emperor. The space feels large again. All I can hear is the swish-swish of brooms and the gurgling of water. The cleaners have finished sweeping all the tiers, and are being followed downwards towards the arena by buckets of water swilled over the stone, sluicing away the stickiness of dried wine, the grease of dropped food. On the arena floor itself the bloodied sand has been scraped up, the last parts swept away. The wooden boards are stained with blood, the stains will only grow darker over the years to come. The trapdoors have all been thrown open, allowing more light below where the disposals are of a more serious kind. I rest a hand on the cool marble, then make my way down under the arena floor to find Marcus.

The staff are gathered in one corner, pouring drinks from several large flagons and munching on sweet cakes piled high on several platters. It looks as though Marcus has allowed them a celebration for having got through today.

I catch Karbo and pull a cup of wine away from him. "Enough of that, you drunkard. Stick to the cakes, will you?"

He gives me a sticky smile. "We did it!"

I smile at his enthusiasm. "We did," I agree. "And tomorrow it has to be done all over again."

He takes a huge bite of cake. "Bigger and better," he manages to get out through the mouthful.

"Bigger and better," I say with a sigh, walking towards the other end of the space, where the animals are being kept. I pause by the lions, who are happily gnawing on the remains of their zebra. One growls when I come too close to the cage.

Marcus and Bestia the beast-hunter are walking past the pens, noting which animals are left to us before the new consignment arrives.

"How many animals still usable for tomorrow?" Marcus asks.

"None of the lions," the beast-hunter says. "You'll not get a damn thing out of them for six days at least. Unless you want them to fight men, of course."

"Got bears tomorrow," says Marcus. "Don't need the lions for a few days. They put on a good show."

"Good quality," agrees Bestia. "You should have paid double for them, you tight bastard. Just water, then. Don't feed them before they're needed again."

Marcus nods.

"Might be worth feeding the two tigers a little. Just enough to keep them interested, don't sodding overdo it. Not a whole body."

Marcus gives him a sideways glance. "Body?"

"Cack, they need to get a taste for men, if you want them to really go for them. Say, an arm each?"

Marcus gestures to Strabo, who has joined the discussion. "Do it." He glances at me and catches my shudder. "They're dead now," he says. "The dying was the worst part."

I nod. The smell of blood is heavy in the air, despite the shafts of light from the open trapdoors above us which should bring fresh air. The tigers pace and growl in their pens, smelling prey nearby, hungry. The newly delivered animals for tomorrow, a combination of African goats and antelopes, tremble, backed into the tightest corners of their pens, sensing their imminent deaths.

"Tomorrow's criminals arrived yet?"

I nod, point behind me at the chained men being led down the other side of the space, into their own pens. No women in this batch, I'm relieved to see. "Are they fighting tomorrow?"

"Yes," says Marcus. "Much chance they have against the Amazons. We've got an all-female troupe from Labeo tomorrow."

"Are they good?"

"Yes. And they have real weapons. That lot will have blunt swords, as today. Their best chance is to be fast on their feet and as brave as possible. You never know, the crowd may feel sorry for them."

"I doubt it." My voice cracks, my eyes filling up.

Marcus steps closer to me. "It's a hard life, Althea," he says simply. "I never told you any different. Now you see what it is. It isn't trumpets and the Emperor being magnanimous, handing out gifts and gold. It isn't rehearsals and costumes to make myths come to life. All of that's the show, the spectacle. But we're the ones left with blood and guts, the smell of fear and a pile of dead bodies to dispose of at the end of every Games."

I nod. "I just..." Just the screaming for mercy that went on and on and on during the executions. A tear rolls down my cheek, then another.

"I know," he says, and touches my shoulder. "I know. Why do you think I wanted to live on a farm instead?"

I nod and try to smile.

He's silent for a moment. "You can leave," he says at last. "I won't hold you back. You're a freedwoman, you may do as you wish. You could be a scribe in the imperial household, Titus likes you, he'd snap you up. You'd be back in the fancy villas with very little to do except look pretty and do a bit of writing here and there. You wouldn't have to mingle with the likes of gladiators and whores or watch the executions every day. You'd be paid well. You could... marry, have children."

I meet his gaze. "Would you manage on your own?"

He gives a half smile. "I've managed for many years," he says, "though it's a lot easier with a good woman at your side."

I don't know if he's comparing me to Livia or Fausta, but either way I'm touched. I look down at the floor. He's right, I could easily find a better position, one which would take me away from the dark life beneath the arena, the grim spectacles above it. It's tempting. But I think of what we've gone through together and more importantly, how he has treated me. He has never laid a finger on me. He set me free. He has treated me almost as a man, his right hand in this strange life. And he is so recently returned from the darkness I thought would swallow him up. I think of Julia and Maria who watch over me every day and how Fausta guided me, how she made me a woman who could stand up to an emperor. I take a deep breath and let it out in a rush. "You wouldn't last an hour without me," I say.

His grin is all the reward I needed for my decision. "I wouldn't," he agrees. "I'd be in the arena within a week."

"A lot quicker than that," I say.

"You're right."

We stand there for a moment, grinning at each other like two idiots.

"Boss! We're leaving. You need anything else?"

Marcus raises one hand. "Check on the elephant on your way home, will you?"

"Will do, boss."

I look up through the trapdoors. The sky is turning a pale pink, with gold and purple streaks. We need to get back to the insula before nightfall. I follow Marcus up through one of the trapdoor ladders onto the arena floor, the two of us standing alone in the vast empty space. I clear my throat and unroll the scroll in my hand, nod to Marcus to begin.

"Animals?"

"Yes," I say, holding my pen against the list. "Woodlands tomorrow. Bears. In the pens. Half trained, half wild."

"Criminals?"

"Yes."

"Gladiators?"

"Ready. The Amazon costumes have been delivered directly to Labeo's barracks."

Marcus nods. "I frightened off two of the worst ticket touts this morning. We might get a few days' peace before they start up again."

"The cleaners have nearly finished. All the tiers have been swept and washed."

"Corridors and toilets?"

"Yes."

"Arena floor?"

I look around me. It's been swept clean, the bloodied sand disposed of. "Yes."

"Fresh green sand for the morning hunt?"

I nod and point. "Sackfuls left at each quarter of the arena, ready for spreading when the wood has dried." I can't bear to say that it's the blood which has to dry.

"I think we're done," Marcus says. "And if not, we'll sort it out tomorrow first thing. The Emperor won't be here tomorrow. He'll only attend some of the shows, so we have a little breathing space. The crowd tomorrow will be less fancy, not so many airs and graces to take care of. Let's get back before dark, I don't care to walk around with this kind of money on me."

We walk through the Forum in silence, too tired for talk. My mind is whirring at all the sights and smells of the day, the sounds of beasts and trumpets still echoing in my ears. Here and there we pass groups of men still discussing the day's events.

"When Priscus struck Verus on the neck, I thought he was a goner, but did you see how swift he came back?"

"Verus has always been swift. There's a man who fights on his toes, I tell you. But you can't argue with Priscus' wits: swifter than his feet. And both given their freedom! Never seen such a thing, screamed myself hoarse!"

"Then you need more wine, here, pass your cup. To Verus and Priscus."

"Verus and Priscus!"

I glance at Marcus, who gives a weary smile. "You were right," I say. "They'll never forget."

"It could have gone either way."

"It went the way you planned it," I say.

"One can never tell with emperors," he says.

We pass through a burnt landscape to reach the insula. It seems empty, the tight streets opened up into gaping holes, the odd building still left, as ours is, the rest gone, smoking ruins and ashes everywhere. The courtyard feels like a refuge from it all. Marcus heads towards Julia, who is coordinating the women, setting up a small cooking area.

Balbus is standing behind me, holding a large bundle wrapped in a cloth. "I m-made what you asked for. We grabbed it when we took our valuables."

"Thank you," I say. I sigh and wipe my hand across my face, bone weariness sweeping over me. "I am not sure he will accept it."

"All homes m-must have a L-Lararium," says Balbus with certainty.

I nod and hold out my arms, taking the bundle with reverence. Balbus gives a jerky nod back and steps away.

I hesitate. Will Marcus be angry with what I have done? Will we even stay here? The building is so damaged, I am not sure it can be repaired. But I asked Balbus for it before the fire and here it is. I use my elbow to open the door of the first-floor apartment we will be sleeping in for the foreseeable future. We have one room of it, sharing the rest with the baker's family, who have warmly offered us the space. The smell of smoke is still heavy in here, unable to escape. I rest the bundle on the bedding mats, clear a shelf of a few odd items, leaving it empty. Then I squat down and undo the bundle. Inside is a wooden shrine, painted beautifully with two spirit ancestors, as well as a bearded snake in the centre as is the custom. This one has been exquisitely coloured. The tail is black and white and grey, but slowly colour emerges, ending with a gloriously bright head and beard in many colours. Balbus has done a beautiful job. I lift the shrine up onto the shelf, where it just fits. As I do so, a collection of tiny figures drops from the bundle. I stoop to collect them, then stand clutching them, tears falling onto their tiny woollen clothes. I take a deep breath and place each one on the ledge of the shrine. A delicate woman, her hair the bright brown of a freshly plucked hazelnut, a child in her arms. Livia and Amantius as I recall them. Another woman, tall and broad, with tumbling black hair. Fausta. And finally, two figures that I did not ask Balbus for, a tall man holding a wax tablet, a woman clasped to his side, her hair dressed in the Greek fashion. My parents, as he has imagined them.

It takes me three fumbling attempts to light one of the two candles I had already bought and kept for this shrine. My tears flow so heavily I can barely see what I am doing. I almost set fire to the curls of the tiny Fausta and have to take a breath to steady myself.

"What is this?"

I turn to Marcus and watch his face as he takes in the Lararium, the candle I have finally lit flickering wildly in the draught from the open door. He steps forward and I move out of his way so that he can reach the shrine. He stands for a few moments, staring at the tiny figures. At last he lifts a hand and reaches out to touch the figure of his wife and son, one finger following the loose hair of Livia, before coming to rest on the head of Amantius. There is something so terrible in his tenderness that I turn away and step out onto the landing, pulling the door shut behind me. Only then do I hear him cry.

I take a few deep breaths, then make my way downstairs to the courtyard. People are milling about, the men pulling down the last small charred parts of the wooden stairs, adding them to a brazier.

"Where is Adah?"

No-one seems to know. I have to use the interior stairs again. They smell so strongly of smoke I am coughing by the time I reach the roof.

She is where I expected her to be, squatting by the ruins of her little hut, poking through the remains. When she sees me coming, she stands, gripping a candlestick with many arms. The candles have long since melted of course, but the metal has withstood the fire, though it is dirty with soot and ashes.

"The Almighty has not forgotten what Titus did to us," she says, and there is a bitter joy in her voice. "He has burned Rome's empire three times over for the burning of the Holy Temple of Jerusalem. First Vesuvius, then the fever burning people up inside so they could feel the pain of the fire and now this, a fire burning up the great places of Rome." She spits. "The Almighty has shown His greatness over your mish-mash of gods, He has burnt the very temple dedicated to all of them together, a crowd of false idols."

I feel a chill of fear at her words. These things may all be coincidences, but still… Titus came to the throne and in just one year these three disasters have occurred, all of them linked to fire and burning… I think of the Pantheon, blackened and still smoking. A shiver passes over me. "Do you think your god has been appeased?" I ask. "If it was all done at his hand, as you say, do you think he has finished punishing Titus now?"

Adah looks away, across the rooftops, at the smoking haze still staining the pink evening sky. "He may have finished punishing Rome," she says. "He will not rest till Titus dies."

I swallow.

Adah is using a piece of her wrap to try and clean the candlestick, rubbing at the dirty metal. "What did you want?"

"Everyone is gathering downstairs to eat together."

"I won't celebrate that place being inaugurated."

"We are celebrating being alive more than anything, I think."

She hesitates.

"Please, Adah," I say. "We will all be together. I do not want to think of you being alone up here."

She shakes her head. "A good child," she says at last. "I will join because you asked. Only because you asked."

I smile, although I am so tired tears spring to my eyes again at everything that has happened: the fire, the inauguration, the Lararium, now Adah. "Thank you," I manage, a little sob escaping me.

Adah comes closer, reaches up to my cheek and wipes the tears away as they fall. "Come," she says, more gently than I have heard her speak before, and it is she who leads me by the hand, as though I were a child, down the smoky stairs and into the courtyard, where tables are being taken from every household and workshop and laid together. Every family and person has brought lamps and whatever food they have to share, little dishes of olives, radishes, a few large pots of bean stew and savoury porridge, cheese, roasted chickpeas, dipping cups of garum sauce, dates, figs and melons, plums, nuts. The baker's family are busy stacking loaves and little fruit buns in a huge pile, Cassia is pouring wine. The brazier has been piled high with logs, and is burning brightly, illuminating our gathering. I gaze at it for a moment. Contained, the flickering flames are cheerful, giving of warmth and comfort.

"Adah is joining us? You're more persuasive than I gave you credit for." Marcus is red-eyed but smiling.

"I must have worn her down," I say.

He nods. We stand in silence for a moment. "Thank you," he says at last.

"It was nothing," I say quickly. I am afraid he will cry, and I don't know what to do if he does.

"You remembered the colour of her hair," he says and his voice cracks.

At first, I worry that the amphitheatre will be toasted, that the excitement and spectacle of the day will be rehashed despite what I told Adah, that she will retreat back up the stairs to sit alone. But I was right. Exhausted and relieved, people embrace one another quietly and eat, sitting shoulder to shoulder, glad for the comfort of our little community, for the mercy shown them. Later there is some music and dancing, the children chase the dogs about the courtyard, there are a few stolen kisses in the shadows between couples or those who would like to be so. There are no noisy toasts, instead one person after another comes up to Marcus and quietly raises their cup, embraces him, speaks softly with him and then makes their way back to the gathering. He nods, smiles, embraces them back, listens to what they have to say.

The children are growing sleepy and even the dogs lie panting under the table, tired of games. Marcus nods to me to join him. I make my way across the courtyard to him. He is sitting with Julia, the two of them a little apart from the others.

"We had a deal, you and I," he says. "That when I was rewarded, I would leave Rome and go to buy my family farm. And I would set you free."

I nod.

"You are free already, but I had intended to give you money to start a new life." He pulls out the pouch Titus gave him, heavy with gold. "Enough to buy the farm already. Plus enough to give you that new start."

I wait.

"I find myself without the heart to go, just yet. The farm would feel without purpose. Perhaps in a year or two I will feel differently. For now, my share will go to Julia, to rebuild the insula."

Julia is shaking her head, her hand raised to stop him, but he pushes it gently away. "I need a family about me and this –" he waves at the gathering "– is all I have for now. Let me help, Julia."

She looks away but nods, then turns and gives him a fierce embrace. "You are a good man, Marcus," she says. "May Vesta bless you."

Marcus is still holding the pouch. "Your share is here, Althea," he says.

"No," I say. "Give it to Julia with yours." I look round the courtyard. "This is my family too. I have no other," I add to Julia. "Use my share to get running water put in and build us a fountain in the courtyard. I'm sick of carrying water from the street."

We laugh.

"I will have a large apartment set aside for the two of you when we rebuild," she says.

"No," Marcus and I say together. He gestures to me to finish, smiling.

"I – prefer the roof hut," I say, and he nods.

Marcus passes Julia the pouch and she shakes her head at it, smiling at us both. "Then I shall build you the finest roof hut Rome has ever seen," she says and we all laugh.

"Don't tell the others it came from us," says Marcus. "Just say there was insurance after all."

"The gods will know your deeds and bless you," she says.

Slowly, in twos and threes, people begin to leave, some carrying sleeping children, a few leaning on one another to steady their tipsy gaits. They make their way into the half-charred building, their voices fading.

"I will wish you a good night," says Julia, when there is no-one else left. She stands and stretches her back before looking down at Marcus and me, sitting opposite one another, Marcus staring into the flames as though about to speak an oracle, my own face tilted up to look at Julia, catching myself mid-yawn. "Today was a triumph brought forth from the ashes of what went before."

I nod and she looks at Marcus, but he doesn't reply, only continues staring into the last flickers amongst the embers. She smiles at me and places her hand lightly on my head in what feels like a blessing, then walks away, her feet quiet as ever, the darkness of the building swallowing her up within a few paces. I watch her go, then look back to realise Marcus has lifted his head and is watching me. I meet his gaze. I wonder if I should say something about how proud his wife and Fausta would have been of him drawing back from the darkness that he was heading for, of what he has managed to accomplish, the triumph of the inauguration. But then I think of the grey fields of Hades we scrambled over, his little son lost beneath them, and close my mouth. We have come a long way together. But not far enough for words of hope. Not yet.

The last flickers of flames have gone out, now there are only dark embers left, a sullen red beneath their ashen coatings.

"Only ninety-nine days to go, then," says Marcus, raising his cup towards me. I am not sure if there is a glimmer of humour in his weary words, but I lift my own cup to him and nod.

"Ninety-nine days."

Author's Note on History

THIS IS THE FIRST BOOK in a series that started as the simple question I asked myself: who were the people who made up the 'backstage team' for the Colosseum? There is hardly any mention whatsoever of them and yet Games on such an immense scale could not possibly have been put on without a very large and permanent team in place. Who were the stage managers, the makers of costumes and scenery, the technicians? I did a lot of research, but the team were still invisible, so I have had to construct them from a combination of historical evidence and common sense. For example, there are mentions of large-scale painted scenery (so someone had to make it, store it, hoist and remove it), of mythological re-enactments (there must have been rehearsals and costumes), beast-hunts (someone had to provide/store/release at the right moment a variety of animals), trainers for the gladiators as well as their remains which show that physicians patched them up, etc.

It has been fascinating. At the heart of the team is Marcus, because there had to have been someone in overall control, and his scribe Althea, because you can't run a show on that scale with nothing written down.

This first book focuses on fire, from the burning of the Temple of Jerusalem to Vesuvius erupting, fever and fire breaking out in Rome, to the sacred flame cared for by the Vestal Virgins. The next three books in this series focus on the same team through the themes of water (*Beneath the Waves*), earth (*On Bloodied Ground*) and air (*The Flight of Birds*).

79 AD was the year in which Vesuvius erupted and wiped out Pompeii. Traditionally the date of the eruption was accepted as the 24th August, but in fact more recent discoveries including autumnal fruits, heating braziers and an inscription (as well as the fact that the original date in a letter was transcribed multiple times with varying dates between August and November) convincingly set the date as the 24th October instead, so I have gone with this more recent historical record. Fausta's description of events is closely modelled on that given by Pliny the Younger, the only person to have fully recorded a personal description of what happened; he was based in Misenum as a teenager. His uncle, the admiral and scientist Pliny the Elder, died of a heart attack while trying to save people in Pompeii with his fleet. Pompeii was buried under 5 metres of ashes, Herculaneum under 20 metres. We know very little about the days and weeks after the disaster, except that an imperial messenger could get to Rome in one day by changing horses every 12 miles and that refugees with Pompeiian names begin to show up afterwards in Cuma (near Puteoli) and Naples (Neapolis), tending to marry one another, suggesting they stuck together in their own communities. The Emperor Titus was considered to have handled the disaster well; he visited the area

twice, put a lot of money including his own personal funds into building up the cities that were not damaged (presumably so refugees could settle there) and appointed two senators to look after the area and get it back on its feet. Looting started very quickly, with looters tunnelling into the houses beneath the ashes. It still goes on to this day.

There are a lot of erotic paintings on the walls of Pompeiian villas, but not all of them can have been brothels. My thanks to Steven Cockings, who suggested there might have been very fast painters at events, for example painting your favourite gladiator as an item of merchandise, which I developed further as an idea for fancy dinners.

80 AD saw both 'pestilence' and a three day fire break out in Rome in the spring/summer and although there is not a lot of detail available, it seems possible that the former was malaria, which was rife during this time period. Up to 10,000 people died during this outbreak. Some people believed that the ashes from Vesuvius had created the illness. Jewish people believed that the three disasters (Vesuvius, pestilence and fire), taking place shortly after Titus became Emperor, were a punishment on him for his troops looting and burning the Temple of Jerusalem. This looting partly funded the building of the Colosseum and it is also possible that the prisoners of war were put to work on its building site. It is not clear when exactly the fire was, so I have used a little poetic licence to have it very close to the inauguration of the amphitheatre.

The Colosseum was formally inaugurated by Titus in 80AD, with one hundred consecutive days of Games. We can't be sure of the date but looking at the Roman calendar of events and celebrations, I have chosen what seems a likely starting point. No-one knows who the architect was. No mention is made of the members of the backstage team.

Some of the specific Games I have written about actually happened. Those that I have invented were based on very similar approaches, such as the regular use of re-enacting myths and legends of the Greeks and Romans.

There is a wonderful vase in the British Museum which shows 'the dwarf assistant to a physician, showing in patients.' I loved this so much I immediately created the physician Fabius and his daughter Fabia.

The area in which Marcus and Althea live in Julia's insula is an in-joke on my part. It is approximately where my mother and I lived in Rome when I was a small child. The main road outside our block of apartments was called Via Arenula and when I looked it up it meant Sand Street (arena means sand, because of the sand scattered across arena floors). I wanted to base my characters here but thought that I might need to move them elsewhere as I didn't know in which region the fire of 80AD would have been. In one of those magical coincidences that happens when you write, when I did the research it turned out they were in exactly the right place. My mother worked in an office by the Colosseum and saw it every day on her way to work. Virgin's Street is a made-up name, many small streets had no formal name and would just have had a local name based on whatever landmarks existed. Few Vestal Virgins married after their thirty years' service and it was considered bad luck to do so as a rather large number of their husbands died.

BENEATH THE
WAVES

For Julia Legg
I love how you've built the joy of music and dance into your everyday
life and shared it with hundreds of children over the years.

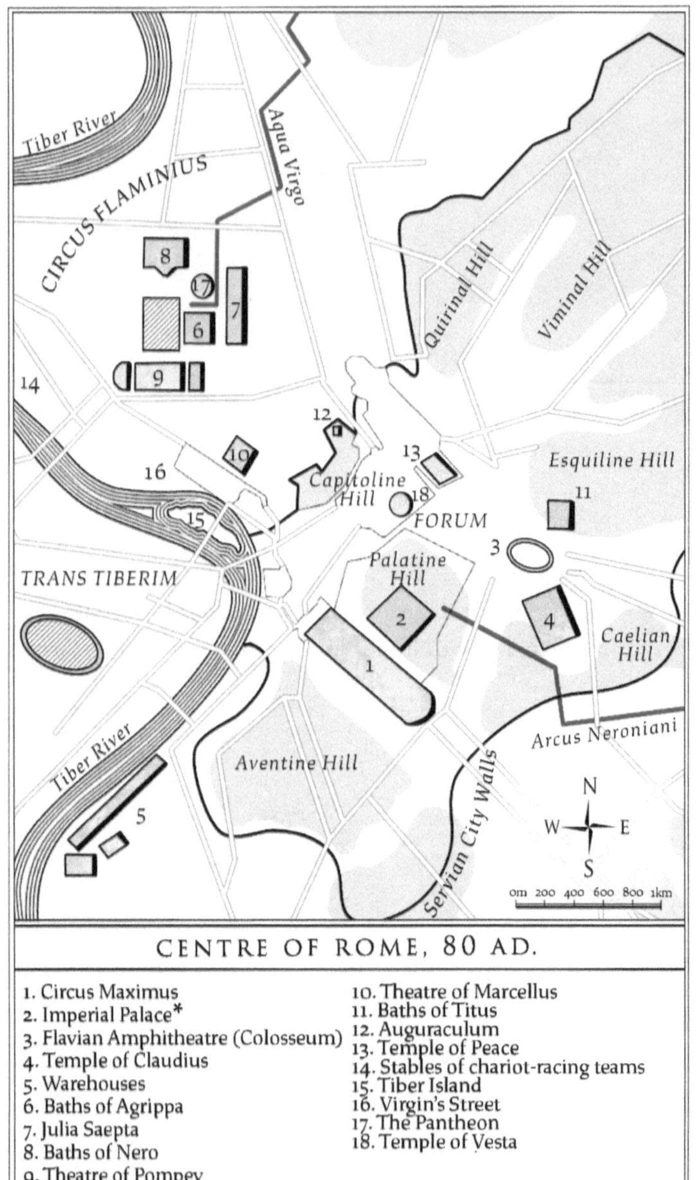

CENTRE OF ROME, 80 AD.

1. Circus Maximus
2. Imperial Palace*
3. Flavian Amphitheatre (Colosseum)
4. Temple of Claudius
5. Warehouses
6. Baths of Agrippa
7. Julia Saepta
8. Baths of Nero
9. Theatre of Pompey
10. Theatre of Marcellus
11. Baths of Titus
12. Auguraculum
13. Temple of Peace
14. Stables of chariot-racing teams
15. Tiber Island
16. Virgin's Street
17. The Pantheon
18. Temple of Vesta

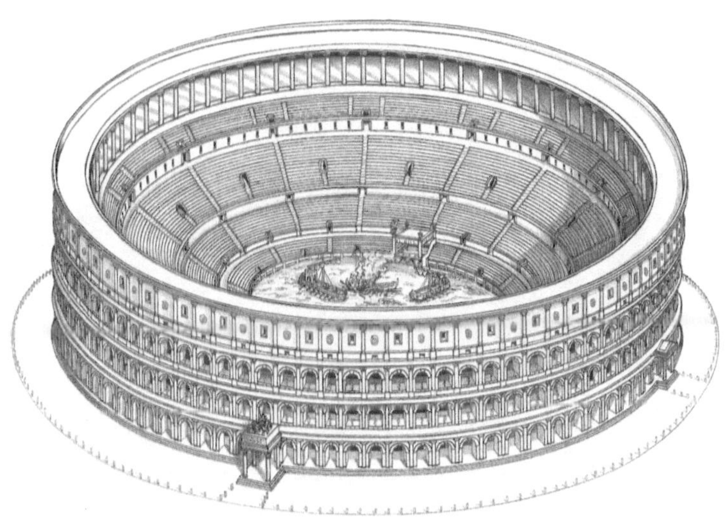

The Flavian Amphitheatre

Rome, early August 80AD

THE AQUARIUS

I'M SPLASHING WATER ONTO MY face when the hammering starts. Marcus curses under his breath and pulls a pillow over his head, in a futile attempt to go back to sleep. I know better than to try. Once the builders start for the day it's best to get out of the insula as quickly as possible. It's hardly light when they start, even though dawn comes early in August.

Our whole life is filled with dust and the sound of hammers. For the past month the entire area around Virgin's Street, turned into a blackened ruin by the three-day fire at the start of July, has had to be torn down. All the wooden buildings went up in smoke and their remains had to be dragged away. Emperor Titus has pushed for the area to be regenerated as quickly as possible, not wishing for people to dwell too long on the multiple disasters that have taken place so far in his one-year reign. Town planners descended and agreed with local landlords where replacement buildings could and could not be built, aiming for the Ninth Region to join the rest of Rome in having larger streets and fewer buildings made of wood, to reduce the risk of fires in the future. The rubble and ruins largely removed, work has already begun on repairing any buildings, like ours, that are still standing. Important properties will be rebuilt and many new buildings will be created, mostly larger insula with more room for businesses on the ground floors. Every builder in Rome has more work than they can keep up with, plumbers and carpenters too. It's probably why they start so early and work long hours; they know they can get another big job as soon as our insula is finished. Still, at least when it's finished Marcus and I can return to our rebuilt roof hut, rather than sharing a cramped corner of the baker's family apartment.

"I'm going to Cassia's. Shall I order for you?"

Marcus grunts. I think it's a yes. He's not going to go back to sleep anyway, he might as well join me for breakfast.

CASSIA ROLLS HER EYES WHEN she sees me. "We'd barely pulled the shutters open, and the builders were here, wanting their breakfast," she says, yawning. "I'd only just got the fire going. Father's not even up yet, I had to manage by myself." She lifts a large pot of dried beans, soaking in water. She's about to make what she calls her weekly soup, a hearty mix of beans and vegetables to which she adds scraps of this and that as she goes along, including the bones of the meat she gets from the amphitheatre, for flavour. She keeps it simmering away over the week. Anyone who is hungry in our Region knows that they can come and ask Cassia for a bowl of hot soup and she will give them a generous portion, no questions asked. She does it without fanfare, her own small way of sharing plenty.

I lean my elbows on the counter as Karbo joins me. "Don't rush on our behalf, I don't mind waiting. I just had to get away from the worst of the noise. It's not as bad if you're not trying to sleep."

Cassia nods and disappears for a few moments, returning from the bakery next door with two large baskets of fresh bread, fruit rolls and cheese pastries, which she places just under the counter, ready to serve her customers. "The fire's hot enough now. Pancakes?"

"Yes," says Karbo. "Three."

"Three? You'll be sick."

"I'm a growing boy," says Karbo.

"You'll be growing width-ways if you eat three pancakes every day. Althea?"

I shake my head. "Too hot for pancakes. Fruit, please."

Cassia pours batter on the griddle, which hisses pleasantly while she chops up fruit. By the time Marcus joins us, Karbo has demolished two pancakes drenched in date syrup, while I'm slowly making my way through a plate of figs, sliced melon, and a large peach.

"Still got a sweet tooth, whatever the weather," Marcus comments, glancing at my plate.

"Have a fig," I offer as he bites into a cheese pastry. I hold one out, already pulled in half, its vivid green skin contrasting with the jewel-like sweet pink filaments inside.

He bolts it in one mouthful. "Good. Pass me another."

"Get your own," I tell him.

Cassia laughs as he tries to filch one from my plate. She pops two next to his half-eaten pastry. "Hungry work, is it, running the Games? You all eat like you spend your days labouring in the fields."

"I'll bring you two deer later," says Marcus. "Today's theme for the morning hunt is the goddess Diana with her hounds. There's over a hundred deer to kill."

"Are the hounds killing them or the woman?"

"Both. She's vicious with her bow, arrows in all directions, fast as you like. We've had to place extra supplies of arrows all around the arena so she can swap quivers."

"Well, venison will be something to look forward to. I'll tell Father when he gets up. He can spend the afternoon butchering."

Cassia's father was older than most when she was born. Now he's getting on, he is happy to spend his days chopping up meat and vegetables for stews to be served in the popina that evening, or decanting wine into jugs that can be poured by customers. He rises later than Cassia, and retires earlier, although he can be relied on to rise again should Cassia need help fending off unwanted suitors, not that she wouldn't be capable of wielding the stick he keeps for that purpose herself.

"Naumachia," I say to Marcus.

He chokes briefly on a crumb. "Must you repeat that word every single morning? You spoil my appetite."

"I'll keep saying it until you find us an aquarius."

"I don't have the time."

"Titus expects a naumachia on the final day of the inaugural Games," I say. "You promised."

"I regretted it immediately."

"You going to pop by the Palantine and let him know that?"

Marcus sighs.

"Time's running out. We've already done thirty days out of the hundred."

"Will you stop nagging?"

"Find us an aquarius, then."

Marcus finishes his glass of cool watered-down wine. "Alright."

"Today."

"I've got Diana's hunt to oversee."

"I can do that."

Marcus' eyebrows go up. "And the execution afterwards?"

I swallow. Thirty days in and I still dislike the executions. "I can manage. There's just one."

"Fine. You manage that, I'll find an aquarius."

"Did you hear about the Jewish queen?" asks Cassia, busy pouring drinks for new customers.

Marcus frowns. "What about her?"

"She's in Rome."

"Titus sent her away when he became emperor last year."

"Well, she's back. Her ship arrived two days ago and yesterday she sailed up the Tiber in a barge. They said it was all covered with flowers and coloured awnings, Berenice was wearing a golden crown and beautiful silk robes."

Marcus shakes his head. "I thought Titus had more sense. The senators won't like it. So far, they're praising Titus to the skies. But none of them want some foreign queen thinking she can claim a place as ruler in Rome if she gives the Emperor a child. Cleopatra was enough trouble back in the day."

"She hasn't given him a child," I point out.

"Tricky to give him a child if she's not by his side," says Marcus. "Hence her visit?"

"She's fifty-two," says Cassia. "Much chance."

"She could adopt some likely child," says Marcus.

I eat the last slice of peach. "Let's go, Karbo. Marcus: stop putting it off. Don't come back without an aquarius."

Marcus sighs. "I don't know why the naumachia couldn't have been held somewhere else."

"Because the amphitheatre is more spectacular than a jumped-up pond."

"Augustus managed to have perfectly good naumachiae in a 'jumped-up pond', if you mean the man-made lake the other side of the Tiber. It worked just fine and it's still there if they cleaned it up a bit."

I shake my head and turn away. "Bye, Cassia."

She waves us off, one hand wiping down the counter, the other pouring wine with practised grace.

The crowd has been seated, gentle pastoral music is playing, and the beast hunt is about to begin. In the gloom of the under-arena, Labeo, owner of the gladiatorial school that has provided our Diana, makes a few last-minute adjustments to her costume before she appears to the crowd. The woman playing the goddess is one of his best gladiatrices, a woman named Alyssa. She's over forty, her face is lined, but she's fearsome. Usually she takes part in the gladiatorial bouts in the afternoons, but her skills with a bow make her an excellent venatore for the hunts, so we sometimes bring her in for those too.

"I'll just pin it in place," Labeo says, briskly pulling her tunic down so that one breast is on show. Alyssa's of a tall and wiry build, her breasts aren't exactly large, but Labeo is now busy tucking the extra fabric tightly under the exposed breast, giving it extra volume and lift.

"Is she supposed to be naked?" I ask.

"Puts a smile on the punters' faces," says Labeo, a brooch held in his mouth while he finishes tucking the tunic into the right place and then fastens it. He tugs at her extremely long and thick hair, large parts of it no doubt bought from slaves and woven into place for these events, checking that it will not come undone. A goddess' hair can never be too long nor lustrous. "Alyssa has followers in that crowd who've lusted after her since she was sixteen and first went into the arena, they've still got a soft spot for her. Or a hard one, eh?" he adds winking. "Plus, it fits your execution story later, doesn't it?"

I grimace. "Yes."

"There you are, then. In you pop, my lovely."

Alyssa shoulders her quiver and steps into the lift. The two lifts either side of her hold twelve panting hounds each, snapping and growling at each other, eager for the hunt to begin.

"You have everything you need?" I ask.

She nods, her face set. I've never yet heard her speak, nor seen her smile in any of the rehearsals, nor on other occasions, but she's a regular headliner, comfortable in both the beast hunts and the afternoon gladiatorial combats, an unusual combination. Today she's wearing a gleaming white tunic, along with the cheaply gilded sandals and jewellery that will indicate her divine status to the audience.

I make my way back upstairs, reaching my designated watching spot, just to one side of the imperial box, today occupied by some distant family connection of Titus'.

Watching me through specially designed grating set into the arena wall are Strabo and his team, awaiting the signals that usually come from Marcus. Today, I'm on my own.

The amphitheatre is two-thirds full, I'd guess. It's a hot day to sit in an amphitheatre that doesn't have awnings, the Emperor will not be attending, and the full crowd usually only turns out for the gladiatorial sessions later. Still, there's over thirty-five thousand people and we have a show to put on.

The space itself looks delightfully peaceful. There's a small grassy hill, various trees grouped into small groves and a pretty pool made with an extremely large, though shallow, wooden circular trough we had commissioned specially. It's coated with pitch, like a boat, to make it waterproof, then lined with blue mosaic tiles, to give a more attractive colour to the water. It's a good prop, we've used it on several occasions, and it hasn't leaked yet. Drinking from the pool, eating piles of grass laid out for them, standing in the shade of the trees, are over one hundred head of deer, mostly females with a few stags and a couple of fawns, just to complete the picture. Nervous this morning when we first sent them up in the lifts, they've had two hours to settle down and get used to the crowds as they entered. The music is mostly soft piping, combined with the trilling of the water-organ, in keeping with the forest idyll laid out before us.

I lift my hand and the music changes, dramatic drumming heralding the arrival of the goddess.

Diana rises from the floor of the arena, the lift trapdoor closing behind her, leaving her to stand on the small hill, surveying her domain while the crowd whistles and stamps at the sight of her, especially her partial nudity, which several shouts from the onlookers indicate has gone down well. She lifts her bow and pauses. She has been taught well by Labeo and her years of experience show, she knows how to work the crowd. When she does move, her arrows are so fast the crowd gasps, three deer already struggling on the ground, legs still trying to run, too late. I raise my hand again.

The hounds pour out, Diana raises her own arm in response as trumpets sound, as though commanding the pack. The deer scatter in alarm, but they have nowhere to run to, no woods to hide in, no streams to jump that might erase their scent. The hounds fall upon one animal after another, ripping at their throats, while Diana strides about, her arrows striking in all directions, one quiver after another exhausted.

The crowd love the combination, the glamorous goddess elevating what would otherwise be a simple hunt. Today I have only allowed a brief pause between the hunt and the execution, just enough time for most of the deer carcasses to be removed and the hounds dispatched back under the arena.

Now Diana drops her quiver and her bow. She makes her way to our blue pool and slowly, provocatively, removes first her golden sandals and then her tunic altogether, leaving only her jewellery to indicate her status. I wonder whether it's blasphemous to have a goddess stripping for a baying public like this, but clearly, she's a hit. She steps into the blue pool and stands, washing herself after the exertion of the hunt, turning on the spot so everyone gets a good view. Time for the music to change, which it does at my signal, the loud hunting music fading away to be replaced by an ominous low-pitched drumming, as a door in the wall opens and a man stumbles towards her. Our criminal for the day is a slave who stabbed his master. Now he finds himself re-enacting the story of the unfortunate young hunter, Actaeon, who saw the goddess Diana bathing naked and was cursed by her to be turned into a stag and hunted by her hounds, dying a horrible death for daring to glimpse her divine beauty.

Our Diana looks up and startles, as though the eyes of this one hapless man are suddenly more than she can bear after the gaze of thirty-five thousand lascivious onlookers. She holds out her hand to stop him approaching, then screams an inaudible curse and splashes water in his direction. The man cowers as she strides towards him and rams down onto his head a metal helmet without eye holes, shaped like a stag's head, complete with vast antlers. He tries to remove it, but he is already too slow. A rope swings into sight and Diana seizes it, is quickly lifted to safety over the wall, taking her place beside a startled senator in the front row as a lift trapdoor opens in the floor and a new pack of hounds are released.

These hounds don't care about deer. They have been trained for other purposes. They leap at the man, who screams and tries to run, but, blinded by the helmet, he stumbles and the hounds go about their business, tearing at his throat and belly. It does not take long. His limbs still twitch, but their work is done. The crowd applaud, well satisfied with this extended mythology linking the beast hunt and the execution. Now they hurry off to the toilets before the queues build up, or wave over food vendors, paying scant attention to the various dancers and actors filling in the time with light entertainment until the gladiators arrive in a procession for the afternoon's bouts. The senator who unexpectedly found himself with a naked goddess by his side looks delighted, even as Diana stalks away and back into the space under the arena, where Labeo will be waiting with her clothes and no doubt a warm welcome should the senator care to send a message asking for Alyssa's company one of these days. Labeo's a showman through and through, no better than a pimp, although a successful one, as the many golden rings on his fingers can testify.

The gladiators in the afternoon are a solid range of performers, we have one 'to the death' bout, dispatching a troublemaker the trainer can't be bothered with anymore, the rest put on a reliable and professional show. They come from Patronus' school and have been highly trained, even the newer fighters are never hired out until they've had a decent schooling in combat. The regular audience appreciates their skill and bravery, point out good technique and daring to one another, cheer on their favourites and, as usual, bet incessantly on possible outcomes. There's little to do during this part of the day other than watch the bouts, make notes about the next day's events, and answer any questions the team have.

When I get home that evening I see Adah's door ajar and look in on her. She's busy dipping candles, so I settle myself on a wooden stool, looking about me. It is a sparse place, her silver seven-armed candleholder the only item of any worth. She has managed to polish away the soot that blackened it during the fire, and it takes up a favoured spot on a shelf, much like the Lararium does in my own hut.

The room smells deliciously of honey. Adah stands hunched over a pot of melted beeswax, set over a portable clay stove in which burns a small fire, just enough to keep the wax liquid for dipping. She has twisted strips of papyrus and now is dipping them over and over again into the wax, building up layers. Her candles are in demand for use in temples, and add a little money to her income from the honey her bees make.

I tell Adah about the Jewish queen arriving. "I'm sorry for Titus," I say. "They say he really does love her but had to send her away. She must love him too, to come back when she knows she's not welcome by anyone but him."

Adah tuts in disapproval. "Why would she love a man who desecrated her own place of worship? She only wants to secure her own status." She makes a dismissive sound. "Enough of these people. We should give thanks we have good people in our own lives." She pats my hand with her wrinkled one. "Time for you to marry," she adds, as if this has been an ongoing conversation between us.

"Oh? Who am I supposed to marry?" I ask.

"There are good men in the world," chuckles Adah, showing a rare glimpse of humour. "If you know where to look."

I shake my head. "Then I must not be looking about me enough," I say. "What I need is sleep. It's been a long day."

"Perhaps you will dream of him," says Adah.

"What nonsense," I say.

"Dreams can foretell the future," says Adah.

"My future is already foretold," I say. "One hundred days of Games for the people of Rome. Nothing else is happening in my life until they have been delivered."

THE TABBY CAT WHO HAS taken up residence in the amphitheatre has given birth to kittens. Karbo is curled up next to the rags the cat has settled into, stroking the kittens with the tip of one finger.

"You'd think she'd be scared of the lions and tigers," says Strabo, "but she doesn't seem to care, lies right next to their cages and hisses at them if they so much as glance at her babies. Helps keep the rats down, anyway. She and her kittens are going to be the fattest cats in Rome. Eh, Domina?" he adds, having bestowed this name on her.

"Will you keep them all?" I ask.

"There's enough rats to go round even if she had another litter after this one," says Strabo.

I make my way up a ladder and onto the arena floor. The spectacle is over for the day, the crowds have departed and now there's only the swish-swishing of brooms and gurgling water as the stone terraces are swept and washed by our cleaning team. Below the arena Strabo will be checking the animals' pens for tomorrow. I consider returning to the insula, but the dust today will be awful. Having removed the ruined top storey of the building, the builders have now started to rip off all the plasterwork, inside and out, including the interior stairs and the walls of every apartment. Nothing else will get rid of the stink of smoke. Meanwhile new waterworks are being plumbed in, which will improve the smell of the block's toilets and allow the plumbers to install a fountain in the centre of the courtyard. I'll be grateful not to have to carry water from the public fountains, but the digging required to lay the pipes means the courtyard is barely passable.

I take refuge from both the building works and the unbearable heat of early August in the shade of the cool stone corridors of the amphitheatre, sitting on the floor, my back leaning against a column with my knees pulled up, so that I can rest my tablet on them and write. A pale green dove wanders past, one of the five hundred birds we had dyed for the opening ceremony of the amphitheatre. A month later, they can still be spotted all over Rome, their once-white feathers now faded hues of the original brilliant colours we chose.

I look back down at the wax, which I'm surprised isn't melting in the heat, and re-read my notes, mostly relating to yet more building works. The barracks for the amphitheatre's slaves, located down by the docks, is in need of a lot of renovation. We took over two decrepit warehouses, one for the animals we cannot store beneath the arena floor, one for the slaves. We have over one thousand in all, employed in many roles including cleaners, toilet attendants, ushers, an animal-handling team, and the teams of men who turn each windlass lifts to bring animals and gladiators up to face the crowds. Strictly speaking, the slaves all belong to the imperial household, as we are all paid for from the imperial purse, but as they have been designated fulltime amphitheatre workers, they come under our jurisdiction. Both warehouses were falling apart, but now that the hundred days of inaugural Games have got underway, and we have a steady schedule in place, they are slowly being repaired and better laid out internally. We have built a cooking station and established a routine which means the slaves work in two shifts. The cleaners are not needed till late afternoons when the crowds have gone home, so they work on repairing the warehouses under the direction of a small team of professional builders, looking after the animals next door and cooking for their peers. The slaves working during the spectacles return to the warehouse once the Games conclude, to find food waiting for them and their own domestic tasks to take care of, including fetching water, preparing the sleeping mats for that night and the tools and materials for the next day's work. Marcus raised his eyebrows at the amount of time I spent making these arrangements, but I reminded him that I used to be a slave myself and he nodded and said no more. Besides, it's in our interest to have a smooth operation we can rely on, with this many people to manage. It's just as well we have a large workforce; we'd never have secured enough builders for a low-paying job like warehouses for slaves and animals when there's a whole Region to rebuild for good money. I could go and inspect the works in the warehouses, I suppose, but it's just too hot.

My eyes linger on the note about an aquarius and the thought of water makes me long for the baths to wash away some of the endless dust. My hair is lank with it. I pull myself up off the cool stone floor, walk back down to the arena, kneel on the sand and put my head down through one of the trapdoors.

"Is Fabia there?"

"Althea?"

"Do you want to come to the baths with me?"

She nods, then makes her way awkwardly up the ladder, her short legs struggling with the depth of the rungs.

"I'm sorry," I say. "I never thought about the ladders being difficult for you. Shall I get one of the carpenters to make one you can more easily use?"

She grins up at me, pulling her tunic back down where it has rucked up during her climb, cheeks flushed pink. "It would help, though I'm used to managing without much in the way of special consideration."

"I need the baths desperately," I tell her as we make our way out. "I stink."

THE BATHS ARE A RELIEF. The hot rooms not so much, although rubbing down with oils and scraping off the dead skin and grime that has collected is satisfying. We help each other. The first time Fabia and I visited the baths together and saw each other naked I found Fabia's little body strange, but I am used to it by now, am more likely to comment on her unruly hair.

"Venus and Juno! How does your hair tangle like this when it's just been oiled? I can't get a comb through it."

Fabia giggles. "I don't know, it's a pain, isn't it? Tell me when your arms get tired, and I'll finish combing it myself."

"How's the work going?"

"Not bad. My father is so happy taking care of wounds again. Stitching away with a smile."

I laugh. "And you?"

She wrinkles her nose in irritation. "I help him, but I'm only an assistant, I never get to treat the wounds alone. The gladiators send for me and then when I arrive at the barracks it turns out they want their women seeing to, there's a baby due or a child with a fever or stomach-ache. They think a dwarf as a midwife is lucky, got the idea from the Egyptians. I want to do the same work as my father, but they insist on having a man to do it."

"Would he let you?"

"Father? Oh yes. I always assist him with the difficult cases, and he sends me on purpose sometimes when he's called for a stab wound or a broken nose, but I can tell they don't want me. They let me dab them with vinegar if they get some tiny scratch, that's all."

"I suppose all you can do is keep trying."

She nods. "Let's go somewhere else. It's so noisy here."

She's right. The baths are an endless source of noise. There are the grunts of men lifting weights and medicine balls too heavy for them, just to show off, as well as those who dive into the pools and then splash about with a lot of huffing and puffing, ignoring those trying to simply relax who end up getting sprayed in the face. There are people lounging in the water who, busy cleaning their ears out with a tiny metal ear scoop, are temporarily deafened and thus speak far too loudly to their friends. That's leaving aside the various cries of people advertising their wares and services, from the hair-pluckers to the cake-vendors. The prostitutes take a quieter but no less active approach, slipping into the water next to potential customers and murmuring in their ears about the delights that are theirs for the asking… and payment, of course.

We walk in the baths' gardens instead, which are cool and shady, then settle under a tree and call over a seller of drinks, sip some well-watered and chilled wine. Out here are mostly people playing board games, a quieter pastime. Fabia is a calm person to spend time with, a thoughtful woman. She tells me about some of the books she reads, educating herself further in medicine, even though the gladiators she would like to care for still doubt her skills.

"I'd better go and find Marcus," I say at last, though with reluctance. "See if he's secured an aquarius for us."

The insula is looking most peculiar. The outer layer of plaster, cracked and chipped as it was, its paintwork fading to nothing and covered with graffiti on the lower walls, has all been chiselled off. The grouting is being refreshed, old mortar chiselled out and replaced with new, strengthening any weak parts. It looks exposed, fragile without its outer layer, even though it's being made stronger.

"Don't even say the word," warns Marcus with a grin when I find him having a drink at Cassia's. He looks fresh and rested, dressed in a clean green linen tunic that shows off golden-brown skin from months in the sun, his hair newly cut, beard trimmed short. "I've found someone suitable, and he'll meet us at the amphitheatre first thing tomorrow morning. Aulus Tuccius Merula's his name."

I make a note. "Strabo will be over soon with the deer," I tell Cassia.

Almost daily we have large quantities of animal carcasses to dispose of. Everything from commonplace hares, sheep and goats, deer, wild boars, and pigs, to the exotic zebra, antelope, rhino and more, all butchered after the day's show is complete. The best cuts and any unusual animals are sent to the Emperor and senators. A selection is regularly sent to the gladiatorial schools, our musicians, and other contacts. Most of the meat is distributed to the poor as a gift from the Emperor, to supplement their grain rations. They queue up outside after the shows. Some of the animals have an odd taste, mostly the carnivores, but the poor aren't fussy about what they receive and the imperial family like to try new flavours. In the past month I've tried bear, wolf, hyena, lion, and tiger. Overall, I prefer regular woodland and farm animals. As Marcus gets first pick, we must be some of the best fed people in Rome. We use the scraps, bones, and poorer cuts to feed the amphitheatre slaves, sending the meat down to the warehouse to add flavour to the thick vegetable and grain stews that make up the bulk of their food. As soon as the Games got properly underway Marcus made a deal with Cassia, he provides her with a generous daily supply of good quality meat, and in return she feeds the insula's inhabitants at a discount. She's a good cook and there's no shortage of meat, at least while the Games are on. Any animals who survive a show stay in pens below the arena overnight or are sent back to the warehouse until the next time they're required. We got through three thousand animals in the past month and no doubt we'll get through the same again for each of the two months to come. The skins end up in the tanneries just across the river from us, we catch whiffs of their working stench from time to time in the insula. Cassia's father has started salting and smoke-curing some of the excess meat we bring back, setting it aside for the leaner times of the year, after the Games finish.

I look down at my tablet. "Also, I need to check the list of animals with you for next week," I tell Marcus.

"No," says Marcus firmly. "I've had enough of work for the day. Tell me tomorrow."

"You work too hard," says Cassia over her shoulder to me.

"Yes," agrees Marcus. "She does. Tell her to ease off, Cassia." He waves as he walks away. "I'm going to see Fabius. See you tomorrow."

"What you need is a bit of fun," says Cassia when he's gone.

"What do you mean?"

Cassia lays down her spoon. "Look," she says, elbows on the counter, her earnest face close to mine. "You were only made a freedwoman less than a year ago. And since then, you've dealt with one disaster after another. But in two months the inaugural Games will end and then you'll have a quiet winter. You've been working so hard you might as well still be a slave. Soon you'll have a chance to have a bit of fun, think about what *you* might want in life."

"Oh, it's that easy? What do *you* want, then?"

Cassia grins, her cheeks a little flushed. "Maybe… maybe a husband?"

I raise my eyebrows. "Oh? Someone we know?"

She giggles. "No, I don't have anyone in mind. But a sorceress could make a charm to bring me one, what do you think? You, Fabia and I, we can go to the sorceress and ask her to bring us what we most desire."

"How do you know where to find a sorceress?"

"*The* sorceress. The one who lives three streets down from here. Just before the fullers'."

"I've never heard of her."

"Well, you haven't been here as long as I have," says Cassia. "But she can help us. She can bring me a husband, make the gladiators accept Fabia as a physician. And…" she gestures towards me "… do whatever you want her to do for you."

"I don't think I have anything I want her to do," I say, uncertain of what I am agreeing to.

"Nonsense," says Cassia firmly. "Everyone has something they want, and the sorceress will help us to get it. I'll get us an appointment, you tell Fabia. But keep it quiet, or we'll get in trouble for using her. She only sees people who are local, in case anyone tells on her for practising magic."

I head into the insula and run into Maria. After the wooden walkway and stairs went in the fire, she took to sitting in a chair looking out of her window, so she can continue to watch any interesting comings and goings in the insula. Occasionally, like today, she brings a chair down into the main courtyard for a better view.

"Sorceress?" she says when I mention Cassia's plans.

"Do you know her?"

"Oh yes."

"And?"

Maria thinks. "She knows things," she says at last. "But it's whether she'll tell you them."

"Meaning?"

"What she says isn't always clear until… later."

"Like most oracles?"

Maria nods. "Better not to know sometimes," she says. "Oracles can make you forget common sense." She folds her arms over her ample bosom with the air of one who can be relied on to keep her wits about her.

THE NEXT MORNING THE AQUARIUS is late.

"If he's not here soon he'll find himself taking part in the beast-hunt," mutters Marcus. "I've got a show to put on, I'm not standing around all morning for someone who can't be bothered to be here on time."

"You're so grumpy," I say.

"I'm fed up with hammers everywhere. They feel like they're in my head."

I nod.

"Marcus Aquillius Scaurus?"

We both turn, then look down. A man's head is sticking out of one of the trapdoors. I consult my tablet to check I'm getting his name right. "Aulus Tuccius Merula?"

"Yes."

"What are you doing down there?" asks Marcus.

"Checking the drainage."

We walk closer and the man climbs out of the trapdoor to meet us. He has a satchel like the one I carry my writing implements in slung across his chest and once he's standing fully upright is revealed to be taller than Marcus but with a skinny frame and an awkward demeanour. He holds out a hand to Marcus and nods warily to me, as though he finds me frightening, then stands facing us, one foot crossed over the other, a position that looks hard to balance in. His eyes and hair are dark, but his skin is very pale, considering it's August. Marcus and I are already summer-brown and Karbo's black skin has gone even darker since the spring. I wonder if the aquarius spends a lot of his time underground, in drainage tunnels and water tanks.

"When did you get here?"

"Just after dawn. I've been measuring the amphitheatre so that I can calculate filling and drainage speeds. Depending which options we use, of course."

Marcus softens, now that he realises the aquarius wasn't late after all. "And what have you found so far?"

"The building's plumbing is excellent. You're using Nero's extension of the Aqua Claudia, it's a good source, nice water quality. Forty input channels where your water comes in, for the toilets and water fountains. Four drains laid in the base, they're very large, can tackle a huge amount of water. You could have a thunderstorm in here and it would cope, no problem, even on top of the usual drainage."

"Let's worry about filling it before we talk about draining it."

Merula rocks slightly on his crossed feet. "How deep does the water need to be, as a minimum?"

Marcus grimaces. "Somewhere close to the height of a man. Otherwise, the show ships won't have enough water to float, even though they're made specially for us, flat-bottomed, with wheels so we can drag them around in rehearsals. And it will look too shallow. But the problem is that if you only fill it to that kind of depth from the current base under the arena, the sightlines from the seating won't be as good. This wooden floor we're standing on sits at least four times higher than a man above the under-stage area, so the performers are usually much higher up."

Merula nods, his face serious. "But if you filled it from that base enough to have the surface of the water where the wooden floor is now, it would be very deep. It would take four times as long to fill – and drain."

Marcus shakes his head. "It has to fill and drain fast, or it won't be impressive."

There's a silence.

"Leaving that aside," says Merula at last. "The current base isn't waterproofed. It's just a big empty space under the arena floor, in a basic brick."

Marcus sighs. "The architect never got round to it, he died in the run-up to the inauguration and there just wasn't time."

"Well, it will have to be done if you want it flooded to any depth at all."

"The problem is that we have to complete one hundred consecutive days of Games, which means putting on a daily show. There are no gaps in the schedule. The whole area down there gets used every day: lifts for all the performers, props, animals kept in pens, people coming and going."

"I would need three days to have it waterproofed, to allow the mortar to be put on and dry. Can you keep that area empty for three days and still put on the shows?"

"I don't have much choice. And it'll be five days. One to empty the area of everything that's down there now, three days for waterproofing, one to put everything back. But Titus wants a naumachia and none of us is going to tell him he can't have one. Tell me you can fill it easily, at least," he adds, fixing Merula with a direct stare.

Merula opens his tablet. "There are several options," he starts.

Marcus' shoulders slump at the thought of extending this conversation and I give Merula an encouraging smile to make up for Marcus' grumpiness, but the aquarius is consulting the notes he has made and doesn't seem to notice either of us.

"Now, you already have a flow of water for your usual use: the toilets and water fountains within the amphitheatre. How many fountains?"

"One hundred," I say.

"So, with that many, if we used your usual water capacity, we could flood the hypogeum, as discussed, in about five hours."

Marcus, who has been looking bored, suddenly snaps back to attention. "Five hours? That's completely unacceptable. It must be *fast*. If it's slow it's just boring. And our toilets and water fountains can't be out of use during a show."

Merula doesn't seem worried. "Another option is to simply divert, for the occasion, all the water from the Aqua Claudia. That would probably fill it in two hours."

Marcus rolls his eyes. "Still too slow. Plus, the new Baths of Titus are opening the same day as us; they're just across the road and will be using the same water source. We can't shut off their water supply. Not to mention the surrounding homes and businesses that all use the Aqua Claudia, what will they have to say about it?"

Merula nods. "There's another option. Nero had a cistern built on the Caelian Hill to allow for a greater flow of water to his own private baths and fountains, as and when required. It's disused now, but we might be able to press it back into service, if it doesn't leak. It's about three hundred paces from here and the elevation in relation to the amphitheatre is substantial. So, we could fill it before the show and then use it to quickly bring in a large body of water. It could be flooded to the height of a man in half an hour."

"That's more like it," says Marcus.

"But it still doesn't address the problem of the sightlines," says Merula.

I walk to the edge of the arena and stand against the stone wall, looking up at the seating. Marcus watches me with a frown.

"What are you doing?"

"Just thinking."

"Thinking what?"

"This wall is higher than a man."

"And?"

I shake my head.

"I'll take any idea," says Marcus. "Whether you think it's ridiculous or not."

"If the entrances to the arena were sealed..." I start.

"We can do that."

"Could the flood start from this wooden floor, going up to the edge of the seating?"

Marcus looks down at his feet. "It's wooden boards," he says. "There are gaps between them. The water would leak away."

"Boats are made of wooden boards," I say.

"They're waterproofed."

I nod. "With pitch."

Marcus waits.

I raise my eyebrows.

"Are you actually suggesting we seal the entrances, waterproof the whole floor with pitch and then flood it?" he asks.

I shrug. "It would make the water level a perfect height. The senators and Emperor would almost be able to reach out and touch the water, it would be very impressive. So that's the sightlines taken care of. Plus, you can be using the arena and then have it flood. It'll start off shallow but get deeper right in front of them. In half an hour, like Merula says."

"And the waterproofing underneath?"

I shake my head. "You'd still have to do that because the water has to drain down into that space. But the drainage would be equally impressive because we can have a large drainage hole, or multiple holes, maybe even use the trapdoors as our plugs. The water would drain very fast when we open them but the audience wouldn't be able to see how. The floor will reappear."

"So, you're suggesting we seal the whole floor, but we'll only have the time between one show ending in the afternoon and the naumachia taking place the next day to apply the pitch?"

"We have over one thousand slaves in our team to apply it."

"It'll never dry in time."

Merula is listening, his head turning between us as we speak. His dark eyes are bright with interest, reminding me of the blackbird for which he is nicknamed. "Actually," he offers, "my father had a little boat, and a coating of pitch could dry overnight. One coating wouldn't last over time for a boat at sea, but for just one show, if it leaks a little it can be topped up. And," he adds with increasing confidence, "you'd only be filling and emptying the shallower depth. It would take half an hour in each direction if we use the cistern to flood and then the trapdoors to empty."

"The timescale and sightlines are good," says Marcus grudgingly, "But what am I supposed to do with boards coated in pitch after that?"

"It will be the last show of the inaugural hundred days of Games," I remind him. "We'll have all winter to replace the flooring with clean boards."

"The gods give me strength. I was hoping to have a quiet winter, with absolutely no building works. Now you're saying we'll have to re-lay the entire floor? Jupiter, the hammering will never end!"

We wait.

"Oh, very well," says Marcus at last, tilting his head back and closing his eyes against the bright sun. "Pitch it is. Let's turn the floor of the greatest amphitheatre in the empire into a poorly-made fishing boat and spend our winter with a constant headache. This will teach me not to say yes to emperors and their ridiculous whims."

I DEPART WHEN THE CROWDS do, leaving Marcus the job of overseeing the post-show work, from the building being cleaned to the butchering and distribution of carcasses. The undertakers are just arriving. One gladiator was killed and will be returned to his school, where his companions will mourn him and arrange his funeral. The six criminals who faced execution today receive no such honour. Their bodies will be loaded onto a cart by means of the same hooks we use on the animals, before being dumped into a mass burial pit, denied the usual rites of death.

Merula has gone to search for the disused cistern, hoping he will find it still waterproof, which will give us a better chance of a dramatically quick filling of the arena, turning it from land to sea before the audience's eyes, as Marcus insists.

CASSIA HAS NOT GIVEN UP on the idea of a sorceress. When I return home a few days later with Fabia, she leads us both down the tangle of back streets at the end of Virgin's Street. The smell of the local fullery is very strong here and even from the street we can see the bobbing heads of the workers through its open gates, still stamping down urine-soaked clothes.

"Here," says Cassia, turning one more corner into a tiny courtyard.

The room we are ushered into by a silent slave girl is full of perfumed incense and lit with only two lamps, the window covered over with a red hanging, which both tints and dims the last of the daylight. There is a low bench with cushions and a large carved chair draped in a dark red throw opposite it, but there is no sign of the sorceress. We are all a little nervous, keeping close together, looking around us as though she is about to appear from thin air.

"I'll sit there, then, shall I?" says Fabia, nudging me and grinning at the chair.

"If you already know what you desire and how to achieve it, why not?" says a deep voice.

We startle. A woman appears, stepping out from behind a red screen set against a wall. She stands still, watching us as we scurry to sit on the low bench, Cassia to one side of me, Fabia on the other. We look up at the sorceress. She is tall, and her hair is a silver grey that falls loose around her shoulders, as though she were a bride. Her tunic is an unassuming and undecorated brown, but her palla, which is draped about her head and shoulders, is a vivid green and embroidered all over with leaves, as though she were a tree come to life. There is something about her that reminds me of Julia; the ability to stand entirely still and upright, without shifting from one foot to the other or finding something for her hands to do. They hang at her sides, relaxed. She does not cock her head to one side or change her expression, only looks at us.

Cassia finds her voice. "We have come for a charm," she says, a little too loudly.

The woman's eyes glimmer with what looks like amusement. "A charm," she repeats, as though this is an entirely new idea to her rather than what she makes her living from. "And what should this charm do?"

"We each of us have something we want," says Cassia, her voice quieter.

"And can you not get it by yourself? Three young, free women, with spare money for charms? It must be something very difficult that you each want."

"It is," says Cassia.

The sorceress moves and the three of us all shift closer so that we are now huddled together. I can feel Fabia and Cassia breathing too fast. The woman sits down in her chair, takes her time leaning back. I notice the subtle showmanship of this seating arrangement, the bench her customers must sit on built a little lower than is usual, the chair a little higher, so that she holds the power in this room, merely through her furniture. Marcus would approve.

"You first," says the sorceress, pointing to Fabia.

"I want to be a physician to the gladiators," Fabia says. "But they don't trust a woman, they want a man to stitch their wounds or amputate their limbs. They only send for me when their womenfolk need tending to."

The sorceress looks Fabia over. "They don't want you because you are a woman, or a dwarf?" she asks bluntly.

"Both, I expect," says Fabia sullenly.

"And are you capable of doing the work you wish to do?"

"Yes," Fabia says, lifting her chin.

"You are sure?"

"Yes."

The sorceress nods. "Then await your moment and when it comes, do not hesitate or it will be too late," she says.

"How will I know when my moment comes?"

"If you are truly a physician who can tend to the wounds that gladiators must face, you will know your moment."

"And if they refuse to let me treat them, even though they are wounded?"

"One will not refuse."

"What one?" asks Fabia, confused.

The sorceress smiles. "You ask too many questions," she tells Fabia. "Know this: when you are certain of your desires in this world, when you can speak their name without hesitation, as you have done to me, your moment will come and all that is required is that you recognise it is your time and step forward to claim what is rightfully yours."

Fabia gives an obedient nod, though she still looks a little confused.

"Now you," says the sorceress to Cassia.

"I want a husband," says Cassia.

The sorceress looks as though she is trying not to laugh. "That's not a desire."

"What is a desire, then?" asks Cassia.

"It is something you long for when it is not there. It is the thing the Fates wove for you the day you came into the world, that which will make you whole and certain of yourself. Your little friend there knows what her desire is, she has known it a long time, that is why it comes so readily from her lips, so certain. She has named her desire out loud, and once your desire is named, it is only a matter of time until it comes to you, for you have summoned it by its name and it will begin its journey towards you. Some journeys take longer than others, but once a desire has been summoned, it will make its way to you for sure."

Cassia looks put out. "I want a husband," she insists. "That's a desire. I desire a husband. There."

"You can open your lips and ask for a husband but then what? Will any man do? Was it any man the Fates chose to be your husband? Do you think them so slovenly in their work as to weave only the rough shape of a man and not name him, not single out the very one to whom your spirit will be bound, if it is a man that is your true desire?"

Cassia is growing impatient, scowling. "I want a charm to bring me a husband. You're a sorceress, you can make a charm for that."

"Words can be dangerous. Be careful how you ask for things. Do not ask for an empty shape, for you may not like what fills it."

"I don't like riddles."

The sorceress laughs out loud. "Think on it, girl. Find your true desire, not some vague thought you had in passing. When you know it, name it. Not just to yourself, not secretly and half-whispered, but out loud. When you know your desire with certainty, speak its name and its journey towards you will begin."

There's a silence. Cassia looks as though she would like to argue further but daren't. "And you?"

The sorceress' eyes appraise me, her gaze unnerving. "I don't – I don't have a desire," I manage. After all, what is there I can ask for? Cassia's romantic notion of seeking a husband has already been dismissed. I have a job, a home, even my freedom, which I would have begged for a year ago, when I was still a slave. As for feeling whole, or seeking something the Fates wove for me… what would that be? Anything I think of would sound foolish, too small, set against such a description.

"A husband?" says Cassia, smirking.

The sorceress laughs again. "Your friend still does not understand," she tells me, nodding to Cassia, who flushes at the jibe.

"I never said a husband," I object quickly.

"She was a slave," Fabia explains. "She was set free less than a year ago, she is still new to life as a freedwoman. She has never made her own choices."

"Then she must learn what it is to be free. One step, one choice at a time. She must learn not to think like a slave. And when the time comes that she knows her own mind, she will name her desire. Out loud," she reminds me, smiling.

"How does one know a true desire then?" asks Cassia, stubbornly questioning.

"Because it will complete you. Because it will not require charms nor curses, only what is in you already. Because you will be certain. Specific. And all those around you will know it is right for you."

"But –"

The sorceress rises, still smiling even as she is clearly dismissing us. "Charms and curses are for those who find themselves powerless and must grasp at that which they do not understand for comfort."

"What do we owe you?" asks Fabia, ever practical, as we shuffle off our bench, keeping a wary distance between ourselves and the sorceress.

"You will pay me when your desire completes its journey. You will know when to come to me and what to bring with you in payment."

"THAT WOMAN IS VERY ODD," complains Cassia, once we are out on the street. It's late, growing dark. "I still think I should have been given a proper charm. Perhaps she's not a real sorceress after all. A *real* sorceress would have taken our money and given us what we wanted, there and then."

"What if I miss my moment?" worries Fabia as we walk back to the insula.

I stay silent. Fabia knows what she wants, even the hard-to-please sorceress seemed to think so. But I cannot name what I want, cannot look ahead into my future and name anything at all, only see what is already in my life: the amphitheatre, the insula, the people I know. I bid my friends goodnight. I think of asking Marcus for advice, but what would I say? And he might laugh at me for consulting a sorceress. Instead, I make my way to the small room I share with Marcus. He is already asleep. I lie down on my sleeping mat and try to recall the exact words of the sorceress, hoping I might suddenly understand her better, but I only confuse myself more and for a moment think I can smell her close to me before I sniff my tunic and realise I smell of the incense that swirled around her room. I fall asleep and dream strange dreams, of perfume and questions to which I have no answers. I try to open my mouth, but nothing comes out. I wake a few times, sweating in the August heat, my tunic clammy, and finally sleep more deeply, though I wake no less confused.

TITUS WILL BE AT THE Games today. We've saved up criminals for the executions for over a week so we can put on a good show at midday. The team all arrived early, and the seating is full. The crowds like to see the Emperor and the senators want to be seen by him.

The trumpets sound and Titus makes his entrance to loud applause, but Marcus' eyes narrow at once.

"What is it?" I ask, under the noise of the cheering.

"Berenice," he answers.

Sure enough, a woman is entering the imperial box and settling herself at Titus' side. She looks well preserved for her age, her dark hair elaborately arranged in towering curls in the latest Flavian fashion, as it's known, with a gold circlet fixed just above her forehead, emphasising her regal status. The crowd is not quite sure what to make of her; the clapping for Titus grows uncertain and fades away.

Marcus quickly signals for the beast hunt to begin. Hyenas chase down unwilling antelope before defending themselves against a team of dark-skinned venatores with spears, dressed in something approximating African dress, a deliberately exotic demonstration of just how far Titus' empire stretches. The criminals are executed in style, forced into fighting lions whom they have no chance whatsoever of beating, since their swords are blunt. The gladiators re-enact some of Titus' most daring military conquests in Judea, although the actual desecration of the Temple has been left out, the painted walls of Jerusalem merely falling in an obliging manner when his "troops" attack them, the inhabitants on the other side putting up a brief but compelling series of bouts and then kneeling in homage to their rightful ruler. Titus generously gives the gladiator playing the part of Titus-as-general his freedom, presenting him with a traditional wooden sword, much to the crowd's pleasure, as he's a well-known headliner with an excellent record of wins, nearing the end of his fighting life. Now set free, he'll be able to earn a comfortable retirement making guest appearances for wealthy patrons to liven up their dinner parties with very little risk to himself. The crowd is happy enough with the day's entertainment that they even give a good-natured small ripple of applause as Queen Berenice rises to leave, then a standing ovation for Titus as he departs.

CASSIUS IS BUSTLING ABOUT THE popina when we go for our evening meal, making small adjustments to just about everything, from where pots and pans are hung to tut-tutting over a chipped jug.

"What's got into your father?" I ask Cassia.

"We've got a cousin of mine coming to stay, name of Rullus. He wrote to say he'd like to visit us for a few weeks, help out in the popina. Father wants to make a good impression, show we're doing well for ourselves."

Fabia has joined us for dinner. "So you asked the sorceress for a husband and now a man is coming to stay with you?" she teases.

Cassia laughs. "He better be good-looking, if he's been sent by her."

WHEN I COME DOWNSTAIRS EARLY a few days later, Julia is standing in the middle of the street looking up at the building. Despite there being plenty of people around, no-one asks her what she's doing blocking everyone's pathway. Instead, they skirt around her, giving her a wide berth, nodding deferentially as they pass. A Vestal Virgin commands respect, even if she is retired.

"The new plaster looks good," she says. "They're going to paint the popina today, so Cassia will get a day off."

"I'll have to get my breakfast elsewhere then," I say. "I can't wait for all the building works to be over."

Julia gives a patient smile. "All in good time. Will you come to mine for dinner, since the popina is closed?"

"No thank you," I sigh. "I need to go down to the warehouses to see some of the repairs that need doing there. I'll be back late. But if you can feed Karbo I'd be grateful."

"Don't walk alone in the dark. Can't Marcus come back with you?"

"I'll be back before it's dark," I say.

"I'll make sure Karbo is fed and goes to bed."

"Thank you."

I DO LEAVE THE WAREHOUSES before dark, but only just, twilight has already fallen and I walk quickly back towards the Ninth. Rome's streets at night are not for the fainthearted, especially down by the docks. I feel better once I am away from them, but by the time I reach the start of Sand Street, it is really quite dark and I am relieved that the safety of Virgin's Street is not far away, although the shutters of Cassia's popina are closed tonight, this being her one night off each week when she does not run an evening service. I hurry towards the dim outline of the insula, grateful to be almost home. I can smell paint in the air and remember that the painters were due today, to start work on the outside of the building, though I can't see their handiwork in the darkness. I can only see the dim flicker of a lamp from Julia's courtyard, she likes to keep one burning till very late at night.

The man's hand is so swift that I do not even open my mouth and already it is sealed shut, his other hand twisting my right arm behind my back, dragging me against the outer wall just on the corner of Sand Street and Virgin's Street, opposite the gateway I was hurrying towards. I can smell him pressed against me, a sour-sweat reek that only seems to intensify as I struggle against him.

"Stay still, pretty, or it'll be the worse for you."

I jerk in his arms, kicking backwards with my right foot, left hand flailing behind me trying to grab at him, mouth still trying hopelessly to open. I feel as if I can't breathe properly and when he tightens his hold against my struggles I claw at his forearm, digging in my short nails as hard as I can.

"Futuo! I'll teach you a lesson for that!" he spits and pulls his arm away for a too-brief moment. I gasp for air, ready to scream but he cuffs my head so hard I stagger and this gives him a chance to grab me around the waist, shoving me hard against the street wall while pulling up my tunic from behind. But to do so he has to let go of one of my hands. I reach behind me and scratch his other arm, as hard as I can and he loosens his grip for one brief second. I turn to flee and he trips over my foot and stumbles, grabbing at my tunic but I kick out and run. The heavy wooden gate is open and I dart through it, not even pausing to shove it shut behind me, running to a corner of the courtyard where Julia is growing a vine and pushing myself against the wall so that I cannot be seen when he comes after me. I am shaking so hard I think he will spot me just from the trembling leaves around me, but he does not come through the gateway after me, as I expected. I wait, still shaking, still panting, but nothing. Nobody. I am alone in the dark courtyard and after a few moments I take one cautious step out from the vine and then another, creeping towards the doorway to the interior stairs and then slowly making my way up, looking behind me so many times in the darkness that I stumble more than once.

In the apartment, everyone is asleep. I tiptoe to the room I share with Marcus and lie down very quietly. The sound of his light snoring, the faint warmth from his body being nearby, is so comforting that I weep, silent tears sliding down my face. I breathe slowly and deeply, trying to calm myself. It is alright. The man did not succeed in raping me and now I am here, with Marcus beside me, safe in our room. I will tell Marcus everything in the morning and he will be on the lookout for the man, whoever he was. If he stays close by we will know him by my scratches on his arms, for I am sure, given his reaction, that I drew blood. At last my tears slow and then stop. When Marcus rolls over and stops snoring I move a little closer to him, to better feel his warmth and listen to his breathing now it is quieter, each breath a protection.

When I wake Marcus has already got up and left, so I cannot tell him what happened. But I will see him shortly, at the amphitheatre and I am not so afraid by daylight. Before I go to work, though, I must find Cassia and tell her too, so she can be careful herself and keep an eye out for any strangers she notices loitering nearby. I make my way out of the gate and am about to turn left but find Cassia right in front of me, standing in the middle of the street, arms folded as she inspects the popina, ignoring the traffic trying to get round her.

"Look at it," she crows, beaming.

The painters have finished their work for Cassius and the large counter that encloses the popina has been painted a strong dark red along the top, marked out with a bold yellow trim all around the side, over which have been painted, in bright colours, a crowing rooster and two mallard ducks ready for plucking, rosemary bushes, as well as a scene of a Nereid riding a horse through the waves, surrounded by all types of fish, placed near to where Cassia keeps her barrels of salted fish for the little saltfish fritters of which her customers are so fond as a snack between meals with a glass of wine. There's even a painting of a dog tied with a lead, into which image a couple of metal rings are set where the popina's customers can tie up their own dogs if they wish to take a seat inside and stay for a more leisurely meal.

I try to gather myself and focus on her happiness for a few moments before confiding in her. "It looks wonderful," I say. "When I think of how it was the first time I saw it..."

Cassia nods. "It was so run down," she says. "I used to think we'd have to move one day. But now that the whole building's been strengthened and replastered and painted... this is where I can spend the rest of my days." She beams at the rest of the building's exterior, the bare dried plasterwork ready to be painted in the usual white with a dark red band on the ground floor, against which her cheerful yellow will stand out, drawing new customers her way. "They'll be done in a few days."

"They're working fast," I say.

"They've got work available from now till next year's Saturnalia and beyond if they get each job done quickly, so it's in their interest to work fast."

"I wanted to tell you something," I say.

"What is it?"

"Shall we go inside?" I ask. I don't want to be talking about what happened last night in the middle of the street. I'm still a little jumpy despite the welcome light of daybreak, looking around me in case I should spot some unknown man, recognise my assailant.

"Of course," says Cassia agreeably, still smiling at the paintwork. "And you can meet my cousin."

"Oh, did he arrive this morning?"

"Yesterday afternoon."

I follow her. It's good there will be another man about, I think, especially for Cassia, who after all often has to work evenings and sometimes has trouble with over-familiar customers, who need to be reminded by Cassius that he keeps a big stick inside the popina for just such patrons. The cousin can help keep a lookout for any unwanted men hanging about.

"This is Rullus," says Cassia.

The man behind the counter of the popina is probably in his mid-twenties, of a sturdy build and with a wide smile. "Ah, you must be Althea, I've heard all about you," he says. "I'm very glad to meet you."

His voice sounds familiar, it must be because he's related to Cassius. I nod and smile. "And I you," I say. "Welcome to the insula."

Cassius comes bustling out of the back part of the popina. "Met our new family member, Althea?"

"I have," I say.

"So good to have another man about to help us," says Cassius. "I'm getting on, after all."

"You should be able to take things easy," smiles Rullus. "I can do whatever is required to help. You sit down, tell me what to do and I'll do it."

"Be with you in a minute," Cassia says to me. "Just sorting out the plates." She disappears from sight, ducking down under the counter. I can hear her shifting crockery about, preparing for a busy day ahead. I stand, shifting from foot to foot, still nervous.

"Excuse me," says Rullus, coming towards me. He is carrying a large pail of dirty water from the back of the popina. It's been used for scrubbing down the tables in the back and washing the floor afterwards, which Cassia does first thing every morning and now he is about to throw it out into the street. I step out of his way but as he passes I catch the scent of him and stagger backwards, grabbing at the counter.

The smell of him.

He smells like the man who assaulted me.

Cassius is burbling on about something from his table, but I can't really hear him. I'm staring at Rullus' back as he throws the water. When he turns back I look down at his forearms, where I scratched the man, where I drew blood.

His arms are scratched.

He is the man who assaulted me.

I hold the edge of the counter and watch him as he comes back past me, catch the smell of him again and swallow. He puts the pail away and tends to the fire but my eyes do not leave his forearms, where multiple scratches have freshly scabbed over since last night.

"I need to go," I say, my voice too loud.

"No breakfast?" says Cassius from the back. "Thought you'd come for your breakfast."

"No," I say.

"Unless you wanted something else," Rullus adds, hands on the countertop, smiling sweetly at me, but his eyes are no longer on mine, they have travelled down to my breasts.

"No," I say, backing away. "No, nothing."

"You said you had something you wanted to tell me?" says Cassia, popping her head up from under the counter.

"No," I say again. "Nothing. It was nothing."

I hurry away from the popina, back into the courtyard of the insula, see the open door of a storeroom the bakery uses and slip inside.

I am shaking. What do I do? I try to breathe.

One breath.

What do I do?

Two breaths.

Perhaps I was wrong?

I clutch at this idea. Yes. Perhaps all I smelled was the sweat of any working man, perhaps Rullus' arms were scratched by a stray cat or…

No.

I know it was him.

And he knows. His too-sweet smile, his words, *Unless you wanted something else…?* Bile rises in my throat for a moment, bitterness in my mouth. I force a swallow. Breathe again, forehead pressed to the cold bare plaster. Think. Think. The man who attacked me, who tried to rape me, is Cassia's cousin. How can I – *what* can I say? He arrives here, is a family member to one of my dearest friends and I must accuse him – without any evidence, only a few scratches on his arms and my say-so?

The cold wall is chilling me. Julia, I think. I will confide in Julia first, she will know what to do, she will understand.

"Althea?"

Julia is calling from the courtyard, like an answer to a prayer. I hurry out to her.

"Julia," I say gratefully. "Hello."

"I have to go, but I just wanted to check something quickly with you."

I want to tell her now, but this is not something I can tell quickly. It will have to wait. When she is back from wherever she is going, I will talk to her properly. "Yes?"

"I meant to tell you before: Adah will not take the second roof hut when it's built. She says she would prefer one of the small rooms on the top floor."

I barely understand what she's saying, it's so removed from what is important right now. I try to focus. "Probably for the best," I say at last. "Especially in winter, if you're coming or going when it's cold and wet. She's pretty old."

Julia nods. "So, there will be a spare hut and it seemed more fitting if Marcus lived in one and you in the other. I will put Karbo in with you, he has need of a motherly figure in his life, with Fausta gone."

I blink. "Did Marcus agree?"

"It was his idea."

She's already moving away with a brisk wave over her shoulder to me, through the open gateway and away down the street. For a moment I stand alone, staring after her.

No.

No, no, no.

I need Marcus near me. I need him, after what happened to me I cannot have him sleeping elsewhere. I hurry back out through the gateway after her. "Julia —"

"Get out of the way!" yells a passing trader and I jump aside to avoid being run over by his mule cart. Clearly, I do not have the traffic-stopping status of an ex-Vestal Virgin. I look about me, but Julia has already disappeared. I try to think my way through what Julia said but it only feels worse. Of course, if Adah is not going to take the second roof hut, it is sensible to suggest that Marcus and I should each have one to ourselves, and Julia is right: we are not a couple, so it is hardly proper that we should live together as though we are. I will have more space and the hut will be mine to manage as I wish. But to lose the comforting shape of Marcus after what has happened, and face whatever each night's darkness may hold all alone…

I ARRIVE LATE AT WORK. The familiar darkness under the arena feels uncomfortable, the vast shadowy space closing in on me. I tell Strabo to open up all the trapdoors. He looks puzzled but doesn't ask questions. Gradually the space lightens and my fears subside a little. I will tell my friends and they will protect me. Fabia is standing in the physician's area, preparing the space for her father.

"Morning, sleepyhead," says Marcus when he sees me. "Bet you're looking forward to not hearing me snore anymore," he adds, grinning.

I open my mouth to speak but he is already halfway up a ladder to the arena floor above us.

"What's he talking about?" asks Fabia.

"Julia is giving us a roof hut each. Adah will move into a room instead."

"You don't sound very happy about it."

"I'm... not."

"What's wrong with it?"

"No-nothing," I say. Strabo is standing nearby, checking animals off a list. I will confide in Fabia, but I don't want an audience.

"But you're not happy?"

"I just didn't..."

"Are you in love with Marcus?" asks Fabia, leaning forward and lowering her voice.

"Oh no!" I say, hastily checking over my shoulder that Strabo has not heard this suggestion. "No, no, I just... we... we got along fine there before the fire, sharing one hut..."

Fabia waits for me to finish a coherent sentence and then shrugs. "Well, you'll have more space," she points out. "And you're unmarried, you don't want word getting around you live with a man if he's not *your* man, do you? It would discourage suitors." She continues laying out instruments, each one neatly lined up in a certain order.

I stare at her tiny hands, not seeing anything, feeling again Rullus' hands on my mouth and pulling up my tunic, hurting me. "Suitors?"

"You might want suitors?"

"I don't... I haven't..."

Fabia laughs. "Are you going to finish any of your sentences today?"

"People keep saying things and asking questions I wasn't expecting!"

AND SO THE DAY GOES on. I stumble from one thing to the next, every time I think I might have a moment to speak with Marcus, or Fabia, there is someone else there or the hunt has started or the gladiators are about to begin the pre-battle parade.

When I return to the insula I skirt around the popina, slipping quickly through our gateway, hoping to avoid Cassia and especially Rullus.

"Met Rullus?" asks Maria as I pass through the courtyard. She's in her usual spot, watching everything that goes on in the insula, missing nothing. I wish she had been there last night but it was too late, she goes back to her rooms when darkness draws in.

"Yes," I say tightly.

"Seems all right," she says. "Polite enough. Won't be here long I suppose, just visiting family. Cassia said a few weeks."

My shoulders relax a little. Yes, perhaps he will stay just a couple of weeks or so and I can stay well out of his way, then he will be gone and no-one need be told anything difficult. After all, I escaped, he did not manage to rape me. I let out my breath in a rush. Yes. I need only avoid the popina and he will leave soon. All will be well.

THE NIGHTMARES START ALMOST AS soon as I have fallen asleep that night. *Hands grabbing at me as I try to open a mouth that is sealed shut, the overwhelming smell of sour-sweat and my own fear.* I jolt awake over and over, but each time I do Marcus is there, one arm over his head, peacefully sleeping, and I can listen to his breathing and sleep again, albeit briefly.

I AVOID THE POPINA FOR three days, eating elsewhere, making sure to come and go from the insula only in the full light of day, even though Marcus calls me a lazybones for not rising at dawn like everyone else. I stay at work as long as possible and when I get home each day I go to my room in the baker's apartment and stay there.

THE PLASTERING TEAM WORK FAST. By the fourth day plaster has been applied to all the inner walls of the insula's courtyard and is awaiting a decorative coat of paint to complete the work. Inside, one apartment and room after another has been worked on; most are now finished. The lingering odour of fire damage is slowly being replaced with the smell of wet earth from the plaster.

"The roof huts are complete," says Julia, appearing in the doorway of my room, where I am darning a tunic of Karbo's. "Do you want to go and see them? Marcus and Karbo are ready downstairs."

She leads the way with Marcus, Karbo and I walking behind her up the inside stairs.

"Will you put a wooden staircase back on the inside of the courtyard?" I ask.

"Yes," says Julia ahead of us. "I liked it the way it was and besides, having two staircases was a blessing during the fire. Then I can plant out my herbs and flowers again."

"They're bigger," says Karbo excitedly as we emerge onto the rooftop. He's right, the two huts are now larger, one set into one corner of the rooftop, the other diagonally across from it. Karbo opens the door of our hut and goes inside, exclaiming at something, but I'm distracted by Marcus, who has disappeared into his own hut. It's strange to be separated after everything that has happened over the past year, when we have slept in any tiny space available together, after we had both lost friends and family and faced the devastation of a volcano, of plague and fire. Julia, who has been looking out over the city, turns to me with her eyebrows raised and I make my way inside the hut, away from her gaze. She will be expecting me to be curious, to want to look inside my new home.

The larger space inside should be welcome but it feels too big somehow. The doorway is too wide, there is space to move quietly around without tripping over anything, without disturbing anyone until it is too late... my breath comes short. I put out a hand to touch the wall to give me back a sense of balance, to take away the dizziness that was sweeping over me.

There is room for the two simple wooden beds tightly strung with linen cords that

Julia has had the carpenters make for Karbo and me, which will be more comfortable than the simple mats we have slept on thus far. There is additional space to keep clothes and any other possessions as well as shelves on the walls. The plaster is still bare but there is a new lararium on one of the shelves. It's very similar to the one I had Balbus the toymaker make for Marcus and me barely a month back. I recognise his painting style in the bearded serpent and delicate images of household gods set into a decorated wooden frame. In front of it are two tiny dolls, symbolising my dead parents. Marcus must have commissioned this shrine for me and put it here along with my ancestral figures, keeping in his hut the figures of his dead wife Livia and son Amantius, as well as the one of Fausta, his best friend and my mentor. Our odd little household of three, the straggling survivors of the past year, is now split in two, each with its own lararium, clearly indicating that we no longer share a common home.

"Going to need a lot of paint in here," says Karbo, who hasn't noticed that my eyes have welled up. "Are we going to decorate our hut?" he adds eagerly. "Can we have pictures on the walls, like a fancy villa?"

"I think a coat of white paint will do," I say.

Karbo looks disappointed. "I want chariot races on the wall," he says. "And a red trim around each picture."

I raise my hands. "If you know someone who can paint a chariot race on our wall for nothing, you can have what you like," I say. I can't face arguing with anyone, my legs feel shaky. I step out of the hut, only to see Marcus already disappearing into the stairwell.

"Are you happy with the hut?" asks Julia, walking over to join me.

"Yes," I say. I'm thinking about whether I can have a lock put onto the door, whether it would be strong enough to withstand a man, if he were intent on reaching me. Rullus could easily find out where I live, I cannot be too careful.

Julia is looking at me, expecting more. I want to talk to her about Rullus but Karbo is still close by and so I force a delight I do not really feel. "It's a wonderful space, so much more room. Thank you for the beds."

"Are you happy..." she begins again, and Karbo or no Karbo, I want to confess to her about Rullus right now. I want to tell her that no, I do not feel happy. I already feel lonely in this new arrangement, cast off from the only person I have clung to for stability over this past year, as all around me people I loved have died and left me to manage alone. I am scared of Karbo being given to me as though he were only my responsibility when I know nothing of being a mother, let alone to a nine-year-old boy who has spent most of his life on the streets. I am terrified to sleep in this new space alone, without Marcus by my side for protection, when there is a man who has attacked me living in this very insula, unknown to all except me.

I open my mouth to try and explain all this, but Julia is already finishing her sentence. "...for Adah to still keep her beehives on the roof? We saved one colony when they swarmed during the fire and someone else has given her a gift of a new colony, along with a hive, so that she can still sell their honey and beeswax candles to make a living. She does not need much, especially with Cassia's deal with Marcus, but the bees bring in a little money so that she can pay her rent and buy food."

"Adah?" I am bewildered for a moment, then gather myself. "Yes, yes of course, there is…" I wave my arms about without indicating anything in particular "…plenty of space, wherever she wants…"

"Thank you, I will let her know," says Julia and she walks away before I can summon up the courage to speak.

On the rooftop, Adah's beehives have been put in place as agreed, two of them, facing out over the city, allowing the bees to quickly rise into the air as they leave their home and set out on their foraging missions. They have a clear path they use, which will not bother us. Karbo watches them come and go for a while, kneeling by the hives, curious about their tiny lives. Inside our hut, I place the extra lamp I bought onto a shelf, glad of the additional light. Our sleeping mats are now placed on top of the strung beds, giving us a luxuriously soft night's sleep. There is no need for covers just now, the nights are too hot. I would like to leave the door open at night but dare not. Instead I have a lock fitted to the door. The lock opens only from the inside, and I wear the key on a string around my neck.

"But shouldn't we lock the roof hut from the outside, for when we're not here and someone might steal something?" Karbo asks. "What's the point of locking ourselves in?"

"Good point," I say. "I'll have it changed one day when I have time to arrange it." But I don't. I don't explain because I don't want to frighten Karbo. His presence at my side provides a little comfort, but he is only a child, if Rullus were to find us, he could not provide any defence and might even be assaulted himself. I lock the door with care each night once he has fallen asleep, which thankfully he does quickly, then check and re-check it. I think that I would scream if Rullus broke in, that Marcus would hear and come running, but then I think of how Rullus clamped his hand over my mouth, how I could barely breathe, let alone scream. I touch the lock, to be certain that it will hold. Then I sleep, but often I have nightmares where I see the lock turning without a key and the door opening, before I wake with a start and have to reach out to touch the door again and be certain that it is closed in the darkness that surrounds me.

THE DAUGHTERS OF THETIS

THE BATHS OF TITUS, JUST over the road from the Flavian Amphitheatre, will soon be ready for inauguration, right on schedule.

"They're not on schedule," objects Karbo. "They were supposed to open the same day the Games did. That was more than a month ago. They're late."

Marcus grins and lays a finger to his lips. "We don't say anything the Emperor puts his name to is late," he says. "We say the Emperor has chosen to inaugurate it on the same day that we put on a naumachia. Water everywhere, by his command, see? A new baths complex for the people, an astonishing water show in his family's amphitheatre to complete the one hundred days of inaugural Games."

Karbo looks unimpressed at this lesson on imperial etiquette. He peers down at the baths from the second storey of the amphitheatre, watching sweating slaves in the burning heat of August transplanting full-grown trees and bushes into the gardens surrounding the building, while others paint the outer walls, transforming them into glistening white with a smart red trim and yellow outlines for doors and windows. "Late," he mutters to himself.

I look around me. The cleaners are sweeping down the tiers, we're nearly finished. Today's Games were less well attended. With no main awning, only the most committed plebs, or the richer audience members with slaves to fan them and hold parasols, fancied braving the heat. I'll be grateful when we get to September and the days cool off a little.

A long whistle draws our attention. We look down at the wooden flooring at the centre of the amphitheatre. A trapdoor is open, and Strabo's head is poking out, blowing his whistle to summon us. There's a cluster of bodyguards standing around a man in a toga, standing in the lower tiers where the senators usually sit.

"Cack," says Marcus. "It's the Aedile. What's he doing here at this time of day?"

The three of us hurry down the steep flights of stairs to find the Aedile and his entourage waiting for us.

"Welcome," says Marcus. "Won't you step into the shade?"

We stand in the cool stone corridor, its paintings thankfully completed, at least on this tier. The topmost corridor is still being decorated whenever we get the chance, although its ceiling is low and dark compared to the lofty elegance of the lower tiers. The important people never have to see the topmost corridor, so it is only the height of an ordinary room, not the double, almost triple, height allowed for the tiers below. The painters get an hour in the mornings if they're lucky, then perhaps an hour or two in the afternoon when everyone has gone home, so progress is slow. Not that the

Aedile cares, he's never asked to see the top tier, not even for the spectacular view of Rome it would offer.

"I am here on a delicate matter," he says, waving away Karbo, who is offering a tray with cold water and cups. Karbo bows with grace and then disappears behind the nearest archway, where I know full well he is listening to every word that is said.

"I am at your service," says Marcus.

The Aedile clears his throat. "The recent… *visit* of the Jewish Queen Berenice to the Emperor has…" he clears his throat again, "possibly been, ah, *extended* beyond what might be considered…" He stops.

"Appropriate?" suggests Marcus. I can see he is trying not to smile; he is chewing on the inside of his cheek.

"Indeed," says the Aedile, looking relieved. "Appropriate, as you say." He pulls a cloth from his toga and wipes his sweating forehead with it.

Marcus and I wait.

"You are holding a naumachia in early October, I understand? A grand finale for the inaugural hundred days of Games?"

Marcus frowns at the change of topic. "Yes?"

"Excellent, excellent. I was wondering whether, as a… a… discreet *hint*, as it were, whether it might be possible to, um, stage something which would, in its, um, subject matter, ah, suggest to the Emperor the advisability of the visit and… and indeed the, er, *relationship*, being, um, concluded."

"You want to me to stage a story about a man getting rid of the woman he loves?"

The Aedile looks appalled at Marcus' blunt summary but gives a wordless nod.

Marcus sighs. "Did you have a specific story in mind?"

"Odysseus and the Sirens?"

Marcus grimaces. "Tying himself to the mast of his ship so he could see their beauty and hear their songs but not be tempted to jump into the sea and join them?"

"It seems suitable?"

Marcus gestures to me and I make a note on my tablet. "I'll see if there's something we can do," he says. "You can leave it with me."

The relieved Aedile retreats, no doubt to lie down in a shaded garden after his diplomatic exertions.

"The stuff these people come up with," mutters Marcus. "So now we have to find sirens? What are we supposed to do, go fishing?"

MORE THAN TWO WEEKS HAVE gone by and Rullus is still at the popina.

"Haven't seen you for ages, are you avoiding me?" calls Cassia as I try to slip out one morning.

Reluctantly, I make my way over to the counter. Rullus, thankfully, is nowhere to be seen.

"I was busy," I say.

"Too busy to eat?"

I try to smile. "How is Rullus getting on?" I ask, his name leaving my mouth with difficulty. "He must be going home soon?" I can't help adding, hoping to hear the answer I want.

"Can't get rid of me that easily."

I jump. Rullus has appeared from the back of the popina, from the storeroom door.

Cassia laughs. "You startled her!" she says.

Rullus gives an easy smile. "Ah, I'm sorry Althea," he says. "I wouldn't want to frighten you. We should be friends. Any friend of Cassia's is a friend of mine." He nods to Cassia. "Just checking on the saltfish stocks, be back in a minute."

Cassia beams. "Thank you, Rullus."

I glance at his arms. The scratches are gone, healed in the weeks I have held my tongue. My only evidence against him is gone because I waited too long.

He steps back through the door and I look at Cassia, who is beaming.

"He's very helpful," she says. "I hadn't realised how much I was doing on my own, now that Father is getting on. I'm glad he's staying."

My stomach suddenly feels heavy. "Staying?"

"He said he'll stay as long as we need him and Father and I agreed we could do with the help. And he's..." she trails off slightly, a blush creeping up her neck... "A good man to have about," she finishes awkwardly.

"I have to go," I say. "I'm late."

My feet are heavy all the way to the amphitheatre. I have left it too long. If I had told everyone what happened, at once, if I had shaken Marcus awake and told him, then Rullus would have been thrown out of here, family or no family. But now the scratches are gone and he has already made himself helpful, pleasant, embraced as a family member by Cassius and Cassia, even, judging by Cassia's behaviour, a possible source of romantic interest. This last thought makes me feel sick. I am not falling for Rullus' act, for his helpfulness and bright smiles. Beneath them is a man whose eyes slide to where they are not wanted, who takes what he wants, violently and in the darkness, while smiling in the daylight.

I sit on the arena floor, loaded with sadness and fear, trying to think what to do.

"I need these Sirens sorting out, Althea, can I leave it with you?"

Marcus' head is poking out of a trapdoor.

"Yes," I say. "Marcus?"

"Got to run. Need to see Bestia about these bears he promised, he sent a note saying they'll be late, I need a replacement. You alright with the Sirens?"

"Yes," I say. When he has gone I sit for a few moments in the empty arena, the vast space blurred by my tears. Then I get to my feet.

I MAKE ENQUIRIES, WHICH LEAD ME, unexpectedly, to gladiatorial owner Labeo.

"I have just the thing. The *very* best. I won't even spoil the surprise. Just visit the Baths of Nero early in the morning, ask for the swimmers and see what you think. I promise you'll be delighted." He beams, adjusting a gold chain round his neck, the latest addition to his ostentatious jewellery collection.

"I didn't know you provided show swimmers," I say.

"I provide *spectacle*," says Labeo enthusiastically. "Which is, after all, what the Games are, wouldn't you say?"

I nod. Labeo certainly knows how to put on a show, though his enthusiasm for the unusual sometimes borders on the obscene. I can only hope that's not the case in this instance.

I set off the next morning in the opposite direction to Marcus, heading north past the heavily damaged Theatre of Pompey to the Baths of Nero, which managed to escape the fire. They stand in a wasteland of construction sites and still-scorched buildings, including the Julia Saepta. The outer walls of the baths are soot-stained but they are still operational. We've used them occasionally since the fire as the Baths of Agrippa that used to be our local were ruined. I've never been to the baths at this time of the morning; it feels empty, only slaves here and there, cleaning for the day ahead.

"You want the Daughters of Thetis," says a male slave when I describe who I'm looking for. "They'll be practising in the main pool. Through there." He gets back to his work, busy mopping the changing rooms.

It's odd being fully dressed at the baths. I remove my shoes and make my way through to the main large pool.

I peer into the room. The pool is empty, the water faintly rippling, perhaps from a breeze. I am about to turn away, return to the man and tell him he was wrong, there are no women in here.

But from beneath the rippled surface, a pair of legs suddenly appear, bolt upright, as though their owner is standing on their head at the bottom of the pool. And behind them are another pair, and then another and another, until there are twelve pairs of legs, now slowly, very slowly, opening wide until they are almost level with the water level. And then, as suddenly as they appeared, all the legs fold, crumple into the depths to be replaced by twelve heads. I step back, startled. In the pool are twelve women, now making their way to the side and climbing out. They are all wearing underwear and breastbands in a vivid red. Most of the women head away, towards the changing room, but one strides towards me. Her dripping wet hair falls as far as her waist in tiny braids like the Egyptians wear, but much longer, her skin is a rich dark brown, beaded all over with glistening water, as though inset with gemstones.

"I don't have room on my team for another girl just now," she says. "I can send you to another team, if you're looking for one." She is very tall, she might almost stand eye-to-eye with Marcus.

"I'm not here to join up," I say.

"Why are you here, then?"

"I wanted to hire you," I say. "That is, your team. Labeo said I should talk to you."

"For what?"

"A naumachia at the Flavian Amphitheatre."

"We don't do fighting. I told Labeo."

"We don't want fighting for this show," I say. "We want to stage Odysseus and the Sirens."

She gives a half-snort. "We don't sing."

"You don't need to. The singers and musicians will take care of that part. What I need from your team is a display of your swimming, after which Odysseus' ship will sail in and you'll re-enact his meeting with the Sirens."

"We don't do nudity."

I look at her red costume. "So I see."

"Gives people the wrong idea when we do private events."

I nod.

She thinks for a minute. "No funny business?"

I think of Fausta. This was a phrase she used to use and there's something in the woman's fierceness that reminds me a little of her, though she's younger.

I shake my head. "No funny business from our side. You'll have to manage Labeo yourself."

"I already do that." She holds her hand out, like a man. I take it. Her grip is strong.

"My name is Althea," I say. "Althea Aquillius."

"Vita." Her lack of a family name tells me she is a slave, owned by Labeo.

"I'm pleased to meet you, Vita," I say. "Your team are extraordinary. How long can you stay under the water for?"

She gives me a wide grin, suddenly less fierce. "A lot longer than most people."

"I've never seen anyone hold their breath for more than a quick ducking," I say.

"Most people can hold their breath for the count of thirty, maybe up to seventy. After that they struggle unless they've been trained. The best of us can hold our breath for over one hundred and fifty counts."

"That sounds like a long time not to breathe," I say.

"Have you tried?"

"I can't swim."

"It's not that hard to learn," she says. "But it's easier if you've been taught as a child, like most things."

"Were you?"

"I could swim like a dog paddles as a little child," she says. "The rest I learnt after seeing a troupe perform for Nero."

"You belonged to Nero?"

"I was one of his slaves. I was only a child, but he liked me because I had a good memory and could recite poetry at his events."

"What was he like?"

"He should have been born to an acting family," she says. "He'd have been happier and better off with less power and a lot more performing in his life. He got obsessed with it. The senators were appalled."

"And you saw a troupe of swimmers?"

"Yes, they came and performed for him once. After that I used to sneak into his private bath area at night and practise holding my breath and standing on my head in the pool. When he died there was chaos in the palace. Four emperors in one year. Slaves running off and all sorts, no-one managing the place properly, barely knew how many slaves they even had. I went to the troupe and begged them to buy me. Nero wouldn't have allowed it, but when Vespasian became emperor, he said there were too many slaves hanging around the palace with nothing to do and sold a bunch of us off. I thank the gods he was a plain-living man."

"And you stayed with that troupe?"

"No. They liked to perform at private functions and then pimp any of us out to the clients, if they fancied a night with a water-nymph." Her lip curls. "I heard about Labeo, how he liked to have unusual elements in his offering, went to him when I was fifteen and suggested he buy me and I'd set up a water troupe for him, train the girls myself. He could see the attraction for his wealthier clients with their own pools, for their dinner parties. We perform as the Daughters of Thetis and Labeo pimps out some of the girls who are willing to earn a little extra, but he knows I won't behave myself with the clients, so he leaves me out of it. Makes it harder to save up for my freedom, but it's not worth it. I've been whored out enough for one lifetime."

I nod, impressed that a slave child found a way to become a skilled performer and claw her way out of prostitution, at least, by coming to some sort of arrangement with Labeo, who can't be easy to manage. "I'll see you at the amphitheatre then, so you can see the space and what we'll need from your troupe."

She nods and walks away without further niceties.

I walk slowly back towards the insula, thinking about Vita and her life. I think of the sorceress and whether Vita's certainty of buying her freedom one day meets her criteria for a desire. I imagine it does. Again, I turn over in my mind what my own desires might be and again, come up with nothing, or at least nothing that seems as important as what other people are striving for. Vita for her freedom, Fabia to be respected by the gladiators as a surgeon, like her father. Even Cassia, whose request was dismissed by the sorceress, seems to me to be clear in what she wants to do. At any rate, she is clearer than I. What do I dream of, wish for? My freedom has already been granted, and yet it has left me confused. I would like to be rid of Rullus, but I cannot think how to do that. I feel I can no longer speak about what happened, that I lost my moment, now lack the confidence to accuse him with no evidence, with the question hovering on everybody's lips; why did I not speak before now? How do free people find the courage to live their lives and make choices? Perhaps the life of a free person is confusing. A slave has no need to ponder their desires, for they will not be fulfilled. They do not have the opportunities to make choices, all choices are made on their behalf, by their owners. I could say I chose to join Marcus in running the amphitheatre, but the truth is that I was given to him, an expensive gift, like a good working mule or an obedient and successful hunting dog. A slave woman cannot even choose how to dress, for her mistress will have a say in it.

Perhaps, I think, I should start with some small decisions, I should make myself braver in small ways. If a slave woman cannot even choose how to dress, then as a freedwoman I could choose what to wear. I have one nice set of a tunic and hair wrap that Maria gifted me, as well as one more set I bought myself, still decent but plain. But I have worn both of them a lot, having little else to wear. I have two pale blue tunics, from my days as a slave, but I dislike wearing them, even though the cloth is still good. They remind me of the time before my freedom.

The popina is closed up for the night and Maria says that Cassius has taken Rullus out drinking. I tell Cassia that I want to make new clothes, half-hoping that finally having some time with her will let me know what may happen with Rullus. She takes me to her apartment to show me her own clothes, pulling them out of the chest in which she keeps them. As a beloved only child, Cassia has accumulated more clothes than most women in this neighbourhood, five long tunics as well as accessories: belts of leather and braided wool, three pairs of shoes, plenty of hair ribbons and a handful of hair wraps, not the large and heavy palla of a married woman, but lighter pieces with which to tie up her unruly curls.

"This was my mother's," she says, pulling out a golden-orange bridal veil, carefully folded away at the bottom of her chest. "Father said I should keep it for when I marry."

"It's lovely," I say, touching it. Someone, perhaps Cassia's mother or even grandmother, embroidered tiny flowers round the edge, in the same colour, so that they can only be seen as the light falls on the veil when it moves, a tiny, delicate touch.

"How good is your embroidery?" she asks me. "If it's good, you can just buy plain cloth and make it much prettier. I can show you how to weave trims and a belt too. And we can refresh the tunics from when you were a slave, then they won't remind you of that time."

"How are you getting on with Rullus?" I ask tentatively. I wonder if I should break my silence now, while the two of us are alone together.

She smiles. "Well enough. Father is happy to have a man about the place. And he's good-natured and helpful."

Hope rises in me. Perhaps my fears about a possible romance are just that. Cassia does not sound as if she is falling in love and Rullus has not attempted to come near me again. Perhaps I am safe after all, I think hopefully. He must leave soon and then I will be safe. Perhaps.

At Cassia's insistence, I take the older tunics to the fullery and have them dyed, changing one to a dark blue and one to a violet. I have money for one more tunic and Cassia steers me towards brighter colours than I would have chosen if I were alone. I find a dusky pink wool but she shakes her head briskly and points to a springlike yellow linen for the summer heat. We buy two light linen hair wraps, one in a soft green, one a stronger blue. Cassia shows me how to braid different trims out of woollen strands that can be added to the neckline and hem of my tunics.

I decorate the dark blue tunic with a woven orange wool belt. To the violet, I attach a wide woven trim in a soft green and blue design, which I wear with my leather belt. They look so different I forget they used to be my slave livery. I go to the cobbler in our insula, too. He is more used to making shoes for soldiers, but he turns out a simple pair of red leather sandals at my request, which I like immensely.

"I never knew you were such an elegant lady," teases Fabia when she sees me. "Cassia tells me you've got whole chests of clothes."

"It's been fun," I admit. "I've never been able to dress how I please, I've always worn livery until I came to Virgin's Street, and there hasn't been much time to think about clothes, this past year."

We buy tiny shells and beads to sew along the edges of hair wraps and Cassia shakes her head at my lack of embroidery skills and teaches me better and neater stitches. She does not have a lot of spare time, for the popina is open most days and most hours, but when she snatches a little rest here and there and I am about, we sit in the shady courtyard together and add decorations to our clothing, twining flowers and leaves, bringing delicacy to the plain fabrics. I have missed her company and I'm grateful to have found a way of spending time with her that keeps me away from Rullus.

"Ah, Cassia, there you are." Rullus is standing in the gateway of the insula, beaming. "Sorry to drag you away from your friend. Need your help with the customers."

Cassia smiles back. "I'll leave this with you," she says to me, dropping her sewing next to me. She hurries past Rullus, turning left out of the gate, back to the popina. I lower my eyes, not wanting to meet Rullus' gaze in case he starts talking to me, take Cassia's hair wrap into my own lap and try to pick up where she left off.

But Rullus comes closer, his voice lower when he speaks so that his words can only be heard by me, not by any random inhabitants of the insula who might be close by. "Trying to make ourselves pretty, are we?"

I don't answer. I can see the dark shape of him standing over me, but I can smell him, too, the smell that makes me want to retch.

Now he squats down in front of me, even closer and his voice is just a whisper.

"I'll look out for you wearing your new pretty clothes then, and I'll know you're wanting some attention when you do. And we'll keep it just between us, shall we? Otherwise I might have to come and visit you one night in that roof hut of yours."

He stands up and walks away. I gather up my embroidery and shells into my sewing basket, crush the hair wraps into it and make my way, shaking, up the stairs and back to my hut.

I put away all my new clothes into the chest I have for my belongings and go back to wearing my ordinary clothes. When Fabia and Cassia ask what happened to the pretty new tunics and hair wraps, I shrug and say I'm keeping them for a special occasion.

I take to leaving the insula early without breakfast, arriving at work before everyone else. I go to the baths in the afternoons and linger longer than usual. I return late, although always before it gets dark. I stop at Cassia's only if I cannot see Rullus. If he is there, I eat a handful of olives with bread and cheese.

"You've lost weight," says Maria as I pass. "You look skinny."

I shrug, don't pause to gossip with her. "Too much work on."

"You still need to eat," she calls after me.

Even when I escape the fear of Rullus' presence in the insula, the thought of the naumachia hangs over us all at work, so that a heaviness seems to follow me no matter where I am or what I am doing. Every day that goes by is taking us closer to the day we have to flood the amphitheatre, which despite all our planning seems an impossible task, especially as we can't test it before the event. Even when I try not to think about it, small things will remind me, like the odd graffiti in the shape of a fish, etched onto a wall beside an ill-fitting door I pass every day on my way to the Forum and the amphitheatre. Most of the graffiti I see is obscene in nature, some of it is political, information about one candidate or another. Amongst it all the fish stands out: too simple in shape to be anything of a vulgar nature, no writing alongside it to explain its purpose, only two curved lines joining together to create a fish. Clearly it has some meaning, but I cannot fathom what it is, it only makes me think of water, which leads me back to the naumachia, round and round.

Marcus has gathered some of our team together, early in the morning before it gets too hot to think. Karbo sits holding one of the growing kittens, which is enjoying exploring the bright wider world beyond its dark under-arena home.

"We need more water-based stories. We've promised Odysseus and the Sirens to help the Aedile, and Althea's already found the swimmers to perform the Sirens. Other ideas?"

"Got a brilliant idea," Carpophorus starts.

Marcus looks doubtful. Carpophorus, a walking mass of muscle, is spectacular and well-loved as a bestiarius, but his ideas are not always to Marcus' taste. "Which is?"

"Pasiphae and the bull from the sea."

Marcus' brow furrows. "The conception of the Minotaur?"

"Absolutely. I've got a trained bull."

Marcus waits a moment. "Trained in what way?"

"It'll copulate with a woman, if you put it in the right position. The carpenters can build something to put the woman at the right level, a platform or whatever."

It's the sort of thing Labeo would come up with. Marcus catches my eye and I shake my head, disgusted. I can just imagine a man like Rullus taking pleasure in such a spectacle.

"I'll get back to you on that," says Marcus, a sigh escaping him. "Anyone else?"

"Horses," says Karbo. "King Neptune arriving in his chariot through the water."

"Very nice," approves Marcus and I jot it down. "We'll visit the racing stables, see what they can do for us. The Blues might want to be involved; their livery will be a nice connection to the water theme."

"Dido and Aeneas?" I offer.

Marcus narrows his eyes. "A story about a Roman ruler bidding farewell to his lover, a foreign queen, before sailing home, leaving her to kill herself? Is that supposed to be a hint to them both?"

"Too heavy-handed?"

Marcus shrugs. "Well, Odysseus and the Sirens is probably a bit subtle," he says. "The Aedile sounds like he wants us to hammer the message home, so perhaps we should add Dido and Aeneas. Titus liked being compared to Aeneas at the inaugural ceremony, so we can keep the theme going. It'll do for now."

When Vita arrives to look round, it is Marcus who sees her first and goes to meet her, I see her extend her hand in her trademark greeting, and Marcus, without hesitating, shakes it. I wonder if he, too, is reminded of Fausta. Vita nods to me as they pass; today she is dressed in a long green tunic with a strikingly bold orange geometric pattern as its trim, made up of tiny beads, something far brighter and bolder than a slave would normally wear or indeed be able to afford, but then she is one of Labeo's best performers and Labeo would never let sartorial hierarchy get in the way of putting on a good show. Vita, in her bright colours and with her eye-catching hair, is a walking advertisement for his services. Marcus spends over an hour showing her the dimensions of the floor, letting her try out various audience sightlines and finally escorting her below the arena floor so that she can see how we manage many of the Games backstage.

"Interesting," she says, emerging through one of the lift trapdoors.

"Has Marcus explained to you how it will work?"

"Yes," she says. "Broadly. But I'll have to come back soon to better understand some of the dimensions of your props. The ships are the most important thing. It depends how tall they are, whether there is space for us to dive, as well as how we get on board in the first place. Maybe concealed rope ladders."

I nod. "I'm sure it'll be very impressive," I say.

"Marcus says he wants me to play the part of Dido, too," she says. "Could you not get a woman who looks like the Jewish Queen?"

"Is it that obvious?"

She shrugs and laughs. "Everyone knows the Senate wants to get rid of Berenice. Stands to reason they'd ask you to throw in a few hints here and there, they've been doing the same at half the theatres in Rome. They'd be better off just saying it to his face."

Now that I'm sharing a room with Karbo, I become aware of his nightmares when I wake from mine. Barely a night goes by when I do not hear him whimper in his sleep, and sometimes he will wake, screaming. In the time I have known him, he has slept first in our courtyard, then in Fausta's room before she died. Since then, he has mostly slept in Maria's room as she had a little extra space while the baker's family took in Marcus and me, and so it is only now that I become aware of how disturbed his nights are. When he whimpers, I reach out sleepily and hold his hand. The whimpers die away into silence and I hope for his dreams to take on a more pleasant aspect. But instead he sometimes screams, his eyes open but staring into nothing as though he sees something I do not, or cannot leave his dreams behind.

"How did you become a slave?" I ask one day, when we have eaten our evening meal on the rooftop and the light is fading.

"Can't remember," he says.

"I used to be a slave," I say, hoping to entice him into confiding in me by reminding him of this fact.

"Years ago," he says, dismissively.

"No," I say, surprised that he does not know my recent history. "I was only set free a few months before I met you."

Now I have his attention. "By Marcus?"

"Yes, after Pompeii... Afterwards."

"Why?"

"We went back to Pompeii," I say slowly. It is not something I often talk about. "We went back a few days afterwards, Marcus was searching for his wife Livia and son Amantius."

"What was it like?"

"Like the entrance to Hades," I say. "Everything was grey. Everything. You could barely see the city for the ashes, but Marcus was desperate to find his home. He dug for hours, and there was nothing I could do to help him. He set me free, there, in all the ashes, amid that devastation. He wanted rid of me," I add, trying to be honest. "I think he wanted to die, and I was only a burden to him."

"You came back to Rome, though."

"That was Fausta's doing," I say and his face changes at the mention of her name, the pain of her death still fresh. "She knew it was the only way for us all to survive. Marcus had a job here, he could earn money, she and I could be his assistants and she thought if he stayed alive long enough, he wouldn't try to..."

"You didn't have to stay," says Karbo. "If he'd set you free."

"I had nowhere else to go," I say. "I didn't know anyone; I would have been alone in the world." I think for a moment. "As you were, before we found you," I add, trying to bring the conversation back round to him again.

"Before Maria caught me," he says.

I laugh. "You had no chance against her."

He grins.

"But before she caught you," I say, persevering. "Where were you living, how were you getting fed?"

"Slept anywhere quiet. Slept in the amphitheatre plenty of times, but not under the arena." He looks away. "There were some bad people down there."

"I'm sorry," I say, touching his hand. "How come Maria saw you often?"

"Found the insula, some of the street kids talked about it, Julia didn't throw us out like other people, looked the other way when we slept in the courtyard overnight, it was safer than most places. The gateway was never locked. The bakery gave out stale bread sometimes. Cassia would give you a bowl of soup if you asked. It was worth hanging around here."

"But before that?"

"I don't remember."

I think of my own childhood before I became a slave, how it comes back to me only in small snatches, perhaps all that I can bear to remember, or all that has been branded into me too deeply to forget. Tiny memories of what was once my home on the Greek island of Kefalonia, *my mother singing, washing hanging out, flapping in the breeze. The sound of the waves on the beach of my tiny island home.* Happy thoughts, yet so few of them left, so much forgotten with the years. And the memories I wish I could forget, *the red of my mother's death, my father on his knees before his new master, begging for me, too, to be enslaved, if he could only keep me by his side.* I don't want to press Karbo too far, probably his memories are like mine, tiny snatches he wishes were more, others he wishes would go away entirely, yet never will.

"Do you remember your parents?"

He shakes his head. "Not my father, don't know who he was."

"Your mother?"

"A slave."

I don't push him further. We sit in the gathering darkness and then his voice comes, his face hidden. "They said I was old enough to be sold. She screamed."

I hold his hand in mine and feel the shaking of his body come through it. "Then they brought me to Rome."

"From where?"

"I don't know. Somewhere down south? I've forgotten the name."

I know what he is thinking. He can never go back. He can never find her again, even if she is still living.

"I'm glad we found you," I say.

"I miss Fausta," he says suddenly. "I thought I'd found a new mother. And then she died."

My tears rise so fast they are spilling over my cheeks before he's even finished the sentence. "I miss her too," I say. "She taught me everything."

"I liked her being on our shrine," he says in a very small voice, and I wonder if he, too, has felt the loss of Marcus, his hero, in this new division of our homes.

"I'll ask Balbus to make us a new figurine," I say. It's not much to offer, but it's all I can think of. "And you have me," I add. "I will look after you."

"Until you get married," he says.

"What?"

"One day. When you get married. A new husband won't want some runaway child hanging around you," he says.

I swallow at how practical his voice is, how certain he is of being left alone again, one day. I want to protest, but then again, I know he's telling the truth. No doubt one day I will get married, although I can't imagine it for now. And Karbo is right, no man will allow his bride to bring some unknown street child into a new marriage, with no binding ties between them of any kind. Silently, I pat Karbo's hand, then keep holding it even after he has fallen asleep.

I don't mention our conversation again, but I listen out more carefully for his whimpers in the night and hold his hand as long as I am awake. I speak with Balbus and he makes a copy of the tiny Fausta from Marcus' shrine, which I bring to Karbo for our own. He holds the miniature doll in his hands, one fingertip touching the messy black curls, then stroking the folds of the toga that had marked her out as a prostitute. He does not say thank you, but he places the doll with loving care on our shrine and glances towards it every night before he goes to bed, seeking comfort from it.

"I feel I should be more of a mother to him," I say to Cassia and Fabia one evening at the popina. "But I don't really know how."

"Three motherless girls," says Cassia sighing. "None of us are going to have much guidance in how to be a mother, are we? I suppose making clothes, keep him clean, teach him manners? At least you can teach him to read and write."

"I try," I say. "He gets bored too easily and runs off to play. Copying out his letters over and over again is hardly his idea of fun. His numbers aren't bad, he listens when we do the accounts."

"Ah, ladies, good evening."

It's Rullus. Fabia waves a cheery hello, Cassia smiles.

"We were talking about what makes a good mother," she tells Rullus.

Rullus pats Cassia's shoulder. "This one will make an excellent mother. So kindly. One day soon, eh?"

Cassia blushes and Fabia laughs. I force a smile onto my face but my stomach turns over at the idea that Rullus does seem to be courting Cassia – and worse, that she is pleased with his comments. I should say something but who will believe me, when Rullus is endlessly pleasant to everyone?

THERE'S A PREACHER IN THE Forum as I go to work most days, calling out to passers-by and addressing the small crowd that gathers in front of him. I pause to hear what he is saying.

"He is your Shepherd, your light in the darkness, son of God, come unto Him and pledge your lives to Him, for He will guide you and care for you in spirit, until His second coming, when He will set you free from the bonds that shackle you. And it will be soon, very soon, prepare yourselves for His glory."

"What about our own gods?" asks one man from the crowd.

The preacher shakes his head. "You do not need them any longer," he says, with certainty. "There is but one God, and His son, Jesus, will be your guide."

"Jews and their mad ideas," scoffs the man, entirely unconvinced. "It's all very well, you saying I should ignore the gods I've worshipped all my life, but what happens when I turn my back on them and they take offence? Eh? I wouldn't want to be the one to insult them. I've seen what they can do when they're upset. My cousin Bassus lost an eye after he offended Jupiter by not praying to him..."

"Can't I pray to your god *and* ours?" asks a woman.

"And what about the Emperor's father?" asks a man.

The preacher shakes his head, almost sadly. "There is only one God," he repeats. "The Emperor Vespasian is no god, he was a man like you and me, as is his son Titus. And the gods you have been raised with are merely false idols, with all too human characteristics. Do you think that a truly divine being concerns themselves with sex and beauty, as you believe Venus does? Do you think that God needs a messenger such as Mercury, when He can speak directly to you through His own son?"

I walk on. If the preacher is not careful, he will be arrested and charged with high treason for suggesting that Titus is not the son of a god, since Vespasian was deified after his death. Not to mention for blasphemy in speaking against the gods of Rome and for spreading dissent by encouraging the crowd to follow his lead and change their ways. And if he is arrested, he will end up in the amphitheatre, probably facing wild animals, crucifixion or a gladiatorial bout he has no chance of winning, should we need to stage a battle scene and not wish to lose a professional fighter. He would do better to keep his mouth shut and worship whomever he pleases, without drawing attention to himself or his religion. The justice system in Rome is mostly lenient in such matters, for Rome is full of people from all over the Empire, worshipping all manner of gods. So long as they publicly bow their heads and make some small effort at worshipping the gods of Rome, any other shortcomings of faith are generally overlooked. But deliberately public displays of blasphemy and treason are another matter.

I ASK ONE OF THE scenery painters for a favour, and he agrees, for Karbo is a favourite amongst the amphitheatre's crew. He spends a day off site, and I only shrug when Marcus asks where he is. I send Karbo on several errands that afternoon, delaying his return to the roof hut, and when he does come back, I tell him that we're having dinner with Julia to buy time.

"Carry this lamp," I say, when it's almost dark and time for bed.

"I don't need a lamp to get into bed," he says. "I can see enough to get upstairs."

"Just carry the lamp," I insist, picking up one of my own.

"What are you, an empress, that needs this many lamps to get to bed?" he asks, stomping noisily up the stairs ahead of me. But when he opens the door of the hut there is a satisfying gasp and I giggle.

"You never told me!" he says, eyes wide over his shoulder, before turning back to look at the walls.

The scenery painter has done a good job. Despite the small scale of the room, I could be back in Lucius' villa in Pompeii, with freshly painted frescoes on the walls, one racing team on each. Wheel spokes and the long legs of the horses appear to move in the flickering light of our lamps, the drivers' faces grimacing at the effort of guiding their teams to victory. The Blues, Karbo's favourite team, take up the largest image, on the wall right next to his bed, and as I doze off to sleep, I have to remind him to blow out the lamp and stop staring at it, afraid his passion will lead to another fire. The next day the scenery painter receives one of Karbo's enthusiastic hugs, nearly knocking him over.

"You made him very happy," I say. "Thank you."

"Anything for that one," says the man, pleased with the reaction to his work. "He'd make a good apprentice, if he had the paperwork. I suppose he's a slave, but you can't prove it either way, can you?"

I shake my head. He's right of course, it is something that I hadn't had time to think about before. If Karbo ran away from a slave trader, then legally he is still a slave, even though no one has come looking for him. And being a slave will shackle him forever to an inferior life, unable to make his own choices or even pursue chances such as apprenticeships, should anyone be willing to offer him one. I wonder what Fausta would do in my shoes, and wish she were here to guide me. I remember the day she insisted that Marcus repeat his manumission of me in front of a lawyer, so that I would have the paperwork to prove I was no longer a slave, the little freedwoman's cap in a fresh green wool she had ready for him to give me. She knew full well the importance of these actions, the difference they would make in my life and the choices I would have as a result. I take down her tiny figurine from our shrine and turn it in my hands. Fausta would have known what to do. For starters, she would have punched Rullus in the face. A few tears fall onto the black curls that top her little head. That night I stay awake long after Karbo has fallen asleep.

FOLLOWING CASSIA'S ADVICE, IN THE quiet moments before or after shows I try to groom Karbo a little. His hair was clipped short earlier in the year to keep him cool, but it's grown quickly, and he won't let me cut it again. I use the comb Myrtis gave me before she died, with her name carved into it, but his hair is impossible to comb through; every day it seems to have more tangles, despite my best efforts. If I can pin him down for long enough, it stands out like a lion's mane around his head, before swiftly tangling again as soon as he sleeps. It is Vita who comes to my rescue, watching me one day when I am trying and failing to manage it, the two of us sitting in the shade of one of the corridors after the crowds have left. She and two other members of her team have come to inspect the model ships, built half to three-quarter size for the naumachia. One has been wheeled out onto the sand so we can see how it will look, the other lies in sections in the darkness under the arena floor.

"When it grows long, you twist it into strands," she says, looking at Karbo, who is wriggling in my hands like an eel.

"Braids?" I ask, looking at her own hair.

She shakes her head. "His hair will just naturally take on the shape," she says. "Try it, you'll see."

I choose small sections and twist the hair under her guidance and sure enough, it quickly and easily forms little locks, which look like braids in the Egyptian style from a distance, it is only up close you can see they are not plaited at all but simply hold together by themselves. Karbo grows vain about them, I catch him twisting them ever tighter so that they will fall just so, quickly reaching his shoulders. The other children in our block try to imitate him, but their own curls are too loose to hold the shape. A few of the girls have their hair plaited into tiny plaits like Vita for a while, pleased with the novelty of it. I find them drawing sooty fingers across their eyelids, trying to complete the Egyptian look, although they give the impression they have been in a fight and received a black eye rather than achieving the exotic elegance they were trying to emulate.

THE SHOW-SHIPS ARE COMING TOGETHER, made by the same carpenters who make real ships. Flat-bottomed and half the usual size, they are still impressive. Once they have been built, our painters descend on them, painting them a bold red and adding extra touches such as shining copper fittings and symbols on the prows such as giant eyes. These are not practical ships that must face storms, they must glitter and shine in sunlight and torchlight, draw the attention of the crowd and leave plenty of room for the men on board to do battle across the gap between two ships. Even their sails are impressive, not just plain white but painted with motifs of warriors to remind the audience of the Trojan War that Odysseus has just left behind him. The only practical element is the wheels fitted onto them, so that they can be pushed around like carts when there is no water on which to float. When we go to inspect them, Karbo spends his time down at the docks jumping off and on them, calling out naval orders to an invisible team of sailors, until I drag him home.

"Will they really float?" he asks.

"They had better do," I say. "If anything about this show doesn't work, it'll be our team that gets in trouble."

Neptune's Chariot

It's the end of August and as promised, now that the insula has been refurbished, Julia has an apartment available for Fabia and her father, Fabius, on the middle floor. I am pleased to have Fabia's company more often. But Fabia moving in has an unexpected effect, which is that I see Marcus even less. We no longer share a roof hut, but we had often eaten our morning and evening meals together, as well as spending the days at the amphitheatre, working closely together. But the amphitheatre team has grown larger, meaning that Marcus is often somewhere else in the vast building, or, if he is briefing the team on what the next day's spectacle will hold, we are a big group, and much of my time is taken up making notes or checking lists, even though Marcus always listens to what I have to say. Now that his old friend Fabius has moved into our building, Marcus has a companion for his evenings, and the two of them often take their meals together, either at Cassia's or further afield. The nights when they go out, I am nervous. I touch my hut's lock more than once and listen out for footsteps. When they return, they will often have an evening drink or two in our courtyard, and I hear them late into the night telling old stories of their time in the army together, or friends they had in common. At least then I know he is nearby. I still see Marcus in the mornings, for breakfast, but he is not a naturally gregarious person when he has just awoken, and frequently all I hear from him is the odd grunt in reply to anything one of us might ask or comment on.

"I miss talking to Marcus," I venture one day in an unguarded moment to Maria, when I have joined her in the courtyard. "I spent so much time with him this past year and now I barely see him."

"Men prefer talking to other men," says Maria unsympathetically. "They don't understand womenfolk."

I don't argue with her, for she has stubborn views on such things, but I disagree. I had grown close to Marcus, I felt as though the two of us were a partnership within the wider amphitheatre backstage team, especially after we lost Fausta and we were the only survivors from Pompeii of our acquaintance, the only two who had been back there, and seen what had become of it. It was a shared bond, and now it has gone. Sometimes, I hear a Pompeiian accent in the street and my head turns fast, seeking out the familiar physiognomy of the city's inhabitants. Sometimes I find myself smiling at complete strangers, who look back at me in surprise, not knowing that I was there, in the lost city, days before its demise. Once or twice, I have spoken with such people, and their eyes fill with tears when they think of it, in grief at having lost many of their friends and family members, but also with guilt at having, somehow, survived, only by the merest of chances, a fishing trip, a visit to family elsewhere, service in the army away from home. Some loudly and frequently give thanks to the gods for having saved them, others only mumble something about how other, better people than they should have been saved. All of them have haunted eyes when they speak of Pompeii, nothing I nor anyone else can say will ever take away that look.

"We should eat together one evening," I say to Marcus, trying to secure his company. He agrees, but somehow one evening and then another is not suitable, for Fabia likes to chat with me and Fabius wants to explore more of Rome. Having not been here for many years, he has old friends to visit, many of whom also know Marcus, and so the days and weeks drift by and I see Marcus less and less. Karbo misses him too, he trails around after Marcus more than usual at work, eager for his attention, though mostly this only results in extra errands, which he undertakes at speed, returning to Marcus' side as soon as possible.

MARCUS SPENDS A GREAT DEAL of time cross-questioning Merula, still concerned about the flooding and whether the pitch coating will suffice. There is no true way of testing the idea beforehand, but he has a tiny amphitheatre built in wood by one of our carpenters, coats it in pitch and then spends time pouring water into it and timing how long it takes to drain out. When he stops messing with it Karbo takes it as his own, dragging it all the way home. He pours sand into the arena, then makes little gladiators out of sticks and puts on miniature Games of his own with the other children in our insula. Merula seems confident enough in his plans, though, so I leave Marcus to worry about it and instead, after much nagging from Karbo, agree to go to the racing stables with Celer as our guide, to try and convince some of the racing teams to take part in our naumachia. The stables are to the north-west of Virgin's Street, laid out close to the Tiber. There are four teams, each beloved to the brink of obsession by their fans, all of whom pledge a lifetime's loyalty to their own faction.

"Celer used to drive for the Blues," gabbles Karbo, so overexcited by the visit that it is all he can do to stay quiet. "Who would you drive for, Althea, if you could drive for one of the teams?"

"I'm not a man," I say.

"Well, who do you support then? The Blues? Reds? Whites? Greens?"

"I'm not really sure," I say, distracted by the vast stable yard into which we have just entered. The colour blue is everywhere, leaving no doubt as to which team is based here. Horses poke their heads out from their stable doors, their names written in bold blue above each doorway, each name known to their supporters as though they were members of their own family.

"How can you not *know*? Blues forever!" yelps Karbo and several of the horses, startled, jerk their heads up.

"Shush now, or you'll frighten them," says Celer gently, his own voice kept low and steady. "Most of them are very highly strung, one loud noise and they'll be off. Speak softly when you're around the stables."

"Sorry," Karbo whispers. "Can I touch them?"

"Certainly, but remember to approach them slowly, speak softly, and watch out for the dappled one, he bites."

"What's his name?" asks Karbo, instantly drawn to the troublemaker.

"Swiftfoot. And he is. One of the best horses in years, but there isn't a stable hand without a scar from him in this yard. They only put up with him because he's so fast. Stay well away."

Karbo chooses the horse right next to Swiftfoot, a black beast, who accepts his caresses in a pleasant enough manner. Karbo strokes it absentmindedly, his eyes fixed on Swiftfoot, who rolls his eyes and stamps his feet in a menacing manner, disliking the smell of unfamiliar visitors.

"He's so beautiful," says Karbo dreamily.

"Not when you're bleeding," says Celer. "Now let's find someone in charge."

We find the stables manager, who agrees he will speak with the owner of the Blues and ask for one of their best quadriga chariots and its driver, along with four fine horses, to take part in the naumachia.

"Will the horses run through water?" I ask.

"Don't know about that," says the stables manager, considering. "Might need a bit of training first. They're used to water being thrown at them to cool them down, so they wouldn't mind that, but they're not much used to their hooves and legs being in water. Are you having the other teams?"

"We thought your livery would go better with the water," I say. "So we were going to use you for the main event, dress up your driver as King Neptune, that kind of thing. But we might end on a small race, nothing serious, one chariot from each team, just showing you all off as the water disappears and we turn the arena back to land."

"A race is never not serious," says the stables manager grinning. "The people are too besotted with their favourite faction to let it be anything but serious."

"I'll bear it in mind," I say. "No managing a win for a particular team then, just for the sake of storytelling?"

"Not if you want to live."

"Point taken."

"Any particular colours of the horses you want?"

"Not really, I'll leave that to you."

"Can we have Swiftfoot? *Please?*" Karbo, standing by my elbow, has his best pleading face on, all wide eyes and parted lips.

"You don't want him, he's vicious. We're only keeping him because he's the fastest. You'd never see his top speed, you don't have the space for it, so it would be a waste."

"He let me stroke him," says Karbo.

"You were told not to go near him!" I say, appalled.

"But he let me," says Karbo. "Watch."

"Karbo! Come back here!"

But he has already hurried back to Swiftfoot, who stamps his feet again but, astonishingly, does indeed allow Karbo to touch him, stroking down the front of his face, ending on his upper lip, while I cringe in fear that Karbo is about to be bitten.

"Impressive," says the manager, looking surprised. "Never seen anyone stroke him. Perhaps the lad has an affinity for horses. Worked with them before?"

"Get back here," I hiss, and to my relief Karbo makes his way back over to me. "*Have* you ever worked with horses before?" I ask, but Karbo only shakes his head. "Well you're not about to work with that horse now," I finish. "We'll take whichever horses are most amenable to being trained to something new," I say. "I can't have them skittish around the water."

"We could take a few of them down to the river," says Celer. "Try them out in the shallows, see what they make of it if they've not been in water before, pick out the ones that seem steady."

The manager nods. "Leave that with you then," he says. "Choose a few and take them down there, test them out and let me know which four you want."

"No time like the present," says Celer, as we make our way down to the river's edge, each of us leading two horses. He's given me the most docile, but it still makes me nervous to be leading racehorses about as though they were pets, rather than highly strung beasts who will startle at the slightest noise and then bolt as though a race has begun, with no hope whatsoever of holding them back. Celer, having worked with horses all his life, is entirely at ease and so, I note, is Karbo, who is murmuring comforting noises to the two horses he is leading, leaning against one a little as though they are friends when we have to pause to let a cart roll by. Looking at him I wonder whether he ever has had dealings with horses, perhaps before he can remember, as a small child, to be so comfortable with them.

Of the six horses, only one is truly uncomfortable with the water, stepping back and flattening its ears in a worrying way. Another is cautious, but does not refuse. The rest seem happy enough, perhaps they find the water cooling on a hot day. They drink a little and then, encouraged by our confidence, trot happily enough a few paces in either direction with the water lapping as far as their knees.

"Not bad at all," says Celer happily as we lead the horses back to the Blues' stables. "Looks like we have our four and one to spare. King Neptune's chariot is ready. We can come back to choose more of them for the other chariots. The other stables might give a chariot each, if you're going to have them race."

"Goodbye, Swiftfoot," murmurs Karbo, pulling away from my restraining hand for one last caress.

"You really are the most disobedient child," I say, still relieved to have escaped a bloody incident involving horse teeth and a skinny child's arm. "Let's go and let Marcus know that we have our King Neptune."

I try to slip past the popina on my way home, but Fabia is there and spots me, waves me over. I approach with reluctance. Rullus is there with Cassia, both serving customers at the busy counter.

"Never see you these days," says Cassia over her shoulder as she pours wine with one hand and stirs a stew with the other.

"You know how it is," I say vaguely.

"Too much work for a good woman," says Rullus. "You should be married and have your husband look after you, then you could stay at home more."

"Oh, is married life so easy?" asks Cassia.

"With the right husband," says Rullus, offering her a broad smile, then ducking through the door into the storeroom at the back of the popina.

Fabia laughs. "Considering it?" she asks Cassia.

I hold my breath.

Cassia shrugs. "Might do. He's a good enough man."

"Good enough? How romantic," says Fabia.

Cassia laughs. "Marriage doesn't have to be all romance," she says practically. "A man who works hard in the family business and is pleasant is a good find. Father dotes on him, Rullus barely lets him lift a finger anymore."

"I'm going indoors," I say. I want to cry at the idea that Cassia is seriously considering Rullus as a husband, that she is so level-headed about it. It makes it feel as though a marriage might really happen and then what? Rullus will settle into the insula for the rest of his life and mine? I will have to spend all of my life, if I wish to stay here, with my head down and my feet quick, always ready to run or hide from him? I'm so caught up in these thoughts I barely hear Fabia, then realise she is standing by my side, tugging at me to get my attention.

"I can't spend the evening with you like I promised. I've been called by one of the gladiators."

"Really?" I ask.

"Oh, not for himself," says Fabia wearily. "For his woman. She's pregnant, the baby's due any day now and he's fretting. It's never the man I'm called for, I might as well resign myself to it."

"The sorceress said your moment would come," I remind her.

"I'm not sure I believe her," says Fabia and she waves me farewell, setting off towards her appointment. I watch her go and wish I could think of an excuse to go with her, to keep someone by my side at all times.

We've spent weeks discussing whether the water for the naumachia should gently trickle in from an unseen source or whether we should use some sort of waterfall effect, but the next morning I become aware that Merula has stopped listening to me. "Who is that?" he asks.

I look over my shoulder. Vita and her team are pacing across the sand, Vita is explaining something to Marcus, gesturing at the imperial box and the top seats, probably something about the sightlines. Her tiny braids are finished with red beads today, swaying around her waist as she strides back and forth.

"That's the swimming team from Labeo. The Daughters of Thetis, they call themselves. They're playing the Sirens in the show."

Merula is still staring. "I meant the woman next to Marcus."

"That's Vita, she's their leader."

Vita shakes her head at something Marcus has just said and grabs his hand, lifting it up in the air. I know she's trying to envision how high the ships will be above the swimmers, there's been a debate about whether they can easily climb aboard, allowing them to the dive off in spectacular fashion at the end of the sequence.

Merula's expression changes to crestfallen as he watches the exchange. "Is she Marcus'…" He trails off, his shoulders even more hunched together than usual, dark eyes sorrowful.

"Oh no," I say at once, but as I watch the two of them, I wonder whether Merula has spotted something I have not. Marcus has started laughing at something Vita has said. She shakes her head at him with a grin on her face and mock-pushes him away from her, before they both step close together again and look down at a diagram Marcus was busy drawing up last night, showing how he expects the sequence to take shape, the entrance and exit for Odysseus' ship, the point where the Sirens can appear. Their heads are almost touching. Something in me feels a little sad. Has Marcus developed fond feelings for Vita? It seems soon after losing Livia, but then he has been alone for almost a year. I like Vita, but the idea of Marcus having a woman in his life makes me feel even more distant from him.

"I am sorry," says Merula suddenly.

"What?"

"I didn't mean to suggest anything if you and Marcus…"

"Oh no," I say hastily. "There is nothing between us. Only –" and suddenly all the thoughts I have been keeping quiet in my head come spilling out. "We spent so much time together this past year and so much happened, we had become friends. And now I barely see him, what with the new roof huts and Fabius and…" I realise I was almost about to mention Rullus, whom Merula does not even know. I come to an awkward stop. "Well, anyway, it just seems as though I hardly see him, or even know what he's thinking about. I mean if he were…" I gestured awkwardly towards Marcus and Vita, "I wouldn't know. And I would have done, before."

Merula nods his head. "I wasn't sure…" He trails off, as incoherent as I am. But his eyes stay on Vita and more than once he loses his train of thought, clearly smitten.

"Can Karbo swim?" asks Marcus, as our working day ends.

"I don't think so," I say.

"Meeting Vita made me think of it," says Marcus. "He should be taught. I'll teach him. Can you swim?"

I shake my head.

"Shall I teach you at the same time?"

"I don't – no," I say, confused by the unexpected offer.

"Well, I'll teach the boy anyway. Tell me if you change your mind," says Marcus. "I'm done for the day. See you tomorrow."

"Yes. Goodbye," I manage. I stand for a moment, uncertain whether to call after him. I'm pleased Karbo will learn to swim, it's a good skill to have. Perhaps I should have said yes, too. I open my mouth, but Marcus has already disappeared through one of the arches, heading to the baths and it's too late. I'll tell him another day. It might mean I see a bit more of him.

"Your aquarius been trying to buy my star performer, eh?"

I look up from my notes on the gladiators that I need Labeo to provide. "I don't know what you're talking about, Labeo. Merula tried to buy Alyssa?"

"Not Alyssa. Vita."

I think back to Merula's face when he saw Vita, his awkward questions about her. "And has he bought her?"

Labeo laughs. "Can't afford her. He went as high as he could, but Vita's not for sale, not at any ordinary price. She may be a nuisance, but she can perform and she can train other girls too, so she's worth a lot more than just the price of a slave girl. I mean, I can see why he wanted to buy her, that's the kind of slave you want in your bed, isn't it? Although having said that, he doesn't know what a troublemaker she is in that department." He twists a gold ring on one of his fingers, an anxious gesture.

"Alright," I say, disliking Labeo's gossiping, knowing he's going to share more salacious details than I want to hear. "I need a fight between dwarfs and giants for one of the myths we're putting on. If we use your dwarfs as ordinary men in the story, it'll make the giants look even bigger."

"Absolutely," says Labeo, distracted at the thought of hiring out a large group of his men.

When I next see Vita, though, I can't help asking about what happened. Her face turns dark with annoyance.

"He only tried to buy me so he can keep me in his bed," she all but spits, "just like they all do. I won't be someone's whore. I'd rather stay as Labeo's slave than that. At least we have an agreement. And he values what I can do, how I can train up other slaves to perform in the water."

"To be fair to him, I think Merula might have a soft spot for you," I say.

"I'm not taking that risk," she says. Her face turns thoughtful. "And anyway, there might be something else I can work towards," she adds.

"What?"

"Can't say yet."

I don't press her but when I see her talking with Marcus, heads together as though they are already the best of friends, I wonder whether Merula was right to ask if there is something between them, if his bid to buy her was a pre-emptive way of getting rid of Marcus as a possible rival. And I feel sad again that Marcus isn't confiding in me, that I have no idea whether he has an interest in Vita, whether his heart is ready to open up again after losing Livia.

"Why were you trying to buy Vita?" I ask Merula. He's kneeling in our under-arena space, measuring the flow of water in one of our drains, adding to his complex calculations. His pale skin flushes scarlet and he stands up suddenly, crossing his feet again, awkward.

"To set her free," he mumbles.

"What?"

"I wanted to set her free."

"Why?"

He swallows. "I thought if she were free..."

"Yes?"

"I might marry her."

I stare at him. "You could just have bought her as a slave and had her," I point out.

He shakes his head hurriedly. "No, I – I wanted her to be free to choose..." he trails off again.

I feel sorry for him. So confident when he talks about water, so certain and full of ideas. And then he turns into a stuttering wreck over Vita, full of fantasies that she might choose him if he were to set her free, like some sort of story from the old legends about a love affair between a poor fisherman and a water-nymph.

"Any-anyway," he says, rocking on his clumsily-placed feet. "She was beyond my means. So..."

"I'm sorry," I say, and I mean it. I can't really see the two of them as a match, but Merula is evidently a good-hearted, if hopelessly romantic, man and Vita would have had little to fear from him. I wonder whether Labeo, cunning as he is, really told Vita what Merula intended for her, or whether he implied to her that she would be kept enslaved and used for sex and nothing more, to discourage any interest on her part in encouraging Merula. Either way, it sounds as though Vita's price is too high, and so it's probably better to let the whole matter drop. Merula will just have to gaze upon Vita from afar.

THE FOUNTAIN

Now that the plasterwork and painting are finished, the new outdoor wooden staircase and balconies around the interior of our courtyard are quickly built and the carpenters finally depart. Julia is delighted, she goes about her days humming, filling new plant pots and placing them everywhere. As it's September already, many of her flowers will need to wait till next spring to bloom, still she prepares their planting grounds and places them where they will catch the most rays of sun. Maria takes up her customary place on the walkway balcony again, cushion tucked over the wooden railing, her breasts on top of her crossed arms, leaning on its softness, her place as guard dog rightfully restored.

"I've no idea what's been going on all this time," she says, ignoring the fact that she has spent all summer watching from her window or sitting in the courtyard, and can hardly have missed anything. "All sorts could be happening and no one the wiser. Has anyone even been keeping an eye on the builders? All they want to do is a quick job and finish, they've probably been cutting corners all over the place."

I laugh, look out from our spot on the new balcony overlooking the beautiful courtyard, the new fountain beneath us, almost ready for use, the bright clean paintwork everywhere. "They've done a fine job, Maria, I'm sure you kept an eye on them even without a balcony."

"Well, somebody had to," she says righteously. "I've had to wake early every day to make sure they're not shirking while everyone's still asleep."

The courtyard is being paved over with fresh cobbles, now that the plumbing is complete. The toilets are already working, made larger by taking over an old disused storage room. They smell a great deal fresher than they used to and now have seating for eight at a time, which makes a change and stops queues forming of a morning. We look forward to the day when the cobbles are complete, the courtyard strangely smooth to walk through compared to its old uneven surface.

Julia holds off the fountain being turned on until we've all come home to witness the great moment, the aquarius in charge of it huffing with impatience, but not daring to argue with an ex-Vestal Virgin, for fear of what Vesta might do to him if he is rude to her handmaiden.

"You can turn it on now," says Julia graciously, when we are all gathered in the courtyard.

The aquarius makes some adjustments to the plumbing in a corner of the courtyard. There's a gasp of air being pushed out of the pipes and then the carved stone face of a stern Neptune spouts water into a wide basin, first in gargling fits and starts, then settling into a smooth flow. Everyone applauds and those nearest the basin splash the others, so that the celebration of the new fountain quickly turns into a water fight, the children shrieking in delight and all but climbing into the basin.

Its installation makes collecting water quick and easy for everyone in the insula. This pleases the women and children above all, as they are usually the ones who must carry heavy amphorae or jugs back to rooms and apartments. The children spend the hottest part of each day splashing each other amidst gleeful yelps, occasionally someone yells at them to be quiet if they are interrupting afternoon naps. Marcus and Celer rig up an awning and Julia leaves a couple of benches out for anyone who wishes to rest under it. The courtyard has become a haven of perfumed shade and babbling water, as Julia fills it with ever more pots of plants and flowers, a far cry from the first time I saw it when it was a crumbling ruin of a space. It still feels homely though, it has none of the stiff elegance of a villa's atrium, rather an easy comfort which is good to come home to each day. A new gate has been fitted, one which actually swings on its hinges rather than drooping from them. It has a large bolt on it, but I notice that Julia still leaves the gate unbarred at night, so that anyone without a home can find a sheltered safe place to sleep. Sometimes, if I rise very early, I'll startle someone who has spent the night under the shelter of the wooden staircase, and I direct them towards Cassia, who is always ready with a ladle of her ever-simmering weekly soup and a piece of yesterday's bread to dip into it. I used to take them there myself, but I don't want to risk meeting Rullus in the half-light of dawn.

THE HEAT OF SUMMER RECEDES, settling into balmy warm days, with a welcome breeze, cooler nights and the odd thunderstorm here and there to break the dry spell. The first grapes arrive from the southern vineyards, and everyone enjoys their rich sweetness, the marketplaces have bunches piled high at every fruit stall, both red and white varieties.

Karbo spends every spare moment that he has with Celer, begging for stories of his days as a racing driver. He wants to know every detail, from how the horses and drivers are chosen and trained, to how the chariots are constructed and the races arranged. Knowing the dangers of the racetrack and that Celer, despite being a kindly man, is only alive today because he spent all his money on women and drank so much that he became a liability and ended his racing career early, I try to drag Karbo away, but it's difficult. He will accompany me to work and do all that is required of him, but as soon as a show is over he'll slip away and I'll find him back in our courtyard, where Celer likes to sit in the shade most afternoons with a jug of wine. Karbo will be sat at his feet, one question after another tumbling from his lips.

"And if a chariot overturns?"

He knows the answer already, anyone who's been to the races knows what happens, but he wants to hear it all again, in lavish and bloodthirsty detail.

Celer shakes his head sadly. "You have to cut yourself free of the reins that are tied to your waist," he says. "Or you'll be dragged behind the horses along the ground. They won't stop, they've been trained to keep going. If you don't cut yourself free quickly, you'll be dead in moments, no-one can withstand being pulled along the ground at that speed. Every driver carries a sharp knife and they have it blessed in the temple as often as possible."

"Did it ever happen to you?" asks Karbo, eyes wide.

Celer pulls up one side of his tunic, revealing scars running all the way down his thigh and calf. "Those scars run the length of my body," he says seriously. "And I was lucky it was only the once."

"What's the knife like?"

"I still have mine," says Celer. He takes a knife out of a fold in his tunic, turns it so Karbo can look at it, but pulls it away when he reaches out to touch it. "Too sharp, little one," he says. "I keep it sharp even to this day, out of respect. It can cut through a rope in one swipe. It saved my life. It never leaves my side, even now I no longer race."

"How long did it take to heal?"

"Many months. The skin is still tight, it pains me sometimes. I raced for one more year after that, but my fight was gone."

"Gone?"

"When you've been badly hurt, you stop thinking you are immortal. The young drivers who've never had a bad fall, they think they are gods, they think they will live forever and ever, that is why they can drive the horses at such speed. Once they have a bad fall, as I did, they realise they are not immortal after all. And the men who have families, you see them grow afraid too, scared to leave their wife and babies alone. They don't drive so fast anymore. It's a young man's game."

"Did you stop racing because you were afraid?"

"I started drinking too much to help soften the pain of healing, and then when I recovered and went back to the track, I drank more to numb the fear before a race, but you can't drive when you're drunk, you make mistakes. I lost too many races, made too many mistakes. My days were over and I had to stop before I died on the racetrack."

"You still drink too much," says Karbo.

"Karbo," I say. "Don't be rude."

"He's right though," says Celer, refilling his cup. "Can't blame the boy for speaking the truth."

"Why don't you stop?" asks Karbo.

"Harder than you'd think," says Celer. "I thought I'd stop when I left the stables. But that was a long time ago." He gulps from his cup. "You should get yourself an education instead of hanging around here with me listening to the old days. A chariot driver's lot is no life."

"But if you win…"

"If you win a lot of races, you'll make more money than you've ever seen in your life. Women will throw themselves at you. You'll be crowned with laurels by the

Emperor himself. You'll even buy your freedom, have your own slaves, live in a villa with every luxury. And then you'll die before you're twenty-five."

"But –"

"No buts. Go and learn your letters," says Celer, pulling himself to his feet and making his way somewhat unsteadily towards the stairs.

I TRY TO TEACH KARBO his letters. I give him one of my old tablets, freshly filled with wax, then have him copy the neat examples I show him. He is reluctant, bored with the slow nature of the task.

"No-one learns to write straightaway," I tell him. "It takes time and patience and a lot of repetition."

"Too much repetition," he says. "I can write all my letters."

"Not neat enough yet," I say, looking over his work. His writing looks like that of a much younger child. "Here's a fresh sheet of wax, copy out the writing one more time for today."

"What's the point?" he asks sullenly. "What do I need to read and write for?"

"So you will know what is going on and no-one will be able to fool you," I say. "You'll know what you're putting your name to, if you make a legal agreement. And if you wish, you could be a scribe. Scribes are paid better than labourers."

"That's a boring job," he says.

"Thank you very much."

"It's all right for a girl," he says. "Girls like to stay quiet and clean. I want a more exciting job."

"Such as?" I ask. I'm hoping he doesn't say gladiator, since he watches them all the time. It's not a respectable trade and it's a dangerous one. I want to keep him safe.

"Don't know," he mumbles. I think of his excitement at the stables and wonder whether he is thinking of the racing life, although he'd never dare say so to me. The racing drivers' lives are very short, even if glorious. Most of them die before they reach thirty, their death rate is far worse than the gladiators'.

"Well, whatever you want to do, if you can read and write you'll be better off," I say firmly. "And you can practise your numbers when we do the accounts tomorrow, work out the wages for the craftsmen. So sit there and copy out that page."

"Who are you to tell me what to do?" Karbo mutters. "You're not my mother," he adds, under his breath.

"Your mother would want you to be able to read and write, I can assure you," I say, a little hurt that he has thrown this truth in my face. "Get on with it," I add, more crossly than I had intended and Karbo bows his head to the work, his face one big scowl. He copies out the words poorly, then all but flings the tablet back at me and races off down one of the amphitheatre's corridors before I can make him do them again. I look down at the tablet and sigh, the words are barely legible. It will take many more lessons at this rate before he will have even a decent script, let alone the fine work of a scribe. To be fair, he does not seem to want to be a scribe, but someone with few prospects in life needs all the skills they can learn. The next day I make him sit through all the accounts, even though he yawns and twists in his seat like an eel, bored with the endless repetitive nature of this task too. But he makes a fair fist of copying out the numbers at least, so I praise him for that.

"I'm going to the baths," says Marcus, when we finish going through it all.

"I need to ask you for something first," I say. "Can you give me a minute? Karbo, you can head for the insula, I'll catch up with you."

Marcus raises his eyebrows when I explain my plan. "You're a woman," he says. "Even my say so as your patron and guardian won't be enough. You'd have to get permission from Titus himself."

My shoulders slump.

"You can ask," says Marcus. "Next time you see him. He liked you and he's fairly amiable."

"I hardly ever see him," I say. "I might have to wait months."

WE HAVE FIVE DAYS OF Games that try our patience to the limits while Merula's team waterproof the under-arena floor and walls, a job that should have been done well before the inauguration, had the architect not died. Running Games on a scale that the crowd expects without any access to our usual under-stage space leads to frayed tempers and hot words. On the first day our team has to dismantle all the animal pens and clear away vital elements such as Fabius' surgical area. We end up roping off one of the corridors so that we have at least a small storage area, closing three entrances to the seating, which makes for delays and more management than usual required for the crowds when they arrive for each day's events. We try to make our lives easier by running what Marcus bills as a 'special event': three days of headline bestiarii pitted against savage beasts, using Carpophorus as our star bestiarius, who is in his element fighting tigers and suchlike. He's brave, I'll give him that. A tiger won't listen to a gladiatorial referee nor follow any accepted rules of fighting, caring only to kill. And from our perspective, two tigers take up a lot less room than a hundred head of deer. But this special focus on one star performer comes with its own problems. Carpophorus is much beloved by the ladies of Rome, who no doubt like to daydream of having him in their bedchambers and sometimes attempt to make their daydreams come true.

"I'm sorry," I tell a veiled and silk-clad lady in a litter being carried by six well-dressed slaves on the second morning of the five days. "I cannot send Carpophorus out to you, he is about to fight."

"I'll make it worth your while," murmurs the woman, holding out a little pouch to me.

"It won't be worth my while if the Emperor finds out I didn't put on a show today," I say, backing away. "Perhaps you can arrange something yourself with him after the show?"

She obviously does, because Carpophorus is late the next morning, looking pleased with himself.

"You be late again, and I'll send you to fight the lions without your sword," spits Marcus. "I've got enough on my hands without you disappearing off with your lady friends."

"She was actually a lady, though," says Carpophorus, pulling on his armour with a grin. "If I told you whose wife she is –"

"I don't want to know," says Marcus. "And I'll deny everything if you tell me. I just want you out there on the sand. Right now."

We get by somehow and spend the fifth day frantically moving everything back into the under-stage space from dawn till dusk, while above our heads a lion hunt goes ahead using a herd of antelope we drove into the arena overnight in pens mounted on vast carts through the Gate of Triumph.

"All this for one naumachia," mutters Marcus, as we look round the under-stage space by torchlight. The smooth waterproofing layer that has been applied over the past few days is almost dry, we touch it lightly, feel a slight damp chill coming from it.

"It's done now," I comfort him. "Merula says it's all waterproofed, we're nearly there."

"Apart from coating the whole floor with pitch and sealing all the doors, you mean?"

"Well, there is that," I admit.

Thankfully Titus saves his next visit to the Games for after our waterproofing, so that we have our usual facilities available and can put on a spectacle worthy of his attendance. He has Berenice with him again and when I see her arrive in the imperial box, I take Karbo aside.

"Get one of the kittens and keep hold of it till I tell you."

"What for?"

"Just do as I say."

"Which one?"

"The black one."

He returns a few moments later with the smallest of the litter, a tiny creature with a little dash of white in the centre of its otherwise black forehead and huge green eyes. "Now what?"

"Follow me."

We make our way through the cool corridors to the imperial box. The Praetorian Guards regard me with suspicion.

"A small gift from the backstage team for Queen Berenice," I say.

"What is it?"

"A kitten."

They hesitate.

"She will love it," I say. "The Emperor will be pleased that she is beloved by the common people."

The guards have obviously already experienced this for themselves. One of them ducks through the drapes. I can hear muttering, then he waves us through.

Titus is watching an ongoing bout between two well-known gladiators, who are making a good show of things, but Berenice has turned to see us enter. I nudge Karbo who, having a good sense of the dramatic, promptly falls to his knees and holds out the kitten almost above his bowed head. The kitten mews, as if on cue.

"Oh!" says Berenice, "Too pretty." She's smiling, her hands already reaching out for the kitten, which Karbo, lifting his head to see better, delivers into her lap. The kitten, feeling silk for the first time in its life, nestles into the folds of her clothes and purrs.

"A small gift of welcome," I say. "Motherless, your majesty. Karbo thought you might care for it."

Karbo looks up at me questioningly, obviously thinking of the plump mother cat who is at this very moment prowling around the amphitheatre, searching for rats.

"Motherless," I repeat firmly and Karbo nods vigorously.

"Poor tiny thing," says Berenice, stroking the kitten. "And you are?" she asks me.

"Althea Aquillius, scribe to the amphitheatre's manager, majesty," I say.

"And is the boy your son?" she asks.

"Motherless, majesty," I say. "Like the kitten," I add, ramming the point home.

"Poor child," she says. "Dearest?" she adds to Titus.

Titus looks over his shoulder at us. "Ah, the scribe, I remember you," he says. "Althea?"

"Your memory is astonishing, Imperator," I say.

"I don't forget someone who beats me," he says. "Beat me at shorthand," he explains to Berenice. "Excellent scribe. Offered her a job, but as she said, who would sort out this place if I took her away?"

"The boy has brought me a kitten as a gift," says Berenice.

Titus looks at the tiny creature and then back at me, his face softening. "A kind gesture," he says. "You are good to have thought of the Queen." As I thought, given the reluctance of those around him to accept the relationship, anyone treating Berenice as his rightful companion is pleasing to him. "What was that about the boy?" he adds.

"Motherless," says Berenice with sympathy.

Titus looks down at Karbo. "Do you want him as a pet as well, eh?"

"We care for him ourselves, Imperator," I say, gesturing to Karbo to leave. When he's disappeared through the drapes I add, "But I have a request, if you would look with favour on it?"

"Speak, speak," says Titus, one eye back on the gladiators.

"Did it work?" asks Marcus when he catches me in one of the corridors as the crowds disperse.

"Yes," I say. "He promised me a scroll within a few days."

"You're a wily thing," says Marcus. "Well done."

I'M PAINSTAKINGLY COPYING OUT A legal document when Karbo interrupts me. I hastily cover over the scroll, but his sharp eyes miss nothing.

"Why's my name on there?"

"Oh, so you have been practising your reading. I thought you'd given up."

"I can read my name," he says. "Why have you written it down?"

"None of your business."

"If it's my name, then it's my business."

I shake my head. "You'll see it soon enough. What do you want?"

"Julia said to tell you she asked at the temple and the most auspicious day is in four days' time."

"Tell her everything will be ready."

"For what?"

"You'll see," I say.

He huffs. "Why is everyone keeping secrets?"

"Why are you so nosy? Go and find someone else to bother."

"Fine," he says and stomps away. I smile and bend back to my work, outlining his name with care.

THE CHOSEN MORNING, HALFWAY THROUGH September, dawns bright and sunny, an auspicious sign. Fabia winks at me when she spots me at the amphitheatre.

"Everything ready for this evening?"

I nod.

"Did you manage to convince the lawyer, then?"

"A whole wild boar made a very convincing case," I say. "The paperwork's all done."

"Paperwork for what?" asks Karbo.

"Never you mind," says Fabia.

THE DAY'S SHOW OVER AND done with, I grab Karbo before he runs off somewhere. He still insists on washing himself in the public fountains, doing so often but not exactingly.

"I think the time has come for you to attend the baths," I say.

Karbo screws up his face. "You boss me around too much."

"No arguing," I tell him. "And look," I add, trying to tempt him. "I've made you a new tunic. You can wear it once I'm satisfied you're properly clean." I rummage in my satchel and hold out a new green tunic. The green is from the same cloth of a new tunic Marcus has been wearing lately, and I can see that Karbo is swayed by this.

He trails behind me to the Baths of Nero, bare feet dragging. I force him to sit in the hottest room, although he wriggles and complains throughout. When I get out a little bottle of oil and a strigil, he screws up his nose. "I don't want all that on me."

"You don't have a choice," I say. I rub him all over with oil, then show him how to scrape it off the parts of himself that he can reach, before finishing the job for him and obliging him to take a dip in the cool pool. When he emerges, his black skin is gleaming with the treatment it has received, I have never seen it look so healthy.

"See how well you look," I say.

He shrugs as if he couldn't care less, but I catch him turning first his arm and then a leg this way and that, admiring the glow.

I add some oil to his scalp and locks, rubbing it in as much as I can before he slips away, demanding to wear his new tunic. I put it over his head and pass him a little leather belt the cobbler made up for me. He puts it on, tightening it with a manly air, imitating Marcus so closely that I have to hide a laugh.

"Now for shoes," I say and pull out a neat pair of new leather boots. Karbo all but grabs them out of my hands, then quickly puts them on, strutting up and down in front of me.

"They'll keep your feet warm and dry this winter," I say. "Just one thing missing," I add.

"What's that?"

"You'll see," I say. "Fabia has gone to collect it."

"Collect what?"

"I can't tell you that," I say. "It's a surprise."

When we reach the courtyard there's a fire built up in a brazier and the smell of roasting mutton from two whole sheep. Tables have been laid out end to end and platters of food are already laid out. Loaves of bread and cheese pastries from the bakery, dipping bowls of garum and olive oil, pickled mushrooms and olives, heaped piles of grapes and blackberries, jugs of wine and sweet wine cakes, as well as a big dish of a spiced milk pudding sweetened with honey, a rare treat and Karbo's favourite.

He stares. "What's the feast for?"

I pretend not to hear him, turning instead to Julia, who is making her way into the courtyard carrying a pot of vegetable stew. "It all looks wonderful, Julia, thank you."

Julia smiles. "It's not every day a child is named," she says.

Karbo frowns. "Who's had a baby?"

Julia rests her hand lightly on his head. "Go and call Marcus, please," she says. "He's upstairs."

Karbo mutters something and disappears into the stairwell as Cassia joins us, wearing her best tunic, a bright yellow and orange, with a red headwrap embroidered all over with tiny yellow flowers, the outfit she lent me on the opening day of the Games.

"I've closed up the popina," she says. "I'm looking forward to a night off."

The residents of the building are gathering, all in their best clothes, a bright and colourful throng. The smaller children dash about, over-excited, and the adults beam as Marcus makes his way down the wooden staircase, with Karbo behind him, the two of them in their matching green tunics and leather belts. Once they reach the courtyard, Julia moves past them and ascends a few steps, so that she can look down on us all. Cassia nudges me, smiling.

"Does he still not know?"

I grin, shaking my head.

Her eyes shine with unshed tears. "He will be so happy. May the gods bless you for doing this."

The whole insula helped me pull strings here and there after Titus gave his permission. It's taken weeks of planning to change Karbo from a runaway slave to my son. First, I drew up false documents indicating that Marcus bought Karbo just over a year ago from a slave trader based in Pompeii, who, having died in the eruption of Vesuvius since then, cannot argue to the contrary. Then Marcus gave a generous gift of a whole wild boar to a careless lawyer who certified that Karbo has now been set free and finally, a higher-class lawyer wrote and certified the legal scroll which names Karbo as my newly adopted son and the Emperor himself as having given permission. Not only will I be Karbo's new mother, but Marcus will now be his legal guardian and patron, as he is to me, since he freed both of us. A woman cannot adopt without imperial consent; the scroll from Titus allowing this is a rare concession and one now securely tucked away in my most treasured possessions.

"Today we gather in this place to witness a new beginning for a child," starts Julia, who has volunteered for the role normally reserved for a priest, since Karbo is too old for the naming ceremony which should take place when a baby is nine days old. From what I can tell, Karbo is closer to nine years old, so we have had to make up our own rite of passage. "Step forward, Karbo."

Karbo stands stock still and I have to gently push him forwards. He looks over his shoulder at me, bewildered.

"The boy Karbo has been legally documented as the slave of Marcus Aquillius Scaurus," says Julia, her clear voice ringing out.

Karbo starts and for a moment I am afraid he is going to bolt, as he used to when we first found him. To be named as a slave, when he thought he had escaped such a future, must be terrifying to him. But Maria, standing close to him, has already grabbed hold of his arm, no doubt anticipating just such a reaction.

Julia smiles down at Karbo. "On this day, the slave Karbo has been set free by his master," she says, and Maria loosens her hold. "Furthermore," Julia continues, "Althea Aquillius today offers to take the boy as her own child, adopting him as her son. Extraordinary permission has been given for this, from Emperor Titus himself, and cannot be contested. Step forward, Althea."

I step forward and stand close to Karbo. He stares up at me.

"You take this boy as your son?" asks Julia.

"I take him as my son," I say.

"Do you accept Althea as your mother and promise to obey her in all matters, as a loyal son should?" says Julia to Karbo.

Karbo gives a wordless nod, his wide eyes never leaving me.

"And what do you name him?" she asks me.

"Titus Aquillius Karbo," I say. I have given him the Emperor's name as his formal first name, since this has been made possible by him, and kept Karbo as his common-use name, which he will continue to be known as. His family name comes from Marcus, since he was supposedly set free by him, and I am pleased that it matches my own.

Julia nods and lifts her hands, palms upwards. "May Nundina and Nona bless this boy child, now named Titus Aquillius Karbo, and give him a long life."

"Long life," echo the onlookers.

From the folds of her tunic, Fabia pulls out and passes to me a fine chain, from which dangles a little gilded amulet, the bulla given to every boy child during his naming ceremony. The lack of a bulla has, until today, marked Karbo out as a foreigner amongst his Roman peers. I slip the chain over Karbo's head, before laying a hand on his black locks in a blessing. Karbo gazes up at me, amazed. His hands, hanging by his side, are shaking. The crowd breaks into applause and blessings, naming Nundina and Nona more than once, as they would for a baby.

"Well, now you have a mother and a proper legal guardian I hope you'll be more obedient," says Maria, sniffing loudly and using her palla to wipe her eyes. "Or you'll get a good beating, I should imagine."

Cassia and I look at each other and giggle. Maria's stern words are fooling nobody. It was she who bought the extra green cloth to make Karbo's new tunic and who took up a place close to Karbo during the ceremony, who knew him well enough to stop him from running off when he was named as a slave. She might as well be his grandmother, the amount of time she spends feeding him little treats and reminding him of his manners.

Karbo throws his arms about my waist, burying his face in my tunic. I kneel down and put my arms around him in a tight embrace, which leads to cheers from the crowd. When Karbo pulls away his eyelashes are wet and I dash away my own tears that have welled up at his happiness.

"Time to eat," says Cassia and everyone moves to take up a place round the long table, embracing Karbo and me as they go. I sit next to Julia and Karbo sits between us, very upright, conscious of all the attention being lavished on him.

The meal goes on for hours, new platters of roast mutton handed round, cups refilled with wine, while olive stones and grape pips pile up on our plates and the children gulp down as much milk pudding as they can. As darkness falls, we light lamps and torches around the courtyard. Someone pulls out a flute and someone else a cithara, tambourines keep the beat and favourite songs are sung, growing louder and bawdier as more cups of wine are drunk. Karbo is now racing about the courtyard with his friends, all solemnity forgotten, excitement keeping him awake long past his usual bedtime. At some point I tell him to go to bed and Karbo, for once, obeys with alacrity, the crowd cheering on this display of motherly care and filial obedience. Cassia and I laugh, our cheeks flushed with too much wine. We hold hands with Fabia and other friends and dance through the courtyard, enjoying the chance to celebrate the joyful things in life. I very much doubt Karbo is asleep, he is probably peeping over the rooftop railing at us all, enchanted enough with his new status as my son to at least have made a pretence at obedience for the past hour or so.

I make my way to the toilets and when I emerge, Rullus is standing in the shadows, blocking my way.

"So you got the Emperor himself to grant you permission to adopt a child?" he asks, his words low and slurred.

"Yes," I say.

"Ridiculous. Can't imagine why he'd do that. Women can't just go round adopting children. Why should they be given permission to adopt some street rat? They don't even have authority over their own children, that's a man's job."

"The Emperor was kind enough to think otherwise in this instance," I say, looking away, hoping someone in the crowd will see me and come over.

"Well, I suppose amongst your lot anything goes."

"My lot?"

"Gladiators, actors, whores, all you lot."

"I'm none of those things," I say and add, lowering my voice, "but I work with them every day and most of them are better than you."

"What did you say?"

"Nothing," I say.

"I won't have Cassia hanging about with disreputable people. You stay away from her. You, that waddling little dwarf Fabia and Marcus. He's probably got his eye on her," slurs Rullus. "But she's mine. My family, and I'm going to make her my wife. Only right. Girl shouldn't be unwed at her age. Running a popina, too. It's not decent, you get all sorts trying it on."

"I'm sure you do," I say. "If you'll excuse me." I try to walk away but he catches at my arm.

"Nothing better than a whore, that's what you are," he mutters. "And I know how to show a whore a good time."

"Althea?"

Fabia is standing close to us, frowning.

"Ah!" says Rullus, with a big smile. "Come here, little one!" With one quick movement, he picks her up and deposits her on top of the nearest table. "Dance for us!"

Fabia's face freezes. "Help me down," she says to me.

I hold out a hand and she climbs back down via the bench set below the table.

"Not dancing? Where's your sense of fun?" cries Rullus. "Cassia! You'll dance, won't you?"

He grabs at Cassia's hands, leads her away in a dance that has others joining in.

"I hate people lifting me," mutters Fabia, glowering as she watches him. "I'm not a child."

"I don't like him," I say, and even this tiny confession feels like a freedom.

"Nor do I," says Fabia. "Father said he's seen him coming home late most nights from brothels. I mean, men do go there, but every night? When he's courting Cassia?"

I sit down heavily on the bench. "Is he?"

"I think so. Laughing and joking with her all the time, making little comments about wives and mothers and suchlike. I thought he was alright at first but I'm beginning to think he's not as nice as he seems."

"He – he put his hands on me once," I say, this watered-down version all I can manage to get out of my mouth.

Fabia looks at me and her face is serious. "Have you told Cassia?"

"You're the only person I've told," I manage.

"She needs to know," says Fabia.

"Will she believe me?"

"I believe you."

Tears of relief spring to my eyes. "I'll tell her," I say. "I just have to find the right moment."

THE STARS HAVE CROSSED THE sky and the songs grown slow, children have fallen asleep and been carried back to their beds. People disperse, calling out sleepy goodnights. I help Julia blow out the lamps and torches, then, carrying a little lamp of my own, make my way up the stairs to the rooftop. I open the door of my hut and see in the flickering light that Karbo has finally fallen asleep, without even removing his new shoes or belt. I'm about to go in but then I catch sight of Marcus' silhouette across the rooftop, standing by the eastward wall, looking out over the darkness of the city, soon to grow light with the coming dawn. We are going to have to get through a whole day tomorrow on barely two hours' sleep.

I walk over to his side. He straightens at my approach, wipes a hand over his eyes. I realise he has been weeping and want to creep away again, but it is too late.

"He was pleased," Marcus says, forcing a smile.

"He was afraid of losing me one day," I say. "He wanted a mother so badly; I could not see him desire something so much and not grant it if I could convince Titus to let me adopt him. And he has your protection now, too, it will be important for him to have a legal guardian and patronage."

He nods.

I swallow. "It must bring back memories," I start awkwardly.

He gives a half-shrug as though to indicate it is nothing, but cannot complete the gesture. "Amantius…"

"I know," I say. My mind fills with the searing image of Marcus on his knees, digging with his bare hands through the ashes of Pompeii, searching for his little son and his beloved wife, knowing even as he did so that they were gone, lying to himself that he might find them alive in that hellscape. And before that, I recall Livia's soft voice and hazelnut-coloured hair as she welcomed me into her home, playing peekaboo with Amantius early one morning. I only knew them for a few hours, their faces have already grown hazy in my memory.

Marcus looks away. He clears his throat. "He should get as much education as possible," he says gruffly. "You'll teach him to read and write?"

"I will," I say. "When he has caught up with children of his own age, he can attend school with a proper tutor. I can't teach him everything."

He nods. "Good work on the bill of sale," he says, attempting some humour. "Don't let slip what you did, though, or you'll have every slave in Rome wanting forged documents. And wide-eyed kittens to offer to foreign queens."

"Karbo was going to leg it when Julia said he was your slave," I say. "Good thing Maria grabbed hold of him."

"He always was fast. Now he's got a taste for the races, he'll be disappearing off there if you let him out of your sight."

"He was good with the horses though. I've never seen him so quiet and patient."

"Just as well. They're going to need all the patience we can muster to get them running through the water when the crowd's roaring. Speaking of which, it's time to sleep or we'll be dead on our feet at the show today."

"Goodnight then," I say.

"Goodnight."

I walk back to my own hut and look back briefly, expecting Marcus to be making his own way to bed, but he is still leaning on the wall, looking out over the darkness, lost in his own thoughts. For a moment, it had felt like the old days, when we spoke about everything, but then he all but dismissed me, cutting the conversation short, while continuing to think about the past without me. Perhaps I should have spoken about Rullus, but Marcus had enough on his mind. I feel lonely again, but the sight of Karbo cheers me. I have made his desire come true even if I cannot settle on what mine is, I think, and that is a good enough start. Karbo is properly documented and has me as his mother now, and no-one will be able to separate us, come what may.

WE VISIT THE STABLES AGAIN. We will need one chariot from each racing team, for the Blues aren't about to wear another team's colours, their followers would be up in arms at the very notion. We take more horses down to the river, try them out in the water, choose those who seem least concerned. Agreements are made, team drivers chosen. We have our four chariots, four horses and a driver each. They're not the very top drivers, the stables aren't about to waste their time on a show where they won't even be able to reach their top speed, but these four are the younger drivers in the next tier down, training to become the future stars of the racetrack. They can drive plenty fast enough for our needs. Mindful that they will be performing in front of Titus in an unusual environment, the stables agree to have weekly sessions to accustom the horses to water. Celer will take on this task, and Karbo begs me to be allowed to be his assistant.

"Fine," I say in the end, exasperated with the constant nagging. "Celer, don't let any harm come to him."

Karbo comes back from the first water-training session glowing with pleasure and gabbling at great length about the names and temperaments of the various steeds. When it becomes clear he isn't going to stop any time soon, I nod along, trying to make notes on the next day's show and occasionally making appropriate noises of disbelief or praise according to what seems to be required from me. I keep trying to find a moment to pluck up my courage and tell Cassia about Rullus. Perhaps I should wait until the end of the season, I think. If I just focus on the naumachia for now, then afterwards there will be plenty of time. Fabia nods uncertainly when I tell her this. "Don't leave it too long," she says.

"I won't," I promise her. "There's only a few weeks to go. What difference can it make?"

"He's good," says Celer to me, a week later.

"Who is?"

"Karbo, with the horses. You should come and watch one day."

I accompany them to the next week's session. We're back down by the Tiber and the horses have moved beyond tentative steps in the shallows. All of them now trot through water higher than their knees, and most of them even go willingly into deeper parts and swim. Karbo is encouraging the most reluctant one beyond the shallows. He whispers to it, he strokes its neck and flanks, all the while pacing along the shoreline, getting ever deeper into the water.

"Is it safe?" I ask, thinking about the currents.

"This part is, which is why we practise here."

The horse gets in up to its chest and Karbo, in one smooth move which tells me he's done this before, slips onto its back, pulling himself up through the water by holding the horse's mane. It jerks its head, trying to decide what to do about this strange state of affairs, but Karbo is already leaning forward, whispering into its ears again and the horse relaxes, takes a few more steps forwards, then changes its gait and begins to swim.

Celer is smiling. "He's done it with all of them," he says. "One by one. That one was the last one, didn't want to go deeper than its ankles at first and now look at the two of them. He's born to work with horses."

"Don't tell him that," I beg.

"You've got one hour," warns Marcus. "I can't have the boards still wet when the hunt's on, the venatores will be slipping all over the place."

Merula nods, his face tense. The wooden trough he's had built, held up by scaffolding to get it from Nero's old cistern to the edge of the amphitheatre, will act as a kind of mini aqueduct, channelling the water three hundred paces across the buildings and roads and to one side of the amphitheatre, far above our heads. It's been painted a sky blue to help it blend into the background of a sunny day and now we're all standing waiting at the far end of the arena, to see if the water really will pour down at the rate Merula has worked out. It will mostly fall into Diana's blue-lined hunting pool, so that Merula can measure how fast it fills, but there's bound to be splashing.

He gives a signal, repeated far away at the top of the amphitheatre's highest wall, which will be seen up at the cistern, where they will open up the water flow, allowing it to reach us in moments. We stand, waiting, craning up at the trough, see a shudder in it and then…

"It's working!" yells Karbo as water streams down from the sky, pouring into the blue pool, Merula watching its progress, nodding to himself as it quickly fills, faster than we've ever managed to fill it for shows. He gives another signal and the stream falters, then stops, dribbles a little more, and is gone. It has spilled over the sides, so fast was the flow. Karbo dabbles his toes in it even as it drips away through the cracks in the boards.

"Fast enough?" asks Marcus.

"Yes," says Merula, his confidence clear. "Yes. It did what it should do. It will fill in half an hour and empty perhaps even more quickly than that, with three of the largest trapdoors open in the centre."

Applause breaks out between us, Marcus claps Merula on the shoulder, smiling, relief showing in his face.

"Thank Neptune," he says. "Speaking of which, Althea: are the costumes ready for King Neptune's arrival?"

"Yes," I say. "All the costumes are complete."

"I keep waking up and thinking I've forgotten something," he says. "Thank all the gods this will be over soon, and I'll never have to run another naumachia again. Right, clear this space. It has one hour to dry and then I've got a beast hunt to get started."

We try to keep the second-to-last day of Games simple, putting on a larger but shorter gladiatorial bout in the afternoon, consisting of the re-enactment of a battle, which allows us to show off one hundred gladiators in a much shorter space of time than the usual sessions, where more of the gladiators fight in pairs. The crowd enjoys the larger spectacle and departs earlier than usual.

The last people have barely left the building when our full team gets ready for tonight's work. We have one thousand slaves in total and for this piece of work we will be using over eight hundred of them all at one time. While the remaining two hundred sweep and wash the seating as usual, making it ready for tomorrow, we dismantle, once again, all the pens and work area below the arena, for fear that the quantity of water that will flow through it would cause damage. We leave only one lift mechanism with one prop, which we will use at the very end of the show, operated by six slaves whom we have checked can swim well in case of accident; the water even at full drainage should only come to a man's waist. We have taken out all our other lifts, breaking them down into their component parts and sending them by wagons down to the warehouses for the time being, so that we do not waste them. They can be refitted over winter. While this goes on, firepits are lit at eight points around the outside of the amphitheatre, and large cauldrons are placed over each, before the pitch starts to be added. It arrives in vast solid slabs, which have to be broken into chunks with chisels, then thrown into the cauldrons to become liquid. We have perhaps overordered, but it was hard to judge how much would be needed to fully coat the wooden boards and we did not dare run out. Three trapdoors are left open. They will act as our plugs, so they cannot be sealed shut, while the rest are fully locked into place.

The smell as the pitch begins to heat up and the solid blocks melt down into thick black liquid makes me feel slightly sick, charcoal and pine resin making for a stomach-churningly strong combination.

Marcus briefs the team. "As each cauldron of pitch becomes liquid over the fire, we use these smaller dipping metal cups, each held with a long rod handle. You dip out a cup, then quickly take it to the boards and pour it on. It'll be brushed over the floor by the sweepers to smooth it out and get an even coating. You have to walk fast, it can't cool too much, or it won't brush on, just be lumpy and sticky." Marcus shakes his head. "I can't believe we're doing this. There'll be two hundred brooms thrown out tomorrow, what a waste. To say nothing of a whole floor only good for scrap in the boatyards after this."

The smell grows thicker in the air. The first few cups of pitch are spread onto the surface of the three trapdoors, to ensure they will leak as little as possible, though we have to leave their edges and hinges undone, so that they can still open and close. Meanwhile some of the doors into antechambers around the arena are being sealed with wax. It won't hold forever, but we can't put pitch on them, it would ruin them. The wax can be removed with boiling water when there is no longer a need for the seal. Usually the antechambers are where our gladiators and other performers wait to enter the arena. The only obvious way in and out now for any performers is the Gate of Triumph. The Gate of Death has also been waxed shut. The water will continue to fall from Merula's waterfall throughout the show, to make up for any leaking that may occur, keeping the water level stable.

Now the pitch is ready in large quantities, the work begins in earnest. We start at one end of the floor and spread it, working backwards towards the other end. There are a few errors at first, the pitch cooling too quickly and being impossible to spread, until we realise we must bring one whole cauldron at a time from outside and apply it quickly, then move onto the next cauldron, setting the first to boil again with fresh chunks of the cold pitch. More than ten slaves get burnt during the exhausting hours that follow and Fabius and Fabia are kept busy seeing to them, applying a lotion of wine, myrrh and honey and administering a draught of thyme and belladonna to ease the pain of the three worst patients.

It is odd to see the familiar wooden boards slowly disappear under the thick black sea of pitch, the smell making several of us feel so sick that we have to leave the building in search of fresh air. I go outside but find little respite, for there are always seven cauldrons bubbling while one is being used, slaves taking turns to stir them with long wooden paddles, a back-breaking job as it is a thick mixture. When I return, Marcus has disappeared.

"He's gone downstairs to see what it looks like from the underside," says Fabia.

I make my way downstairs and find Marcus standing in the growing gloom, holding a flaming torch for light. Usually, a little light comes in from the fine cracks between the boards, but they are slowly being filled in, so it is darker than usual and feels larger, now that it is all empty.

"Seems to be holding," he says. "There are drips on the floor, but you can't see sunlight through the boards, so it must be filling the gaps. Let's hope the leaking is far less than the flow of water."

"I feel sick," I say. "The smell is disgusting."

"My shoes are ruined," says Marcus, looking down regretfully. They have several splatters of black on them. "That's not coming off, is it?"

"We're making good time," I say.

"It's not so much the applying it, it's the drying. Is it going to be dry enough for chariots to run over it by late morning tomorrow?"

"The gods will help us," I say.

"Neptune better be on our side, it's his realm we are representing. If we do it badly, he will not be pleased. I'll offer a prayer at his shrine tomorrow morning. Where's Merula? How are the water chambers coming along?"

"Well, I think," I say. "Shall we go and check?"

Five entryways into the arena have been left unsealed. One is entirely empty, a simple stone passageway. The other four each contain a replica ship, sitting on the stone floor, awaiting their moment to shine. Most are the length of six men, one, heavily decorated, is even longer and each can hold more than twenty men aboard.

"Will they float well enough with the weight of the crew in?"

"They're flat-bottomed, they should do. Hard to steer, but then they don't have to do much and there are no waves. So long as they stay together and the men aboard row smoothly, it'll look impressive enough. The sails will come up as soon as they move out, it'll make them look bigger."

THE WORK FINISHES AS THE sun goes down, the fires finally extinguished, one thousand slaves slowly walking back to their warehouses to eat a brief meal of bread and cheese as there has been no time to cook anything, the rest of the team left to stand in the imperial box, looking out over the now entirely black floor.

"It looks ominous," I say, shivering.

Marcus says nothing, but I notice his hand shape into the gesture against evil spirits. He is as nervous as I am, even if he is trying not to show it.

"I want everyone here at dawn tomorrow," he says. "We have to know if it's going to work."

"The horses and chariots will arrive first thing," says Karbo.

"There are guards tonight watching over the amphitheatre and the water scaffolding," says Strabo. "Just so there are no silly accidents. That floor would go up like a torch if you put a flame to it. And we can't have any idiots thinking it would be fun to climb up the scaffolding."

Marcus takes a deep breath. "I'll be sleeping here tonight," he says.

"You'll sleep so badly," I say.

"Why? Do you think I'm going to sleep well back at the insula? My dreams will be full of unending waves and fish."

I'm half-tempted to suggest that we both sleep at the amphitheatre, so that I will have the comfort of Marcus close to me, free of fears about Rullus. But such a suggestion will make Marcus ask questions and I still don't know how to tell him when I have not even told Cassia.

DIDO AND AENEAS

THE SUN IS JUST RISING. Marcus and I are standing on ladders poking through two of the three remaining open trapdoors, our heads just above the newly pitched wooden floor. The smell is still overwhelming. We each tentatively prod the surface. It feels very slightly tacky, but not sticky.

"Jupiter be thanked," says Marcus, huge relief in his voice. He has dark circles under his eyes. "I thought it would never dry. I checked it in the middle of the night when I woke up and it wasn't dry at all. That was the end of my night's sleep." He pulls himself up the last few steps up onto the floor itself and takes a couple of careful steps. "Not bad," he comments as I join him.

I lift a foot and examine the sole. There's a little marking from the pitch, nothing too bad.

"Can we test the chariots?" Karbo's eager face is looking up at me from the trapdoor ladder.

"Yes," I agree. "Just quickly though."

Merula joins us as Karbo disappears. "The pitch is holding," he says. "I had the slaves throw several buckets of water down on it and there were no drips on the underside, at least not for now. So it should hold for the duration of the show." He looks anxious, this is his moment after all, if the water system doesn't work as planned, the whole event will be a disaster.

We stand back as the newly arrived chariots are quickly driven round, then await the verdict.

"Bit sticky," says the lead driver. "Can feel the wheels dragging. But nothing bad. Not for what you want, anyway. No good for a real race."

"Good. Now leave," says Marcus. "The longer it has to keep drying, the better. I don't want the wheels damaging the pitch."

"More likely to be the other way round," says the driver, guiding the horses away from us.

THE TRUMPETS ARE SOUNDING.

"Right," says Marcus. "Titus has arrived. Everyone ready to start?"

Nods all round.

"Then get to your posts."

There's a final blast of trumpets and the singers burst into a chorus praising King Neptune. The Gate of Triumph opens, drawing attention to a steep ramp which leads from the arena to the gate itself, then down again into the outside world. Four blue chariots make their way up the ramp, lifting them high into the gate's vast archway, then down and into the arena. The lead one is picked out in gold amongst the blue, its driver wears a golden crown as well as magnificent blue robes and carries a trident. By his side is Karbo, dressed in a blue and green tunic. The crowd applauds the appearance of King Neptune, as the other three chariots, full of additional blue and green-dressed attendants, array themselves in a line behind the chariot as it draws to a halt in front of the point where Merula's blue-painted trough hangs above them. In the crowd, Merula gives a signal, passed on up to the very edge of the top tier, even as Neptune raises his trident.

From the sky, a glistening column of water falls at his command, the sunlight sending dancing rainbows through it. The water hits the black floor and splashes, ripples out as the chariots move on, first at a stately speed, then gathering pace as the water pours on and on, the chariot wheels spraying up arcs of water which throw cool drops onto the first few rows of seating. And then the crowd gasps as all over the amphitheatre a fine mist is sprayed over the audience. Scented water cools and perfumes the crowd, the effect achieved by our teams pumping the usual water supply for the fountains through additional tubing installed under Merula's direction this past week, with flattened ends forcing the water to emerge as a mist rather than a flow, perfume added through the specially modified tubes. The audience applauds this delightfully refreshing touch, even as before their very eyes the water deepens, the horses, trotting happily, slowing a little as it reaches their knees. At a gesture from Marcus, Neptune salutes Titus, then directs his chariot back up the ramp, through the Gate of Triumph and out again, the water lapping further up the ramp but unable to flow out of the gate.

The water is not yet very deep. The singers break into the story of Theseus and the Minotaur, how Zeus, disguised as a bull, rose from the sea and impregnated the wife of King Minos, leading to the birth of a monstrous child, half-man, half bull. Marcus has skipped over the suggestion to have a real woman copulate with a bull, though it has been done before. Instead, he has found one of the largest bulls I've ever seen and it is driven over the ramp the chariots have used to exit. The bull stamps about, mystified by the water coming up to its knees, and suddenly finds itself face-to-face with Carpophorus, who swings over the wall and into the water on a rope, sword in hand, bare-chested. There's applause and a lot of high-pitched cries of admiration, suggesting it is the ladies in the top tiers who are most pleased to see him in action.

The bull stamps again, irritated by the glinting sword and Carpophorus' direct stare and stance, which signals aggression. It begins to approach, evidently believing the man will back down, show some signs of deference, but when it does not see them, it speeds up.

I have to admire the bravery on show. Carpophorus stands entirely still, allows the bull to all but reach him and then swipes, cutting at its jowls, an instant line of red appearing. The bull bellows in pain and rage and attacks, its black horns clanging against the sword that harmed it, then it turns to try and catch the bare chest, so vulnerable. But the glinting, glistening sword is too fast, it slices again and now the bull's shoulder bleeds, blood flowing down into the water. The bellow this time is deafening, the blade even faster, Carpophorus cuts the bull again and again until he permits it to come perilously close, its own momentum driving the sword deep down into its chest, its own attack turned against it. The beast sinks to its knees as though paying homage to the bestiarius' skill and strength, even as it slowly dies and the crowd cheers. Carpophorus turns a full circle to soak up all the praise, then pulls out the bloodied sword and washes it in the deepening water, striding away to where he's pulled up over the wall into the first row of seating. The bull is dragged away with hooked poles, put onto a wheeled cart and taken through the Gate of Triumph to be butchered.

The audience has barely finished chanting Carpophorus' name when four doors are pushed open by invisible hands and, on a rush of additional water, four beautiful ships float into the arena, each full of gloriously dressed gladiators in parade armour, who set to and hoist the sails. I can see Merula beaming. The passageways containing the ships, empty this dawn, have been filling up for hours, so that slowly, slowly, each ship began to float. They sail in, the sudden boost of water increasing the depth considerably, so that it is now deeper than a man's waist.

The musicians play a bold military theme, then the chorus tells the story of Odysseus, of his turbulent journey across the seas after the fall of Troy, seeking to return home, yet meeting one disaster after another.

"And so he came to the Island of Sirens and bade his men to plug up their ears with wax, and bind him to the mast, that he alone amongst mortal men might hear their song and yet resist their charms, living to tell the tale."

The man playing Odysseus is bound to the mast of the main ship, the ships follow one another through the water, music playing, the singers singing, and from the water emerge Vita and her swimmers. They are dressed in short tunics, painted as though they were feathers, to show the bird-like nature of the Sirens. Vita and the other women follow the ships, draw close and stretch out their hands to Odysseus, who in turn reaches out to them, desperate to join them and yet unable to do so, as his men, immune to the song of the Sirens, row on, their faces turned away from the terrible temptation of the women below.

The ships position themselves as much out of the way as they can, each of the four in a different quarter of the vast oval, tucked against the wall as the Daughters of Thetis take centre stage. There are forty girls in all, Vita's largest team. They create a circle between them. As delicate lyres and citharas play a rippling tune, they move to the music, each one rising and falling in perfect coordination with her fellow performers. The circle becomes a trident and then an anchor, a simple straight line suddenly takes on the shape of a ship and then a star. The women move as though propelled through the water by an unseen force, barely seeming to make an effort and yet every move they make brings applause, for all the spectators watching know how impossible their shapes are, as woman after woman disappears under the water for extraordinary lengths of time, only their legs or arms visible, before they rise to the surface with joyous smiles, as though what they have done is nothing, a mere child's frolicking. The water grows deeper all the time, now comfortably the depth of a man. As the women finally complete their piece, bowing their heads to Titus, he leads the rapturous applause.

Now comes the most elaborate part of the storytelling. The swimmers make their way discreetly aboard the boats, taking their places on the rowing teams in plain tunics which make them blend in as the men take over, the ships sailing round again as, opposite the imperial box, just to one side of the Vestal Virgins' own seating, a purple and gold banner falls over the edge of the front row. Vita, swiftly re-dressed as a foreign queen, her head crowned in gold and brightly coloured robes falling about her, holds out her hand to the lead ship, which makes its way to her. Once close, a man in golden armour leaps ashore, clasping her in his arms.

The chorus reminds us that Prince Aeneas, freshly escaped from the fall of Troy, knew he was destined to be the founder of Rome and so, despite his great and enduring love for the Queen of Carthage, Dido, he chose to follow his destiny rather than his heart, leaving her behind for the good of the yet-to-be Rome.

The golden-armoured man makes his farewell to Vita, who clutches at him even as he re-joins his ship, which sails away to Titus' side, as a singer gives Dido's grief a voice, lamenting her fate and insisting that she would rather die than love another. Vita plays Dido's tragic end well, taking up a sword and enacting her suicide, finishing the scene draped lifeless over the edge of the wall, long braids touching the water below, while a group of maidens weep over her. There is vast applause. In the imperial box, Titus puts a hand to his eyes, wiping away tears as many of the women in the top tiers are doing. It looks as though he has understood the message.

The music dies away and Marcus is about to give a signal when, without warning, Titus stands and there is a sudden silence. The audience crane their necks to see what he is about to do. Is he displeased? The crowd is well aware of the relevance of the story, they wonder if Titus has been offended. Will there be a punishment for someone? I hold my breath.

"Come, Queen Dido, sail to me," he calls out loudly across the silent amphitheatre.

There's a flurry of activity. The lead ship reverses its journey, taking Aeneas back to his swiftly revived beloved. Vita turns towards Marcus for guidance, wanting him to tell her what to do, but he is too far away and cannot do anything. The silence of sixty thousand people is deafening.

The ship reaches Vita, who steps aboard and is brought to the imperial box, her body regally upright, her face set to a stillness I am sure she is not feeling. The height of the water means that Vita is almost face-to-face with Titus when the ship reaches him.

Titus leans from the imperial box, reaches out a hand and Vita holds out hers. He takes it and leans forward, kisses it, then lets it go.

"An affecting performance," he says loudly. "It shall be rewarded. You have shown true skills in recalling our glorious history and the needful sacrifices made by those who came before us. Therefore, this is yours."

The crowd gasps, for he is holding out a wooden sword, the item ritually given to a gladiator to set them free. Vita has been given her freedom.

There is rapturous applause. Vita falls to her knees in the ship, clutching the sword, tears falling down her face as the ship departs. The four doors around the arena open and the ships return to their secret passageways.

It's time to drain the arena. Below are six slaves, who will unbolt the three trapdoors, allowing a rush of water to pour away. Once again, I hold my breath as the Gate of Triumph opens and Neptune's entourage of chariots re-enters over the ramp, shining in their blue and gold, Neptune holding aloft his trident. This time the drivers are alone, no attendants. They drive slowly through the deep water, which comes to the horses' shoulders, so that they are a hand's depth from having to swim. But three central whirlpools have opened up; the water level is visibly lowering even as the chariots canter on. One by one, three of the chariot drivers pull away their sea-trims, the chariots now revealing the colours of Rome's four racing teams even as the water, like a divine miracle, slowly disappears, the floor losing its watery glow altogether, now becoming a racetrack. A model obelisk, our only prop, rises up from the centre of the floor, mimicking the Circus Maximus. The crowd recognises it at once, along with their favoured racing teams, and scream their approval as the horses gain speed, the water all but gone and the aquatic display now become that most earthly-bound sport, beloved of Romans everywhere, chariot racing. Our choice of drainage in the very centre works to our advantage, for the teams' route takes them in a wide oval, so that there is no danger of being caught in the gaps into which water is still pouring, disappearing into the hypogeum below.

The audience are on their feet, chanting the names of the teams.

"Reds, Reds, Reds!"

"Go the Blues!"

"Come on, the Greens!"

"Whites! Whites for the finish!"

Karbo's smile is ecstatic as he leans over the wall to watch the Blues driver, released from his gravitas as Neptune, urging his team on.

The show is about to end but a signal from below has summoned Marcus and me from our places in the crowd. Strabo meets us in a corridor.

"Titus has asked to see both of you," he says, worried.

"What if he's annoyed, now he's thought about it?" I whisper to Marcus as we hurry towards the imperial box.

"Too late now, we've done it," says Marcus, but he sounds nervous. It's one thing to devise a suggestive show at the Aedile's wishes, but if Titus does take offence, he'll take it out on us, not the Aedile, who will plead ignorance.

We make our way through the drapes. Titus turns to face us, smiling, though his eyes are still red-rimmed from his earlier tears. "A delightful spectacle," he says. "A perfect finale to the inaugural Games."

Marcus' shoulders drop with relief. "Imperator."

"And excellent storytelling, most... most affecting, certainly. You know your history."

"The history of how Rome rose from the actions of one Prince is a glorious reminder of its power today," says Marcus.

"You must tell me exactly how it was done. It filled so fast and drained even faster, a marvel, as though the gods themselves helped you. How was it done? Was the water the full depth of the under-arena? Surely not in so little time?"

"The floor was coated in pitch like a sailing boat, then the trapdoors used as plugs for swift drainage. We used an... old water storage tank to have it fill quickly," says Marcus, carefully avoiding any mention of Nero.

"Most impressive."

"I am glad to have pleased you, Imperator," says Marcus.

"Of course, now that we know it can be done..." begins Titus.

I see Marcus stiffen and he goes so far as to interrupt Titus in a desperate attempt to stop what he can tell is coming next. "The audience will have been delighted to have seen a once-in-a-lifetime spectacle. They will be able to say they have seen something no-one else will ever see."

"Ah but now that you know it can be done, and done so well," says Titus, "it would be an excellent thing to do to end the season each year, do you not think? And perhaps next year you could have it even deeper, to allow for creatures of the sea to be displayed. No need to fill and drain it so quickly, if a greater depth is achieved, but... crocodiles? Sharks? Perhaps a night-time show... it would be very dramatic, even frightening. A magnificent spectacle. I will leave it with you."

I can feel Marcus' horror even though I can't see his face, the stiffness of his shoulders has spread to his whole body. "Imperator," he manages, his voice somehow staying steady and polite. "We will turn our minds to what is possible."

"Excellent. I look forward to next year's naumachia to complete the season. It can become a tradition. The crowds love a tradition, as you know." He looks at me. "I saw the boy playing his part. You must be proud of your son."

"I am eternally grateful for your kindness in allowing me to adopt him," I say. "You have made us both very happy."

Titus nods. "If only happiness were so easily won in all matters," he says with a sad smile. "You may go."

We make our way out of the imperial presence, Marcus striding down the corridor so fast I have to run to keep up with him, trying to come up with something comforting to say, but I can't think of anything. Marcus has detested everything about this naumachia, it has caused him worry for months. The idea that he will now have to deliver one on an annual basis is going to put him in a foul mood. By the time we reach the entrance to the under-arena, I have a pain in my side, and I let him go. We still haven't spoken to one another. The evening should have been a celebration, marking the end of the inaugural Games, one hundred days in which we have delivered a spectacular show every single day without fail. Instead, it is a gloomy one.

Julia has a bountiful meal waiting for us, but Marcus goes drinking with Fabius, no doubt to drown out the bitterness he feels. He does not come home till very late, for I lie awake a long time and do not hear him. The next day he stays in his hut, perhaps sleeping off the wine, till past midday and then sets off for the baths, so Celer informs me. We should be celebrating our freedom: no shows to put on for many months, no more continuous Games. A whole winter where we need only plan ahead and manage the upkeep of the amphitheatre, far less work with far less pressure. But Marcus stays out of sight.

AFTER A FEW DAYS OF rest I go to inspect the amphitheatre. The water drained away quickly, as Merula promised. It's still damp, but it has plenty of time to dry out, especially once we start removing the wooden flooring, letting in more air from above. I climb up one of the ladders, stand in the deserted, still-black arena. It's strange not to have to put on a show every day. The amphitheatre is empty of life without the sounds of the Games and the screams of the crowd.

"Haven't you got the winter off?" It's Vita, standing in one of the archways. She makes her way down the steps, leans over the wall to look down at me.

"Shouldn't you be out celebrating your freedom?"

"I still can't believe it. I've come here every day since then, gone through it all again in my mind, what he said, how he looked, trying to be sure it's real." Her voice wavers a little. I've never heard her so emotional.

"What did Labeo say?"

She snorts. "He was livid. Never heard so many curses out of one mouth. But you can't argue with an emperor, can you? Now he'll have to pay me properly if he wants me to keep on doing shows for him."

"Will you?"

"For a while, I suppose. While I think what to do. We've got plenty of bookings. And lots more coming in, now I'm Titus' favourite… that's how Labeo's billing me. He's hiked up the price for us."

"Will you take Labeo's name, now you're a freedwoman?"

"I will do no such thing," she says. "The paperwork's being drawn up and I chose Vita Africanus."

"Very nice," I say.

"I want to be my own woman. Although Labeo will be my legal guardian and patron until I marry, since he was my last master."

"Do you want to marry?"

"Now I'm free to, perhaps."

"Who to?" I ask, wondering if the answer is going to be Marcus.

"Don't know. Although most men would be better than being under Labeo's thumb. You're lucky, you have Marcus."

I nod.

"He's not happy, though?"

"Titus said we have to flood it all again next year – and every year, as a finale to each season. Marcus thought it was going to be a one-off. And next time the pitch won't be enough. Titus wants the full depth, dangerous animals, a night-time show, all sorts. It'll be challenging for anyone who can't swim well."

She shrugs. "Well, the Daughters of Thetis are at your service, if you need us. I owe you my freedom."

"We only chose your part," I say. "It's you that performed it well enough to earn your freedom. Did you see what the poet Martial wrote about the day?"

"Some drivel about sea nymphs?"

I laugh. "How did you know?"

Vita rolls her eyes. "He likes to put in a divine touch when he writes about the Games, it pleases the imperial family. What did he say?"

I pull open a scroll and read from it. "A well-coached team of Nereids frisked across the calm surface, their shifting formation giving colour to the waters. The trident threatened us with straight tooth, the anchor with curved; a mast, a ship, we took for real; the star of the Spartan boys, the sailors' friend, seemed really to shine, and sails to swell in a gauzy curve. Who devised such techniques amid the limpid waters? Either Thetis taught him these ploys, or she was his pupil."

Vita laughs. "I told you. He knew perfectly well who we were, that's why he mentioned Thetis. He's seen us perform before, he's a frequent guest at some of the best villas in Rome. He just likes adding a touch of poetry to his commentary, and of course he likes to please the Emperor by suggesting no one's ever seen anything like it before."

"Do you know him?"

"Only in passing. He writes well about the Games, plenty of grovelling, you must have seen all the stuff he wrote about the opening day, praising the amphitheatre as one of the wonders of the world and suggesting the animals obey the Emperor's command when he knows perfectly well the animal trainers have spent weeks and months getting them to do their bidding. Have you read his other stuff? Much bawdier. There isn't an affair in Rome he doesn't know about, and he never keeps the gossip to himself, writes it all down and publishes it. He must be responsible for half the divorces in Rome. Mind you, people ought to know better than to tell him anything at all, they know it'll end up in writing. Maybe they just use him as their messenger boy or maybe they think if they share their secrets, he'll tell them everybody else's. In unrelenting detail."

"I'll be sure not to tell him anything I want kept secret, then."

She grins. "So how many shows will there be next year?"

"Maybe one hundred and fifty? It seems like a lot more than this year, but they won't have to be consecutive, so that gives us more flexibility. We'll probably start earlier, April or even March through to September, which gives us the odd day where we don't have to do a show. We can do things like move the flooring for the next naumachia without crazy night shifts."

"That will help. Have you tried the Baths of Titus yet?"

I shake my head.

"Not a bad size," she says. "It's mixed bathing, instead of men and women at different times of day. Looks very elegant, seeing as it's just opened. Not like the crumbling ones you use."

I laugh. "They are a bit scruffy."

"We can go together now if you like. It'll be your local baths once you start putting on shows again next year. You can fall out of work and into a nice bath, think of that."

"Fine," I say. "Let's try them."

The Baths of Titus, only a few paces away from the amphitheatre, gleam with newness. Underneath, their construction and heating may have been cobbled together from Nero's private bathing rooms to give a quick result, but they are elegant enough. Outside, the gardeners are still frantically watering all the plants and whole trees they transplanted to give the illusion of an established garden, but there is still the smell of paint close to the outer walls as we enter. Inside, brand-new mosaic floors greet us, including a vast entryway motif of a hunting scene from the Games, no doubt a nod to the amphitheatre, a reminder of all the works the Flavians have commissioned since coming to power.

We make our way to the changing room to discard our clothes. Rows of brand-new niches await, so we have no trouble finding two side-by-side to leave our tunics and shoes.

We sit in the hottest room for a while although, given the time of year, I'm more inclined to hurry through this part and get into the cooler pools. We oil each other and scrape away the accumulated dust and dead skin, then make our way to the cooler rooms. The pool here is very pretty, with fresh mosaics depicting sea-scenes. The baths I usually go to definitely feel scruffy, now that I see a newly decorated version.

The cool is delightful. I sink into the water gratefully, and Vita and I lie beside each other, she floating, I holding lightly to the edge to keep myself afloat. After a few moments she rolls her head towards me.

"I forgot, you can't swim, can you?"

"No," I say. "I must seem strange to someone like you."

"Shall I teach you?"

I think about it, then nod. "I'd like that."

"Let's start you with floating."

"We're starting now?"

"Why not?"

I shrug. "What do I do?"

"Float."

"I'm not sure I know how."

Vita shakes her head. "You float without doing anything. In fact, the less you do, the better."

"But I'll sink!"

"No, you won't. Look." She demonstrates, lying on top of the water as easily as though lying on a bed. "You just lie still, and the water will hold you up."

I try, but the water goes in my ears, and I jolt my head, my belly sinks immediately, and I end up spluttering.

Vita laughs.

"I'm sorry. You looked so startled. Try again. Trust the water. It will hold you; I swear by Thetis. Just lie down as though you are sleeping, let your arms come out a little, I will put a hand under your back until you can feel yourself floating."

I splutter several more times, my nose and ears repeatedly filling with water, but after a few attempts there is a brief moment when I feel Vita's hand come away from my lower back and the water, as she promised, really does hold me up. I lift my head to tell her so and promptly sink again.

"I felt it!" I say as I come back up and she grins. I try again and this time I remember the sensation and when it comes again I remain still, even when Vita's hand moves away from me. I keep my eyes closed, the better to concentrate, trying to steady my breathing, gaining in confidence as the water continues to hold me, even daring to move my arms and legs a tiny bit. When I open my eyes, Vita is smiling down at me.

"You're doing it! You will be one of my team in no time."

"I doubt it," I say, standing up again.

"Of course you will. Carry on floating, it's good for you to trust the water. If you remember the feeling, next time we come here it will be even easier for you. I'm going to do some practise."

She sets off to the other side of the pool, plunges under the water and her legs appear. She must be standing on her head. I can't help staring at her for a while before I lie back and, after a fumbled attempt, find my floating ability again. It's quite peaceful, the growing certainty that I will not sink, that the water does indeed hold me up.

"I see you found a swimming instructor after all."

I go under immediately, jam my feet down to the floor in a panic, come back up coughing and spitting out water, open my eyes to find Marcus standing right in front of me in the pool, amused at my performance. My hands come up without thinking to cover my breasts, but then I feel foolish and have to lower them again. We are surrounded by naked men and women, why should I be shy? My cheeks and neck feel hot, though.

"Didn't mean to interrupt your swimming lesson," says Marcus. "Is that Vita?" he adds, looking down the pool to where her legs are going through various formations.

"Yes," I manage.

"Not bad, the baths, are they? They might become my new after-work favourites, since they're right next door."

"Yes," I say. "I mean – not bad. I like the decorations."

"Fresher than the Baths of Nero. I suppose no Flavian emperor is going to refurbish those in a hurry, are they? Not without their name on the door, so we know to whom we should be grateful."

I nod. For some reason I'm finding this conversation very difficult. I feel as though I am standing too close to Marcus, am too aware of the wet skin of his chest. I step backwards slightly, bumping into the wall of the pool.

"She's a quick learner." Vita has reached us by swimming underwater, so that she suddenly appears right next to us.

"I'll leave you to your swimming lesson, then," says Marcus. He wades to the steps at the side of the pool and climbs out. I look away, somehow embarrassed though I'm not sure why.

Vita is floating, watching me. "Do you get on well with Marcus?"

"Yes," I say. "He's a good patron," I add more formally.

"The gods know how Labeo will be. He's not yet over not being my master anymore. A patron has to be more respectful. Not like the old days when he first bought me. He tried to take me into his bed."

"What did you do?"

"Bit him," she says.

"You didn't!"

"Did so. Got whipped for it. Worth it. Warned him I'd do it again and I'd do it every time. Only solution was to pick someone else to bed or sell me. And I was worth too much to him in fees for events. So he picked someone else."

"Brave."

She shakes her head. "Stupid, really. But I knew Labeo cared more about making money than which specific slave he bedded; he had plenty of others to choose from, men or women. It was a risk worth taking."

"Well, now you're free."

She splashes backwards onto the water, floating easily. "I have to remind myself all the time. And every time I do, I smile. I've kissed that wooden sword every night before I sleep, it's getting more time in my bedroom than Labeo ever managed."

I look about me as we wander back to the changing rooms, wary of bumping into Marcus again, but there's no sign of him. I'm glad to have seen him smiling though, perhaps he has recovered from Titus' insistence on a future naumachia. Now we have a whole winter to recover before our season starts again.

When I reach the insula, there is a table laid out, with jugs of wine and cakes. Most of the inhabitants of the insula have gathered, including Cassius, Cassia and Rullus, all of whom are smiling.

"Althea! Come join us!" calls Cassius. "Drink a toast to my daughter and Rullus, they are to be married!"

Cassia embraces me and Cassius pushes a cup into my hand.

"To Cassia and Rullus!"

Everyone echoes the toast. My mouth silently shapes the words, while in the crowd, Fabia meets my eye, her face serious.

WHITE WATERS

Now there are no daily Games I find myself without enough to do, without enough excuses not to be more available round the insula. Cassia will find my behaviour odd.

I arrange for the amphitheatre to be given a thorough clean in every part over several days, any repairs made good. We finally finish the paintings in the top tier corridors. The warehouses where the slaves and animals live still need plenty of work, since they were not our priority during the summer, so I set in motion a plan of works for the autumn and winter, including substantial repairs to both roofs, since they leak with the slightest drop of rain. The last few animals are killed for meat or sent back to Bestia to sell on if they're of any value. Once their warehouse is empty it is easier to clean it and complete any necessary adjustments to the building. Next season, we will have stronger and larger pens available. We're also building a permanent ramp so that carts can be rolled right inside the warehouse, loaded with cages and rolled out again, which will make the job of transporting the animals a lot easier. The place smells better now that we only have mules stabled there. They pulled our carts of animals for the Games in summer and are used for various smaller tasks the rest of the year: picking up food supplies at the markets, transporting building materials, carrying their own hay and straw for food and bedding.

"Looks like the show worked, then?" says Maria from her spot on the balcony. Karbo has already bolted his food and run off to play in the twilight with his friends, I can hear them all yelling as they chase each other round the nearby streets.

"What do you mean?"

"Titus has sent the Queen away for good."

"Really? Berenice?"

"Didn't think you had that much power, did you?"

"I'm not sure it was entirely us."

"He was crying at the show, wasn't he? That's what I heard. He knew what was being hinted at. He's not a fool."

I grimace. "I'm sorry he can't marry whom he chooses. He looked like he really did love her."

"Well, she wasn't a good choice, was she? Too much like Cleopatra. Foreign, likely to cause trouble. He could have picked some nice Roman woman, couldn't he? Not exactly short on the ground. Would have made life easier for everyone. Marry close to home, keeps things simple. Look at Cassia."

I don't answer, only make a fuss over calling Karbo back from his playtime and putting him to bed.

"I'm TAKING YOU AND FABIA to the baths for a treat," says Cassia. "I hardly ever see Althea, she works too hard," she adds to Fabia. "We're going to have our nails dyed."

"Ooh," says Fabia. "I've always wanted to do that, it does look pretty."

After baths, we make our way to the beauty room, set aside for women only, filled with cosmetae and their customers, surrounded by the tools of their trade: dozens of little pots containing coloured powders and rich creams, as well as miniature mortar and pestles for combining ingredients and tiny tools that hang from hoops on their belts. Our cosmetes cuts and files our nails to an acceptable oval shape, tutting over how short they are. Then she mixes a strong-smelling green herbal paste and meticulously coats each fingernail and toenail with it, careful not to let it touch our skin.

"Stay still for one hour, until it has completely dried, like a crust," she says. "Then call me back to scrape it off. Don't let it get on your skin, or you'll spoil all my work. And don't get near water or it'll be too pale."

She makes her way to her next customer while the three of us sit and wave our hands and feet about, trying to make the squidgy paste dry faster.

"I've only ever seen it on rich ladies," says Cassia. "Mind you they've got their own personal nail slaves; they can have fancy designs and all sorts. But we deserve a treat."

The cosmetes returns to us when the green sludge has dried to an unpleasant-looking stiff crust. She pulls out a tiny spoon-like instrument and scrapes it off, revealing our nails dyed a dark glowing orange, like burning embers. We admire them all the way home, almost tripping over our own feet as we peer down at our toes.

"Very pretty," says Rullus to Cassia, who smiles and makes her way through the back door of the popina into the storerooms.

Fabia walks ahead of me into the insula and I turn to follow, but Rullus leans across the counter, looking down at my feet.

"Such pretty feet," he says, keeping his voice quiet. "I've been thinking: I'm marrying Cassia for her business but I can have you on the side for a bit of fun, eh? After all, once we're married it'll be too late, I won't have to be careful what I say and do around her, the man's the master, everyone knows that. And no-one's going to marry a whore like you, who works at the amphitheatre with the likes of gladiators. So you might as well have a taste of a real man now and then."

I back away, then all but run after Fabia.

"I've GOT AN AUNT IN Tibur," says Fabia soon after our trip to the baths. "She's invited us to go and stay a few days, enjoy the hot springs and celebrate Fontinalia. Will you come with Karbo? Father has already invited Marcus." She lowers her voice. "I'll ask Cassia as well, perhaps if the two of you have some time away from Rullus you could tell her before they make the betrothal legal?"

I nod, feeling my heart start to beat faster at the very idea. But being with Fabia will give me confidence, I think. Cassia needs to be told.

But it turns out that Cassia cannot come, for Rullus has other ideas.

"He says we should keep the popina open during the festival, that it will be good for our profits," she says, a little disappointed.

"Can't you say no?"

She shrugs. "He's right," she says. "Father and I always took the festival off as a holiday, but a popina that wants to do well should really be open during festivals, when people have more time to eat and drink and spend a little more enjoying themselves."

"They were getting along fine," says Fabia when she hears. "She's just trying to be loyal because she's going to marry him. But he's already showing some of his true colours, all he cares about is getting his hands on their business and making Cassia work harder. You need to tell her."

I nod. "I know," I say. "When we get back."

The Acque Albule, the White Waters, have been famous for centuries. Augustus himself used them for his aches and pains and soldiers wounded in combat are often taken there to recuperate and be cured. They're less than a day's journey outside of Rome, to the north-east.

Marcus borrows a cart from the racing stables and reclaims his two horses, who live there. They're mostly used for transport, not being anything like fast enough to compete in the races. They are treated well and stabled at no cost to Marcus, allowing him to keep the two of them, as they occasionally come in handy for such journeys. The five of us climb aboard early in the morning, well-wrapped in cloaks and with a few bed mats on board to soften the ride. Marcus strokes the horses' noses and speaks gently to them, offers each a handful of grain, before climbing up and taking the reins. Karbo watches him as though memorising every move.

"Can we gallop?" he can't help asking, knowing full well Marcus will refuse.

"No," says Marcus. "But you can hold the reins for a while if you like, here, like this."

Karbo's face lights up with joyful responsibility. Marcus looks over his shoulder at me.

"Hold tight," he says laughing.

It's a pleasant enough day, the horses alternate trotting along good stretches of flat roads, walking on the hillier terrain or when they get tired. We stop in the morning to relieve ourselves and once more in the middle of the day to eat the food we have brought with us. As we come closer to the town of Tibur we pass several large and imposing villas. Many rich families keep a country home here, conveniently close to Rome but with all the benefits of the healing waters.

By late afternoon we reach Fabius' sister's house and are welcomed by her. Her house is not large, but we find enough space here and there for the bed mats we have brought. Sabina is a good host to us. She is a widow now, but her husband was a physician like Fabius, so she has been left well-provided for. Her children are grown and married, her son and daughter-in-law live with her and there are three grandchildren, who, being younger than Karbo, see him as an excellent source of new games. We have only been there an hour and he is already pretending to be a horse, carrying them on his back in turns, neighing and rearing to their obvious delight. We are well fed and spend an enjoyable evening cracking new-season nuts and telling stories.

The next morning we make our way to the hot springs, eager for a day of bathing. The strong smell of sulphur reminds me briefly of the smell in Pompeii's ruins after Vesuvius erupted, and I look to Marcus, whose face is tight. He turns to Fabius, who is making some joke, and manages a smile. I feel a little less awkward around Marcus this time; it helps that we are part of a group, but also the water covers us better than at the baths. It's an odd greenish white, hence the name White Waters. The colour is a little off-putting at first, especially when combined with the strong smell, but once we get in, the gentle warmth is relaxing. I float alongside Fabia while Karbo splashes about, practising his underwater swimming as well as diving, popping up here and there, often unexpectedly. Marcus joins us after a while and leads Karbo off to a quieter area to practise, so that we won't get splashed so much. Fabius joins us and lies back in the water.

"I wish I could send all my injured gladiators here," he says. "It does wonders for wounds and muscle pains. Marcus was a different man after he'd been here."

"Marcus has been here before?"

"Oh yes, after his injury."

"I didn't know that."

"I insisted on it. He was a good soldier and my friend. Once I saw the wound was healing I sent him home to Rome from Egypt with strict instructions to come to my mother's house, stay with her for a month and bathe in the waters every day. I came home myself a little while later and he was so much better."

"How did he get injured?"

"Oh, some thug with grand ideas about Egypt being free of the Romans. An attack from behind, cowardly. They wouldn't have had a chance if they'd fought him face-to-face. Shame though, one stroke of the sword and it ruined his leg, he's limped ever since."

"And after he'd recovered?"

"He had found Julia's by then, was living there but getting restless, wondering what to do with his life."

"Was that when he went back to Pompeii?"

"Yes. They were just about to re-open the amphitheatre after the ban and wanted someone to run it. He thought he had nothing to lose, so he applied for the job and they were delighted to get an ex-army man still in his prime. And he did a good job of it."

"Did you keep in touch all these years?"

"Oh yes. Marcus isn't a bad letter writer. He'd send me stories of gladiators and beasts and all sorts. People looked down on him for having that kind of job, dealing with the sort of people you get in that world, but he didn't care about stuff like that. He'd had people whispering about his grandfather's gambling for years, so perhaps he saw anyone can rise or fall. When he told me his right hand for the amphitheatre wasn't just a woman but a prostitute, I confess I was a bit shocked. But I met Fausta once, she was a formidable woman."

"She was," I agree. "I still miss her."

"And when he met Livia, well, that prompted a lot of letters, I can tell you. I could tell he was smitten from the very first one. All these details about the colour of her hair in the sunshine." Fabius laughs. "And then of course they had Amantius so then there were fewer letters, he was too busy."

I think of hazelnut-haired Livia and Amantius, a tiny copy of Marcus. "The anniversary's coming up," I say.

"I know."

"I thought recently, maybe, he was…"

Fabius raises his eyebrows. "What?"

"Thinking of… moving on?"

Fabius shakes his head almost immediately. "Doubt it. He doesn't drink much, but if he ever gets tipsy, all he talks about is Livia." He shrugs. "I mean, we've visited the odd she-wolves' den of an evening, but mostly at my suggestion, not his. Marcus is a man who doesn't forget easily."

"How's your swimming coming along?" Marcus is wading over, the water swirling around his hips, addressing me.

"Nothing like as good as Karbo's," I say, wondering if he heard Fabius mentioning visits to prostitutes.

"Want a lesson, while we're here?"

I follow him through the water to where he had been teaching Karbo, a quieter section of the pool.

"Let's see you float, then."

I lie back in the water, but I am finding it hard to relax and so my middle keeps dipping down, as though seeking to hide under the milky waters.

"You need more lessons," he says, putting one hand under my back, his touch gentle but sure, holding me upwards. "Right, do some strokes."

I turn over and begin swimming, a clumsy movement.

"Smoother," says Marcus. "Your legs and arms need to coordinate."

"I'm trying!" I protest.

"Try harder."

"My turn again," says Karbo, suddenly appearing out of the water.

"You've had your turn," says Marcus.

"I want to learn more!"

"You're better off teaching him," I say, "I'm nowhere near as good."

"That why you need more lessons," says Marcus, but he gives in to Karbo's pleading, taking off through the water using smooth, certain strokes, while Karbo follows enthusiastically behind him, fast but splashing water everywhere. I watch a little enviously. Vita will need to give me more lessons, I think.

On our third day at White Waters, the thirteenth of October, it is time to celebrate Fontinalia, Festival of Springs. The guardian god of wells and springs, Fons, must be honoured and where better to do it than here? The day is a holiday, so there are crowds of people with garlands of flowers making their way round the town, some locals as well as plenty of people from Rome and even further afield. The garlands are laid on the tops of wells and floated in the waters of the hot springs. By midday, the whole of the main pool is covered with flowers, so that the water itself has all but disappeared and the bathers emerge from their dips with petals clinging to their hair and skin.

We arrive at the pools holding our own garlands, bought at the market. Fabius and Marcus murmur Fons' name and throw their garlands into the water, before following them into the warmth. Fabia and I take ours to the very edge and gently push them into the pools, watching them float off for a while. Karbo, meanwhile, is scattering petals wildly.

"Perhaps Fons would like his garland still whole?" I suggest.

Karbo shakes his head. "This is prettier," he says, and I leave him to it. Certainly the petals are pretty as they gently come to rest on the water, colours intertwining like elaborate mosaic pieces.

All I can see of Karbo is his toes, pointing out of the water.

"I wish he'd stop trying to hold his breath," I say. "He's seen what Vita can do and he wants to copy her, but it can't be good for him not to breathe for so long?"

Fabia giggles, watching the toes collapse and Karbo's gasping face suddenly emerge. "He's getting good at it though," she says. "I'm sure that was even longer than he managed yesterday."

"You have to gulp lots of air before you go under," says Karbo, joining us, still gasping.

"Yes," I say. "It's what keeps you alive. So don't forget to do it occasionally, will you?"

"When I get back to Rome tomorrow, Vita will see I've got better," he says, with a hint of hero worship.

Back in Rome shortly after our trip, I wake up and, remembering what day it is, feel a sinking in my stomach and a chill that has nothing to do with November being almost upon us. Today is the day that Vesuvius erupted, one year ago. I think back to the nearly built amphitheatre, to Marcus and its architect standing talking. How

I looked down at my sleeve and saw ash, could not understand where it came from, did not know the horror that had already happened, did not realise the cloud of ash had drifted from Pompeii and all the other destroyed cities to Rome, the dark clouds heralding the news that would devastate so many.

"This will be a hard day for Marcus," I remind Karbo. "Leave him alone if you see him, please don't ask difficult questions or make a nuisance of yourself."

"Will we visit a temple and make sacrifices?"

"You and I will," I agree. "I don't know what Marcus will do." Privately, I hope that we can spend time together today. I know nobody else from Pompeii, certainly no-one who saw the aftermath of the eruption. The images of it come back at odd moments, at night is the worst, when I dream of ash everywhere and Marcus, digging and digging through it, finding nothing, turning to me with empty ashen hands. Even a few specks of ash from a fire often make me swallow, feel again the rush of fear as we raced back to Pompeii.

Julia and Maria both nod when they see me, solemn. Julia holds out a cage with two white doves in it.

"Take them to the temple in sacrifice," she says.

"Thank you."

She's holding three roses, the very last of her autumn blooms, delicate pink. "I'll leave them for Marcus' lararium," she says. "You said Livia used to wear flowers in her hair."

I've been keeping an eye out for Marcus, but I've not seen him anywhere today and have to conclude he doesn't want company. Karbo walks with me to the temple of Vulcan, where we hand the doves to a priest and light incense. I stand for a little while, praying for everyone I knew who died in Pompeii, hoping that despite the lack of funerary rites at the time, they somehow found their way across the River Styx and into the fields of Elysium, to dwell in peace.

On the way back, I tell Karbo about Felix the gardener, who never said much but was kind-hearted, and Myrtis the cook, my friend, who talked faster than anyone I knew and made the best honey cakes I've ever tasted.

"Let's make some to honour her," says Karbo, enthused at the idea of a treat.

"I don't have the recipe," I say. "She always said she wouldn't share it with anyone." But the idea appeals, and I tell Cassia about the little cakes, and the secret mix of spices Myrtis kept to herself.

"The popina's quiet today, Father and Rullus have gone off to the baths. Let's do a little baking. If it's spices you need to get right, I should be the one to help you, don't you think?" says Cassia. "Maybe you just need my namesake."

I nod. "Let's start with that then."

We make one small batch after another. We chatter to each other and for a while it feels like the days before Rullus came, the fun of spending lighthearted time together. We try both cassia and its sweeter cousin cinnamon, we add nutmeg, mace, cloves, ginger. We end up with some honey cakes that are barely edible, they're so heavily spiced. Only Karbo, leaning on the counter and watching with great interest, wolfs them down, willing to eat anything with honey in it. When Marcus finally appears, late in the afternoon, and we tell him what we're doing, he grimaces, having no sweet tooth at all.

"They're not right, are they?" I say.

He shakes his head. "Too much of everything," he comments through a mouthful.

My head droops. "You and I are the only people left who ate them," I say. "No-one else knows what they tasted like and Myrtis always said she'd never tell anyone. Perhaps I'll never get it right." My voice turns unsteady, and tears well up. I turn away, unwilling for him to see how much it matters to me, such a silly thing to be upset over, so insignificant compared to his loss.

"Pepper," he says.

I turn round. "What?"

"Pepper. I think she used pepper." He waves and walks away, back inside the insula.

Cassia and I try another batch and there it is at last, a hint of the taste I remember. We bake two more rounds and suddenly I really am in tears, choking on a mouthful of honey cake, back in Myrtis' tiny, smoky, gossipy kitchen in Pompeii. Cassia puts an arm around my shoulder.

"We'll make them for Saturnalia, give them to our friends, what do you say?"

I nod, swallow.

"Been baking?" Rullus is back. He stuffs a few of the cakes in his mouth. "Always said you were an excellent cook, Cassia," he says with his mouth still full.

"We're going to give them away for Saturnalia," says Cassia. She passes me the batch we made, then moves away, clattering with jugs and cups at the back of the popina.

"Wasting my profits?" says Rullus to me in a low voice. "You might have to compensate me. I'll think of what I might like in payment."

I TAKE A DOZEN OF the little cakes and walk down Sand Street, past the local urine collection point, till I reach a corner shrine to Libertas, where I offer up the tiny morsels that taste of the past, as well as a prayer for my old friends Myrtis and Felix and all those who perished in Pompeii.

When I return, thinking to try and find Marcus, I see, as I walk up the stairs, Julia's door open and inside, Marcus, sitting at her table, head down, shoulders heaving. Julia stands over him, her face solemn, one hand on his arm. She looks out at me and nods as I pull the door closed so that no-one will hear him sob.

I feel sad as I climb the stairs. Not just because of those we have lost, but that I did not manage to share that pain with Marcus, today of all days, that he went to Julia to be comforted, rather than come to me. I wonder if I have failed him as a friend, if I should have found a way to help him through the pain he is still suffering. I lie awake, wondering if I have lost him altogether as a friend, if we are now nothing more than two people who work together in a pleasant enough fashion, who once, through fate alone, shared a horror that has now faded away, as has the bond it created.

The next day Marcus seems his usual self, he says something about having chosen a day when our team can begin to dismantle the wooden floor, now made unusable with pitch, so that we will be able to rebuild it with fresh timber in the new year. I want to say something about Livia and Amantius, but I don't know where to start and it seems too late, and so I say nothing.

BETWEEN US, CASSIA AND I keep Karbo busy during Saturnalia. The streets ring out with loud seasonal greetings of, "Io, Saturnalia!" while we make batch after batch of Myrtis' honey cakes and I ignore Rullus' scowls when he thinks Cassia is not looking. We put handfuls of the cakes in small woven baskets with festive mottos and riddles written out in my best hand on tiny scrolls, then send Karbo to our many friends and acquaintances. These include the gladiator schools, the butcher who carves up our animals, the undertakers, as well as suppliers of everything from sand to the stallholders who surround the amphitheatre every day. In return, many gifts arrive, some of them overly lavish, especially those which arrive for Marcus. As manager of the amphitheatre, there are plenty of people who want to maintain his favour, hoping to continue supplying us next season, not to mention those who would like to become suppliers themselves and are angling for the opportunity to show off their wares to impress Marcus, rather than giving the traditionally un-ostentatious gifts among friends. Daily, we receive gifts of honeyed nuts, scarlet pomegranates, elaborately layered and spiced pickles, the very finest olives and bottles of garum and even more expensive gifts, such as bundles of reed pens for myself and a finely woven piece of yellow cloth dyed with expensive saffron for Marcus, which he passes to me with raised eyebrows.

"Don't you fancy dressing in yellow then?" I ask him, knowing full well that he prefers simpler colours, with a preference for blue or green.

Bestia, who must be delighted at having supplied us with almost ten thousand animals this past year, goes so far as to send us a lion cub, and although Karbo begs to keep it, embracing it with delight, Marcus shakes his head and instead regifts it to Titus, hoping that it may live out its life as an imperial pet rather than face death at the hands of a bestiarius.

Marcus gives Karbo a hunting knife and Julia some beeswax candles with a little joke about her guarding their flames. I have already given Karbo a box of marbles and I give Marcus a set of glass drinking cups decorated with moulded grapes that remind me of his family farm. Marcus gives me a delicately painted basket, which, when I open it, reveals a branch of gilded dates, still on the stem.

"They're too pretty to eat," I say.

"I'll help you," he offers.

We sit on the wooden stairs and make our way through a good half of the stem, the rich sweetness making me almost dizzy.

"You don't usually like dates," I say.

"Saturnalia," he says, spitting out a stone. "Everyone eats more than is good for them."

"How's the arena floor coming along?"

"If I never hear another hammer in my life it will be too soon. But it's getting there. We're more than halfway through ripping it up. When we rebuild it, we can make better trapdoors, to open more quickly, so that will help next year."

"And we can still move it away to deep fill it for the next naumachia?"

"I think so. We'll make it in sections, so we can lift them out more quickly. We'll have to store it all down at the warehouses. At least next time the Games won't be one hundred consecutive days, so we can have no shows for a couple of days beforehand, give us a chance to remove the floor, fill it up with water, get the animals in."

"Shall I come down one day? Can I help in some way?"

He shakes his head. "No. Have fun with your friends and when Saturnalia's over, you can start devising some shows for next season. Make a list of any well-known myths we haven't used yet; they always go down well with the crowd. And we can repeat a few of the most popular shows. Two of our musicians have resigned, one's too old and the other one's joining a theatre, so we need to replace a trumpet player and a water organist. Look into that, will you?"

"I will do. We're going to hold a Saturnalia feast for the slaves, down in the warehouse."

"I'll be there."

MARCUS PLAYS HIS PART WELL at the Saturnalian feast for the slaves. There's a big meal and Marcus and I, Strabo, Fabius and Fabia, Karbo and others in our management team, including Merula and Vita who have joined us for the fun of it, wait on the slaves, bowing and scraping as we bring them their plates of food, much to everyone's merriment. We have brought our musicians with us for the evening, and the noise of everyone talking and the loud playing is raucous. Marcus throws dice to determine who will be named the Lord of Misrule and one of the slaves who has a twisted spine is chosen. He's crowned with a golden circlet used in the parades at the Games and takes to his new role with pleasure, making Marcus serve at tables for the evening, Strabo tell riddles and jokes and Fabia and I sing a duet, which we do very badly, to much amusement.

"It's my first time on this side," says Vita, laughing after she has been told to walk on her hands, which she has done with admirable dexterity.

"Me too," I say. "We didn't really celebrate last year."

"We used to make Labeo do all sorts," says Vita. "Fighting, swimming, you name it. We chucked him in a fountain once, in someone's villa on the outskirts of Rome. He practically drowned, he's a very poor swimmer."

"What was he like as a master?" I ask.

She shrugs. "You've seen what he's like. It's all about the spectacle, how much money he can make and he doesn't care how he gets it. He'll do anything for money."

I make a face.

"He was born into a very poor family," says Vita. "He grew up thinking money would solve everything. It doesn't. But it does make life a lot smoother. He doesn't have status, but he does have money, and it offers him some protection and peace of mind."

"Is he splitting fees with you, now you're free?"

"After a lot of arguing. He was afraid to lose me. My team brings in a lot of money, there aren't many slaves who can do what we do."

"And now a dance!" proclaims the Lord of Misrule.

Strabo and I end up clinging to each other as the music plays faster and faster, tripping over each other's feet. Meanwhile Marcus and Fabius pretend to show off elegant dance steps as though they were a couple, while the Lord of Misrule takes Fabia's hand and they dance around all the tables, urging everyone to join in. I see Merula dancing ever closer to Vita, but not daring to reach out for her hand, catch his look of disappointment when she is whirled away to a larger circle of dancers.

"This year you're learning to cook," says Cassia as the year draws to an end. "It's absurd you don't know how."

"I was a body slave to a rich girl by the time I was ten and a scribe to my next master. I lived in rich men's villas, other slaves did the cooking. I wasn't required to learn."

"Well, no time like the present. Help me make the weekly soup."

I spend a week chopping vegetables, soak beans and barley, learn to make pancakes and flatbreads and Cassia even teaches me how to make her famous saltfish fritters. I keep close to her and avoid Rullus where I can, but any time she leaves my side he makes comments under his breath.

"Waste of time, her teaching you cooking," he hisses. "Not about to get married any time soon, are you? Although I suppose you have to feed that street rat you've adopted."

"His name is Karbo," I say. "And Titus himself knows his name, so you might want to learn it."

"Don't take up too much of Cassia's time," he says. "She's as good as a married woman now, she has to think about my profits. She can stop making that ridiculous beggars' soup and teaching waifs and strays like you her skills, for a start."

"Does she know you're so uncharitable?" I ask. "Does she know what kind of man you are?"

"It'll be too late when she finds out, won't it?"

He stands a little too close when I am in the popina, brushes past me once too often when there is no need to. I'm glad when I can claim that our new season of Games will begin again in March, and that I have to prepare for them.

Diana's Spring

THE NEW YEAR FEELS LIKE a threat rather than a promise.

"WILL YOU BE MY MATRON of honour?" Cassia asks me, in a quiet moment.

It's a role of huge importance. I will not only help prepare Cassia for the wedding day when it comes, I will also give her away to Rullus during the ceremony. I'm both flattered that she has asked me and sick at the idea of giving her to Rullus. "Of course," I say, embracing her tightly. "I'm honoured."

"YOU HAVE TO TELL HER," says Fabia. "You can't be her matron of honour and not tell her."

"I know," I say miserably.

"You want me to be there too?"

I shake my head. I know that Fabia has lost faith that I will tell Cassia, can see how afraid I am of what has to be done. But I need to do it alone.

"It has to be before the betrothal is made legal," insists Fabia.

"I know."

I DON'T KNOW WHY I choose that particular morning. I wake and know it must be today. After all this time, too much time, it must be today. I have waited too long and now I must find the courage to open my mouth, whatever it takes. Cassia will be unhappy for a while, I think. She will be sad that the wedding is not to be. I don't think she has fallen head over heels for Rullus, but she is a practical woman, she sees, in Rullus, a pleasant man, from her own family and therefore, to her mind, trustworthy. He has worked hard in the business and given her father a rest, he has plans for the business to do even better and has offered honourable marriage. But I cannot let her marry him.

"Of course," says Cassia, when I say I need to talk to her and could it be in her apartment. "Rullus, will you mind the stove?"

"Anything for my betrothed," he says. "Althea, look after my Cassia, now." He is all smiles, but there is a warning in his eyes, I know he does not like the idea of my speaking with her somewhere away from him, somewhere private.

Inside Cassia's apartment, she offers me wine, some little biscuits.

"No, thank you," I say. I sit down and then stand up again immediately.

"Sit," she says.

"I need to tell you something about Rullus," I say very fast. There. Now I cannot say 'nothing,' if she asks, I cannot get out of it, I have made a statement that is odd, that will be questioned.

"What is it?" She is not concerned. She cannot think of anything I could have to say that would be bad about him.

I talk about how late I was that evening, how the streets were already dark, how – how foolish I was to risk the streets of Rome at night. I talk of seeing the gateway and the dimly lit safety of the courtyard beyond it and then. And then.

"Then?"

The man's hands, how I could not scream nor hardly even breathe, how I struggled. I struggled, I fought, I scratched. That is the important part. I scratched. And his cursing and stumbling and my running running running.

"I'm so sorry," she says, kneeling close to me because I am shaking. "You should have told me."

I want to push her away because she does not understand what there is to be sorry about. "I didn't tell you, because."

"Because?"

Say it quickly. Say it and it is done. Say it. "Because it was Rullus."

"She won't talk to me anymore," I tell Fabia. My stomach feels sick with the thought.

"She didn't believe you?"

"She said I was jealous that she was getting married and that I was trying to ruin her happiness. That she'd never seen Rullus behave badly and I was just making things up."

"Should I talk to her?"

"No. She needs to keep her friends about her. If she won't have me as a friend, she needs to keep you for when it all goes wrong."

There is a betrothal party, at which Rullus gives Cassia the traditionally lucky iron ring to wear and a wedding date is set for September. June is a luckier month for weddings, but the popina is often busy that month, not least with catering for the weddings of better-off families which Rullus says they should be mindful of. September is a little quieter. Cassius insists on giving a dowry, as though Cassia came from a wealthy family, I think it makes him feel proud to offer it, so legal documents are signed agreeing it and Rullus kisses Cassia in front of the lawyer.

Cassia punishes me by naming Fabia as her matron of honour, without explaining her change of choice, but Rullus smiles broadly at me when I hear this, no doubt he can guess what happened and now I have nothing against him, for I have not been believed and he has triumphed.

Everyone in the insula gives Cassia gifts, intended to help her set up house. Fabia and I buy her a length of good cloth for swaddling her future babies, as well as a tiny glass vial to keep perfume in. A grand wedding would have ten witnesses, but Cassia chooses the important older women in her life: Julia and Maria.

Rullus is often at the counter of the popina now, serving customers, always with a bright smile on his face and often waving away Cassius, telling him to rest, that an old man deserves to take life easy. If I catch Cassia's eye she only turns her face away and has Rullus serve me instead, so that I frequent the popina only when absolutely necessary.

"She'll come round," says Fabia, but she sounds uncertain.

We open the season in March, which will give us seven months to offer one hundred and sixty-five Games, the number agreed with the Aedile for this year. The extra days we have available this year are heartily welcome, they mean we do not have to put on a show every day, allowing us to take breaks when needed, especially before the end-of-season naumachia and any other particularly complex Games.

We get off to a good start in the first two weeks, showcasing a vicious battle of Carpophorus against a rhino, which he manages to kill using only a spear, and a huge re-enactment of the Battle of Zama where the crowd enjoys watching Roman general Scipio Africanus defeating the Carthage general Hannibal, for which we even provide elephants, one of whom kneels to Titus to show Rome's superiority. There are tiger fights, acrobats bull-leaping as part of a story about Theseus and the Minotaur, and a display of Amazons fighting which uses Labeo's entire selection of gladiatrices and which Titus seems to find very compelling, no doubt helped by them all fighting bare-breasted.

In order to fill the year's programme, we've also looked back at the previous season and will be repeating a few of the most popular Games. One of these is our Diana deer hunt followed by a criminal execution, featuring Alyssa. Labeo is pleased when I book her.

"Still got it, hasn't she? Does well for me, that one. I thought she might be getting past it, but you can't see the wrinkles from a distance, I suppose. Plus, she helps the newbies with their training, especially on their archery skills. No-one shoots like her. Might make a good trainer when she's too old for the arena. But there's a few years still left in her, I'd say."

Fabius is out of town for a few days. His brother is unwell with a fever and he wants to see him for himself, doesn't trust the local doctor. Fabia is standing in for him. There have been two minor injuries from fights and the gladiators have sullenly submitted to her ministrations. But her stitching and dressing of their wounds has been neat and they are healing well. Both they and their managers have expressed a reluctant acknowledgement of a job well done.

"They'll give in to you in the end," I say.

She nods and gives me a smile, although I can see she is a little afraid at the weight of responsibility resting on her shoulders. She lays out her tools with great care before every show, a little stove with boiling water by her to clean her instruments, preparing for any and all eventualities. Her body tenses when Marcus gives the signal for our team to take their places before the show begins and she steps up onto a little wooden platform one of the carpenters knocked up for her, so that she will be the right height to treat any gladiator laid out on the table in front of her.

Diana's Hunt is our opening piece this morning. The hundred-odd deer are in place; we'll eat venison for a few nights. I look forward to it, it's one of my favourite meats. Our pool, symbolising the sacred spring in which our goddess will wash herself, is a sparkling blue in the bright March sunshine. The eyeless helmet with stag's antlers for the hapless criminal lies ready, the two groups of hounds are panting in their cages. I steer clear of the second pack, their taste for human flesh frightens me. Labeo is here again, arranging Alyssa's divine appearance. One naked breast, as before, is already on show.

"Bought a new head of hair," he says, running his hand through golden tresses bound into Alyssa's own darker blonde. They tumble down to her waist. He fixes a gilded circlet onto her head, ties it tightly into the hair with small strands of thread so that it cannot fall off while she is hunting. Satisfied, he steps back to survey her and nods.

"Bow," I remind him.

"Of course," he says, passing the bow. Alyssa takes it in her left hand, rolls her shoulders, checking the quiver is safely strapped to her back.

"Places," calls Marcus. The morning hunt is about to begin. The first pack of hounds are in their lifts.

"Ready?" I ask Alyssa.

She nods.

I open the door of her lift and she steps in, face impassive, her gilded shoes and jewellery gleaming in the dim light.

Marcus walks away, up the dark stairs leading to his place in the amphitheatre's level of seating, by the imperial box, from where he will watch the Games, give signals as needed. I nod to Labeo and follow him, take my own place in the tiers, on the other side to Marcus, close to the Vestal Virgins' box. The music begins, the water organ bringing its delicate sound to the peaceful pastoral music, appropriate to the scene we have created.

Marcus' hand lifts and the drumming starts as Alyssa is lifted into view to the applause of the audience. Some have seen this show before, others heard about it last year and wished they'd had a chance to see it. Either way, the crowd like a divinity, especially a partially naked one.

The hunt is perfect. Alyssa's skill with a bow is without compare, her arrows flying faster than seems possible, one deer after another falling. When the first pack of hounds are released, the tempo of the hunt increases still further, until the floor is littered with the dead and dying herd.

There's a brief pause as the carcasses are dragged away, the hounds returned to their lifts, disappearing beneath the floor. Alyssa takes her time, slowly pacing around the perimeter of the arena, gradually disposing of first her bow, then her quiver. She pauses, looking up over her shoulder at the audience, turning round on herself as they bay for her to undress. She walks towards the blue pool, undoing her belt with care, then slipping her tunic over her head, dropping it to the floor, entirely naked except for her gilded adornments. The applause is deafening. She bends over to undo her sandals, the shouts from her admirers bordering on the obscene. Barefoot, she steps into the pool and washes herself, the water glistening on her skin as it trickles down her body.

She's a good performer. I've been caught up in her storytelling but realise, as the music changes again, that Marcus has given the signal. We are about to execute today's criminal.

A young man stumbles into the arena, pushed by hidden hands. He turns back to the door immediately, trying to open it, but it opens only from the inside, there is no escape. Turning back to Alyssa, he sees her play out the moment when Diana is seen by a mortal, her anger and the raising of her hand, cursing him to a terrible fate for having dared to glimpse the divine.

The trapdoor at the other end of the arena, behind her, opens up; the second pack of hounds is about to be released. They hunger for the man, they will tear him to pieces in moments, even as Alyssa escapes unscathed. She strides towards the criminal, the eyeless helmet surmounted by a stag's antlers in her hands, rams it down on his head as the bars fall, the hounds racing towards them across the already-bloodied sand.

But the blinded man grabs at where Alyssa was, manages to clutch at her golden hair and pulls her towards him. She should be grasping the rope dangling just out of reach, the rope which will lift her to safety, without which she will share in his gruesome fate.

I'm on my feet, Marcus is on his feet, the crowd is roaring.

Alyssa jerks away from the man's desperate clutches as the hounds reach them. Her right hand finds the rope as one of the hounds closes its jaws around her left hand. The rest of the pack have fallen on the man, his throat is already spewing blood, his entrails spilling out. The slaves above Alyssa are pulling her upwards but the hound will not let go of her, its jaws move even as it is lifted onto its back legs and Alyssa's mouth opens in a scream as her hand comes away into the hound's mouth and blood spurts from her arm.

I am running, running along the corridors, down the steep steps to the dark space below the arena floor, screaming for Fabia to be ready, to clear everyone and everything out of the way. Just ahead of me in the dark space is Marcus, roaring for more light, for torches to be moved to where Fabia is waiting, her eyes wide, Labeo turns in horror as

Alyssa is carried into the space, eyes closed, her naked body covered in slippery blood, the team members gripping onto her, their faces pale with horror. They all but throw her onto the waiting table, so eager are they for her to reach Fabia's hands.

Marcus is by her side. "Anything you need. Anything."

"More light," gasps Fabia and already she is lifting a scalpel, is cutting Alyssa's arm still further. Alyssa's eyes open and she screams.

"Hold her," says Fabia. "I have to find the blood vessels and tie them off, or she'll die. I don't have time to give her anything for the pain." Her face is pale, but her hands are steady and her voice is firm. "Talk to her, Althea," she adds, without looking at me, all her focus on the bleeding stump.

"I have to go," says Marcus to me. "The Games must continue; I can't leave the arena empty." He's gone before I can answer, dragging Labeo by the arm after him. Karbo appears in the doorway, having made his way down from the upper tier where he was sitting, and Marcus grabs his tunic and pulls him, too, with him.

Strabo and four of the men hold Alyssa down. I can't see much of her from where I am, only her head, still crowned with the gilded circlet and golden hair, purchased from some northern slave, now streaked with red, dangling down from her head to the floor. I step closer to her, look down at her face which is scrunched up in agony, an unearthly moaning coming from her mouth.

"Alyssa."

She tries to focus on me, eyes wildly moving about until she fixes on my gaze.

"You're a gladiatrix," I tell her, almost hissing into her face. "The best Labeo has. You're a warrior. There is no woman who can bear pain like you. What Fabia is doing to you, it's nothing. Nothing you haven't borne before." I don't dare to look at what Fabia is doing; I don't dare to break eye contact with Alyssa.

Alyssa's open mouth moves for a moment. Then her jaw clenches shut and silent, her eyes grow hard. I shudder. This is what it must be like to look into the eyes of a gladiator before they kill you.

"Yes," I say. "Yes. See? You are a warrior. This is nothing to you. Nothing. I could put a sword in your hand right now and you would fight on."

I keep talking. I don't know what I'm saying half the time, repeating reminders of how brave she is, how little she cares for any pain, how she has terrified every opponent who ever came near her, man or beast, because of her reputation, her fierceness, her skills. All the time I can hear the breathing of the men, of Fabia, Alyssa. Once, Alyssa's eyes roll up and I think she will faint, but she recovers and then Fabia speaks.

"I've tied off the blood vessels. I'll give her opium for the pain so I can finish." She steps away for a moment, her hands dripping red, plunges them in a basin of water, washes them, then wipes them on a clean cloth and takes up a small cup, into which she pours a mixture from a tiny bottle, then takes it to Alyssa, forces it between her lips.

It's a relief to see Alyssa slowly blink, her jaw loosen, the fierceness drift into confusion and then her eyes close altogether. Above us I can hear light-hearted music, the actors and dancers putting on a comedic show. Marcus returns briefly to see how we are doing and Fabia nods.

"I think the arm bones are safe," she says. "They are smooth. But all of the hand is lost." She is using tiny forceps and hooks now, prodding for chewed fragments of wrist bone, dropping them with a tiny clink into a bowl beside her. Her face is intent, and Marcus touches her shoulder lightly and leaves us again.

Gladiators have come and gone for their bouts before she's finished, each one glancing towards Alyssa and touching their hands to their chests in a salute to her as they pass, their other hand making a gesture against bad luck by their sides, each afraid that today may be inauspicious for their own fight. But there are no more casualties. A couple of small cuts will be taken care of back at the barracks.

"Done," says Fabia.

The men move back. Where Alyssa's hand was is now a stump, ending where the wrist once was. Fabia has cut and pulled together flaps of skin to create a covered end, criss-crossed with rows of tiny stitches. The arm has been wiped clean of blood and Fabia wipes it again with vinegar, the smell sharp overlaying the heavy scent of blood in the air.

"I'll dress it with honey," she says.

I nod.

Marcus returns with Labeo. "You saved her life," he says to Fabia.

"How is she supposed to fight like that?" asks Labeo, appalled, looking down at Alyssa.

"You'll be compensated," says Marcus.

"I want the price for her if she'd been killed. She might as well have been."

"You'll get it. Now shut your mouth and get out of here," says Marcus. "I'll have her brought back to your barracks as soon as Fabia is done, and I'll send a slave to look after her from our own team."

Labeo has finally left, and the Games are over for the day. Alyssa has been taken back to the barracks on a litter by Marcus and three other men. I have made sure the crowds are gone and the cleaning team have started their work.

I come back to find Fabia putting away her instruments. She is boiling each one in the water to clean it, then lifting them out with little tongs and wrapping each in a cloth, for storage. She looks as though she's in a trance, her movements slow and her eyes unfocused.

"You were wonderful," I say.

She looks up as though she's only just become aware of anyone else in the space. "I was so scared," she says in a tiny voice and suddenly she drops the scalpel she is holding to the floor, her whole body shaking.

I kneel down and take her in my arms, feeling her small body shuddering, her teeth chattering. I wait a few moments, holding her as tightly as I can, until the shuddering slows and then I pull back to look in her face. "You were wonderful," I say again. "You saved her life."

"Her hand —"

"No-one could have saved her hand," I say. "It was on the arena floor with a dog chewing on it." I gag at the thought of it, then swallow and focus on Fabia again. "Let's go home," I say.

"My tools —"

"Leave them. There's no show tomorrow. We can come back and get everything then."

We walk home in silence, Fabia's hand in mine. Sometimes I feel a shudder pass through her again. When we get back, I tell Julia what happened and Julia gets honey from Adah, mixes it with unwatered wine and gives it to Fabia, who first sips a little, before draining the cup.

"And now sleep," says Julia and Fabia follows her like a child back to her apartment and lies down on Julia's own bed, her eyes closing almost immediately. Julia pulls up a stool next to her.

"I'll watch over her. Do you need a cup of wine too?" she asks me.

I shake my head. "I think I need to sleep though," I say.

"Sleep. I'll tell Marcus where you are when he gets back. Where is Karbo?"

"Went with Marcus to take Alyssa back to the barracks."

I sleep as though dead, waking in the late evening. Marcus has left a plate of food for me outside the door, Karbo is asleep on the bed next to me. I sit in the dark and eat, then kneel under the stars and pray to Apollo, god of healing, and his son Aesculapius, god of medicine and physicians, that Alyssa will recover.

IT'S BEEN A MONTH SINCE Alyssa's accident.

"How is she?" I ask Labeo, on a visit to his barracks.

"Useless," he says in his usual brutal way. "Sits around with a miserable face on her. I thought she might at least train some of the other women, since she knows what she's doing, but she won't even do that. Might have to sell her. Won't get a proper sum for her though, not with her bow arm gone, now she's just a one-handed slave, and who wants one of them?"

"I meant how is the stump?"

"Oh, that's healed well enough, looks like. Fabia knew what she was doing, saved her life I suppose. But she can't perform anymore, so what good was it?"

"I thought you said she was a favourite with the crowd?"

"Only if she can use a bow. She's no good otherwise, is she? That stump's off-putting. I could have sold her to one of her older fans, perhaps, as a bed companion for old time's sake, but no-one's going to want her looking like that."

I look out into the courtyard, where the women are being trained. Alyssa is slumped in a corner, knees drawn up, her eyes on the ground, not even watching the fighting going on right in front of her. Her right hand cradles her stump, as though holding a broken kitten. Labeo need not concern himself with selling her off. If she is as unhappy as she looks, she'll die of her own accord within the year.

Worried, I report back to Fabia, but she only smiles as though she is not concerned at all.

"The stump looks good," she says. "It is healing beautifully. I had Father inspect it and he was so proud of me." She glows with the remembered praise.

"But Alyssa seems…"

"I know. Don't worry. I have something planned. It's taking a little longer than I thought, but you'll see."

She won't tell me anything else and I worry about Alyssa for days before Fabia sends a message via Karbo, asking me to meet her at Labeo's barracks.

When I get there, Fabia is standing by Alyssa, looking at her arm.

I get closer and stare. Where the stump was, there is now a hand in the shape of a fist, made of gleaming bronze, attached to her arm with a leather brace.

"What is that?"

"Her bow hand," says Fabia grinning with pride. "I had a man make it for me. I told him about General Marcus Sergius Silus, in the Punic Wars. He lost part of his left arm and they made him an iron hand, just like this one, so he could still hold a shield. Now Alyssa can hold a bow, so she can still shoot. See, the thumb can open and close, to insert the bow and close around it. Once it's in place, she can shoot."

"As well as before?"

"Not quite as fast as she used to. But better than most people."

Alyssa opens her mouth. Her voice is softer than I expected, with a hint of a foreign accent to it, I'm not sure where from. "Labeo is keep me now: as trainer for the women." Her lips curve into something approaching a smile.

"I'm so pleased," I say. "Fabia, you're amazing."

Fabia is grinning. "Maybe the other gladiators will let me near them now," she says.

"I spoken with Labeo," says Alyssa, addressing Fabia. "Physician we use, he old now. Retire. I ask for you to be physician to our barracks. Labeo say yes, if you willing. He hire you."

Fabia's mouth hangs open.

"You don't want job?" Alyssa looks disappointed, but Fabia grabs her round the legs and hugs her and Alyssa breaks into a broad smile and bends down to hug her back, the bronze hand caught in Fabia's untameable hair.

THE PORT OF OSTIA

IT'S ONLY MAY AND ALREADY Julia is having to water her plants every morning or they will wilt by the end of the day.

"We've had no rain for a month," she says. "It's not right for this time of year. What will we do in summer if we haven't had the spring rains?"

"Good thing we have our own fountain," I say, "or you'd be traipsing back and forth to the public fountain down the road."

"We have you to thank for it."

"It was a good use of the money," I say, scooping up a handful of the gurgling water spouting from Neptune's mouth and gulping it down. It's cold and fresh. My share of Titus' reward for making the opening day of the Games a triumph has been well spent.

MARCUS SAYS HE WANTS MERULA to join us for breakfast and discuss the naumachia for this season. I go to the local market and fill a basket with breads, cheese, fruit and bring it to the amphitheatre, thus avoiding the popina. It's been months since Cassia has spoken to me, it hurts when I think of it.

We sit in the senatorial seats and share out the food. Merula's eyes are bright with enthusiasm, as they always are when he discusses anything to do with water. "The added depth will mean that you can have any water animal that you care to add to the spectacle," he says. "Even quite large animals."

Marcus' shoulders slump and he takes another gulp of wine. "Such as?"

"Crocodiles? Rays? Sharks?"

"Oh, may the gods have mercy on me. I knew it would come to crocodiles."

"I've never seen one," I say.

"I have, in Egypt. Vicious creatures. You can see them plotting to kill you, it's in their eyes. Merciless. If you could train them to fight in a battle your opponents would be wiped out in moments."

"Can they be trained?"

He snorts at the idea. "There are three ways to make an animal do your bidding. You can make it trust you so it will do what you want out of loyalty and a desire to please you, you can keep it hungry until it learns, or you can frighten it into submission. They can't be frightened, I wouldn't care to keep them hungry and they'll never trust you. I'd rather go up against a full-grown lion than a crocodile."

"I shiver. "How big are they?"

"Length of a man, even the smallest ones. But they can be three times that. I've seen them take down a leopard with barely a fight."

I've seen leopards in the arena, their powerful wiry bodies, their merciless killing of prey. The idea of an animal who could dispatch one with ease is terrifying.

"Will they go for people?"

"If they're hungry they'll go for anything. Book us a meeting with Bestia, let's see what he can get hold of."

Bestia is not impressed with our latest shopping list of animals.

"I don't do water stuff," he says, coughing and then spitting phlegm. "Waste of bloody time. The transport's a pain, half of them die if you take them out of sea water, even the good bestiarii can't train the buggers. I stick to land animals. Or birds. Don't mind birds, you can train them and the big ones look impressive when they're flying. I've got some nice eagles in, good wide wingspan. One of them will rip out a man's intestines, no problem."

"You mean I have to travel to Ostia and find a new beast hunter to provide this lot?" prods Marcus, evidently hoping Bestia will change his mind at the idea of a possible rival for his business. "I have to hire a new beast hunter just for one show?"

"Jupiter's dick, do what you like, just keep me out of it," says Bestia. He has another coughing fit, doubling over and making a hacking noise that sounds none too healthy.

"Don't you die on me," says Marcus. "I've got enough to do without changing supplier for the rest of the shows."

"By the Furies, who said anything about dying?"

"Go and see a doctor then," says Marcus. "Tell him to sort out that cough."

"They're all shitting quacks," says Bestia.

"And you're a stubborn old goat," says Marcus.

"Is he alright, do you think?" I ask Marcus as we leave.

"I expect so, he's a tough old thing. Although he must be getting on by now, I've known him a long time. Send Fabius over to him, will you?"

Fabius tries, but Bestia roundly refuses any medical help and Fabius retires defeated from the attempt.

"Ostia it is, then," says Marcus. "I swear this one show is causing me more trouble than the hundred days of Games last year. Remind me, why did we say yes?"

"Because you did such a wonderful job last time and the Emperor himself asked for it," I say.

"Oh yes, that'll be it. Neptune help me then. We'll go in June. Got to plan ahead to get the best stuff."

June brings the unwelcome anniversary of Fausta's death. Karbo and I light candles Adah has given us and put flowers near the tiny doll in her image, we visit the temple together and offer sacrifices and prayers. When we get home, Maria calls to us.

"You're eating with me," she says, more of a command than an invitation.

She has made a beautiful meal, including a dish of thin flatbreads layered with herbs and fresh curd cheese cooked in the baker's oven, along with a fresh green salad and tiny cakes topped with a sweetened cream and fresh strawberries. Julia and Marcus have joined us, and there is an unexpected guest, a woman dressed in a toga, a prostitute.

"Acca," I say, recognising the woman who used to talk to Fausta about anything the local prostitutes wanted, such as having members of their informal guild dressed as gladiatrix near the amphitheatre, to titillate the crowd as they came out of a show. It's her professional name, referencing the she-wolf or prostitute who suckled Romulus and Remus. I'm amazed that Maria, usually a pillar of propriety, has invited her here to dinner, but she had come to a reluctant respect for Fausta, during the time they knew each other, especially when she saw how Karbo treated her like a mother.

Acca lifts her chin at me by way of greeting.

"Fausta would have been glad to have you here," I say to her, as we make toasts to her memory.

She gives a brusque nod. "Me and the girls, we sacrificed for her today," she says. "Down at the temple of Venus."

"Thank you," says Marcus and he sounds moved.

When the evening is over I embrace Maria. "Thank you," I say.

She gives one of her shrugs. "Thought it was important. For Karbo," she adds. "He's got you of course, but..."

"Yes," I say. "Thank you."

This time I'm not going to let Marcus get away with not talking. I follow him to the rooftop and find him, as I expected, looking out over the city.

"I miss her," I say.

"Me too."

We stand in silence for a few moments. It feels companionable and safe. It is a long time since I stood here in darkness without feeling afraid.

"When I first started as manager of the amphitheatre in Pompeii, she used to come and sit in the stands to watch rehearsals," Marcus says after a while. "And she'd make these really loud comments about all the mistakes I was making, how the sightlines weren't good enough, how a different bestiarius was more popular with the women and ought to be given a bigger part. How one of two gladiators in a bout wasn't up to the skill of the other one and they made a poor match together, that the gambling wouldn't be any fun because you could see the outcome right away."

I start laughing. I can imagine her loud voice and raucous laugh, a younger, inexperienced Marcus struggling to cope with this strange new job and being harangued by a prostitute who knew all the ropes.

"In the end I said just shut up or come and work for me," he says. "She got up and walked out and I thought she'd buggered off for good. Next morning, there she was, in the arena before me, telling me if I was going to be late every morning she'd find it very hard to respect me as a manager."

We laugh together in the dark and when we wish each other good night Marcus touches my arm and I'm glad I followed him, that I forced him to talk about her rather than grieve alone for his best friend.

A WEEK LATER WE TRAVEL by river barge to the port of Ostia, following the Tiber down to its mouth, leaving Rome in a dark dawn and arriving in the heat of the day at the bustling harbour, where ships and barges cram into a limited space, bringing everything Rome needs from across the empire. Huge sacks of grain from Egypt and endless amphorae of olive oil from Hispania are being unloaded from big ships and loaded onto the river barges, along with noisy livestock and live fish in vast barrels of fresh or salted water. Customs officials are everywhere, scowling as they make notes on their tablets, trying to keep up with the flow of goods.

"I saw an elephant being put on board a ship once," says Marcus as we walk towards the town centre. "It hardly seemed possible the ship would hold such a beast without sinking, and it did not much wish to board the vessel, either, but they managed it in the end."

"Where was it going?"

"To take part in Games somewhere, I expect. It had been trained a little, but it still disliked the heave and swell of the water."

"I don't blame it," I say. I am relishing the firm land under my feet myself, having felt nauseous at the motion of the barge. I am not a natural sailor.

In the centre of Ostia is the Merchants' Forum, a large paved square set all around with a portico divided up into little cubicles, their fronts shuttered or open for business. Each one is marked out on the pavement in front of it with black and white mosaics indicating their wares: sailing ships for chandlers; barrels with wheat sheaves for grain shipping, mostly from Egypt; leaping dolphins and Nereids for garum sauce and fresh or preserved fish; an olive branch for olive oil.

"Look for the elephant," says Marcus.

"Elephant?"

"Mosaic of an elephant. It's the agency of Sabratha, based on the coast of Africa. They ship wild animals for Games, I've heard they have a good beast hunter. Quality merchandise and he can get difficult items. Which is what we'll need."

We spot the elephant and the name of Sabratha picked out above it, but the cubicle is shuttered.

"He'll be back shortly," says the trader next door. "Probably gone to get something to eat."

"Not a bad idea," says Marcus. "Come on, let's get some food and come back later."

We wander down a few streets to find a local popina and purchase bread, cheese, olives and wine, then sit under an awning and watch Ostia bustle by. We hear more than one foreign language being spoken; a port town brings people from all over the empire and beyond.

I enjoy being in Marcus' company. It's been a long time since we spent time together like this, without constantly being interrupted or worrying about work matters. I take a sip of wine and close my eyes to the sunshine, for once enjoying its warmth without fretting about something that has to be done.

"You were looking for me?"

I look up. The man speaking is tall and slender, with hair growing in the same locks as Karbo's. Both his skin and hair are a soft brown though, unlike Karbo's far darker tone, and each of his locks ends in a tiny sun-bleached golden curl. I wonder where his parents are from. His clothes are unusual. He's wearing a blue skirted loincloth, something like Egyptians wear, with a white top to his waist like a very short tunic, tied with a red sash. Attached to his loincloth, at the back, is a tiger's tail, the black and orange fur silky-bright in the sunshine. He has wide brass armbands over his upper arms and a string of small white shells around his neck. The skin on his cheeks and nose has been deliberately scarred in a pattern.

Marcus stands. "Marcus Aquillius Scaurus. How did you find us?"

The man grins. "The manager of the Flavian Amphitheatre? Every beast-hunter in Ostia has been watching you, hoping for your business. If I hadn't come to look for you, they'd have told you I was unavailable in the hopes of winning your interest for themselves." He holds out a hand. "Funis."

I note both that his nickname means rope, no doubt in reference to his hair, but also that he has omitted the rest of his name, unusual at a first meeting.

Marcus indicates me. "Althea Aquillius. My scribe and right-hand woman at the amphitheatre."

Funis turns his dark eyes on me and gives an open smile. "Althea."

I nod.

"I think you're going to regret meeting me," says Marcus. "Can I offer you a cup of wine before I make your life difficult with what I need?"

Funis takes the seat by my side. "There aren't many demands you can make of me that would prove especially difficult. The Games are my speciality."

Marcus waves to the serving girl. "More wine here."

Cups filled, Marcus raises his. "Your health."

"Health," echo Funis and I.

We raise our cups and drink. When we set the cups down Marcus takes a deep breath. "So."

Funis leans forwards expectantly. "So?"

"I have to put on a naumachia this autumn, on the last day of the Games in the Flavian Amphitheatre. We did one last year but now they want something bigger, the water has to be deeper, the events more spectacular, more dangerous. The trouble is that we've also been asked to showcase the battle between the Corcyreans and Corinthians, the one that led to the Peloponnesian War. It's dull as you like, they only want it because Augustus had it. We could have had something much more interesting. I don't know why the Aedile always has to poke his nose in, he has no idea what the crowds like or what looks good in the arena. Which means that everything else has to be even more spectacular, or everyone's going to sit there yawning. So it's down to the animals to provide the danger."

Funis laughs. "Ah, I see your difficulty. All water animals?"

"Yes. Last time, we had horses running through the water. It worked well enough, but now Titus wants more."

"Dangerous animals?"

"Yes."

Funis nods, unperturbed. "I can get them. If I have enough time."

"We have a few months. What's possible?"

"Crocodiles from Egypt are no problem, even hippos if you want them. They may look like fat cows, but they can kill a man, they've got a temper like rhinos. Sharks if the water's deep enough. Rays. Vipers, they can swim. Eels."

"The water's plenty deep," says Marcus. "It's half the problem though. It's no good if a man just gets dragged under the water and eaten without anyone seeing the struggle, it doesn't make for a spectacle."

Funis thinks. "The sharks are good, their fins stick up when they're circling, adds tension. The crocodiles kill their prey by rolling them in the water, it's pretty spectacular. Rays and vipers, if they attack, less so, but it all adds interest."

Marcus nods. "And you can provide them all?"

"Of course. It'll be expensive though. They're not just dangerous, they need transporting differently to most animals or they'll easily die."

Marcus shrugs. "What the Emperor wants, the Emperor gets."

"Do you have bestiarii to fight them?"

"Some. I don't know how used they are to water animals."

"Do you want me to send you some water-trained bestiarii to go with the animals?"

"That might be useful. Do you fight them yourself?"

"I used to. Not anymore." He pulls away one of the armbands, showing a large, scarred area, a clear bitemark where a chunk of his flesh has been bitten away. "It would happily have eaten the rest of it, if I hadn't put a spear in it."

"Crocodile?" asks Marcus.

He nods.

I shiver at the thought, and he catches my movement, laughs. "I still shiver at the thought of it myself, on dark nights. I thought my time had come. After that I decided not to tempt the gods any longer. So, no, I no longer fight in the arena. But I know a few men who are good beast hunters, no doubt they would be delighted to fight in front of Titus himself, they will brag of nothing else. If they survive, of course."

We make our way back to the Merchants' Forum, trying to stick to the shade offered by umbrella pine trees along the way. At the sign of the elephant, Funis pulls up the shutters of his trading cubicle and gets out his ledgers. He and Marcus put their heads together, discussing numbers of animals, adding a few extra in case some of them should die in transit, the prices of each. I take notes on the care of each animal, what food they must be given and how each must be kept. The sharks, in particular, must be kept in saltwater until we release them into the freshwater we will be using.

"They won't live long in freshwater," says Funis grimacing. "I've had too many die on me to risk it for long. They'll stay alive for your spectacle, but only if you keep them in seawater until just before the show starts."

I make a note.

"Keep the crocodiles hungry," he advises me.

I think of the hapless gladiators who will risk being drowned while clamped in the hungry jaws of a deathly monster.

"Quicker death than some," says Funis, watching my face. "Lions will eat you while you're still breathing."

I nod.

"Time to see some of the animals you're thinking of showcasing?"

"You have them here?"

"A few. Not all of them."

We follow him back to the docks, where he leads us to a warehouse similar to the one we have in Rome, only smaller. Inside there are three huge tanks and over twenty barrels of water, spread around the room. Funis takes us to one of the larger barrels and dips into it with a net on a pole, swiftly bringing up a pair of grey snakes, who writhe in the net, their mouths open, hissing.

"Vipers," he says. "They can swim and they are venomous." He lets them back into the water and closes the lid.

"I've got an octopus in that one," he says, pointing at a larger barrel. "Gets out all the time and tries to eat the fish if you don't catch it. No good to you though, not very dangerous."

"Who will you sell it to?"

"Oh, they make interesting additions to the pools of big villas. I sold one to a man once who liked to throw jewels into the pool for it to catch, found it amusing. And you can eat them, of course."

We walk to the first of the large tanks, built higher than my shoulder, I have to tiptoe to look in.

"Moray eels," says Funis. I can just make out rippling yellow grey through the water, but when Funis pulls one out, I step back. The eel has spotted grey skin and it opens its mouth at once, baring many long narrow teeth, like needles, at us. "Carnivorous," says Funis. "If you frighten them, they'll attack."

The second tank contains stingrays, whose tail barbs are both sharper than swords and venomous.

The final tank is the largest, taking up half of the warehouse floor space and it appears empty. There is a wooden platform halfway up the height of it and it has a heavy metal grid fitted over the top.

"Crocodiles," sighs Marcus, without even seeing the contents.

"Indeed," says Funis. From a hook close by he takes the carcass of a hare and throws it into the tank, onto the wooden platform. The carcass has barely come to rest when the water explodes and a crocodile has leapt onto the platform and snatched the hare. It lies on the platform as it crunches its prize, tail still dangling in the water. It is longer than Marcus and its yellow-green eyes watch us even as it swallows.

"Just as I remember," says Marcus. "I'm grateful it won't be me in the water with any of them but especially not those. We should be going."

I can't help but feel relieved once we've left the warehouse behind, a heavy bolt drawn across the door to keep its inhabitants from escaping.

"Thank you for your help," says Marcus. "If you wish to bring the animals yourself, you are more than welcome at the amphitheatre."

Funis smiles. "I am not overly fond of Rome," he says lightly. "Ostia suits me better. I miss the sea if I am not near it."

Marcus shakes hands with him and begins to walk away.

"Thank you," I say.

"It was my pleasure," says Funis. "I am sorry not to have the pleasure of getting to know you better, Althea," he adds, taking my hand with a smile that brings a little heat to my cheeks. "Should you ever wish to leave the amphitheatre, I am always in need of an assistant. There is no lessening in Rome's demand for animals; if anything it is growing now that the Flavians have invested in the Games so greatly."

I swallow. "I am glad to have met you," I say. "Goodbye, Funis." I catch myself. "What is your full name?"

"Ah, I am afraid it would be hard to say, it comes from my mother's country, the Kingdom of Kush. You know it as Dodekaschoinos," he adds, seeing my frown.

"I'd like to hear it."

"My given name is Arikakahtani. It was the name of a king, long before my mother's time, but she must have taken a fancy to the idea of having a son with a regal name. No-one can pronounce it here, so they have nicknamed me Funis, for my hair."

"Arikaka… Arikakahtani," I manage.

"Impressive."

"I have to remember a lot of names. You said it was your mother's country? Not your father's?"

"Too many questions for a first meeting," he says, not losing his easy smile. "You will lose sight of your companion if you do not hurry."

Marcus is already striding away towards the barge that will take us back to Rome.

"Oh, I – Goodbye."

"Goodbye," he says, and lets go of my hand.

I turn to leave and stumble over a loose paving slab, gather myself and hurry after Marcus.

SHIPWRECKS

IT'S JULY NOW, AND WE have all given up hoping for rain until the autumn thunderstorms come. Dust gathers in the streets, sticks hot and grimy on our skin, kicking up into the air if there is ever a breath of breeze, which there is less and less often. The whole city feels like an oven. I dread to think how the baker's family manages their work. Mostly they try to do all the baking by night, when the temperature drops, if only by very little. In the early dawn they mix and knead, by day they leave the dough to rise and make up for their night-time labours with sleeping in the daytime, leaving only one of them by turns to look after customers.

Next door to them, Cassia sweats through the day as she makes and serves food for her customers, though her offerings have cooled with the growing heat. Now she has cold salads of salted cheese and beans with herbs, garlic-herb curd cheese to spread on bread, boiled eggs and green beans with olive oil and pickles, fresh green salads and balls of spelt, flavoured while cooking into a thick mush and then shaped into little balls to be eaten cold, dipped in garum. Olives and fruit, fresh summer cheeses and cool wine make up the rest of her offerings. I mostly send Karbo to buy food for us now, but it makes me sad to eat Cassia's food knowing her warm smile no longer comes with it and often I send Karbo elsewhere, to local popinas whose food is not so good but at least does not come flavoured with sadness.

A RARE DAY OFF FROM the Games leaves us free for the day. Celer has invited Karbo to see the races and I have gone with him, anxious to keep him safe, anxious to avoid the insula.

"We need to get there by sunrise," says Celer the night before.

"So early?"

"One hundred and fifty thousand spectators. It takes hours to get everyone in, the entrances are not as well organised as the amphitheatre, not to mention it's almost three times as many people."

"Glad it's not mine to manage," I say.

We get there early, but still the crowd is already huge and Celer is right, it's not as well organised. There are, supposedly, lines one should queue in, but no-one is staying in their own lines and there's a lot of elbowing for the top tier seats, which are free of charge. Celer has already procured tickets for us, so we do not have to sit so far from the action, we are somewhere more mid-range. A few wealthy patrons of the races make their way through the crowd only by dint of surrounding themselves with heavyset bodyguards. There are soldiers everywhere, some of whom carry large clubs to quell the crowd in no uncertain terms should things get rowdy.

Just as we have at the amphitheatre, as well as the usual stalls of snacks, drinks and sweet treats, are other stalls selling portraits of the charioteers, as well as tiny wooden replicas of their chariots and horses, toys for the more privileged children or perhaps their fathers, the sort of thing Balbus the toymaker creates.

We struggle through the crowds, Celer being approached more than once by she-wolves in gaudy-bright tunics pinned to allow a more than usually abundant view of cleavage, who tug at his arm and make lewd suggestions about what he can do to them for a very cheap price. He nods and grins at a few who greet him by name, but pushes onwards, Karbo and I in his wake. Occasionally I clutch at his tunic so we will not be separated. Karbo has his arms full of cushions we can use to sit on the seating area, should we ever get there, which I'm beginning to doubt.

Finally, we get out of the throng, as everyone, one way or another, finds a place to sit, we put down our cushions and try to settle ourselves. I give Karbo water and a peach pastry to eat as a belated breakfast, but he is too giddy to think of anything so prosaic as hunger. His head turns this way and that as he tries to take in everything.

"How do you bear coming here often?" I ask Celer. "I felt as if I couldn't breathe."

"Oh, I usually help out one of the stable hands when they bring the horses down here before dawn in return for watching with them from the starting gates," he says. "This a different view. Didn't Marcus want to join us? He was more than welcome."

"He's gone down south to Puteoli," I say. "With Vita," I add.

"Really? What for?"

"I'm not really sure," I say. "He said he was going to visit the manager of the amphitheatre there. But he has friends in the area, it's where his family was from before they ended up in Pompeii. He said he wanted to introduce Vita to some people there."

Celer nods. "The family farm's there, isn't it?"

"Yes." I think of Marcus taking me there, the sweet strawberry grapes we tasted, the deal he made me as we left: that I would work hard for him and be loyal, that in return he would free me one day and then return to the farm with his wife and son. They are gone now, swept away by Vulcan's wrath. I suppose the farm is still there, abandoned and waiting for its master to return. I wonder whether Marcus feels the time has come to return, whether he is ready to begin a new life, perhaps with Vita. Perhaps he is introducing her to a distant family branch, a first step towards marriage? I didn't feel I could question him before he went. Perhaps when he returns, he will explain. I am not sure how I feel about Marcus remarrying, I worry that we will drift further apart. It might lead to him leaving altogether, if he wants to go back to the family farm, and that thought makes my stomach turn over with fear of losing him altogether when he is so much a part of my life and work. He is also my protector. If he leaves, I will have no choice but to leave the insula and live elsewhere. I would be too afraid to do otherwise. If Rullus saw me without a protector nearby, he would not hesitate to do as he pleased with me. Nor did I need to ask how Merula felt about the trip, his face was a picture of misery at the idea of Vita going on a mysterious journey with Marcus.

"About time he found some happiness again," says Celer. He takes a gulp of wine he has brought with him and nods to a man currently walking through the tiers of seating, stopping to chat here and there. He has a broken-off branch of laurels stuck in his tunic and Celer gestures him over. I gather from their conversation that the man is a roving bookmaker, taking bets, illegally of course, as gambling is not strictly permitted, although it goes on everywhere and in plain sight. Celer consults with the man for a little while.

"…on the *third* race, mind you. No, nothing on the first two or the fourth, don't fancy any of them. Now, the fifth…"

For his part, the bookmaker, knowing Celer's connections, is asking a few questions, in case he should find out something interesting. "How is Golden Laurels doing, anyway? Heard he was limping, is that right? And has Sergius gotten over that girl or is he still moping? He drove like a ploughman last time I saw him, no spirit at all."

The pompa circensis is about to begin, a vast ceremonial procession heralding the opening of the races. Karbo's eyes surely can't get any larger, he leans forwards staring as the procession makes its way onto the track. First horseback riders from the very best families, followed by more young men on foot, who will join the infantry. The crowd erupts as the top charioteers appear in their four-horse chariots, followed by those less well-known or still young and working their way up the ranks in chariots drawn by two or three horses. Having finished with the bookmaker, Celer takes on the role of commentator for Karbo.

"Ah that's the dancers and musicians, along with the choir of satyrs, then behind them are servants, their jobs is to carry the statues of the gods and incense burners. Here comes the Emperor."

Titus is in full regalia for once, not his usual modest toga. He's riding in a four-horse chariot, and I'm reminded of the day I saw him, as a much younger man, riding through the centre of Rome in his celebratory Triumph over Judea, when he burnt the Temple of Jerusalem to the ground. Today he is not showing off Jewish slaves and loot from the Temple, only waving to the crowd to acknowledge their cheers. As the procession continues round the track and Titus makes his way to the imperial box, three bulls are taken to a temporarily erected altar and sacrificed. Celer is busy explaining the day to Karbo, who has never seen a full day's races, only caught little bits here and there when he lived on the streets and would try and sneak a glimpse between the tiers of seating.

"There'll be thirty races today. Used to be twenty-four, but the Flavians prefer a fuller day. Seven laps round the track. If you're fast, you can keep a tight line and the horses will run less distance, see? If you're slow and there's other people in the way, you have to go wide and your horses end up running further and getting worn out, so then you fall even further behind. Look, they're drawing lots to see who will go in which starting stall."

Karbo cranes his head to look. The chariots for the first race, painted in the bold colours of the four racing teams, red, blue, white and green, are being guided to their starting stalls, the horses already struggling against the stable hands' attempts to move them, eager to be off. They toss their heads, manes plaited to keep them from going in their eyes at the wrong moment, distracting them or obstructing their vision, either of which could spoil a race.

A sudden blast of trumpets accompanies the presiding magistrate dropping a white cloth. The stall doors open, the chariots are already halfway along the track before I've drawn a second breath. The speed down the straights is breath-taking, the tightness of the cornering has me wincing, certain that the drivers will make a mistake, that they will collide with not just each other but sections of the building. By the third lap, drivers and horses are visibly sweating and the sparsores along the racetrack are throwing water over both, as well as the chariot axles to stop them over-heating.

"What are they doing?" screams Karbo to Celer, indicating horseback riders who are galloping alongside the chariots, each dressed in the same colours of the chariot they are keeping abreast of.

"Telling them how the race is going!" yells back Celer. "They can't see behind them, and they don't always know how many laps someone's done, or who's gaining on them. The hortatores are telling them anything they need to know."

The riders Karbo has taken an interest in are leaning perilously from their horses so they can be closer to the drivers and though I cannot hear them above the roar of the crowd, I can see them yelling at the drivers, passing on information. The drivers do not look at them, only at the track ahead, but they can hear them and change their tactics accordingly.

As the seventh lap of the first race approaches its conclusion, it becomes clear the Greens will win despite the other supporters' cheers and Karbo's urgent screams of encouragement to the driver of the Blues. When the Greens driver holds up his arm to claim victory, Karbo very nearly weeps, but Celer whispers in his ear and Karbo pins his hope on the third race, which obligingly delivers a Blues win to fill both Karbo's heart and Celer's pocket.

The elite four-horse chariot races give way to those pulled by two or three horses, showcasing the younger drivers working their way to stardom. In between races, there are acrobats on horseback, or a few unusual races such as those featuring chariots pulled by ten horses, more of a demonstration of the skill required to manage such a number of steeds than a standard race.

I have to hide my face when both the eighth and fifteenth races end with crashes between chariots, where a driver has miscalculated how much room he has to manoeuvre or grown too ambitious. Two horses are led away limping, their racing lives over.

"Stud farm," says Celer to Karbo, who asks what will happen to them.

The third horse is not so lucky, a broken wheel spoke pierces its side as it falls onto it, blood spurting in a wide arc that hits some of the closest spectators. A hammer to the head finishes it, just as Charon does at the amphitheatre and men with hooked poles drag it off the racetrack as the pieces of chariot are gathered up and the track swept clean of debris for the next race, the programme and spectators' enthusiasm continuing unabated, death or no death.

Crashes in the sixteenth and twenty-second races only lead to broken chariots, the horses and men escaping damage.

"We call them shipwrecks," says Celer to Karbo, indicating the shattered remnants of chariots, their racing colours now mixed together on the tracks.

In the twenty-third race a chariot overturns and the driver must cut himself loose from the reins with his knife. He survives, but only just, carried from the track with blood pouring out of him all down one side of his body. I can only hope he will recover, that the Whites have a good physician ready and waiting for him.

"Can he race again?" asks Karbo.

"Doubt it," says Celer. "If he's had a bad injury, especially on his arm, he'll not have the strength or flexibility. And he'll have the fear. Once you have the fear in you, you can't race anymore."

THE VISIT TO THE RACES has a not wholly unexpected consequence. Karbo is now certain that he wishes to be a charioteer.

"Absolutely not," I say, thinking of the dead horse, the bleeding charioteer.

"Fabia said people should name their desire and then work hard for it, and look at her now, she is physician to one of the biggest gladiatorial schools in Rome! And my desire is to race chariots! For the Blues! And I will, no matter what you say, Althea."

"Mother," I remind him.

"You're not my real mother," pouts Karbo, though the provocative statement lacks the vehemence and volume of his initial outburst.

"I've been as good as since the day I met you," I say sternly. "And you know it. And you are my adopted son now, you owe me obedience. Titus himself made me your mother."

"When you won't let me do what I want to do?"

"My word is final," I say. "I am afraid for your safety. Charioteers die young, everyone knows that."

"Celer's still alive."

"He ruined himself with women and wine," I say. "It's all that helped him survive, he said so himself, or weren't you paying attention then, either?"

Karbo gives a wicked glance at me. "I could ruin myself with women and wine," he suggests and ducks as I swat at him.

"Dea Bona! You think talk like that will win me round?"

"Nothing will win you round. You're so stubborn."

I snort. "Says the boy who won't listen to anything but his own desires."

August is coming to a close and the pleasure of having our own fountain in the insula's courtyard is dimmed by a city-wide declaration that private fountains must be turned off most of the day to avoid wasting water, due to the drought. Every day we scan the sky, hoping for a glimpse of clouds or the distant rumble of thunder that might indicate the end-of-summer storms that would break the heat and bring the much-needed rain, but each day dawns sharp-blue clear and the sky is silent. Even the city birds are too hot to sing, they huddle in the shady corners of rooftops, sheltering from the heat. The tiles on the rooftop are so hot that bare feet are impossible, I have to keep my sandals on until I reach the shade of my hut, which is also too hot after a day baking in the direct sun. I want to leave my door open at night to try and cool the roof hut and sleep better, but I daren't, instead each night I lock the door as usual, feeling as though I am locking out not just Rullus but Cassia's friendship, too.

"I've had enough of this heat," says Marcus, wiping sweat off his face in the dark and smelly under-arena space after the show is over for the day. "It's ruining the water-clocks, they're all evaporating too fast. I'm going to have to bring in the clockmaker again to make some adjustments to them or the timings of the shows will be a mess, the clocks down here aren't matching my sundial in the seating upstairs at all. I'm going down to the river for a cold dip. Who's coming?"

Fabius, Karbo and Fabia are eager, three of the gladiators who have not sustained any injuries today nod agreeably to the idea. We make our way upstairs and out into the bright heat of the afternoon. Strabo lumbers along behind us, a few dozen slaves join us. After making our way through the hot back streets we clamber down a steep side of the river to a grassy bank much favoured for swimming. The water is already full of people who have had the same idea, especially young boys who take turns leaping in with a huge splash.

"Be careful to stay out of the current," I tell Karbo.

"He's a fish," says Marcus proudly. "Don't you worry about him."

"Even fish get caught in currents," I say. But Marcus is right, Karbo is turning into an excellent swimmer and soon enough he is flinging himself off the bank with the other boys, their yelps, taunts and cheers so loud that in the end we move further away to where the river slows briefly in a little curve, allowing those of us who cannot swim well to paddle safely.

The men strip off at once and dive in, Marcus amongst them. The female slaves peel off their tunics and wade in the water; a few can swim and strike out into the deeper part, others tread water and gratefully dunk their heads under the water to cool themselves, emerging dripping and smiling at the freshness they have not felt these past months.

I undress, then tentatively enter the river. It's blissfully cool and I lie back and float in the shallows, then, feeling braver, strike out a little, my swimming motion clumsy but, to my pride, keeping me above water. I smile to myself, pleased with my progress, but then, dipping one foot down, find I can no longer feel the bottom and panic, lose my rhythm, instead feeling again and again for a foothold and finding none, now paddling like a dog, but splashing more wildly, frightened the current pulling at me will drag me away without anyone seeing me or being able to help.

"Got you." Marcus has a hold of my arm, pulls me hard backwards, and suddenly my feet touch something under me and I am safe, find the riverbed under the water, stop struggling and stand up, turning to him. He's shaking his head.

"Thank you," I manage, still gasping. "I – couldn't feel –"

"The Tiber is not like a still pool at the baths," says Marcus, one hand still on my arm. "The currents can grasp at you when you least expect them. You were doing well, though. More practise and you'll be like Karbo," he adds, letting go of me and looking to where Karbo is trying to do handstands under the water, as Vita and her team do. "The boy's a natural."

"Fish and horses," I manage. "He must be beloved of Neptune, since he looks after both."

Marcus nods. "Are you alright now?"

"Yes. Thank you."

"Stay in the shallows. Lucky I was watching you."

I stay in the shallows, but I envy Marcus' comfort in the water, how he lies back in the water and allows it to carry him a little way off, before returning to shore with smooth, fast strokes through the water, his golden-brown skin glistening. Meanwhile Karbo is joyfully leaping into the water again and again, certain of his ability to return safely to dry land. I must keep practising.

"They've chosen a prisoner for us to use at the naumachia," says Marcus.

"Just one?"

"For the Hero and Leander scene," he amends, looking over some plans for the water rafts.

"Why choose this one in particular? We usually pick the most suitable one for a specific scene."

"This one's a troublemaker, they want to make a point."

"What's he done?"

"He's a Jewish preacher. Refuses to worship the gods or acknowledge Vespasian as a divinity. He's one of those followers of that preacher that died, Jesus of Nazareth. Troublemakers, the lot of them."

I nod, only half listening.

"Go and see him," says Marcus.

"What?"

"He's being held in the Tullianum."

I look up. "Why?" Most prisoners are not held for long, they are sent straight to us for their public punishment if that is what they have been condemned to. Occasionally we will hold a group over a few days to make the numbers larger at a particular Games. The Tullianum is an underground dungeon where Rome keeps some of its most dangerous enemies, usually leaders of a conquered land. It sits at the bottom of the Capitoline Hill, close to the Forum. Its walls are rumoured to be three times thicker than a man's outstretched arms. It used to be a water cistern, now used for darker purposes. It's a dark and frightening underworld to be banished to.

"They want to make an example of him, they don't want him lost in a crowd of other criminals being executed."

"And why do you want me to visit him?"

"I need to know if he can swim or not. And I don't just mean whether he's been taught. I mean whether they've broken anything. I can't have a big swimming scene with a man who can't swim, it'll look ridiculous."

"He's going to be drowned anyway," I say, swallowing at the thought of it.

"He has to at least start out swimming," says Marcus. "Check whether he's able and warn the jailors not to damage him before the event."

I nod. I don't much fancy the task, visiting the most frightening prison in Rome puts chills down my back, but if I can save the man from being tortured in advance of the Games he will appear in, I suppose it will be a kindness to him, even if he has been condemned to die.

HERO AND LEANDER

THE FINAL DAYS OF AUGUST are draining the last drops of energy from me, the heat unbearable.

"I'M SO SLOW," I COMPLAIN to Vita, as she outstrips me again and again along the length of the pool.

"You have to keep moving."

"I was moving!"

She laughs at me, lying back in the water and floating.

"Tell me what I'm doing wrong."

"Nothing. It's just practise, you'll get faster without even thinking about it."

"Easy for you to say."

I sigh and float beside her.

"You're not practising."

"I'm resting."

"I'll be glad when the autumn rains come. This whole city is drying up. They said they might even have to close some of the baths, or shorten the opening hours. Never known a drought like it. Not a drop since April. It was practically cooler down south."

"How was your trip there?" I ask. I've not worked up the courage to ask Marcus the same question, am not sure I even want to hear Vita's reply. But it seems absurd not to know whether Vita is Marcus' new chosen companion, as though I were only a minor acquaintance of his.

"Good," she says enthusiastically. "He showed me round Puteoli and the amphitheatre there, and further afield."

I think of Marcus' family farm near Puteoli, wonder whether she means he took her there, a place so full of meaning to him. I wonder whether he even suggested to her they might live there together, one day, since I know that being there is his ultimate desire. Is he ready to move back yet, to leave Rome and his role at the amphitheatre behind? What would I do if that happened? Who else would or even could run the Games?

"Did he —" I start but a woman leans over the edge of the pool and hails Vita, who swims over to answer her, greeting her like an old friend. They start chatting together, so that my opportunity to ask her anything must be abandoned and I am left to practise my slow, clumsy swimming again, passing the same part of the pool, over and over again.

THE WALK TO THE TULLIANUM in the hottest part of the day leaves me panting by the time I reach the large wooden door.

The guardroom is hardly the frightening place for which I had braced myself. Sunlight streams in from the open door. A couple of bored guards are throwing dice in a spacious if plain room, the walls raw stone, unadorned by plaster.

The guard at the doorway looks disconcerted at my visit. "Why would you want to see the prisoner?" he asks.

"I have to make sure he can swim," I say.

He looks baffled.

"The Emperor wants a naumachia," I clarify. "He's going to be in it."

"Thought there already was a naumachia," he says. "Last year, final day of the opening Games. You couldn't get tickets for love nor money."

"Titus liked it so much he wants another one," I say. "You going to let me see this prisoner or what?"

"I can't bring him up to see you," says the guard. "You have to be lowered down to where he is."

"What?"

"I have to lower you down. On a rope. There isn't a lot of room down there and we're not allowed to leave our posts, so it'll just be the two of you. I can't be held responsible if he attacks you."

I try to think of an alternative but find none. "Fine," I say, feigning a bravery I certainly don't feel. "Lower away."

He waves me in and the two other guards look up from their game, curious at my presence.

"Seeing the prisoner. For the Games. Works at the Flavian Amphitheatre," says the door guard.

They go back to their gambling, uninterested.

The opening in the middle of the floor is only as wide as my outstretched arms and below me everything is dark. There is a smell of damp. The rope is coarse between my hands. One of my feet is held in a loop at the bottom of the length, with the other I feel desperately for the floor as I am lowered ever further into the darkness below. I hope the guard will not loosen his grip on the other end of the rope.

My foot touches the floor and I tug at the loop, trying to get my foot out, afraid of falling. The room is very dark, and I blink, waiting for my eyes to adjust to the lack of light. The smell of damp is mixed with another smell: of unwashed human, not the sweat I am used to from many of our labourers and even myself on a hot day, but a smell of abandonment and despair, of uncaring, a sweetish smell that makes me nauseous.

"Who are you?"

I startle at the voice, even though I have been expecting to hear it since I know there is someone down here in the dark with me. I am still holding onto the rope, as though for safety. I peer into the dim corners of the room and see a man, huddled on the floor, his knees pulled up, bare feet resting on the cold stone floor. He has long hair and a beard. His head is up, his eyes watching me.

"My name is Althea," I say.

"Alon."

I'm still holding the rope. Slowly, I let go of it, steadying myself without it. "I work at the Flavian Amphitheatre," I start, unsure of how much he knows about his fate.

He says nothing.

"You have been condemned to the Games," I say, getting the words out quickly.

"I know."

"We are telling the story of Hero and Leander." I pause, hoping that he knows the story, that it will be obvious what his fate is.

"Tell me the story," he says.

I don't know if he is forcing me to tell the story to highlight the cruelty he will be facing, or whether he truly doesn't know it. It's a famous legend, surely everyone knows it?

"There was once a beautiful priestess of Venus named Hero, who dwelt in a tower in the city of Sestos," I begin slowly, aware that I am using the style of a storyteller, perhaps to make the story seem more distant than it will be for this man. "A man named Leander saw Hero at her duties during a festival and he fell in love with her, as she did with him. He persuaded her that Venus, being the goddess of love, would look kindly on their intimacy, and so they lay together. Leander lived on the opposite side of the strait of Hellespont, at Abydos, but the strait is very narrow there and Leander was a strong swimmer. By night, he could see Hero's tower, and she would set a light in it if it was safe for him to visit her. He would set out in the darkness, using her light as a guide, and swim to her tower, where she would meet him on the rocky coast and help him ashore. And so their lovemaking continued, all summer long."

The room is very quiet. I can hear the drip-drip of water somewhere.

"Were they found out?" Alon asks at last. "Punished?"

I swallow. "The end of summer brought a sudden storm," I say. "Hero had lit the torch at the top of the tower, but then she fell asleep and did not hear the wind rise. Leander, for his part, saw the light in Hero's tower and was so filled with love for her that he felt he could brave any storm, for had he not swum the strait many times that summer and always reached her arms safely?"

The dark room's damp has cooled my hot skin. I am shivering. "Hero awoke and realised a storm was in progress, but the high wind had blown out her torch, leaving Leander to swim without a guide, through the darkness rent only by thunder and brief flashes of lightening when he could see the tower and hope not to lose his way. Hero re-lit the torch and waited anxiously. But the rocky shore proved Leander's undoing, for, exhausted from battling the waves, he was flung against the rocks, unable to escape the sea's wrath. He died and Hero, seeing his dead body surface, climbed to the top of her tower and threw herself into the sea, to join him in death. Their bodies were washed ashore in a lovers' embrace and they were buried together, united at last."

"You're holding a naumachia?"

He has caught on quickly. "Yes."

"You are going to cast me as Leander? Drown me?"

"Yes."

"How?"

I think of Merula and Marcus, their faces concentrating over diagrams, adding notes or elements to sketches of the mechanism to be used. "It is something like a small raft that will allow you to swim at first, then drag you under the water. Once – once you have drowned, the raft will re-surface so that Hero will see you."

"Do I need to swim at all, or merely pretend?"

"The mechanism will hold you up a little, but you will need to swim at the beginning, across the arena a few times. As part of the story." It feels strange to be discussing the details of how this man will die with him, as though he were one of our team, considering how something must happen rather than whether it should happen at all. I have never discussed their death with a criminal before: they arrive in our space under the arena, we dress them according to our needs, occasionally we tell them what they are to do and whether they have a chance of saving themselves, if they fight well, for example. I have never had a conversation with one of them.

"And who is to play Hero? Another prisoner?"

"A show-swimmer."

"Ah. She is able to merely enact the part?"

"Yes."

There's a silence. Then he speaks quietly, almost as though to himself rather than to me. "So be it. As my Lord requires of me."

"You are Jewish?" I ask.

"Yes. But I also follow the teachings of Jesus."

I frown. "The Nazarene preacher? You are a Nazarene?"

"Indeed."

"Why were you sent here?"

"For refusing to worship false idols."

I think about this for a moment. I'm aware there are some followers of the Nazarene who refuse to offer even a basic show of worship to the Roman gods and the Emperor, as their leader did and that such refusal does not go down well with the Emperor nor the priests of Rome, who consider it treason, as well as blasphemy. "Surely you can worship both your own god and ours? You need only offer incense to the gods and say, 'Caesar is Lord,' and you would be released."

"Only?"

"Rather than die?"

"If I must die, then I must die."

"Why did they single you out? Plenty of your people get away with little or no public worship. What did you do to draw attention to yourself?"

He gives a very small chuckle. "Preached once too often and far too loudly in the Forum."

I take a step closer, look down into his face. "I remember you!"

"Do you?"

"Yes. I've seen you preaching in the Forum, answering questions."

"Then you know why I am here."

"I thought at the time you were pushing your luck."

"I do what is needful for the Almighty," he says.

"Your god is not being very helpful to you right now," I say. "Shouldn't you be praying for him to get you out?"

"His own son was crucified by the Romans, yet did not protest. How may I refuse what has been laid before me?"

"If he was the son of your god then he was divine," I say. "It's hardly a fair comparison, is it? Expecting a man to do what a god does?"

"Jesus was a man," he says.

"You said he was a god."

"Both."

"You can't be both."

He smiles but doesn't answer.

"So," I say, trying to gather myself. "You didn't say whether you can swim."

"I can swim."

"Well?"

"Not as well as your show swimmers. Well enough for an ordinary man."

"More than once across the length of our arena?"

"I daresay."

"Then that's all I needed to know."

"Can I help you in any other way?"

Something has caught my eye. "You can tell me what this means," I say, indicating the rough outline of a fish, scratched onto the stone wall just by his head. "I've seen it before, on walls. And it was drawn on the ground by your feet when you were preaching."

He smiles. "The fish is a symbol for our Lord Jesus," he says. "We use it as a sign for meetings, or to show that one of us who follows Him lives in a certain place, so that we can find one another."

"Why a fish?"

"We call Him a fisher of men, since He drew believers to His side, out of the waters of our former lives."

"What were you, then, before you were drawn up into his net?"

"A potter. Nothing out of the ordinary. But I left everything when I heard His call."

"And it led you here?"

"Where He leads, I follow. Even here."

I spread my hands. "Is there anything I can do for you before the show?"

"Before killing me?"

"You might as well not suffer any more than you have to."

He thinks for a moment. "Paul asked one of his friends to send his cloak," he says at last. "Perhaps I, too, might make such a request without failing in my service?"

"Who is Paul?"

"One of the Lord's followers, who took leadership upon himself after His death. A great man. Wise. Dead now, he died after the Great Fire, it's hard to believe it is almost twenty years back now."

"And he wanted a cloak here in Rome?"

Alon smiles. "Here in the Tullianum. He was kept here under Nero, before he was condemned to decapitation. A quicker death than the one I have been promised, it seems."

"I think your lives as followers of this preacher would be a lot easier if you would only agree to worship Roman gods alongside him," I say.

"They would," he agrees with a smile.

I sigh. "I'll send you a cloak," I say. "And I will tell the guards you are not to be harmed while in their care."

"I'm grateful to you."

"You won't be grateful come the naumachia," I say.

"I will remember your kindness in saving me from the cold and any harm caused by uncaring guards while I am kept here."

I nod, uncertain how to end this conversation. There should be something more, but what else can I say? He has been judged a criminal, and I put criminals to death every single day in the Games. It may be the part of the job I like the least, but I do it anyway. But I have never stood in a room and spoken with a criminal like this, knowing full well what his fate will be and that it rests in large part in my hands to carry out. Usually, the criminals arrive in a group, the evening before their execution. They are put into one of the pens in the under-arena and they are fed, for I consider it unnecessary cruelty to keep them starving. Then they must find a way to sleep. And during all of this time, wild animals around them roar and grunt and screech in their own pens, waiting for the chance to kill, while other creatures huddle, bleating and whimpering, afraid of the fate that awaits them the next morning, when their known or unknown predators will make short work of them. I walk past the pens sometimes, making notes as I go, counting the occupants the better to plan their use, or directing one of our team as to how to care for them while we have the brief management of them. I do not look into the faces of the criminals or single them out. This man, Alon, has only been singled out to be made an example of. He has gone beyond simple crimes between people and instead committed treason, threatening Rome herself rather than one of her citizens. It is only this that has brought me face-to-face with him, to hear him speak.

"I must go," I say at last. "I will send you the cloak."

"Thank you," he says.

I fumble with the rope, finally getting my foot into the loop and tugging. It grows taut in my hands as I am lifted upwards and I pull my shoulders together as I pass through the hole above, rising into bright sunshine that makes me blink. Feet firmly on the ground again, I look back down into the hole, but it is so dark down there compared to the light here that I can see nothing at all.

"He is suitable for the Games," I say. "He will perform on the last night of this season, in front of Emperor Titus himself. You must take good care of him, I need him fit and healthy."

"He's not going to be very fit and healthy, staying down there till then," says the guard and the other two shake their heads dolefully.

"Feed him better and I will send him a cloak to keep him warm," I say. "Make sure he gets it. Can't you pull him up here and have him walk about under supervision?"

"Oh no," says the guard, looking shocked at this idea.

"Breach of protocol, that would be," adds another. "We'd get in a lot of trouble."

"Once they're in the Tullianum, they stay in the Tullianum until execution day. Everyone knows that," says the third.

"Fine," I say and leave the room without bidding them goodbye, the heat as I step outside almost rocking me backwards, my dampened lungs dried out within two breaths. I make my way along the street, trying to stick to the shade, confused and saddened by the encounter. When I return to the insula, I take the brown woollen cloak Livia gave me, with its little patch of darning where a hole used to be, and tell Karbo to take it to the Tullianum right away.

"Can't I go tomorrow?" he whines. "What does anyone want a hot woollen cloak for in such a hurry? I can barely wear a tunic in this heat."

"Just take it and be grateful you're not in the Tullianum yourself," I say.

He makes his way down the stairs, still grumbling, and I go to join Adah, who has just finished looking after her bees, burning cow dung to create smoke so that she can safely handle them. I keep my distance until she replaces their wicker-work cover and comes towards me, a few chunks of honeycomb in a bowl.

"Not gathered a lot today," she says. "Just a little for myself. I'll do a full harvest soon." She holds out the bowl and I break off a small piece and put it in my mouth. It is sweet and richly, intensely floral.

"It's delicious," I tell her.

"Where's Karbo? He loves honey."

"Gone to the Tullianum."

"Why?"

"There's a prisoner there. A Jew."

"What's he done?"

"He's a follower of the Nazarene preacher."

She grimaces. "Not one of ours. They let all sorts in."

"I thought they were Jews?"

"Used to be. They still follow some of our laws. But they wanted to convert people. At first they made everyone fully convert to all our laws if they wanted to follow the Nazarene's teachings. But they wanted more people and Gentiles were a lot easier to convert if they didn't have to be circumcised, or follow all of our laws. So they grew looser and looser. I wouldn't call them Jews now."

"But you both believe in the same god? And you only have one god?"

"Yes. One. The Almighty. But now they're worshipping a man they call His son. Sounds like idolatry to me. He may have been a preacher, I don't argue with that, there's been many good preachers. They said the Nazarene was a Jew, upheld all our laws, was a good man. But now all these Gentiles…" She shrugs, puts another piece of honeycomb in her mouth and offers me some more, which I take. "What did he do, anyway? Refuse to worship the Roman gods?"

"And preached about it. In the Forum."

She shakes her head. "He should have known better, if he is a Jew. We keep quiet. We don't draw attention to ourselves, it only leads to trouble."

"He won't give in."

She nods. "Then he'll die. But the Almighty will bless him for standing true to his faith, once he had spoken out. I don't agree with worshipping the Nazarene. But the Almighty is a different matter. I will pray for this man."

STRABO IS WAITING FOR ME the next morning when I arrive at the amphitheatre. "Bestia has died."

The old beast-hunter. He's provided us with thousands of animals since the amphitheatre was inaugurated, and Marcus has known him for years. He was a foul-mouthed grumpy old man, but I'd grown used to his ways. "Have you told Marcus?"

"Yes."

"I'll miss him. Never thought I'd say that when I first met him. He should have let Fabius look after him, foolish old man. So stubborn."

Marcus has gone to attend the funeral, so I run the day's Games. He arrives back at the amphitheatre late in the afternoon, when I'm supervising the cleaning.

"How was it?" I ask.

"Well-attended. Most of the bestiarii in Rome were there, many were trained by him at one time or another and they all knew the quality of his animals was good; made their work harder but they respected him for it. No-one wants a mangy old tiger limping around, makes the man fighting it look weak."

"And now?"

"I don't know. His assistant can finish what we need for this season, everything's already been ordered and dispatched, we're nearly done on the regular shows and Funis is providing everything for the naumachia."

"Could Funis become our beast-hunter?"

"He'd have to move to Rome, we need to have someone close to hand, can't be travelling to Ostia every time we have to discuss things. I got the feeling he didn't care for the big city. But it's worth asking. When all this is over, write him a letter. He'll have part of the winter to think about it before we have to look elsewhere."

"He'd be politer than Bestia, at any rate."

"That wouldn't be hard."

Vita is back at the amphitheatre; this time we have to consider how she will play the part of Hero, requiring her to seem to fall from a tower into the water below. One idea is for her to have a length of cloth wrapped around her middle, so that it unravels as she tumbles, an illusion of falling while being safely held. It's something we've seen acrobats do.

"Can Merula talk you through how it would work?" I ask. "I've got to go to the Baths of Nero, Fabia asked me to book a bridal bath for Cassia."

Vita nods. "Can't you talk me through the falling illusion? I feel awkward around Merula. He stammers all the time and there was that misunderstanding…"

"He's still in love with you," I say. "He'd marry you in an instant, if you said the word."

"I'm afraid of marriage," she says. "I got myself out of being whored around by my masters, by getting Labeo to buy me. But I was lucky."

"You were brave," I say.

"And lucky," she says. "If my former master had found out that I approached Labeo, or if I hadn't found ways to manage Labeo… a marriage can be as bad as being a slave, if you're not careful. A husband has as much power over you as a master."

"Merula's a good man," I say. "He works hard and he's kind. It wouldn't be like having a master."

She looks away to where Merula is measuring one of the ships to ensure it will fit through the passageways once they're filled with water. Her face is full of doubt, but there is a little longing there too, as though she glimpses something but does not quite trust herself to see true.

"I have to go," I say. "Merula will talk you through it."

It's the afternoon before Cassia's wedding to Rullus and most of the women of the insula are helping Julia decorate the courtyard with flowers, both her own and bought specially for the occasion. There's much chatter and giggles, occasionally everyone breaks into songs, mostly romantic, sometimes bawdy, leading to more laughter and some ribald jokes.

"Here," Julia says, passing out little basins, "fill them with water and then we can put flowers in, that way they'll keep well overnight. Otherwise, they'll die in this heat."

We do as we're told, passing basins filled with water to Julia and Maria, who are filling them with flowers, then we suspend them in knotted strands of fine rope, so that they dangle all over the courtyard, hanging above Julia's existing plants and flowers.

"Pretty," says Fabia, but her voice is flat.

I take a break from helping out and sit with her on the rooftop. "I hate that I'm her matron of honour," she confesses. "I have to give her in marriage to Rullus!"

I nod. "Is everything ready?"

Fabia shrugs. "The baker's making the unleavened bread for them to eat during the ceremony. I'm taking her for the bridal bath at dawn, while Cassius, Marcus and Fabius go with the priest to watch for omens and make the sacrifice before sunrise, so everything will be auspicious."

I snort. "How *can* it be auspicious? The minute she's bound to him, he will show what he's really like. And it will be too late."

"I know. I did try to tell her to listen to you, but she wouldn't have it and I was worried she'd stop speaking to me, too."

We sit in silence a bit longer, neither of us feeling there is much else to say, as twilight grows over the city. At last we bid each other goodnight and go to our beds, though I stay awake a long time, wondering how I can get Cassia out of this marriage. But I can't think of anything.

I'm up before dawn and so is Marcus, I meet him on his way to join Cassius and the priest. Fabius appears as we go past his door.

"Morning."

"Morning."

I follow them further than necessary and touch Marcus' arm. "If there's any doubt about the omens, any at all… you will speak up?"

He looks up at me, hovering on the stairs. "Why?"

"Just… I want to be sure." I try to smile.

He nods. But he's there out of custom and tradition, it will be the priest who declares whether all is well. I think of the multicoloured doves we released to fly over the amphitheatre the day it was inaugurated to suggest an auspicious event. Perhaps if I'd told Marcus what had really happened, all those months ago, he would have put a stop to this wedding, would have thrown Rullus out with a beating. And if Cassia had still refused to listen, we could have staged something that would have indicated the marriage was doomed, but it already is doomed and it's going ahead anyway. I stand in the dark courtyard, building up my courage.

Maria appears, taking up her usual spot above the courtyard. "Big day," she says.

"Yes."

"I knew her mother."

I nod, looking up at her dark shape.

"Good-hearted. Like Cassia. A good word for everyone, helped out anyone, even strangers. And light-hearted, too. She used to sing all the time, you could hear her from here."

I never met Cassia's mother, but now I feel her taking shape through Maria's words and the idea that Cassia is marrying a man who will take away all that is good and kind about her makes my heart sink even further. I stand in silence, waiting for Maria to say something more, but she doesn't. I wonder what Cassia's mother would say if she knew what Rullus was like.

What can I do to make things better for Cassia? Nothing. She does not even want me as a friend. But she will be in need of friends if she marries Rullus.

I think of what the sorceress said about learning to be a freedwoman and wonder whether I am in fact free at all. I have lost my friendship with Cassia. I have avoided the popina for months and so have had to eat food that is not as good or plentiful as Cassia's fare. I wear my plainest clothes, walk quickly with my eyes down, even in the insula, where I should feel safe. I have been assaulted but kept my mouth shut, as though I were a slave who might well expect to be used by her master and not complain about it. I have become a slave again, my master the fear I have of Rullus.

Enough. I will not allow Rullus to take from me the thing I value the most.

I take a deep breath and go to knock on Cassia's door.

"Come."

I push open the door and see her sitting, her bridal clothes laid out, a single flickering lamp and Fabia by her side.

"What do you want?" she asks, looking up but not meeting my gaze

"To be your friend," I say. "Can I walk to the baths with you and Fabia?"

She jerks her head, not a no, not a yes.

THE THREE OF US WALK together in silence. The baths are empty, the ceremonial bridal bath has been specially booked to take place before public hours begin. She is steamed, a plucker is let loose on her, which causes her to wince but not cry out. She is rubbed down with oils and scraped by a professional, before being put into a beautifully presented bridal bath, all perfume and rose petals, then her nails and toenails are dyed. Throughout it all, the plucker and cosmetes made chattering conversation, to which all three of us answer in painful monosyllables. I feel like the dark-hooded Charon, taking a hammer to the head of any fallen gladiator who must be put out of their misery.

We walk back to the insula, the sun now risen, which means that the auguries will have been taken, the decision already made. A priest reading omens for a wedding would need a drastic sign before they put a stop to a pre-planned event such as this, where the father has already given his consent and all the legal arrangements have been made.

"Did you find out what the Fates had spun for you, then?"

The three of us startle. Standing in the middle of Sand Street, ignoring the early morning traffic, which is weaving around her, is the sorceress. Her palla embroidered with green leaves is wrapped about her and once again I'm reminded of a tree.

Cassia gestures at her loose hair and dyed fingernails. "A husband. As I requested. Though you did nothing to bring him to me."

"And will he complete you?"

"He's a good man," says Cassia defensively, but her eyes flicker.

The sorceress follows Cassia's eyes to me.

I say nothing.

The sorceress smiles. "I wish you well on your wedding day," she says.

"I don't want your wishes," says Cassia and she walks past the sorceress and towards the insula. Fabia moves after her.

"One more thing," calls the sorceress.

Cassia stops in the middle of the road, but she does not turn round. "What?"

"There is a beggarwoman waiting at your popina for a bowl of soup. I told her the popina is likely to be shut today, but she said she'd heard you never turned anyone away."

Cassia looks round at the sorceress, her eyes a little wary, but then she nods.

"She's getting married," says Fabia. "She can't be looking out for beggars today, she has to be dressed for the wedding."

Cassia shakes her head. "Will you go and feed her, Althea?" she asks me. "I've never let a beggar go hungry yet. It wouldn't be right on my wedding day. The soup will be cold, but there's bread and cheese and fruit."

It's the most she's spoken to me for months and I give an eager nod, glad to feel I am doing something for her.

Cassia and Fabia walk onwards, turning into Virgin's Street and disappearing through the gateway of our insula.

I stand, facing the sorceress.

"Did you find your desire?" she asks me, smiling.

"Right now, my desire is to get Cassia out of this marriage," I say. "The man she is marrying is not a good man. But I don't suppose you can help with that." I'm speaking more rudely than I normally would, but the sorceress is annoying, the way she is smiling and still speaking in riddles when a bad thing is happening, right now, in our lives, not some far-off legend.

"The right thing will happen for her," she says. "Trust me."

"Why should I trust you?"

"I've known Cassia all of her life," says the sorceress. "I know everyone around here. I see what the Fates wove for her, even if she does not."

"And was it this marriage?" I ask.

She shakes her head.

"What then? Go and tell her, if you know! Or tell me and I'll tell her!"

She shakes her head. "She must see it for herself."

"She's about to get married! Time has run out for seeing what Rullus is like!"

She shakes her head. "The Fates wove their story for her. And no mere mortal can warp their threads."

"You speak in riddles," I say, angry now. "You're just making fun of people, teasing and saying things no-one understands. Like oracles that led to tragedies in the legends because no-one would speak clearly. I spoke up about what happened and I lost a good friend. I should have spoken sooner, she might have believed me then. When she marries this man, I may have to go and live elsewhere, just to escape him. But she will be stuck with him."

She takes hold of my arm and brings her face very close to mine. "Go back to the insula," she says.

I pull away from her hold. "That's what I'm doing."

"Do what your friend asked of you. And stay alone while you do it."

"You leave us alone," I say and push past her, hurry back to the insula and through the gateway.

I expect Cassia and Fabia to have already gone to get dressed, but instead they are standing in the courtyard with Rullus. He's dressed in a toga, as befits the occasion, but it does not look elegant, only hangs poorly on him, crumpled and bulky. Fabia is standing with her back against the wall, Cassia is face-to-face to Rullus. They seem to be arguing.

"I always feed beggars," Cassia is saying. She looks shocked, eyes wide.

"I know. And that stops today. Wasting my profits."

"*Your* profits?"

"Mine. As are you, from today. And you'll do as I say."

I glance at Fabia, who gives a tiny shake of her head, a warning to stay out of it. I step back a little, press myself against the wall as Fabia has done, keeping a wary eye on Cassia and Rullus.

"I will be your wife," says Cassia slowly. "But that does not mean I will stop doing what is right. What I have always done, and my mother before me. The beggars will be fed."

"Get to your room and get dressed," says Rullus. "Before I make you."

Cassia stands still for a moment, and I think she is going to argue, but then she looks to Fabia. "Come with me," she says.

Rullus follows them to the apartment, closing the door with a slam. I am left alone.

I feel tears spill onto my cheeks. Here it is, Cassia's future, played out in front of me. Rullus showing his true colours, knowing full well it is too late for the marriage to be revoked, Cassia realising she is beaten, her good heart about to be broken. I want to go and cry in my hut on the roof, but I have a task to do. Cassia asked me to feed the beggarwoman, and I will do it, even if it is the last beggar she will ever feed.

I use the courtyard door which leads into the popina's storeroom, from where there is a door leading into the popina itself. It is all empty, and very dark, for the dawn light is still weak. I fumble my way through the room, then undo and lift one of the shutters, allowing light to come in. I find bread and cheese as well as a couple of ripe plums and a plate to put them on. I look this way and that but I cannot see a beggarwoman on the street. I pull the shutter back down and carry the plate back towards the courtyard through the storeroom, thinking that at least I can have the plate ready if the woman comes into the insula gateway to ask for food.

"Going against my word?"

Rullus, blocking the doorway into the courtyard. I feel my breath start to come short at the sight of him, my escape route barred in both directions. I wish I had left the shutter of the popina up, so that I could have run from him into the open street. Why did I think I would be safe?

"I'm feeding the beggarwoman for Cassia," I say.

"When I told her there'd be no more of that nonsense?"

"I am not yours to command," I say, but my voice comes out too high, like a scared child.

"We'll see about that, shall we?"

I step back as he advances, one step after another, further and further into the darkness of the storeroom.

He's still fast. A lunge, the plate of food shattering on the floor at my feet, his hands on my body, his face pressed close to mine although this time I have time to scream before his hand covers my mouth. My tunic pulled up, his hand rough on my thighs.

"One more move and you'll feel this across your backside!"

Cassia is standing in the doorway. Dressed in her bridal attire; a white tunic with an elaborately tied knotted belt, her black curls covered over with her mother's flame-coloured bridal veil, floating down her back. In her hands she is holding the thick stick Cassius keeps to use on anyone who thinks they can take liberties with his daughter. Behind her is Cassius, also wearing a toga, which I've never seen him in before. Both of them look shocked and angry.

"Cassia – Cassius," stammers Rullus. He lets go of me, tries to rearrange his toga as though nothing has occurred.

"Get out here," says Cassia, her voice low.

"I –"

"Out!" she yells.

Cassius and Cassia walk backwards, Rullus slowly following them into the courtyard. When he is well clear of the door I follow. Fabia is just outside, she grabs at my legs and I squat down with my back to the courtyard wall, shaking, tears trickling down my face. She stands by my side, her short arms wrapped as far as she can round me, cheek pressed to mine.

Curious about the noise, the inhabitants of the insula begin to appear from the courtyard windows and doors, in their best clothes or half-dressed, some coming out into the courtyard or onto the balconies, others poking their heads out from upper windows. I see Karbo's face appear over the rooftop railing, followed by Marcus.

Cassia grips the stick in her hands and lifts it up high. I don't think she will do it, but she does. The full weight comes down on Rullus' left shoulder, he buckles under the blow.

"Have you gone mad?" he shouts at her, staggering back to his feet.

"No! I have come to my senses!" yells back Cassia. "I'm not marrying you."

"Just because I said Althea couldn't feed that beggar a bowl of soup?"

"Because you assaulted Althea for a second time, while showing a sweet face to father and me so you could get your greedy hands on the business. Father and I, we look out for people round here. I feed people who are hungry, I look after my friends who are loyal to me even when they've been poorly treated by my own family. I won't lower myself to marry a pig like you. Not today, not ever!"

"You can't do that!" yells Rullus. "What will happen when your father dies and you're still unmarried, eh?"

"What makes you think I'll never get married?"

"You're refusing to marry me!"

"And why would that be, do you suppose?" shouts Cassia. "Oh, I know! Because you're a mean-hearted letch of a man, who only wants a wife who can work all the hours of the day and night for him while he goes drinking and whoring and gambling! You don't care for me! You don't care about the popina or the people I feed every day. These are my people. I grew up in this insula, I know everyone who lives here and all our neighbours. I look out for them, and they look out for me. More fool me for wanting a husband, any husband, when I will always be safe and loved, whether I marry or not. Because here we care for each other, and we are good people. My friend tried to tell me the truth about you, and may Venus and Juno forgive me, I didn't listen, because I wanted to be married and I thought you were a good enough man. And you're not. You're not worthy to marry me. Go back to the miserable little village you came from and leave me alone. Leave us alone. You don't belong here."

There's a long silence and then, clapping. Everyone looks up. Maria, perilously leaning over her balcony to get a really good view, is applauding. Grins start to spread and slowly, one by one, the rest of the inhabitants begin to clap too, until the courtyard is full of loud applause from all levels. Cassia, her cheeks pink, looks at me, her eyes filling up with tears, although her mouth has widened into a smile.

"That's all very well," blusters Rullus, awkward now that the crowd has turned against him. "But your father has given his permission to this marriage. And you are subject to your father's rule. So you will be marrying me today, whether you like it or not. And when we are married, you will be subject to *my* rule. And I will go about teaching you some manners, my girl. With the aid of that stick you're holding. None of this giving food away, or consorting with people who are no better than whores."

The crowd, silent now, looks towards Cassius.

"No, Rullus," he says quietly. "You will not be marrying my daughter. Not today, not ever. You will leave us now, and return to your own town. You are no longer welcome here."

There's an approving murmur from the crowd.

"You gave your permission!"

"I withdraw it. I won't have my daughter marry a man who dishonours her friends, who threatens to beat her for showing kindness, who just wants the profits of a business we have worked hard to keep going all these years. I thought that you cared for her happiness. I only wanted to know she would be cared for after I was gone."

"And who will care for her, old man?" shouts Rullus. "When you are dead, which can't be long now. Eh?"

Cassius ignores the jibe. Instead, he spreads his hands like an orator, taking in all of us gathered in the courtyard, from Marcus and Karbo on the rooftop, past Adah and Maria, down to Julia, standing at the foot of the stairs. "They will," he says quietly. "Come, now, Cassia."

Cassia hesitates before she moves towards him, the stick still clutched in her hands. When she reaches him, he looks at her for a long moment, reaches up and lifts away the bridal veil from her head. He looks down at it in his hands, then meets Cassia's gaze and smiles. "You will be married one day, a happier day," he says. "To a better man."

Cassia gives a little sob and leans against her father, loosening her grip on the stick, so that it falls to the ground with a heavy clatter, lost in loud applause and cheers from us all. We fall silent only when Julia steps past Rullus as if he doesn't exist and makes her way to Cassius. She puts a hand on Cassia's shoulder and nods to Cassius.

"You are a good man," she says.

Cassius swallows, but nods in return. He looks tired, an old man shaken by what has happened.

I join Fabia in hugging Cassia, who is crying. Over her shoulder I see Rullus, his face sullen and crimson with humiliation, making his way out of the courtyard and through the gateway. I suspect I will not see him again.

"I'm sorry," says Cassia into my hair. "I was a fool not to believe you."

I shake my head. "You believe the best of people," I say, tears falling. "I should have told you at once, before he had a chance to worm his way into your lives."

I MAKE WAY FOR OTHER people to embrace Cassia and find myself face-to-face with Marcus, his face serious.

"Why didn't you tell me?"

I shake my head and swallow. "I didn't... there was never a moment and then it was too late..." I trail off.

"You should have told me!" says Karbo, bouncing indignantly at Marcus' side. "I would have made him sorry. Marcus, go after him and beat him up!" he adds, enthusiastically. "Make him sorry for what he did to Althea."

"I am not sure he deserves a man's beating," says Marcus. "Cassia delivered all the humiliation he was worthy of." But his face is still serious. "Althea, you should not have held such a burden in your heart, nor ever thought it was too late to tell me. And I will not forgive myself for not seeing that something bad had happened to you, for not realising that you were not safe in your own home."

I try to say something but my tears only fall faster and I find myself held tightly in Marcus' arms, Karbo joining our embrace till I have gathered myself a little.

The rest of the day is a strange one. We sit in our best clothes in the decorated courtyard and eat the wedding feast as though it were a picnic, we tell stories of brave deeds overcoming the dark things of the world. There is laughter and more hugs to reassure us all that we are safe here, amongst our friends and neighbours.

Two days later Cassia tells me that Cassius paid Rullus off to dissolve the marriage contract, that he packed his bags and left. Her last sight of him was as he trudged away, shoulders hunched, his bag slung over his shoulder.

"He can go and find some other wife," she says. "And I hope for her sake she's got a big stick somewhere."

"You were brave," I say. "I was afraid you'd be lost to a horrible marriage for the rest of your life and there was nothing anyone could do."

She shakes her head. "It was when he said I couldn't feed the beggar, that I had to stop making my soup," she says. "And I knew. I knew right then I couldn't marry him, that the soup was what I do, what I am. That I look out for people. That it was what the Fates wove for me. And it might only be a pot of soup to anyone else, it might not be important or grand, no-one will remember my name, but it is the thing I am certain of, it is what completes me. Then I came looking for him, to tell him I couldn't marry him, and I found him with you. And then I knew I'd been a fool not to believe you. That he was a bad man in every way."

I laugh, although I'm wiping tears off my face at the same time. "Every mouth you feed will remember your name, Cassia," I say.

"I owe the sorceress a thank you," she adds. "She saved me."

"Saved you?"

Cassia smiles. "Did you see a beggarwoman that day? Anywhere near the popina?"

I stare at her, thinking back. "No," I say. "No, there was no-one there."

"I'm taking her this," she says with a grin, reaching under the counter and pulling out a little roll of cloth. Inside, a sturdy wooden stick, delicately crafted in silver miniature.

TITUS' TEARS

IT'S DAWN ON THE TWELFTH day of September and it's already too hot, even a long night has not done anything to cool the city. We keep hearing the rumbling of thunder, but the sky is clear. I dread to think how hot the stone seating will be by the time we start the show tonight, when the sun will have blazed down on the amphitheatre for hours. Despite the oppressive heat I feel light, a burden lifted away from me with Rullus' departure as well as the truth being told about what he did to me, the comfort of Cassia's arms about me, our friendship renewed. Last night I unbolted my door and let what little breeze there was enter and it felt like a breath of freedom.

"I could do with being in that water right now," says Vita longingly. We're standing together in the top tier, looking down. The arena is an impressive sight from here, full of water so deep it has a rich blue-green colour and looks very inviting.

"If you want a dip, you better have it now," I say. "It won't be much fun once we put the animals in."

Vita raises a hand to shield her eyes from the glittering water.

"I'll have my chance when we do the show-swimming. Although that's less relaxing. Can't just float about and have fun. And then we have to get out sharpish, so you can get the animals in. Eels, vipers and crocodiles?"

"With rays and sharks. They don't like fresh water, so the less time they spend in it the better. The barrels they're in now may be a tight fit, but at least it's sea water. The plan is to put them in the fresh water just before we start, so that they'll still be lively."

"I wouldn't want to be the bestiarii today."

I shake my head. "Me neither. Most of the time you won't even be able to see these creatures coming towards you, at least on dry land you see the lions and other animals before they attack. Anyway, let's get back downstairs. We've got one section of a corridor cordoned off, that's where all the barrels are and where the prisoner will be kept."

We start walking down through the seating, then make our way into one of the cooler corridors.

"You're really just having one prisoner executed?"

"They want to make a spectacle of him, so they're keeping him as their star."

We reach the ground floor corridor, where an area has been roped off for our use, since we have lost our usual space below the arena. Cages and barrels are crammed together. We've sent costumes out to the gladiator barracks so they can dress there before arriving.

"What time will he be brought here?"

I hold up my small sundial. "Two hours?"

"That's early."

"We have to know we have everything and everyone in place. He'll be under guard until the performance starts."

I SPEND THE NEXT TWO hours checking everything is ready, making notes on scroll after scroll of lists. I catch Karbo loitering near the crocodile pens. They lie in their cages, glinting eyes half-closed, watching us as we move, remaining absolutely still themselves.

"Get away from that cage," I tell Karbo for the third time. He's squatting down next to the cage which holds the largest animal, a beast longer than a man.

"What is it thinking?" he asks.

"How nice you would taste if it could sink its teeth into you," I say. "Get *away*."

I hear the marching of feet and turn as four guards enter. Between them, they hold up Alon.

I grimace. He looks pale and wasted, tired even from the short walk here. How is he supposed to convince the audience he is the bold lover Leander, strong enough to brave the strait's waves to meet his beloved Hero?

"We meet again," he says.

"Are you well?"

"Well enough to drown?"

"Well enough to play your part?"

He nods.

"One of you needs to stay," I tell the guards. "He must remain under guard until he's taken into the arena. I don't have a pen to lock him into, they've all been dismantled for the naumachia."

"I'll stay," says one, younger than the others.

"Fine," I say. "There's a barrel of clean water there, a tunic and shoes, a belt. He needs to look like a brave, confident man. I've got a barber waiting: have him trimmed, shaved, washed and dressed. He looks like a prisoner, and I need him to look heroic."

I leave them to it, go and inspect the ships, waiting in their passageways. The water level is almost at their doors, as they sail out it will rise that little more, bringing it to its full depth. The ships look good, a little smaller than last time, but more of them: eight, four for each side. These ones are not flat-bottomed, which means they can steer better, making the fighting easier and more realistic. We have borrowed some sailors from the navy who will take care of managing their smooth movements on the water, leaving the actual fighting to today's gladiators, whose ceremonial armour is already laid out for the parade, which will take place on the water just before the battle proper begins.

I pass Celer in one of the corridors. He doesn't usually attend the Games, even though we often invite him to join us in watching from the side-lines.

"Come to watch the show?"

He smiles. "Karbo said I had to see the crocodiles. They're all he's talked about."

"I swear, he's going to end up with an arm missing, if he gets too close to their cages."

"I'll try and keep him away."

"Thanks."

Rounds done, I make my way out into the seating, looking down on the water. The sun has sunk, it will be twilight soon. I can hear a babble from outside, growing in volume. The crowds are waiting to enter, held back only by the ropes leading to each entrance and our staff manning each archway. Marcus is standing in the imperial box to my side, his usual final inspection point. It won't be long till Titus' servants arrive to set up refreshments and final touches such as silken cushions for the seats, brought directly from his own dwelling.

"All good?"

I nod. "Just need our audience and we're ready to start. The musicians, singers and actors are about to take their places."

Marcus nods back. "Good. I'll tell the staff to let the audience in, might as well get them all settled before Titus arrives and we have to start." He ducks out of sight behind the draped exit, I hear a muffled shout and then the noise of the crowd escalates. People begin to stream into the corridors on the ground floor, making their way up the higher tiers.

Marcus reappears. "We better get out of the way," he says. "You're standing in front of some senator's seat."

"Marcus. Marcus! Althea!" Strabo is leaning out of one of the corridors above us, his usually placid face panicked.

"What?"

He hesitates, looking about him for listening ears. "The man's gone."

"Man? What man? What are you talking about?"

"The – the drowning man." He opens his eyes wide, trying to tell us without speaking.

I gape. "He can't have done. There was a guard with him."

"The guard's been knocked out."

We make our way with difficulty through the corridors, fighting against the tide of the crowds entering the amphitheatre. Finally, we reach the ground floor and the section we've kept roped off. The stacked barrels are all in place, but the guard we left with Alon is sitting slumped on the ground, cautiously feeling his head.

Marcus yanks him to his feet. "Where's the prisoner?"

"I don't know," whimpers the man. "He attacked me and ran off."

Marcus looks as if he's about to punch him. "Ran *off*?"

I step in. "We need to organise people to look for him," I tell Marcus. "We still have over two hours of the show to get through before it's his part, even once it starts."

Marcus and Strabo set off at a run, Marcus blowing on his whistle to summon staff.

"So the prisoner just attacked you?" I ask the guard.

"Yes," he says. "Punched me." But his eyes flicker to one side and I know something is not right. I think back to my conversation with Alon in the dark and damp of the Tullianum, his strange acceptance of his fate, his quietness and calm. I stand closer to the guard, look at his face, which seems undamaged, and then into his eyes, but he will not meet my gaze.

"You're lying to me," I say softly. "He did not attack you. He was willing to follow whatever fate brought to him. You let him go. Why?"

"I don't know what you mean, I swear on Jupiter, by Mars, I –"

"Be careful," I say. "The gods do not like those who use their names for false oaths."

"I swear by –".

"Be quiet. Or I'll let Marcus get his hands on you."

He falls silent. I think about his flurry of oaths and a certainty comes over me. "You have converted to his religion," I say and watch his face change. "You didn't care about swearing false oaths," I add. "You don't care about our gods or their wrath."

"They are nothing but false idols," he mutters.

"You converted," I say. "He converted you and you let him go so he would not die?"

"Why should he die?" bursts out the man. "He speaks the truth! He says the son of God came to us, here on earth, and that if we follow His word, He will come again and take us –"

"Shut up," I say, keeping my voice low. "Shut up. If anyone hears you, you're a dead man, because you'll be taking his place. The Games must go ahead tonight, and someone must be put to death in front of the Emperor. He expects it, the whole crowd expects it. What am I supposed to do, now you've let the prisoner escape?"

Marcus is back, with Strabo. "We won't find him," he says. "He could be anywhere, there's no chance. How did this happen?"

I pull him away from the guard and explain what happened.

"I'll throw him in with the crocodiles myself," says Marcus, enraged.

"We can't tell Titus we let that happen, he was under our care as much as the guard's. It'll be us in with the crocodiles if we're not careful. So we can't put the guard in instead or there'll be questions asked which we don't want to answer."

Marcus mutters something blasphemous under his breath and glowers at the guard.

"We could get another criminal?" asks Strabo.

Marcus shakes his head. "There isn't time and we used up a whole batch of them the other day, remember?"

I nod. It's the end of the season, we were given everyone left who had been condemned to death. And time is running out. If we had a day or two, there would be a way to find someone, but now? "If we tell…" I start, but Marcus is already shaking his head.

"No, you were right," he says. "If we tell what happened there's a good chance we'll be blamed and that will mean being condemned to death ourselves, both for letting a prisoner go who was treasonous *and* for trying to lie to the Emperor by covering it up."

Merula joins us. "I heard," he says. "What do we do?"

I look about me, as though a likely-looking criminal might helpfully wander in off the street and offer themselves up to us. "If one of Vita's team were a man we could try and fake it," I start, then trail off, unconvinced.

But Marcus' eyes light up. "Yes," he says.

"Yes what? They're women, they won't look right."

"I'll do it."

I stare at him. "What?"

"I'll be Leander."

"No."

"Vita's playing Hero's death, why can't I play Leander's?"

"Because Vita has a linen ladder to 'fall' down and all she has to do is lie still at the bottom of the tower! Leander has to drown, actually drown. Under the water!" My voice is getting louder, and Marcus shakes his head at me, touches my arm. I lower my voice. "No."

"I'm a good swimmer," says Marcus. "All I have to do is swim the arena a few times, then –"

"Then you get tied to a raft that will pull you underwater and only release you to the surface when you're dead. No."

"I can hold my breath."

"I can't believe I'm having this conversation," I say. I'm having a nightmare, one of those where people say garbled things and nothing makes sense, but you know for sure things are going very, very wrong. "How long can you hold your breath for?"

He thinks. "Sixty breaths? Ninety?"

"You're just *guessing*? No."

"You keep saying no," says Marcus. "But we don't have a choice."

"Titus will know it's you."

Marcus shakes his head. "It's dark. He expects to see a prisoner, that's what he'll see."

I'm about to cry, I can feel it, the sobs pushing up in me, my voice growing shaky. I stand still for a few moments, breathing, trying to think of what it will be like, what will need to happen if we go ahead with his plan. "Show me."

"What?"

"Show me how long you can hold your breath."

"Now?"

"Yes, now."

"But —"

"But nothing. You have to swim the arena which has crocodiles and sharks in it. Then I have to give the signal to drag you under the water," I say, and my voice goes shaky again at the thought of it. "And I have to give the second signal, to pull you out of the water, when you have been convincingly drowned. Not a quick ducking. It has to be convincing. So how long do I leave you underwater with the crocodiles?"

We stare at each other, then Marcus nods. "Barrel of water, Strabo."

Strabo and Merula roll a barrel over. Strabo opens the lid, then uses a net to fish out a huge moray eel, which thrashes about violently, its mouth open, showing rows of pointed teeth. It snaps at the net as Strabo and Merula between them transfer it to another barrel.

"I have to check the crowd is seated," says Strabo, his face worried.

"Yes, go," says Marcus. "Merula, stay with us."

The three of us stand by the barrel of water.

"Don't do this," I say. "There has to be another way."

"Count," says Marcus to Merula. "Steadily." He takes a gulp of air, then leans into the barrel, submerging his whole head.

"One," says Merula. His already pale skin has gone white, one of his hands is trembling, the other is gripping the edge of the barrel, almost touching Marcus' fingers, pale underground skin against burnt brown. "Two. Three. Four. Five."

There's a sudden burst of trumpet fanfare. Titus is making his way into the imperial box.

"Twenty. Twenty-one. Twenty-two. Twenty-three."

We hear the crowd burst into applause.

"Thirty-eight. Thirty-nine. Forty. Forty-one."

The show must start in a few moments, we never keep the Emperor waiting. How many breaths will Marcus manage? Will it be enough to convince the crowd that he has drowned in that time? I look at his body, the back of his neck, his hands tightly holding on to the side of the barrel, his back tense with the effort of not breathing.

"Sixty."

Marcus said sixty breaths. But how did he know? Has he ever tried this before? Did he say sixty because it was easy, or very hard? I have no idea, I have never tried it myself, my own breathing is too fast. And is it long enough to fool a crowd? It feels like eternity to me, the steady counting in Merula's shaking voice, but is it long enough?

"Seventy. Seventy-one."

A stream of bubbles rises from the barrel and I look at Merula, our frightened eyes locked together as he keeps counting.

"Seventy-nine. Eighty. Eighty —"

Marcus' head jerks out of the barrel, water splashes on Merula and me as we step back. He gasps for air, breathes heavily for a moment, then looks to Merula.

"Eighty-one."

"Did it feel long enough for a man to drown?"

"I don't know," I say. "It felt horrible."

Marcus ignores me. "Long enough?" he asks Merula.

Merula considers. "I think so," he says at last. "You should probably move under the water, so they think you're struggling. But that may need more air than keeping still. And if you struggle, it may draw the attention of the crocodiles."

"We could feed them?" I suggest.

Marcus shakes his head. "Can't do that. People will be expecting at least one kill by a crocodile, if we feed them they won't bother going for the gladiators if they fall in. As it is the sharks might just eat the rays, easier for them, it's all underwater." He pushes back his wet hair, wipes drips from his forehead. "No choice. I'll do what I can. Count to eighty, then pull me out. I won't be able to lie completely still when I come up, though I'll try, I'll be gasping for air, so Vita has to draw attention to herself by falling from her tower and doing her dying scene. Someone needs to tell her what's happening. Then extinguish the arena-side torches, faster than we had planned, have a slave ready in front of each one, put them out all in one go rather than one by one. The less time people have to look at me, the better."

I nod. I'm full of questions, but there's no good in asking them. What if the animals we put in the water attack Marcus, when he is swimming or when he is lashed to a raft from which he cannot escape? What if we mis-time the count to eighty, or if Marcus cannot hold his breath as long after he has swum the arena several times? But none of these questions will give courage to Marcus. They are my fears to hold and no doubt he is asking himself the same questions.

"I'll go and tell Vita now, she'll be taking her place for the start of the show."

There's a tug at my arm. Strabo is at my side, his expression strained. "Titus has asked for either you or Marcus to attend him."

"Attend him?"

"He wants you to sit with him throughout the show."

I gape. "What, all of it?"

"Yes."

"But doesn't he have…"

"He's got some distant members of his family in the box tonight, not Domitian or anyone like that. He says he wants company."

"From one of us?" I look at Marcus.

"Yes. Now. There's a Praetorian Guard waiting to escort you."

I hover, uncertain. With Marcus risking taking the place of Alon, we had relied on me being available to direct the show. I can't send Marcus to Titus, nor can I explain what is going to happen, so I have no choice but to go to him myself. I look about me.

"It has to be you," says Marcus to me.

"But —"

"I'll give the signals," says Merula.

"But you —"

"I've watched enough rehearsals. I'll manage."

I think of his dark eyes watching Vita, his stammering approach to her, his crushed demeanour after her rejection. At least I know he has a vested interest in all of this working out well. "You'll look after them both?" I ask.

He nods, serious. The team moves a little closer to him, acknowledging the new leadership. Karbo looks worried and Celer puts a hand on his shoulder.

I make a move towards the corridor where I can see an impatient Praetorian Guard waiting, then turn back. "Celer?"

"Yes?"

"Keep an eye on Karbo."

"I will."

I FOLLOW THE PRAETORIAN GUARD down the dark corridors, now empty as the audience have taken their places. The opening music plays; in only a few moments the first part of our spectacle will begin. My heart's hammering at the idea that we are about to put on a show in front of Titus, a naumachia no less, without either Marcus or myself able to influence events. And as for what Marcus is planning to do…

We've reached the imperial box and the drapes are pulled aside for me. Towards the back of the box a few men and women are seated, elegantly attired but clearly not important enough to be any closer to Titus, who is sitting right at the edge of the box, where the audience will have a good view of him. A few servants hover in the background in case they are needed. A narrow table set to one side holds various platters of delicacies: exquisitely presented figs, grapes and gilded dates, little bowls of olives, roast chickpeas and pickles, tiny rose-shaped pastries piled high and scattered with pink and white rose petals, glass jugs of wine and water alongside little glass cups decorated with gladiatorial scenes.

"Ah, Althea. Come in, come in," says Titus, waving a hand towards a seat placed by his side.

I lower myself cautiously into the chair, wondering what the spectators will make of a commonly-dressed woman appearing at the Emperor's side as though I were his wife or a member of his family. I'm conscious that my hair leaves much to be desired, being in no way elegantly arranged in the fashionable Flavian curled style, only bound up in a hair wrap. "I am very sorry, Imperator," I begin, barely allowing my behind to make contact with the chair, expecting to be rapidly sent away again. "Scaurus is unable to attend you at this particular spectacle, the naumachia requires his direct supervision, it —"

"Oh, I don't mind in the least," says Titus. He winces. "I have a headache today, a ringing in my ears. It comes and goes, drives me to distraction. Sometimes I even have men with hammers come to my rooms and make a din. It eases the pain, would you believe." He sighs. "I wanted someone to talk to me, to lessen the ringing. You'll do," he adds, giving me a pained smile.

I'm surprised the roaring and cheering of the crowd isn't helping, if the sound of hammers does. But I try to settle into the chair and give what I hope is a bright smile. "Of course, Imperator. It is my honour. What would you like to speak of?"

A servant offers me a cup of wine, which I accept, although I hold it awkwardly without drinking and shake my head when I am offered the tiny pastries, afraid of choking on a crumb and inelegantly spluttering. It's strange and frightening to be the guest of the Emperor. I look over my shoulder. His other guests are staring at me with undisguised astonishment and horror.

Titus puts a hand to his head and groans. "Such pain," he says. "They seem to grow worse with time. Do you get headaches?"

"No, Imperator."

"Give thanks to the gods who have spared you such suffering."

"Yes, Imperator."

Titus gulps down his wine and holds his cup out to be refilled. He does not even look round to see if a servant has caught the gesture, simply assumes they are watching him at all times, ready to fulfil even the most subtly expressed desire. Which they are, of course. He is the Emperor. Fear ripples through me again, the strangeness of sitting here beside him as though I were one of the great matrons of Rome. If he knew that we were planning to deceive him, deceive fifty thousand people... I stroke my wrinkled tunic down over my knees with one hand, still holding my cup out as though I'd just taken it from someone's hand.

"How is the boy? What was his name again?"

"Karbo," I say. "I am – we are so grateful for your intercession –"

"Yes, yes," says Titus, waving away my protestations. "Only right the boy should have a mother. Berenice said –" He stops. "Never mind."

"Her majesty seemed very kind-hearted," I say.

Titus turns his face away a little. "She is," he says.

I wait in silence, unsure how politic it is to say anything else about the queen.

Titus clears his throat. "The flooding is very impressive. The depth must have been hard to achieve."

"We have had the power of Rome's mighty aqueducts and a very able aquarius on our side," I say.

"What beasts will be in the water?"

"Crocodiles from Egypt, eels from the south, sharks and vipers. There are rays, too, they will be easy to spot, they come to the surface frequently."

"Are they dangerous?"

"They have barbs that can kill a man, Imperator."

IT'S DUSK. FOUR MEN CARRY burning torches around the front row of seating, lighting dozens and dozens more torches, taking their time, tension building as a soft glow spreads across the dark waters. It's time for the show to begin. A blast of trumpets and the doors swing open, the eight ships rushing out on a wave of water, the increase in volume lifting them all higher. The men aboard raise their weapons, and the eight ships begin to row, while the audience applauds this water-based version of the usual costumed parade.

Once they have shown off sufficiently, the eight ships pull back, siting themselves tightly against the walls, the better to draw attention to what is happening in the centre, where Vita's women have appeared. Desirability has triumphed over modesty; they are all naked, twisting through the water, creating formations which mimic not just shapes and objects like stars and the sun, but also test the strength and bravura of the team, from holding their breath for an unfeasibly long time while their legs perform above the surface, to rolling their whole bodies through the ripples, sometimes using their power to lift a performer right out of the water, allowing her to shine above her sisters. Music plays delicate songs with moments of tension, including when they manage a triple-height structure with Vita at the top, before she leaps from the human tower they have created, diving gracefully into a circle created by the other performers.

This brief interlude complete, Vita disappears under the water, followed by her team. They do not reappear, or at least, the audience supposes they have not. In fact, the sails of the eight ships, not yet hoisted, conceal their return aboard, creeping up the sides closest to the wall, pulling on dark tunics and tucking into position among the men, so that they will not be spotted, while the sails rise up the masts, drawing attention away from them.

Before the ships begin their war, the waves beneath them must be made more dangerous. An actor dressed as King Neptune announces that his army must be assembled before we mere mortals fight our own battles. He calls for the beasts of the deep and as each one is named, our team lowers pens fastened to the wall and releases their clasps. Moray eels are followed by rays, then sharks and vipers. The most frightening are saved till last. Six crocodiles remind the audience of Rome's power over Egypt and their appearance is greeted with a round of applause. They are not dropped into the water, rather their cages, complete with solid floors but open bars, are lowered close to the water's edge, allowing each animal to stay on its open raft or dive into the water, their slinking movements causing shudders in the audience. Two crocodiles instantly dive into the water, four stay on their rafts, wary of this new place. All of them are longer than Marcus, one of them is both double his length and broader than the others. It lies very still on its platform. King Neptune warns us that from this moment on, should anyone enter his realm, they take their life into their own hands.

The water now made perilous, the chorus begins the story of the sea battle we are about to observe, between the Corcyreans and Corinthians, leading to the Peloponnesian War, over five hundred years ago. It's not a tale I have much interest in, especially as I've been obliged to listen to the chorus rehearsing it over and over again until I am sick of it, but the crowd enjoys it, cheering on the battle as the ships move about the arena, coming close enough to each other that the men on board can reach out with their swords and clash weapons, the odd victim falling overboard with a satisfying scream and splash. Two, not too badly harmed, swim back to the nearest ship and climb aboard, continue fighting. One is dispatched into the dark waters and does not re-emerge, a quick glistening fin is all we see close to where he disappeared, a silent death in the dark waters. Then a man falls and out of nowhere appear open jaws, gripping the man round his belly and I watch in horror as what Funis described happens before us; the crocodile rolling the man in the water, his arms flailing, screams drowned and then re-emerging over and over until he falls silent and the crocodile swims easily into the shadows of the water to feast on its prey.

Cruelly, I am praying that more gladiators fall in, for if Marcus enters these waters before the beasts we have sent into them have been fed to satiety, his life will be at even greater risk. I shift in my seat, wishing I could leave the box, go and tell Marcus to change the plan, even if it means confessing that we have lost a prisoner, rather than risk losing his life to one of these monsters in an agonising death. I risk a sideways look at Titus, wondering if I dare ask to be excused, but he is leaning over the edge of the box, gripped by the scene.

There is a splash and then a sudden scream that has even the fighting gladiators hesitate. The man who has fallen in is twisting in the water, thrashing against an unseen foe. A crocodile slips off its raft and swims towards him. It reaches him and its jaws open wide, close over his desperately waving arm, separating it from his body in one easy bite, as though it were a soft roll of bread. There is one more scream from the man and then he is pulled down, beneath the water and gone. The crocodile swims leisurely back to its platform.

The remaining gladiators, forced to keep fighting despite the fate of their comrade, proceed with more caution now, I can see their expressions grown fearful rather than bold, faced with this unaccustomed risk.

THE SEA BATTLE IS OVER, there is applause. The ships pull into the sides, clearing the centre of the arena. They lower a large raft into the water. Onto it step two men, bestiarii sent to us by Funis. They have been equipped with the armour and swords of Roman soldiers. They are about to fight the largest crocodile, representing the Egyptian crocodile-headed god, Sobek, strongly associated with pharaonic power.

Three members of our team, using long poles, push the huge crocodile's platform towards the men's raft. The beast does not move, it stays as still as though dead, even when the two rafts bump together.

The men approach the crocodile, swords out. The crocodile stays still until one of the men slashes at it and then it opens its vast jaw, revealing a terrifying array of white teeth that has the crowd oohing in interest.

The two men proceed to taunt the beast, first one then the other stabbing at it from different sides, so that as it snaps and twists at one, so the other will gouge at its hide from another angle, blood welling up and the enraged animal turning away towards this new attack. Finally, it lurches forwards at one man, its teeth just grazing his leg and his partner, sensing real danger, plunges his sword deep into the beast's head. The crocodile gives one last writhing lunge, but it is already dying. The men, representing Rome, have triumphed over this beast, just as Rome has triumphed over Egypt and made it her vassal state. The audience is pleased by the symbolism and claps with enthusiasm as the vast creature's corpse tips over the side of the raft and has barely time to float before grey fins begin to circle. The sharks are hungry and there is blood in the water, the two bestiarii are barely pulled to safety before first one and then another set of gaping jaws open up and crunch down through the tough hide without any difficulty.

Silently, I urge the sharks on. Let them feast on the dead monster. Let their bellies be full, one less threat to Marcus. I try to count them, hoping that all of them have eaten their fill, that there are none left who are still searching for a helpless victim.

It's grown fully dark now. Above us the sky is lit up with stars. I squirm in my seat as the music changes to a romantic ballad heralding the story of Hero and Leander. The singers finish their rendition, then the chorus step forward, ready to tell the tale. It is too late now.

A banner unfolds at one end, the pointed tip of it raised into the air, the base slipping into the water near a platform piled high with scenic rocks. Painted on the banner is a tower. By its side, in the front row of seating, appears Vita, lit by the flaming torches, her delicate white dress in the Greek style billowing in the evening breeze.

"…though Hero lived across the strait, yet Leander could by night see the shining light from her tower, a beacon of love to him and he, being a strong swimmer and full of desire for her, braved the dark waters and swam to her one night…"

Vita stretches out her arms, beckoning to her beloved Leander. I swallow.

Opposite her, a naked man appears, stands a moment, then lifts his arms, hands briefly touching together, before diving gracefully into the water.

I watch as Marcus swims towards Vita, his wet arms glistening in the torchlight as they curve through the water. I scan the water for the creatures that I know are lurking there, praying with every stroke that they will not attack him. The snakes, rays and eels, I believe will not attack unless provoked. But I am afraid of the crocodiles and sharks, what if they have not eaten enough? I try to think of what Funis said about how much we should feed them and whether that is the same as having feasted on the giant crocodile and the gladiators. Is it enough? My thoughts are muddled, I am unsure. As Marcus reaches Vita's side, she helps him out of the water with the aid of a dangling rope part-hidden in the water. They embrace, Marcus first pressing his lips to hers, then bidding her farewell, before plunging back into the waters. My hands are in fists, my nails digging into skin.

"He returned home safely that night, through the dark waters, yet his love was so strong that the following night he stood on the edge of the shore and looked towards her tower, before taking once again to the water."

Marcus dives again. Again, he swims the arena, again, he climbs to Vita's side, again, they embrace. One of the crocodiles shifts on its platform, but does not dive.

"Their passion forbidden, the world arrayed against them, and yet unable to stay apart, such was the depth of their love…"

I become aware of an odd gulping noise to my side. To my horror, Titus is openly weeping as Marcus returns to his own side, his strokes now slower. He is getting tired. Tears are running down Titus' face and he makes no effort to stem them, wiping them away with a fold of his toga. I try to give the impression I have not noticed, staring fixedly down, seeing nothing but Marcus' body. But Titus reaches out a hand and puts it on my arm, deliberately drawing my attention. I turn to him and affect faint surprise, as though a weeping emperor is a common sight and only to be expected.

"Imperator? Is – is something wrong?"

Titus gulps again. "Some of the demands of office are very hard," he says at last.

"I'm sure they are, Imperator," I say, uncertain of how to proceed. Do I pat his arm, as I might do with a friend? Or would that have the Praetorian Guards on duty seizing hold of me? I look around. The crowd has noticed Titus' obvious display of emotion and have started applauding him for it, enchanted by him being so caught up in the storytelling.

"Personal choices in particular," says Titus, his voice still choked. "When one's own desires must be put aside for the good of the Empire."

"No doubt the Empire recognises your sacrifices and applauds you for them, Imperator," I say, grasping at polite platitudes. He must be talking about Queen Berenice, perhaps prompted by Marcus embracing Vita again before he turns back to the water.

Vita lifts one arm, bidding Marcus a fond farewell.

"I have only made one mistake during my reign," Titus says, looking down at his hands.

I want to scream at him to be quiet. My fists are clenched with fear at what is about to happen. I need to watch Marcus and pray for him, I am afraid that if I don't watch him with all my concentration that something will go wrong, that he will die and no-one in this box will know but me. But I cannot scream. Instead I have to unclench my fists and smile, turn my head towards Titus and respond.

"Imperator?" I say, trying to give the impression I might be asking for further details if he wishes to divulge them but also that I am absolutely not asking, if that is more correct. I don't want him to talk anymore, I don't care about what minor thing he thinks he has done wrong when I am shaking with nerves at what we have done, what I agreed to.

"Ah, never mind," says Titus, raising a hand to acknowledge the crowd's applause. "I will not burden you with my woes, Althea."

I give a relieved nod, it is all I can manage by way of acknowledgement. Marcus has reached his own side again and now comes the part I have been dreading. The audience makes a low sound, half fear, half approval, as he is reached by members of our team. I watch as he is tied to the narrow raft, all but covered by his body once he is fully bound to it. Titus watches with interest, leaning over the edge of his box. I give thanks he has not seen Marcus in over a year, has met him only a few times. If he recognises him, we are done for. We will be in the arena immediately, probably thrown to crocodiles as a punishment befitting our crime. If he does not and the performance continues, I may have to watch Marcus being attacked, probably by one of the evil-eyed crocodiles, their vast toothed jaws closing around him, his blood staining the water as the crocodile rolls him to his death. Or the raft will sink under the water and I will watch him drown. I have a sudden memory of the beast hunter Funis in Ostia, of the missing flesh on his arm after just such a crocodile attack, one from which he was lucky to escape alive. I clutch the stone ledge of the box, but there is no comfort from its cold hardness.

This time as Marcus sets off across the flooded arena, he is lying face down on the raft, his arms and legs bound, pulled across by a mechanism operated by a team of our slaves who usually operate the lifts. Almost as soon as it starts to move, it is also pulled downwards, and the water rises over his body. I can see his back lift as he takes in his last gasp of air, and then the water closes over his head. Silently, I start to count, struggling to keep to the same rhythm Merula used, while the chorus continues to tell the tragic tale of the two lovers.

One, two, three, four...

"But on one fateful night..."

Ten, eleven, twelve, thirteen...

"Little did they know, those two lovers, that a great storm was brewing..."

Twenty, twenty-one, twenty-two, am I counting too fast? Too slow?

Only a faint ripple in the water shows where the rope meets the raft, indicating where Marcus is underwater, the speed agonisingly slow.

Sixty-one, sixty-two, sixty-three, sixty-four – eighty, he said he could stay under for eighty, but can he, when he has swum the arena over and over again?

"Anxious Hero looked out across the strait for her beloved and yet could see nothing through the great storm."

Cymbals clash, drums keep a racing heart-beat going, the audience cranes forwards, silent in expectation.

Seventy-seven, he will be up soon, seventy-nine, eighty... eighty, now he will be lifted to safety...

But there is no sign of Marcus, the rope stays still. Something is wrong. The mechanism is jammed or the counting has been done wrong.

Why is he not up? Eighty-one, eighty-two, eighty-three... how long can a man not breathe and still live, how long, how long? Or has he already taken his last breath, have jaws closed around him without even a ripple, is he dead already?

One of the crocodiles slips off its platform, disappears into the water. The audience's heads swivel towards it, they gasp. But something else has caught my eye, a tiny motion on the opposite side, close to where Marcus should be now, a shadow, a darkness, slipping over the wall and into the water... Karbo? Have I just seen Karbo enter the water? It can't be, Celer would never have allowed...

Celer. Celer's sharp, sharp knife. Is Karbo trying to cut the rope holding the raft underwater?

Ninety-five, ninety-six, ninety-seven...

And the raft comes to the surface, Marcus tied to it. There is barely time to see him, for above him Vita cries out and leaps downwards, hitting the water with a splash.

And every torch is suddenly put out, the amphitheatre plunged into darkness as we had planned. The audience erupts into cheers.

A few moments of darkness, then the torches are relit by the imperial box and the Vestal Virgins' box, followed by all the others in sequence. Vita is now lying sprawled over Marcus on the rocky shore, the two of them are lifted by gladiators onto one of the ships, which is guided carefully back into the underground passage it came from, disappearing from sight as the chorus finishes their tale.

"Buried in one grave, Hero and her beloved Leander, united in death even as they were separated in life..."

Is he dead?

Is Marcus dead?

He was lying so still – but he had to lie still, he could not cough and splutter, he was playing the part of a criminal, condemned to die in the Games. But he was so still...

Titus is talking, I think he must be commenting on the sentence that was passed for Alon. "Of course, treason must be punished harshly. I don't understand these people, insisting their god is the only god. No tolerance of other peoples and their beliefs, no sense of compromise. We don't ask much of them, they are free to worship their own gods, so long as they also worship ours... and have respect for the divine nature of the imperial role, when after all my father was deified..."

I try to nod at everything he is saying, try to look as though I understand and agree, but I can't speak, I can't even make sounds, I must not cry, must keep breathing, my head nodding, nodding, nodding.

"Well, it has been an excellent spectacle. As always. You will tell Scaurus so from me, I am sure he is busy managing everything. I shall be leaving now," says Titus, standing.

I stand up so fast I feel dizzy. The torches flicker, the darkness ripples before my eyes and I put out a hand, touch the stone edge of the box to steady myself, while Titus raises his arm in a salute to the crowd. They give him a standing ovation. He nods acknowledgement and waves for a moment, then moves away.

I move to follow him.

"You must remain in the box until the Emperor has left the building," a Praetorian Guard reminds me.

"Goodbye, Althea." Titus smiles from the doorway. "I shall not forget your kindness in keeping me company."

I manage to bob my head and say something, I don't know what, as he exits the box. As soon as he's done so, I make a move forward, but another guard holds up a hand to stop me.

"The Emperor's guests must also leave the building," he says.

"But I need to –" I start, but this is an argument I'm not going to win. I stand, shifting from one foot to the other, my hands clenched into fists at the slowness of the imperial party's departure. The ladies' delicate pallas, in shining shades of silk, have slipped here and there and must be gathered up, straightened, wrapped about them against "the night air" of the unbearably hot evening. A little chit-chat is engaged in, noting that Senator so-and-so didn't seem to have attended tonight, perhaps he had other more pressing engagements, giggles breaking out at what those engagements might or might not be, did you *read* Martial's latest? Oh, it's all in there, if you know where to look, you can tell *exactly* who it's about...

I feel as though someone is crushing my head with a mortar and pestle. Titus' headaches can be nothing compared to this.

The relatives, uncertain of what sort of status they ought to be granting me, given that I've sat next to Titus all evening as his personal guest, despite being dressed like one of their servants, finally mutter something in my general direction, uncertain half-smiles on their bemused faces, then make their way through the silken drapes, followed by the servants, leaving me alone.

RAIN

I RUN.

THROUGH THE CORRIDORS, PUSHING THROUGH the departing crowds, against the cleaners arriving for their shifts, down the steep steps, clutching at the bannisters for fear of falling.

I reach our holding area and see a crowd of staff gathered into a huddle, Vita, Merula and Strabo among them. In the shaky light of flaming torches, they all look stricken. In front of them, waiting for me, the last person I want to talk to. The Aedile.

"Marcus – Karbo –" I gasp. Behind the Aedile, Vita nods hastily and holds up her hands, a forced smile on her face, indicating all is well, the rest of the team too, nod fervently. I try to nod back, to believe them, but I am trembling all over and I still cannot see Marcus or Karbo, I have to see them for myself to believe they are safe.

"Your team outdid themselves," says the oblivious Aedile, beaming at me. "A magnificent spectacle."

"We're never doing a naumachia again," I say. My hands are clenched into fists, I'm shaking with shock. I keep looking over the Aedile's shoulder, straining to see the only two faces I need to see.

The Aedile blinks. "But it was so well-received –"

"Never again," I say.

"But if the Emperor should wish –"

"Then he'll have to get someone else," I say, and push past him, into the crowd of slaves, looking around for Marcus and Karbo. There is nothing behind them except barrels where the animals were kept.

"It's been a difficult day," Merula is saying to the Aedile behind me. "There were some – technical hitches – behind the scenes. The flooding and draining of such a space, not to mention managing performances within the water is very demanding, as I am sure you can appreciate."

I turn back on myself, pacing like some wild animal caught in its pen, back through the huddle.

The Aedile is nodding. "Of course, of course. But if the Emperor were to demand…" He sounds worried.

"Let's worry about that if it happens, shall we?" Vita says, stepping to Merula's side, blocking me so I can't reach the Aedile. "For now, everyone's happy. The Emperor was so pleased with the performance he was moved to tears, as everyone saw, and now he's going off to the countryside for a holiday and the Games are done for the season. Everyone can have a rest."

The Aedile seems reassured. "Yes, yes, of course," he agrees. "As you say, very technically demanding, understandably tiring for the team. Delightful spectacle!" he calls to me, looking past Merula and Vita to where I am standing, my hands twisting in fear.

I don't answer him. He waits and then nods awkwardly, before walking away.

Merula turns to me. "It's all right," he says, his voice low. He puts a hand on my shoulder, and the shaking of my body slows under his comforting touch. "Marcus is well. I saw him for myself. He spoke to me, he could walk. He has been taken back to the insula to rest."

"Karbo –"

"Karbo too. He was very brave. They have both been taken back to Julia's, I arranged a litter so that they would not exert themselves any further, after all that happened. Celer went with them. You can go back yourself, if you wish. I will manage everything here, if you tell me what to do."

I shake my head, close my eyes and take a deep breath. "You can help me, so it gets done quicker and we can all leave this place."

"I am at your service. Vita too." He looks to her and she nods, her face serious.

"Nobody suspected?" she asks me.

I shake my head. "I thought they were dead," I say, my voice coming out hoarse now that the Aedile has gone. "I thought…"

She nods, puts an arm about my shoulders. "The ropes to move the raft were stuck, Marcus had to try and get free and he could not, I could see him struggling but if I had intervened…"

I nod. "I know."

"Karbo took Celer's knife and slipped into the water, saying he would cut him free by diving underneath. Merula had the crocodile pushed in on the opposite side to create a diversion. Karbo was very brave, he risked his life for Marcus."

I shake my head, still unable to let go of my fear.

Merula takes over the story. "We tried to persuade him against it, but his small size and the colour of his skin made him less noticeable in the dark. We told him that he must not try beyond his breath, that all our lives were at risk if we were found out. But he succeeded and then Marcus played his part well, no-one knew. The Aedile asked where the body was before you arrived, we said we had already thrown it to crocodiles in pens on the other side of the building. He seemed happy enough, as you saw."

My shoulders heave as I try to breathe deeply, to let go of the fear. I feel first Vita and then Merula embrace me and then, slowly, all of our team gathers into a huddle, arms about shoulders all around us, and we weep with relief.

I stagger back through the gateway of the insula, the stars bright above me, the sky soon to change to dawn. I've left Vita and Merula to finish the last few small tasks of the day and walked back through the Forum and the local streets with two male slaves carrying torches to keep me safe, barely seeing where my feet were placed, head still swirling, my body weak with shock.

"Julia!" calls Maria somewhere above me, from her perch. She is lit by a single wavering flame from a lamp, she must have waited all this time for my return. "Althea is back!" She looks down at me. "Don't worry about Karbo, he's in my room and asleep."

"I heard what happened," says Julia, appearing on the balcony above me. She walks down the stairs towards me, puts both hands on my shoulders, looks into my face. "All is well now. All is well. We will celebrate and give thanks that they are safe tomorrow. Marcus must rest. As must you."

"I didn't do anything," I say, "I was trapped in the imperial box, I couldn't help, I couldn't…" Tears start to fall, my hands are shaking. I try to wipe my face.

"You must rest," says Julia. "Go and see Marcus, it will set your mind at ease. He is well, only very tired after such an ordeal. Fabius visited him and gave him a strengthening tonic. He wanted to give him a sleeping draught, but he will have no need of that, his eyes were half-closed by the time he had told me what happened."

"I don't want to wake him if he is asleep."

"He said I must send you to him as soon as you got home. He said to wake him if he was asleep."

I CLUTCH AT THE BANNISTER all the way up the stairs, it is the only thing keeping me on my feet. At Maria's apartment, I look in on Karbo, needing the sight of him. I kneel by the bed in the dim lamplight, place my hand lightly on his chest, feel him breathe for a few moments, with Maria's hand on my shoulder. When I reach the roof, it is so dark I can barely make out my hut, which is in total darkness. There is a faint light from Marcus' hut, though, and I make my way over to it, hesitate before opening the door without knocking. He must be asleep, I do not want to wake him, whatever he said.

His eyes are open, fixed on the door as I open it. "You're back."

"You're awake."

"Couldn't sleep without knowing you were well."

I stare down at him. "I was sitting on my arse in the imperial box watching a spectacle," I say at last, my voice shaking. "You were fighting for your life, and you want to know if I am well?"

He lifts himself onto one shoulder, eyes serious. "You were sitting on your arse in the imperial box, as you put it, unable to move while you watched someone you care about drown and your son die trying to save him, or so you thought, while having to make polite conversation with an emperor," he says and I sink to my knees by the bedside, shoulders heaving. He sits up, wraps his arms about me and I sob into his tunic.

"I thought you were dead. I thought Karbo…"

"I know," he keeps repeating. "I know." He rocks me and I continue to sob until in the end I have to pull away to wipe my nose inelegantly on my tunic.

"Is Karbo well?" he asks.

"He's asleep in Maria's apartment."

"He was very brave."

"I thank Neptune you taught him to swim."

"If I hadn't, he might not have risked his life trying to save me."

"Then you'd be dead."

He gives a half-snort of laughter, the sort of sound he used to make when Fausta amused him. "True. Just as well I taught him, then."

I rest my head against his chest and breathe in the smell of him, comforting and familiar. I relish the few words we have spoken, the quick banter in the face of fear that made us friends over these past two years, the certainty of the other person being in our lives. When my breathing slows, Marcus pushes me lightly away.

"You're falling asleep," he says. "Go and get in a proper bed."

"Promise you'll still be alive tomorrow," I say.

"I promise not to drown in my bed four storeys up in the air," he agrees.

I WAKE TO BRIGHT SUNLIGHT and when I squint to examine my sundial, it is halfway through the morning already, I haven't risen so late in years. Outside the bees hum about their business, calm and certain of their work, as ever.

"I've made fresh honey wine for this evening," says Adah. She's standing by one of the hives, one hand resting protectively on it. "You'll take a cup later, it will settle your nerves after the upset."

"I thought I was watching Marcus die," I say. "I thought Karbo would die too, that I would lose them both in one night."

She nods.

"I thought my world would end," I say.

"Marcus is well. I saw him this morning, he woke less than an hour ago, went to the baths. Said he needed a shave and a haircut, that he'd be back later today."

"I'll do the same," I say. "Karbo and I both need to get clean. I'm not sure I want to see a pool of water ever again, though."

"Wash the fear away," says Adah, turning to go back downstairs. "And I'll have that cup of honey wine waiting for you later today."

I STAND FOR A WHILE in the hot sun, eyes closed, face turned up to it, trying to let its bright heat take away the cold fear and dark of last night, the slithering creatures of the deep waters and the endless counting still echoing in my head. *Seventy-five... eighty-five... ninety-five... how long can a man not breathe and still live, how long, how long?*

"What time is it?" Karbo, arriving at the top of the stairs, yawning and squinting in the sun.

I grab hold of him and squeeze him to me.

"I was a hero," he says, his words muffled in my tunic. "Everyone said so. Marcus said so."

"You were."

He pulls away and looks at me, large eyes a little wary. "Aren't you going to tell me off?"

"It's not the right time for that."

"What time is it?"

"Time to get a stack of pancakes in you and go to the baths together," I say.

"Where's Marcus?"

"Already gone to the barber."

"I think I need four pancakes today," says Karbo, hopeful.

"Me too," I tell him, taking his hand in mine and leading him down the stairs. "Me too."

WE WOLF DOWN ALMOST NINE pancakes between us, eating till we are heavy with date syrup and gulping down more than one cup of fresh grape juice, the sweetness upon sweetness bringing us back to life. We laugh together at a stray dog's pleading eyes, begging for our remaining pancake. We know full well it belongs to the local butcher and is hardly short of food, only as fond of pancakes as we are. Karbo feeds it the scraps bit by bit and strokes its fur with lovingly sticky fingers.

"Can I have a puppy?" he asks.

"Perhaps," I say. "But right now, you need a bath, not a pet."

WE EMERGE HOURS LATER FROM the baths, my nails freshly stained orange, our skin glowing, my hair washed and his oiled. Once back in our hut, I dress him in clean clothes and have him put on his belt and boots, nod admiringly at him.

"You've grown this summer," I say. "That tunic used to go well below your knees, I know it did."

"I'll be taller than you, soon," he says proudly.

"You will."

"I'm hungry again."

"We'll be eating as soon as it's dusk, wait till then," I say. "Or you'll grow between now and tomorrow morning."

"Can I go and see Celer?"

"Before you go, I have something to tell you," I say.

"What?"

I take a deep breath. "I've made a deal with the stables."

"The stables?"

"The Blues, specifically."

"What about them?"

"You can work there, starting next month. One day a week, as a stable hand. They'll pay you."

Karbo's face lights up. "Thank you!" he bursts out, hugging me wildly.

"You'll be shovelling horse shit and polishing leather, not racing horses," I say. "Don't say I didn't warn you. It's not a glamorous job, you'll be begging me to get you out of the deal in a month."

"I'll be in the Blues stables," says Karbo, whirling round in glee and falling onto the bed. "I'll be the happiest boy in Rome."

"If horse shit makes you happy, then you most certainly will," I agree. I'm trying to sound stern, but his smile is too broad for me to do anything but smile back. "I'm glad you're happy," I finish, abandoning my attempts to dampen his enthusiasm. "You did seem to have a gift with the horses," I add.

"I love them," says Karbo, his voice almost serious. "I'll be the best stable hand there ever was and one day –"

"Yes, yes," I say hurriedly. "Never mind 'one day'. For now, you're a stable hand and we'll see what comes of it if you work hard and behave yourself. No-one is making any promises. I can only pray the gods look after you and keep you safe from harm."

"I will pray for their blessing and guidance," says Karbo, making pious eyes.

"That'll be a first," I say. "Go and tell Celer then, and say thank you. He put in a good word for you with the stable master."

Karbo scrambles over the bed and bolts for the stairs, leaving me to gaze at the bright chariot-racing scenes on our walls, hoping I've done the right thing.

I SIT BY THE BEEHIVES for a while, where they cast a little shade.

"Here you are." Marcus is standing over me, freshly shaved and groomed.

"How are you feeling?"

"Oddly well. Perhaps I should spend more time getting half drowned."

"You've been gone all day."

"Gave thanks at a temple and went to the baths. And dropped by to see how the water was draining, it's all gone, those drains are pretty reliable. Place smells like a fish tank, though. I've asked Vita and Merula to tonight's celebrations before they run off making their own plans."

"Their own plans?"

"Vita wants to buy some of her girls out, go on a tour of the empire showing off their skills. They'll have a lot of demand."

"What's Merula got to do with it?"

"He's going to be part of the team, their own aquarius. As well as her husband, as soon as they can arrange the wedding."

"Husband?"

"You didn't know?"

"I knew he liked her. I thought she didn't care for him."

"She wanted to be his wife, not a slave girl for a bit of fun on the side."

"How do you know all this?"

"She told me. When we travelled down south."

"I thought you were…"

"What?"

"Showing her the family farm," I manage, looking away.

"Why would I want to do that?"

"That's not where you went?"

"I took her to meet the manager of the amphitheatre in Puteoli. He might do a naumachia with her as the star, in Lake Avernus. I vouched for her. I visited the farm on my own, though."

"How was it?" I ask, thinking back to the day I saw it, the sweet strawberry grapes we ate from the tumbled-down vine.

"As it was. A few more tiles have fallen off the roof." He shrugs.

"Do you want to go back there?" I ask, a little afraid of the answer.

"Not yet. I've barely had a moment to think, we seem to stumble from one problem to another. I'd like a couple of peaceful years, build up some money, know I've done all I can here. Though I might change my mind if Titus keeps insisting on sodding naumachiae."

"Did you go back to Pompeii?"

He shakes his head. "Didn't have the heart."

"I'm glad you're staying," I manage. "I…" my words trail off. "I don't feel I've seen much of you, this past year."

He laughs. "You miss me? Is that what you're saying?"

"Yes," I say.

He squats down so he's facing me directly, speaking more seriously. "I'm sorry. I should spend more time with you and Karbo. I'm your patron, I should be helping you both make your way in the world. Keep Karbo out of trouble at the stables for starters, when he's stopped being giddy with joy at the prospect of shovelling horse shit." He suddenly laughs. "And finish teaching you to swim properly. You never know when you might have to dive in and rescue me."

THE DAY TURNS TO DUSK, and I pull out my best clothes, free at last to wear them without Rullus' comments to frighten me, then go to help with the preparations for the evening celebration. Tables have been laid out, Julia has hung garlands of red and orange autumn flowers everywhere. I'm standing, admiring it all, when a little boy comes into the courtyard, carrying a bundle of brown cloth. I've not seen him before.

"I'm looking for Althea Aquillius," he says.

"That's me."

"I was told to give you this." He holds out the cloth.

I take it, let it unfold. It's my cloak, the one I sent to Alon. Something falls from it, clinks on the courtyard cobbles. I stoop and pick it up. It's a shard of old pottery. I turn it over. Scratched into it are two swooping lines, together making the simple outline of a fish.

"Who gave you this?"

"A man. He said to say thank you."

"Where was this man?"

"Near the gate to the Appian Way. He gave this to me and then climbed on a cart heading out of Rome."

I give the boy a sweet cake from the feast we're about to have and send him on his way. I put the cloak away in my hut, then consider the little terracotta fish lying in my hand. I could be angry, I suppose. Alon escaping put Marcus and Karbo in great danger. But then again it brought me closer to Marcus than I have felt this past year, it reminded him to spend more time with Karbo and me. And Alon struck me as a good man at heart, whatever his strange views on the gods. In the end, I lay the tiny shard on the rooftop wall looking out over the city. Perhaps a fish will summon rain, I think with a smile. And we could all do with the drought finally breaking.

CASSIA IS HARD AT WORK frying batches of her salted fish fritters. I sneak one from a dish and she slaps my hand.

"Out of my kitchen, you."

"I'm glad it is still *your* kitchen," I say, and she grins and waves me away.

Women from the different rooms and apartments of the insula make their way in and out of the courtyard with contributions to the meal, everything from roast pumpkin and mashed turnip fried with garlic to an aromatic herb salad served with hot freshly-made flat breads. The baker's wife hurries by with loaves of bread while her eldest daughter balances a vast basket of blackcurrant buns in one hand and a large sweet pastry overlaid with a plum preserve in the other. I help her lower both safely to the table and she follows her mother back to the bakery to fetch cheese pastries and sweet wine cakes, a staple at any celebration. I sent Karbo to fetch fruit earlier and now I arrange it on large platters: grapes, melons, early apples and pears, none of the dainty presentation of Titus' fare, but a bountiful and colourful harvest nonetheless.

Julia is standing at the entrance to her apartment. "We have been blessed," she says. "It has been a year of renewal after so many terrors." She looks me over. "And escapes from dark futures."

I nod. "It would be nice to have a peaceful year," I say.

"May the gods send us one," she agrees.

Cassia allows me to fetch and carry on the strict understanding that I'm not to help myself to any of the foods she is entrusting me with. I'm carrying a platter of venison to the table, one last meat-filled meal. We will have to rely on Cassius' smoked and salted meats over winter, but tonight we feast on the last fresh meat from this year's Games. When Karbo comes running into the courtyard and grabs at my arm, the platter rocks precariously.

"Hey!" I yelp. "You'll have this all over the courtyard!"

"Titus," he gasps.

I put the platter down on the nearest table. "What about him?" A horrible thought strikes me, and I look over my shoulder at the gateway Karbo's just pelted through. "He's not making a visit to us, is he?" That would be all I need, I think, an impromptu visit from Titus just when we were all looking forward to a relaxing evening.

"Dead," manages Karbo. He's holding his side and panting, there are beads of sweat on his face.

"Dead?" I stare at him. "What are you talking about, dead? I was just with him yesterday evening, he was fine. He's only forty-one. He went to his countryside estate for a holiday. How can he be dead?" My skin suddenly crawls. I drop my voice to a whisper. "Was he assassinated? Poisoned?"

Karbo is getting his breath back, shaking his head. "He was sick with a fever. He said his head hurt, he was clutching at it, they say. He only made it to the first staging post, he never reached the family estate."

Marcus is halfway down the wooden stairs. "What's going on?"

"Titus has died," I say.

"Titus?"

"The Emperor."

"Assassinated?"

It's worrying that both of us thought it. "Karbo says not. Sick. A fever."

Marcus' shoulders slump. "We could do without a new emperor," he says.

"Will it be Domitian?"

"I suppose so," says Marcus. "Better him than another civil war. I doubt he'll be as easy-going to serve as Titus though."

I nod, thinking of Domitian's narrow, sullen face, his stiff posture and lack of conversation. His wife Domitia, her hair arranged in impossibly stacked curls and the rest of her draped in the finest silks and jewels. She'll enjoy being Empress, I think.

THE COURTYARD IS ABUZZ WITH the news all evening. More dribs and drabs of information reach us, some of it very odd, such as Domitian immersing his dying brother in ice to make his fever abate, which may or may not be true. Titus' body is returned to Rome and some people head towards the Forum to see if they can watch the procession go by, but most of us stay put. The Games are over for another year, we can relax a little. There are toasts made and promises of sacrifices to various gods, hoping that they will bless us with peace and stability in the coming change.

Late at night news comes that Domitian left his dying brother's side, hurrying to the Praetorian Guard's barracks to ensure their loyalty, possibly with promises of payments. They in turn have sworn their allegiance to him, perhaps because there are no other firm favourites, perhaps swayed by his promises. Either way, their allegiance means that he will be Emperor, as we thought, but there's some tutting at the lack of brotherly love he displayed. There's a perfunctory toast to the new Emperor, more to show willing than anything else.

"What was the hurry?" asks Cassia. "Who else would have claimed the title?"

Her father shakes his head. "You're too young to remember how frightening the Year of Four Emperors was for all of us," he says. "You were only a child. But there could have been real trouble. Domitian will have known he needed to be declared Emperor quickly, before anyone else got any funny ideas about laying claim to the title. So be it. At least there will not be any civil war this time. He has a sturdy claim and he's made it swiftly. He doesn't seem such a bad man either."

"He has a surly face," says Cassia. "Looks like someone slapped him."

"I've heard nothing bad about him. No doubt he felt sidelined by his father and brother until now, perhaps being Emperor will put a smile on his face," says Cassius amiably.

"And on his wife's, she'll have fun being Empress," says Cassia. "I've never seen a woman who enjoys her status so much. Though her ornatrix will be hard-pressed to fit any more or higher curls on that head of hers. How many slaves' hair is she wearing, anyway?"

I giggle but it turns into a yawn against my will. "I need to sleep." I say. "We've finished the Games for the season, we have a new emperor. I'm going to sleep like the dead."

In the shadows of the courtyard, I catch a glimpse of Merula and Vita, standing very close together, her head tilted to one side as he speaks earnestly to her, before she turns back to him with a smile. Her hand reaches out to clasp his and he wraps one arm about her waist, pulling her close to him for a moment before they move further into the shadows, where I can no longer make them out.

"Who'd have thought it," murmurs Cassia, following my gaze. "Him so shy and her so bold. I never thought he'd work up the courage to even speak to her."

"Perhaps they are learning from one another," I say.

"They certainly share an affinity for water. Their children will be part-fish."

"Here's to their future little fishes," I say, raising my cup.

"Little fishes," echoes Cassia.

"Why are we drinking toasts to fish?" asks Fabia, joining us. She's unsteady on her feet.

"You're not toasting anyone," I tell her. "You can't even walk straight."

"I'm celebrating my desire coming true," she says happily.

"I'm glad for you," I say. "What did you take to the sorceress?"

"My first wages from Labeo."

Cassia and I nod at the appropriateness of the payment.

"Time for bed, now," I say and the other two protest, but only weakly.

"You still have to find your desire," Cassia reminds me.

"Well, yours took a stick to come true and Fabia's took knives. Maybe I need a weapon of some sort. Enough of your nonsense. Goodnight."

"Goodnight," they chorus.

I start climbing the stairs but am waylaid by Adah, peeping out of her door along the walkway.

"I promised you honeyed wine. It's a good batch, the new honey is very sweet from the drought."

I don't really want to delay sleep any longer but I like to sit with Adah and so I follow her to her little room.

"You heard about Titus," I say.

She nods, murmurs something under her breath.

"You're glad he's dead," I say.

"The Almighty has punished him," she says. "He did not forget what Titus did to my people. He sent Vesuvius, the plague and the fire to Rome and now he has taken Titus." She passes me a cup of honeyed wine. "Did you hear what they found inside him?"

I take the cup, frowning. "Inside him?"

"There was an autopsy this afternoon, when they brought his body back to Rome. Inside his head they found a giant insect that had been growing in his brain ever since the Temple was destroyed at his hand."

I think of Titus clutching at his head and talking about trying to drown out sounds in his head with hammering and the roar of the crowd, his tears. "I haven't heard this anywhere else."

"It is not something the imperial family would like known. That their actions were punished by a greater deity than their own."

"How do you know about it then?"

"One of my people performed the autopsy."

"A Jew?"

She nods. "A doctor. The word spread quickly amongst us. We will be giving thanks for this sign of the Almighty's greatness."

I nod. Titus' death will give Adah and her people a sense of justice for his desecration of their holy place. But I will say a small prayer for Titus, for his kindness in allowing me to adopt Karbo and his unhappiness at not being allowed to keep Berenice by his side.

"Goodnight, Adah."

"Goodnight, child," she says.

When I reach my hut, I barely have the energy to undress, kicking at my sandals to get them off without having properly undone them, tugging at my headwrap and belt, both of which try to resist me. At last, I do as already-sleeping Karbo has done and lie down in just my tunic, pulling it up a little so my legs are mostly bare against the heat.

I can hear rumbles of thunder somewhere in the distance, but I don't get excited about them. No doubt tomorrow will be just as dry and dusty as today and all this summer has been, though at least I can leave the door open to get any small breeze that might help cool the hot night. I murmur my prayer for Titus before my eyelids grow heavy, and I drift into sleep.

I WAKE AT DAWN, TO a soft pitter-pattering sound on the roof. I lie still, frowning, confused for a few moments, until I realise what the unusual sound is.

Rain.

It is raining.

The drought has finally broken.

I make my way to the door, which stands ajar, stubbing my toe on the threshold. I put out a hand to push the door and as I do so the pitter-patter turns to a heavy drumming, my arm already wet even with the door only half open. Rain. I step out into the downpour, uncaring that I am getting drenched. It is such a wonderful feeling to be rained on again, to feel the fresh cool water pouring out of the sky. I turn and walk barefoot through the rain to the very edge of the wall, looking out over Rome as the thunderous clouds split with flashes of lightning. I should be scared by it, but instead I feel elated. I catch one last sight of the tiny shard with the fish on it, just as the rain tips it over the edge of the wall, falling into the street below. The rain soaks my crumpled tunic to my body in moments and the cold chill is delightful. I peer down into Sand Street and see the dust dissolving, the dirt and grime of these past months being swept away down the street as tiny streams form, already running towards the Tiber. I find myself laughing out loud, delighted at the sight of them, then turn to go back indoors but stop abruptly.

Across the rooftop, his back to me, Marcus is standing outside his own hut, facing out across the city. He is naked. The rain pours down over his bare skin, his neck, arms and lower legs burnt brown by the sun, the rest of him untouched, pale golden. His head tips back. Face raised to the rain, he slowly stretches out his arms, palms up as though he were praying, revelling in the rain as I have been.

Standing in the rain, my hair and clothes dripping, I stare across the rooftop, my eyes drinking in the sight of him, from his broad shoulders down to the old scar that still marks his right leg. A flash of lightning flares out across the city and finally, finally, I know what will complete me, the name of my desire. My mouth opens without knowing and I allow my lips to speak its name, my voice lost in a boom of thunder.

"Marcus."

Author's Note on History

This is the second book in a series that started as the simple question I asked myself: who were the people who made up the 'backstage team' for the Colosseum? There is hardly any mention whatsoever of them and yet Games on such an immense scale could not possibly have been put on without a very large and permanent team in place.

Beneath the Waves focuses on water, from naumachiae to the baths, aqueducts and running water of Rome, to hot springs and the early symbol of Christianity, the fish. The other three books in this series focus on the same team through the themes of fire (*From the Ashes*), earth (*On Bloodied Ground*) and air (*The Flight of Birds*).

From varied sources, it seems that the Colosseum hosted at least two naumachiae but possibly no more, before the building of a brick maze-like hypogeum beneath the arena floor which did not allow for any more flooding. It is possible that the second naumachia was during Domitian's time, but I have kept both events in Titus' time, mainly because the hypogeum and other related building projects were very much Domitian's.

The decoration of Cassia's popina is a direct copy of a beautiful recent find in Pompeii, I have posted a CGI video restoration on my Facebook author page. It is exactly how I imagine my fictional popina, right down to it being placed on the corner of a building for best customer footfall.

One of the only direct historical references to the backstage work that would have gone into creating Games at the Colosseum is the epigram I have quoted by Martial, in which the poet marvels at the show-swimmers taking part in the naumachiae put on in the amphitheatre, asking whether they learned their skills from the sea-nymph Thetis, or she learnt her own skills from them.

The Romans were capable of amputation and there is also evidence of prosthetics, from an Egyptian big toe 3000 years ago (so that the person could continue to wear thonged sandals) to General Marcus Sergius Silus, who had an iron hand fitted after amputation so he could hold a shield with his right hand and switched his sword to his left hand, continuing to fight and win many battles in the Punic Wars (264 to 146 BC).

There is no clear evidence of what caused Titus' death, which was officially blamed on a fever (possibly malignant malaria). There were various rumours. One was that Domitian poisoned him, which is unlikely, although he did not show a lot of brotherly concern for Titus' wellbeing, instead focusing on staking his own claim as Emperor. Jewish tradition claims that having been punished throughout his reign (with the eruption of Vesuvius followed by a 'pestilence' and a three-day fire in Rome) for destroying the Temple of Jerusalem, Titus was then killed by a gnat going up his nose by the Almighty's command and causing a growth in his brain, found during an autopsy. According to historians Dio and Suetonius, he did seem to suffer from sadness (including the recorded public weeping at the closing Games) and did not do a lot of work just before he died, so it is possible that he had a brain tumour. Apparently, his last words were that he had made only one mistake, although no-one knows what this was in reference to, possibly in relation to allowing his brother to plot to take over as the emperor.

The Kingdom of Kush was located in modern Northern Sudan and Southern Egypt.

Professor Crapper of Northumbria University wrote a very helpful article, titled 'How Roman engineers could have flooded the Colosseum,' while a 2015 NOVA production with Adriano Morabito (Director of Subterranean Rome) looked at naumachiae and how ships (of ten to fifteen metres long) could have been brought into the Colosseum from side passages pre-filled with water. Both sources considered many solutions for filling and draining the Colosseum, most of which my aquarius Merula runs through and which I have drawn on. The idea of putting pitch on the existing wooden arena floor, as the team choose to try for the first, shallow, naumachia, is mine.

The average person, without training, can hold their breath underwater for thirty to ninety seconds (the Romans did not measure time in seconds). Many of the specific Games I have written about actually happened. Those that I have invented were based on very similar approaches, such as the regular re-enacting of myths and legends of the Greeks and Romans. The poet Martial marvelled at horses and bulls behaving as normal in the water.

Why did a Muslim emperor pick the son of a Christian slave as his heir?

The Moroccan Empire series. 11th century Morocco and Spain. An epic journey of complex choices and opposing faiths told by the voices of forgotten women.

ON BLOODIED
GROUND

For Steven
You have been a constant reassuring presence as I wander
through the backstreets of Rome. Thank you.

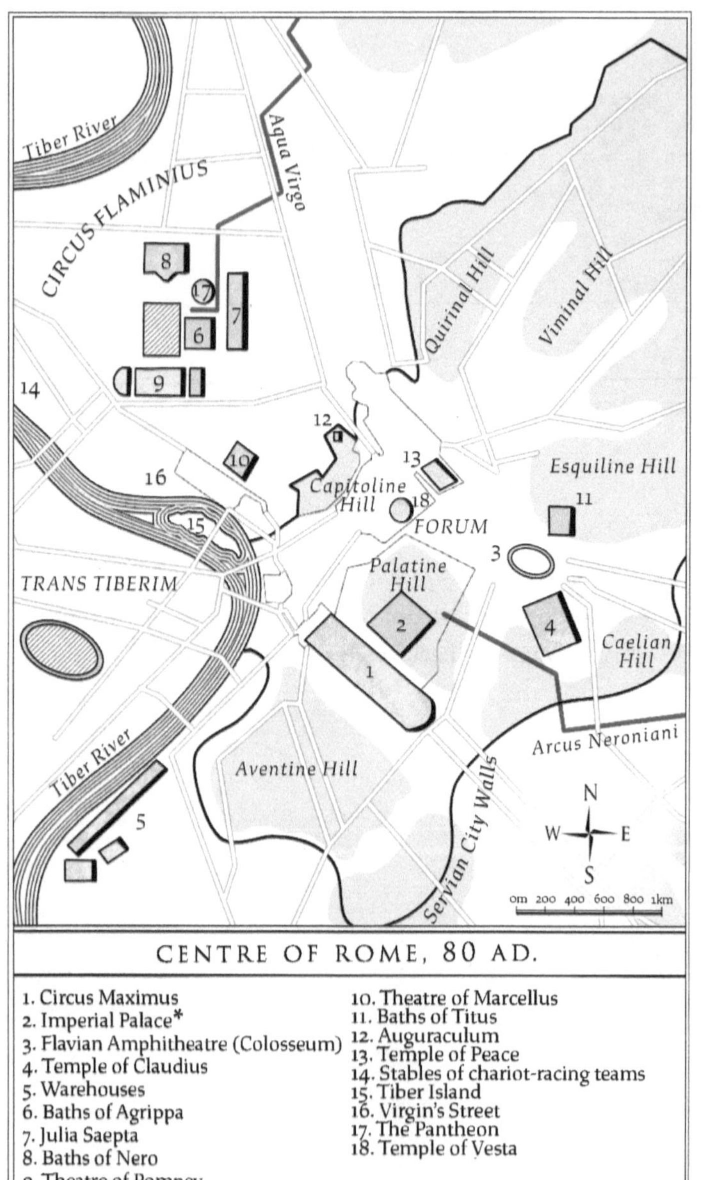

CENTRE OF ROME, 80 AD.

1. Circus Maximus
2. Imperial Palace*
3. Flavian Amphitheatre (Colosseum)
4. Temple of Claudius
5. Warehouses
6. Baths of Agrippa
7. Julia Saepta
8. Baths of Nero
9. Theatre of Pompey
10. Theatre of Marcellus
11. Baths of Titus
12. Auguraculum
13. Temple of Peace
14. Stables of chariot-racing teams
15. Tiber Island
16. Virgin's Street
17. The Pantheon
18. Temple of Vesta

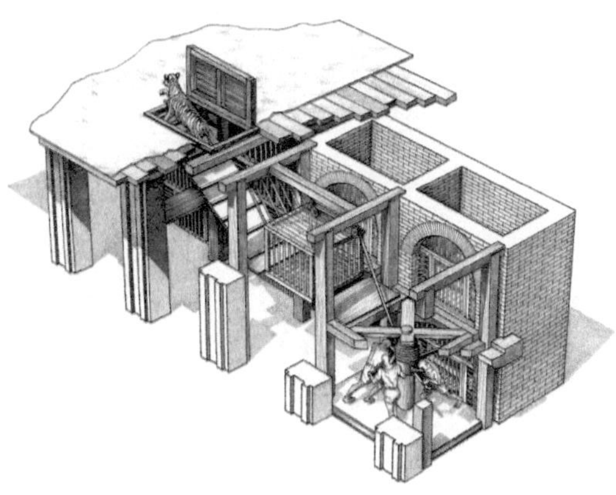

A section of the under-arena space (hypogeum), with working lifts and trapdoors.

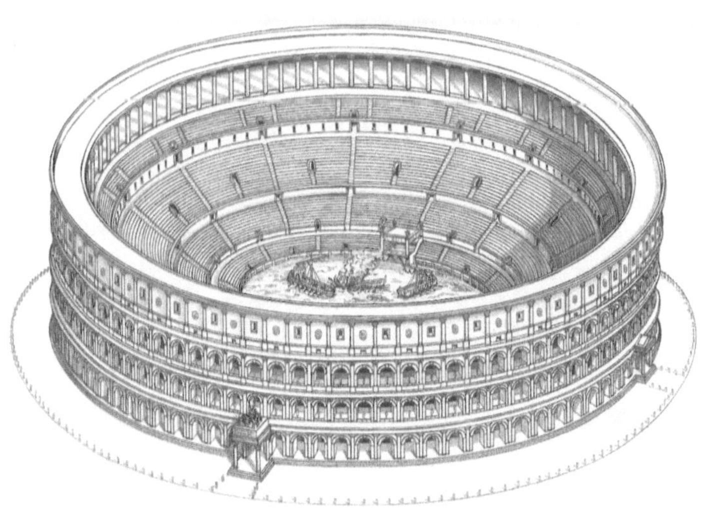

The Flavian Amphitheatre

Historical Background to 81AD

I n 66AD the Roman province of Judea rebelled against Roman rule and drove the Romans out. Fearful that this might spark further rebellions in other provinces of the Empire, Emperor Nero recalled General Vespasian from exile (he had fallen asleep during a poetry reading by Nero) and sent Vespasian and his son Titus to quell the rebellion. This took four years, engaged one quarter of the entire Roman army and ended in Titus' troops looting and burning the Temple of Jerusalem in 70AD. Hundreds of thousands of Jews were killed or enslaved during this period.

Emperor Nero died in 68AD, the last emperor of the Julian-Claudian dynasty. His reign started well but his later years are mostly associated with extravagance and cruelty, which mainly affected the aristocracy. He remained popular among the lower classes which made up the majority of the population. He had a large area of central Rome cleared to create his Golden House, a vast palace complex with a lake. Rumours said the Great Fire of 64AD had been deliberately started by him to enable this project.

Following Nero's death came the Year of the Four Emperors, which culminated in Vespasian taking power in 69AD and founding the Flavian dynasty, which lasted twenty-seven years. He was the first emperor to come from the Equestrian rather than Senatorial rank and he set in motion a large number of building works, including the Flavian Amphitheatre, known to us as the Colosseum, which was located on Nero's now drained lake and largely paid for with loot from the Temple and the sale of Jewish slaves. Vespasian died in June 79AD and was succeeded by his son Titus. In October 79AD, Mount Vesuvius erupted, destroying multiple cities including Pompeii. In spring and summer of 80AD, Rome suffered first a "pestilence" (possibly malaria) in which 10,000 people died, and then a three-day fire. The Flavian Amphitheatre was inaugurated that summer, with 100 days of consecutive Games including water-based spectacles, for which they flooded the arena. Titus ruled for only two years, then died, possibly of a brain tumour. He was succeeded by his younger brother Domitian in September 81AD.

ROME, OCTOBER 81AD

BROKEN SHARDS

"LUCKY PECKER, DOMINA? VERY BEST quality, very affordable. Wood, bronze, even silver or gold if it takes your fancy. Lucky pecker, Dominus? Brings vigour in the bedroom, lots of sons, wealth in all your business transactions…"

"Morning Secundus." I say to the bustling man currently working the crowds in the Forum.

Caius Didius Secundus makes his living selling pendants in the popular shape of a phallus, a highly auspicious symbol found all over Rome. His merchandise is small and portable, which does make it prone to stealing, so he wears a normal tunic but also a cloak, even in summer, into which are stitched the many pendants he offers for sale. When a customer has chosen the one they like best and paid for it, Secundus will cut the thread and hand it over, along with an ongoing monologue about the many benefits it will bring his new customer in every possible aspect of their life.

"Virility of a gladiator, Dominus, I swear – Morning, Althea. You well?"

"Not bad."

"You're heading the wrong way. The Flavian Amphitheatre's just there, if you hadn't noticed. The great big building at the end of the Forum?"

"Been summoned by Domitian," I say.

"The new Emperor? Already? He's barely got settled in."

"I know."

"Ooh. In trouble, are you?"

"Hope not."

"Tell him if he's feeling nervous about his sudden rise to power I can do him a very good price on a lucky pecker, get his time as emperor off to a good start."

I grin. "I will do."

I'm almost at the imperial palace, where Marcus will be waiting. We got the summons last night that Domitian wishes to see us. I left Marcus at dawn, cursing over the folds of his toga, Karbo trying to help him put it on elegantly. My own smartest tunic and headwrap feel overdressed, but you probably can't be too smart to meet an emperor. Titus used to just turn up at the amphitheatre if he felt like talking to any of us, which was alarming in its own way, but at least you couldn't fret about it in advance. This summons by Domitian feels far more formal and is frightening. I tug at the shoulders of my tunic and the brooches holding it in place, trying to make it feel more comfortable. I've sent word down to the warehouses by the docks to inform the cleaning team that they'll have to do without me this morning, instead appointing two supervisors to manage the work we had planned. The Games are over for the year, our workload therefore considerably reduced from the strain of producing vast daily spectacles to the simpler task of repairs and cleaning programmes. However Marcus and I are still supposed to be on site overseeing the end of season cleaning and refurbishment works; our absence will throw the teams into disarray, but then no-one would consider refusing an imperial summons.

The Forum is busy. I'm not sure I've ever seen it quiet in all my years in Rome. There's always something going on. Road-sweepers and carts at dawn followed by stallholders setting up for the day to sell everything from trinkets to street food, priests on their way to the temples. The drifting smoke above the Temple of Vesta assures all of Rome that the sacred flame is burning as it should, cared for by the six Vestal Virgins. The lawyers are setting up for the day, there's the odd tutor leading their pupils to find a good quiet spot in which to sit and carry out their learning for a few hours. Men hasten to attend the morning salutatio with their patron. Later there will be senators and other men of importance strolling together, having heated discussions or heading to the baths for a relaxing afternoon. And as the day goes on Rome's she-wolves will be on the prowl for rich customers. The Forum is always lively.

There's a cool breeze in the air, the desperate heat of the drought-dry summer washed away by the early October rains. It's been more than a month since I stood on our rooftop and laughed out loud with pleasure at the sensation of heavy rain falling on me, before I turned to see Marcus doing the same and…

And nothing.

I tug at the shoulder-brooches again as my stomach turns over. The feelings that rose up in me at that moment, the sudden realisation that I… that I am in love with Marcus… the dizziness and desire that swept over me… I have done nothing about them. In that moment of realisation I spoke his name out loud like a spell, an incantation that would bring him to me, but the thunder drowned me out, took the spell and threw it away in the wind. I stood there one moment longer, gazing at him as he, unknowing, looked out across the city, and all my certainty left me. I ducked back into my own roof hut just as Karbo woke and shrieked with glee at the rain, then ran out to play in it. I heard Marcus' laugh, Karbo's joyful yelps as they danced about the rooftop like madmen together, bare feet splashing in new-made puddles, while I sat drenched and shaking on my bed, trying to make sense of what I was feeling.

It took me two whole weeks to even look Marcus in the eye again when speaking to him, suddenly, ludicrously, shy in his presence. He asked more than once if I was well and I had to give hurried reassurances, heat rising up my neck and into my face.

"I knew it," was my friend Cassia's shrieked response when I finally broke and told her.

"Hush," I begged.

"I will not hush," she said, beaming. "I knew it! You two are made for one another. When's the wedding?"

"There is no wedding! He knows nothing about how I feel!"

"Tell him then."

"He might not… he…"

"Venus and Juno! He might not what? Want a lovely woman like you as his wife? Nonsense. Lucky to have you. You do everything together. He says you are his right-hand woman, that he could not do his job without you."

"That's *work*."

"Oh and he wouldn't like you in his arms? A pretty one like you? Snuggle into his bed one night, see if he asks you to leave."

"Cassia!"

She laughed, black curls bouncing. "Get on with it or someone else will. Handsome man like that." She grew serious for a brief moment. "A good man, too. He'd make a good husband, Althea."

"He's *been* a good husband," I said sadly. "He's still grieving for Livia."

"He'll grieve for her all his life. My father still misses my mother and that was many years ago. But that doesn't mean Marcus can't love a new wife. How long's it been?"

"Nearly two years."

"Tell him."

"I…"

"You want me to tell him?"

"No! Don't you dare!"

"Well, don't come crying to me when he comes back home with a new wife one day just because you didn't speak up."

THE PRAETORIAN GUARDS ON DUTY nod without interest at the small scroll I present, which names me and allows me to enter the imposing building. I'm directed to a vast atrium where a tinkling fountain plays in the sunlight. There are marble benches set around the walls, where people, mostly men, are waiting to be called in. They must all have appointments, whether to see Domitian himself or one of the high-ranking senators and officials based here. I look around and spot Marcus, who, I'm glad to see, has successfully put on his toga. He doesn't look comfortable though.

"Hate wearing this," he mutters, rolling his shoulders.

"You look very smart," I say. *Handsome*, is what I want to say, but I can't bring myself to.

"Wish he'd just turned up on site."

"Do you think he's dissatisfied with something?"

"Who knows."

The large sundial near the fountain indicates that we ought to be called for at any moment. Swallowing, I sit up straighter, the marble bench chilling my behind.

THE SUNDIAL'S SHADOW MOVES ON and on. Marcus, who is reading through scrolls and occasionally huffing to himself, puts one foot up on the bench and leans against me, trying to find a more comfortable position. Once I would have leaned back against him, would have thought nothing of it. Now I sit stiffly, feeling the weight of him against my arm and shoulder. I am conscious of every part of our bodies and how they are touching. When I breathe in I can smell his scent, the fresh toga and his own clean sweat, a trace of horse from his visit to the Blues stables last night to collect Karbo from his work as a stable hand, the apple he was munching on when I arrived here.

I try to ignore the scent of him, roll my shoulders.

"Sorry," says Marcus, straightening up.

"I – don't mind," I say.

"Good," he says, slumping back against me, the warmth of him heavy, his arm pressed against mine, bare skin to bare skin. The hair on his forearm brushes against me as he lifts the scroll back up. "Mercury help me, what *is* this drivel? Can no-one explain themselves properly? All I asked for was a simple list of how many gladiators and of what type they have in the training school of Puteoli and what is this? A lot of nonsense about prices and suchlike. As if I don't know what a gladiator costs and as if the Emperor doesn't have the wherewithal to pay. Write back and tell them I just want a list."

"I already have," I say.

"I'm glad someone knows what they're doing."

Once, I would have smiled, pleased at the praise. Now I only wonder whether this is how he sees me: a comrade to be slumped against, his right-hand woman in the role he carries out as organiser of the Games. Nothing more. And yet there is so much more it could be, *we* could be. The warmth of him against me...

"I'm supposed to be overseeing the repairs to the lifts," he mutters. "The carpenters were due this morning. Jupiter knows what I'll find when I get back on site."

"Do you think they're going to call for us at all?"

"The gods only know." He fishes out another scroll. "Ah, you wrote to Funis. Has he replied?"

"No answer yet."

"We need to know by Saturnalia at the latest or we'll be left without a beast hunter and good luck to us if we have to start a new season of Games in March without one of those."

Funis, the beast hunter we met in Ostia last year when we needed water-based animals. His unusual clothing, the pattern of scars on his dark-skinned cheeks. The evil-eyed crocodiles he delivered to us when we took on the near-impossible task of flooding the amphitheatre for spectacular water-based Games. I shudder at what happened afterwards, the moment when I thought Marcus had drowned. But afterwards, when he held me while I wept... I should have said something then, should have touched his face...

Marcus is waiting for an answer. I clear my throat. "He said he wasn't fond of being in Rome; perhaps he doesn't want the role."

"Anyone with ambition would jump at the chance. Beast hunter to the Flavian Amphitheatre? Doesn't get more lucrative than that."

A Praetorian Guard is waving us over. "Marcus Aquillius Scaurus?"

We jump to our feet and follow him through a door and down a corridor. Halfway down is a lofty double door, this one flanked by more guards, who push it open at our approach.

We're shown into a large chamber, well-lit by windows down one side. In the centre of the room is a wooden table, at which are standing two men in togas, one of which is trimmed with purple. So this is Domitian. Thinner and taller than his brother Titus, a long face, short hair.

"Marcus Aquillius Scaurus, manager of the Flavian Amphitheatre, and his scribe, Althea Aquillius," announces the guard.

Domitian doesn't move. He's staring down at the table, on which is laid out a model of Rome, meticulously rendered in pottery.

The other man looks up at us. Slight of build, he is holding a quill in his right hand, while his left holds down on the table a partially unrolled scroll. There's something owl-like about him, with his large gold-hazel eyes and dishevelled brown hair sticking up like rumpled feathers. His skin is very pale, untouched by the sun. He stares at us for a moment, then looks to Domitian for guidance.

Domitian pays no attention. Very slowly, he squats down, bringing his eyes level with the table and the model, peering through the tiny streets of his toy Rome, gazing at something we cannot make out. He reaches out one finger and prods a building, straightening it up. I realise that each edifice on the table is a little block which can be moved about.

I glance at Marcus, who gives a miniscule shrug.

"Ahem."

The sound comes from another person in the room. A tall thin man, elegantly attired in a toga, standing unseen in a far corner. He has grey hair and, although he looks our way, he does not smile, only coughs again, a discreet sound.

"Ahem. Imperator."

Domitian looks up at the man, who flicks his eyes in our direction. Domitian follows his gaze to us and stands up.

"Who are you?"

Marcus inclines his head politely. "Marcus Aquillius Scaurus. Manager of the Flavian Amphitheatre, Imperator."

"Who's she?"

"Althea Aquillius. My scribe. You sent for us, Imperator."

Domitian doesn't offer any kind of welcome. Instead he sinks back into his squat. "Look."

We approach the table.

The model of Rome is exquisite. Every building I can think of, from the amphitheatre, Forum and great temples, down to the most insignificant and run-down insula, is represented, each made like a little toy house, moulded out of pottery, then painted in minute detail. The river Tiber has been painted onto the table, in a winding green-blue. I spot our own insula in Virgin's Street, close to the island in the middle of the river, which is occupied by the temple of Aesculapius, god of healing.

Domitian stands up again. "My architect Rabirius is preparing the designs for a large-scale programme of building."

The owl-man nods fervently and gestures towards the half-open scroll. Marcus and I shuffle closer, peer at what he is indicating.

The area around the amphitheatre is clearly marked out, but the arena floor is not shown as one smooth surface, but rather as some sort of odd maze-like structure. Outside the perimeter, four new buildings have been sketched. I frown, trying to make sense of what I'm looking at.

Marcus is looking from the model to the scroll. "You have... plans... for the amphitheatre's arena, Imperator?"

Domitian answers without looking up. "Yes. A brick-built hypogeum, two storeys high, sitting beneath the existing arena floor. It will be better than the current layout, which is really just a big empty area. It's a waste of space and doesn't allow for efficient management of lifts and so on. This will be better, more organised."

Marcus doesn't say anything but his eyebrows go up. "And these?" he asks, indicating the four new buildings on the scroll. One of them is quite large.

Domitian lays his finger on the drawing. "Gladiator schools. With barracks and arenas of their own, as required. This one," he points to the largest, "will be the Ludus Magnus, the Great School. Three storeys, one hundred and thirty-five rooms, a three-thousand-seater arena for practise so that the fans can watch the gladiators training. That one right next to it," he points to a smaller but similarly shaped building, "will be the Ludus Matutinus: the Morning School. For beast-hunters, venatores and the more exotic fighters, women and such, with a five-hundred-seater arena. Then two more schools in due course, the Ludus Dacius and the Ludus Gallicus, for the gladiators of those styles and provenances." He talks fast, but his facial expression remains strangely blank, though his eyes are bright with enthusiasm.

I look down at the model and then glance at Marcus who gives me a tiny nod, knowing what I'm going to say.

"The new gladiator barracks," I say tentatively, "according to the drawing they would need to be..." I gesture to the pottery model, which clearly shows that the designated area is already full of buildings, both large and small. There is certainly no space for four large new edifices to be constructed.

Domitian tilts his head. "Of course," he says. He reaches out with swift movements, picking up one tiny creation after another and letting them drop to the floor, where they smash, pottery shards skidding out across the marble floor, the noise echoing round the empty room. I gasp and step back, but Domitian, after breaking perhaps ten miniature buildings in this way, turns his head and gives me a sudden odd smile, teeth bared, which vanishes again in an instant. "I have these, you see."

He fumbles in the folds of his toga and pulls out four little pottery pieces, neat replicas of Rabirius' architectural drawings of the gladiatorial schools, then places each one into the new gaps on the model, tutting when he finds one more building that will need to make way for what he has in mind, casually dropping it as he did the others, one last crashing destruction.

"See?" he says, looking down at the revised model.

I steal a glance at the architect, who is staring down at the model, eyes wide.

"And there's so much more I want to build," says Domitian. "A new Circus, a villa for the Vestal Virgins near the Temple of Vesta, a new imperial palace here in Rome as well as one outside in the country. Temples. And, of course, there's all the reconstruction that needs completing after the fire in the Ninth Region. The Pantheon, Saepta Julia, Baths of Agrippa, the stage of Pompey's Theatre, the Diribitorium and the Theatre of Balbus." His words spill out so fast I can barely keep up, his finger moving above the model, indicating locations. Rabirius is nodding with enthusiasm at the catalogue of works, fumbling through a tub of scrolls as Domitian speaks, ready to produce drawings of everything being listed.

"Ahem." Again the quiet man in the corner.

Domitian looks his way.

"Your next appointment."

Domitian hesitates, then gives a reluctant shrug. "Very well." He looks at Marcus. "I would like to meet the animals."

"Imperator?"

"You have animals. For the Games."

"Yes, Imperator, they are delivered weekly, to the warehouses by the docks, but only during the Games season, they –"

"I would like to meet them. When shall I come?"

Marcus makes a quick recovery. "Were there particular animals you wished to see?"

"Antelope."

I was expecting something like lions or tigers, but Marcus smoothly agrees. "Next week, Imperator? I can send word of a good day for a visit to your secretary?"

Domitian waves a hand towards the quiet man's corner without looking at him. "You can let Stephanus know. He takes care of everything."

Marcus glances at the man, who gives a short nod.

"That was odd," I say, taking a deep breath as soon as we are outside and far enough away from the building that I can risk speaking out loud.

"Very," agrees Marcus. "All that building? That's how Nero started. It sounded like a good idea till he started behaving strangely."

I lower my voice. "He's already behaving strangely. Smashing those models? What was that about?"

A voice comes from behind us. "The Imperator has his own way of doing things."

I freeze, then slowly turn, as does Marcus. Behind us is the tall quiet man. Stephanus.

I swallow. "I didn't mean —"

The man waves away my untruthful protest. "The Imperator behaves… unusually sometimes. But he is not mad. You will come to know his ways, as I do."

We wait for him to continue.

"You will likely see a lot of him over the coming months. He is fond of the Games. He also has a passion for building and now that he has the power to do as he pleases, he will indulge it. He likes to manage things very closely and in person, he will not just give the command for the work to be done and walk away."

We nod.

The man gives a very small smile. "He also likes animals. As he has mentioned. He will be with you at the animal warehouse in six days' time, at midday. He rises late, since he has difficulty getting to sleep. I will see you then."

He turns and walks away briskly, without a farewell.

We look at each other, breathe out. My heart is still thudding.

"Find out who this Stephanus is," says Marcus. "I don't trust him. He's too quiet on his feet, for starters. And we've got to find a herd of antelope, off-season? With no beast-hunter?"

As I make my way back towards the insula that afternoon a man asks me for directions.

"Virgin's Street is just off Sand Street," I tell him.

"Full of virgins, is it?" says the man, winking.

"It's named for my landlady Julia," I say. "She served for thirty years as a Vestal Virgin."

The man swallows. "No offence intended to Lady Vesta," he says, making a sign to ward off the ire of the gods. He mutters thanks and hurries down the street when I indicate it to him while I turn into our insula's gate smiling to myself at his sudden respect.

Julia is pruning the vines that snake up the wooden courtyard staircase. Below her the children of the insula splash water from the fountain at one another and the adults gather after the evening meal, making the most of the last light of the day to chat between themselves. Among them are the tall gangly framed Fabius, physician to the amphitheatre and his dwarf daughter Fabia, one of my closest friends and physician to the second largest gladiatorial school in Rome. By the time I've got a plate of stew from Cassia's always-busy popina and eaten half of my meal, Marcus joins us, in time to hear me tell Fabia and Fabius about our morning's meeting with Domitian.

Fabia frowns at us. "He threw the pottery models on the floor? Do you think he's going to be trouble?"

Marcus shrugs, spooning up another mouthful of his own stew. "Not sure. He's strange, for sure. He seemed enthusiastic about public buildings for the good of Rome, but –"

Fabius chimes in to finish the sentence. "– but that's how Nero started."

"As long as he doesn't start raiding the temples to pay for them," says Julia from above, clipping away at the vine. "If he starts that, we'll know to be careful."

Karbo is following along behind Julia, picking up the fallen clippings. "If I put one in a pot, will it grow?" he asks.

"You want to grow a vine?" she asks.

"Yes. I want a garden on the rooftop."

"I'll help you. Marcus, you have a farmer on your hands. You need to buy back your family's farm so you can take him there with you."

Marcus laughs. "I could do with a strong boy," he agrees cheerfully, pouring more wine for Fabius. "The farm will be falling apart and overgrown, it's going to take some hard work when I return there, whenever that day finally comes."

I sit quietly, listening. Marcus speaking of leaving his life here as manager of the Games makes me anxious. Will he leave soon? And if he does, will he ask me to go with him, or simply leave me here? I imagine for a brief moment what it would feel like if Marcus were to turn to me and say that it is time to start the life he has always dreamed of; that he will buy back his family's long-lost farm and return to Puteoli to live there, but that he cannot think of doing so without me by his side, that he...

"Time for bed?" says Marcus.

I choke on my wine. "What?" I ask, spluttering.

Fabia pats my back ineffectually. Being a dwarf, her tiny frame is unable to put enough weight into the action and it takes me a few moments to recover.

"I need some sleep," says Marcus, standing up. "Tomorrow we need to request a copy of those drawings from Rabirius. I've had to put all the lift work on hold till we know what structure they'll need to fit into. I was hoping for a quiet winter. Why do we never get a chance to rest properly?"

I watch him making his way up the stairs.

Karbo appears at my side. "Can we have a cat?"

"What?"

"A cat. Domina has had kittens again. Can we bring one here? The little tabby one? I've called her Letitia. Can she live here with us? She would enjoy exploring the rooftops. Especially if I plant her a garden."

I set aside my own half-built daydream. "Very well. But she is to be your pet, understood? You must save her scraps and feed her every day until she can hunt for herself. And right now it is time for bed."

I WAKE TO A SOFT singing, which turns out to be Adah tending to the bees. She disdains protective clothing or smoke when caring for them, her gnarly wrinkled hands unafraid as she lifts up the wickerwork lids of the hives, shuffling from one to another through a cloud of buzzing with no apparent harm. Karbo and I keep a more wary distance.

"Can I try some, Adah? Please?" begs Karbo.

"In good time," murmurs Adah between snatches of song. I don't understand the words, it must be a song of her own Jewish people. She always sings to the bees, claiming that it makes them calmer than the usual burning of cow dung.

"It looks like a good harvest," I say, as she lifts out several chunks of heavy wax, dripping with golden honey and lays them carefully in a large platter.

"It is," she says. "Here, boy."

Karbo creeps up to her, crouching down in the vain hope the bees will not find him and sting him for stealing the fruits of their hard work. He takes the chunk of honeycomb from her and slips back to me, a couple of bees following the scent and weaving around our heads. Karbo breaks the chunk in two and honey drips down his fingers as he offers me some. We pop the honeycomb in our mouths and lick our fingers, while the bees continue to circle, wondering at the sudden disappearance of the honey they'd traced as far as us.

Karbo makes happy noises through his mouthful.

"It's delicious, Adah," I say and she smiles, satisfied.

"After this they can sleep for the winter," she says. "Rest and be strong for the spring to come," she adds over each hive in what sounds like a blessing as she closes them up again.

"That's what we ought to be doing," I say. "Resting over the winter to be ready for spring and the next season of Games. But it doesn't sound like we're going to get much rest if Domitian has his way with all these building works he has planned. The amphitheatre's going to be one big building site."

Adah spits, not unexpectedly. "Cursed place," she says, referring to her long-held resentment over the amphitheatre built with money and slaves from the destruction of the Temple of Jerusalem, the most holy place of her people. "You should not work there any longer. Do something better with your life."

"Such as?"

"Get married and have children," she says promptly, a smile playing around her mouth.

"I'll think about it," I say, not wishing to develop this conversation any further in case she starts making suggestions of possible husbands for me to consider. "Karbo, you're supposed to be at the stables and I'm supposed to be at work. We'll see you later, Adah."

I can hear Adah chuckling to herself from the rooftop, before she drifts back to her beekeeping song. I run down the wooden stairs, only to be met by a dark figure standing in the gateway of the insula.

"Althea."

It takes me a moment to realise it is Funis, the beast hunter from Ostia. If anything he looks even more unusual here. By the docks his brown skin marked with facial tattoos, the armbands and the tiger tail he wears, as well as the Egyptian-looking top and skirt he favours fit in better, filled as the area was with people from across the Empire. Here, in our insula, he looks like a visitor from another world.

"Funis! You came to us after all. I thought your silence after my letter of invitation was a refusal."

He gives a chuckle. "It was. But then I thought better of my plans. Why deny myself Rome when she has called my name? My own prejudices towards her from the past should not cloud my judgement when looking to the future and what it may bring."

"I am glad to see you," I say. "And Marcus will be too. He was keen for you to join our team."

"I am at your service. I wondered if I could call on you to show me the amphitheatre?"

"Of course," I say. "I was about to go there. Do you need a place to stay? I can ask Julia if there are rooms free here in the insula."

He shakes his head. "I will be staying at the gladiatorial barracks run by Paternus," he says. "He's an old friend and has been good to me."

"Gladiatorial barracks are hardly luxurious," I say.

"I'm used to them from the old days. They make me feel at home."

We walk to the largest gladiatorial barracks, where Funis embraces the gladiator owner and trainer Paternus, leaves his travelling bag and promises to meet him at the baths later. Then onwards through the Forum and to the amphitheatre.

"Impressive," murmurs Funis, tilting his head back to look up at the third floor. "And you say Domitian has further building plans? I thought it was complete."

"He wants a different layout under the arena floor," I say. "I'll show you the plans."

We make our way to the arena floor, where Funis turns around on himself, looking up at the vast white expanse of seating. "Sixty thousand?"

"We can do. Usually about fifty thousand, but it's possible to squeeze more in."

He stands silent for a moment. "I can hear the roar of the crowd," he says at last. "It must be an extraordinary place in which to perform."

"You were a gladiator yourself, you told me."

"A long time ago. Beast-hunting is a lot safer as a career."

"Not tempted to take up gladiatorial combat again?"

He laughs. "No, thank you. Rome is dangerous enough, I don't need to add extra danger to my life."

I frown. "Is Rome a dangerous place for you specifically?"

"It is," he says, turning away to look at the Gate of Death, still locked up from the night.

"Why?"

"Oh, a very long story," he says.

"I'd like to hear it if you'd like to tell it."

He turns back to face me. "I will. One day."

"If you had misgivings about coming to Rome, what overcame them?"

He looks steadily at me for a moment, his brown eyes warm, a smile on his lips. "A letter."

My cheeks grow hot. "Being the beast-hunter for the Flavian Amphitheatre is a hard role to turn down," I say. "It's very prestigious. And lucrative of course," I add.

"Some things are worth pursuing, whatever your misgivings," he agrees. "Can you show me the space under the arena?"

We make our way through one of the hidden doors in the arena wall, through a stone tunnel and down a dark wooden staircase to the vast empty space underneath, the ceiling far above us. Tiny streams of daylight filter down between the arena's wooden boards, cutting up the area into tiny strips of light and dark, hard to see clearly in.

"Usually there's a lot more down here," I say. "The lifts which take the animals and gladiators into the arena, the physician's area, the morgue. If Domitian's plans are put into place, this whole area will be split into two storeys and lots of smaller spaces. Marcus doesn't much care for it."

"Does he still enjoy the role?"

"Yes. Although he gets frustrated when things are changed without warning, on the Emperor's whim."

"Understandable. Has he remarried?"

The sudden change of topic leaves me flustered. "N-no."

Funis looks directly at me. "And you?"

"Me?"

"Married?"

My cheeks are burning, I'm glad the light down here is so poor. "No," I say and then, my voice too loud, "Let me show you outside the amphitheatre. You can see where the new gladiatorial schools will be built."

I lead him back up to the exits, grateful to feel a cool breeze on my hot face as we come to the top outside but conscious of him walking right behind me up the stairs.

"You'll need to find us some antelope," I say, grateful to have thought of a matter of business to talk about. "Domitian wants to feed some animals and we don't have any in storage. We didn't get much warning."

"Of course," says Funis. "You have only to name the day and they will be there."

Two days later, a pale dawn wakes me. I could sleep in; our days in autumn and winter have far less work to do than when we have to provide the near-daily spectacle of the Games. But I'm too used to rising early and besides, I have news for Marcus. I wash and make my way to Cassia's popina, rubbing my bare arms. The summer warmth has well and truly gone. I'll need to air my winter cloak and Karbo's; they've been packed away for months.

"I'm making pancakes," Cassia says.

She knows me well. The fresh fruit that I am fond of in the summer is coming to an end, though there are still some late grapes. It's time to return to her griddled pancakes with date syrup, which both Karbo and I are fond of. "I'm going to need to get our cloaks out again soon. Although Karbo's boots will be too small, the way he's shooting up."

Cassia pours wine for two customers and flips my first pancake over. "It's the anniversary soon."

"Fifteen days." Fifteen days till the morning two years ago when ash fell softly over Rome and we found to our horror that Pompeii had been obliterated beneath its smothering weight, taking with it Marcus' wife and baby son.

"Has he said anything?"

"No. He didn't say anything last year either. He just disappeared all day and then went to see Julia." I glimpsed him sat at her table, head down, shoulders heaving.

Cassia serves me my pancakes and pours more batter onto the hissing griddle as she sees Karbo approaching. "It'll be easier to speak to him when the anniversary has passed."

The piece of pancake is too big in my mouth. I take my time chewing to avoid answering. By the time I've swallowed, Karbo is telling me in minute detail how he plans to take care of Letitia the kitten. I nod along without really listening until it's time to wave goodbye to Cassia and make our way to the amphitheatre.

MARCUS INTERROGATES ME AS SOON as I arrive. "Tell me what you found out."

"His name is Gaius Petronius Stephanus. He's a cousin of Gaius Petronius Arbiter."

Marcus' eyes narrow. "Nero's 'arbiter of taste'? The one who people said wrote the *Satyricon* under a pen name?"

"Yes. But I don't think they were very close."

"Arbiter came to a sticky end anyway, didn't he? Can't imagine many in his family would have wanted to acknowledge him."

My notes say that Arbiter's preferential treatment eventually made the commander of Nero's guard jealous. Arbiter ended up being accused of treason and arrested for it at Cumae twenty years ago. He didn't wait to find out what his sentence would be, instead taking his own life. "How come his cousin's been hired then? If Arbiter ended in disgrace?"

"That whole clan are well in with the Flavians, they're not going to let one bad apple taint their chance of being cosy with the Emperor. What's Stephanus' actual job, did you find out? Is he Domitian's secretary?"

"No. Everyone was a bit vague about what exactly he does. Someone called him

Domitian's 'handler', as if Domitian were a wild animal being trained up for the Games."

"He could do with some handling if he's going to be chucking pottery around and pulling apart half of Rome to add in the buildings he fancies." Marcus runs his hand over his hair and I have to stop myself imagining what it would feel like on my fingers. "Any luck getting the antelope?" he asks.

"Funis has sourced twelve. They'll be at the warehouse when he visits."

"As if we need Domitian treating our warehouse like a private zoo."

I shrug. "If it keeps him happy with us it's a small price to pay. It'll be easier once the season starts again in spring, then there'll always be animals down there for him to visit if that's what he likes to do."

"Funis is visiting us this morning," says Marcus. "Ah, there he is. We're glad to have you join us."

Funis offers a wide smile. "It's my pleasure to be here," he says. "Although I hear there's a building programme to get done before we can start a new season?"

Marcus tuts and strides over to the edge of the balustrade, waving down at the arena below us. "I've been sent a copy of Rabirius' drawings. This hypogeum he wants under the arena floor; it's like a labyrinth, two floors of it. Hardly any air flow, or light. So we'll need torches and lamps everywhere, which will turn it into Vulcan's furnace during the summer. And a fire hazard."

I offer Funis a copy of the drawings and he examines them with interest.

"It looks like a labyrinth," he comments. "Two floors of it?"

I nod.

"You don't look happy with it," Funis tells Marcus.

"I'm not. It's a waste of space. All those archways and corridors, they're only made possible with a lot of walls. Which means we lose space. And flexibility. We used to be able to put things wherever we wanted. Now the lifts will be fixed in place and you can't move a few out of the way when you need the space for something else. It's very elegantly designed but it's very rigid too. And complex. And it's... hidden."

"Hidden?"

"You can't see what's happening in another part of the hypogeum: everything's in tiny little spaces. So something could be going wrong somewhere and I won't know until someone gets a message by running to me, which will take time, or by signals like our whistles, which can interrupt music or the chorus." He looks worried and I want to rest my hand on his arm to reassure him.

"So remind me: did you like the design or not?" grins Funis.

"Will we still have the same number of lifts?" I ask, bringing matters back to practical considerations.

"Yes," Marcus acknowledges. "So that's good. Just less room overall and smaller, tighter spaces for everything."

I groan. Nothing is ever easy. "Right now I need to look over the merchandise the stallholders are preparing for next season. And it's time for the morning salutatio, you'll have people calling on you. Are you coming?"

Marcus shakes his head. "I'm heading to the Aedile's salutatio session to try and get some guidance out of him. But there's probably no arguing. The current Aedile doesn't stand up to the Emperor, anyway, never has done. So you'll have to run the salutatio here." He grins. "You do it so much better than me, anyway."

I laugh. The morning salutatio, when people who consider Marcus a valuable contact and patron visit him to proffer their greetings and mention what they may be able to do for him, or what they'd like him to do for them, is a regular part of Roman life for a man of means or, like Marcus, a man who can offer valuable opportunities. But Marcus finds the whole process tedious and manages to wriggle out of it most days, leaving the formalities of the process to me instead. His suppliers and other contacts found it peculiar to deal with a woman at first, but have given up trying to locate him, settling for me instead, knowing that their messages and presence (or lack thereof) will be duly noted and passed on. They find it odd, but then we're seen as a strange lot at the amphitheatre anyway, falling somewhere between the imperial power that funds us and the glamorous, but still lowest, dregs of society with whom we associate, from prostitutes and dancing girls to gladiators and wild beasts.

"I'll leave you to your work," says Funis. "I should get back to the gladiator barracks. There was a break-in last night, perhaps robbers looking to steal weapons. The entry guard was stabbed, but nothing was stolen as far as we can tell, perhaps they got disturbed. Paternus is in a bad mood and could do with a friend about the place."

We wave him off, the three of us going about our separate ways for the day.

When I reach the ground-floor corridor Secundus is hanging round with the other stallholders.

"I didn't know you wanted a stall next season, Secundus?"

"Oh, I don't, I prefer working the crowd while they're queuing. People buy on impulse when they're bored," he says, winking. "But I always like to see what everyone else will be offering."

I try to get some semblance of order out of the jostling crowd of men I need to get through. I point to the narrow table we've set up and take a seat behind it, Secundus hovering by my side like a keen assistant. I've got a scroll with stall spaces marked on it so that I can write in each name and where the stall will be when we re-open next season. Although the crowds can approach and enter the amphitheatre from all directions, there are certain favoured places for stalls. The imperial entrance of course, since some crowds gather just to watch the emperor arrive. The Baths of Titus, since some spectators will want to head straight there after a hot and dusty morning spent at the Games. Most popular is the area close to the meta sudans fountain, favoured by crowds and hawkers alike because of the way the waters cool the air during the heat of summer. These favoured spots go to the best traders, who have proven their wares are good quality and of interest to spectators, season after season.

"Right, let's start at this end, queue up in the order you arrived this morning and lay your wares out here on the table so I can see what you have in mind. What've you got for me on your second stall, Brocchus?"

Brocchus has more than one stall promised to him this year, having done a roaring trade last year. He specialises in models of gladiators which are always popular merchandise, but this new stall is something different. He unrolls a cloth wrap, carefully laying out the items inside it for me to look at. "Children's toys, Althea. Go down ever so well with the parents, especially if the children nag."

I look down at the clay and carved wooden or bone models of wild animals and gladiators, posed in fighting stances. Next to them sits a small green glass cup with a tiny spout. "What's that?"

"Ah, new for the season, very proud of this one, had the mould commissioned specially. It's a baby's bottle."

"With *gladiators* on it?"

"For the proud father who loves the Games."

"Brilliant," says Secundus. "They'll love that."

I hold up the little green glass cup. "I hope they do well for you. I don't need to see the other merchandise, I remember it from last year. I'll try and find you a good spot." I dismiss him and wave forward the next in line, a squat bald man, who is empty handed. "Calvus?"

"This is going to require a contract with Paternus from the gladiator school, but I'm thinking of a premium offering next year, not available to just anyone, but worth the price for the blessing it will provide to the happy couple."

"Which is?"

"Bloodied spears for weddings. Straight from the Flavian Amphitheatre itself, I mean you can't get more prestigious than that, can you?"

Secundus nods wisely. "Oh absolutely. Very good luck for the bride, that, having her hair parted by a gladiator's bloodied spear before they put on her veil."

I grimace. "I'm not sure I'd want that put through my hair."

"'Course you would. The blood will be dry by the time they actually use it, won't it?"

I shake my head. "Whatever the customer wants. But you'll have to talk to Paternus, or Labeo, if you want to get a bloodied spear. Normally all the armour gets sent straight back to the barracks at the gladiator schools, where they clean it up."

AFTER A MORNING SPENT INSPECTING ever more outlandish ideas for Games merchandise, I send a messenger to find out if the antelope are safely installed and make my way to the Baths, where I meet Fabia for a well-earned soak.

"Labeo's beside himself at the idea of moving to a big new gladiatorial school right next to the amphitheatre," she tells me. "He can't wait. We'll be able to have a lot more gladiators once we have a large barracks like that."

"Will you be able to manage by yourself?" I ask. "Being physician to a big school like that was enough already. If they expand, will you be able to look after even more gladiators?"

"I'll get an apprentice," she says. "Or maybe even two. I could do with them."

THE DAYS PASS QUICKLY AND down at the docks, at midday as promised, we're awaiting Domitian. The warehouse where we store animals is finally complete, having undergone significant repairs to the leaking roof. Once waterproof, it was cleaned and then laid out to enable us to receive deliveries of animals more easily and to keep them apart. Storing animals like antelope next to lions is always a poor idea. The antelope cringe in fear and end up not eating; the lions spend their time growling and swiping through the bars, maddened by the proximity of their natural prey. Instead we subdivided the giant space available so we can keep predators and prey separate. We built bigger and better pens too, and left corridors of space so that pens can be lifted straight onto carts to be taken to the amphitheatre. We will use the large pens for keeping the animals, then move them into much smaller, closed ones for transport. The heaviest ones have their own wheels mounted to the bottom so that they are simply hitched up to a cart and pulled through the streets to the arena.

Today the slaves stand to attention, as Marcus makes one final check. The warehouse looks ridiculously clean and neat; the floors have been washed for the occasion. Usually the air is thick with the smell of animals; today it smells fresh in a way I've never experienced before.

"We're ready," Marcus says finally, although with reluctance. "I don't know why he'd want to see the animals when they're not doing anything interesting. If he's keen on animals, why doesn't he just attend the Games in the mornings, when we do the hunts, come springtime?"

Only Funis is calm. "Who knows how great men think," he says.

Karbo dashes in. "They're here," he says.

"Keep out of the way," advises Marcus, hurrying out of the door to go and greet Domitian.

I expected a vast entourage: the Praetorian Guards, officials, hangers-on. But Domitian enters with only the tall shadowy figure of Stephanus behind him.

"Imperator," I say, bowing my head as Domitian strides past me.

He doesn't reply, though his eyes flicker towards me and away as he passes, intent on the cage of antelope ahead of him. Reaching it, he stops close by the bars, snaps his fingers and holds out his hand without looking behind him.

"Grass."

Marcus and I look at each other and both of us look to Funis, but Stephanus has already stepped forward and produces a clump of fresh grass from the folds of his toga, which he places in Domitian's outstretched palm.

Domitian pokes the grass through the bars of the cage, but the antelope huddle at the far side, uncertain of his intentions. They have been caught and made captive, brought to this frightening, echoing place. They can scent past predators who have been held here. Besides, they are no strangers to being seized by friendly hands offering just such temptations. Whatever trust they once had is long gone.

"What's wrong with them?" demands Domitian over his shoulder.

I stare at Marcus for help. He frowns but before he can speak, Stephanus smoothly intervenes.

"Timid, Imperator. You will have to show great patience."

Domitian sinks to the floor in a cross-legged position like a child about to receive tuition, arranging his toga folds so that he is comfortable. Once settled, he holds out the grass again and waits.

I glance at Stephanus, who is waiting in silence, hands behind his back. Catching my gaze, he gives a small nod, politely acknowledging a distant acquaintance, and returns his focus to Domitian.

Marcus looks at me and opens his eyes wider, a tiny comment on the absurd situation. Karbo peeps round a dividing wall at me, his face asking questions I am not at liberty to answer. I make a tiny gesture with my hand, a quick *go-away*. Karbo sticks out his tongue and disappears, no doubt to report to the rest of our hidden and curious team that something peculiar is going on.

It takes over an hour before the antelope trust Domitian and feed from his hand. Marcus, Funis, Stephanus and I stand in silence watching his back. He never speaks or moves in all that time, never sighs with irritation or moves his hand, only keeps the grass held out, resting his forearm on his knee to keep it steady. Eventually, a brave antelope moves forwards and reaches out its neck as far as it will go, its muzzle so close that its breath ruffles the grass. For a moment I wonder whether Domitian will grab at the animal, but he stays still and the antelope gathers its courage and eats. It is joined by another and when the grass is gone they retreat and Domitian stands up and turns to us, his previously blank expression lit up with a joyous expression which makes him look both younger and more handsome.

"They ate from my hand," he says. "I had to wait a long time but I knew they would come if I stayed still."

"Exemplary patience, Imperator," says Stephanus.

Domitian's smile broadens at the compliment, then turns to Marcus. "I will visit often," he says. Next time I would like to feed meat to lions."

Marcus opens his mouth to answer, but Domitian is not waiting for a response, he is already striding away, stepping out into the sunshine beyond the warehouse door, his shadow Stephanus following him.

We reach the door a few paces behind them and sure enough the entourage I had expected is gathered just outside, a few dozen bodyguards, officials and litter-bearers with a large litter, into which Domitian climbs, the drapes pulled around him for privacy, the whole group already moving away, curious bystanders scattering out of the way.

"Did he just sit there for the whole hour trying to feed the antelopes?" demands Karbo from behind us.

"Yes," says Funis smiling.

"Why?"

I look at Marcus. "I really don't know," I say, starting to laugh.

I'm EATING AT CASSIA'S THE next morning when one of our slaves arrives from the barracks, white-faced and shaking with news that the slave who does the cooking for the amphitheatre's slaves has been killed. His body was found only paces from the barracks, throat cut, limbs stiff, blood congealing.

"It must have happened last night," they say. "Siro's body was found at dawn by a road sweeper."

"Siro?" I ask, horrified.

They nod, wringing their hands.

I try to wake up. "Karbo, run to Marcus and send him to the warehouses. I'll meet him there. You're not to come."

"But I –"

"No," I say and my tone makes it clear there is no room for argument. "Go. Cassia, I'll see you later." I'd promised to have dinner with her and Fabia. It's hardly an auspicious start to what I had hoped would be a quiet day with friends.

I follow the slave through the streets down to the docks. I know most of our slaves by sight, but Siro I knew by name. A Syrian, hence his allocated slave name, he was a lopingly graceful man, with two missing front teeth and a quiet disposition. That changed when I discovered he was a good cook and assigned him to the slave kitchen in their barracks situated in a large warehouse by the docks. Slowly he came out of his shell, singing to himself first quietly and then loudly in his own language as he turned out vast pots of vegetable porridge, loaves of bread, stews with scraps of meat from the amphitheatre. His fellow slaves, discovering his talent for cooking, would shyly request food from their own countries, food they were homesick for and he would try to recreate it from their descriptions with the few ingredients at his disposal. He used to call out to me when I inspected the barracks, offering to feed me along with the cleaning crews and other teams of slaves assigned to the amphitheatre.

There's not much to see. His throat is cut. Someone who knew what they were doing. A violent and bloody end. I shake my head, tell two of the women to clean him up, send a runner for the undertakers. Marcus arrives shortly after me.

"Why would anyone want to kill Siro?" I ask. "He's a cook. He looked after everyone."

"Unlikely to be anyone in our own team," says Marcus. "Rome is dangerous at night. He shouldn't have been out so late. What was he doing wandering round Rome at that time, anyway?"

It takes a while before a slave admits that Siro had fallen for a slave woman belonging to a family of merchants who live close to the docks and had sneaked out late to meet with her. We try to follow up on the information but no-one knows the merchant's name, so we can't find trace of them.

"Robbers. Street thugs," says Marcus. "They must have thought he had money on him and when he said he didn't they probably thought he was lying."

"Not the owner of the woman?"

"Cut Siro's throat? Doubt it. If they didn't want him around they'd have given him a thrashing or sent word to us. I'll send word to the Aedile so they can update their records."

The slaves we manage belong to the emperor, so it's his administrators that have to be notified, not that they will know or care who Siro was. He had no family here in Rome, so his only mourners will be his fellow slaves.

I PROMOTE SIRO'S ASSISTANT TO our head cook and try to reassure the team as the undertakers take the body away. We're unlikely to find out any more information and meanwhile, a thousand slaves need feeding every day. I'm sad for Siro, but Rome's streets are treacherous at night. My own experience last year, when coming home alone at dusk threw me into Rullo's clutches has already taught me this lesson in no uncertain terms and Siro's fate has been a forcible reminder. I'm sorry for the unknown slave woman he has been courting and her confusion and sorrow when he no longer comes to see her, but there is no way of sending word to her.

AFTER THE UNSETTLING EVENTS OF the day, the familiarity of the insula and the surroundings of Cassia's warm popina are welcome. It's Cassia's night off, so the shutters are drawn close, but she invited Fabia and me to dinner and the popina has more room than her small apartment, so we agreed to gather there. Her father Cassius has already retired to his bed, so we will not disturb him with our chatter.

"It's your evening off and you're still cooking?" I say as I arrive.

Cassia grins. "Can't help it."

Fabia arrives with a gift of rich black grapes and adds it to my own offering of spiced apples baked into a rich pastry case. "You made that?" she asks, eyebrows raised.

"Less of the surprise," says Cassia. "I taught her well."

"Had to make it twice," I confess. "I burnt the first one in Maria's oven. Didn't stop Karbo from wolfing most of it and Marcus finished up the rest."

Cassia's eyes gleam. "And?"

"And?"

"Did you say something?"

I pretend not to know what she means. "About what?"

She huffs at Fabia. "Still hasn't told Marcus how she feels about him."

"It's impossible," I wail. "How do I even start a conversation like that?"

"Just tell him," says Cassia.

"Oh yes, that's excellent advice. Very detailed. Thank you. 'Marcus, you know how it's the anniversary of your wife and child dying? Well, how about you marry me? Because I've just realised I'm in love with you.' That sort of thing?"

"Yes," says Cassia, lifting out a tray of roasted pumpkin from the oven. "But without the reference to his dead wife. That will not set the right tone."

"Oh really? Hadn't realised that. Juno have pity on me."

"There's always that handsome man who turned up here asking for you."

"Handsome man?"

"Your new beast hunter."

"I'm not interested in him," I say.

"He couldn't stop looking at you."

"Never mind anyone else," I say. "I like – I love Marcus."

Fabia pours us all wine and adds water to the cups. "Maybe wait till the anniversary has passed," she says. "He will make an offering at the temple and pray for them, but it's been two years and perhaps the pain is no longer so sharp. You could..."

"Yes?"

"Spend some time with him?"

"I spend every day with him!"

"Not at work. Here. Invite him to dinner. Get Karbo out of the way. I'll have him at mine for the evening. Talk to Marcus about the future, about the family farm, see if he still thinks of going there one day. If he does, you can say how lovely you thought it was, how much you, too, would like to live in such a place. Plant the seed in his mind of going there with you."

"There you go," says Cassia approvingly. "There's a detailed plan for you. Venus herself couldn't do better. Now all you need to do is carry it out."

"I don't have the courage. My mouth goes dry when I think of saying… anything."

"Well, if you don't, someone else soon will. A handsome man like that doesn't stay a widower long. I'm surprised he's lasted two years. You better nab him quick, or you'll be coming weeping to me and Fabia when some woman who's not as shy as you steps up to the challenge."

"But what if he doesn't… if he doesn't like me in that way… it would be so awkward having to keep working together."

"Cross that bridge when you come to it."

"I suppose."

"No suppose about it. Get on with it."

"You're putting me off my food," I say. "It makes my stomach roll to think of him… of saying…"

"Ooh, she does have it bad." Fabia laughs. "You better start visiting Venus and Juno's temples and see if they can help your cause."

We settle round the table. Saltfish fritters and roast pumpkin are the main dishes, but Cassia has also laid out a collection of tiny bowls, filled with spiced chickpeas, little balls made of breadcrumbs flavoured with nuts and herbs, fried mushrooms and pickles. There is also fresh bread studded with olives, which is hard to stop eating.

"So good," says Fabia indistinctly through a mouthful, while I make noises of agreement, mouth too full to speak.

Cassia leans back against the wall behind her bench. "It's nice to sit down and eat," she says. "I'm usually eating with one hand and serving customers with the other."

There's a sound outside, beyond the courtyard's gate, a whimper which fades. We glance at each other, shrug. But it comes again.

"Baby," says Fabia.

There must be a woman and her baby somewhere in the street, passing by. Though it's getting dark. I hope they have someone to accompany them. A chill comes over me at the thought of Rullus last year, how he grabbed me in the darkness and how lucky I was to escape. Fabia sees me twitch and gently touches my arm.

"Anyway," says Fabia, "I meant to tell you. Father was saying that there will definitely be more physicians needed if the gladiator schools are to be extended and he knows a man who –"

The cry is louder this time, more indignant. There is a loud hammering on the popina's shutters.

Cassia frowns. "Who's there?" she calls out.

"Open up!" A man's voice.

Cassia stands on our side of the shutters, hesitant. "We're closed."

The hammering comes again. "Open up. Please!"

Fabia and I get to our feet.

"I said, who's there?" Cassia repeats.

"Quintus."

Cassia's frown deepens as she thinks. "From the fullery?" she asks at last.

"Yes. Let me in."

Cassia glances at us, but undoes the shutter and pulls it open. A young man takes a step forward, hesitating on the threshold. He's of average height, with black curls to rival Cassia's unruly mop and olive-toned skin that has been burnt dark brown by the long hot summer. I've seen him occasionally in the area; he's the local fuller's fifth son. Their fullery is a few streets down, easy to find by the stench of human urine used in the washing process and the rhythmic sound of soaking clothes being stamped on by slaves to rid them of dirt and stains. Right now he looks anxious.

"I was hoping someone would be here."

"What do you want?" asks Cassia.

The man gestures to the shadows outside. "Have you seen it? I wasn't sure what to do."

"Seen what?"

"The baby."

Cassia stares into the gathering darkness. "Baby?" She glances over her shoulder at us. "We heard something, we thought someone was passing."

Quintus shakes his head, his expression anxious. The cry comes again, louder now that the shutters have been opened.

Cassia peers out into the dark. "Where is it?"

Quintus gestures. "Just there. On the ground."

"Pick it up," says Fabia.

Quintus hesitates but our expectant faces convince him. He steps into the darkness and returns a moment later, gingerly carrying a large woven basket. He holds it out at arm's length to Cassia.

"Put it there," she says, stepping back from him and indicating the countertop from which she serves her customers food and wine.

He places the basket down gently enough but the movement upsets its occupant. The baby cries again and this time it does not stop. Cassia and Quintus hover, but Fabia, ever practical, drags a stool over to the countertop and climbs onto it, which brings her up to our height. She looks into the basket.

"Hello, little one."

The wailing increases in volume. Fabia puts her hands into the basket and lifts out the wriggling bundle, pulls away the cloth wrapping it and reveals a furious, red-faced baby, who screams louder than ever.

"What's the matter with it?" asks Cassia.

Fabia gives her a look. "It's cold, hungry and its mother's nowhere to be seen?" she suggests. "Get some milk," she instructs. "Help me down," she adds to me.

I assist Fabia down from the stool. Still holding the baby, she sits and pulls away more of its wrap, nods. "A girl." She refastens the wrap in place.

Cassia is standing staring.

"Milk?" says Fabia again.

Cassia brings some goat's milk and Fabia uses a spoon to get it into the baby's mouth. She's eager, mouthing into the air and whimpering when the spoon is withdrawn, sucking frantically when it is put back in her mouth.

"Where did she come from?" asks Cassia.

Quintus shrugs. "How would I know? I was heading home and heard her, thought it was a kitten at first but then I made her out, wriggling in that basket. I didn't know what to do."

Cassia's eyes narrow. "Is she yours?" she asks bluntly.

"What? No!"

Cassia keeps her eyes on him. "Might be she's your baby but you don't want a baby. Or a girl. So you got the mother to leave her here so you get off without marrying her or a mouth to feed?"

Quintus raises his hands. "I'd never do such a thing. Bona Dea! What are you accusing me of? If it wasn't for me noticing her as I passed she might have died out there tonight."

"Why's she outside my popina?" asks Cassia to the room.

"You're known for feeding beggars," I say. "Maybe her mother thought you'd look out for her."

"I can't keep a baby! What will Father say? What will people think? They'll think she's mine. As if I haven't been shamed enough with a marriage falling through on the very day of the wedding!"

We all watch in silence as Fabia continues spooning milk into the baby. "We'll need a proper baby bottle," she says, calm and unflustered as ever.

"Are you *keeping* her?" asks Cassia.

"Are you throwing her out?" asks Fabia.

We all stand silent while the two women glare at each other, neither breaking eye contact.

"Julia," says Cassia at last, dropping her gaze. "I'll fetch Julia. She'll know what to do."

Moments later, Julia arrives and proves as practical as Fabia. "For now, we'll make sure she's fed and clean. Tomorrow we can decide what to do. Cassia, can you have her in your apartment? Fabia and Fabius will be out all day from dawn, your work means you'll be here all day."

Cassia splutters but Julia's calm request sounds like a command. Reluctantly, she acquiesces.

We all follow her back to her apartment, where her father Cassius has to be woken. Julia explains the situation as though it is entirely normal to bring an abandoned baby back to one's home after an evening with friends.

"Only for tonight," says Cassia more than once.

It is Fabia, still practical, who finds an old tunic, rips it up to create a clean wrap for the baby girl, spoons more milk into her and lays her gently on Cassia's bed. Cassia lies down, keeping a wary distance.

"Wouldn't it be better if she were with you?" she asks me. "You already have a child, you know what to do with them."

"Karbo came to me already a boy," I say. "I know as little as you do about babies. And tomorrow I have to go to work."

Cassia looks downtrodden but doesn't answer, only edges slightly further away from the baby, leaving her most of the bed.

I climb the stairs to the roof hut, where Karbo is already lightly snoring. It takes me a long time to fall asleep. Where is the baby from, and what is to be done with her? It's common enough for a baby to be left on the streets and found by strangers, when for some reason its family cannot care for it, or perhaps the head of a family has refused to welcome it into the family on the ninth day of its life, when it would be laid at their feet to be accepted and named. Sometimes a family without children of their own adopt such a child; sometimes, unfound or unwanted, they simply perish. This one has found its way to our insula and into Cassia's bed. Whatever is to become of her?

DUST AND RUBBLE

I CAN HEAR THE BABY CRYING as soon as Karbo and I approach the popina for breakfast the next morning.

"I CAN'T KEEP FEEDING HER with a spoon! It takes ages and she just cries," says Cassia, flustered by the crying baby in her arms and the curious, waiting customers. Some look annoyed with the delay in being served, others are asking questions about who the baby is or giving their conflicting opinions on how to quiet her.

I turn to Karbo. "Karbo, run to Brocchus. Tell him I need that baby bottle with the gladiators on it. Tell him his stall can be by the meta sudans fountain when we reopen next season if he'll send it straight back with you, no questions asked."

"Run!" begs Cassia as Karbo disappears down the street.

"I'll hold her," I say.

Cassia hands over the squirming angry bundle.

"She's wet," I say, holding her away from my clean tunic.

"I can't change her now, I've got customers!"

I take the wailing baby to our courtyard fountain. The cold water turns her scarlet with shock and outrage, but the sound of her cries brings the baker's wife out to investigate and, when she's done exclaiming over the story of how we found her, she goes into her apartment and returns with some strips of cloth. "Mine are done with such things. Lucky I still had a few," she says.

She teaches me how to wrap the baby and I return to Cassia's where Karbo, panting, is holding the little green glass cup. Once filled with milk, the baby struggles for only a moment to understand what she must do, then sucks with desperate hunger, emptying the cup in moments, before making small grumbling noises which break out into a loud cry.

"*Now* what's wrong?" asks Cassia.

"I have to go to work," I tell her, passing the crying baby over the counter.

"Don't leave me with her!"

"How is she?" a voice asks from behind us.

We both turn to find Quintus standing outside the popina.

"Good, you're here," says Cassia. "Take her."

She hands the baby back over the counter and Quintus obediently moves forward and takes the little bundle. I expect him to drop her, but he looks surprisingly confident, holding her pressed against his shoulder. He pats her back a few times and she lets out a loud belch, then closes her eyes drowsily, letting her head rest on his chest.

"How did you do that?" asks Cassia.

Quintus grins with pride. "Got two younger siblings," he says. "You get the knack of these things."

"You're looking after her during the morning rush."

Quintus doesn't argue. "You might need to feed me breakfast, if I can't go home," he says.

Cassia pours half a cup of wine from the dregs of a jug and bangs down a plate with a piece of stale bread in front of him. "There you go."

"Thank you," he says politely.

"I'll leave you two to it," I say, grinning. "And someone needs to think of a name. We can't keep calling her 'she' and 'her'."

"Emilia," says Quintus.

"What?"

"I've named her Emilia. I thought about it last night."

"Are you keeping her?" asks Cassia.

"I'm not going to dump her back on the street," he says indignantly.

"Is she going to live with you?"

"I thought she could live here, but I'll help out."

"Oh you did, did you?" starts Cassia, outraged.

"I'm late," I say, grabbing Karbo by the tunic and pulling him with me. "See you later."

Karbo trails behind me. "What will happen to her?"

"I don't know."

"Can't you adopt her? You adopted me."

"And you're a handful," I say, smiling. "I couldn't even if I wanted to. That took special dispensation from Titus before he died. I don't see Domitian being so easy to get favours from. Women can't adopt children. It has to be a man."

"Will Quintus adopt her?"

"I don't know," I say. "Perhaps. But his family's big enough as it is, I'm not sure his parents would want to take in a foundling, with eight grandchildren of their own."

WHEN WE GET TO THE amphitheatre Marcus has a face like thunder. "He actually wants the hypogeum built before March. *Before* our new season starts."

"He? Domitian?"

"Yes."

Four months is not long to build a two-storey brick building, complete with lifts that fit within the structure, trapdoors and so on. "Can't it wait till next year?"

"Do you want to ask him that?"

"No thank you. So they'll build the hypogeum this year and build the gladiatorial schools next year?"

"No. All of us together."

"What?"

Marcus expands. "The amphitheatre first, to complete before the season opens in March, while they rip down the buildings to allow them to build the two largest gladiatorial schools by summer, the Matutinus because it's smaller first. The Magnus will probably take a bit longer as it's so big. But he's not holding back. Practically every builder in Rome has been hired for this and he's talking about bringing in building teams from further afield, or even drafting in soldiers for extra labour. He's not being patient about it."

It's a huge workload, but the imperial purse is deep and it looks like Domitian is a decisive person, not given to delays when he wants something. He's a great fan of the Games as well as chariot racing. No doubt the stables will also get some imperial attention soon enough.

"And what is the theme for next year's Games? Have you decided yet?"

Marcus shakes his head. "I was trying to spend some time planning before all this got thrown at us." He shrugs. "I'll think of something. Let me know if you had something in mind."

LATER I FIND FUNIS, BUSY inspecting the mechanism of the lifts and taking measurements so that he can work out how many differing animals each one can hold.

"Time for the baths," he says. "Want to come, Althea?"

Although I've happily bathed with most of our team on one occasion or another, something about the idea of bathing with Funis is too intimate. "I promised Cassia I'd give her some help with the baby," I say.

Funis smiles. "I heard. Not every day a baby is dropped on your doorstep. Would you like children of your own one day?"

Once again, he has steered the conversation towards me and my future and again, I find myself flustered by his interest, his attention. He has a knack for asking about the very things I long for but cannot see a way towards. "I have Karbo, the gods know he keeps me busy enough," I say with a laugh that sounds false, even to me.

"Sounds like you and your friend Cassia both have kind hearts," says Funis smiling, and turns back to his measurements, calling out the numbers to his assistant, a young slave boy.

I'M ROCKING A SLEEPY BABY Emilia for Cassia during the supper rush while Marcus sits at a table nearby. It should be a quiet evening in the insula's courtyard, but Karbo and his friends are engaged in a game that involves a lot of roaring from one boy in the middle of the group and much swordplay and elaborate death scenes from everyone else.

"Be quiet!" bellows Marcus after a while. "Trying to think!"

"They're playing at Theseus and the Minotaur," I say.

"They need packing off to bed," he grumbles. He has scraps of papyrus and a couple of empty scrolls in front of him, as well as a quill pen and ink waiting for ideas which, clearly, are not forthcoming. "All I've got so far is we need to showcase Carpophorus," he says. "He's been one of the finest bestiarii Rome's ever seen and now he's retiring, it's his final season and he'll be a huge draw to the crowd, everyone will want to say they saw him fight. But all he likes doing is stomping about killing animals. He's not all that for gladiatorial bouts, not his specialism." He crumples up another scrap of papyrus, dissatisfied.

"Karbo," I call. "Too much noise. Shall I tell you the story of the Minotaur instead?"

"NO," says Karbo, still dashing about an invisible labyrinth.

"It's that or bedtime," says Marcus firmly.

Reluctantly, the children gather at my feet.

"Long ago on the island of Crete," I begin, "the king died. As he was childless, his stepson Minos declared himself as the next ruler. He called upon the king of the seas, Poseidon, to send him a bull from the sea, which would prove his claim to the throne was looked upon with favour by the gods. If such a bull were sent, he declared, he would sacrifice it to Poseidon, to honour and thank him for his favour.

And a bull did come from the sea. It was huge and white and perfect and at this sign of favour from the gods, Minos was acknowledged and crowned King of Crete. But he did not stand true to his word. Instead he sacrificed a lesser bull and Poseidon, angered at this slight, made Minos' wife, Queen Pasiphae, fall in love with the white bull, feel lust as she might for a man. So besotted was she that she went to the palace inventor Daedalus and asked him to make for her a wooden cow, in which she could conceal herself and thus mate with the bull."

I grimace. Marcus grimaces back at me.

"Go on!" says Karbo.

"Months passed by and Pasiphae bore a terrible creature, which had the body of a man with the head of a bull, and which she named Asterius. Ashamed, King Minos ordered Daedalus to design a labyrinth in which to conceal the beast forever and there it grew up into a vicious monster, the Minotaur. It had a taste for human flesh. Afraid of not fulfilling its dark desires, King Minos ordered that Athens, his vassal state, should send each year fourteen youths, seven men and seven women, to be thrown into the labyrinth and torn to pieces by the Minotaur. Three Twice the terrible orders were given and twice a ship with funereal black sails set sail from Athens to Crete, carrying with it the sacrificial victims who perished at the hands of the grisly monster.

"But Athens had a hero warrior as its prince. Theseus, son of King Aegeus of Athens, had already proven himself time and again against many terrible dangers and had even gone with other heroes on their adventures, such as Jason in his quest for the Golden Fleece, and Hercules to conquer the Queen of the Amazons and had always been victorious. He told his father that the next time the sacrifice was to be made, he would join the youths and maidens selected. He would enter the labyrinth, slay the dreaded Minotaur, and –"

"That's it!" says Marcus.

"What?" I ask, startled.

"We'll take the story of Theseus and the Minotaur as our theme for the Games next year. We'll work our way through the whole story at key events during the season. We can have demonstrations of bull-leaping for the Minoans and some of Theseus' first heroic deeds, like fighting alongside Hercules against the Queen of the Amazons. Then we can have the Minotaur killing the sacrificial victims and finally the moment when Theseus kills the Minotaur. Perfect."

I nod. It will give us a strong theme for the season, which will help us develop more spectacular events in all the Games we put on. It will allow us to draw on legendary feats and stories with which the audience is already familiar and which will lend themselves well to the gladiatorial battles and animal hunts we need to provide. Having a story running throughout the season makes people want to come back over and over again, keeping the amphitheatre full and the Emperor happy.

"Good choice," I say, and Marcus grins back, his previous grumpiness erased.

"I'll make some notes about the different elements," he says, pulling a scroll, quill and ink towards him with more enthusiasm.

"Only," I add, "the bit with Pasiphae and the bull… it really has been done in the arena before, but…"

"We'll fake it," he says.

"Go ON!" says Karbo, bored with our sudden enthusiasm for planning the Games when he and his friends want to hear the rest of the story.

"Yes! Go on!" cry the others, tugging at my tunic. Emilia startles, hiccups and then, as I hush the other children, she grows softer in my arms, slowly falling asleep.

I try to remember where I was and speak more gently so as not to wake her. "Umm, so… so, Theseus' father, King Aegeus of Athens, afraid for his son's safety, begged him not to go. But Theseus was adamant and when the time came he took his place aboard the tribute ship with black sails, together with seven maidens and six other Athenian youths. As they set sail, he promised his father that he would return in a ship with white sails, to signify his victory over the beast. And so they reached Crete. There were many rituals to be undertaken before the sacrifice was made and in the days that followed, Princess Ariadne, daughter of King Minos, fell in love with Theseus. She went to him in secret one night and told him that she would help him defeat the Minotaur if, in return, he would take her with him back to Athens as his wife, and this Theseus agreed to do."

I imagine myself as Ariadne, whispering with a Theseus-Marcus, our heads close together. Perhaps they sealed their bargain with a kiss, although I'm well aware their romance does not end well…

"AND?" demands Karbo.

"And," I say hastily, "Ariadne, being very clever, gave to Theseus a ball of red thread she had spun with her own hands and told him to tie one end to the entrance of the Labyrinth, so that he would not get lost inside its maze of corridors. The next morning, the fourteen Athenians were taken with much ceremony to the opening of the Labyrinth, and sealed up inside it. The others were terrified, of course, fearing that at any moment, around one corner or another of the impossible maze, they would be found and eaten alive by the monster that dwelt within. But Theseus used the ball of red thread given to him by Ariadne, tied it to the entrance and made his way to the centre of the Labyrinth, where he found the Minotaur. In the desperate battle that followed, Theseus was at last victorious and returned safely to the door to the outside world, where his fellow countrymen and women stood huddled together, waiting for him to return a hero or for the beast to find and kill them. When they emerged in triumph, Ariadne joined Theseus and the whole company set sail for Athens. But alas, Theseus did not honour his promise. Instead he abandoned Princess Ariadne on the island of Naxos, where she married the god Dionysus. But Theseus was punished for this deed, when, in his haste to return home, he forgot to…?" I pause, to let the children complete the story.

"Change the black sails for white!" they yell back at me.

"Indeed. And so his father, seeing the ship returning with black sails, and despairing at the thought of his own son being dead, jumped into the sea and drowned. And so Theseus lost his own father, even as he returned victorious."

"Couldn't be better," Marcus mutters to himself, still scribbling. "Battles with Amazonian women and centaurs, Golden Fleece adventure, culminating on the last night of the Games with the Minotaur. Carpophorus can be Theseus. Perfect end to his public career." He looks up, beaming at me. "Well done, Althea. It's a perfect theme. We can work so much around it. Tomorrow we'll start proper planning."

BUT AS THE DAYS GROW cooler and the anniversary of Pompeii's destruction approaches, Marcus grows noticeably more irritable, disappearing for long stretches of time, muttering every time he sees anything to do with the new plans, even snapping at head of the under-arena area, Strabo, who lets it wash over him, unbothered.

"I'm sorry he got cross," I say, when Marcus has stamped away over some minor misunderstanding about where the props will be stored overwinter, since the whole of the under-arena space now has to be fully cleared for the builders to move in.

"He didn't mean it," Strabo says, lumbering over to a group of slaves and indicating which items are to be taken to the warehouse at the docks we have secured. "Hard time coming up. He'll be better afterwards."

I nod, glad of Strabo's calm understanding.

Funis watches the exchange. "I was going to ask Marcus about some of these animals I need to source," he says. "But perhaps it would be better if I spoke with you, for now?"

"Yes," I say. "What did you need?"

"The overall theme is Theseus and the Minotaur. What other elements are you including?"

"We've had a fantastic helmet with horns made for the Minotaur and we'll do a few shows of the beast's conception, birth, early years, the festivals and culture of Crete, the maze itself of course and the Minotaur killing anyone who enters. Theseus will go on some adventures: with Jason for the Golden Fleece, with Hercules to battle the Queen of the Amazons. There's a hint of romance with the Queen and also with Princess Ariadne because Carpophorous is a bit of a favourite with the ladies in the audience."

"So I've heard. Is he a favourite of yours, too?"

"He's a great bestiarius, but not really my idea of a handsome man."

"And what is your idea of a handsome man?"

"So," I say firmly, refusing to answer and feeling my cheeks grow hot, "the grand finale will be Theseus against the Minotaur. That's when he will kill the monster. Last day of the Games for the season."

Funis looks amused at my refusal to answer, but takes the hint to keep the conversation focused on business matters. "I've met Carpophorus. He's an impressive bestiarius. He'll be bored when he retires. He may be getting too old to fight but he says he would consider being a beast hunter. I might need a man like him, perhaps we can work together. How many times will you run each element of the story?"

"Hard to tell. Once for each of them at least, but if something is really successful, it'll get run several times. The Golden Fleece quest and the battle with the Amazons will be popular."

"And the bull-leaping of Crete."

"Yes. Not many people will have seen that, but I've heard it's spectacular."

Funis nods. "It is. It requires extraordinary skill not to get hurt. I better start training bulls and round up a larger team of bull-leapers."

"I've never seen bull leaping," I say.

"It's what it sounds like. Men and women, although the crowd usually prefers women. In the arena with bulls. A bull comes running at you, you leap towards it, grab its horns, vault over the back of it and land unharmed. Acrobatic."

"Sounds dangerous."

"It is. One moment you're safe, the next you could be dead. The crowd loves it."

QUINTUS IS ALWAYS CARVING WHEN I see him, finding small bits of scrap wood and turning them into toys. He gives tiny wooden horses, cats, pigs and sheep to the children of our insula and a horned bull to Karbo when he hears about our theme for this year. He is ready with a smile for everyone he sees and will lend a hand with whatever anyone is doing. He has quickly come to feel like part of our community and it's strange when he speaks of "home" and means somewhere else.

"Does your father mind that you spend so much time here?" I ask.

"There's enough people to run the fullery, that's mostly what he worries about, so I can slip away if it's quiet," says Quintus. "My mother frets more. She wants me married off and giving her more grandchildren, though you'd think with eight already born that would keep her busy."

"What does she make of Emilia?"

"Thinks I'm mad, picking up some unwanted baby off the street." He looks down at the gurgling baby, who is currently examining her toes with great interest. "But we could hardly put her back there, could we?"

I shake my head. "But she'll have to be adopted one day," I say.

"I'll find a way."

"Good lad," says Maria from above us. As usual, she's been listening to anything that goes on. Ever since I've lived in this insula, Maria has been at her self-allotted post every day, sat on the walkway just outside her own room, vast bosom resting on a cushion to make the balustrade more comfortable. From there she can watch everything that goes on in our courtyard and the inhabitants' lives, commenting as she sees fit.

I twist to look up at her. "But who is she supposed to belong to as she grows up?" I ask. "No-one's formally adopted her."

"All in good time," says Maria. "And you're doing a fine job, young man."

Quintus picks up Emilia. "Looks like I have more work to do," he says. "This one is wet."

He leaves the courtyard to change her and Maria smiles at me. "Don't fret. Althea," she says. "Bona Dea looks out for babies. She has a plan."

"Does she?"

"Oh yes," says Maria with satisfaction. She winks and adjusts her bosom on the cushion. "You'll see. Let fortune run its course."

THE TWENTY-FOURTH OF OCTOBER COMES and I wake very early, uneasy memories of the past dragging me from sleep even though it is not yet dawn. The day when, two years ago, the sky darkened across Rome and grey ash fell all around us in the amphitheatre, silent and soft. Delicate and, as we came to find out, deadly. I lie awake for a while, then slip out of my bed and walk out onto the roof terrace, my feet cold. Marcus is already there. He is standing close to my roof hut, looking out across still-dark Rome to the south, where, far away, a lost city he once called home is buried under a smothering blanket of ash and lava and where, somewhere within that dark embrace, lie the bodies of his wife and baby son.

I want to creep back to bed, want to avoid the awkwardness of grief, but this only made me feel worse last year, when Marcus avoided me all day, even though only we two shared the horror of the aftermath, when we returned to Pompeii and he dug through the ash in desperation while I prayed to every god I could think of and none of them heard my call, trapped as we were in the realm of Hades. Seeing him turn last year to Julia instead shamed me. I take a deep breath and make my way to him, stand by his side. My sorrow at what happened is made harder because he is mourning his lost love and, if I could have my own desire, it would be to take her place as his wife. But now is not the time for those feelings. Above all else, Marcus and I have been friends. We have stood by one another through horrors such as others can only imagine. I think of the short hours when I knew his family, try to recall what I saw of them, how they looked, how they behaved.

"He looked so like you," I say. "But with her hair."

He nods, does not turn to face me. But his right arm wraps around my shoulders, he lets it rest heavy on me, sharing his burden.

"You must see them always in your dreams," I say, my voice shaky.

He is quiet. I have overstepped our moment of confiding, I have said something foolish, starkly set against the grim reality of their fate and his loss. I try to think what I can say to take back such nonsense, am about to open my mouth, but he speaks.

"Their faces are fading," he says, voice low and hoarse, and his shoulders heave. "I cannot see them clearly anymore when I try."

He sweeps me into his arms. His head lies heavy on my shoulder as he sobs and sobs, his tears rolling down my skin. It takes all my strength to stand upright against him. My arms meet tentatively around his broad back and tighten to hold him as he weeps. My tears fall, not for the darkness that crushed Pompeii but for the guilt crippling Marcus because he can no longer recall the exact outlines of his wife and son's face. This man who would know the scent of them, the touch of them, their voices, in an instant, is broken by the loss of their faces, fading from his memory despite his enduring love for them. He has no portraits of them, only the tiny dolls made of wood and wool that stand on his household shrine, made with kindness by Balbus the toymaker, a skilled man who never saw the woman and child whose likenesses he tried to craft.

Marcus pulls back, though I would have held him forever, wipes his eyes and nose, looks down at my wet face. He brushes away the tears on my cheeks.

"I'm sorry," he says, clearing his throat when his voice croaks. "It is not your grief to bear. Though you have helped me bear it all this time."

I want to say something important in return, but I do not know what.

He takes a shuddering breath in and blows it out in a rush. "Did you make Myrtis' spiced honey cakes to remember her by?" he asks.

"Not yet."

"We should," he says. "Wake Karbo and we'll go to Cassia, beg her for some kitchen space this morning. I'll mix, if you'll tell me what the ingredients are."

"And work?"

"Never mind work today," he says. "This is more important. Wake Karbo."

When I've woken Karbo Marcus takes his hand and leads the way to Cassia's. She is waiting for us, a basin and little bowls already laid out, filled with ingredients.

"You remembered," I say.

"How could I forget?"

"Emilia?"

"Still asleep," she says, laying a finger to her lips. "Try and be quiet. That girl can cry to wake the gods."

And so we spend the hour before dawn and the arrival of customers in the dimly-lit popina, mixing up Myrtis' spiced honey cakes, with the addition of pepper which made hers different from every other cook's. I tell Karbo and Marcus how I used to sit with her in the kitchen in Pompeii when we were both slaves together in a rich merchant's household, how we'd eat cakes and chatter together before the rest of the day's work faced us. We eat the warm cakes straight from the oven and share them with the first customers and passers-by, before taking some to the little shrine at the end of the road in gratitude for having been spared, in sorrow for those who were lost.

"I'll be out most of the day, but I'll make a sacrifice at the Temple of Jupiter later," says Marcus. His eyes are still red-rimmed but he manages a smile of sorts, gives me a crushing one-armed embrace around the shoulders before striding away, leaving me alone, my fingers still sticky-sweet from the cakes, wishing I could run after him and slip my hand into his, follow him everywhere.

"I'll keep an eye on him," says Fabius when I pass him in the courtyard. "He said we'd meet at the baths later."

"Thank you," I say. "It's a hard day for him." I'm grateful to Fabius and his long friendship with Marcus, his calm knowing that today his friend will need him, to sit in silence or talk of the past, to laugh or perhaps even to cry.

Later I will find Marcus again and sit with him on the roof, in the dusk, let him talk about Livia and Amantius, as I am the only one left who knew them when they were alive. And perhaps that shared bond we have will strengthen further, will lead to something more, to...

But it goes as it always does. Fabius and Marcus go to the baths and to dinner. They come home late and another moment that I have half-planned slips away and I am left to dream again, dreams that fade away before I can make them real.

ROME IS AGOG WHEN THE news is finally released about Domitian's ambitious building programme, not least because of the speed at which he is putting it into action. There's uproar in the neighbourhood surrounding the amphitheatre when the plans are displayed in public. More than ten large buildings will be pulled down to make way for the first two gladiator schools, as well as the odd smaller building, a roadside shrine that will have to be moved, a few decrepit shops, tatty enough but whose owners and proprietors have enjoyed the benefits of heavy footfall and passing trade that comes with being situated so close to the Forum and the Flavian Amphitheatre. Shopkeepers and landlords alike are outraged at the idea. The landlords are soon silenced when the imperial purse turns out to be more generous than expected, but the people living or working in the buildings are resentful at the sudden change. No-one dares to challenge Domitian, of course, at least not in public.

"What in Hades is this?" Marcus roars when we arrive in a cold dawn light a few weeks after the announcement.

The pristine white stone of the amphitheatre around the Emperor's entrance has been daubed in mud… or possibly something worse, as there are also several cartloads of manure dumped in front of it, blocking the way in.

"Looks like the locals aren't happy," I say. "Karbo, get down to the docks. I'm going to need a bigger cleaning team this morning. I need thirty extra slaves, with brooms and shovels. Tell them to bring the mules and the cart. Run."

He darts away while Marcus and I survey the mess, the anger of those whose buildings will be knocked down having spilled out against the towering symbol of the Games rather than their imperial patron.

"They must have worked through the night," mutters Marcus. "Good thing we were here early."

When the Games aren't on we don't come here every day, and often arrive late in the morning, rather than our usual dawn arrivals when the season is in full operation. But today we had arranged to meet our aquarius to shut off most of the water supplies for the building overwinter, leaving only the ground floor water system working. The work planned for the day included wrapping some of the spouts and pipes in cork and wool lagging to avoid any freezing during the coldest parts of the winter. But this silent, stinking protest is unacceptable; placed right in full view of the Forum, it must be made to disappear immediately and preferably before word gets back to Domitian. Should word get back to anyone, there should be no trace of what happened by the time he or anyone important comes to check on the amphitheatre.

The team of our slaves gathered by Karbo arrives and within an hour, as the late autumn sun slowly rises and the Forum begins to grow busy, the worst is gone; there only remains the daubing on the walls. We use the water fountains inside to fill buckets, which half the team pour down the sides from the first floor, while below the other half of our crew use brooms tied onto poles to reach the offending splatters and scrub the wall back to its pristine white, a task which thankfully soon looks as though we are simply carrying out normal cleaning routines, rather than an emergency correction. Marcus has stomped off somewhere muttering about night-time guards being required from now on, while I oversee that the work is done to a high standard. The Emperor's personal entrance cannot be anything but perfect. The odd person passing glances up at our work, but I'm glad that no gawping crowds have gathered, as they would surely have done had we arrived later in the morning. The aquarius and his team arrive but I tell them they will have to start the lagging on the upper floor while we maintain the water supply down below until the job is finished. They look bemused but make their way up to the third floor.

"Handled with aplomb, as expected."

I startle. Stephanus is standing just behind me. Does the man have Mercury's wings on his feet, to always creep up so quietly?

"Word came to you already?" I say by way of greeting. There's no point pretending he doesn't know what happened, I'd lay a large sum of money he knows every detail already. I can only hope he can see that we have worked very hard to keep the matter as little gossiped about as possible.

"I find it is better to let the populace express themselves in unimportant but symbolic ways and feel that they have had their say, won a small victory, than let resentment build too high, don't you think? Especially when one is confident that any such 'expression' will be taken care of discreetly."

I blink in confusion. Is he really suggesting that he allowed this protest to happen, maybe even encouraged it? Or perhaps actually arranged for it to happen? Surely not. "Did you –" I begin, but I don't even know how to complete the sentence.

He looks amused. "The common people will feel they have had their say. The more exalted will barely know it happened. The Emperor is still asleep. Your team are very reliable. I commend you for your excellent management of the situation."

"We might not even have been here," I protest, still appalled by what he's suggesting. "It's not Games season, we're not here at dawn every day."

"Your aquarius was keen on an early start," he says.

"How did you even know he was due –"

"It's been a pleasure speaking with you," he cuts me off. "Until another time."

I open my mouth to say something else, to ask another question, but he has already turned away, striding past the giant golden Colossus Sol statue glinting in the early rays of the sun, making his way back through the Forum, no doubt returning to Domitian's service before he even awakes.

"I'll have to have a guard on here every night from now on," calls Marcus, appearing through the now-immaculate imperial entrance. "What a waste of a morning this was. Anyway the aquarius is here now and the cork lagging is ready for the lower pipes. We've wasted enough time today. Keep the extra cleaning crew, they can help us catch up. We need this job done before we get a hard frost. Come on."

I stand thinking for a moment. Did Stephanus actually arrange the "protest" himself, to make the locals feel that they'd had their say... without having protested at all? Did he set everything up, even our arrival here early this morning so that everything would be taken care of, allowing just enough protest to be effective? Here and gone again, to be whispered about with satisfaction by those who are angry without causing real offence? I shake my head. It's too early and too much has already gone on this

morning. But Stephanus is a wily one, that I am increasingly sure of. "Coming," I call
back to Marcus.

If I thought last year's demolition and rebuilding work in the insula and around
us in the Ninth Region was noisy, dusty and impossible to escape, it's nothing compared
to what is happening now. It's extraordinary what an emperor can command. Whole
buildings tower above us one day and come crashing to the ground the next, curses
and bricks flying though the dust-filled air as vast teams of builders, recruited not
just from the whole of Rome but all the surrounding areas, descend on the shops,
apartments and other edifices that Domitian has indicated must make way for his
first two gladiatorial schools. I watch from the upper levels of the amphitheatre as the
buildings are swiftly demolished, echoing the tiny pottery counterparts that Domitian
smashed on the marble floor of his palace. The air is barely breathable, I have to hold
my hairwrap in front of my mouth and Karbo refuses to accompany me after the first
few days. But it is mesmerising work, one moment a building whole and complete,
within a few hours standing without its roof, its walls rapidly shrinking downwards,
pulled by unseen hands (or rather, more accurately, by the giant sledgehammers the
builders wield without mercy) until it reaches the ground and meanwhile endless
carts take away the ensuing rubble. Some will be reused, such as the roof tiles, which
will top the gladiatorial schools. Others, such as the broken-up bricks still clinging
stubbornly to the concrete, will be broken up still further for use in the construction of
roads, or ground down to make a waterproof plaster to help repair the many fountains,
aqueducts and baths in the city. The endless noise grows wearying to all, people trying
to hold conversations in the Forum scowling and leaning closer to one another to hear
better, before rapidly deserting the area, if they are able to go elsewhere.

"It's ruining trade," says Secundus. "Customers don't buy trinkets if all they can
hear is hammering and their clothes are gathering dust. Especially the richer women,
they worry about dust in their hair… or hairpieces, I should say."

"They'll start the building work soon, I hope," I say.

"Hardly going to be quieter, is it?"

"A bit, perhaps?" I say hopefully.

"Now you'll like this story, Althea," Secundus says, grinning. "Sold a lady one
of my peckers last year, finest quality bronze. Week later, she comes back and says
she's lost it, wants to buy another. I say, Domina, I assure you, it'll still be working its
wonders on you, even if you've lost it. No, no, she says, I must have another, I want
to conceive a child, a son. Well, I'm not going to refuse the sale, am I? So I sell her
another. Don't see her for almost a year. Yesterday she comes to find me in person.
Secundus, she says, I've borne twin sons, my husband is delighted with me!"

I laugh. "You're going to be telling that story all over Rome now, aren't you?"

"Of course. I've already sold ten peckers off the back of that, three of them to the same lady for her sisters and cousins. Might you be in the market for a lucky pecker or even two, should you be wanting twins?"

"Need a husband first," I say.

"Got one in mind?"

I shake my head.

"Ah, now, you're blushing, Althea, I can always tell when a woman has her eye on a man. My lucky pecker will get him to look your way, you know?"

I push him lightly away on the shoulder. "You're incorrigible, Secundus."

KARBO'S TINY KITTEN LETITIA ARRIVES in our lives. The amphitheatre's cat, Domina, is growing weary of her new brood, who have grown large and now pounce on her out of the shadows to chew her tail and ears, learning to hunt and fight using her as their training ground. She swipes at them from time to time or hisses, brings them dead lizards and half alive mice to encourage their killing instincts and show them the way towards independence. Karbo swoops in to choose his favourite kitten and take her away to a new life in our insula, hurrying her through the ever-busy courtyard and up the wooden staircase to our rooftop world. He makes a space for her on his bed and watches over her like a mother as she explores her new surroundings, first our hut and then further afield. Named for the goddess of gaiety, she lives up to her name, bounding around the rooftop and playing with anything that moves, from her own tail, which has Karbo in fits of giggles, to the discarded feathers of doves or even a wisp of straw carried to us on the wind. At night, she sleeps on Karbo's bed with him, as close to his face as she can, while he curls a sleeping arm around her, protective even in his sleep. She chases pigeons and shadows, sleepy lizards and even ants, when she finds a column of them busy about their own affairs.

"You'll have to hold her or this will never get done," I tell Karbo. I'm trying to sweep the rooftop clean, but Letitia is certain that this is a game invented for her alone, and so follows me around, pouncing on the broom, tumbling over when she tries to ride on it.

Karbo clutches Letitia to himself, cooing over her, while I briskly finish sweeping the rooftop which is heavy with leaves that have twirled across the rooftops of Rome throughout the autumn and found their resting place here. "There, that should be the last of them, the trees are all bare now," I say.

WE MAINLY STAY AWAY AS the building works proper begin. Carpenters swarm across the arena and rip out most of the wooden flooring, leaving a gaping hole in the centre of the space. They're followed by the builders, whose work demands that carts full of bricks arrive daily.

On a rare visit to the amphitheatre I stand with Marcus in the imperial box, looking down into the vast dark hole from where red brick dust and curses rise, together with endless scraping sounds as mortar is laid and the first floor of the hypogeum begins to take shape, the maze-like pattern from Rabirius' meticulous scrolls turning into reality, our simple open space now shaped into something different.

"Don't like it," Marcus mutters. "It's going to cause trouble."

"How?"

He shrugs. "I don't know,' he admits unwillingly. "I just feel it."

"We're going to number all the lifts and all the rooms and cages," I try to reassure him. "We've worked out a system of signals as well, both with the whistles and with bells which can be rung on a different floor if there's a really big problem."

"I know."

"What else can we do?"

"Nothing."

"It'll be alright," I try again. I touch his hand lightly, wanting to clasp it but not daring. "We'll get used to it." I watch his face, brown eyes moving and forehead furrowing as he looks around the whole amphitheatre, then back at the dark hole that will become the hypogeum. For a moment my heart beats faster when I realise he has not moved his hand from under mine. Perhaps he will clasp my hand in his now, perhaps he will say he is tired of this life and…

"Getting used to things isn't the same as them being right," says Marcus and he turns to leave, his warm hand gone from under my fingers, leaving them cold.

We barely see Funis during November. Occasionally a messenger boy will run to me with a note checking something: the space available, whether the bulls can be penned in somewhere within the amphitheatre or will have to wait outside, what animals we're likely to need in the first week of the season when we open. Evidently he is busy, but he does not respond to invitations to join Marcus and me at the insula for a more relaxed meal or at the amphitheatre to see how the hypogeum is shaping up. I wonder sometimes, with an odd flutter in my stomach, whether he would come if I alone invited him, but that is not a path I want to venture down, when I have eyes only for Marcus. It would feel like teasing and I do not want to do that.

We are all growing used to both Emilia and Quintus becoming part of the insula's community. At first Quintus comes by only in the mornings, to feed and rock Emilia while Cassia serves customers, then he returns to his own home, where he works alongside his brothers and sisters in his father's fullery, managing the business of keeping the clothes of the Ninth Region's citizens clean. Sometimes he will return in the evening, to pace our courtyard with Emilia in his arms until she falls asleep. But, as time goes by, he returns more often in the evening and even sometimes, when he can get away, in the afternoons when she is often restless, carving a small wooden horse and singing old songs to her. Cassia mostly ignores him, but I catch her glancing his way once or twice, when he is rocking Emilia or speaking softly to her.

"He's kind," I say quietly, watching him one evening.

"And what am I?" bristles Cassia, chopping vegetables for the next day's savoury porridge. "Taking in a baby I know nothing about, and not even married?"

I laugh. "I already know you're kind-hearted," I say. "Everyone knows it round here. It's probably why Emilia was left outside your popina." I lower my voice so Quintus can't hear us as he pauses by the steps where Julia bids him goodnight. "But Quintus could have told us about her and not looked back."

Cassia shrugs, but her eyes rest a moment longer on Quintus when he lays Emilia down at her feet in the wooden cradle the baker's family donated when it was decided Emilia would be staying. He straightens up slowly as the baby snuffles and turns, her eyelids fluttering at the change of position. He keeps one hand on her belly until the last moment, a comforting touch, and after a moment, she subsides and moves deeper into sleep.

"Long day?" I ask.

He nods, brushing back his dark curls and straightening out his back. "Fullery's hard work," he says. "I'd rather have my own trade but it's not easy to move away from the family business."

"What would you like to do?" I ask curiously.

"Make toys like Balbus does," he says without hesitation. "I asked to be apprenticed to him when I was younger but my father said he needed all his children in the business. Of course now several of my siblings are married and even have half-grown children, so there are plenty of us. He could easily do without me, but I'm too old for an apprenticeship, so I'm stuck in the fullery." He gives a warm smile with a hint of sadness to it.

"I'm sorry," I say.

"Ah, it was only a dream," he says. "And now I have a better doll than any that could be carved from wood or made on the potter's wheel." He gestures down at the sleeping Emilia. "I must go. My mother will not be pleased if I'm not there for the evening meal."

"I'll have your breakfast waiting," says Cassia without looking at him.

"I'll be here," he says. "Goodnight, Cassia. Goodnight, Althea."

"Goodnight, Quintus," I say.

"'Night," says Cassia, chopping another carrot at ferocious speed.

"He likes you," I say, when he has disappeared through the gateway to the darkening street outside. "He's been here every day since Emilia was found."

"Nonsense," says Cassia, but her knife slips and she cuts her thumb.

"I won't say anything else," I tease. "Wouldn't want you to be bleeding over him."

"Get to bed," says Cassia, chopping faster than ever. "And stop with your nonsense. Man doesn't even have a trade. That fullery will go to his eldest brother when his father dies. It would cost a lot to set up one of his own and he doesn't even like the business."

"Oh, so you have thought about the practicalities?"

"Don't know what you're talking about," says Cassia, bringing the knife down too hard. A carrot slips and rolls away.

"Just promise me you'll still have all ten of your fingers when I see you tomorrow," I say, giggling. I bend to stroke Emilia's tiny head, covered in silken black hair and start up the staircase. "Goodnight, Cassia."

"Umph," is all the response I get.

THE BULL-LEAPERS

SATURNALIA ROLLS AROUND AGAIN AND we decorate the courtyard and our rooms with branches of greenery and dangling ribbons in bright colours. I buy all of Adah's stock of beeswax candles, wrap little scrolls around pairs of them with jokes and riddles I have spent a few evenings writing out in my best hand. I wrap each one with red leather strips and Karbo and two of his playmates deliver them to our friends, suppliers and acquaintances all over Rome. They spend the rest of their time begging for festive cakes and biscuits from Cassia or wistfully mentioning certain gifts they might like to be given, should I be feeling generous.

Marcus gives Karbo a finely tooled belt, which he swaggers around with, and I give him a blue cloak in honour of the Blues racing team. His old cloak is too short for him, he's grown so much this past year. I spent some time cutting and resewing the good woollen fabric, adding an embroidered sun to the centre, turning it into a cosy blanket to lay over Emilia's cradle, a shining reminder of the warm summer days to come after the dark of winter. She clutches at it, having only recently discovered her own hands and what they are capable of, pulls it right up to her face, mouths at it with interest.

"You funny girl," I say to her. "It's been a strange entry to the world for you, hasn't it? But the gods smiled on you when they saved you from the streets."

Quintus brings her a life-size wooden mouse he has carved, nibbling on an acorn, which she in turn chews on with enthusiasm. It fits neatly in her small hands.

"You're very skilled," I tell him and he ducks his head at the compliment.

"She deserves good things," he says, mimicking her earnest expression.

Later I notice a wooden brooch Cassia has taken to wearing, a flower with twining tendrils and leaves. "Where did that come from?"

"Quintus," she says, face turned away.

"He's a wonderful craftsman," I say.

"He's alright, I suppose," she says.

I grin at Fabia, who winks at me.

"Did you give him a gift for Saturnalia?" she asks Cassia.

Cassia shrugs. "Just a basket of biscuits for his family," she says. "Nothing special. Sent out lots of them to acquaintances, thought he might as well have one too."

We nod, lips pursed together so as not to laugh.

"What?" she demands, looking at our pinched mouths and shaking shoulders.

"Nothing," we chorus.

"Better be nothing," she warns. "You're in my way, be off with the pair of you."

"How are we in your way when we're on the other side of the counter?" asks Fabia.

"You're being noisy," amends Cassia.

"Barely said a word," says Fabia.

I'm half asleep on the first day of the festive season. The cold mornings are not conducive to early rising or quick wits, but even I notice that when Quintus arrives and Cassia feeds him breakfast, it's no longer stale bread, but rather a freshly baked fruit bun from the bakery and, this morning, a hot spiced wine to warm him. I raise my own cup to him in festive salutation.

"Io, Saturnalia!"

"Io, Saturnalia!" he replies cheerfully, bouncing Emilia on his knee and tearing off a chunk of his bun to give her. She gums it with interest, dropping most of it on the ground and beaming at him as she rubs some of the mush into his tunic.

"She will need to be adopted one day," I say.

"I intend to, but I need my father's permission and he wants me to marry first. My mother says a new bride won't want some foundling given to her to bring up."

I glance at Cassia, who is pouring wine and apparently listening to some endless anecdote by one of her customers. "And do you have a wife in mind, Quintus?"

"Oh, I don't know," he says. "These things are tricky, aren't they? Finding the right wife? How does one know you're suited? How do you know whether you just like a girl for her good looks and then it will turn out she's ill-tempered or… or something?"

But his neck has flushed and he is very carefully looking anywhere but at Cassia.

I give him an encouraging smile. "A good start is probably someone you already know, someone you see every day and work happily with on… something." I stroke Emilia's hair. She reaches out for my hand and chews on my knuckles, dribbling enthusiastically.

Quintus risks a quick glance at Cassia. "I'd want to set up by myself," he says. "There are enough of my siblings and their families working at the fullery. I'd like my own work, my own place. But I'll have to find a trade of my own and I've always worked in my father's business, I'm not sure what else I'd be good at."

Fabia, Cassia and I go shopping together on one of Cassia's rare days off and exchange gifts of embroidery threads, shells and beads, so that we can all sit together and update our tunics and headwraps with new decorations.

We receive gifts from friends and from our own team, including candles and gaming dice as well as foodstuffs; beautiful red pomegranates and little honey cakes, small sacks of lentils and jars of olives. Our suppliers send more lavish items, especially to Marcus, keen to impress and maintain our lucrative Games business over the next season. We are sent glass cups decorated with gladiators from Paternus and perfume in little glass vials from Labeo. Gilded dates still on the stem, Syrian figs, the best garum sauce and smoked cheese, as well as truffles and honeyed mulsum wine, arrive in large quantities. More toiletries than we can think what to do with, from elegant strigils and tiny ear scoops to soaps and oils. Marcus keeps the odd item, such as a drinking flask and a new strigil, but mostly distributes the goods onwards to me and Karbo, as well as other people in the insula. Lamps and candles are popular gifts and well-received. Secundus, who is fond of Karbo, sends him a tiny collar and a feather-filled leather ball for his cat Letitia, who is annoyed with the collar but delighted with the little ball, chasing it so wildly that I insist she must only play with it in the courtyard, I am afraid that if she plays with it on the rooftop it will one day be thrown too far and too fast and Letitia will follow it over the wall and fall down onto the street, four storeys below, a leap I'm not sure even a cat can walk away from unscathed.

Karbo brings me a bracelet he has woven himself, made from long horsehair strands, interspersed with blue beads. "From the Blues team's four best horses," he tells me proudly. He is still as devoted as ever to his work at the stables, still a natural, by all accounts, at looking after the fastest and most highly strung horses in Rome, used in the Circus Maximus' chariot racing events. Thinking of last year's races that we attended together, I can hardly hold back a grimace at how close the charioteers come to death every time they drive the chariots.

"I don't want to think about how you managed not to get kicked when you gathered these," I say, embracing him. "But thank you."

He has made a matching one for Marcus and we raise our hands in a kind of salute when we spot them on one another's wrists.

"He's growing up fast," sighs Marcus, examining the beads. "Has he asked you if he can be a charioteer yet?"

I grimace at the thought. "No."

"You know he will do soon," says Marcus. "As soon as he thinks he stands a chance at being chosen for a trial drive."

"The answer is no," I say.

Marcus raises an eyebrow. "Are you ready for his tears and fury when you tell him that?"

"Are you ready to watch him die on the racetrack?" I ask.

"It's a risk. But he does have an affinity for horses."

"Good, then he can carry on being a stable hand," I say. "They don't get killed. Or a trainer," I add, grasping at any possible ways out of the dilemma coming closer every day.

"They don't earn glory and vast sums of money either."

"There's no glory in dying," I say.

"Better start practising your refusal speech," he says. "He's going to take some persuading out of it."

It's strange to have conversations suited to the parents of a child and yet not be a couple. I want to lay my hand on Marcus' arm, to beg him to help me persuade Karbo against the life of a chariot racer, and a year ago I would have done just that, but now touching him is too intimate, I cannot bring myself to do it, to move closer, to plead while gazing up into his eyes. The very thought of it makes me awkward. "I'll expect you to back me up when the time comes," I say, overly brisk. "You don't want harm to come to him any more than I do."

He gives me a rueful smile. "This is for you, before I forget." He holds out a cloth bundle and when I open it there is a new wooden writing tablet, intricately carved.

"I asked Quintus to work it for you."

"It's beautiful," I say, delighted. My old one is battered and stained, having been clutched to me every day for years now around animals, dust, food and drink. It has also been dropped more than once, so that one leaf was developing a worrying crack down the side. I trace the delicately tooled and polished lines which depict a trailing vine covered in flowers, like the one Julia has in our courtyard. "I shall think of you when I use it," I add, shyly.

Marcus laughs. "All the time then?" he asks. "You're hardly ever without a tablet in your hand. I'll never be out of your thoughts."

I laugh but my stomach turns over. *Yes. Yes, I will think of you that much. I do think of you all the time. You are never out of my thoughts.* "This is for you," I say, holding out my gift to him.

He opens the little pottery jar and looks at the contents. "Raisins?"

"A special kind," I say.

He tastes them and his eyes brighten at once. "Strawberry grapes? You found raisins made from strawberry grapes?"

I smile, pleased that he can taste the difference from the usual raisins one finds in Rome. "I ordered them specially from the Puteoli region," I say. "To remind you of the ones that grow on your family's farm."

"They make me homesick," he says shaking his head. "I thought I'd have left Rome by now, be done with the Games. And yet, here we still are."

I cling to that *we*, take a deep breath, thinking I might say something, though I'm unsure of what exactly, perhaps something about what I remember of the farm, keep him talking about it, see if he will mention his plans and whether they might include me. "I –"

"Here," he interrupts me, holding out some of the raisins pinched between his fingers towards my lips, expecting me to open my mouth.

Heat rushes up my chest and into my neck, my cheeks, as his fingers brush my open lips and I bite down on sweetness, catching his fingers in my mouth.

"Careful!" He laughs. "You nearly bit me!"

About to choke on a raisin, I turn my face away and duck my head to stop a coughing fit. Julia appears in the courtyard and Marcus offers her some of the raisins, which she accepts.

"Althea remembers your family farm as fondly as you do, Marcus," she says smiling over at me as I recover from coughing. "She will retire there herself if you do not make haste."

For a breathless moment I wonder if she can see into my heart. I stare at her but she raises her gaze up to where Maria is sitting on her balcony. "Have you tried these raisins, Maria? You must, they are wonderful. Marcus will bring some up to you."

Marcus climbs the stairs, offers the jar to Maria, who tastes them suspiciously but then takes another few. "Good," she pronounces. "You should grow a vine like that here, Julia."

"Marcus will have to promise me a rootstock when he finally retires. Which will be when?"

I hold my breath.

"Ah Julia, I don't know," says Marcus. "Every time I think I might be able to leave the amphitheatre complete and in good hands, some other crisis comes up, some other demand, some other project. I'll be glad when this building nonsense is over, it might mean a chance to leave."

I glance at Julia to see how she has taken this idea. She gives her usual calm nod.

"You never meant this to be a long-term job," she reminds him. "One day the memory of the farm will draw you home." As she turns to go back to her apartment she catches my eye and in her smile I see her knowledge of what I long for. Perhaps it is her decades as a priestess that has given her knowledge of what people want, what they pray for when they go to temples, or perhaps Julia knows me too well to not see how I look at Marcus. Which makes me wonder why he cannot see it for himself and with that comes the fear that perhaps he does not want to see it.

I send a standard gift of honey cakes and the traditional candles with riddles to Funis, and he appears in our insula one day with gifts for everyone, from little model animals for the children to jars of spiced figs in honey for the adults.

"Something for you, Althea," he says.

I look down, expecting a jar like the ones he has been handing out to Julia, Maria, Cassia and others in our insula. But instead it is a little cloth bag and when I open it, there is a bronze bracelet in a twisted design. At one end is a bull's head, opposite it the mid-vault body of a bull-leaper, so that it appears the space between them which will allow it to fit onto my wrist is part of the flying body's journey which will lead it over the bull's head. It is beautifully and intricately made, I have never seen such a design.

"A commemoration of this coming season and our work together," he smiles.

"This – this is too much," I stammer.

"Nonsense," he says firmly. "It gave me pleasure to see how the jeweller created what I asked for. And I wanted to invite you to come and see the bull-leapers. They will be arriving in a few weeks and I want them to try out the arena space."

"I want to come!" says Karbo, jumping up and down at my side.

There's a tiny flicker of disappointment in Funis' eyes and I can tell he wanted this to be a private outing, time for us to be alone together watching the spectacle he is arranging. But he is too good natured to deny Karbo.

"Of course," he says with a smile. "I will send word when they are ready."

I MAKE MY WAY TO the amphitheatre every few days, drawn to watch as the intricate outline of a maze of passageways and pens, rooms and lift-shafts, begins to take shape, only a few bricks high. The chief builder waves when he sees me, his leathered brown face creasing still further as he consults the complex drawings sent by Rabirius, ensuring they are re-created in the real world.

"I'm not giving the order to build higher till we're sure this is right," he says in passing. "Picky bugger, he is."

"Rabirius?"

He gives me a look and lowers his voice. "Domitian."

"Did he brief you himself?"

"Oh yes. And turned up at my actual house, three nights in a row, because he couldn't sleep for worrying that some minor detail wasn't right. Made me come and look at it, right away."

"Here?"

"Yes. A hammering on my door in the middle of the night and me and him down here in the dark, surrounded by flaming torches held by the Praetorian Guard. Can you imagine? My wife thought I wouldn't come home alive. Fretting over the exact measurements. I'd have liked to tell him I've been building for longer than he's been alive, but I wasn't sure that would go down well. There's something odd about him. Middle of the night and that's what he's thinking about? Why isn't he asleep like the rest of us?"

I shrug. "Who knows."

The builder looks around, lowers his voice even further, so that I have to lean forward to hear him. "D'you think he's dangerous?"

I think back to his calm patience with the antelope. "I'm not sure," I say. "He certainly gives all his attention to things he's interested in."

"You can say that again. My wife was worried sick."

He walks away, skirting a pile of bricks that have been delivered from the brickyards. On top of the pile is a freshly-made brick with the imprint of a child's foot in it, which makes me smile. The thought of a brick-maker's son, barely half Karbo's height, running about the yard, chosen to place his foot on this brick as a symbol of good luck for his family having secured a huge order, for an imperial building no less, the brick arriving here to be built into the hypogeum of Rome's greatest public edifice, is touching in an odd way. I wonder how many hands, how many people, have been involved in the making of this vast space, from the Jewish prisoners of war brought back here by Titus after the Judean rebellion, to the slaves, builders, the now-dead architect who planned its original structure, followed by Rabirius and his labyrinthian designs to be added into its existing structure, and even this unknown child, whose small foot has nevertheless set its mark on the amphitheatre for all eternity.

"MORNING, CASSIA," I SAY. "THE usual, please. Morning, Quintus."

Quintus waves with one hand while shaking the rattle for Emilia with the other, who stares up at it, amazed. But he looks serious today, there's no bright smile or warm greeting. His sturdy shoulders are slumped and his dark curls are dishevelled.

Cassia ignores my order and leans on the counter, bringing her face close to mine. She, too, looks pale, anxious. "Have you heard?"

"Heard what?"

"The Vestal Virgins."

"Did the fire go out?" Very occasionally the sacred fire that the Vestal Virgins tend goes out, which is supposed to signify the end of Rome itself, so it's a terrible omen and the Emperor himself is supposed to whip whichever Vestal was responsible. Although it's happened a few times and Rome is still standing, which suggests it can't be as ominous an event as everyone makes out.

Cassia's eyes are wide. "No. Worse."

"Worse?"

"They were caught."

"Caught doing what?"

"With a man."

This is much worse. Above all, a Vestal Virgin is a virgin. Pure, untouched. They are absolutely not allowed to lie with a man. "Which one?"

"Two of them."

"*Two?* With – with the same man?"

"No. Each one with a different man. Once one was discovered, she told on the other. They were sisters."

The punishment for a Vestal Virgin who is found to have been with a man is death. And the death enshrined in Roman law for them is very cruel: they are locked alive in a small underground chamber and left to die from starvation or, more likely, a lack of air. It is forbidden to harm one of the Vestals, so they are put into the chamber with food and water and sealed up, so that it can be said no-one harmed them, everyone's conscience clear.

"Will they be entombed alive?"

"I suppose so."

"Wine and bread over here, Cassia!" a customer calls.

"I've got to serve customers," says Cassia hurriedly. "Will you go and see if Julia is alright? She will have heard already. She may have served alongside them. Here," she adds, thrusting a plate at me with small plum pastries on it. "Take this to her. You can share it for your breakfast."

I take the plate and make my way back into the courtyard. Marcus will be waiting at the arena but this is more important. I hesitate outside Julia's door but gather up my confidence and knock.

"Enter."

Julia is standing in front of her household lararium, deep in prayer. I stand in the doorway, awkwardly holding the pastries, a foolish offering given the seriousness of what has happened.

She lowers her hands. "Althea."

"I heard – I'm sorry…"

She must have prayed all night, there are dark shadows under her eyes. "Thank you."

"The pastries are from Cassia," I say, not wishing to claim the kindness as my own. She nods. "Sit."

I sit down. She pours me a cup of watered wine and pushes the pastries towards me. "I cannot eat just now. Eat on my behalf, keep me company for a while."

I don't think I've ever heard Julia express a need for company, for comfort. I take a small bite of the plum pastry, find it hard to chew and swallow, harder still to speak. "The Vestals that have been found… did you know them?"

"One of them. She was twelve when I left. A new woman and only just understanding what already was lost to her. The other had not yet joined us. She is still very young. They covered for one another, a dangerous game. And sure enough they have not been able to keep their secrets."

"One told on the other when she herself was found out?"

Julia sighs. "It was too late. The first moment, a first glance, even allowing themselves to daydream of such a thing and they were already lost. You cannot keep secrets in the House of the Vestals, it is impossible. There are servants everywhere. You are accompanied wherever you go." She gives an involuntary shudder. "I thank the gods I was never tempted during my years of service. Once you are tempted, it is already too late." She sighs. "But *two* of them."

"What will happen now?"

"Domitian will give the order for them to be executed."

"By the – in the burial chamber?"

"That is the law."

We sit silently for a while after that. There is nothing else to say. I finish the pastry when urged, though it tastes of nothing in my mouth. In the end Julia touches my hand and says that Marcus will be waiting for me. I nod and get to my feet, still sombre.

Julia embraces me before I leave. "Thank you for coming," she says. She has maintained her upright posture and her level voice, but when I look back one time through the half-open door she has returned to the lararium, palms up, ready to pray again for her sister Vestals.

PERHAPS HER PRAYERS WORKED. By the end of the day, Rome is both shocked and relieved. The Vestal Virgins must be executed. Everyone expects this, though they shuddered at the method demanded by law, the Vestals to be entombed alive. But Domitian has surprised everyone. He has said that the two culprits may choose the manner of their deaths, they will be able to pick something a great deal quicker than a long slow starvation or suffocation, alone and underground.

"Looks like he's not a bad sort," I hear one of Cassia's customers say. "New Emperor. With that sulky face on him I was expecting worse. But he's been generous, allowing them a choice like that."

Domitian's reputation, at least, has done reasonably well out of the incident. Coming so early in his reign, it has allowed him to appear sternly wedded to the law and an upholder of Roman values, but surprisingly merciful in carrying it out.

Julia's face remains white and still. She spends her days in prayer for the two women but she is relieved that they will meet a quick death. When the day comes there is a subdued atmosphere, not just in our insula, but across Rome. The streets are quieter and few people attend any public events. Today is the day the two Vestals will be taken privately somewhere and killed by whatever method they have chosen, for it has not been made public knowledge, nor will the execution fall to us to carry out. We put to death many criminals as part of the Games, public executions serve as a warning to the common people of what will befall them should they ever break the law. Even when disgraced, the Vestals are treated with greater care than common criminals. Despite this, their names will be chiselled away from their statues, they will not be remembered, only taken away and disposed of somewhere secretly, nameless, lost to future memories. New girls will be chosen to serve Vesta; Rome's divine flame will burn on in their shamed absence.

TODAY THE ARENA IS EMPTY, as is the amphitheatre. The endless dust from the works all around us and in the hypogeum below hangs in the chilly air. I wrap my cloak tighter about me. Funis sent a message yesterday, carefully naming both Karbo and me, asking us to come and see the bull-leapers try out the arena. Although a small part of the arena floor is still open for the building works, most of it is slowly being put back in place. So there is more than enough space for the bull-leapers to test out their routines.

"Are the bull-leapers here?" asks Karbo.

I point across the arena to the Gate of Death. "They're going to come out of there."

"Wrong gate," says Karbo automatically.

"The Gate of Triumph is blocked by rubble this morning," I remind him.

Karbo shivers.

"I told you to wear your cloak."

"Didn't want to."

"Regretting it now?"

"No."

"You're shivering."

"N-not."

"You silly," I say. I wrap part of my own cloak around him and he huddles closer to me. He feels large, solid, nothing like the scrawny child he once was. "How are the stables treating you?"

"They work me like a dog," he says, delighted. "I cleaned out five stalls yesterday. Five! All by myself. Feel my muscles."

I squeeze his proffered arm. "Hercules, that's what you are."

"*And* I polished eight saddles. Then they let me saddle up a horse and said I did it really well. I did up the harness, then I poked the horse in the belly so it would breathe out and tightened it up again. That's what you have to do, else it's too loose, you see, the horses try to fool you, but now I know what to do." He is bursting with pride at his new skills and knowledge.

"Excellent," I murmur, trying to sound admiring rather than worried about Karbo poking a temperamental racing horse in the belly.

"Ready?" Funis has arrived behind us without our noticing. His dark skin has grown lighter in these cold winter months without much sun, but he still favours his foreign clothing, although today he has conceded to the weather and is wearing a thick woollen cloak in a dark green. He pats Karbo on the shoulder, who returns his warm smile with a grin, before turning his attention back to the arena. "Now you'll see something special," Funis promises me. "Watch."

I look where he indicates, though I am aware even as I do so that Funis is not following my gaze but rather watching my face, his whole attention on me. I feel awkward knowing I am so closely scrutinised, but as soon as I turn to him his attention is elsewhere, on the team of ten men and ten women that make up the bull-leapers.

They stand in the chilly dawn air, huddled in long cloaks, talking amongst themselves. The women have their hair worked into tiny tight braids plaited flat against their heads, pulled back from their faces, then twisting into one thicker plait. Around their heads, keeping any loose strands of wayward hair away from their faces, are colourful bands of cloth.

"Can't risk hair getting in your eyes when a bull is coming at you," says Funis, looking them over.

The bull-leapers shed their cloaks, both women and men bare-chested, wearing only tight-fitting loincloths in bright colours that match their headbands. The women's thick plaits are tucked into the back of their loincloths, so that they will not swing loose and cause a distraction.

"They work in teams," says Funis.

The leapers begin to run around the arena floor, first slowly, growing faster and faster, swinging their arms as they go. First one, then another and another throw themselves forwards, performing handsprings and cartwheels, with their hands on the floor or sometimes without using their hands at all. Some even go backwards.

"They're like spring lambs!" says Karbo and he's right, their legs have a bounce no human normally possesses. "Won't they get tired out?" he adds.

"They need to be warmed up before they leap the bulls," points out Funis. "If they fall while they are warming up, there is no harm done. If they miss their timing when there is a bull present… they could lose their lives."

"Does it happen?" asks Karbo.

"Occasionally. And it's why the crowd watch, really," says Funis with a small sigh. "It's not the beauty or the skill of the leaping they are here to admire so much, as the possibility that they'll see someone gouged to death. The crowds are always bloodthirsty," he adds, making his way over to the team. He speaks with them for a few moments, returns to us and raises his hand in a signal to Strabo.

The Gate of Death slowly opens.

I find myself clutching Funis' arm without thinking. The bull standing in the gateway is huge, the largest I have ever seen. Dark brown, with horns as long as Karbo's arms, it stands silhouetted for a moment, then steps forwards, unafraid of the group of humans it faces.

"Is it good-tempered?" I whisper to Funis.

"He's finished off two men and one woman in his time," says Funis.

I gape up at him. "And they didn't kill him?"

"He'd be hard to replace. He makes it look even more dramatic. They make sure to tell the audience he's a killer."

"I wouldn't have the courage to face him," I say.

But the bull-leapers have already moved into their positions. The first woman runs towards the beast. Karbo is on his feet. I am still clutching at Funis' arm and he puts his hand over mine, warm and confident.

The woman leaps as the bull turns towards her. Her hands clench around his horns and he, annoyed, tosses his head – and the woman – backwards, but her hands have released him, her body turns on itself, her feet touch lightly on his rump but already her knees have bent to allow her to push away from him and down to the ground, landing safely. The bull turns, angered at this taunting use of his body and his horns graze her skin as she bends her back impossibly in an arch that saves her. His prey is gone, skipping to one side like one of our dancing girls, risking nothing but her modesty. I take in a gasp of air, I had forgotten to breathe in watching this extraordinary demonstration of skill and fearlessness.

The bull snorts, looks this way and that, turns about on itself. It spots a man in a bold yellow loincloth, who waves his arms. The bull does not hesitate. It charges wildly, Karbo shouts and the man twists backwards and to one side but not far enough, the tip of the bull's left horn scrapes against the man's ribcage, a line of blood showing at once, while the rest of the team immediately move to draw attention to themselves. The man moves out of the way, one hand to his side, blood seeping through his knuckles but already two more women have leapt through the air, one man has dodged and dodged again the searching horns and all are unscathed.

"Is he alright?" I ask Funis.

"He is well," he says with confidence. "That is a common injury, there is not one member of their team that has not been caught in that manner more than once."

"Too dangerous," I say. "Karbo, you are never, ever to take that up," I add, for his eyes have a gleam to them that usually only comes when he talks of horses.

He gives a shrug, half relieved, half regretful. "But the thrill of it..." he says, his voice trailing off with uncertain longing.

"No," I say more firmly.

"See?" He grins at me, "Chariot racing not so dangerous now?"

"Why must you like anything that's dangerous?" I give him a little push. "Get out of here, back to the stables or you'll be late for work."

"Ah, the cry of all mothers," says Funis. "Why can their sons not choose a quiet life?" He strokes my hand with a gentleness that reminds me that I am still clutching his arm and I pull away, blushing.

"Your mother can't have liked you being a gladiator," I say, hoping to move on to a story from the past rather than our present closeness.

"She thought it might be a way out of slavery, and that was all that mattered to her," he says, looking away.

"And she was right."

He makes a gesture that is neither a nod nor a shake of the head, something oddly in-between, unreadable. "For me. Not for herself."

"She stayed a slave till she died?"

His jaw goes hard at the memory. "I tried to buy her out as soon as I began making money."

"Her master wouldn't let her go?"

He shakes his head, abruptly walks away from me, across the arena floor to speak with a member of the team. I watch him go, wondering what happened. Most masters are not averse to a slave having their freedom bought by a family member, even by the slave themselves if they have saved enough money, a difficult but not impossible task. Rome is full of freedmen who were once slaves. It would take a master with a grudge against a slave, or a stubborn mind, to insist on a man or woman staying enslaved even when offered their full value. And it is unlike Funis to break off a conversation with me, he is usually more than willing to seek me out, to engage me in conversation. This memory, of his mother being enslaved and he unable to free her, despite his success as a gladiator, must be both distressing and something he does not wish to divulge further details of, at least for now. I'm curious, but I won't probe further. Past memories can be painful.

THE COLD DAYS OF THE new year come upon us and we wrap up warm in thick cloaks, wear boots against the cold wet streets. Married women all but disappear under their winter-weight palla shawls, draped about them and pulled up over their heads for warmth and protection against the unpleasant weather. Not having a palla, I layer up my headwraps, sometimes wearing one on top of another to keep my head warmer.

"The horses were behaving oddly today," says Karbo one evening. "One of them nearly kicked me, and he never kicks. And when we locked them up for the night in their stables they kept whinnying, two of them even struck out with their front hooves at the gates, they wanted to be let out."

I frown. "Did the trainers say anything about it?"

"They'd gone for the night, it was just us stable boys."

I shrug. "Maybe they just get grumpy where it isn't peak racing season. Fewer races might mean they don't get as much exercise and it's what they've been bred for, isn't it?"

Karbo nods, rolling the tiny leather ball for his cat, who ignores it for a moment and then pounces, not at the ball, but at Karbo's hand, and bites.

"Ow!" he yelps, swatting the cat away. She hisses back at him, baring her tiny teeth. "You bad cat!"

"Looks like all the animals are grumpy," I say. "I'd be nervous about earthquakes but it's hardly the time of year for them. Spring and autumn, I'd be more worried. Maybe the windy day has just annoyed them all. Let's go and eat some dinner. Cassia's made a really good vegetable porridge, I could smell it on the way past earlier today." I shiver. "I could do with something hot. I wish spring would come faster."

"When spring comes we'll be working again," says Karbo, following me down the stairwell.

"I'd rather have the Games start again and some warmth to go with them," I say. "I'm bored of winter."

It's dark when I'm shaken awake.

"Too early," I mutter, but the shaking continues and when Karbo shrieks I'm awake in an instant. I reach out to him, find a flailing arm in the dark, realise the shaking is going on without anyone's hands on me. It is the floor swaying under us, the walls creak. Something smashes outside.

"Earthquake!" I scream and yank Karbo to the door. We run out into the first glimpse of dawn. A roof tile crashes at our feet, one shard hitting my bare calf. We both scream as Marcus' door bursts open. He runs across the roof towards us and as he does so the tremor stops, the lurching from under us gone.

"Earthquake," I gasp again as he embraces us both.

"Downstairs and out," he says. "There's likely to be another tremor."

We follow him down the wooden staircase, which creaks under the weight of all the inhabitants who have hurried out of their rooms and apartments, children crying in fear or asking endless questions which their parents ignore as they call out to one another – is everyone safe? Anyone injured? Is everyone out?

We gather outside the insula's courtyard, as far away from buildings as we can get, standing in the middle of Sand Street, shifting from one space to another, our feet uncertain of finding any stability. The insula has survived well enough, since it was only strengthened and rebuilt recently. There are a few roof tiles in the street, smashed terracotta shards here and there. Julia, calm as ever, is doing a headcount, ensuring everyone is safely out of the building. There are clouds of rising dust to the east and west so she sends Karbo and one of the baker's children in the two directions to find out what's fallen. They run back in a few moments to say that a small insula has collapsed, although it was a crumbling wreck anyway and no-one has been hurt. The other cloud of dust was a group of three little shops, which had been poorly built. One man has received a blow to the head and a woman has broken a finger when she reached out to grab something and was hit by a falling tile, but otherwise the area has been lucky.

"Thanks be to Neptune," murmurs Julia when she hears the children's reports. "We will sacrifice to him."

"That's why the horses and the cat were behaving strangely!" says Karbo.

"You're right," I say. "We should have trusted our instincts. And theirs."

Marcus looks anxious. "The gods only know what will have happened to the foundations of the hypogeum," he says. "They've only just started building. We need to go and inspect it."

He sets out with Karbo and I trotting after him, he is walking so fast.

"Slow down a bit," I beg after a few streets.

"Sorry," he says, briefly slowing his pace before speeding up again two streets later, as we come to the Forum and he has a wide-open space to stride through.

"Why are we rushing?" complains Karbo.

"Be all we need if there's damage and they have to slow down the works," Marcus mutters.

We circle the building on the outside, but cannot see cracks or any other signs of damage. Inside, we dash down the steps leading to the lowest level of the hypogeum. The head builder is there, also inspecting the building and looking pleased.

"Works every time," he says with satisfaction.

"What does?" I ask, grimacing as I catch my breath, Karbo and I both clutching at our aching sides.

"Trade secret," he says, winking.

"Tell us!" begs Karbo.

The builder grins, leans in confidentially. ""When you build a really big structure, something important like this amphitheatre, you don't want it falling apart next time there's an earthquake, do you?"

"But you can't stop earthquakes," says Karbo, confused.

"What happens when you throw a stone in the water?" asks the builder.

"It sinks."

The builder laughs. "What happens to the surface of the water?"

Karbo frowns. "You get ripples. What's that got to do with earthquakes?"

"Earthquakes are the same," says the builder. "The tremors are ripples but in the earth instead of in the water and each one that comes, rocks the building a little more, a little more, till it can't stand against it, and it starts to crack. Now, look about you, and tell me, can you see any cracks?"

Karbo looks closely. "No."

"So what we do when we have a large building, is you build in holes."

"Holes?"

"Gaps in the building. Like the big arches of the amphitheatre that you can see above ground, we do the same kind of thing below the ground. And when a ripple comes, a tremor, there's nothing for it to pass on to. It can't keep pushing, it just loses its power. Of course some of the ripples get through, but not all of them, so the earthquake *loses its power*." He speaks the last sentence very quietly, avoiding Neptune himself hearing and being offended at a mere mortal, a common builder, having found a way to outwit his divine wrath.

Marcus' shoulders have come back to their usual resting place and he's smiling. "I hoped it would work," he says. "But you never know."

The builder grins. "It always works," he says confidently.

"But an insula fell down near us," objects Karbo.

"You can't do it for smaller buildings," says the builder. "There's not as much room to build like that. You need big buildings, so that there's space to have the holes as well as the foundations. We always do it for amphitheatres. You don't want them falling apart, they're a big job to fix and they're a lot more dangerous if they fall down. You don't want fifty thousand people running screaming during an earthquake and some of those big arches coming crashing down on them, do you?"

Karbo is wide-eyed. "Who invented it?"

"Ah, who knows? But we pass it down, builder to builder. And now I've told you, you'll have to be an honorary builder and swear yourself to Vulcan, eh?"

Marcus grimaces. In his mind, Vulcan is the god who crushed Pompeii, who stole his wife and son. He might not demean the god out loud, for that would be foolish, but I doubt he sacrifices to him or speaks his name with praise.

WE SPEND THE REST OF the morning at the insula, cautiously awaiting further tremors, but there is only one more, very light and quick, a fleeting moment. Karbo and Marcus visit the stables in the afternoon and find a priest conducting a hastily arranged sacrifice and blessing. Neptune rules horses as well as earthquakes, so the stables are concerned that he is in some way offended with them and think it wise to sacrifice to him so that he will be appeased. Horses panic during earthquakes, they try to kick down their stable doors and can damage themselves in the process, which is highly undesirable when they are the finest racehorses in Rome, perhaps in the Empire. Marcus takes the opportunity of this visit to the stables to look over his own two horses. They are certainly not the finest racehorses in Rome, just ordinary beasts that receive free stabling in return for use in more prosaic jobs like pulling cartloads of straw or hay or feed about the place, as well as spare harnesses and saddles to the races. He returns satisfied that they are well and calm enough, perhaps happier for being stabled together. Few of the racehorses benefit from this. Each is kept in its own stable, to discourage fights between them, high-spirited as they are.

"We had to take each horse out and let it run in the training ground," Karbo reports back. "So they'd calm down after the earthquake."

"I hope you were careful," I say, worried by the thought of Karbo around powerful, frightened horses.

"They trust me," he says simply.

"They do," chimes in Marcus, patting Karbo's hair. "He must be blessed by Neptune. Like kittens with him, they are."

"Letitia!" says Karbo, reminded of his cat and running upstairs to find her. He comes back down with her purring in his arms, all forgiven.

But when Fabius comes home in the evening he has brought Funis with him, his head heavily bandaged.

"Funis! What happened?"

"Roof tile," he winces. "Caught me good and proper."

"In your barracks?"

"Not even during the earthquake," he says, accepting a cup of hot wine from Cassia. "Happened this afternoon."

"But there weren't any aftershocks,"

"It came loose on the roof during the quake, fell off later in the day."

"Lucky not to have been killed," says Fabius. "It caught him on the side of the head, if it had come down straight on top of his head…" he grimaces. "He's staying the night in my apartment so I can keep an eye on him."

After the earthquake, the building of the hypogeum proceeds at pace. With its foundations in place and a team of builders, the first storey is rapidly completed. Standing above it on the arena floor, all I can see below is a curved grid of brick passageways, with walls rising upwards, and many small chambers. Some will be fitted with wooden lifts that will rise through two storeys, other lifts will only rise one floor before delivering their occupants, be they human or beasts. There will be space for Fabius, our physician, as well as a morgue where dead gladiators will be stripped of armour before being taken back to their respective barracks. Executed criminals will also be stripped of any armour or weapons, blunt or otherwise, with which we have seen fit to provide them. Their bodies will not be returned to grieving fellow gladiators, to be treated with comradely honour, but instead will be dragged away with metal-hooked poles by our undertakers, who will dispose of their bodies in a mass burial pit as instructed.

Meanwhile the endless rubble around us swiftly disappears, cartload after cartload loaded up and taken away for sorting and cleaning, while more valuable items like rooftiles have been neatly stacked for reuse. Piles of earth appear as the foundations are dug, the workmen slowly disappearing underground as they dig deeper and deeper, spadefuls of earth lifted by buckets. The more senior builders stand over the slaves who are doing most of the hard labour, occasionally lecturing their apprentices on important building tips, mostly admonishing them for being too soft to do a proper hard day's work, which, the builders claim, they did much better in their own younger days, making audacious claims for how high a wall they could build in one day. The apprentices roll their eyes when their masters aren't looking or make sly comments and laugh between themselves. The slaves keep their mouths shut, knowing better than to talk when they're being worked so hard, a useless waste of energy.

Day by day the outlines of the two new schools grow clearer as the foundations are laid and they begin to rise up from the ground.

TUNNELS

T HE HYPOGEUM IS TAKING SHAPE well, the first floor is almost complete, only one more to go and the final sections of the arena floor will be re-laid. Marcus begins to relax, assuming that we are on schedule for the opening of the new season's Games. But one morning I find him staring wide-eyed at a new set of drawings, being held for inspection by the owl-like Rabirius.

"Good morning," I say, joining them. I'm huddled in my cloak, the damp days of February are cold and I'm looking forward to some sign of spring weather to come soon.

"Tunnels," says Marcus, without greeting me. He rubs his eyes, looking tired.

"Tunnels?"

"Domitian wants to have tunnels joining up the schools and the amphitheatre," says Marcus.

"What for?"

"So that the gladiators can arrive from their schools straight into the hypogeum of the amphitheatre without being seen." Marcus gives me a brittle smile, eyes indicating Rabirius. Presumably we are not at liberty to comment unfavourably on this new element of the plan, in case our lack of enthusiasm is reported back to Domitian.

I turn to Rabirius and try to emulate Marcus' smile. "Why?"

Rabirius shakes his head without commenting.

"Thank you for letting us know," I say politely to Rabirius, now packing away his scrolls, leaving me with a copy of the diagrams.

"I'll be over the road briefing the builders," he says, and sets off.

I turn back to Marcus. "We don't know Domitian's reason for it?"

Marcus shrugs. "Probably thinks it's more efficient or something. Or more dramatic that you don't see the performers until it's time for the Games? Or fewer opportunities for armed gladiators to revolt while they cross the road?" He sighs. "I don't pretend to read the mind of emperors. They don't think like ordinary people."

Our own builders will have to accommodate the tunnels, and there's a fair amount of cursing when they hear about it. The entrance points will come in on the lower floor of our hypogeum and so digging starts all over again, this time creating two large tunnels between each school and the amphitheatre. A whole new building team is assigned to this job, as our own team flatly refuses to take it on and Marcus backs them up with some force. If they don't continue with the hypogeum we won't be opening the season on time, and that's not something he can allow.

"So this year there's no flooding of the arena required?" I ask Marcus, teasing. "Blue cloth for a sea, as usual? Sure you don't want some real water like last year?"

"Don't even joke about it," he says.

Vast strips of blue-dyed cloth ripple across the length and breadth of the arena, pulled up and down by dozens of our slave team to create the illusion of water as three half-scale ships are wheeled in, bearing the doomed tributes to the Minotaur. Later in the season the heroic Theseus will also make his arrival in them. We practise hoisting the sails, which make the ships look more realistic. I stand back and consider the black sails against the blue ripples. The effect is good, it brings the sea voyage to life. I'm glad there is no real water demanded this year, in this regard Domitian has been easier to work with than his deceased brother Titus.

I've taken it upon myself to appoint Celer as the amphitheatre's chief chariot driver and manager for horses. He drinks less when he has something to occupy him, and his old skills as a charioteer come back to him. He recruits other retirees, those who escaped the racing arena with their lives and bodies sufficiently intact. We have developed our own chariots for shows; they are plain wood with easy to change decorations made of flag-like cloths, so that designs can be applied and removed. This season the chariots will be primarily used for the Amazon scenes, and the set designers are busy creating colourful patterns which will be used when the fearsome women warriors meet Hercules and Theseus in battle.

Now that we have our theme and it looks like the arena will be ready in time for the opening, it's time to begin choosing our performers for the season. Paternus is busy dealing with the building of the new Ludus Magnus and transferring from his old barracks to the new ones, while maintaining a strict schedule of training for the gladiators performing at the Games in a month's time, so he puts us off as long as possible.

"Let's visit our new neighbour Labeo," suggests Marcus one morning, looking out from an archway on the middle floor across to the gleaming new gladiator schools. "Have a look round his Ludus Matutinus, see how it's shaping up. We can start discussing what we need and what he has available."

The Morning Gladiator School has been so named because it will include the training of animals, which are usually showcased in the mornings, but it will also house and train the speciality acts that Labeo has always provided for us: the bestiarii who fight animals, the venatores who hunt them, as well as those gladiators who require special training not always available in a regular school: women, dwarfs, giants and other such unusual performers. There will be some space provided at the larger school if required for training with larger animals than usual or particularly impressive hunt scenes, but most of these acts will be managed under Labeo.

The Ludus Matutinus, being significantly smaller than the Ludus Magnus, is already close to being finished; the main structure is in place and now it's only a matter of completing the interiors and paintwork. Its inhabitants have moved into the new accommodation and the gladiators are already training even though they are surrounded by plasterers and painters, who are spending a lot of their time watching the training bouts rather than getting on with the work in hand.

Owner of the school, Labeo, laden with gold rings, neck chains and bracelets as usual, greets us as old friends. "Marcus! Althea! I was thinking, do they even *know* what I have in store for the Games this year? You wouldn't credit some of the women I have. And dwarves of course, giants, always got them in stock," he adds affably, as though speaking of items in a shop rather than people. "But my women are the best, as I don't even need to tell you. Alyssa has been training them all winter, they're fighting fit and gorgeous. I've had a new set of hair pieces bought in last week. We like our gladiatrices with long tresses, don't we? I hope you have a wonderful theme for us this year?"

"The Minotaur and Theseus," I say.

Labeo has a quick think. "*Tell* me you're going to include the Amazons?"

"Of course."

"The gods above, you cannot even imagine what my girls will be like. Bare-breasted of course, long hair, perhaps some face paint? Tattoos. Properly savage."

"Won't they need some armour, if they're fighting?" I ask, wincing at the thought of the women going into battle scenes bare-breasted, no matter how accurate to history the look is.

"Some, yes," says Labeo casually. "But not too much, not in the wrong places, eh?"

We make our way into the central yard, which is shaped around a miniature amphitheatre that can seat five hundred spectators. It's surrounded on all four sides by the barracks, containing the usual armouries, a medical centre, sleeping quarters, kitchens, toilets, a large room for eating and other such amenities.

"Dreadful, isn't it?" says Labeo. He indicates the team of plasterers working their way from cell to cell in the sleeping quarters of the barracks, joking and whistling as they go about their work. In other areas there are painters daubing the building inside and out with whitewash, while a deep red trim is being added around the edges of the yard and the amphitheatre. "Can barely hear ourselves think. Not that most of that lot need to think," he adds, waving disdainfully at a group of ten gladiatrices, who are engaged in learning sword fighting. They look new and inexperienced, their moves clumsy. Two of them are already tired out, not displaying the kind of stamina necessary for long-term success in the arena.

"You've got a fantastic building though," I say to Labeo.

He strokes the gold chains round his neck and gives a pleased shrug. "Unbearable, having all these builders about," he says, but I can see he's delighted really. He has a magnificent new school to house his wares, right by the amphitheatre, built by imperial command. His school is even going to be completed before the supposedly more important Ludus Magnus. For now, he is relishing being the centre of attention.

"There's two more schools going to be built on the other side of the amphitheatre," he says. "Dacian and Gallic apparently, but they're not going to get round to those right away, they're too busy with these first two plus the tunnels and special ramps so Domitian can arrive from his palace underground and all sorts." He's proud to have one of the two larger schools, for his contributions to our spectacles to have been noted and rewarded in this way.

"And now you have your own amphitheatre," I say.

"It makes the fans happy," he says. "And whatever pleases them pleases me."

The seats of the tiny amphitheatre are half occupied with fans of the Games, the rest of the space is taken up with she-wolves on the prowl and vendors of food and drink. The women who have already found their targets lounge in the laps of their customers or lean against them as they watch the women training, whispering filthy jokes and sharing sweet or savoury snacks they order from the vendors, their clients paying for whatever they order: wine, olives, bread and garum sauce to dip it in, spiced roasted chickpeas, dried figs, nuts, small honey-cakes. The she-wolves take the opportunity of the men being distracted to ensure they get a solid meal inside themselves, ready for their own performance later. The men watch the gladiatrices with hungry eyes, rubbing the thighs of the women sat next to them, squeezing their waists tighter. They drink more wine than they can handle, some of them lurching to their feet when it comes time to leave, unsteady but certain that they are going to have a good time with their chosen companion.

"They won't be able to perform," scoffs Labeo. "They shouldn't pay for services up front, but the women know better than to let them get away with that. More fool them."

"Not tempted?" I ask him. "Considering how many of them hang about here?"

"Oh, I'm tempted by other goods," says Labeo with an easy smile. His eyes drift over the crowd to a young man who waves back at him. "My assistant. A good lad."

I nod. Clearly the assistant's role goes beyond the standard tasks required in running a gladiatorial school.

"So," Marcus begins, when we have settled down with drinks and cakes, "the theme this year is the legend of the Minotaur and we'll be focusing on Carpophorus as Theseus, as it's his final year."

"Such a shame," laments Labeo. "Best bestiarius Rome's ever seen. Martial even writes poems about him, you know. *Had the ages of yore, Caesar, given birth to Carpophorus, barbarian lands would not have boasted of their monsters.* That's one of them. I'd have kept him going a few more years but he says he wants to retire from the arena and be a beast hunter instead, supply animals to amphitheatres. I blame that Funis of yours for putting ideas in his head."

"Funis?" asks Marcus.

"Oh they spend all their time together. Carpophorus follows him about like a lost puppy, I'm surprised he doesn't sacrifice to him."

"And he wants to be a beast hunter?"

"Apparently they're planning to go into business together. Funis wants a good man to work with, and there's no-one better than Carpophorus when it comes to animals, we all know that. Can hunt them, train them, kill them if needed. Brave, I'll give him that. Not much on the brains front, but I expect Funis will make up for him in that regard. They've already got a pretty lucrative contract supplying you lot at the amphitheatre, it'll easily keep two men in business."

"We'll make the most of Carpophorus while we still have him," says Marcus. "Keep him in good condition, Labeo."

"Always, of course. He's one of my best performers. No barracks for him, he has his own villa. Though he's not proud. Trains with the rest of the men here in the school, hangs around here even when he's finished. He's used to the camaraderie. His wife tries to put ideas in his head but he's a simple creature, bit like the animals he spends all his time with."

"I'll go and have a word with him," says Marcus. "Althea will talk you through what we need for the rest of the season." He makes his way out of the seating, heading towards the barracks in search of Carpophorus.

We sit in silence for a moment, watching the women training. I spot expert gladiatrix Alyssa adjusting the shooting pose of one of the women who is learning to fire arrows. When she catches my eye she raises her hand to me in a kind of salute and the sunlight glints off the bronze it is made of. I still shiver at how Alyssa lost her own hand to a pack of slavering hounds in the arena, but I also swell with pride at Fabia's expertise in saving her life, how calm she stayed in the panic that ensued. When Alyssa's fighting spirit was lost along with her hand, Fabia found the solution, the bronze prosthetic hand allowing Alyssa to handle a bow again. Fabia herself, I see, is busy inspecting a fellow dwarf's ankle, crouching to look at it more closely, turning the foot this way and that while the gladiator tries not to grimace with the pain. She straightens up, gives directions. The gladiator tries to argue with her but her firm shake of the head means he will be out of action for a while at least.

"Knows what she's about," says Labeo, watching my gaze. "Softy though, I'd make them perform even if they are in pain. No-one said being a gladiator was going to be an easy life, did they?"

"I'd be grateful to have a physician as good as her for your school," I say.

"Oh I am," says Labeo. "I wouldn't be rid of her. Though she'd rather be the chief physician at the Flavian Amphitheatre." He winks. "She'll make it one day, you mark my words. Never known a woman with such ambition."

I acknowledge a brief wave from Fabia who has noticed my visit. "Did you find her an assistant?"

"Ooof, the trouble we've had on that front."

"Why?"

He shrugs. "She's a woman and a dwarf. The ones that don't mind one thing object to the other. She's had assistants and apprentices come and go for weeks. They start all humble and turn disrespectful to her in a matter of days. She won't have it. Sacks them right away." He grins. "Told you, ambitious. She won't let anyone stand in her way. Least of all some jumped-up assistant or know-it-all apprentice. Anyway, these last two have worked out. Her father sent for an apprentice from Egypt. And the assistant is a slave girl, but she shows some aptitude for herbs, apparently. Knows a good chance in life when she sees it. Here comes Fabia. I need to have a word with one of the trainers. I'll leave you to have a chat with her." He rises and makes his way towards the training area.

Fabia is followed by two people. A young girl, her dark hair neatly plaited, her skin still winter-pale, and a tall young man with golden-brown skin and black hair arranged in the Egyptian style. He hovers behind Fabia, attentive to her every move. As they reach us Fabia directs the girl elsewhere and she hurries away.

"Watch out for arrows," says Fabia as Labeo crosses paths with her. "They're supposed to stick to their own target area but you never know, some of them are new and aren't very good at hitting the target. But Alyssa will sort them out."

"She looks happy," I say, rising to greet Fabia.

She beams. "She is. She can still shoot faster than any recruit and as well as most of the venatores. And she makes a good trainer."

We embrace each other.

"Was that your new assistant?" I ask, pointing at the girl in the distance.

"Yes. Decima," says Fabia. "A good girl, very careful with preparing remedies. And this is Sadiki, my new apprentice," she adds gesturing upwards at the young man standing behind her. "This is Althea, you've heard me speak of her."

He bows. "My honour to meet a friend of the Physician."

I smile at hearing Fabia spoken of so formally. "Good to meet you," I reply. "You're from Egypt?"

Sadiki nods. "I trained there under my father, he is a physician also."

"An old friend of Father's," says Fabia. "Sadiki wanted to come to Rome as an apprentice and Father wrote and said that I was looking for one." She notices one of the women clasping her hand after a mis-timed blow with a wooden sword, her face twisted up in pain. "Excuse me, I need to check on her."

Left alone with Sadiki I can't help asking the question that came to mind. Or at least part of it. He's attentive to Fabia, as well as deeply respectful in the way he speaks of her, but I can't help wondering how he feels about being apprenticed to a woman, and not just a woman but a dwarf, given Labeo's earlier comments. "You were happy to be apprenticed to a woman?"

He turns his attention back to me from watching Fabia crossing the yard. "I was unsure at first," he says. "I did want to be a physician to gladiators, so of course I was interested in the opportunity. It was odd to be apprenticed to a woman. But my mother had always worshipped Bes. She gave me her figurine of him before she died last year, so I thought it a sign from her."

"Bes?"

He pulls out a little figurine. It's a model of a dwarf, with a large head and bowed legs, wide eyes and a protruding tongue. His head is crowned with a feathered headdress. "He is the god who protects mothers and children. We place him on the outside of birthing houses to drive away evil spirits and protect those within. And because he drives away evil he also symbolises the good things in life – music, dance… umm," he blushes slightly, "…sex." He clears his throat. "Anyway. My mother was a midwife and in Egypt many dwarf women are midwives, it is considered good luck. So I am… accustomed, my mother had several colleagues who are dwarves. Although I had not yet met one who is a physician to gladiators," he adds.

"Fabia is special," I say, laughing.

"She is," he says solemnly, watching her tend to the injured gladiatrix. "She is one the best physicians I have ever met."

Labeo arrives back. He waves Sadiki away, who bows to me and makes his way back to Fabia's side. "Now," he says, settling back. "Tell me everything."

I begin to describe the season's plans.

"No, no," says Labeo, cutting me short. "The Emperor. Is he mad?"

"Labeo!" I hiss.

"Oh, everyone's wondering. Funny old fish. Face like he's been slapped and can't do anything about it; annoyed but hasn't worked out how he's going to punish you yet. He likes the Games though, thank the gods."

"He's odd," I agree. "But not dangerous… I don't think."

"Not dangerous *yet*," says Labeo. "You can't trust them. They go funny in the end, most of them."

I don't answer, instead take a sip of my wine and turn the conversation back to safer topics.

"So first of all, we need a lot of gladiatrices for the Amazons."

"Done," says Labeo. "Easy. Do you want one of them dressed up as Queen Hippolyta?"

"Paternus is supplying the queen."

"A gladiatrix? Why does he have a woman? *I* do the women."

"He just has the one," I say. "She's pretty special, he says, or he wouldn't have taken her. A Briton. Name of Billica. She was sold as a potential gladiatrix because when they attacked her village she killed three armed men, despite only being sixteen."

"No-one offered her to me," says Labeo. "What colour's her hair?"

"I don't know."

"Red," he says. "Only good colour for a Briton woman. Dye it if it isn't, add some extra if it's a bit thin. You have to build her up, make a name for her if you want her to do well, have a long career. She has to be recognisable in the arena even at a distance, sexy, get a reputation as a savage so men like the idea of taming her in the bedroom. Paternus doesn't know how to manage a gladiatrix. He's going to under-sell her."

"Apparently hardly anyone can manage her," I say. "She's kept locked in her sleeping quarters unless she's in the training ground and no-one gives her real weapons till she's about to fight, they don't trust her. But Paternus says she's fierce when she's let loose in the arena."

"See, that sort of information ought to be all over Rome by now, it'll make the crowd keen to see her. Should have been mine," says Labeo, sulking. "But tell Paternus, I'll help prepare her for the Amazon scenes. Can't have her letting down the side when my girls will look spectacular."

"I'll tell him. Now what I really need is something more difficult. An outstanding *damnato a munera* gladiator. Actually I'll need several who've been given that sentence. Paternus has a few and I need them all, but none of them are really special. I need a leading man to set against Carpophorus. Do you have anyone?"

Damnato a munera. Damned to the Games. It means a criminal who has been condemned to die in the arena, but will be fighting as a gladiator before their end comes. Some must die at once, others are given a specific sentence to serve, during which they will be trained as a gladiator and fight in formal bouts. But all the time they fight, time is running out, for they must die within a certain period, also set by a judge. It can be up to a year, but no longer.

I've caught Labeo's interest. "For what?"

"First of all there are two rounds of Athenians being fed to the Minotaur," I say. "We need men and women who will fight, but they need to die. They can't give in to the Minotaur, but they can't win against it either."

"How many?"

I make a face. "I need fourteen women from you. Seven for one event, the first time the Athenians send tribute to Crete, then a second group of seven. The matching men will come from Paternus' school."

"Don't have that many," he says. "I think I've got nine. You'll have to share them into the two groups. But you can chuck some criminals in there with blunt swords. They'll swing at the Minotaur if they get desperate, it'll do. The other ones will make up for them, they'll fight harder. But we can blunt their weapons too. And a female gladiator with a few months of training behind her is not going to make it against a man with years behind him. Who's your Minotaur?"

"I don't have one yet," I say. "That's why I need someone special. He needs to be *damnato*, because he'll be the Minotaur through the whole season and have to fight properly all the way to the end. Then in the closing Games Carpophorus-as-Theseus will kill the Minotaur. It'll be the big finale."

Labeo lights up. "Oh, I have just the man. Wait till you see him. *Damnato.* Really good with a sword and a fierce fighter, makes an excellent gladiator, you wouldn't credit it. He should have been a gladiator from his first days as a slave, then he wouldn't be condemned to death, he'd be one of Rome's favourites, raking in the money with girls falling at his feet."

"What did he do?"

"He killed his master, said he tormented all the slaves in their house, men and women, beat them, starved them. A poor sort of master. But you can't have slaves going round killing their masters, whatever they've done. He's handy with a sword, so they gave him to me. He has to die by the end of the year, which will coincide with the end of the season of Games."

"He can't earn his freedom if he fights well?"

"No. Has to be dead by the end of the season. You'd think he wouldn't bother fighting, but he says it's about honour, showing that he isn't a coward."

"If he can be relied on to do as he's told he could be the Minotaur."

Labeo is enthusiastic. "He'd be excellent for that. Happy to kill other people if needed, but he's also mindful of the referees during a proper bout, no silly stuff behind your back or anything underhand like that. And he's young, good looking. The ladies are fond of him already, wait till they find out he's going to die at the end of the season and they'll be swarming all over his barracks of a night-time. Nothing a noble lady of Rome likes more than a gladiator who's going to die soon. Tragically romantic. And more importantly, can't tell tales to your husband if he's dead, can he? Or anyone else. No nasty gossip to ruin a lady's reputation."

"They won't be able to see his face much," I point out. "He'll be wearing the Minotaur's mask any time he's on the arena floor."

"I don't think they're that bothered about his face," says Labeo, making an obscene gesture. "It's other parts of him that'll put a smile on their face, won't it?"

"If you say so," I say.

"Ah, don't fret about him. He's got his pick of the ladies, he's being trained by the best in the business and has a full belly every night. He's killed the man that did him wrong and he's still alive to tell the tale."

"For a few months."

"Better than being killed off straightaway, isn't it?"

"I suppose."

"Carpophorus has taken him under his wing anyway, looking out for him, showing him the ropes. He'll do you proud. I swear."

"What's his name?"

"Felix. That's him. Second from the right."

The man he's indicating is talking with Marcus and Carpophorus. He's nothing special to look at, decently broad-chested and a good height, shorter than Carpophorus, but that will be easily remedied with a spectacular horned helmet.

Felix. *Happy.* A common name for a slave, the sort of name handed out by a master who likes the idea of their slaves being cheerful and well-disposed. Poorly named, in this case. But there it is. One season of glory, fighting for his honour, then killed as required by his sentence. By the time Marcus has re-joined us, the deal has been struck and Felix is now damned to this season of Games and the dark role of a monster.

WHEN WE VISIT PATERNUS a week later, the Ludus Magnus, the Great Gladiatorial School, is supposed to be complete. There's to be an opening day for it shortly, which Domitian himself will attend. Paternus has asked Marcus to help him design a suitable theme and programme for the day.

In reality, the wooden amphitheatre and its arena are in place but the barracks are still being built all around it, the builders laying roof tiles while carpenters work on gates and windows. There's dust everywhere, the plasterers haven't even started and the painters won't be able to get near the place for weeks. Paternus looks weary, I'm sure his hair is whiter than last year.

"Marcus," he says with some relief. "Thank you for your help with this."

They've settled on the twelve tasks of Hercules, with a different gladiator taking on the role for each of the twelve feats. In this way Paternus can showcase his very best fighters, gladiators whose names are known by everyone in Rome, giving each one a chance to shine.

"Most of Hercules' tasks involve killing animals," comments Labeo, who has joined us to look round. Despite his own impressive new school, he knows full well that it's seen as secondary to this one. "That's venatores' work. *My* school's speciality. Why's he using that as a theme?"

"The animals are all being portrayed by gladiators or criminals," I tell him. "The nine-headed hydra is going to be one gladiator against nine criminals, and we're giving them real swords. Not that they've been trained," I add. "Paternus is having spectacular helmets commissioned for the event. Snakes, lion, boar, stag... the drawings look beautiful. The armourers are working on them already. And it crosses over nicely with our theme at the Flavian Amphitheatre. We've got Hercules trying to steal the Minoan Bull, the father of the Minotaur, as well as Hercules and Theseus fighting the Amazons, so we'll repeat a section of that show here. And if today's programme goes well, we might show it off again during the season."

The amphitheatre that holds the Great School's training ground is impressive. Seating three thousand spectators, it would not disgrace a small town and right now the arena is noisy with the thunk thunk thunk of wooden training swords hitting each other or stumps of wood. Here the audience is markedly different, fewer she-wolves are prowling, most of the seats are taken by die-hard fans who are earnestly watching as their favoured gladiators practise their moves, muttering to one another about technique or past glories. The most ardent supporters have already made it their habit to stop off on their way to or from the baths to watch their favourites. The street food and wine vendors have added the venue to their regular trade, wandering up and down the seating offering everything from cheese buns and pickles to dried figs stuffed with a honey-nut paste and cups of hot spiced wine on colder days. Paternus takes a cut of their profits and everyone's happy.

Also evident are the bookies, who are taking notes, jotting down in inscrutable shorthand their views on the form of each gladiator and adding odd symbols of their own invention: are they getting a bit old for this game? Are they hungry enough for the win? How are they looking physically? A good gladiator needs muscles, yes, but also, preferably, a bit of fat here and there, which will protect them from the lighter cuts they receive and make the heavier wounds easier to bear. A younger gladiator will have better speed, probably less fat on them, but also less cunning. They do not have years of knowledge on their side. A gladiator who has won many battles over the years may have put on a bit of weight, may be less fleet of foot, but they also know every trick possible in a bout. They can see a younger man's ideas before he even enacts them, dodge blows that would have landed on someone less experienced. They can afford to wear out a younger, hungrier competitor, before delivering a blow that might well prove fatal in the arena. The older men also know how to put on a show. Most of their movements are larger than they need to be, the sword arcs wider so that they can be seen from the back of a sixty-thousand-seater amphitheatre like our own. When a retiarius, a 'fisherman' gladiator, catches his opponent in his net, he does not hesitate to show off his capture, forcing the secutor or 'fish' gladiator to his knees to humiliate him further, so that the crowd has time to applaud and jeer.

A small group of new recruits have been gathered together and now they are led into the arena. They will take their oath as gladiators in public, adding a bit of showmanship to the moment. The fans lean forward, casting their judgement on the newcomers. They would like to say that they were here the day a future star was sworn into the gladiatorial life.

They repeat the time-honoured words, their voices, a mix of accents from across the Empire and tones, from bravado masking as confidence to resentment and terror. "I will endure to be burned, to be bound, to be beaten, and to be killed by the sword."

Marcus and Paternus appear at my side, Marcus looking weary. "Domitian's sending me notes again about the Games."

"For the battle with the Amazons?"

Marcus rolls his eyes. "Yes. He sent a note to ensure they would definitely be bare-breasted. I'm not running a brothel."

Paternus chuckles. "Labeo wouldn't care. I'm pretty sure he pimps them out willingly, don't you?"

"Certainly. Good money in it," says Labeo.

Marcus shakes his head. "That's your business. How many are fighting in the Amazons' battle, Althea?"

"Two hundred for the biggest scene. About one hundred and fifty proper gladiatrices who will take part in the fight. The other fifty, some of them are dancers, some of them will ride in the chariots. They won't fight but they add to the numbers, make it look more impressive during the fight. We've colour-coordinated their outfits, anyone in blue isn't actually fighting, the men won't engage with them. Everyone else is fair game. Twenty criminals marked out with a red dot on their foreheads, they've got blunt weapons, they're for killing."

"Who's playing Queen Hippolyta?"

"Billica."

Marcus shakes his head. "Don't know her."

Paternus gestures at the barracks. "She's a Briton. A mad crazed bitch. Kills anyone you put in front of her. Won't take orders. We're going to have to put in a group of male criminals so she has someone to kill. But she's sensational in the arena. She's tall too, she'll look even taller if you put her in a chariot." He nods to Labeo, one trainer to another. "I had your Fabia and Alyssa come and look her over to see if she needed training in anything."

Labeo snorts. "They said she was terrifying. Spat at them and tried to bite Fabia. Didn't dare unchain her. You have to sort out her hair though. That mousey colour isn't impressive. If you've got an advertised Briton as your lead gladiatrix people will expect blonde or red, and red's more impressive."

Paternus raises his eyebrows. "What would you do with it?"

"Dye it red and add some extra hairpieces."

"She'll bite anyone who tries that."

Labeo shrugs. "Keep her chained while you do it."

"Why's she so wild?" I ask. It may be common for gladiators to kick up a fuss at first, but they usually get punished for bad behaviour and learn not to resist their fate.

"They slaughtered her whole village, as I heard it," says Paternus. "She hid and came out fighting, killed three Romans in full armour before they caught her. Hardly ever talks, but I've got another Briton and he says she just wants to kill Romans. Which she does, very ably. But keep her away from your prize fighters, because she's a savage."

Marcus frowns. "She wouldn't have a chance against Carpophorus or any of your best gladiators."

"You say that, but they listen to the referee and also, they'd rather not die. She doesn't care if she lives or dies. Makes you fearsome in the arena, if you don't care about living."

THE LABYRINTH

I T'S EARLY MARCH, ONLY A couple of weeks to go till the opening Games of the season, when Rome will watch the creation of a monster and the birth of a hero. Everything should be ready, but I am anxious and sometimes I have to force myself to leave the amphitheatre rather than staying later and later. I retreat to the rooftop of the insula with Karbo, carrying bread, cheese, olives and fruit, and enjoy the delicate return of spring warmth.

The roof terrace is changing. It was bare when the builders finished last year, save for the two rooftop huts, one belonging to Marcus, one to Karbo and me, which were then joined by Adah's beehives. Now it is a garden.

I started with the lower half of a broken amphora, filling it with earth and planted seeds in it, offered by Julia, who has an abundant supply from her many years of gardening. They grew well and now I have pale yellow primroses to welcome the returning sun. Karbo spent time poking at them, before asking to grow other things. Between us we made a rough structure from old planks of wood, taken from the offcuts as they replaced the arena floor at the amphitheatre. It is raised up off the rooftop like a bed on little legs, filled with earth, most of it carried bucket by bucket back from the loose soil on the riverbanks of the Tiber. Karbo found an old bucket with a hole in it and a cracked cooking pot Cassia was going to throw away. He is using them as tubs for peas, finding the odd branch to stick in the pots for them to twine up and poking the little shrivelled green seeds down into the ground. I doubt I will actually get to eat any of the peas when they are grown, for Karbo is very fond of them.

Our main vegetable bed contains broad beans sown last autumn and their strong shoots are already reaching up for sunlight. We should be able to harvest the beans in early May. They are considered a delicacy, eaten fresh from the pod with strong salty sheep's cheese.

I close my eyes to enjoy the last rays of sunshine. The beans are Ripe and I invite Marcus to eat with us. We sit in the golden May sun and eat fresh beans and cheese, with warm bread from the bakery and good wine. Karbo eats with us and then wanders away to play with Letitia.

Marcus makes a joke about Karbo and me evidently being born to be farmers, if we can grow such good crops even here, on a rooftop in Rome.

I ask about the farm, just lightly, wonder out loud whether he still intends to return there one day, and Marcus' voice changes, it becomes husky as it does when he feels something strongly and he turns his face away and mutters something. I have to ask what he said and he turns his eyes on me, his direct gaze making heat rise up my neck and he says that he will only return there if he can take me with him, as his wife… and I…

"Your farm is coming along well," says Marcus.

I open my eyes to find him standing over me, smiling.

"I – I didn't hear you coming up the stairs," I say, flustered by his sudden appearance and blinded by the low sun's fading rays. I stumble to my feet, awkwardly resting one hand in the soft earth of the bed and then having to brush the earth off my hands.

"I want a fruit tree," Karbo announces. "Can we grow one? And a vine for grapes?"

Marcus laughs. "A fruit tree might break through the roof into the rooms below," he says. "But perhaps a vine. It'll be a long time till it's too heavy for the roof and then it can be moved elsewhere. You should grow the strawberry grapes from my family's farm, they were delicious."

"Do you still intend to go back there one day?" I ask, clutching at the remnants of my daydream, trying to make the moment that I was lingering over happen in real life.

Marcus shrugs. "Who knows," he says, with little emotion. "I can barely think through the next two weeks. Ask me again some other time, when this season is properly underway. For now all I can imagine is some catastrophe on the opening day. And all I can hear is scraping from the tunnel digging or hammering from the arena floor finally going back into place. My whole future comes down to a matter of days, not years ahead. Have you eaten? I'm famished."

I mutter that we have already eaten. He pats Karbo's shoulder and strides away, clattering down the staircase towards Cassia's and a hot meal.

"A vine!" says Karbo. "He said we could grow a vine."

I try to show enthusiasm for Karbo's gardening plans, which moments ago had been a pathway for my desire and are now nothing but mud and fading light.

The road sweepers have either grown lazy or have deliberately allowed straw and dung to build up in the immediate vicinity to the amphitheatre, perhaps paid to 'forget' by those who are still angry about the buildings that have been torn down to make way for Domitian's vision. I send out a team of our own cleaners to sweep up, while making a comment to one of the official sweepers, currently leaning on his broom, about how I'll be meeting with Domitian personally very soon and how very particular he is about cleanliness. I've no idea if that's true but note to my satisfaction that the official sweeper is taking his role more seriously the next day.

Interspersed throughout our ongoing story of Theseus and his many adventures, we will also be weaving in the story of Ariadne. Princess of Crete, daughter of Minos, sister to the doomed Minotaur, she will help our hero Theseus escape, having fallen in love with him. For this role we've chosen a dancer who goes by the show name of Luna, famous throughout Rome as a performer at the best private villas, a rarefied she-wolf available for more intimate encounters, if the (very high) price is right. She has black hair that falls well below her knees, possibly with the assistance of bought hair from previously shorn slaves. She is not very tall, but she moves like a snake, leaving onlookers wondering whether she actually possesses bones in her spine, so far backwards can she bend her body when dancing. Her costume for this season is a magnificently painted and decorated dress in the Minoan style, with long skirt ruffles and an entirely open chest, so that her bare breasts are on display, nipples outlined in gold. Despite her reputation for being hired by the most noble men in Rome, her mouth is a latrine, not sweetened in any way by the fragrant mastic resin she constantly chews.

"It's all about moving your arse," she says matter-of-factly when our resident choreographer tries to alter her dance routine.

Our choreographer prides himself on his classical knowledge, even if he does spend most of his year creating routines that will be shown in the amphitheatre as light-hearted breaks from the more bloody elements of the Games. "Ariadne was said to have a dancing floor made for her by Daedalus himself, designed to mimic the shape of the labyrinth he created to imprison her ill-fated monstrous brother," he points out loftily. "It's described in the *Iliad*. The steps you take are supposed to be reminiscent of a maze. You see?" he adds, demonstrating a few twisting turning steps of the dance he's attempting to teach the troupe of dancing girls. "It's said to have been depicted on Achilles' shield."

Luna rolls her eyes. "If you say so," she says, still chewing. "But if you don't move your arse and jiggle your tits a bit, the men get bored. And a bored man is a limp man. And you don't want them. They don't pay well. You got to get them a bit *interested*, that way, when you've finished all this dancing nonsense for the day, there'll be a nice evening invitation to one of the villas up on the hill waiting for you, won't there?" She winks, lasciviously. "I'm sure the girls know what I mean."

The other dancers nod. Dancing for the Games is only a side-line. The real money comes from wealthy men, who might spot you and be persuaded to give generous gifts as well as the money they owe for services rendered.

The exasperated choreographer turns to me for support.

"Don't look at me," I say, hiding my laughter at their exchange. "I'm sure both of you know what you're doing, in your own ways. I'll leave you to come up with a compromise."

A voice calls out. "I'm looking for Marcus Aquillius Scaurus?"

I turn and immediately bow my head at the sight of a senator standing behind me, surrounded by not only assistants and scribes, but also bodyguards. "Aedile. We weren't told to expect you."

The Aedile looks flustered, as usual. Despite officially being the senator in charge of all the imperial Games, and therefore the Flavian Amphitheatre itself, he is not a naturally commanding man. He gestures vaguely in the air and an assistant presses a scroll into his hand. "Yes, yes, didn't know myself… ah, well it appears the Emperor likes all administrative matters to be carried out *very* correctly, so it has come, ah, let us say, ah, *forcefully,* to my attention that in fact Scaurus' contract as manager of this amphitheatre ought to be renewed, it is too vaguely stated in the first one he signed, you see, ah, er, where is it? Ah yes, here." He indicates a section of the scroll. "You see, it states that Scaurus is appointed as manager 'up to the inauguration of the amphitheatre and for one hundred days of Games afterwards,' during which time he may neither resign nor leave Rome. But of course that was… some time ago and ah, the Emperor is, ah, displeased that our contracts are not up to date. He wishes Scaurus to agree to another season, after this one is complete." He hesitates. "In actual fact, he, ah, would prefer to agree on several years of service, being, ah, not *fond* of changes in personnel related to important administration. But in the meantime, we must definitely ascertain that Scaurus will be continuing as the manager here for the remainder of this season, and all of next season as well. Where is he?"

I hesitate, but there's no stalling the Aedile, no way of escaping this meeting. "I'll send Karbo to fetch him, Aedile." I gesture to Karbo, who bounds away.

I try to make polite conversation, although my head is whirling. I had completely forgotten Marcus' original contract and that it only bound him for the first hundred days. He is free! He could leave at any time and no-one could force him to stay. For one wild moment I imagine him leaving right away, but try to calm myself. The season will have to be completed. "You must be looking forward to the season?" I ask, growing aware that I should fill the awkward silence.

"Oh, er, yes, yes of course," agrees the Aedile vaguely, leaving me with the distinct impression that he has absolutely no interest in the Games and barely frequents them. Certainly I never saw him much after the opening day last year, until the closing event. He always strikes me as more of a scholarly man, someone who would be happier in some dusty study somewhere, reading the ancient poets and making notes to himself. How he ever got chosen as Aedile for the Games is beyond me.

Marcus is striding towards us. I want to intercept him. I should have gone to fetch him myself, how stupid. If I had found him alone, I could have explained what the Aedile was here for and suggested that he at least ask for time to consider what he wants to do. I might even, given the circumstances, have had the courage to remind him of his desire to return to the family farm, encouraged him to make this his last season. Of course, there is a risk that he would simply leave and go to his farm without me, but if nothing else he is my legal protector, and Karbo's too, I would have more time to persuade him…

"Aedile."

"Ah, Scaurus, good to see you again, you are, ah, well? Confident with the season's plans?"

"Yes," says Marcus. "It's going to be spectacular. Bigger and better than ever. It's taking up every moment of our working day. Was there something you needed to discuss?"

I watch, anxious, as the Aedile re-explains the matter of the out-of-date contract to Marcus. I hope to see a flicker of reluctance, even think he might outright refuse. He might state that this is his final season, that he wishes to return to the family farm and that as such he cannot agree to further service. But his face stays serene.

"Of course," he says.

A weight sinks in my stomach. How many more years does Marcus intend to run the Games? He said, when I first met him, that one season was enough, that he would inaugurate the empire's greatest amphitheatre and run its first one hundred days of Games, as contracted, then he would retire, buy back the family farm and live there, content as a farmer. He delayed only because he lost Livia and Amantius, and even in the depths of grief, he suggested it would be only for one more year. Is this what will happen? He will go on and on, one season of Games rolling into another, the farm slowly rotting away? Will I be stuck in this world too, unable to leave because I want to be close to him, but unable to live the kind of life I would really like because he will not leave the Games? Will he remain oblivious to what else he could be doing with his life, oblivious to me? Perhaps he thinks I will always be here too, but I am growing tired of the Games, beginning to hope for something else in my life. I watch, my face carefully blank, as he presses his seal onto the soft wax of the new contract, signs his name. He is bound, not just to this season, but to the next as well; that small piece of papyrus is a year and a half of commitment, of choice taken away. I bow my head as the Aedile departs, but cannot bring myself to say goodbye, my throat feels constricted. If Marcus is bound here, am I bound too? Or must I break the bond between us in order to be free of this place? If I were to leave this job, would I lose Marcus too? The thought makes my stomach turn over. Clearly Marcus does not feel the need to leave this role, nor has it occurred to him how I might be feeling, he has barely glanced at me during all of the conversation, has not even silently raised his eyebrows to ask, *Will you be here too, are you committing to this too?* My shoulders slump as a wave of weariness washes over me.

"At least that's out of the way," says Marcus, as the Aedile and his entourage wander out of view. "Can get back to what I was doing. Why do these people never ask for an appointment?" He turns away, about to leap down the final tier of seating and make his way down the steps back to the hypogeum.

"Are you happy doing another year after this one?" I ask, the words coming slowly, sullenly, out of my mouth.

He turns back, surprised. "We need that contract to keep the team safely employed with us," he says. "There's over a thousand of us reliant on this amphitheatre. Those who are paid need to know they'll keep being paid, and the slaves we've been loaned from the imperial household probably get better treatment from us than they could expect elsewhere, thanks to your work on their barracks and food," he adds with a smile. "So I doubt they want any changes to personnel."

I nod.

"Did you need something?"

"No," I say.

"Right, back to it," he says cheerfully. "At least we can sleep easy knowing we all have jobs for the foreseeable future. You never know when you get a new emperor. I was worried he might not renew the contract, but apparently he likes what we're doing enough to keep us for now. So you can spread the good word to the team."

And he's gone, leaping three seats at a time and disappearing down into the gloom of the hypogeum.

I do what I have to do, one task after another, but a weight is pressing down on me. He didn't ask me if I was happy staying. He didn't even *think* to ask. He assumed that I would want to carry on here. He never mentioned his own retirement, not even as a far-off possibility.

"IDIOT," SAYS CASSIA THAT EVENING after hearing my mournful account. "Want one of us to have a word with him?"

I gulp more wine than I'd usually take, draining the cup. "What's the point?" I ask. "It didn't even occur to him."

Fabia tickles Emilia under the chin and the baby giggles, trying to keep her balance and failing, rolling over onto her blanket on the floor with a surprised air, unsure how she got there. "Perhaps he was thinking of keeping everyone around him safe, rather than his own desires," she says.

"Yes, exactly," I say. "That's what he said, more or less."

"Well, that's what a good man would do, isn't it?"

I sigh. "I *know* he's a good man. I don't need another season of the Games to prove that to me. I want to leave."

"Leave," says Fabia.

"With him."

"Then speak to him."

"Can't find the words," I say, a miserable groan escaping my lips. "Why is it all so hard?" I demand.

"Because you're making it harder by not telling him how you feel."

"He didn't hesitate! Nothing! He just said, oh yes, no problem, here's my seal, good to have seen you, Aedile!"

"Perhaps he doesn't want to leave till he's sure *you* want *him*," says Cassia, wiping the countertop.

"Very funny. He's shown no interest in me that way at all."

THE LAST PIECE OF WORK the builders do, at my request, is to set small plaques into the walls, which create a complex numbering system identifying every pen, trapdoor, passageway and lift. Larger areas, such as Fabius' medical area and the spoliatorium where the armour is stripped off, are named rather than numbered. I add the numbering to our diagrams and encourage the team to familiarise themselves with it. We need to be able to refer to lift twenty-two and have people use the correct lift, or say that pen six contains lions that need to be sent into the caged lift numbered three and know they will not end up in the wrong place, perhaps loaded in with gladiators who are not expecting them. Not being able to see each lift at a glance means we are more reliant on planning every show's exact sequence in advance and sticking to those plans, to avoid any errors. I spend time each evening studying the plans, trying to commit the layout of each floor to memory. When I close my eyes all I can see are endless corridors, animal pens, lifts and labelled drawings.

"THE WORK'S DONE," ANNOUNCES THE head builder to Marcus a week later. "I'll need you to sign it all off, agree that we've completed the works as requested, to the proper standard and that you are satisfied, on behalf of the amphitheatre, as its manager."

Marcus never wanted the works, but he has nothing much to say about how they've been completed. The building has been done at speed, to a good standard, and has even weathered an earthquake along the way, proof of its quality. He makes a show of walking through the whole of each floor, checking that the work matches the diagrams sent by Rabirius at the start of the works, checks that every one of our twenty-eight lifts rises and falls smoothly, that the thirty-six trapdoors of the arena floor can open and close, unimpeded by any of the new brickwork. It takes most of the morning. Finally, he affixes his seal to the scroll proffered by the head builder, stating that the works have been approved.

There are handshakes and farewells as the head builder and his apprentice leave. Marcus and I are left standing alone in an empty corridor, next to one of the lift shafts. We are silent for a few moments.

"I don't like the feel of it," I say. It feels like a stupid thing to say, given there's nothing here that wasn't here before: the morgue, the lifts, the physician's area, the gladiators' entrance and the undertakers' exit, but before it was one wide empty space with a high ceiling, which even when full you could see across it, through the jumbled but organised chaos of equipment, performers and our own staff. Now the ceilings feel very close and you can't see anything except the area you're in, can only hear noises from other parts. I find it hard to breathe here.

Marcus chews his lip. "Enough to make you want to leave, isn't it?"

I can't believe what I'm hearing. "What?"

He clears his throat. "Sometimes I think it might be time to pack it all in."

"Leave the amphitheatre? Go back to your family farm?"

He shrugs. "Maybe."

Is this it? Is this the conversation I have been dreaming of? Is it my moment to speak, to encourage Marcus towards making some kind of declaration?

"When?" Too blunt, too awkward, too much to ask.

He looks away. "Oh, who knows? I've signed that contract…" He clears his throat again. "Anyway, I can still hear the noise that lift's making upstairs, it's irritating. Someone needs to oil it. I'll go and sort it out."

He's striding away before I've opened my mouth again and so I stand watching him walk down the tight corridor, before he takes a sudden right and disappears from view.

IT'S DAWN AND MARCUS SETS off to visit Paternus, to spend a morning finalising which gladiators will be used on which days to ensure an even spread of skills and experience, styles of combat and levels of fame.

I head to the amphitheatre. I need to familiarise myself with its final form. I know every part of it above ground, the high-ceilinged corridors of the larger floors and the endless entrances of the ground floor, the darker narrow top tier corridor, seen only by slaves and women. I know the seating tiers, have sat in all of them, including the Emperor's own imperial box, to understand what can be seen from each space. And until last year the hypogeum was only an empty area under the arena floor, barely worthy of the name but fully my domain. But now it is a wholly different place. Two storeys where there was only one, intricate passages where before there was only one wide-open space. I must make it my own even though I dislike it. I must grow to know it intimately, because once it is put into full use it will only grow more complex. There will be noise, there will be doors and cages that must be kept securely locked or lead to certain danger, even death. There will be our numbering system, which I believe I have learnt but still worry about in anxious dreams where I call out a number and a lion leaps out from what should have been a safely closed cage, or I hear a number followed by laughter and ridicule from the crowds when they should be gasping in awe, because dancing girls have appeared rather than wild beasts. So today, in the quiet before we begin the season, I have decided that I will walk the hypogeum alone and make my peace with it.

I make my way through the Forum, which is slowly coming to life, and enter the amphitheatre with confidence, lighting a large lamp with brisk fingers before I descend into the hypogeum's lower floor.

But down here, all alone, the darkness unsettles me. The lamp has five wicks, it is plenty bright enough, yet I hesitate before I set off down the central passageway of the lower floor. I look left and right at each junction, noting the numbers are indeed as I recall them.

"Sixteen." A whisper, echoing in the dark passageway.

I freeze at the junction labelled twelve. Sixteen is another four plaques away, it is in full darkness, I would have to take more than twelve paces to be closer to it.

"Fifteen."

I can't move. The lamp shakes in my hand. I could raise it above my waist level, could hold it up and beyond me, at arm's length and I would see further, might see who is ahead of me, who is down here in the dark with me, but I don't dare. I take a step back, try to steady my breath. I daren't even ask who is there. There's a light ahead, but it's tiny, like a glimpse of sunlight from a crack in the floorboards of the arena, but that is a whole floor above us. It has to be a lamp, but if it is the person should be so much further away from me… I am growing even more frightened in my confusion

"Fourteen."

I don't recognise the voice that whispers the question, other than it sounds like a man. They are moving towards me but I cannot yet make them out, although shadows are shifting now, I can see the shape of a person, but only when they move. Fourteen? My mind is whirring. If that is what they can see they are… walking backwards? Towards me?

I am bone-cold with fear from trying to work out too many things at once. I want to turn and run back up the passageway, back towards the stairs which will take me out of here, but I am afraid that if I do the unseen person, the man, will follow, that I will hear footsteps running behind mine and they will come closer and closer and –

I take one step back and another, trying not to make a sound, open my mouth so that I will breathe more quietly and bring my lamp down lower towards me so I can try and see their light better.

"The morgue?"

I let out a gasp of fear and the person turns, their lamp held up high.

"Who's there? Answer now!" There is no trace of the soft sibilant whisper, it is a loud command. The raised lamp illuminates a tall man with a longish face, bright eyes fixed on me. Domitian? It cannot be. Domitian?

"Speak your name!"

"I – Althea."

"Althea who?" He comes closer. I am face to face with the emperor of Rome. Domitian. His eyes are wide, perhaps he is even frightened himself. "The scribe. What are you doing here?"

I'm amazed he's remembered who I am, he never gave any previous trace of interest in me or my role here.

"Inspecting the hypogeum, Imperator."

I try to step back and bow my head and in my confusion, I stumble, clutch at the bare brick wall to try and stop myself, mindful of the lamp in the other hand, and find myself falling on my backside, a sudden and humiliating bump to the cold floor. I scrabble back to my feet, where Domitian is standing, watching me like an odd performance, something gone confusingly wrong. He makes no move to help me as most people would when someone falls in front of them, only raises his own lamp to inspect me more closely.

"Your hand is bleeding," he remarks, as though commenting on the weather.

I look down. He's right. I have scraped my hand and it is bleeding, though not badly. It stings, though. "It's nothing, Imperator."

He doesn't reply, but looks expectant. "You may continue," he says after a long pause, irritated.

"Continue?"

"With whatever you were doing," he says. "You were inspecting the area?"

"Yes," I say.

"Proceed. I will go on with my own work. You will not be in my way," he adds as a sort of gracious afterthought.

"Your work, Imperator?"

"My own inspection of the building works." He looks at the nearest plaque. "I like the numbering system, it is very orderly. Did you invent it?"

"Yes, Imperator."

He nods, satisfied.

I don't know what to say. "Should I… attend you?" I stammer at last.

"No," he says. "Continue your work."

There is an awkward moment when I have to pass by him in the tight corridor, twisting myself to avoid any contact, but he simply pushes past me and continues down the passageway, whispering again to himself as he moves away from me, his voice echoing through the darkness. "Ten. Nine. Eight."

I stumble down the corridor and take the first turning to my right, finding myself inside the room where the animals will be butchered after the games. I lean against the cold rough wall, my whole body shaking with shock at the encounter. After a few moments, I quiet my ragged breathing, then make my way through the side passages towards the Gate of Death. I do not wish to be in the hypogeum alone with Domitian wandering around. His behaviour leaves me unsettled every time I am near him, wondering whether he is about to praise me or grow impatient. And after last year being alone in the dark with a man I do not know well is frightening in and of itself.

The key for the Gate of Death is in a tiny antechamber at the far end of the hypogeum. I make my way there as much by touch and memory as my lamp, which I hold very low. I change the lamp into my left hand, reach tentatively up the wall, rubbing my hand across its rough texture till I touch the cold metal of the hanging key, and lift it down. Strabo likes to joke darkly that he doesn't need Charon's hammer, this key alone could finish off a fallen gladiator. He's probably right, it is twice as long as my hand and very heavy, with Cerberus, the three-headed dog that guards the underworld moulded into the bronze of one end while its three prongs at the other end are as thick as my fingers.

I follow the last part of the corridor, make my way up one flight of stairs, still listening for Domitian, but I can't hear him, which makes me more nervous. The crack of light ahead of me at the end of the second flight of stairs is a welcome relief, and I push hard on the door leading to the arena, make my way through it. I've never been so glad to see the cold light of dawn in my life, it feels like the full midday sun compared to the darkness below. I step further out, shove the heavy door behind me, make my way to the Gate and use the heavy key to unlock it for the day before hanging it back up on its hook. I heave on the low-set handle to open the Gate and slip out into the welcome hustle of the day. It may be cold but there's life and noise around me, street sweepers, carts making their way out of the city having made their deliveries, and guards... the Praetorian Guards who should have been with the Emperor, a small cluster of them. They are not in their formal uniform, rather in togas, clothing designed to let them slip unnoticed through crowds, looking out for troublemakers and protecting the Emperor from them. Domitian must have told them to wait here and make themselves unnoticeable. Despite being half-hidden by the Colossus Sol statue, they still look highly conspicuous, even from here I can see their gladius sword hilts poking out of their togas and their short military haircuts, but knowing that the Emperor is all alone inside the amphitheatre is making them nervous; they don't want to be blamed should any harm come to him.

"You!" bellows one of them, not doing a very good job of being discreet. "Come here!"

I indicate myself, eyebrows raised.

"Yes, you, you stupid girl! Come here."

I make my way over. There's twelve of them, trying to maintain their usual intimidating presence while hiding at the base of the statue. The absurdity doesn't make me want to laugh though, it only makes me more anxious. I wish Marcus were here.

"Were you inside the amphitheatre?"

It's not something I'm able to deny, seeing as they've watched me emerge from there. "Yes."

"Doing what?"

"Inspecting the new hypogeum," I say.

The Praetorian Guard looks uncomfortable asking this next question, it makes him look like he isn't doing his job very well. "Have you... did you see the Emperor?"

"Yes," I say.

"What was he doing?"

"Inspecting the hypogeum."

The Guard looks me up and down, evidently beginning to suspect that something else was going on... an assignation? But surely not. I'm clearly a nobody, not showy enough to be a she-wolf, only slightly too well-dressed to be a slave girl. But a nobody, nonetheless. If the Emperor wanted me in his bed, he would have sent for me and I'd have had no choice in the matter, would have presented myself at his villa to be done with as he pleased. He wouldn't have come creeping round the Flavian Amphitheatre at dawn to meet with me in secret. The Guard's trying to formulate a question that will clear all of this up, but he can't think of one.

"Has – has he finished?" he says at last.

"I don't know," I say truthfully and my own confusion must shine through because the Guard blinks once or twice, shrugs and finally makes a vague gesture of dismissal which has me all but running back to the insula.

Marcus stares at me when I relate what happened later that day. "All on his own? Not with Rabirius or the chief builder?"

"All alone."

Marcus shakes his head. "I don't understand him. He's too strange for my liking. I worry we'll see a darker side to him one day."

"He frightened me," I confess. "I didn't know who was down there with me and I –"

Marcus puts an arm around my shoulder at once. "I'm sorry," he says. "You shouldn't be there alone in future. I would never forgive myself if something happened to you."

Held against his chest, I breathe in his words and the scent of him, the warmth of this embrace. I lift my other arm to hold him closer, but he has let go of me, is already moving away.

"The opening Games are one week away and we're behind. Three of the lifts aren't operating smoothly, we'll have to make adjustments to their mechanisms and half the scenery and props are still down at the warehouses. I don't fancy getting any of it down those stupid corridors, but we don't have a choice. Draw up a plan for the shifts the slaves will be working, Althea, we may have to do later hours than usual, maybe even work into the nights. The gods only know how much lamp oil we're going to burn through in the hypogeum just to keep it well-lit enough to see what we're doing."

And he's gone, striding out of the courtyard. I raise one arm and smell it, his scent on my skin, drop it with a sigh. I never think fast enough, move fast enough, to hold him to me, to speak the words that would make him understand my feelings. Because you're too afraid, I berate myself silently. Because you think he will not feel the same way. "Coward," I mutter.

A voice comes from above. "I thought that's how it was with you."

I startle. Maria is in her usual watching place above me, but I'm so used to her I hadn't even noticed her presence. "I'm a coward," I say, face tilted up to her, helplessly honest in the face of her certainty. "I don't think I'll ever find a way to tell him."

"You didn't used to mind telling him things to his face, as I recall," she says.

She's thinking of the day, years ago, when I turned on Marcus, screamed truths into his face that were honest but also too cruel, borne of fear, my own and the team's need to survive. "I was desperate."

She lets out a chuckle. "Perhaps you'll get desperate enough again."

I shake my head. "I imagine it when I'm alone and it's always easy. When he's in front of me, it isn't."

"One day you'll find the words. Venus will guide you."

I let out a deep sigh. It feels about the right weight for what I'm holding inside me, day after day. "If you say so."

"Are you questioning what a goddess can achieve?"

"I'm sure Venus could find the words," I say. "But I don't think I can."

"Venus cannot resist a lovestruck mortal," says Maria, making herself more comfortable on her balcony cushion. "She will seek you out one day when you least expect it and lend you her voice."

"I hope so," I say. "I can't do it by myself, that I do know."

"Do what?" asks Karbo, appearing through the gateway after a morning at the stables.

"Lunch," I say. "Are you coming with me?"

We leave the courtyard and make our way to Cassia's popina. We usually eat breakfast and dinner there, managing with bread and cheese for lunch, but I want to stay in the light, to see Cassia's friendly face and keep Karbo close to me.

"What you doing here?" she says by way of greeting. "Didn't I see you leave as I was pulling up the shutters?"

"Yes," I say. "But it was only a quick trip. I had to unlock the Gate of Death so deliveries can be made, that's all."

"Lunch?"

"Yes," Karbo and I say together.

By the time I've eaten, the trembling in me has died down. Domitian's behaviour is unusual, we've all realised that already, but so far he hasn't done anything worrying, other than appear when we're not expecting him. And he seems pleased with our work, or at any rate not displeased, which is all one can hope for with emperors. I spend some time playing with Emilia, and her chortles and embraces calm me further.

EMILIA MAY NOT HAVE BEEN formally adopted, but it's clear by now that she's here to stay. I make my way to Balbus' toyshop and spend some time looking at his beautiful collection of toys. Most are not priced for the likes of insula-dwellers, they are instead put into carefully arranged wooden trays and leather carrying-cases and taken, on command, to the fine villas of Rome, where wealthy matrons and fond senators will have them laid out for their young children to choose, price no object. Some pieces, such as large-scale wooden toy horses or wooden swords, exquisitely carved and jointed dolls dressed with care by Balbus' wife, are made on commission. Other smaller pieces are there to catch a child's eye, to make them beg their parents for a set of marbles or a painted board game, a little wooden cat or tiny pottery jug and plate for a beloved doll.

"They're lovely," I say. "I was looking for a rattle for Emilia. Something pretty."

He shows me carved wooden pieces, or painted gourds to be held with both hands, dried seeds shaking inside when moved.

"That one," I say, taking a fancy to a tiny bright orange gourd with little black figures painted on it, like a vase. The figures are cats, stretching, curled up, pouncing after mice. Karbo will like it too, he can shake it for Emilia as she is too small to hold it properly yet.

"A good choice," says Balbus. He charges me less than he should, waving aside my protests. "I shall have to retire soon," he confides. "My eyes aren't what they used to be, the smaller pieces are getting harder to make. One slip of a carving knife…"

"What will your clients do?"

"Ah, who knows? I am sure there are other toymakers who will take my place. I have no sons to pass the business onto. The shop will have to close."

I nod, pay for the little gourd, bid him farewell, then turn back at threshold as a thought strikes me. "Balbus, did you never take on an apprentice?"

"There was a lad many years back who showed an interest, but his father wouldn't have it. I had an apprentice before that, but he moved out of Rome to set up his own business in his wife's town."

I come back to the counter. "Would you take on an apprentice now?"

"I'm too old to teach a child," he says. "I wouldn't have the patience. Or the years left to me," he adds with a resigned shrug.

"I'm not thinking of a child," I say.

I catch Quintus the next morning at Cassia's popina.

"Put Emilia down," I say. "I need to take you to Balbus."

"Excuse me?" says Cassia, pouring wine with one hand, turning my pancake on the spitting griddle with the other. "Who's looking after this baby while I serve the customers?"

"You'll thank me for this one day," I tell her. Emilia starts to cry, but I ignore her and pull the bemused Quintus with me, making my way round the side of the building to where Balbus is pulling up the shutters of his shop. "Balbus, this is Quintus."

"The man who found the baby," says Balbus.

"He's more than that," I say. "He's the boy who wanted to be your apprentice. Quintus, show him that little horse you've been carving."

Quintus hesitates. His neck flushes, but he pulls out the tiny carved horse from a fold of his tunic and holds it out to Balbus with a hand that trembles slightly, betraying his feelings.

The two men talk, Quintus growing in confidence as he speaks, Balbus' gnarly fingers stroking the little horse, feeling without looking how Quintus has worked with the grain of the wood, not against it, turning little knots into the dappled hide of the animal. After a while I turn away, to let them talk more seriously and when eventually Quintus and I return to Cassia's popina, we are both beaming and not even Emilia's loud wails and Cassia's thunderous expression are enough to sober us.

"Are you even going to tell me where you've been?" she demands.

"I'll leave that to Quintus," I tell her.

When I next see Cassia, she stops serving customers and puts her hands on her hips.

"So you've set up Quintus as an apprentice for Balbus?"

I grin. "Yes. He'll have a room in their insula apartment, be apprenticed to Balbus for one year, then take over the shop. He can spend some of each day looking after Emilia while he does his carvings, like before. And in a year's time, he'll have his own business, right next door to yours. You can thank me later."

Cassia splutters. "What do I care what job he does? I only care whether someone is going to help out with the baby."

"And he will."

"Well…" She struggles to think of something to reprimand me for and instead gestures at her customers, who are watching, amused. "I'm very busy, Althea. I don't have time to chatter with you right now."

"You're most welcome," I say, making her a mock bow.

BLOOD ON SAND

We crawl home the night before the opening Games, three burly slaves accompanying us to the insula with burning torches to ensure our safety. The hypogeum still smells damp from the fresh brickwork. But everything is laid out correctly, or at least I keep telling myself so, running through lists in my head even as we trudge home in the dark. Animals grunt and roar in their cages, the arena's sand has been scattered, the lifts have been tested and oiled, the dancers' costumes hang in multicoloured rows, the armour and elaborate helmets have been sent to each gladiatorial school. Tomorrow Domitian will arrive to an amphitheatre filled to bursting capacity.

Cassia has left a covered pot filled with vegetable porridge and a loaf of bread on the doorstep of my hut, the porridge is lukewarm but we are grateful for it. Marcus, Karbo and I sit around the pot with spoons, eating in exhausted silence by the light of a small lamp. Letitia mews and licks up the scraps she is offered, but mostly she wants stroking, although even Karbo is not willing to play. Instead he curls up on his bed with her and they fall asleep together almost at once, I can hear little snores from him.

"Sleep well," says Marcus when the pot is empty and we have sat in weary silence for a few moments, too tired to get up and go to our beds.

"I'm not sure I'll sleep at all," I say.

"Everything is ready," he says. He stands, rubs his lower back, offers a hand to lift me to my feet. I take it, feel the warmth of him, the firm strong pull he offers, but even though I would willingly stumble into his arms if he offered, right now I am so tired I don't even feel the rush of desire at his touch that has welled up in these past months.

"It will all go well," Marcus says.

I nod, because there's no point admitting I'm nervous, we both are. I make my way into my hut and lie down on the bed, try to match my breathing to Karbo's, reach out a hand to stroke Letitia's warm fur in the hopes her calm will soothe me.

My dreams are a confused whirling, where naked dancers stumble out of malfunctioning lifts and dangerous animals escape, rushing past me into the imperial box, to the horror of Domitian and his guests.

I wake in darkness, but when I come out of my hut a tiny glimpse of pale sky on the edge of the horizon at the other end of Rome tells me it will soon be dawn and I couldn't sleep if I tried. I wash, shivering at the cold water, then dress. When I finally wake Karbo and we stumble downstairs, Marcus is ahead of us, irritably massaging his neck and carrying his toga.

"I've got a crick in my neck," he complains, "and I'll have to put this stupid thing on in case Domitian wants to see me. Karbo, you'll have to help me. Not now, when we get there."

"Let's have breakfast," I say. "There's really no point being even earlier than we have to be. Everything is arranged."

"Is it?"

"Yes," I say, as confidently as I dare. When he is anxious, Marcus barely eats, while Karbo and I get some comfort and confidence from having a meal inside us. "You need food. So do I. We're not going to get any lunch today, are we?"

"No," agrees Marcus. "Come on."

Cassia is opening the shutters, but she knows what day it is today and already has the fire going. "I made you something heartier than pancakes and bread," she says. "Eat this."

She's made a thick barley porridge and filled it with dried dates, figs and nuts. Marcus wrinkles his nose at a sweet breakfast, but eats it nonetheless. The heat and sweetness is filling and warming and Cassia gives each of us a hot spiced wine to go with it. It's more of a winter drink, but in this cold dawn and with a long day ahead, we're grateful. Marcus twists his neck from one side to the other, trying to loosen up the muscles.

"Someone should massage your neck for you," says Cassia, looking meaningfully at me.

"Can't get to the baths today," says Marcus. "Though that's where I'll be spending most of tomorrow, I'll tell you that right now."

"Massage his neck, Althea," says Cassia more firmly, seeing that her hint has not been sufficient to get the result she was hoping for. "You can't spend a day in agony, Marcus."

My cheeks grow hot, but I move over to stand behind Marcus, place my hands gently on his neck and shoulders. "Where – where does it hurt?" I ask, afraid to move my hands now that they are in contact with his skin, warm beneath my cold fingertips.

He reaches up and takes my right hand, moves it higher up his neck. "There," he says.

I use my left hand to support his head while I massage his neck. His muscles are hard, knotted up.

"Aaargh."

"I'm sorry," I say at once, stopping.

"No, no, it was a good pain," he says, grimacing. "Carry on. It was helping."

More confident now, I continue, enjoying the chance to touch him without him seeing my face, stroking and pressing his neck and shoulders. I make sure not to catch Cassia's eye, who is smirking mischievously at me.

"Right. No more putting it off," says Marcus, tipping back the last swallow of his wine. "Thank you, Althea. At least I won't be hunchbacked today."

He's already walking away. Karbo trotting after him.

Cassia winks. "It's easy to find an excuse to touch a man if you're looking for one," she says. "If you're going to try and arrange my love life," she adds, "I shall arrange yours."

"Shush," I hiss back, but I can't help a grin as I walk after Marcus and Karbo.

THE AMPHITHEATRE LOOMS ABOVE US in the pale light. Slaves are already positioned around the entrances, some busy setting up the rope walkways that will control and guide the crowds as they approach us, others standing in each entranceway to deter any would-be spectators who have not been issued with a token to the first Games of the season, a prestigious day when only the best people in Rome get seats for our opening spectacle. Even we, the team, must show the small, red-painted tokens that Marcus devised to indicate staff. Stallholders are getting ready, the opening day of the Games is a busy day for merchandise.

We make a tour of the hypogeum, ticking things off interminable lists, Karbo carrying a whole bucket of scrolls as he trails behind me and I tell him what I need to check next. Scrolls detailing animals, timings, gladiators and their bouts with matching referees, dancers, singers, extra sand for the arena floor and when it needs to be laid. On and on. Marcus has disappeared somewhere, muttering about insufficient lighting, demanding more lamps, more torches. I can only hope we don't set fire to the place. A burning arena floor would certainly look spectacular, but not in the way that Domitian and his guests will be expecting. Most of the senate is here today so the seating will take longer than usual: the more important the attendees, the more fuss they cause.

By the time I eventually make my way upstairs again the sun has fully risen and I stand blinking in the bright light.

"Thanks be to Apollo it's not raining," says Marcus as he strides past me.

It's rained off and on these past two weeks and we really don't need rain on Games days. It spoils scenery and people don't like sitting in it, so we end up with half-empty seating, which dilutes the atmosphere. Today's fresh spring air and bright sun bodes well for our opening day; it will put everyone in a good mood.

We carry on with preparations as our performers arrive, the singers and musicians settled into their places around the amphitheatre, mostly close to the imperial box so that the Emperor can hear everything perfectly, but also at strategic locations around the seating, so that everyone will hear the stories and songs which will add to the excitement of the fights they will be witnessing.

Now the crowds, who have been building up for over two hours, are allowed in. I make my way up to the first floor and look out, feel the familiar thrill at the sight of so many people, all of them about to enter the amphitheatre, expecting to be entertained. They will only see the performers, but it is we who entertain them really, it is our team that has spent months preparing these spectacles, conjuring these stories for their amusement. I catch sight of Secundus, bustling along the queues, making his pitch. I can't hear him from here but can imagine his patter all too well, *Lucky pecker, Dominus? Domina? Untold wealth… sons… women…crops…the blessings of the gods.* His jovial demeanour is already making him a sale as the crowds stream inwards, entering the vast arches. Time to go to the very top of the amphitheatre, to the women's section, to take up a position where I can intervene, should a noble lady of Rome wish to make a fuss about how many slaves she can have with her, or the lack of an awning to protect her from the gentle warmth of the spring sun. The lack of an awning annoys Marcus, too; he had hoped to have one installed this past winter but the idea of that being done at the same time as the hypogeum was too much to bear.

THE SEATING IS FULL AND trumpets sound as Domitian and his party arrive. Marcus and I meet in the corridor leading to the imperial box, standing by as they pass to ensure all is well. The Aedile, anxious and flustered as ever, is supposed to be in charge of these Games and is therefore standing in front of us, but only wringing his hands, rather than making a gracious gesture of welcome as Domitian comes striding down the corridors at a fast pace, the rest of his group hurrying to keep up. His wife Domitia is a floating cloud of colours, a whisper of silks and perfume as she keeps pace with him, head high, one disinterested flicker of her eyes in our direction as we bow our heads. Ahead and behind them the endless tramp of feet as the accompanying Praetorian Guards sweep by. The silk drapes of the imperial box swish open, Domitian and Domitia enter, along with family members and hangers-on who have been given the honour of sitting with them today. Already in the box are their personal attendants, who arrived more than an hour ago to add the final touches necessary for imperial comfort; cushions, gilded glassware, trays of exquisite morsels of food, fans, even boardgames should the Games not be of sufficient interest.

"The gods help us if we're boring enough for those to be necessary," Marcus muttered when he saw these being carried in.

"Maybe Domitia isn't a fan of gladiatorial combat?"

"She better learn to be. He's obsessed with the Games. He's going to be here for practically every show. As if we don't work under enough pressure as it is."

The drapes of the imperial box close, the signal that the imperial party are seated and ready to be entertained. "I need to go below and get ready," I say.

He nods. "Good luck. Be careful."

My nerves are growing. I want to touch his hand, to be embraced, even if only for a moment, but he is already striding away, making his way to the nearest entrance to the seating areas. He must take up his place, give the signal for the Games to begin. I watch him disappear, then turn and make my way down into the hypogeum, glimpsing the empty arena floor, ready to be filled with spectacle.

The two levels of flickering torch-dark rooms beneath the arena are pulsing with life. Lift doors open, men and animals are taking their places, willingly or otherwise. I make my way from one dark archway to another. On the lower level, Funis is standing by the team of bull-leapers, the gigantic bull in a cage behind them. He nods, serious as I pass, all his attention on the next few moments. Strabo is watching over a pure white bull, its horns painted gold. A cage is being closed up, containing three men, shaking, clutching at the bars. Criminals, our executions for the day.

The upper level. Gorgeously clad dancers and singers, the court of Crete. Amidst them stand two figures even more ornately dressed, destined to receive crowns and become King Minos and his ill-fated Queen Pasiphae. And finally a man, dressed in odd swirling robes, stands by a wooden cow containing one of the two star performers of this season's Games.

This year we are trialling a new approach. Marcus is somewhere above me, as ever, sitting near the imperial box. I used to sit in the opposite part of the amphitheatre, close to the box for the Vestal Virgins, each of us able to see half the amphitheatre perfectly as well as each other. But I am bowing my head to a dresser, who fits me with an elaborate ruffled dress in bold colours and laced sandals. This time I will be standing in the arena itself during the opening crowd scene, able to see everything at close hand, to direct events with a gesture, a low voice which the crowd cannot hear. In theory, it will give us better control in large crowd scenes requiring complex instructions. In practice, it will put me rather closer to the arena action than seems desirable. I will be barely five paces away from those about to be executed.

The doors into the arena are each held by a slave, ready to pull them open on Marcus' command, which will be communicated with a long low whistle.

Bursts of light fill our dark space as door after door opens. On cue, loud music fills the amphitheatre and over three hundred of us emerge into the empty arena: dancers, slaves, singers, bull-leapers. As we do so, a palace frontage appears from the floor and narrow seating arises on both sides of it. We are in Crete of long ago, the court and its performers. I walk with the other courtiers, slaves who usually sweep and clean the amphitheatre's seating, now brightly arrayed in costumes that our tailors have spent all winter making. We take our places, seated safely above the arena's still-clean sand. Our first king takes his place amongst us, golden crown glittering.

The bull is released, the crowd gasping at the size of him, the leapers already spread out across the arena so that all parts of the audience will be able to see the show about to unfold.

The bull snorts, confused by the bright light after darkness, the loud music. But when he spots movement he does not hesitate. He gallops towards the first bull leaper and the crowd gasps as his sharp horns come within a fingernail of the leaper's bare skin.

Again and again the bull attacks and each time the leapers, men and women, arch out of the way with their perfect, life-or-death timing and begin to show off their more elaborate skills, the first leap bringing a resounding cheer from the audience, unable to believe the acrobatic strength and speed on display. All around the arena floor they perform, certain to die, before, unbelievably, surviving. The court of Crete applauds, the king grants a laurel wreath to one bull-leaper. But as he completes the gesture his crown falls, golden light rolling over the arena floor and he sinks to his knees as the bull is led away, the leapers taking their place among the rest of us, chests heaving from the exertion.

"*When the old King of Crete died,*" recites the chorus, "*many men claimed the throne, but Minos made a vow. That if Poseidon should send a bull to show his favour for Minos being King, he would sacrifice that bull to show his gratitude.*"

There is an expectant silence.

"*And Poseidon sent a bull from the sea.*"

Rippling blue cloth spreads across the arena floor, pulled by invisible hands and in the midst of it, in front of the Cretan court, a hole opens up and the white bull with golden horns steps out. Well trained, as I lower my hand amidst the crowd, it sinks to its knees, acknowledging Minos' claim to the throne. I sigh with relief. Our hours of rehearsals with a docile ox standing in for the mighty bull of the tale have paid off.

The man playing Minos picks up the golden crown and fits it to his own head, before crowning the woman beside him, creating Queen Pasiphae. Together, they accept applause from our own court and the crowd around us, taking their places on the top tier of seating in front of the painted palace.

"*But when the time came, Minos would not give up the bull for sacrifice. Instead, he sacrificed a lesser beast.*"

A laughably small and mangy-looking bullock is led out and its blood spilt. The crowd murmurs. They know this moment signals the downfall of Minos and all his court. The gods cannot be treated like this, cannot be lied to or made fools of. There will be a retribution, and it will be terrible.

"*And Poseidon was angered.*"

The blue cloth whispers, rises to almost cover the painted palace like a vast wave, but subsides, as though the god had shown mercy at the last minute. As it lowers, it ripples across the lap of the Queen. The cursed touch of Poseidon, seeking vengeance for the offences of her husband.

"*He made Queen Pasiphae desire the bull, filling her mind with crazed lust.*"

Our crowned queen makes her way down the seating. King Minos tries to hold her back as she kneels before the white beast, kissing its muzzle, stroking its flanks. Then she summons the man in the long robes.

"*She demanded that the King's chief inventor and architect, Daedalus, build her a cow of wood, that she might mate with the creature.*"

Daedalus gestures and the model cow is wheeled out, to many ribald shouts from the crowd as Pasiphae climbs inside it. I gesture and the docile ox is led towards it, where it obligingly simulates mating with the unresponsive model. In past seasons Carpophorus has been known to suggest that a bull should really mate with a woman. I grimace at the thought, raise my hand and the man holding the wooden cow unfastens a latch and from the belly of the cow emerges, not the still-concealed Pasiphae, but a man, who drops to the ground in a crouch, as the cow moves away and our crowd of courtiers step back with gasps of horror.

"Now Minos knew the true horror of what he had done, for Pasiphae, his queen, having given way to a bestial lust for the sacred animal, was delivered of a son. But not a human son. A beast. A monster."

Painted black all over, naked muscles rippling, Felix stands. He is a good height, made taller still by the magnificent helmet he is wearing. Glowing silver, surmounted with two vast horns in black, the front covers his face entirely, moulded into the shape of a bull's face, its muzzle protruding. Two large eye holes have been covered over in a dark fabric, so that the man inside can see out, but his opponents cannot see his eyes.

The crowd oohs and leans forwards, but falls silent at the sight of his hands, which he has raised up into a fighting stance. Black leather gloves cover his hands up to the elbows. But where his fingers end, there are glinting silver knives, sharp and awaiting their first victim as a lift ascends and the door opens. A screaming man is pushed out and into the merciless arms of the horrifying figure. The blades are quick, the man has no weapons, can only writhe in agony as they slash at his arms, chest, finishing with his throat, blood cascading onto the sand of the arena. The spray of it hits one of my feet, the warm blood landing on my bare toe. I swallow down a wave of nausea. The deaths, seen this close, are different. From the seats in the amphitheatre, they are a play, a story, even if grisly. Here, they are very real, the warm blood of a dead man touching our living skin.

"The Minotaur."

The black figure moves, paces first to one side to meet the man emerging from the second lift, then to the other to meet the third and final lift. Three men lie on the now red sand, their blood spilt and spilling, their lives lost, their last sight a monster from a dark myth brought to life for the pleasure of their Emperor.

"King Minos, horrified at what had come from his actions, called on Daedalus to make a maze, a palace of so many rooms that no man could find his way through it, that the monster might never emerge."

Every lift we have operates in unison, the arena floor trembling with their movement, delivering up black walls from the ground, taller than a man, which create the fabled maze across the entirety of the arena, trapping the silver-knifed killer in the centre as the palace sinks away and we, the court of Minos, shrink back, trembling, into a small huddle. There is a huge round of applause from the audience at the impressive structure.

"The Labyrinth."

At the centre of the labyrinth, our Minotaur stands on a raised platform, making him taller than the maze itself, taller than a normal man. He lifts his arms to show once more his glinting knife-claws, still dripping with blood. The chorus open up their throats in a bellowing roar, giving the monster a terrifying, echoing, inhuman voice.

There's a deathly silent pause, all of us frozen in place, before the chorus speaks again.

"But across the seas another queen gave birth to a child with an equally fearsome destiny. A man. A prince. A hero."

The maze sinks, disappears into the floor, taking with it the entrapped Minotaur. The court of Crete disperses through the arena doors. I follow everyone, kneel by a grate in the arena wall to watch the next part.

"Theseus."

The crowd erupts into cheers and applause as, in the centre of the arena, a trapdoor opens and Carpophorus emerges. Naked to the waist, his well-scarred skin gleaming with oil, sword in hand, in every respect the famous bestiarius that he is. I can hear higher-pitched cries of admiration from the upper levels of seating, Carpophorus has always been one for the ladies and they in turn have never held back from showering him with gifts, as well as granting him admission to their bedchambers whenever they can get away with it.

Carpophorus turns this way and that, sword held aloft, enjoying the absolute focus on him by the crowd, the empty arena his stage.

"He was trained for glory and destined to be a hero."

I can rest for a while. What follows is first a brief interlude of dancing girls and actors, then a series of gladiatorial bouts, using high-class gladiators, designed to show off Carpophorus' fighting skills and those of others. There will be no deaths here, the sequence is supposed to show his training period as a young prince and impress the crowd with a showcase of superb gladiatorial combats. These will last at least two hours, made up of multiple bouts of different pairings, many conducted simultaneously. Everything is proceeding smoothly.

THE FINAL PART OF THE afternoon's combats includes a demonstration of archery and a return to our theme of Crete and bulls. While pairs of gladiators continue to whirl about the arena floor with their weapons glinting and clashing, Funis and his team of handlers release bulls, who, confused and irritated by the movement going on around them, try to attack the gladiators, only to be shot down by archers. A dangerous sequence for the gladiators who need to keep out of the way of both bulls and arrows, but the crowd loves the mayhem and threat of it all. We finish the day on cheers and applause as well as a delighted smile from Domitian, who leaves at a fast stride again, leaving us to manage the exit of the other sixty thousand people, which goes smoothly, always something of a surprise. Marcus is beaming over a job well done; he raises his arm in a salute to me from a distance and I grin back, relieved and happy that all has gone well. It's a good omen for our new season. I hurry down the steps into the hypogeum, nodding at everyone, praising the performers and our own team, but as I reach the lower floor and the medical area, I see Fabius outside it, looking worried. He hurries over and takes my arm.

"Come with me."

"What's wrong?"

"A gladiator has died."

None of the gladiators died. "You mean a criminal?"

"No. A gladiator."

I'm following him down the central passageway to the medical station. "Who?"

"Primus."

It's a show name, *First*, belonging, I dimly recall, to a young gladiator who made a name for himself last season, tipped for great things. From Paternus' school. "I never saw him killed?"

"He took an arrow to the arm."

"He can't have died from that."

"He was spitting blood."

"From an arm wound?"

We've reached the medical station. Draped over Fabius' table is the body of Primus, his helmet fallen to the floor. Clearly dead, and yet his body is untouched, except for a small wound, no longer bleeding, on his upper arm. Fabia is holding the arrow that caused it gingerly in her hand,

"Poison," she says, grim-faced. "It has to be."

We stand over the body, looking down at Primus' face. He can't have been more than twenty years old, with a long career still ahead of him as a top gladiator, if he fulfilled his potential.

"Does Paternus know?"

"We've sent a messenger."

I'm trying to recall the sequence of events. "There were four archers."

"Five," says Fabia.

"I hired four," I say.

"There were five in the arena."

It takes a while and we have to consult several witnesses in our team. But eventually it is confirmed that yes, there were five, not four, archers in the arena today, and we can only account for four. The other has disappeared, slipped away somewhere in the darkness of the hypogeum and no-one can give a good enough description to make me think we have any chance of finding them.

"Why would they want to kill Primus?"

No-one can think of a reason. Gladiators don't kill their rivals, they train alongside them, see each other as comrades in arms. They kill only if they are ordered to, and only in the arena. Primus was well-liked, a good fighter.

"A mistake?"

"Who was the fifth archer aiming at?" challenges Paternus. He has arrived and he is angry. We will pay for Primus, of course, but still, he has unexpectedly lost a good gladiator and he is not best pleased. It takes years for a gladiator to be trained well enough to perform at a venue as prestigious as the Flavian Amphitheatre and had we wanted a man to die as part of today's performance, he would never have offered up

Primus. If not a criminal, some poor-quality fighter would have been chosen instead, one with no promise, or one who had caused trouble by being rebellious.

Marcus is grave. "We don't know," he says. "We've been looking at where the arrow was fired. There were six people in the vicinity. Primus and three other gladiators were the closest together. Funis was there to direct the bulls, although he was partly obscured by a piece of scenery. Another animal handler was just visible, we think, because they were by the trapdoor where the bulls were emerging. And Strabo was in the nearest doorway, but it would have taken a master archer to even try and hit him."

"It was right below the imperial box," says Strabo.

Marcus turns to him, horrified. "Are you suggesting it was an assassination attempt on the Emperor?"

Paternus is shaking his head. "If so it was a very poor shot. No archer with even a small amount of training could miss so badly."

"But they didn't hit Primus very well either," I reason. "The arrow almost missed him, it just caught the edge of his arm."

"It didn't need to do anything more than that," says Fabius. "Not if the tip was poisoned."

Marcus heaves a sigh. "We'll probably never know what really happened," he says. "The archer slipped out, and no-one can think of any identifying marks or even anything particularly noticeable about him. No-one was looking at him." He touches Paternus on the shoulder. "I'm sorry, Paternus. You will be compensated for Primus, of course. I will attend his funeral myself. And our team will be told to be on the alert for anything like this happening again."

He speaks with confidence and Paternus reluctantly departs, his assistants carrying Primus' dead body and the other gladiators from his school silently trailing behind their fallen comrade. But I'm wary of Marcus' certainty. In the busy arena we didn't notice the extra archer today and with a team of over one thousand of our own, as well as a few hundred extra performers appearing at each show, how can we possibly be sure that no one else will be able to infiltrate our events in the future? I can only hope that the death of Primus was intended. Some quarrel or trouble he'd managed to get into without anyone knowing of it, now brutally settled.

"It's a bad business," says Marcus. "Send the celebratory drinks and cakes down to the warehouses. I don't have the stomach for them and we don't even have a big enough space to gather everyone together here anymore, except for the arena floor and that's covered in blood. But that shouldn't stop the team celebrating. Aside from Primus, it was a successful opening day. Domitian was pleased."

I make the arrangements. The rest of the day and evening is subdued. Usually we would have celebrated with the team and gone back to the insula to share stories of the day, eaten a good meal, perhaps arranged for some of the butchered bulls to be made ready by Cassia for a shared feast, signalling the start of a plentiful supply of fresh meat for the season, which everyone looks forward to after a long winter of less exalted fare. But instead we morosely eat a vegetable porridge at Cassia's counter and retire quietly to our own huts. Even Karbo, who usually chatters on incessantly after exciting events, is downcast.

"Do you think someone wanted to harm one of our team?" he asks in the darkness, his voice cracking. "Would they come after us, to where we live?"

"I doubt it," I says reassuringly. "They wouldn't have to wait for a Games day to target one of us, would they? Perhaps Primus was involved with something dubious."

"Like what?"

"Gambling. Throwing a fight. Maybe a love affair... who knows, Karbo, go to sleep. Don't worry yourself about it."

Eventually Karbo's breathing slows and tiny snores emerge. But I lie awake for many hours, tired but unable to sleep, reliving the day over and over again, trying to recall any small detail that will help us understand what happened to Primus. And why.

CHARON

Now that the fuss of the opening day is over, we settle into the season and the rhythm of the days – most days are a show day, with the odd respite, and Domitian attends far more regularly than his brother Titus used to. We get used to welcoming the imperial entourage rather than it being a novelty. We've done about fifteen shows when Luna performs for the first time.

The morning hunt and executions over, it's time for something lighter, but still linked to our theme and relevant to this afternoon's gladiatorial bouts.

Twenty slaves freshen the pale sand that covers the arena floor, then fetch buckets with special holes in the bottom, each bucket filled with sand of four different colours, specially tinted for us. Orange, green, blue and black. They walk in a pre-agreed pattern, creating an outline on the sand of Ariadne's famous dancing floor, a maze across our arena. No sooner are they done then the musicians strike up a lilting tune and the arena doors swing open, our dancers take their places, Luna amongst them, in her much-anticipated starring role as Princess Ariadne of Crete.

"Spit that out," hisses the choreographer, who can see her chewing away at mastic gum as usual.

Luna rolls her eyes at him and spits out her mastic with fearsome accuracy, landing the little white ball at his feet, before winking at me and stepping through the door, to be greeted with cheers from the crowd.

She's no slouch, she has in fact learnt all the steps the choreographer requested of her, a twisting turning dance with many quick steps, so that the women appear to dance their way through a labyrinth of their own, the music growing faster all the time, and yet none of them scuff the sand or disturb its intricate pattern. Luna's role requires her to reach the centre and then dance her way back out of it, which she does, although I note that she has made sure to include her own elements. Her breasts tremble with every step, her hips sway seductively from side to side and the mostly male audience sits rapt with attention, leaning forward, clapping and cheering her name when she's finished. She bows and waves, then leaves the arena floor, bringing her past me in the darkness as a messenger reaches her, holding out a tiny scroll. She pauses briefly to unroll it, frowning at the writing in the poor light, then winks at me and waves the scroll in the air.

"Straight from the imperial box. Told you… arse and tits." She gives a wiggle and laughs. "See you, Althea."

"Goodbye Luna," I say, wondering whether the summons has come from Domitian or one of his guests. "Enjoy your evening."

"Not as much as he will," she calls over her shoulder.

THE LIGHTER PART OF THE entertainment over, we settle into the gladiators' rounds. These require less in the way of management, as the referees make sure everything proceeds smoothly.

I make my way down into the hypogeum. I'm still not used to how many rooms there are, the maze-like feeling hasn't gone away with familiarity. Closed doors, glimpses through open walls, little alcoves, the built-in cages and their occupants meet you round every corner. It keeps me jumpy, which I dislike. There is something unsettling about never knowing what is behind some of the doors, of not knowing who or what you might come across. More than once I jump when I come round a corner and find myself facing a gladiator made half-human by an elaborate helmet, many shaped like animals.

A towering black-cloaked and hooded figure steps out of the darkness, blocking my way. A masked face shows only the glitter of eyes behind it.

"Strabo!" I yelp.

The figure pushes back the hood and lifts away the mask, revealing our stolid team manager Strabo's kindly face and squint.

"Sorry, Althea, didn't see you there."

The role of Charon regularly falls to Strabo, a good-hearted quiet man. He's an unlikely person to take on such a dark part. Charon, ferryman to the underworld, will emerge onto the arena after a bout where gladiators have died or been half-killed and take them out of their misery and into the darkness by slamming a hammer down onto their heads, then dragging their body out of the Gate of Death.

"You gave me a fright," I say, trying to smile, my heart beating faster than it should do.

"Ready to go on, if I'm needed," says Strabo. He nods down at the long-handled, heavy hammer he's carrying.

I grimace. "Sure you're alright doing that?"

"I don't mind," he says. "It's better to finish them off if they can't be saved. Unkind to let them linger when there's no hope."

He has always taken this view, unflinching and dutiful, seeing the task as a kindness, which in a dark way I suppose it is.

He lifts the mask back onto his face, pulls the hood over it. It's still only Strabo underneath, but I step back. To stand face to face with Charon, alone in the darkness, is disconcerting. "I'll see you afterwards," I say and he walks away, the long cloak making it seem he is floating, adding to his otherworldliness.

There are two bouts today where it's possible that a gladiator will die, hence Strabo standing ready. Usually the battles are intended to demonstrate the fighting skills and excitement of a well-matched pair of gladiators. The crowd has its favourites, bets are made, the odd wound here or there will be seen to by Fabius and no-one will perish.

But extra excitement from time to time does not go amiss and so some bouts allow for something more dangerous, for the chance to actually kill an opponent, perhaps when a gladiator has displeased their trainer or is weakening and no longer a star performer, or not loved enough by the crowd to be protected from a bloody end.

I'm still down in the hypogeum when there's a triple whistle followed by a long single note.

Our carefully established protocol begins. Our physician Fabius hurries past me, a slave opening the door allowing him into the arena. I stand in the doorway, out of sight but able to see the fallen gladiator, who is lying jerking in the sand, his feet and hands scuffing up little gusts of sand while the victor soaks up the applause of the crowd. Fabius bends over him for a moment, then looks up into the seating area and locks eyes with Marcus, shakes his head while gesturing, a strong quick hand movement from one side to the other, a clear agreement of what is to come, then retreats.

The chorus has been watching Marcus. Now he gives a low whistle and they spread their arms wide, then speak, deep-voiced and solemn, summoning a being from the other world.

"Charon."

Another doorway opens and the hooded masked figure advances, sunlight glinting on the hammer it carries.

Fabius has returned to the shadows of my doorway and we stand together in silence as the crowd grows quiet, watching each slow step. Charon stands over the fallen gladiator, whose body is still jerking in a way that is making my stomach churn. He pauses for dramatic tension but does not hesitate, the hammer rises and falls, a sickening crunch and the gladiator lies still, while the crowd lets out its breath in a collective sigh, which turns to applause.

"I never get used to it," I confess, as the door to the arena closes, leaving us in the flickering torchlight. "It's worse than the other deaths."

Fabius nods. "There was no hope for him," he reassures me.

"I know," I say quietly. The protocol we have is strict. Fabius must inspect the gladiator. He must clearly indicate to Marcus that there is no hope whatsoever of anything being done for him medically. Then and only then will Marcus summon Charon. Usually there is no need, a gladiator will be killed outright. If he is badly wounded but still conscious, the crowd or the Emperor may be asked to decide whether he should be dispatched by the victor, an honourable death. But to kill an unconscious gladiator, there is no honour in that, it would make a poor spectacle, and yet they must be dispatched. Hence Charon. The dark ferryman who takes souls across the River Styx from our world to the underworld. This is the role Strabo must sometimes play.

"Well done," says Marcus, as he passes Strabo later. He pats him on the back.

Strabo bows his head. He is not distressed at these moments, seeing it as a duty and a quicker release of a suffering man than allowing him to twitch alone on the sand. There is an orderliness and righteousness to what he does.

DOMITIAN IS IN ATTENDANCE FOR the much-publicised show in which Hercules and Theseus will face the Amazons.

Our first glimpse of Billica is certainly impressive. With or without her consent, her mousey-brown hair has been dyed and interwoven with additional hair pieces to make it both spectacular and wildly excessive, a scarlet that would rival any soldier's shield, stacked and cascading from her head to well past her waist, surmounted with a magnificent golden headdress to indicate her place as Hippolyta, Queen of the Amazons, though I'm not sure the stories say anything about the Amazons having red hair. She is wearing a skimpy loincloth, attached to decorative leather straps which cross over her chest, the same as all her women are wearing, which have no purpose other than to draw attention to their bare breasts, now helpfully outlined for the audience's benefit.

They carry multiple weapons, from bows and arrows to swords, clubs, battle-axes and more. Billica-Hippolyta wears knee-high boots in scarlet leather, her women lighter shoes along with trousers in bright colours, under which, Labeo has helpfully informed me, is protective armour. I don't bother pointing out that it's hardly very protective if it's only protecting their legs, rather than their heads and chests, surely more vulnerable to weapons. Five of our scene-painters have spent the past two hours painting black tattoos on their arms, backs and thighs, an element that makes them look particularly exotic and savage, though I am unsure how authentic any of them are. I suspect the scene-painters have let their imaginations run wild about what a tribe of wild women would have decorated their skin with. At any rate from a distance it looks very dramatic.

A quarter of the women are on horseback or in chariots, the rest are on foot, although many arrive in the arena sitting behind the main riders, so that they seem more of a horse-bound tribe than is the case for real Amazons.

Labeo's women do not hold back; the male gladiators from Paternus' school are highly trained but are not getting an easy afternoon of it. Both sides sweat and rage, swearing and mocking one another as the fights go on. The better-known gladiators are given their moments to shine, sometimes within a ring of shouting minor gladiators, the better to draw attention to their bout while giving the illusion of one vast battle.

At last it is the turn of Theseus and Hercules to fight Queen Hippolyta. Billica's chariot whips round the arena, circling the two men, who are elevated onto a piece of scenery resembling a large rock. Her sword glints as she slashes at them with it, her women returning to their chariots and horses. The two men are in danger of being overcome. When she eventually leaves her chariot and battles with the two men face to face, I think Carpophorus really might not complete the season, which would be awkward, given that it revolves around him. Billica is fearsome and as Paternus said, does not care about being wounded, receiving cuts, one to her arm, one to her leg. She fights on, bleeding, but she is slowly overcome, despite the shouts of encouragement from her warriors below the rock. At last Theseus grabs at her hair and holds her down, while Hercules disarms her with a passionate kiss and claims her golden belt, given to her by her father, the god of war Ares, and endowing her with superhuman strength. Billica is not willing to play along with the mythology. She has to be forcibly obliged to accept the kiss but legends are legends and the crowd cheers the finale. Three gladiators drag Billica out of the arena so that Carpophorus can take a bow and the Amazons join Paternus' gladiators in a victory lap of the arena.

"Domitian says it was delightful and wants to know if we'll be having the Amazons again," reports back Marcus.

"Not so different from other men as everyone keeps implying, then?"

THE NEW HYPOGEUM HAS A special butchering room on the ground floor, close to an exit for easy access. With close to one hundred animals killed every day, the after-show butchering is always a long job. Skins are removed and sent over the other side of the Tiber to the leather-workers' district for fur and leather; we get wafts of the tanning work from time to time near the insula; it's an unpleasant smell. If there's something unusual or of good quality, like a fine leopard skin, it'll eventually make its way to the imperial palace, freshly tanned and ready to be included as part of Domitian or Domitia's winter wardrobes or made into an elegant rug. Meanwhile the carcasses are butchered for food. Marcus brings home something every day for Cassia to feed the insula. Good quality specialities are sent to the palace, the rest is given away outside the amphitheatre at the end of the day, an eager queue growing as soon as the show finishes, waiting for the handout. Some people skip the Games entirely, keen to be at the front of the line and receive the best or largest pieces available to feed their families. Meat is a keenly anticipated rarity for plebians and the Games season brings the best chance of having it at the table.

I poke my head in at the door of the butchering room. There's a pile of dead animals, perhaps twenty still left. The butcher and his three assistants are sweating; it's a hot day and even away from the sun the rooms within the hypogeum are getting warm now that we have poorer air flow.

"Nearly done?"

"Yes. All smaller animals now, easier."

I nod. "Send one of your lads for the cleaning crew when you're done, won't you? They'll need to wash the room down."

"Yes, yes."

The butcher is a grumpy old thing, but fast with a knife. He doesn't care about the stink that surrounds his work, but I do and so we have the room washed down with several buckets of water whenever we get the chance, sluicing it into the drains. One of his assistants heaves up two large buckets of pieces of meat and hurries past me to the exit where the queue will be waiting, each person holding a container to carry home whatever they are given, a leg of a sheep or deer if they are exceptionally lucky, more usually ribs and offal, sometimes meat from strange animals like lions or hyena, which have an odd taste about them. Still, once they're in a stew with plenty of seasoning they'll be a welcome change from the usual vegetable and grain porridges.

"Billica looked amazing," I tell Paternus, finding him about to lead his gladiators back to the barracks.

"She was furious," he says. "Raging and crying when they pulled her off the arena floor. The Briton slave we have who understands her says she was screaming about being dishonoured by making it look like she lost to the men and she didn't like being kissed by them, either."

"The crowd loved her," I say. "If she could calm down enough to receive more training she'd have a great future as a gladiatrix. She's already a good fighter and the audience likes something a bit different."

"I've tried telling her that," says Paternus. "She spits and hisses when I try to talk to her. The slave says he can hear her muttering about killing us all at night, pacing up and down in her room, barely sleeps till she's exhausted."

I wave him off, sad for Billica, hoping that her successes in the arena may begin to assuage her rage.

BEING NEW AND DIFFERENT, THE bull-leaping becomes one of the season's must-see element of the Games, something people have heard of but not often seen. We make room in our schedule for more events featuring the performance. The female leapers, in particular, are favoured, whether because of their partial nudity or simply their skill and daring, I'm unsure. But certainly the days when we advertise their appearances are very well attended and I see fashionable women about Rome copying elements of the clothing they wear, adding a flounce to the bottom of their tunics to imitate our court of Crete, or having hand-painted elements added to their ordinary tunics, this last very popular as the simple pigments they use are not water-fast and so can be washed away, then added anew in different combinations. Instead of the usual hair wraps we all wear, young girls are plaiting their hair into tight rows or tying wraps tighter around their faces and in brighter colours, so as to emulate the bull-leapers' style, which was born out of practicality but has become something of a fad.

THE DAYS GROW WARMER AND the ladies of Rome insist on bringing parasols to the Games, complaining about our lack of an awning, fearing that the sun's rays will darken their carefully cultivated fair skin. The parasols block the view for anyone behind them and Marcus and I are regularly called on to settle disputes.

There's a burst of trumpets.

"That'll be Domitian," I say. "Places, everyone." We never keep the Emperor waiting once he arrives. Inside the Emperor's entrance I stand unobtrusively out of the way and watch Domitian and the procession that moves about with him. I take up my place as members of the Praetorian Guard and bodyguards sweep ahead, then Domitian and his wife Domitia, followed by a couple of dozen servants and slaves.

Domitia is magnificent in flowing jewel-toned silks, her hair towers, if possible, even higher than the last time I saw her at the opening Games, back in March. There's more than three heads' worth of hair in there, so gossips whisper, held on a wire frame to create the pyramid of curls rising above her face. Her ornatrix must be kept even busier than the one preparing Billica for the arena. This is certainly a woman who is enjoying the trappings that come with being an empress. Her face has been powdered very pale with chalk. Cassia keeps some in her apartment but she can't wear it except in the very depths of winter; her skin goes too dark in the summer, chalk over the top of summer-brown skin looks odd. Domitia is careful to stay out of the sun, like all rich women. Behind her, in her retinue, is a slave carrying a parasol.

The procession makes its way to the imperial box and there's a lot of coming and going as everyone gets settled into their proper places, whether in the box, left outside as bodyguards or waiting for further tasks, should they be required. I give a small impatient sigh.

"It always takes a while to settle everyone," says a voice behind me.

I jump. In the shadows of one of the archways is Stephanus, his long frame clad in a toga blending into the white stone all around him.

I'm silent, unsure what to say.

"Attention to detail," he comments with an approving air, looking at my wax tablet, which I had been consulting while waiting for further trumpets to indicate that we could start the show. "I'll not keep you," he adds. "We all have places we are supposed to be."

He turns and walks away, towards the imperial box. I watch him go, frowning. He never says hello or goodbye. Appears from the shadows and then leaves again. It's unsettling. Not for the first time, I wonder how much influence he has over Domitian, what exactly his shadowlike role consists of.

Today I won't be in the arena. I make my way to an area which will give me a view of the imperial box and the Emperor. It always takes longer to seat important people. Aside from getting all their accompanying bodyguards, slaves and other hangers-on organised and in their places, it's the fussing over whether the cushions are to their liking and the re-draping of their togas and pallas once they've sat down, making sure they've been served a drink and a snack if they'd like one that adds time. Domitian has a glass of wine in one hand and picks up a small cake with the other. Domitia also has a glass of wine but is shaking her head at any food, instead summoning a slave girl with a fan. That will be a boring afternoon for the girl, fanning the Empress hour after hour. Though as a result, the girl does have a front row seat in the imperial box at the Games, so I suppose that's something.

Marcus gives me a nod and we make our way in different directions, he to watch from his place near the imperial box, I to oversee the workings down in the hypogeum for most of the morning.

Come the afternoon, the black-sailed Athenian ships are setting sail across a rippling cloth sea. To liven up the voyage, today's sailing is the setting for many gladiatorial bouts, including the classic secutor gladiators whose helmets appropriately recall a fish. Additional gladiators are dressed as sea monsters and even a few in crocodile-leather armour. All of these are being valiantly fought off by the Athenian 'sailors', or rather some of Rome's finest retiarius gladiators, who traditionally have a sea-like aspect to their weaponry, fighting with a weighted net, a three-pointed trident, and a dagger. There's no mention of sea monsters in the original myth, or indeed any difficulties at all on the voyage to Crete, but we are always happy to add some embellishments.

I should be able to watch this part, the gladiatorial sessions require little from me, but instead I am in the very highest seating area, trying to convince a lady to be reasonable about her parasol.

"How dare you?" she hisses. "My slave will hold my parasol where I tell him to. And no-one will tell me otherwise. Hold it higher," she adds and her slave obeys.

"But it is blocking the view of the two ladies behind you," I say. "Perhaps if it could be lowered, at least?"

"Certainly not," she retorts. "And those are not ladies. They are plebians and should know their place."

The two women behind look furious.

"Perhaps you'd like to move to a different part of the arena," I suggest. "There is more shade on that side?"

"Absolutely not," she says. "And you're blocking *my* view. Move. I want to see Charon finish off that man."

"Charon?" I frown. I've not heard the whistle signal, nor the chorus summon Charon. I turn, looking down into the arena.

Through the rippling waves, now growing still as our slaves slow their actions, comes the dark figure of Charon, striding across the arena to where a fallen gladiator is holding up his hands to ward him off, yet appears unable to stand.

"*Move*," says the woman, pushing me to one side.

I lose my balance, teetering on the stone terrace seats, watching in horror as Charon's hammer falls and the gladiator is dispatched to the underworld.

"Do you *mind*," says the outraged lady as I shove past her.

"No," I throw over my shoulder, taking the stone steps at a run, making for the nearest exit, tearing down through the narrow corridors and steep steps followed by more steep steps, rushing back into the darkness of the hypogeum, half-falling down the last steps in my rush to reach our team and find out what has gone wrong.

"Where is Strabo?" Marcus is yelling. "What in Hades happened out there? That gladiator wasn't supposed to die! He only had a minor cut to his leg, he would have been fine."

"I don't know," I say, still shocked. "Karbo, find Strabo, immediately." I wonder what has happened. Has Strabo lost his mind? Is he killing people with no warning, wielding his hammer against anyone in his way?

Marcus has already gone striding down the corridor and Karbo rushes away but from behind me comes a familiar voice.

"Althea?"

I turn in sudden fear but Strabo is wearing his usual clothes; a scruffy tunic belted over his substantial middle. His face is anxious.

"Why is everyone yelling for me?"

"Where have you been?" I ask, my voice shaking.

He looks bewildered. "Helping Fabius in the physician's bay. There was a gladiator in the first bout needed stitching up. We've only just finished."

I stare up at him. "The first bout?"

"Yes."

"And you just finished now?"

"Yes. What's happened?"

I swallow. "The third bout had a young gladiator in and he got cut on the leg, couldn't get up. Charon came out and finished him off."

Strabo stares back at me. "Charon?"

"Yes."

"But I was with Fabius."

He is confused, anxious. I can't see any dishonesty in his face. "I have to ask Fabius to confirm you have been with him," I say, my voice shaking. "I don't want to disbelieve you, Strabo, but no-one else plays Charon except you."

"But I wasn't called on to be Charon," he says.

"No-one gave the order. We need to go to Fabius."

We make our way to the physician's bay and Fabius confirms, confused that I am even asking, that Strabo was with him, from midway in the first bout until now, helping with the young gladiator they have been patching up and who is about to be taken back to his barracks. A few extra people nod, confirming what I'm being told.

"Strabo!" Marcus' roar has people cringing. It's rare to see Marcus this angry and I step in front of him, hands up. He only stops because I am in the way, my palms pressing against his chest.

"It wasn't Strabo," I say. "It wasn't him, Marcus."

"How can it not be? No-one else plays Charon." He glares at Strabo and Strabo, shaken, stares back, his own hands rising to protest his innocence.

I push harder against Marcus' chest, afraid that in his appalled anger he will go for Strabo, despite our protestations. "It wasn't him. He was with Fabius all the time."

"He was," confirms Fabius again.

"Then what's going on?" demands Marcus.

"I don't know," I say, lowering my hands as I see him gain control of his initial rage. "We need to find out. Strabo, where's the outfit?"

"And the hammer," adds Marcus.

Strabo blinks, then recovers. "In the chest by the fourth door into the arena," he says. "Where we always keep it."

We make our way there, Marcus striding ahead, while I half-run behind him and Strabo, Fabius and a group of slaves follow us.

The fourth door into the arena, always used by Charon, is closed, as it should be. Beside it is the chest, its lid thrown open. It's empty.

"Search the hypogeum," Marcus orders. "Everyone. Now. Every part of it."

With over one hundred people scouring both levels, the search doesn't take long. Close to the end of the arena by the Gate of Death, someone lets out a call that brings us all running. In a dark niche, sometimes used for smaller animals, but today unoccupied, its metal gate unlocked and swinging half open, is a bundle of black cloth, Charon's cloak. Marcus pulls at it, revealing not only the discarded mask but also, with a heavy scraping across the brick floor, Charon's hammer, covered in blood.

There are whispers down the crowded corridor, gestures against bad luck as the news is passed along. Marcus holds up his hand and everyone falls silent.

"Someone took the opportunity of hiding their evil intentions in plain sight," he says. "They used this costume to murder a man who should have lived and thought they could pin the blame on Strabo, who fortunately was with Fabius all the time and can be vouched for. You are all to be careful until we find out who did this."

It takes a while to dismiss the team, to send everyone about their business and I note that they leave in little groups, no-one wanting to walk alone through our dark underworld, now grown darker. I have to give orders to make everyone do the work they should be doing, sending the cleaning team about their business of washing down the seating areas, sweeping the arena clean of the sand bloodied by a man who should not have died today. Strange that we see death every day and yet still are shocked by it when it is unexpected, when it comes unbidden and unplanned for. When I've made the rounds and can see everyone doing their work, I go back to Fabius, who is comforting Strabo.

"Who would do that?" asks Strabo. "And they thought you'd think that I –"

"Do you have enemies I don't know about?" I ask him.

He looks shaken by the very idea. "No! What have I ever done to anyone?"

The men he has dispatched to the underworld over the years, standing over gladiators taking their last dying breaths, before swinging down the hammer... but they were beyond saving, he was doing them a kindness. Still, perhaps they had family members who did not see it that way or... but why not accost Strabo somewhere, a quick knife between his ribs on a dark street? This smacks more of shifting the blame onto someone else, of concealing the true murderer, than of a punishment specifically for Strabo. "Go and have a drink," I say. "We will find out what is going on here," I add with far more confidence than I currently feel, but I have to do something to cheer him.

Fabius frowns. He knows I am putting on a false front of certainty, but he pulls Strabo by the elbow.

"A drink is what we both need," he says jovially. "Come along, now, if a physician tells you that you need a drink, you don't argue."

Strabo follows behind him, shoulders heavy.

"I don't know what is going on," says Marcus, his voice strained. "Two gladiators killed by someone and we can't find them, can't stop them? Last time there were six people it could have been aimed at. This time there were dozens of gladiators and two of them were down, then Charon comes out of nowhere, unsummoned, no checks made and kills one of them."

"What did they have in common?"

"I keep asking myself that. I've no idea."

I think of the gladiator being stripped of his crocodile-leather armour, the helmet in the shape of a vast-jawed beast crumpled like the skull within it and shudder. "Who was he?"

Marcus shakes his head. "A slave. Name of Eros. Even more minor than the last one. A nobody, he'd barely finished his training, they put him in this scene because all he had to do was make up numbers and not disgrace himself. Paternus is furious, he's threatening to stop supplying us."

A horrible thought sweeps over me. "Siro."

"What about him?"

"What if he was part of this as well?"

"Why would he be? He wasn't a gladiator. Primus and Eros were gladiators."

"All of them were slaves linked to the amphitheatre."

"Someone has a grudge against the amphitheatre?"

We're both silent for a moment. "The manure daubed on the front..." I mutter.

"It's a long way from a bit of manure to three murders," says Marcus.

"The Urban Cohorts need to be informed."

"They're all slaves. The Urban Cohorts wouldn't care unless their owners made a fuss. Domitian was hardly likely to care about a slave he didn't even know the name of. Paternus will be compensated for Eros, just like he was for Primus."

"So we do nothing?"

"We'll have to draw up plans to keep everyone safe. For starters, no one goes anywhere alone."

"The whole team? Over a thousand of us?"

"Everyone," says Marcus firmly. "You and Karbo especially. Go everywhere with someone else or not at all. Same rule for everyone. I need witnesses if this happens again."

"Again?" I feel cold at the idea.

"We don't know who did it, so we haven't stopped them," says Marcus, his face grim.

"The rule goes for you, too," I remind him. "Don't go anywhere alone."

It's been a long day and Marcus and I are standing side by side in exhausted and worried silence, elbows on Cassia's counter, eating a richly seasoned stew of antelope. Quintus is rocking Emilia and the popina is busy with customers, eating alongside us or dropping by to collect their dinners to eat in their own homes. Karbo has been picking the first broad beans and now he comes running down with an armful of the fresh green pods, which he proudly shares out to all the customers. Cassia finds a sheep's cheese to slice up to go with them and everyone compliments Karbo and me on our successful gardening as they pod the beans and eat them with the salty cheese. Karbo strokes the inside of the pods, admiring the soft white lining.

"It's furry like Letitia," he says.

Even Marcus smiles. "They're delicious, Karbo," he says. "A real taste of summer to come. Well done, the pair of you. You're practically farmers."

My fantasy moment: the beans were to lead to a conversation about his farm… but it seems inappropriate after what has happened today.

Quintus stands, holding Emilia.

"I have an announcement to make," he says and the popina falls quiet. "Now that I am working towards owning my own business and live here in the insula, I feel I should take care of two things that are important to me. I am going to adopt Emilia."

Everyone applauds and Cassia puts a hand to her chest, tears welling up.

"Also, I would like to marry Cassia," says Quintus. "If you'll have me?"

Cassia's cheeks turn a hot pink and she looks towards her father Cassius, who nods his approval. He doesn't look surprised, Quintus must already have asked for his permission.

"I – I suppose," she says, shrugging, her tone suggesting she's agreeing to an extra loaf of bread being delivered rather than a marriage proposal. But her eyes are very bright and when a cheer goes up from the customers and Quintus approaches her, she holds up her face to be kissed and then, flustered, takes Emilia from him and busies herself with the baby while the men slap Quintus on the back and the women embrace her. I hug Cassia amidst the hubbub, my arms entwined with several other people's. Emilia stares at everyone, astonished at the sudden noise and finding herself in the midst of a crowd, but pleased at all the smiles and pats she is receiving as part of the celebratory fuss.

"He's a good man," says Cassius, when I finally reach him to congratulate him.

"He is," I agree, turning to Quintus. "You look after her, now," I say, in a teasing tone.

"You know I will," he says, his face earnest.

I hug him. "I know," I say.

When the hubbub has died down, I make my way to Cassia for an extra embrace, just the two of us instead of a cluster of people.

"Did you know he was going to ask?"

"No! Father did. He'd already given his blessing."

"Are you happy?" I ask.

She tries to shrug again. "He'll do," she says. "He's a good man, he's been kind to Emilia and he didn't have to be."

"Your cheeks are too pink and your eyes are too bright for 'he'll do', you know," I say, laughing.

"I've been burnt once," says Cassia fearfully, her voice low.

"He's not like Rullus," I say, embracing her more tightly. "He's kind and he loves you, we can all see it."

"Thank you," she says in a whisper, her smile returning.

"For what?"

"His apprenticeship," she says.

"It didn't take much doing," I say. "Balbus is delighted with him and Quintus… he was made for that job. When's the wedding?"

Cassia is beaming again. "He said he asked me now so that we can get married in June."

It's a lucky month for weddings, a good choice. "Only a few weeks to get ready then, we'll have to rush all the preparations along. You ready to be a wife?"

Her cheeks get, if possible, even pinker. "Not much choice, have I?" she says, her voice a little hoarse.

Now that Quintus has made his feelings and intentions clear, Cassia unbends. He showers her with tokens of his affection, from flowers to carvings he has made, and she glows with his attention, offers first her cheek and then her lips for kisses as he passes, nestles into his arms, beams on him when he plays with Emilia. She looks after him in her own way, cooking little treats, weaving him a colourful belt, tutting over the state of his shoes and ordering new ones from the cobblers. She spends time preparing her white wedding tunic, adding embroidery, also in white, to the hem and neckline.

Fabia is delighted with the news. "Now my little one will have a proper mother and father," she coos. She sits on the floor of the courtyard and allows Emilia to crawl over her lap, tickles her and then strokes her hair as the child grows weary and falls asleep. "Someone lift her off me, she's getting so heavy."

Cassius comes to take her, carrying her drowsy over one shoulder back to their apartment.

"You should have your own baby," I tell Fabia.

Fabia laughs. "One day," she says, getting stiffly up from the position she's been stuck in for the past hour. "I have enough to be doing with the new school. We've got twice the number of gladiators we had before."

"How is Sadiki working out?

"Good," she says, nodding. "He works hard and he's respectful. I could do with two of him."

"You'll manage," I say. "You always do."

Billica's turn as Queen Hippolyta of the Amazons has been a raging success and we ask Paternus and Labeo for more bookings to re-run the battle regularly over the season. Labeo is delighted. Paternus agrees, reluctantly mollified over the unexpected gladiator deaths by the higher price Billica now commands as a popular, billed gladiatrix. Painted images of her, red hair flying as she wields a sword from her chariot, adorn advertisements for the Games and I see plenty of obscene graffiti around the amphitheatre mentioning her name and what men would like to do with her in the bedroom. Labeo was right, she is beginning to make a name for herself, whether she wishes to or not.

Meanwhile the deaths of Primus and Eros have been reported, but there's been little interest from the authorities. They were both slaves, they were both gladiators. Their owner Paternus has been compensated by the imperial purse, they clearly feel that this sort of thing is to be expected amongst the low-life of the Games performers. Marcus gives instructions that there should be a guard at each door leading to the arena floor during shows, so that the Charon episode cannot be repeated. Strabo must show his face if he is called upon and Fabius must escort him to the arena door to show that his service really has been requested. All of us try not to walk about the place alone, although with the endless corridors and side rooms this is sometimes difficult. I can feel the nerves amongst the team and am glad when the programme shows a space of three days without shows, one of which will be Cassia's wedding. It would be nice to stop looking over our shoulders for a few days.

THE THRESHOLD

Cassia's wedding day in late June dawns with a bright blue sky and the promise of heat to come later. For now, there is a light breeze and the courtyard is full of women with flowers in their hands, following Julia's orders while over-excited children dart in and out, part help, part hinderance.

"Morning, Althea."

"Secundus! What are you doing here?"

"Brought a gift for the bride, of course." He holds out a bronze phallus on a chain. "Lucky pecker, can't have a bride getting married without one, now can I?"

"Thank you," I say, taking it. "Will you be with us for the festivities?"

"Got to get home," he says cheerfully. "But wanted to make sure I wished her luck."

"You're a kind man," I say, giving him a quick hug. "I'll give her your blessings."

"Enjoy the day," he calls out. "May Juno bless the bride."

"Juno's blessings on the bride," echo the women, still placing pots of water filled with flowers on every available surface.

Marcus clatters down the stairs to go with Fabius and Cassius to the auger, who will say whether the day is auspicious for the wedding. This time there is none of the dread in my belly as there was when Cassia almost married her horrible cousin. I run up the stairs to Cassia's apartment and find Fabia already dressed in a pink tunic trimmed with beads and flowers tucked in her hair, worn loose for once. It makes her look younger, less like her usual scholarly self. She is rocking Emilia in her cradle.

"I'm washing," calls Cassia from the other room.

"I'm so happy for her," says Fabia. "She deserves Quintus, after…"

"Yes. I woke up joyful today, not like that awful day last year."

Cassia appears, skin still pink from being rubbed dry, her eyes bright with excitement. I embrace her, getting wet from her still-dripping hair.

"I'm so happy for you," I say.

"I'm happy I didn't marry Rullus," she says with feeling. "Juno saved me for a better man."

I take the towel from her and rub her hair dry, pull a comb through it as it dries, then help her dress in the white tunic of a bride, adding the elaborate knot of Hercules to her belt and her mother's flame-gold veil to her hair. I can already hear noise from the courtyard, the inhabitants of our insula gathering to celebrate. A cheer goes up.

"That'll be your groom arriving," I say giggling. "Better not keep him waiting."

I lift out Emilia and give her to Fabia, who staggers slightly under her growing weight. "Ready?"

"Ready."

"Cassia?"

She beams at me as I take her by the hand. "Ready."

I open the door and let Fabia out, then lead out Cassia to whoops and cheers. I cannot help laughing with pleasure. To see our whole community gathered here, the courtyard filled with flowers and happy people, is a lovely sight. Opposite stands Quintus. His face lights up at the sight of Cassia. He holds out his hands towards her and I lead her to him. He does not stand on ceremony, clasping her in his arms and whispering something to her, which makes her smile even wider. Then he lets her go.

"Sorry, Althea," he says, still beaming. "I could not resist."

"I'll forgive you for loving her," I say, taking her hand back. "You need only wait a few more moments."

The priest declares that all the signs are good, the bridal pair have the blessing of the gods on their wedding day and for their marriage. He pours a libation of wine to the gods. Then he turns to face the crowd. "Who gives this woman to be wed?"

"I, Althea Aquillius, give this woman, Cassia Umbrius to be wed," I say. I squeeze Cassia's shaking hands in mine and place them gently in Quintus' outstretched palms. His hands are steady, warm as I close his fingers over her hands, his face alight with love, his eyes only on Cassia's face.

"Now you must swear your oaths," says the priest. "First you, Cassia."

Cassia's eyes are brimming as she repeats the traditional vows, invoking all the marriages of the past as she creates her own. "When and where you are Gaius, everyman, I then and there am Gaia, everywoman," she says.

"When and where you are Gaia, everywoman, I then and there am Gaius, everyman," echoes Quintus. He puts an iron ring onto the third finger of Cassia's left hand, then takes a loaf of unleavened bread from the priest and breaks it above her head, before passing it to the priest who takes a chunk of it and places it on the altar.

"I am part of your family," says Cassia, completing the words of the ceremony.

Applause and cheers break out. Cassia and Quintus are seated on little stools before the altar and feed each other pieces of the bread. But we are impatient, we call for kisses and, giggling, they acquiesce, at which more cheers break out and the feasting can begin.

A pig has been slaughtered for the occasion, stuffed with fennel seeds and herbs and slowly roasted in the baker's oven overnight. Within moments a long table has been laid out, made up of every table in the insula. Julia hands flowers to the children, who lay them down the middle under Adah's direction as the women carry in great platters of food. For once, Cassia is not the caterer, but there are many delicacies to be eaten. Wine sweetened with honey and fresh green salads filled with parsley, onion, mint and coriander accompany the fragrant roasted pork eaten with bread rolls studded with olives and nuts. A traditional wedding cake made with grape juice is ready to be shared out. We also have a peach cream, which is Cassia's favourite, blackcurrant tart with a thick custard and figs in a richly spiced syrup. There are many toasts made, offering good wishes, which inevitably lead on to bawdy songs as the afternoon wears on, and later on there is dancing round the courtyard, hands clasped as circles weave in and out of one another.

Before dusk comes we take care of another important matter. Fabia places Emilia on the floor at Quintus' feet and he adopts her, lifting her up from the ground as he did from the street and naming her, to much applause and blessings from the crowd. He gives her a tiny crescent moon-shaped protective necklace, and Fabia fastens it about her neck. Emilia stretches up inquiring fingers but cannot grasp it and is distracted by Quintus handing her to Cassia, who covers her little face with kisses.

"Making Cassia a wife and a mother all on one day? You are quick, Quintus!" calls out a wit and everyone laughs.

It is time for the bride to leave for her husband's home. Quintus is planning to come and live in the insula with Cassia and Cassius, as they have a large apartment, but the rituals must be observed. Two of Quintus' brothers make for Cassia and grasp her arms.

"We're kidnapping you, Cassia!" they shout jovially. "You're part of our family, everyone heard you say it, and so now you must come with us!"

Cassia is laughing but trying hard to hide it, instead pretending, as she should, to be afraid of leaving home. "Oh, oh," she cries out rather weakly. "Father! Althea! Fabia! Julia! Maria! Save me! I am being taken against my will!"

Trying to keep a straight face, the other members of Quintus' family lay hands on her and begin to drag her towards the gate, Quintus leading the way, Cassia's hand held tightly in his. We all follow them out into the street, where a larger crowd has gathered. It is good luck for as many people as possible to see the bride, so our neighbours lean out of windows and come out of their homes as we turn down Virgin's Street, clapping and cheering as we pass.

"I am being kidnapped!" cries Cassia in a louder voice, getting into the spirit of the occasion, widening her eyes and reaching out to Marcus. "Someone save me! Marcus!"

Marcus laughs at her poorly disguised giggles and throws handfuls of nuts into the crowd, followed by everyone from our insula. Children scatter to catch them and the crowd responds with shouted obscenities which will convince any evil spirits not to harm the happy couple.

Quintus' family home is only two streets away, so our procession there is quick. The door is opened to receive Cassia and now she gives up her feigned fear and outrage and turns to face us all to repeat her consent.

"When and where you are everyman, Gaius, I then and there am everywoman, Gaia," she says, beaming up at Quintus. "I am part of your family."

We cheer as Quintus sweeps her into his arms and carries her across the threshold. A few of us follow inside, where Quintus' mother and father greet Cassia with a bowl of water and a burning brazier, indicating that she will be mistress of the home and hearth, before leading the couple towards Quintus' bedroom, where the bed has been draped with brightly coloured blankets and strewn with rose petals.

Shyly Cassia sits on the bed and is joined by Quintus, who pulls her into his arms and kisses her, to a final round of applause and bawdy shouts. I wink at Cassia as I close the door and she smiles back, cheeks pink.

"All right, back to the insula, there's a lot more wine to be drunk!" calls out Marcus and everyone follows him back to our courtyard. "Music!" he cries when we get there and grabs my hand and Fabia's, leading us all into a wild dance round the courtyard.

After several rounds I break away and collapse, laughing and panting, onto a bench where Marcus joins me.

"That was well managed," I say, filling up our cups with wine.

"Oh, you have to control these things or everyone gets silly and starts insisting on staying outside the door while the marriage is consummated," he says. "It's not really what you want is it, everyone giggling outside the room on your wedding night? I had an uncle who took care of such nonsense for me and I was grateful."

Heat creeps up my neck that has nothing to do with the dancing. "Yes," I say, "I mean no, not what you want." The idea of a wedding night, of what Cassia and Quintus will be doing now, flusters me, the thought of Marcus and his bride... The first night I went to Marcus' house as his newly acquired slave, I heard him in the bedchamber with Livia, he kissed her lips as we left, never to see her again. I am torn, as always, between desire for Marcus and the sad memories of Livia and his tiny son Amantius, feeling a guilt I have not even earnt, and wondering if this is how Marcus feels when he thinks of being with another woman, if it is part of what holds him back...

"What are you thinking of, all serious like that? Sad to have lost a friend? She'll be back tomorrow morning you know, looking after customers like always. You won't even have time to miss her."

I force a smile. "Oh, I know. We're lucky not to be losing her. And she is so happy with Quintus, he is a good man. Not like..."

I don't even say his name, I don't want it to pollute this happy day, but Marcus reaches out a hand and places it over mine. "I thank the gods he is gone," he says. "I never wanted to hurt someone so much in my life as when I heard he laid hands on you. But he wasn't even man enough to deserve that, he was better off being humiliated by Cassia."

I sit rigidly still. The warmth of Marcus' hand on mine, his words of protection and care, are leaving me breathless. I want more. I want him to say something else, something about me deserving better, deserving a man who loves me, a man like...

"Quintus is a good man," says Marcus, removing his hand from mine and sitting back, taking a sip of wine. "He'll make Cassia a fine husband. And a baby already," he adds chuckling, "no doubt with another one in a year or so."

His fingertips are so close to mine. I could reach out myself, could take his hand and say…

"Dance with me?" Funis is standing over me, hand outstretched.

I hesitate, hoping for a brief moment that Marcus will intervene, will offer himself as my dance partner, but he has been distracted by a toast called out by Fabius, who has joined our table.

"The happy couple!"

"The happy couple!" says Marcus, raising his cup.

"Come," says Funis and I rise, take his hand and follow him to the other side of the courtyard, where we join the dancers. We clasp hands and enter the circle, taking steps first one way and then the other.

"It must be a happy day to see your friend wed to a man she loves," says Funis.

I smile up at him. "It is," I say. "She deserves every happiness. They both do."

"Knowing who the right person is to bring you happiness is a gift of Venus," says Funis. "When we see that person, we should take them by the hand and make them our own, without hesitation."

We turn in the dance, our steps taking us one way and then another. Funis is a graceful dancer, he guides my direction with ease as the circle of revellers attempts a more complex sequence. I realise, stumbling with shame, that I am not gazing at him as he is at me, but instead twisting my neck in an effort to spot Marcus. I look at Funis and he meets my gaze with a serious look in his eyes.

"Does it make you think you would like to be married yourself, one day soon?"

He's hinting. If I were to clasp his hand more firmly, smile more widely, he would guide my steps away from the crowd and to a quieter part of the courtyard, into the shadows of Julia's tumbling vines and flowers, where I would be embraced. He would be kind, I would be treated lovingly, not just now but in the future. I look across the courtyard, to where Marcus is laughing with Fabia, and although Funis can sense my longing he knows it is not for him. He is no fool and I do not want to lie to him or give false hope. Gently I pull my hand away, touch his arm but with a sad smile rather than the flirtatious one he is hoping for. "It does."

THE GATE OF DEATH

WE ARE USED TO PLENTY of strange sights at the Games. But even the audience is whispering at the drunken ex-senator in the front row of the amphitheatre and his chosen companion.

"Have you seen her?" asks Strabo, eyes wide.

I nod. "Unbelievable."

The she-wolf chosen by the ex-senator as his companion for the day is wearing an outfit that has everyone gaping. She is clothed only in a breast-band and briefs of tightly fitted pale leather, decorated with a leopard pattern, which then extends over the rest of her bare skin, so that every part of her is painted with dark brown spots. Her hair hangs loose, but a hairband is wrapped round her head, from which poke sewn-on ears of leather, the whole headpiece also decorated as a leopard. Her face has been painted, her eyes in the Egyptian style, her nose in black, her cheeks with sweeping strokes to illustrate whiskers. Her feet are shod in delicate sandals and from the back of her leather briefs swings a real leopard tail.

The prostitute has imbued herself with the spirit of the large cat she is embodying. Sinuous, she drapes herself against her client, bends backwards over his knees, slinks along the walkway in front of his seat, crawls up his body, her arms draped about his neck, licking his face with an enthusiastic tongue. He, delighted, holds onto her via a bejewelled leash and collar. He rubs her leather ears, tickles her under her chin, rubs her belly. The audience looks on, part amused or bemused, part outraged that a senator, even one no longer in office, should stoop so low in public.

"We have to get them out of here before Domitian arrives," I whisper to Strabo.

"Can Marcus get rid of them?"

"I suppose," I say. I'd like to deal with the matter myself but I doubt that any senator will listen to a woman, let alone one as drunk as this one appears to be. But Domitian has made it pretty clear already that he does not care for sexual misconduct even in people's private lives, let alone a public display like this. "Where is he?"

"I'll go and find him."

Marcus is not impressed when he spots the couple. "What is that?"

"They've been like that since they got here. And the show has to start shortly."

Marcus looks appalled. "I'll deal with it. If Domitian sees that we'll get in trouble for allowing lewd behaviour at the Games."

Marcus' intervention has the ex-senator leave fairly promptly, but only after the leopard-woman has rubbed herself against Marcus' knees, winking up at him as he argues with her client.

"Thanks the gods Domitian didn't see that," is all he says when he gets back to us. "Come on, let's get the show started and hope nothing else like that happens," he adds, rolling his eyes at our helpless giggles.

TODAY BILLICA IS BACK AS Queen Hippolyta. The crowd cheers when her name is announced, the plebians stamping their feet as the first chariots come hurtling out of the arena doors. I kneel by a grate to watch as Billica makes her entrance, tumbling red tresses surmounted by her golden crown, face contorted in a violent grimace.

She's unstoppable. Labeo's gladiatrices are well trained and are putting on impressive battle scenes, they're not there just to be pretty, but even they look nervous when she's close to them, jerking away from her or looking over one shoulder when they should be concentrating on their own bouts. But Billica ignores the women. It is the men she goes after, sword in hand, teeth bared, lunging and swiping at them. They fight back, but she almost stabs one to death, he escapes with a severe cut to his side and has to be taken at speed to Fabius below. She fights every minor gladiator she can get close to and kills two criminals, one by cutting his throat and one who she runs through with her sword, but her eyes return again and again to Carpophorus and the gladiator playing Hercules. It's them she wants, the heroes of the arena. She gets closer to them and even though Carpophorus is very experienced and so is his fellow gladiator, still my hands clench as she finally enters into combat with them. Paternus is right. Carpophorus is mindful of the referee, aware he is there to put on a good show. Billica just wants to kill. She snarls at the referee when he tries to intervene and her sword comes too close to comfort to his leg. He steps back, alarmed, but the crowd is loving this, the savage woman turned loose, wild and untrainable. They shout her name, they shout encouragement and cheer her on. Marcus, seeing that things are about to get out of hand, makes a gesture and the chorus announce that Hercules and Theseus overcame Queen Hippolyta, claiming a kiss from her as well as her sacred belt. Carpophorus and his co-gladiator take the hint and nod to two other gladiators and the referee.

It takes five men to hold her down and wrest the sword from her hand, during which the referee gets a cut on his arm, before today's Hercules is brave enough to lean over her for a kiss and even so he is careful to put one hand on her forehead, pushing her down so she cannot suddenly lunge forwards to bite him. He kisses her lightly and the crowd cheer, but Billica, heavily restrained, still manages to spit in his face as he holds up her belt. Her chariot arrives and she is forced back into it, now weaponless, and swiftly driven to the exit door. A more docile performer would have been granted a victory lap of the arena with their sword still in their hand, I think, a chance to soak up the applause, but no-one trusts this woman.

The exit door is right by my grate. I stand up as the chariot is driven in. Four men are waiting in the shadows and before the wheels have stopped turning they have laid hands on Billica, gripping her tightly and pulling her out of the chariot, then forcing her to an open lift, into which they throw her. she falls, landing hard on her knees as they slam the door shut, but she's immediately back on her feet, reaching through the bars to the man who is locking the lift door, running her nails down his arm so hard she draws blood.

"Stupid bitch," he swears, raising his hand as though to strike her back, but then thinking better of it when her face shows nothing but eagerness for his hand to come inside the cage where she can grab it and bite him. Instead he shouts for the lift to be lowered and receives an answering shout. He makes an obscene gesture at her and then walks away with the other men.

There's a tiny pause before the ropes tighten, indicating that the lift is about to move. I step out of the shadows and Billica's head jerks with fear at the unexpected movement. When she sees me she swallows and stands still.

"You're a good fighter," I say softly. There is something so animal-like about her that it's like admiring the strength of a tiger, while fearing it.

Billica does not say anything. The lift begins to move down to the lower level, where she will be chained and taken back to Paternus' barracks. As she fades out of sight I see that her eyes are full of tears.

It's late in the afternoon of the same day and I should already be gone, but after the cleaning shift was done and the arena made ready for tomorrow's hunt, Funis has arranged for a large herd of zebra to be brought through the Gate of Death and across the arena floor, to a pen we have erected where they can sleep the night and eat the cut grass provided. I wait for everything to be done and once the animals have been locked up in the pen Funis and I settle down in the seating area to ensure they grow calm and don't try to escape, though I'm fairly sure the enclosure is solid enough to contain them. I don't want the conversation to stray into marriage territory again, so I bring up something I have been curious about.

"You never told me who your father was," I say.

He's very quiet for a moment. "I don't talk about him much," he says at last. "He is a senator."

I stare at him. "A senator?"

He gives a short laugh. "Didn't think I was that well connected, did you?"

"Um… gladiators aren't… usually…"

"I know. Slaves, prisoners-of-war and misfits. Not the sons of senators, as a rule."

"Then… how?"

He gives a sigh, the story is a heavy burden he carries. "My mother was enslaved as a child, just as you were. She came from the Kingdom of Kush."

"Dodekaschoinos."

"That's right. She was brought to Rome very young and sold to the kitchen of a fancy patrician villa. She peeled vegetables and washed dishes, she cried for her mother at night and ate whatever was put in front of her. That was her whole life until she was nineteen. By then she was the assistant to the cook, she'd learnt to cook and make herself useful and some other child peeled the vegetables and cried at night. The old master died and his son took one look at the slaves in his household and decided he'd have his sport with them. There wasn't a slave he didn't bed in that household, male or female. But he took a particular liking to my mother and she was called for pretty regularly. When she told him she was with child, he stopped calling for her. I grew up in that villa, slaves are expensive to buy so if you can breed them yourself, why not? I had my mother with me, but it was a cowed household. Whippings came easy and any slave could be called on to warm the master's bed."

There isn't very much I can say.

Funis sighs again. "He became a senator. His family background made him believe he was superior to everyone, better than even most of the senators in Rome, he was obsessed with how high class he was, his public image was everything to him, never mind what went on behind closed doors. He married a wife from one of the best families, then mistreated her while obliging her to go about in public as though she were the happiest woman in the world. And while most masters would not care if there were a few slave boys about the place with a passing resemblance to themselves, I saw the look in his eyes when I stood in front of him, the recognition and then the hate, how repulsed he was to see his own features in a slave boy."

"But you're free?"

"I waited. Learnt to fight. Found a gladiator trainer and asked him to buy me. My mother begged me not to do it but it was the only way out. The trainer made the offer to the household steward, who was fond of my mother. He agreed a price for me and sold me, the senator was only too willing to get me out of his house. But when he found out who had bought me he was furious: rather than disappear quietly into Rome I was going to be a gladiator? The lowest of the low? He felt it would be degrading for him if it were known I was connected to him, though I doubt anyone but him would have cared. He said he would make it hard on my mother out of spite, so I said I was an Egyptian, used the fighting name Sobek. I trained harder and longer than any other gladiator at the school, started to make a name for myself."

"Sobek the crocodile god?"

"Yes. I wore a suit of crocodile armour and a helmet with crocodile-shaped jaws."

A cold shiver runs down me. "You wore crocodile-leather armour? Like Eros, the gladiator that was killed by Charon?" My mind is whirring. "You were close by when the first gladiator was wounded with a poisoned arrow. Have these attacks been meant for you? Is your father aware of you being here? Wants to harm you?"

"Who knows?" he says, apparently unconcerned. "If that was the plan, they didn't carry it out very well. I'm still breathing."

"Be careful," I say, shaken by his revelation. "It's a dangerous life to be a gladiator, let alone one who is an enemy of people in power."

He nods but his mind is still on the past. "I never got what I wanted. I asked over and over to buy my mother. I offered a ridiculous sum for her. But he stuck to his word and wouldn't allow her to be sold. She got ill and still he wouldn't allow it. She died a slave." His voice is very bitter.

"Did you keep fighting?"

"For a while, but then I started training other gladiators, and the animals. I had a knack for working with them, so I did well and after a while I was worth more out of the arena than in it. I was glad to have made it to the end of my fighting career without suffering a bad injury or losing my life. One of the beast hunters needed an assistant and when he died I moved to Ostia and took over. I've been one of the top animal providers to all the arenas in the Empire for years. I'm proud of what I've accomplished."

"You weren't sure about coming to us, though."

"That was for other reasons."

I wait, but he does not speak again. I say it for him. "Your father?"

"He's still a senator here in Rome."

"Does he know you are here?"

"He'll find out, I expect. He's had spies keeping an eye on me for years. I've been warned more than once not to come back to Rome, not to be too visible. He preferred me in Ostia."

"Warned?"

"At knifepoint. In dark alleyways."

"Why?"

"He does not want his bastard son by a slave woman being famous for being involved in the Games. He worries someone would find out, ruin what he likes to think of as a spotless reputation, though his whole household knows better. If Martial got his hands on it he'd have it written up and circulated round Rome before you could blink, a tasty bit of gossip."

"Plenty of senators have illegitimate children scattered about. And most of them slaves."

"Not ones who were gladiators and now supply the Games as beast hunters. Disreputable trade."

He's right, the work we do places us in an underclass side by side with gladiators and whores; something of the glamorous and desirable about us, yes, but still disreputable. Desired and disdained, all in one.

"But you came back to Rome anyway?"

He looks at me, dark eyes serious. "I came because you asked me."

"You said that once before."

He smiles. "Ah, so you did hear me."

"I did."

"But you didn't ask what I meant by it."

I look down; his gaze is too direct. "I knew what you meant."

"And?"

I look up again. "I don't know."

I have told him much more than I have said out loud. "Is there someone else?"

My head moves, but it is neither a nod nor a shake.

"You're not sure?"

I sigh. "Neither is he."

"Ah."

We stand in silence for a moment.

"I should go," I say.

"Wait," he says.

I wait.

"I *am* sure," he says. "I am sorry he is not and that evidently it is painful to you, so painful that you cannot see who else you might turn to, who else you might have feelings for. But I am sure. I want you, Althea. I saw something in you on that day in Ostia and it drew me back to Rome, a place I am rightly wary of, because I told myself I would be a fool not to see you again, to see if I was right. And I was. I have grown to love you. You are a rare woman. You have a good and kind nature, you work hard and you are quick-witted. And I see you yearning for something greater, for someone to love you."

I look at him. I am not trembling, not swept away with desire as I am when I daydream of Marcus making a similar declaration. Instead it feels like a friend speaking to me, like speaking with Fabia or Cassia, someone I can trust to tell me the truth, someone with whom I can speak truthfully. "I don't love you," I say. "I do not mean that as an unkindness, but as a truth. I could not make you happy."

"I thought you might say that," he says, not distressed by my refusal. "But perhaps if you were not yearning for something that cannot be, you might open your heart to something that could be, to something that is already waiting for you."

"But what if I never love you and you love me?"

He smiles. "You see? Already you are imagining what could be. You are imagining what it would be like if we were to walk through life together, if you would become my wife. If you wish to work with me in my business, we could do that. If you are tired of the Games, as I think you are, then I will sell the business to Carpophorus and you and I can live quietly somewhere on a farm, or in any business you choose."

"Is that what you would want?"

"Yes," he says, with absolute certainty. "I want you to be my wife. I do not care what work I do, I have proven myself already, now I want something new. A different life. A happy life, away from the harshness that is Rome and the Games. Family. Friends. The small joys."

"And if I never loved you?"

"I would still love you," he says. "And there are plenty of marriages where love is never thought of, never planned for at all. So we would already have more love than those."

"Perhaps."

"But?"

I shake my head. "I cannot marry you, Funis. I love –" I stop myself. "I love someone else, as you have already realised, and I cannot marry someone else while... while there might be a chance."

"And is there a chance? That Marcus will stop being an idiot and see what is right in front of him?"

I'm hot. "I –"

He chuckles. "You cannot think I don't see how you look at him. I don't know how he doesn't see it, but I am not blind."

I swallow. "He doesn't see me because I'm always there," I say at last. "He doesn't think of me that way."

"Then he's a fool."

"Cassia and Fabia would agree with you," I find myself saying.

He laughs out loud, a big laugh, startling a passing dove, which takes off with a flutter of wings. "Oh, so everyone sees it except him?"

"Apparently."

"Not blessed by Venus to see what's right in front of him?"

"No."

He sighs. "I cannot believe I'm even going to offer to do this. Do you want me to tell him?"

"No!" I say hastily, horrified.

"No? You'd rather wait until he comes to his senses, one day? After not doing so for – how many years have you known him now?"

"More than two years."

"And you'd rather wait? Or keep waiting, I should say?"

"Yes."

His eyes are sad, but he forces a smile. "Then know that I will keep waiting too. For you. We will see who can be the more stubborn. Marcus, for not seeing you, or me, who sees you every day in my dreams."

"You should find someone else," I say.

"So should you."

We laugh together. I touch his arm quickly, wanting both to comfort and to show gratitude for his declaration and acceptance of my refusal combined, but not wanting him to take it for anything more. "Thank you."

"I have done nothing."

"It is not nothing to offer your heart," I say. "I have not been brave enough to do it."

"Then perhaps you should."

"I don't know how."

"When you are desperate enough you will," he says. "The words will come out of your mouth because you can no longer bear to hold them in."

A voice comes from behind us. "Funis, my friend! You still owe me a drink!"

It's Secundus, who has finished selling for the day.

"So I do," agrees Funis, grinning. "You told me your life story and I promised you mine in return. We're going to need several drinks this evening." He looks at me and lowers his voice to a quiet tone. "I will keep waiting."

"I'm sorry," I say.

"I may win yet," he says, getting to his feet and holding out his hand to pull me up. "I can be stubborn too."

I watch them go, unsure of my feelings. Why is it that Funis can offer everything I want from Marcus, when Marcus is unable to offer the same? Perhaps he just doesn't feel the way I hope he does, and never will. Perhaps he sees me as someone with whom he works, at best a friend and nothing more, neither now nor in the future. And if that is the case… would marriage to Funis be the right choice? Should I accept that plenty of marriages are based on practicalities and a respect that might grow into friendliness and care, yet still without thoughts or hope of romantic love ever flowering?

My steps back to the insula are slow. I walk through busy streets without hearing the noise of daily life around me, my mind uncertain. Have the dice of fate already fallen this way or that, showing what path will be followed? Funis' words, *when you are desperate enough*, make me wonder whether I will know that moment when it comes, whether I will find it in myself to speak to Marcus, to tell him that I love him and find out, at last, what his own thoughts and feelings about me are.

I make my way to the popina, dandle Emilia, eat a platter of olives and salad, scoop up soft fresh cheese mixed with herbs using fresh bread, pass the time of day with some of Cassia's regular customers. Karbo arrives and wolfs down his evening meal before dashing off to play with his friends. I am too tired for much conversation. I pass Emilia back to Cassius, who has been entertaining her by playing peekaboo behind an old dishcloth, wave goodnight and make my way upstairs.

I lie awake for a while, thoughts still turning over, but it is all too confusing and eventually I drift to sleep.

When Karbo and I arrive at the popina the next morning, Emilia is wailing and Cassia is rushed off her feet.

"She's teething," she says.

Karbo and I pull faces to distract her but Emilia is grumpy, with flushed cheeks and a sullen tiredness about her we don't often see. She chews voraciously on a piece of stale bread, evidently the only thing giving her gums any satisfaction.

"We have to go," I say to Cassia. "I'll try and leave a bit earlier and come back to help you, once the gladiators start."

"Thank you," she says. "I'd be grateful for that. I don't know what to do with her when she's like this."

"It's hot," I say. "I'll take her to the courtyard fountain later and she can play in the water, she'll like that."

THE WALK THROUGH THE FORUM, though familiar, is always interesting. There's such a mix of people; from the lawyers and senators to street sweepers and shit carriers, she-wolves making their way home, soothsayers and priests…

"Can we go swimming in the river this evening?" asks Karbo.

"After I've helped Cassia with the baby," I say.

"Can I go with just my friends?"

"Only in the shallows," I say. "The current's too strong, I don't want you getting swept away."

At the amphitheatre, the zebra are calm; none have escaped, one is even lying down, most are chewing grass. There's no sign of Funis.

"Shall I check if he's in the hypogeum?" asks Karbo.

"Yes," I say. "You won't need a lamp if you leave the arena door open, you can call down and he'll hear you if he's there." I'm always a bit anxious that Karbo, or indeed any of our team, might leave a lamp burning and start a fire. Hidden in our maze of rooms and corridors, no-one would know until a blaze had built up.

Karbo makes his way to the arena door closest to the Gate of Death, pausing to try and stroke the zebras, who are having none of it, retreating to the edge of their pen, as far away from him as they can. Disappointed, he pulls open the arena door and disappears inside. He appears again immediately.

"Althea!" His voice is a desperate whisper.

"What?" I ask, already hurrying towards him.

"Come quick!"

I break into a run, join him in the doorway. His face is grey as he points down into the darkness, trying to edge away from whatever he has seen.

"I can't see –" I start and then stop.

On the brick floor, in the dim light, lies Secundus, one arm stretched out so that his cloak is pulled back to reveal the tiny phalluses with which he made his living. He is very still. His head is covered in blood which have come from three holes, neatly spaced out in a small area of his temple. I don't understand what kind of weapon would make such a wound.

Karbo, who has seen all sorts in the arena, is whimpering. I kneel down, touch Secundus' neck, but he is already too cool to be living. I snatch my hand away, stare down in disbelief.

"What if someone wants to kill us? What if they're here?" whispers Karbo.

"They're gone already," I say. "Whoever did this, they're gone. Go and get Marcus. Now."

I WAIT WITH THE DOOR propped open so that I can see Secundus from the arena. Despite my certain words to Karbo, I'm too scared to be alone in the darkness with a corpse. I stare out at the vast amphitheatre all around me, wonder at how calm the zebras are. My world is growing darker and I am afraid.

Marcus arrives at a run, followed by a panting Karbo. He does not even speak to me, just looks down at Secundus in disbelief and silence.

His presence gives me courage. I squat down next to the body, trying to see the wound better. Secundus' eyes stare up at me, empty of the laughter that always accompanied his presence.

"I know what it is!" says Karbo.

"What are you talking about?" Marcus snaps.

"What made those three holes in his head."

"How could you possibly know that?"

"The key!"

"Key?"

"To the Gate of Death, it has that shape. And you could kill someone with it if you hit them hard enough."

I look down at Secundus, his face pale in death. The holes. "Bring it here," I say.

Karbo is up and running before I've finished talking, disappearing down the long corridor, his footsteps echoing.

"I'm sorry," I whisper down to Secundus, patting his shoulder, hoping he might still feel my touch and find it comforting. His jovial smile and the constant patter that tripped easily off his tongue, the jokes and puns, the endless innuendos his merchandise allowed him to make… tears well up, trickling down my cheeks.

"It's gone!" I hear Karbo yell before he's even got back to us.

I knew this already, I expected the key to be gone as soon as I realised it had been used for this purpose. Something very dark is happening and I cannot bring it into the light, cannot work out what is going on. I am afraid, because someone is killing people and I have no idea how to stop them, nor who else might be in danger. I had feared for Funis, because of the crocodile armour and his past, but I must have been wrong, I cannot see how Funis is involved here. Unless… he was going drinking with Secundus last night. They were going to share life stories. Funis would have told him everything he told me. Is he dead because of that knowledge? I can feel the back of my neck grow cold. I know the story too. Am I next? But why kill Secundus and not Funis, if they were both out late, surely it would have been just as easy to kill Funis or indeed both of them. I am growing more and more confused, but no less afraid.

"I'm sorry," I whisper again, and close Secundus' eyes. I stand and stare directly at Marcus.

"What is going on?" I ask.

In the shadows his face is more lined than usual. "I don't know," he says.

"I am going home," I say. "With Karbo. You will have to complete today's Games by yourself. Send a messenger for the Urban Cohorts. They will have to investigate what happened. They will take what's been going on seriously now it is a Roman citizen and not some slave they don't care about. And you can go and tell Secundus' family."

He doesn't argue, only steps aside so that we can leave. I take Karbo's hand in mine and we walk, in silence, back through the Forum, up the stairs to our roof hut, where I lie on my bed and listen to Karbo whispering to Letitia as they play in the sunshine.

I SLEEP, EVENTUALLY, WHEN MY thoughts have gone round so many times that I am dizzy and sick. When I wake the heat tells me it's already afternoon and I sit on the edge of my bed, head in hands, more weary than if I had not slept at all. At last I drag myself to my feet and push the door open. Karbo is in the doorway.

"We need to eat," I say, my voice croaky from sleep.

"Already have. Marcus brought some food." He points in a vague direction behind our roof hut then leaves. I can hear him clattering down the stairs.

My feet drag. For the first time since I realised my feelings for him, I don't want to see Marcus. I don't want to discuss what is going on. I hope he has left some food and gone away.

He is there. Looking out over Rome, his back to me, hands on the wall. I wonder if I can pick up the plate of food at my feet and return to the hut without him noticing me. My stomach rumbles at the fresh salad, flatbread and a crushed chickpea dip thick with olive oil on the plate, as well as the ripe peach sat by its side. I crouch down as quietly as I can and place the peach on the plate, then grimace. My throat is dry with thirst but in order to pour water from the temptingly-full jug into the empty cup sat by the plate, I will most certainly draw Marcus' attention.

I start pouring and Marcus turns at once.

"Althea —"

"I don't want to talk," I say.

"What?"

"I don't want to spend hours going over and over it, how it could have happened, what's going on. I don't want to hear what Secundus' family said when you told them or how they'll get by without him."

"They —"

"Something bad is happening, Marcus, and I'm afraid. For me, for you, for Karbo, for all of us. This life — it's too dark. It's too much. And you have —"

"I have what?"

"Willingly signed up for another year. Without asking me if I wanted that! And will there be another year after that? And another? Will you just keep saying yes, while the roof tiles fall and your family farm becomes nothing but a memory, something in your imagination?"

"The farm?" He looks bewildered and it makes me angrier.

"Your family farm! The one you told me about when I'd barely met you, when I was still your slave. You told me it was all you wanted, it was your dream for the future and you'd go there as soon as you could. The amphitheatre, the Games – that was just to have enough money. You couldn't wait to be rid of this job and now you can't get enough of it, no matter how dark it becomes, no matter who dies or who is in danger!"

"Livia – Amantius –"

"I know! I know they died and took away everything you cared for. But I hoped you might care about – about Karbo," I fumble, putting his name before mine, like a coward, "– about me, that you would take us away from here, that we…"

I stop. Marcus is staring at me while I rant, his face showing confusion at my sudden rage. "Never mind."

Marcus takes a step forward. "I do mind. I do care. I did not know you were so unhappy."

"You think I can be happy with all this going on?"

"No, of course not, but aside from this matter…"

I wave him away. "You don't understand anything. I shall make my own arrangements. I will find a different job, a safe place for Karbo and me to live. You won't have to worry about us."

"But I thought… one day… that we…"

"You thought what?"

His words stumble out. "That I… we… that one day I would return to my family's farm and that you and Karbo…"

"Yes?"

"Would be there too."

"Would we?"

"You are always there," he says.

I almost gasp. "And I would be *what* to you? On the farm? A farmhand?"

He blinks. "Of course not."

"Then what?"

He half-shrugs, searches for words. "My wife, I suppose."

"You *suppose*?" I'm half-laughing, half horrified, tears welling up, the anger burning my neck and cheeks.

He knows he has made an error. A bad one. "I didn't – I meant…"

"You assumed I'd tag along, wherever you went, whenever you felt like going," I spit out. "You assumed that because I always do tag along. Because I'm 'always there', as you have just so perfectly phrased it."

"I –"

"You don't even know how I feel for you! You don't see me as someone to fall in love with because I'm always by your side. You suppose I'll have to be your wife because you can't think of what else I would be. You take me for granted and more fool me for letting you do that, for hoping for a life by your side even without any hope of love. This is my last season of the Games, with or without you. I'm not living like this anymore. And I'm taking Karbo out of this world. It's not safe." I've been speaking so fast I'm gasping for breath, my voice wavers.

Marcus is staring at me. "You feel…?" His voice trails away, he cannot believe what I have just said.

"Yes!" I say, my voice bursting out too loud after being held in for too long. "Yes, I *feel* for you. I love you! I desire you. I can't stop thinking of you. I can barely breathe when your arm brushes mine. And everyone knows it! Everyone but you. How can you not see it? How can you not feel it? Funis wants to marry me, but I turned him down because of wanting you and you don't even know or care or look at me, I'm just there, just always *there* and you don't see me except as your right hand, sorting out messes and doing what I'm told. I've had enough. I want more. I deserve more. I'm done with moping about for you. I want happiness and fun like Cassia, I want a husband who loves me and children who are safe and happy like Emilia."

"But I –"

"But nothing. I am not wasting my time and love on a man who doesn't even see me when I'm standing right next to him!"

I hear him calling my name over and over as I run across the rooftop and down the stairs. I make my way, eyes blurred with tears, through the courtyard and out into Sand Street, run down the street and spend the rest of the afternoon until dusk, sitting by the edge of the slow-running Tiber river, crying until I can cry no more.

THE NEXT DAY WE STAND side by side at Cassia's and eat in silence. Cassia looks at my red eyes and Marcus' stony face and her cheerful morning chatter fades into uncertain silence. Emilia cries and neither of us coos at her. Marcus does not swing her in the air before work, as he usually does, I do not sit on the floor to tickle her tummy.

We barely talk in the following days. We speak only to carry out our work and our voices are flat. I make sure other people are always around us, including insisting that a slave accompanies me everywhere while I am at work and when Marcus asks for me to go somewhere where we can speak alone, I refuse, until he stops asking. I carry out my tasks and leave as soon as I can each day. I forbid Karbo from being at the amphitheatre and hire another messenger boy to take his place. He grumbles, but spends his days at the stables and playing with his friends.

I hurt every day. I cry every night, silently, so that Karbo will not hear me. But there is nothing more to be said. I have spoken my heart and Marcus does not feel the same way. So I go about my business and he goes about his and I harden my heart. I will finish this season of the Games and then I will leave this job and Rome itself and take Karbo with me.

THE BURIAL CHAMBER

THE HEAT OF ROME IN August is unbearable. Stray dogs pant on street corners, desperate for shade. Only the lizards bask in the sun, their bright green bodies whisking away if you get too close. Broad-brimmed hats of straw or felt protect anyone who must work in the middle of the day and by the time the gladiatorial bouts are on, the crowd in the amphitheatre is thinning, women and children and anyone who isn't an ardent fan losing their will to stay any longer without an awning. But our Games are no longer the focus of daily life.

Rome is whispering a name.

Cornelia.

The Virgo Maxima, chief amongst the Vestal Virgins.

Found with? Seen with? Named by?

A man.

No one is certain of the details, she proclaims her innocence. But her name has been spoken by Domitian and now it is muttered across Rome. Her fate is already chosen, no grace given this time, no quick and simple execution of her choice, rather a fate worse than death. Domitian may have been kind the first time this happened but his patience has been tested and he has decided that only the punishment enshrined by law will do. The Virgo Maxima is going to be entombed alive.

I go up the stairs and see Maria settling herself on her balcony for the day, large breasts resting on a cushion. She looks sombre when she sees me, indicates the porridge I have brought with me from Cassia, guessing it is for Julia.

"I'm not sure she'll eat. She was crying last night."

"How did she hear? I thought it was only announced this morning."

"The Vestals know anything that happens to their sisters. They watch out for each other."

Julia's apartment is dark, there is only a faint light coming from the still-shuttered window. I cannot make her out in the gloom.

"Julia?"

"Althea."

Her voice guides me to her location. I pull the door open wider to let in more light and she is there, on the floor in front of her lararium, not so much in a position of prayer as of crumpled despair.

I put the porridge on the table and crouch down next to her. I have never seen Julia like this. She is always composed, even when events around her call for fear or anger. She is always upright in her bearing. If I'd been told she was at prayer I would expect to find her standing in front of the lararium, arms outstretched, palms upwards, her voice clear, carrying her prayers to the gods as she did for the first two Vestals condemned to die. Instead here she is, shoulders heaving, slumped sideways on the cold floor.

"Julia," I whisper, frightened by her loss of control. "Julia."

She sobs, a snotty, gulping sound, lacking all her usual grace. I open the window shutters, then light two lamps, my fingers clumsy. The room filled with light, I look back at her, hoping she will have pulled herself upright, but she is where I left her. I crouch down again and pull at her arm, like a child aghast at its mother weeping.

"Please come and sit, Julia."

She pushes me away, but gently, then puts one hand on the floor and heaves herself upright, her body slow and heavy. She follows me to a chair and sits in it. I bring her a glass of well-watered wine.

"Have you eaten?" I gesture towards the porridge but Julia only shakes her head. Her face is streaked with tears, there is snot beneath her nose. She does nothing to wipe them away. Thoroughly unsettled, I fetch a towel, dip it in water and wipe her face with it. She does not stop me, only sits still, staring at nothing.

"You heard," I say at last, unable to think what else to say.

She blinks so slowly that her eyes stay closed for a moment and fresh tears seep from under her lashes. When she reopens her eyes her gaze moves to meet mine.

"To be a Vestal is a hard life," she says. She swallows, her shoulders tight. "So hard. You are chosen when nothing but a child. What does a child of six know of thirty years' service? How would a little girl know she is giving up the chance of love and family? She knows only the fear of being taken from her mother and given to a household of women who serve some higher purpose which means nothing to her. A household fire that must be tended. A job fit for a slave and yet of such great importance that Rome will fall to dust if you fail? What nonsense is that to a child?"

She stares away again, back into her own past and that of every Vestal chosen, since the first times.

"A house full of women who grow more bitter with every day that passes and they understand more fully what has been taken from them. Or instead grow so proud of their sacred duty that they become insufferable, that they preen and go about in public as much as they can, relishing the only thing that has been given to them in exchange for their snatched lives: the reverence of plebians. They attend the Games, are taken to the box reserved only for them, see the Emperor himself bow his head, feel the crowd's veneration and tell themselves that it is worth it, that their crippled lives are worth it after all, for are they not respected? Are they not given freedoms any woman in Rome would beg for? Do they not live in luxury, with slaves to wait on them and a sacrosanct destiny?"

"Cassia said…" I begin.

"One or two look beyond pride and bitterness. They yearn for something denied to them and when they see its form, they bring such danger upon themselves, unable to resist what is forbidden."

"Were you…?" I don't dare ask the question.

"Oh, I was one of the proud ones," says Julia. "I found my pride early and it sustained me when I wanted to cry for my mother. I held my head high, I spoke to my slaves with all the rudeness a child has in them and grew only ruder as a grown woman, whipped them for the slightest error, the slightest sign of disrespect. If there was a chance to be seen in public, I would go. My hair must be braided just so, my robes had to be whiter than white. I *felt* how sacred my very person was and I revelled in it. Thank the gods I did not see what I could have yearned for until I was freed from my service."

"Your husband?"

"I was thirty-six and I returned to my family's villa, a retired Vestal. Those first days, that first month, oh, I missed my former life. From one day to the next I was nothing, a shadow of my former glory, my place taken by a mere child, six Vestals just as there had always been, as there will always be. My family were proud, of course, such an honour to have given a daughter to Vesta's service… but it is a greater honour when she is a distant, white-robed figure in a temple. When she is nothing but a spinster in your household who used to be a Vestal, it is not the same, is it? When you see that she must eat and wash and use the toilet like everyone else, her sacredness dims."

I try to imagine Julia in her family's villa, the inviolability of her former life drifting away from her, day after day, as she became a woman for the first time, no longer a priestess.

"Is that when you met your husband?"

Julia gives a half-laugh. "Can you imagine my family's horror? A carpenter? It was their own fault, I suppose. They barely spoke to me, weren't sure whether I was to be treated like a Vestal or just a spinster, neither of whom you'd spend time in idle chitchat with, would you? So they mostly left me alone while they decided what to do with me. They didn't even consider marriage."

"Vesta does not share her handmaidens," I murmur. It's a common phrase; it's considered ill luck to marry a retired Vestal Virgin, so if they leave Vesta's hearth when their time is up, these women of thirty-six who have lived such a strange life, accustomed to freedoms and riches, then find it hard to settle back into normal life. And of those few who have married, rather too many lost their husbands early, adding to the superstition, not taking into account that if you marry after thirty-six, your husband is likely to be fairly advanced in years himself.

"Indeed," says Julia. She has gathered herself; the thought of her husband has revived her; she sits upright again, sips some wine, but still refuses the porridge.

"How did you meet him?" I ask. I've never heard the full story of Julia's marriage.

A faint smile emerges at last, the memory of him still making her happy. "Woke up late to a half-empty house, everyone had gone about their business for the day, mostly keeping out of the way because they knew there would be noisy building works. No-one bothered to tell me. The whole house echoed with hammering. I followed the noise out to the garden and there was a man up a ladder, taking an ancient vine down from its pergola, which was half-rotten and about to fall on someone's head. I demanded to know what all the noise was about. He didn't know who I was, had no idea about my past. He looked down at me from up there and said, 'I am here to rescue this lovely vine, Domina, and make a new home for it, so that it can flourish once again.' I stood there and watched him. He didn't speak to me again, only gently, gently took the vine away from its support. It lay over half the garden while he took apart the collapsing pergola and rebuilt a fresh one. Then he took the vine and twined it back onto its new home so that it would be safe and have space to grow. It took him two days and I sat in that garden and watched him all the time. He didn't speak to me. He whistled, he patted our family dog and he talked to the vine when he'd finished, said a few words of blessing over it and wished it many more years of happiness and fertility, of growing grapes for our household. And that was all it took. When he was leaving I asked his name and he told me his nickname. I said no, he must tell me all of his name. He paused then and looked at me and he told me all of his name and asked for mine. I told him. The next day he returned. He asked one of the slaves who answered the door if he could speak with me and when I arrived he looked at me and said, 'You were one of Vesta's handmaidens,' and I felt my heart sink because I thought, he will never marry me and already that was what I wanted. I said nothing, only nodded, and he smiled and said, 'I knew it when I saw you move. But I would like to marry you anyway.'"

We laugh out loud and both of us have tears that have risen up at the same time, the thought of this man, this carpenter-nobody, daring to say such a thing to a woman from a well-off family, a retired Vestal Virgin no less and yet the romance of it, the simplicity of what had been felt between them, the power of it. If Marcus said such things to me… I push the thought away.

"How did he know you wouldn't slap him round the face for insolence?" I ask.

"My mother did," says Julia. "But it was too late by then. I insisted on marrying him and my family cut me off with no money. I had money from my time as a Vestal, some people leave money to Vestals in their wills. So I bought the insula and we moved here. My family were appalled. No-one of their class lives in the Ninth Region. They never spoke to me again, not to this day."

"I'm sorry," I say.

She shrugs. "I hadn't lived with them since I was six. They hardly felt like family. And I was tired of taking care of a make-believe hearth to look after the people of Rome. I thought there must be better ways to do that. The insula was already crumbling then, but I rented out rooms and kept the rents as low as I could so that soon enough the place was full of waifs and strays. Cassia's mother was one of them and even when she found a good husband she refused to leave, opened up the popina downstairs instead and started making her weekly soup for beggars alongside the food trade. She understood what I was trying to do, it felt like we really were providing a home and a hearth for the people of Rome, not just pretending, even though that sounds blasphemous from a Vestal Virgin's mouth. Marcus was one of the strays, an injured soldier from a penniless shamed family, wondering what to do next in his life. I could see what a good man he was and he became a good friend. He came to visit me when my husband died, sat with me while I cried and cried, went home and wrote letters to me, each one with a pressed flower from Livia."

She has skimmed over her husband's death and I don't know whether to ask about it or whether it is something she would rather not tell me, even when she is telling me more than I've ever heard about her life. We sit in silence for a moment.

"It was quick," she says at last. "The marriage and his death. He died on a sunny day, his hand to his chest and gone. I know everyone whispered afterwards that Vesta does not share her handmaidens, that he died because he loved me. But we had such happiness together. Three years we had, one year for every decade I served Vesta. And it was so much, after so little, it filled my heart after all those lonely proud years."

My eyes well with tears again. I have never heard Julia sound like a woman. She always sounds like a Vestal; certain, complete, inviolable. I have never thought of the loneliness a child would feel on being thrust into that life and all the things they would have been forced to leave behind, from their family to the chance of ever making a family of their own…

"Did you know her?"

Her shoulders slump, heavy. "Cornelia was in my care. Came to the Vestals after me and you were supposed to care for the one that came after you, to be her guide. When I left she said she would leave too, when her time came, but when it finally came she was on her way to being the Virgo Maxima, greatest among equals and she couldn't resist the honour, the importance of it. So she stayed past her time, stayed for the glory." She gives a half-sob again. "She could have left and been free, she could have lain in the arms of a man and no harm would have come to her and instead she stayed for the supposed glory – there *is* no glory, she should have known that by then – and because she looked, because she looked out beyond Vesta's hearth and saw a glimpse of what she might have been, what she could have claimed in life and was tempted, reached out for what was forbidden…"

"They say Domitian has decided there will be no mercy this time."

"The burial chamber."

"Perhaps he could be persuaded? With the other two he –"

She shakes her head. "He's making an example of her. She is a warning to the senators of what he can do, of the power he wields. That he will not always be gentle, not always find a kinder way to proceed."

"Why is it a warning to the senate?"

"Most of the Vestals are daughters of senators."

"You don't think he'll change his mind?"

"No."

"What can we do?"

"Nothing."

"What will you do?"

"Be there when it is done. It is all I can do."

"We will be there too," I promise and she touches my hand, her eyes full of suffering only she fully understands.

CASSIA, FABIA AND I MAKE our way early to the Temple of Vesta. There is a crowd waiting outside, despite the heat already rising. Marcus has gone with Fabius to another part of the route. I am glad we do not have to stand together in silence, witnessing yet another dark moment.

I spend my life looking after crowds in the amphitheatre, I know what they are like. They are raucous: talking, singing, shouting, jeering. Even when they think they are quiet and attentive, they are not. They whisper to each other, adjust their clothing or give a cough, all sixty thousand of them. They cannot help but make noise.

This crowd is silent. No-one speaks, no-one coughs or adjusts their clothing. They are cowed in a way our crowds never are, not even when we dispatch criminals. This is no common criminal, this is a Vestal Virgin being put to death in a way that even a hardened soldier would blench at, for they expect to die by a quick blade in the glory of battle, not by the slow, slow lack of food, water and air. And a Vestal is a sacred being, they cannot bring themselves to think of her as impure after bowing their heads all their lives any time they saw one of the six white-robed figures. They are afraid; they know that this is right and proper, what they are doing, she must be punished, but also they know that you must not harm nor kill a Vestal and in their stomachs they know that this death she will be put to is a lie, that leaving her alive in that tiny room, sealed underground with a lamp and a couch, a few days' worth of bread and water, milk and oil so that all can claim they never hurt her is nothing but deceitfulness… and who is the deceit for? Not the crowd, they know it is a falsehood, not the Vestal who is going to her certain death. It surely cannot be for the gods, for the gods see all and know all, they would not be taken in by this pretence. And so if everyone knows it is a lie and yet we are still going ahead with it, then we are indeed harming a Vestal Virgin and perhaps the gods will be angered with anyone who was there, who took part in this sham? The crowd's deepening sense of dread weighs down their feet and tongues, keeps them still and silent.

Today's procession will leave the House of the Vestals and make its way north-east, to the Colline Gate, one of the great gates of Rome. The burial chamber will be on the inside, in the area known as the Evil Field, Campus Sceleratus. Cornelia will be interred within Rome, but only just. A dead body should not be buried within the gates of Rome, but she will not be dead when she is buried, so all is well, another law will have been upheld by this performed pretence.

"Julia said she would be here," whispers Fabia. "Where is she?"

We look about us but we cannot see Julia anywhere. I wonder whether she has entered the Temple of Vesta to pray but I am not sure anyone is allowed in today.

The crowd finally makes a noise, there is a brief rustle and low murmur as she emerges. The chief Vestal Virgin, the Virgo Maxima, once the most revered woman in Rome, even above the Empress. The woman once named Cornelia, condemned by the college of pontifices, is now named the empire's most reviled, shamed, despised being.

She is tall, with the perfect bearing of a Vestal. Pale skin from the decades tending a fire indoors, long dark hair. She has served beyond her thirty years, but, chosen as a child of six, she is not yet old. She is wearing a plain, undyed tunic, like something a poor woman would be buried in, her hair is not bound with red ribbons into the elaborate braided hairstyle that Vestals wear, instead it falls loose down her back. But these deliberate debasements only serve to echo her robes of office, the yellowed-white of undyed linen recalls the white robes she would have worn, her fine loose hair is still crinkled from the braids she has worn every day during her service. Her red hair ribbons and the red band that would have encircled her head are gone, but in their place we can see plainly on her arms and legs, glimpse from the neckline of her tunic, the thin red lines where she has been whipped by Domitian himself, as the law demands.

The crowd shuffles backwards and more than a few bow their heads without realising and then jerk them back up, remembering that she is no longer sacred. She was a bride of Rome, she committed adultery by lying with a man and so she is guilty of treason. They could jeer at her if they wished, could spit and curse and name her a whore, but they cannot bring themselves to do that.

We see her only briefly. The quick tramp of feet brings a litter close to her, into which she climbs, the plain drapes falling about her, hiding her shame from view. The bearers lift the litter with ease, she is a slim woman and there are four of them. There is a brief pause, a slow swirling of positions as the procession forms. At its head, Domitian, in his role as the pontifex maximus, Rome's leading male priest. His face is tight with what looks like anger, but from the way his hands are opening and closing by his sides, I wonder if in fact he is anxious. To have yet another Vestal fail in her sacred duty may be seen as a bad omen for Rome. He looks quickly behind him, to where the executioner, whose role it will be to seal up the burial chamber, and a whole group of additional priests stand. Behind and around all of them, the twenty-four bodyguards assigned to the Emperor in case there should be any trouble during this difficult ceremony. Beyond them, the closed litter. Behind it four sullen but well-dressed people, two men, two women. They must be Cornelia's family, once boastful of having given up a daughter to Vesta's service, who became the Virgo Maxima, now shamed by attending this false funeral, their daughter's body not an honoured corpse but very much alive, streaked with the whipping she has brought upon herself. Behind them, the gathered crowd becomes the main part of the procession, there is much shuffling and jostling, albeit quietly, for a good position, for no-one wants to be at the back of the crowd when we reach the burial chamber and miss seeing the ritual. Indeed some people have gone ahead to line the route and others even further on, are waiting in the Evil Field.

Fabia, Cassia and I find ourselves a little behind the family but there is a sudden murmur, a falling back.

Out of the crowd ahead emerge three women. Julia is the youngest, the other two are more wrinkled and shrunken than she, though they are still upright. Each one carries a burning lamp. I have never seen the other two women, but there is no doubting that these three are surviving Vestal Virgins, those who served out their time and were released, set free to live their lives as they saw fit. They have come today to escort their sister to her place of death, the only ones to give her honour when all honour has been taken from her.

Domitian turns to see what the commotion is and looks appalled at the sight of the three women, looks for a moment to his bodyguards, who tense, waiting for his instructions. But his hesitation means he has lost before he even opens his mouth. He closes it again and pretends he has seen nothing. There is no law to cover this moment, no ruling that says who may attend the entombment of a Vestal and who may not. Domitian jerks his head and steps forwards, the family step back, confused, and so it is Julia and the two women who walk just behind the closed litter, not speaking, holding their burning lamps, the little flames flickering at each pace the procession takes through the silent Forum, north-east to the Colline Gate, the route lined all the way with hushed crowds who gape at the sight, making signs against evil spirits and bad luck, for who knows what gods may be angered, what spirits may be woken by such a sight, such a deed?

The walk feels longer than it is, partly because of the sombre, funereal pace, partly because we cannot chatter amongst ourselves. Behind us, the procession is growing, the people we pass mostly falling in behind us, so that by the time we reach the Colline Gate there is a huge crowd. Ahead of us looms the vast arched stone gate, just before it are built-up ramparts, into which has been dug out the burial chamber. All we can see of it is a large square hole, as wide as a man's outstretched arms, descending into darkness, a wooden ladder joining the world above to the world below.

The procession stops and those of us who were close to the head of it find ourselves grouped in a half circle around the litter, placed on the ground, its bearers stepping away from it. The crowd behind us is vast, I am not even sure what anyone would see from the back. Perhaps people just want to feel the solemn nature of the occasion, and they are right in this, for even if it is soundless and even if nothing can be seen, there is something amongst us all that cannot be described, that can only be felt.

I watch Julia and the other two retired Vestals. They stand upright, they hold their lamps, they do not look about themselves, only wait to bear witness to what is about to come.

Domitian steps forward. He should pray out loud, as would be normal in a ritual or even at a funeral, but he does not, he holds up his hands, palms turned upwards to the sky and prays in silence, I can see his lips move but no sound escapes. I wonder what his prayers consist of, whether they are a prayer for Rome, defiled by this woman's actions, or a prayer for this woman, about to be executed in a manner which even I, who play a daily part in executing criminals, find horrifying.

He has finished praying, turns to the still and silent litter and draws back the drape. The litter shudders as Cornelia emerges to meet him. Her height means she stands almost eye to eye with him. She does not weep or fall at his feet to beg for mercy. She looks into his eyes with an expression of dignified curiosity, who is this man who dares to block the pathway of a Vestal? And after a moment it is he who lowers his eyes, who steps aside and brusquely indicates to her the ladder, forgetting to move with the ritualised care suitable to this moment.

She stands still for a moment, looking at the ladder and then she glances over her shoulder to where Julia and the other two women stand, one last sighting of her sisters. They raise their lamps in tribute to her. She holds their gaze, then turns her face away from them and steps forward to where the ladder descends into darkness. By the hole stands the executioner and his three assistants, who carry shovels.

She grasps the ends of the ladder, then takes her first careful steps down it, her feet disappearing from view, but then she pauses. Her loose tunic has caught on the ladder, she takes one hand off to free it. The executioner, seeing her difficulties, goes to help her but she pulls away, shrinking from his touch which would defile her sacred person. I see Julia's description of herself, the excessive pride she carried to make her strong, to rise above fear and loneliness, reflected in Cornelia's face as she continues to step downwards, the rigid proud bearing the only thing keeping her from crumpling, from weeping in terror. Perhaps she will weep when we are all gone, but she will not allow herself to do so in public, to be further dishonoured by weakness. She will take each step as though it were her choice; it is all that gives her strength.

She is gone.

The executioner looks downwards. He must see her disappearing into the chamber and closing its door behind her, for he gives a signal and two of his assistants draw up the ladder. His face is pale; he has been shaken by her disgust. He points, not speaking, and the three assistants pick up shovels and begin to fill in the pit that leads to the burial chamber.

We stand in silence, all of us, no-one daring to protest, no-one able to walk away until the thing is done. The only sound is the shovelfuls of earth hitting the ground below and it is deafening. Cassia and Fabia take my hands and they are both shaking. They will feel my own winces each time the heavy thud of earth drops a little less far.

The scraping, shaping sounds are almost worse, as the mound is smoothed. Can she hear them, I wonder? Can Cornelia, buried in a tiny room below us, hear these sounds? She cannot hear the crowd, even though there must be more than three thousand of us here, because we stand still and silent, afraid of what we are seeing, unable to look away.

The assistants look to the executioner and he, sweating without having done any of the work, gives an uncertain nod, turns to Domitian and stands waiting to be dismissed. Domitian, face pale, hands still clenching and unclenching, gives a small gesture to release him, his work discharged. Then he turns away and walks through the crowd with the bodyguards and the swaying, empty litter following him.

No-one dismisses us, the crowd. We stand a few moments longer, caught in the spell of what has been done here, then a few people recover and begin to move away, making gestures against evil spirits as they do so, hoping none will follow them home from this most ill-omened event.

I look for Julia, but she has melted back into the crowd with her two sister Vestals. Cassia, Fabia and I walk slowly away, taking a longer route than is necessary to get home, so that we may avoid the crowds. We are walking through a tiny backstreet alley before Cassia opens her mouth. Her voice is hoarse, she has to clear her throat before she continues.

"How – How long do you think?"

Fabia's answer comes so fast it must be all she has thought of. "Maybe three days. At the most."

"She has food and water," protests Cassia.

"She doesn't have enough air," says Fabia.

"Could anyone have given her…"

"Doubt it," says Fabia. 'Where would she hide it?"

WE DON'T TALK ABOUT IT in the insula, we don't gossip about how it all happened or speculate who will be chosen to replace Cornelia. The whole of Rome waits to see who the replacement will be, a child substituted for a Virgo Maxima, starting the cycle again, innocence taking back what was defiled. Only our insula does not take part. Each household leaves food outside Julia's door for many days, our offerings to Cornelia. Julia stays indoors, barely seen, nodding wearily to any of us if we happen to meet her in passing, going to the toilets or to collect water from our courtyard fountain, her face pale and her eyes rimmed red.

One day, a week after Cornelia was entombed alive, Julia finally emerges when it is dusk, takes up a little pot of red flowers and disappears for some time, returning when the streets are dark, carrying the now empty pot back to her apartment.

THE NEXT MORNING A MESSENGER from Paternus arrives at dawn, panting, to tell me that this afternoon's Amazons scene will need a new Queen Hippolyta. Billica has committed suicide. I send Karbo to Labeo to tell him to prepare one of his gladiatrices to take on the part and go myself to the Ludus Magnus, which is very quiet. A guard on the gate is particularly careful about checking who I am, sending word to Paternus, who comes to collect me himself, a far cry from the usual freedom I have to enter whenever I wish.

"Althea," says Paternus heavily when he sees me. His face is drawn. "What a season. Never had so much ill fortune." He makes a superstitious gesture to ward off further evil. "Two gladiators killed before their time and now this?"

"Where... how...?"

"She said she needed to relieve herself. It's the only thing we allowed her to do alone and without being chained. The rest of the time she was chained or in her own room in the barracks. Couldn't leave people in with her and she had a guard outside all the time. She was worth it, her price was rising all the time, but it was a lot of trouble to go to and she wasn't getting any easier to manage."

I hardly care about how she was to manage. "She was relieving herself and then?"

Paternus has to take a deep breath. "She took the toilet stick and shoved it down her throat, so that the sponge suffocated her."

I stare at him in horror. "She suffocated herself? Is that even possible?" I can't help thinking of the other murders. "She wasn't killed by someone?"

Paternus shakes his head. "She was all alone, she died by her own hand." He grimaces. "The undertakers had a struggle to get it out of her." He's quiet for a few moments. "Brave though," he admits at last. "Not many men would have the courage to do what she did."

I swallow. An ending shrouded in secrecy and fear, violent and obscene in its desperation. I think back to Billica's wild fury in the arena set against her eyes filling with tears as she was returned to her enslavement, humiliated time and again for the cheering crowds, forced to simulate submission to men she hated and could well have killed, had she not been held down and disarmed.

"Labeo can find someone to fill in, I suppose?" says Paternus. "I'll send him the crown we used and the hairpieces. She was always ripping them out anyway, we had to put them in fresh for each show."

There's not much I can say or do. I make my way to the Ludus Matutinus where Labeo is shaking his head.

"Told you, they don't know how to manage women. Wild thing like that, you have to tame her somehow, you can't have her chained up forever holding a grudge. But don't you worry. I've got one of my best girls on the job. Dyeing her hair right now, she'll do you proud this afternoon."

BUT THE GLADIATRIX WHO PERFORMS as Queen Hippolyta is not the same as Billica. Her hair and golden crown are magnificent, she can fight, but the wild rage that used to emanate from Billica is not in her and she submits all too willingly to being kissed by one of Rome's celebrity gladiators.

On my way home I take a detour. On the still-fresh mound of earth by the Colline Gate, in an inconspicuous corner, is a little flowering plant, blooming red like Cornelia's hair ribbons, like the streaks of the whip on her skin. Like Billica's false hair, taken from some other nameless slave, crowning her as queen of the Games against her will.

THE MINOTAUR

SEPTEMBER HAS SOMEHOW ARRIVED, THE stiff politeness between Marcus and me making every day a struggle. I might have relented, might have given way to my feelings, but first Cornelia's death and then Billica's were further steps into the darkness and it only made me more resolute in my decision to get away from the Games, to find another life. I have attended each day of the Games, done everything required of me, but I have kept myself aside. I have taken a slave everywhere I go, I do not stay late to chatter or go to the baths with various team members. I no longer stand in the arena for crowd scenes, instead I take my place opposite Marcus in the amphitheatre or watch scenes through a grille in the arena wall. I said I would only complete this season and here it is, the morning dawns, the finale of the last Games I intend to be part of. I expected to feel excited, but instead I'm weary and sad. Part of it is the lack of warmth between me and the man I love, but I also feel sorry for Felix, whose last day it is today. He has played our Minotaur all season and is a favourite in the arena, despite his grisly battle style. Today his monstrous stage persona will be laid to rest alongside him.

The team is gathered in the centre of the sand-strewn arena, making the most of the light before plunging into the hypogeum. Marcus is consulting a scroll of the day's events, his brow furrowed. At last he straightens his shoulders and looks up at everyone.

"Last day," he says and there's a cheer. "We have a lot to get through before there's any cheering," he reminds us. "Domitian will be attending and there's a very full programme. Everyone be careful today, stay with other people, look out for any trouble. Today we tell the whole story of Theseus and the Minotaur in the correct order. Ready?" He tries to catch my eye but I look down at my own notes, nodding without returning his gaze. "Right then. Carpophorus, enjoy your last day."

Carpophorus puts his fist to his chest in a salute. "I just want to say," he says, his deep voice wavering a little, "that I've been honoured to be the lead this season. I never thought when I was a slave boy that I'd be standing in the largest amphitheatre in the empire, playing one of the greatest heroes there's ever been. I'm grateful."

Marcus gives a warm smile and pats Carpophorus' vast shoulder. "We've been proud to have you," he says. "You're one of the best."

THE AMPHITHEATRE IS AT FULL capacity, close to sixty thousand crushed together instead of the fifty thousand it can comfortably hold. I shake my head when the inevitable complaints are brought to me about ladies and their parasols. I don't care. Let them argue amongst themselves. I don't care about how fair their skin is, how many slaves they've brought with them, whose view of the bloodshed to come is obscured. I'm nervous something will go wrong today. It's the closing show, if the murders so far were somehow linked to the amphitheatre then this is the killer's last chance to strike.

Trumpets. Domitian's entrance.

The court of Crete emerges, a riot of colour and music. Minos makes his ill-fated decision, gaining the crown of Crete and losing the favour of the gods. The crowd gasps as the Minotaur rips apart today's unlucky criminals and applauds the appearance of their hero, Theseus-Carpophorus.

"You would not believe the number of women we've had begging for a night with those two," says Labeo, standing next to me as we watch the spectacle from the grille. "I don't think either of them have had a night without a companion this whole summer."

I roll my eyes. The labyrinth appears and disappears, taking with it the Minotaur. Felix will be downstairs, locked into a cell until the final scenes of today's spectacle.

"Sorry to lose him," says Labeo. "He's been an excellent performer. But can't change the rules. Gave him a good send-off last night. Big feast, some noblewoman in his barracks who paid handsomely for his time. Then I left him to drink with Carpophorus and Funis."

I see movement in the gloom. Funis, nodding as the bull-leapers stream out to give their final performance. The crowd roars at the sight of them and minor gladiators follow them out. While the bull-leapers perform at the centre of the arena, gladiators in bull-helmets are killing off criminals who are fighting blind, their heads and eyes fully covered by helmets. They've been given real swords, but they haven't got a chance. They are fighting in a terrifying darkness, symbolising the darkness of the labyrinth, taking the part of the Minotaur's victims.

Ships sail across the arena, our rippling sea of cloth appearing and disappearing twice, before the time comes for our hero to make his mark. In the darkness, Funis is speaking with Carpophorus, who embraces Felix standing beside him, wipes his eyes, then steps out to a roar of applause. The chorus tells how Theseus convinces his father to let him take his place amongst the Athenians given in tribute, and sets out the agreement that if he is victorious, he will return home with white sails in place of the black ones billowing in the breeze. Below us, Felix is guided into a lift which will bring him into the centre of the labyrinth.

The bull-leapers retreat, the court of Crete takes their places, the labyrinth, containing its legendary monster, rises up from the hypogeum to greet Theseus on his arrival. The sea recedes. Luna, as Princess Ariadne, performs one more lascivious dance before handing a ball of thread to Carpophorus, who takes the opportunity to run his hands over her body, encouraged by the crowd, while the chorus creates the roars of the expectant Minotaur, pacing in his labyrinth.

Funis passes me on his way to the bull-leapers, heading downstairs to the lower levels.

I catch hold of his hand. "Funis."

He turns back to me at once, all his attention on me. "Yes?"

I take a deep breath, ready to make the speech I have been preparing, but all that comes out is, "No."

"No?"

I try again. "I thought – about what you said, what you – offered."

He takes a step closer, his hand tightens on mine. "Yes?"

"I – my answer is no, Funis. I'm sorry."

"Why?"

"Because…"

Below us, I hear the grinding of the lifts as the labyrinth reaches its final position. Only the truth will do, only the truth will finish this conversation.

"Because I love Marcus."

Funis smiles. "I know that," he says. "Everyone knows that except Marcus himself. What if he does not love you, Althea?"

I look down. "Then no-one else will do instead," I say.

"Are you sure?"

"Yes."

"For the rest of your life, even?"

"Yes," I say with more certainty, raising my gaze to his.

His eyes are sad. "Then speak to him," he says. "A life spent waiting is not a life. We must step forward to claim what we most desire."

I nod and he lets go of my hand, turns away into the darkness.

"Funis?"

He pauses but does not turn his head to me. "Yes?"

"What will you do?"

"Take another step. When we misstep, we cannot stop. We choose another path, we walk on. We make our peace with the past, we do not allow it to claim our lives forever. Else we give it too much power over us."

He waits to see if I will reply, but I don't. He walks down the corridor without looking back, disappearing into the darkness.

Now comes the moment we have spent a whole season leading up to: the final battle between Theseus and the Minotaur. Reluctantly, I turn my attention back to the grille. Any members of our team who are not actively employed at this moment join me in watching. We stand silently in the dark, peering out at the sunlit arena, as Carpophorus, urged on by a screaming crowd, enters the labyrinth holding his ball of thread as required by the story. He abandons it when the Minotaur rounds a corner and the labyrinth sinks into the ground, leaving Carpophorus and Felix at the centre of the arena, clearly visible for their final battle.

They're well-matched. The crowd howls encouragements as the two fight, the

Minotaur's swiping claws skimming Carpophorus more than once, so that he is bleeding, but these are light cuts and he fights on, sword glinting, body dripping in sweat in the bright heat of the sun and then – with perfect timing from years of performance – the blade slips between two ribs and the Minotaur sinks to its knees before our hero, blood gushing. Carpophorus twists his opponent's body and holds Felix up to face the imperial box, slices his blade across the black-painted throat.

My shoulders drop. It is over. All over. I will never have to stand here again like this. I am done. I can leave. I take a deep breath. Only a few last tasks to complete. Everyone is safe, the season is complete. Thank the gods. Carpophorus drops Felix's body neatly over a trapdoor, which opens to claim his body and lower it back down to the ground level in a lift. I make my way down the stairs, under the flickering light of torches.

As I arrive at the central room of the lower floor, I hear Fabia scream.

The lift has stopped, Fabius is at its door, staring down, aghast. In the lift is, as expected, the dead body of Felix, still wearing his Minotaur helmet.

But Funis is there also, eyes wide, hand to his throat, blood spilling over his fingers as he sinks to his knees.

"Open this door!" roars Fabius.

There's chaos. All lifts are locked to keep everyone safe, to stop criminals and animals escaping. The lock must be fumbled with while I stand in rigid horror and Fabia tries to reach inside, to grab at Funis' arm and pull him closer, but it's too late. He falls sideways just as the lock is undone, his eyes closing.

They try of course. Strabo drags Funis' body out of the lift cage, Fabius and Fabia bend over him, trying to stem the blood, but a cut throat is not a quick sword-swipe to a limb. Funis is dead.

We stand in the space, blood everywhere, thick red pools of it on the floor, soaking Fabia and Fabius' hands, Strabo's shoulder and face.

"Find Marcus," I say.

He will be in the seating area just by the imperial box, entirely unaware of what has happened here. From his vantage point, all he will have seen is a magnificent spectacle and Domitian's engrossed face, the cheering crowd.

We wait in silence. More and more of our staff hear what has happened and appear from one corridor and another, forming a crowd around Funis, whispering down the corridors. Above us we hear Carpophorus-Theseus claim his status as a legendary hero and Luna-Ariadne as his bride.

The crowd parts and Marcus is standing opposite me, his face grim.

"How did this happen?"

Fabius shakes his head. "We don't know. I saw Funis briefly after the bull-leaping. Someone must have attacked him and shoved him into the lift just as the trapdoor above opened to drop down Felix's body."

"The lift was unlocked?"

"It must have been, but then locked again once he'd been forced into it."

Marcus looks at me. "I have to return upstairs," he says, his voice low. "Today's Games must be concluded without Domitian knowing anything is amiss."

"Put him – put Funis in one of the side rooms," I say, gulping back tears, trying to keep my voice steady so I can be understood. "I'll stay with him."

Marcus hesitates for a moment, his mouth opens but then closes again and he strides away.

The spell is broken. Our team begin to disperse, Felix's forgotten body is carried away.

I follow two gladiators as they carry Funis down the tight corridor to the room that we use for the dancing girls' costumes. Hung on the walls are flowing tunics in reds, oranges, yellows, blues, violets, greens, all in vivid shades and made of the lightest linens, so that they will easily flutter about the whirling bodies of their owners.

I want to turn away, to say the room is too bright but that would be absurd. Instead I set down my lamp on a shelf well away from the costumes and sink to the floor, receive Funis' head into my lap.

"You can go," I say. "I will – look after him."

They look down at me, two fighting men lost for words, stricken at the fate Funis has met.

"On your own?" says one of them.

"Yes," I say. "Yes, I'll be – fine."

They back away into the dark corridor, still uncertain. I nod to them, try to appear certain in my intention so that they will not linger any more.

They turn and head back, slowly disappearing into the gloom.

Above us I can hear the low groan of the crowd as Theseus sails home but forgets to change his sails, his father believing his son to be dead, leaping to his death. And then the final roar of applause as Carpophorus is given a laurel wreath by Domitian and praised for his exemplary years as a bestiarius, honoured as one of Rome's great performers in the Games.

I sit, shoulders sagging, over Funis. Hot tears run endlessly down my face and on to his.

"I'm sorry," I say to him, the words coming out slowly and then faster. "I'm sorry you came here and we did not keep you safe. I should never have written to you, should never have asked for you to be our beast hunter. You should have stayed in Ostia where you were safe." I think back to the first time we met in Ostia, his sharing with me his real name, which no-one ever used. "Arikakahtani," I whisper. The name of a long-ago king, he said, a name bestowed by his enslaved mother, perhaps hoping for a brighter future for her slave-born child. "Arikakahtani. May the gods of your homeland find you and take you to your mother's shade, to walk with her in peace."

From far away the trumpets blast out. Domitian will be leaving, his brisk walk keeping his entourage hurrying as he exists the building. When he is gone the vast crowd will also be allowed to leave, the stairs and exits will be packed with people, eagerly discussing the spectacle they have just witnessed, comparing it to previous seasons, wondering what will be planned for next year.

A voice comes from the doorway. "Is he dead?"

I look up, startled. The older, portly man is dressed in a toga. I do not know him, but there is something familiar about him. Perhaps a senator that I have seen in the Forum? Behind him loom two bodyguards.

"Are you lost?" I ask.

He doesn't answer, just looks down at Funis's face in my lap.

"Did you know him?" I ask.

"No."

His response comes so fast it sounds like a lie. I am very tired, my mind feels slow. I wipe away tears and snot. "Why would you come to see him if you didn't know him?"

He turns to go without replying and as he does so I see his face from a new angle and suddenly I know who he is. I move to stand up but Funis' body slides down from me. I bend to let his head down gently so that it will not bang down onto the brick floor. When I stand my hands are red with his blood and I look down at them in new horror.

"Wait!"

The senator turns back to me and as he does so I launch myself at him, press my two palms against his chest, then wipe them on his pristine white toga, two red handprints on his chest, blurring downwards in two scarlet streaks of accusation.

"Make your way out of here with his blood on you," I say, "so that everyone will know you are a murderer. Whoever held the knife, you held their hand. You're a monster. You disgust me. There is no beast in this arena so low as you. I'll spend the rest of my life telling people he was your son."

His bodyguards step forward, blocking me from any further contact while the senator stares down in revulsion at his soiled toga. "Be careful how you speak to me," he says from behind them. "Be careful what you threaten me with."

"You're a filthy coward," I spit at him.

One of the bodyguards hits out, his hand landing squarely on my chest, shoving me to the ground. I land hard on my backside, the second bodyguard stepping forward, one hand on the hilt of a concealed dagger in his tunic.

"Senator." A quiet voice, calm, a polite greeting amongst equals.

The bodyguard hesitates, steps back from the doorway, revealing the angular frame of Stephanus.

The senator turns away without speaking, his footsteps and those of his bodyguards quickly fading down the dark corridor.

I struggle to my feet, look down at the broken body in disbelief that it should still be there, that Funis has not risen from the dead or simply disappeared, that all of this was only some dark nightmare brought on by anxiety the night before the final Games of the season.

"I regret your loss." Stephanus' face is grave when I turn back to face him.

"This was murder," I say. "Not a mistake during the Games."

"I know."

I put my face close to his, my voice uneven with rage. He does not flinch, does not step back from my anger and proximity.

"So? Will something be done about it?"

"It was deliberately planned as a murder. It would be hard to prove."

"That's not good enough!"

"Leave it with me."

"Will you have him accused?"

"I will have him punished."

"For murder?"

"For whatever I can arrange."

I stare at him. "Whatever you can arrange? What does that mean?"

"You must leave it in my hands."

"How do I know I can trust you?"

"I believe in justice."

I look back down at Funis. "There was no justice here. He did not deserve this, he did not cause anyone harm. He—"

"He will be avenged."

I shake my head, tears falling again. "I wish I shared your confidence."

"It no longer concerns you," he says. "Bury your friend with honour and leave justice to me."

I wipe my face, sweat from the heat of the room and tears mingled, the taste of salt in my mouth. "I am done with this life," I say.

"The arena of the Games is a brutal place in which to dwell," he says. "Few can survive it for long. Most exit through the Gate of Death, eventually."

"For me it has been a place of loyalty and friendship," I say. "But it has grown too dark. I cannot bear it any longer."

"Perhaps it is time to leave."

I look down at Funis, at the patterned scars on his cheeks, one hand outstretched, the shining arm cuff hiding past scars beneath it. "He wanted me to. I intend to."

Heavy footsteps approach in the corridor. When I look back, Stephanus has disappeared; once again I have not seen him come or go, his footsteps always silent.

Carpophorus emerges from the gloom, the bulk of him filling the narrow doorway. "I heard," he gasps. "Is it true?"

I step back so that he can see Funis and he sinks to his knees beside him, a hoarse wail emerging from him. "Funis! My friend!" He shakes the body as though there is a chance that we have all been mistaken, that Funis can be woken from his bloodied sleep.

I grasp his arm, the vast muscles tensed in distress and growing rage. "Carpophorus –"

"Who did this?" he bellows. "Who did it? Tell me and I'll kill them with my own bare hands!"

"We don't know," I say, afraid that if he were told the truth he would kill the senator and then be executed for murder. "We don't know, Carpophorus, they got away –"

Carpophorus breaks into noisy sobs. "He was my friend," he howls. "He said we'd work together when I retired, he'd teach me what he knew and I'd be a beast hunter, like him. He didn't think I was an idiot like the rest of them do."

"Carpophorus –"

"Everyone thinks it. Dumb old Carpophorus, only good for a show in the arena and giving the ladies a good time, like a prize bull. That's what everyone's said about me, my whole life. But Funis didn't. He was my friend, he talked to me man to man."

"I'm sorry," I say. I have said nothing else these past months, one sorry after another.

"He knew how it is," sobs Carpophorus. "He knew what it is to kill your barrack-mate, your fellow gladiator. He came with us last night, me and Felix, we drank together and he said there was honour in a gladiator dying well. He made Felix proud to die and he told me he knew I would kill him properly, that I wouldn't hesitate, wouldn't cause any unnecessary pain or suffering. We faced today with our heads held high because of him."

One grief piling on top of another fills me. I will never hear anything good again, only wretched hopes and lives being dashed to the ground, shattering one after another like the tiny pottery models Domitian cast aside so carelessly when I first met him.

A year gone so fast and so much gone with it. Funis, Secundus, my dreams of a life together with Marcus, not one but three Vestal Virgins, Billica and the two gladiators who took blows intended for Funis, Siro, Carpophorus' hopes… nothing good is left. Only Cassia, Quintus and Emilia, the three of them shining amidst the rubble all around us. I do not even try to comfort Carpophorus. He is right to cry. I stand over him and my tears fall onto his heaving shoulders, trickling down to join his on Funis' empty face.

THE FARM

THERE IS ASH FLOATING IN the air, tiny fragments of grey thrown upwards in the hot air from the flames, then drifting outwards and away, slowly making its way towards the earth. Specks of it fall onto the men's funeral togas, the soft grey touching their black. The whole of our insula's community is gathered here on the road outside Rome where burials and funerary burnings take place, along with half the gladiators of Rome. They look strange without their armour and weapons, a motley crew of all shapes and sizes, scarred faces and bodies solid with muscle, expressions grave. They don't talk, only stand together like family, exchanging heavy embraces.

Carpophorus lumbers towards me, his face wet with tears. "I should have protected him. We knew there was still someone out there and –"

I shake my head and touch his arm. "There was nothing anyone could have done," I say. "We didn't know Funis was a target."

"But I could have –"

I put my arms around him, as much to make him stop talking as out of pity for his grief. Carpophorus is a good-natured man but I cannot go through it all again, what happened and why. I have enough of my own grief and guilt to live with. Funis was a marked man as soon as he left Ostia. And he left Ostia, despite his misgivings, in part because of me, because he thought there might be some future for us together.

Carpophorus sniffs, then pulls away. "Thank you, Althea," he says gruffly. "You don't know how it feels, when a fellow gladiator falls. We live and train together, but we have to kill one another too, or watch our friends fall to another's blade. It hurts."

"He admired you," I say. "He said he'd never seen such a fine bestiarius."

"He was the best beast hunter I've ever met," he says, tears falling again. "No-one like him. I'll sacrifice for him at the temple. Me and the lads, we all had a lot of respect for him. He was one of us."

I embrace him again, look over his shoulder to where Marcus is watching us. He looks exhausted, dark circles under his eyes and a slump to his shoulders I have rarely seen since our early days together. He catches my gaze and holds it a moment, then gestures to send Carpophorus his way.

"Marcus wants a word," I say, gently pushing the still-weeping hulk of a man away from me.

"You take care," mutters Carpophorus, patting my shoulder. I don't think he knows how strong he is, it's like being patted by a pile of falling bricks.

"How are you doing?" asks Cassia, appearing at my elbow. "When we get back to the insula I've got food ready for us all, made it last night. Everyone will be too tired to think about cooking." Emilia, on her hip, stares with interest at me, one dimpled little hand twined into Cassia's black curls.

"May Juno bless you," I say. "You are the mother of our whole insula."

Cassia looks down. "It's been a hard time. We need some good news. Got any for me?" she adds, making a tiny gesture towards Marcus.

"No."

"Then he's a fool."

I shake my head. "He's not ready. He doesn't know what he wants."

"Well, he better think about it, hadn't he? Or someone else will know a good thing when they see it."

I look at her and she shrugs. "Did you think I wouldn't notice the way Funis looked at you?" Her face is serious again. "I'm sorry."

"We didn't – I wasn't –"

"I know," says Cassia. "But you felt something for him?"

"He was a good man –" I stop. My shoulders slump a little further. "He wanted what I want. Love. A peaceful, safe life." I sigh. "I'm so tired I can hardly think any more."

"Come on," says Cassia. "We're done here. I've told Father to round everyone up and get them back to the insula. And you should get some sleep."

"It's the middle of the day," I protest.

"You're exhausted," says Cassia. "Don't argue."

We walk ahead of the others and when we reach the insula I hesitate but Cassia is right. I need sleep so badly. I make my way up the stairs and into my roof hut, where I lie down on the bed and sleep comes instantly; I sink gladly into it.

WHEN I WAKE IT'S STILL light. I lie for a while, watching shadows on the wall. There is a lost bee in the room, buzzing helplessly round the walls. At last I sit up and rub my face. I don't know what will happen next, I only know that this life has grown sullied in my mind. There is too much death, too much sorrow, one way or another. I glimpsed something else when I spoke with Funis, the idea of another life away from all of this, and I liked it. Except... except it is Marcus I have longed for, all this time. The life Funis promised was the one I wanted to live with Marcus. But I cannot force Marcus to see me. If his eyes and heart are still full of his past life then I cannot wait and hope for a life together that is never going to happen.

I let the bee out and follow it to the hives and the vegetables. I have money. I can leave the amphitheatre and live somewhere quietly in the countryside, perhaps near a stables to make Karbo happy, for I would take him with me. Marcus can arrange the buying of a little house, nothing grand but enough for us to live in comfort, he would do that for Karbo and me.

I will leave. The amphitheatre. The insula. Marcus.

I swallow. How can I? How could I leave all the life I have built here? I don't know what to do. I want to leave but I can't imagine it. I can't imagine being without my friends. And without Marcus. But the very thought of him makes my feelings for him well up again. His face when he smiles and the warmth of his skin…

Jerkily, I kneel and start to weed the vegetable bed, angry with myself. What is all this whining? I have decided I am no longer happy yet I will not do anything about it because Marcus has not fallen at my feet and declared his love? What would Fausta say, if she were still with us? She would laugh at me for being a hopeless romantic, tell me to stop waiting on Venus, for she is a tricksy goddess and cannot be relied on. She would tell me to make my own way in life for men cannot be relied on either, they –

"Althea."

I twist to look up at him. "Marcus."

He has obviously not slept while I did; he still looks bone-weary. He is holding something wrapped in cloth, a small bundle, which he sets down as he lowers himself to the ground, sitting with his knees pulled up. I hesitate, but it feels silly to continue weeding, so I sit down a few paces away, my back against the hut. I want the sun on my face, am in need of its warmth and light. I tilt my face up to it, close my eyes.

He doesn't speak for so long that I open my eyes again to see what he is doing. He is staring down at the bundle with unseeing eyes, staring at something beyond it, that only he can see. I close my eyes again. I will not waste my days staring at him. I won't be some foolish girl who spends all her time fretting over whether the boy she likes looks her way or not. I am older than that, wiser than that, beyond that. I will turn my face to the warmth and the light and choose a happier life than this one has become.

"It's for you," he says.

"What is?" I ask, opening my eyes again.

He's looking directly at me, serious, about to share bad news or something that we will have to address. "The –" He jerks his chin towards the bundle, lying between us. "It's yours. Open it."

I lean forward, pull at the edge of the cloth so that the bundle shifts in my direction. Once it is close enough, I pick it up. It's a rough square shape, about as wide as my body and lighter than I expected for its size. I fumble with the cloth wrap and as I pull it away I see the maker's mark; Balbus the toymaker has made whatever it is.

It is a toy farm, made from wood. A house and stables set around a courtyard, complete with tiny wooden animals and even beehives. It is Balbus' very finest work, intricately carved, the sort of expensive toy for a child that the noble families of Rome buy for their offspring, who will certainly never be farmers. But…

"Oh, it's broken," I say. The tiny wooden pergola that should be holding up a woollen vine, delicately woven in brown and green with embroidered purple bunches of grapes, is broken, it lies flat and the vine tumbles over it.

"Yes," says Marcus. "I want you to help me fix it."

I frown. "Balbus would be better suited to that task than me. I mean it's his…" I trail off and look up. Marcus is watching me intently. I look back down at the farm, heat rising up my neck. It is not just the pergola that is broken. There are four tiny roof tile pieces lying in the courtyard when they should be on the roof. One of the beehives is lying on its side, the stable door is hanging off its hinges and the tiny wooden pigs have escaped from their sty. I look fixedly down at the little model, unsure whether I can meet Marcus' gaze again. The heat is in my cheeks. I make an effort and raise my eyes to Marcus.

"It's your family farm," I whisper.

He smiles properly, it lights up his tired face. "No," he says. "You're making the same mistake I made."

Flustered, I look back down at the tiny tumbledown vine. "But…"

"It is our farm. Yours and mine. If you say yes to marrying me."

I'm struggling to hold his gaze. In all my daydreams of this moment, I never struggled to look into Marcus' eyes. I was so confident, so self-composed. I said everything elegantly, I didn't whisper or trail off halfway through what I was saying. I couldn't feel my cheeks burning. "Yes?"

He reaches out and lifts the farm out of my lap, sets it aside. He's kneeling in front of me, his face only a hand's breadth from mine. "You were right, I said it all wrong before. I need to say it better."

"You –"

He puts one finger onto my top lip and brushes down to the bottom lip and the touch of it is so deliberately intimate, so unlike how he has ever touched me before, that I stop talking and stare up at him. Suddenly I can meet his gaze, I cannot look anywhere but into his eyes.

"I asked myself the question you asked me," he says, his voice very soft. "How did I not see you for all this time? How did I have such a woman standing by my side and not see her for what she truly is to me?"

His finger has gone from my lips, but his hand is in my hair, he strokes down the length of it, looking at the very tips of it in his fingers before returning his gaze to my eyes. "After Pompeii… I thought I had lost everything and everyone. But I was wrong. All the way through that horror, you followed me. You followed me to places no-one else would go to, through ashes and down dark streets. And when I thought I couldn't take another step you went ahead of me and pulled me by the hand. You stood up to emperors and you told me to my face when I was wrong… and still I did not see you, not really."

Very slowly, I lift my own hand and move it towards his face. He catches it in his own and presses my palm to his rough-stubbled cheek, his skin warming mine. I stare at him. My daydreams were nothing compared to this.

"I found my courage again because of you," he says. "That stupid naumachia we were forced into, I dived into those waters and I was afraid, but because you were watching me I felt safe, against all the odds. Then Domitian…" He takes a deep breath. "He's a strange one, he's had me worried at times, but I'd found myself again.

I thought if all else fails, there is always the farm and when I thought of it, I thought of you there, without even thinking what that meant for how things were between us. You were just there, every time I thought of it. It was unthinkable for you not to be there."

His eyes drop to the tiny model farm. "I'm sorry I said it wrong, though. I knew by your face, before you said anything."

I try to pull my hand away, but he keeps it in place. "I –"

He shakes his head to stop me speaking. "It came out wrong because of Funis, the way he looked at you. It made me afraid and then I knew why. I tried to speak but it came out all wrong. I tried to say how much a part of me you felt, how it was unthinkable to be without you. But it sounded like I took you for granted, that I did not see you for what you are."

He takes his hand away from where it has been holding my palm to his cheek and my hand hovers in mid-air, uncertain. But he leans closer to me, puts both his palms on my cheeks, and his voice is soft and warm, full of tenderness. "I do see you, Althea. From the first day I met you I saw your courage and quick wits, your loyalty. Now I see the touch of Fausta on you, of Julia, Maria and Adah, Cassia and Fabia, how they have shaped what was already in you. I see the woman you have become in the years I have known you and how you shape those around you." He takes a deep breath. "How you have shaped me, from broken shards into a man again, who cannot imagine his life without you beside him because I *feel* you beside me, always, no matter where I am, you are there. I know your scent, I know what you will say before you even say it, I know the way you look when you are trying not to laugh or are about to cry. The only thing I do not know is how your lips feel when I touch them with my own, and I have imagined it so often since we last spoke like this that it has driven me mad."

Perhaps he moves, perhaps it was me, I do not know who breaches the tiny space left between us, but his lips touch mine and my arms slip about his neck, our bodies press together so that we end up kneeling, entwined among the flowers and vegetables, the sun's warmth shining down on us just as I imagined so many times and what I imagined is nothing compared to this.

I'M NOT SURE THAT WE speak much after that, little soft words perhaps, nothing that makes any sense except to the two of us. Marcus stands after a while and holds out his hand and I follow him to his hut without speaking. He undresses and there is one moment, one tiny moment where his back is turned and his face is obscured by his tunic, when I reach out to the tiny doll with hazel hair who sits above us on his household shrine. I touch her with one finger. I do not say anything, neither out loud nor in my head, it is not a proper prayer or even a speech. It is only an acknowledgement, from one woman to another across the years, of a shared love for one man. And then Marcus turns back to me and takes me in his arms.

He sleeps, afterwards, and I watch him, not touching him because I do not want to disturb his sleep, he is so tired. I stare at him. *He is mine.* It is such a wonderful thought that a smile grows on my face until I give a tiny giddy laugh, then pull my tunic back on and creep away, so that he can sleep on.

I make my way barefoot to the stairway, peer over the side to see what is happening in the courtyard below. The meal Cassia prepared has ended, the tables contain mostly scraps. There are still people sitting about, talking to one another, though their voices are low, the courtyard feels like a shelter where we have huddled to be safe from a storm.

I tiptoe down, nod to people here and there and go to find Cassia. She's in the popina, Emilia asleep in a corner, Quintus beside her, carving one of his little toys. They both look up at me, take in my lack of a belt, ruffled loose hair and bare feet.

"Say the word and my wedding veil is yours," says Cassia, in a falsely bored voice. "Been waiting long enough to pass it on to you."

I laugh out loud and she shrieks, runs and throws her arms about me.

"Yes! I knew it! Days I've been waiting for him to take that farm up to you! Quintus carved the pigs. I knew when I saw what Marcus commissioned that he'd bring it to you, I knew it! I saw him walk up the stairs carrying it, I've been holding my breath for *hours*, so don't think I don't know what you've been up to!"

Quintus joins in our laughter but Emilia stirs in her sleep and we all subside into whispers.

"What's all the noise?" asks Karbo at the doorway, munching on a bread roll left over from the meal.

"Marcus and Althea are going to be married," says Cassia.

"Oh, good," says Karbo.

"You say it like it doesn't matter!" says Cassia.

"They're always together. I thought it was already agreed," he says. "But will there be a feast, like there was for your wedding?"

"An even bigger one," says Cassia.

"With cream pudding?"

"With all your favourite dishes," I promise him. "Come to the roof and see something with me."

A curious lizard has been exploring the tiny farm. It lies in the miniature courtyard, basking in the last rays of the setting sun. When it hears me coming its tail swishes away two escaped pigs, almost but not quite returning them to their sty, while the lizard makes good its escape across the warm roof and hides somewhere in the wall.

"Is it for me?" asks Karbo, kneeling over the farm, carefully replacing the fallen roof tiles to the roof and the pigs to the sty.

"It is for you to come to with Marcus and me," I say. "It will be a new adventure."

"When?"

"I'm not sure yet. We will make plans."

"But the racing stables?"

"I don't know," I say. "But I know they are important to you."

He nods, setting the hives back in their proper places.

"I can see you will be a great help," I say. "A proper farm boy."

"Can I bring Letitia?"

"Of course. She will be a real farm cat and catch mice for us and have lots of kittens of her own."

Marcus appears, the weariness gone from his face, instead his hair is ruffled and his smile warm. "I woke and found you gone from me already."

I scramble to my feet and nestle into his arms. It feels easy and at the same time I am astonished by it happening at last, by the warmth of him and the certainty of my place in his arms.

"Ah, back where you belong," he says and kisses me. "When shall we hold the wedding, Karbo?"

"Right now?"

"I would agree with you," says Marcus laughing, "but it is my understanding that women like more notice for these occasions. Mostly so that they can enjoy the anticipation."

"And prepare the food?" I ask.

"That, too."

"And make ourselves more beautiful?"

"That's not possible in your case," he says, tightening his embrace. "But planning a feast, that *is* important. So I will allow a week or two. That should be enough. You have Cassia to help you, after all, and Cassia can make a feast appear out of nowhere. Now come down to Julia, I promised I'd bring you to her for her blessing as soon as I spoke to you."

"You told her you were going to speak to me?"

"I told her I had been a fool and said everything wrong. And she told me to do better next time and to bring you for her blessing when I did."

"She had faith in you doing better."

"More faith than I had in myself," he says. "Come."

Julia is standing in her doorway when we make our way along the walkway to her apartment.

"About time," she says, smiling when she sees us walking hand in hand.

We follow her into the flickering light of her rooms, softly burning candles placed about her household shrine. She stands before it, Marcus and I behind her. She takes a deep breath, then lifts her hands, palms upwards. She speaks in her priestess voice, the certain clear voice of a Vestal.

"To the spirits of this insula for whom I keep this shrine and to all the gods of Rome. I thank you for having kept Marcus safe all these years since he first came here, no matter how far away he has travelled. I thank you for having saved him and kept him from darkness when he lost all that was most precious. I thank them for sending a woman to stand by him when the realm of Hades called but he still had a long life left to lead. I thank you for giving him the courage to love again, for he is a man of great good heart and such a heart should not be wasted."

She bows her head and her voice grows quieter, softer. "I send word to the shades of Livia and Amantius, who walk hand in hand amidst fields of flowers, that the husband and father they left behind stands always true to them, but that they should rejoice, for he has been blessed once more by Venus and Juno, in finding a second wife worthy of his heart. May your shades walk always in peace and may Marcus be free to love again. May Marcus and Althea be joyful in their new love, built as it is on a rock of friendship and loyalty which has outlasted all darkness."

Tears fall down my cheeks. I am grateful to Julia for her wisdom in having spoken Livia's name out loud, for taking away the fear of not knowing how to say something of the kind myself to Marcus, for assuaging whatever guilt he may feel at loving another woman.

She turns to both of us, her face lit up. "I could not be happier for you both," she says. "When is the wedding?"

"Very soon," promises Marcus. "I will travel to secure the farm while Althea arranges the day and we shall be married as soon as I return. There is nothing to wait for. And once we are married, we will plan everything for the farm and leave next spring."

"Won't you have to give notice to the Aedile that you no longer wish to be the manager of the Games?"

Marcus shrugs. "They have plenty of time to find a new manager, everything works well, there's more than five months to choose someone before a new season starts. There's no more building to be done, the team is complete. Whoever takes over will have an easy life of it. When I return I'll give notice. It will all be settled."

He is so certain that he makes me feel confident. Yes, he signed an agreement to continue as manager for next year's season, but that can surely be changed. There are plenty of men who would be eager to take over the largest and most prestigious amphitheatre in the empire and be known by name to the Emperor himself. I lean my head against his shoulder. All will be well.

"I am sure you will find a way," Julia says. "But you will not be gone from here until the spring, I hope."

"It would be better to take possession of the farm in springtime," he says. "It would be a hard life to begin in wintertime, with the roof full of holes and no food stores in place. We will be here till spring."

When I see Maria and tell her she nods approvingly. "Bona Dea send her blessings over you," she says. She turns serious. "I will miss the boy," she confesses.

"He will miss you," I say. Karbo is all but a grandson to Maria. "But I can't leave him here all alone, he's my son and too young to live by himself. Farm life will be good for him."

"You hear that, scamp?" calls Maria to Karbo. "You'll be a farm boy. None of your city softness. Farm boys know the true meaning of hard work."

Karbo grins at her. "I could always stay here and live with you and be a charioteer," he suggests.

"You are not going to be a charioteer," I say. "It's much too dangerous."

"Celer says I'm gifted with horses." Karbo pouts. "He says I'm touched by Neptune."

"Well, if Neptune cares about you at all he won't make you a charioteer," I say. "He'll keep you out of danger."

Fabia's face lights up when she hears the news. "Oh Althea! I am so happy for you."

"I should have followed your advice and spoken up sooner," I say.

"All things come in their own time," Fabia says. "Venus and Juno were watching over you, ready to make you a bride. But I will miss you all so much!"

"If you wish to be a country physician, come with us," I say.

She laughs. "Too late, I have a taste for wounds, just like my father. I would be bored giving out herbs for low fevers and tending to the odd small cut, attending upon women in childbirth. Rome is the place for me."

"Then we must spend more time together this winter, before we leave in the Spring."

"That, I will willingly agree to. We shall have the best Saturnalia in Rome, a huge feast. And I will help you prepare for the country. It will be such a different life!"

"Marcus thinks I am a good farmer only because I grew some beans and peas and flowers. I have never lived on a farm."

"Ah, you will have Marcus by you and it can't be a harder life than running the Flavian Amphitheatre."

"That much is true," I say. "I'll be grateful not to be overseen by the Emperor himself."

"Tomorrow we're spending the whole morning at the baths," says Fabia, pulling my hand. "We'll get a massage and you can tell me every word Marcus said when he asked you to marry him."

WHEN I RETURN FROM THE baths the next day, loose-limbed and sweet-smelling, I climb to the rooftop and find Adah looking after the bees. Singing softly under her breath she lifts the lids of the hives and pokes about within them with her bare hands, while Karbo clutches Letitia to stop her trying to chase the displaced bees and watches from a safe distance, anxious not to miss the golden treasure about to be excavated.

"How are you, Adah?" I ask.

"Aching," she replies, mid-croon. "My back, child, my back."

"Is there no remedy for it?" I ask.

"Dying," she says.

"Adah!" I say reprovingly. "You're not dying."

"It comes to us all eventually, as the Lord commands," she says, extracting a chunk of honeycomb and holding it out to Karbo, who approaches tentatively, cat tucked under one arm, takes the honeycomb and hastily retreats.

"You're not to die any time soon," I say. "Who would look after the bees?"

She smiles up at me. "Not clever enough, child," she says. "You could look after them by yourself."

"I wouldn't know where to begin," I tell her. "And I'm not going to learn, either, so you'll just have to stay alive."

She gives a small laugh. "A little more clever," she concedes.

"Marcus and I are going to be married soon," I say shyly.

"A good man," she says approvingly. "Though he shouldn't work in that cursed place."

"We're going to go and live on his family's old farm instead."

"Much better."

"I had a – a request to make of you."

She pauses in what she is doing, looks curiously at me.

"Would you give me away? On my wedding day?"

Her shoulders hunch up further. "I don't believe in your gods, child," she says, but there is a sadness in her refusal.

"Please," I say. "I would like you to place my hand in Marcus'. That's all you have to do."

She looks away. "Because you ask it," she says. "Only because you ask, child."

"Thank you," I say, not sure whether she is happy or not to be asked. I stand uncertain for a moment, wondering whether I have done the right thing, whether I have offended her, which was not my intention, but then Adah leaves the hives and shuffles over to me, pats my arm and holds out a broken chunk of honeycomb with her other hand, poking it into my mouth. My mouth full of sweetness, I smile down at her. When she tilts her face up, her eyes are full of tears.

"Good child," she says, her voice tremulous. She turns away before I can embrace her, back to the hives, surrounded by the bees, singing her old song again.

I look at Karbo, and we grin at each other, our mouths full of honey. I never knew happiness tasted so sweet, nor that there could be so much of it to look forward to in the days ahead.

Author's Note on History

This is the third book in a series that started as the simple question I asked myself: who were people who made up the 'backstage team' for the Colosseum? There is hardly any mention whatsoever of them and yet Games on such an immense scale could not possibly have been put on without a very large and permanent team in place. *On Bloodied Ground* focuses on the element of earth, from the creation of an extraordinary under-arena area (the hypogeum) and a vast building programme across Rome, to the legend of the Minotaur and its labyrinth, earthquakes and a Vestal Virgin entombed alive. The other three books in this series focus on the same team through the themes of fire (*From the Ashes*), water (*Beneath the Waves*) and air (*The Flight of Birds*).

One of the ideas I have used in this book is that Emperor Domitian might have been on the autistic spectrum. This was first suggested to me by my historical consultant Steven Cockings, who is himself autistic, and is based on the preliminary work of Jen Cresswell, *Domitian and Asperger's Syndrome – a retrospective diagnosis*, which draws attention to Domitian exhibiting certain characteristics linked to autism, including a preference for solitude, some difficulty engaging with people, obsessions (including a huge building programme and the gladiatorial Games/chariot racing), and a love of routine. There can also be obsessive attention to detail leading to a tendency to micro-manage, as well as a rigid adherence to the rules, which results in a certain amount of inflexibility when applying the law (given this last point, it was actually more generous than it sounds for Domitian to have allowed the first two Vestals their choice of how to die). As my own son is autistic, and I found the historical evidence interesting and compelling, I have built in this concept and used examples of behaviour from people I know who are on the spectrum. The interest in wild animals and the vast patience in approaching them comes from my son. Domitian seems to have been judged overly harshly by historians in comparison to other emperors and I thought perhaps he lacked some of the social skills required to endear himself to people generally or to explain and promote his actions and choices. I also thought that the more positive aspects of his reign (such as the vast public building programme he undertook) might have made people nervous because of Nero's similar interests. Nero's madness would still have been very much in living memory and I thought that any odd behaviour at all coupled to a similar building programme would have made people around Domitian wary of history repeating itself and therefore quick to judge him.

I have used one of those irresistible tiny historical mentions you find from time to time during research, but brought it into my own era, even though the era it is from was more dissolute than Domitian's. In 197 AD Septimius Severus addressed the Senate in Rome and said:

> *"For if it was disgraceful for him (Emperor Commodus) with his own hands to slay wild beasts, yet at Ostia only the other day one of your number, an old man who had been consul, was publicly sporting with a prostitute who imitated a leopard".*

Domitian had an architect named Rabirius, who probably undertook most of Domitian's many building works. Very little is known about him, although he is mentioned with praise by the poet Martial.

The two sister Vestal Virgins put to death were approximately in 82AD, so the timing of this is correct. But I have used poetic licence to bring forward the death of the Vestal Virgin Cornelia, as her entombment alive was such a close fit to the earth theme of this book. She was in fact put to death in approximately 90AD, so about 8 years later. Pliny the Younger felt strongly that she was innocent and gives this description of her last moments before the burial:

> *"... when she was let down into the subterranean chamber, and her robe had caught in descending, she turned round and gathered it up. And when the executioner offered her his hand, she shrank from it, and turned away with disgust; spurning the foul contact from her person, chaste, pure, and holy: And with all the deportment of modest grace, she scrupulously endeavoured to perish with propriety and decorum."*

The Kingdom of Kush, where Funis's mother is originally from, was located in modern Northern Sudan and Southern Egypt.

People often ask whether I base characters on people I know and the answer is very seldom, but past pets often seem to worm their way in. It was only after I'd named Karbo's cat Letitia that I thought about our pet cat in Rome having been called Titi…

Recent scientific research has discovered that the Romans had actually worked out how to make buildings earthquake proof, by creating holes in their foundations and structures, which meant that the seismic waves could not travel on to the next piece of the building because there was a gap. This created a sort of 'invisibility cloak'. We are not sure if this was applied to all buildings, but it has been confirmed in the Colosseum (perhaps contributing to its longevity in a very earthquake-prone country) and other amphitheatres. Perhaps it was used in very large public buildings which would have been difficult to rebuild, or perhaps a large size was required in order to leave enough of the gaps. Earthquakes are very common in Italy, especially in spring and autumn, when the weather changes.

Archaeologists found a baby's bottle with gladiators on it, an irresistible piece to mention… I had to find a baby to use it and so Emilia arrived and brought Quintus with her! Unwanted babies were often simply abandoned. Some died, the luckier ones were adopted.

In approximately 64 AD, so about twenty years before the events of this book, Seneca wrote about a gladiator who committed suicide:

> *"In a training academy for gladiators who work with wild beasts, a German slave, while preparing for the morning exhibition, withdrew in order to relieve himself — the only thing he was allowed to do in secret and without the presence of a guard. While so engaged, he seized the stick of wood tipped with a sponge, devoted to the vilest uses, and stuffed it down his throat. Thus he blocked up his windpipe and choked the breath from his body… What a brave fellow. He surely deserved to be allowed to choose his fate."*

While many of the gladiators I have depicted in this series were professionals (whether slaves or free) and lived many years in their line of work quite happily and if very successful were lauded as celebrities, like Carpophorus the bestiarius, there were others who were forced to fight and would have been unhappy and so I used Billica as one of these examples and gave her the fate of the unnamed gladiator mentioned by Seneca.

Many of the specific Games I have written about actually happened. Those that I have invented were based on very similar approaches, such as the regular re-enacting of myths and legends of the Greeks and Romans. The legend of the Minotaur was one of my favourite stories as a child (I was genuinely afraid of the dark because there might be a minotaur lurking about) and so I took this chance to build a story around it.

Chosen for imperial service, some concubines rise to power. Others fall to madness.

<u>The Forbidden City series.</u> 18th century China. An extraordinary lost world of exquisite beauty, hard-won power and deeply emotional choices.

FLIGHT OF BIRDS

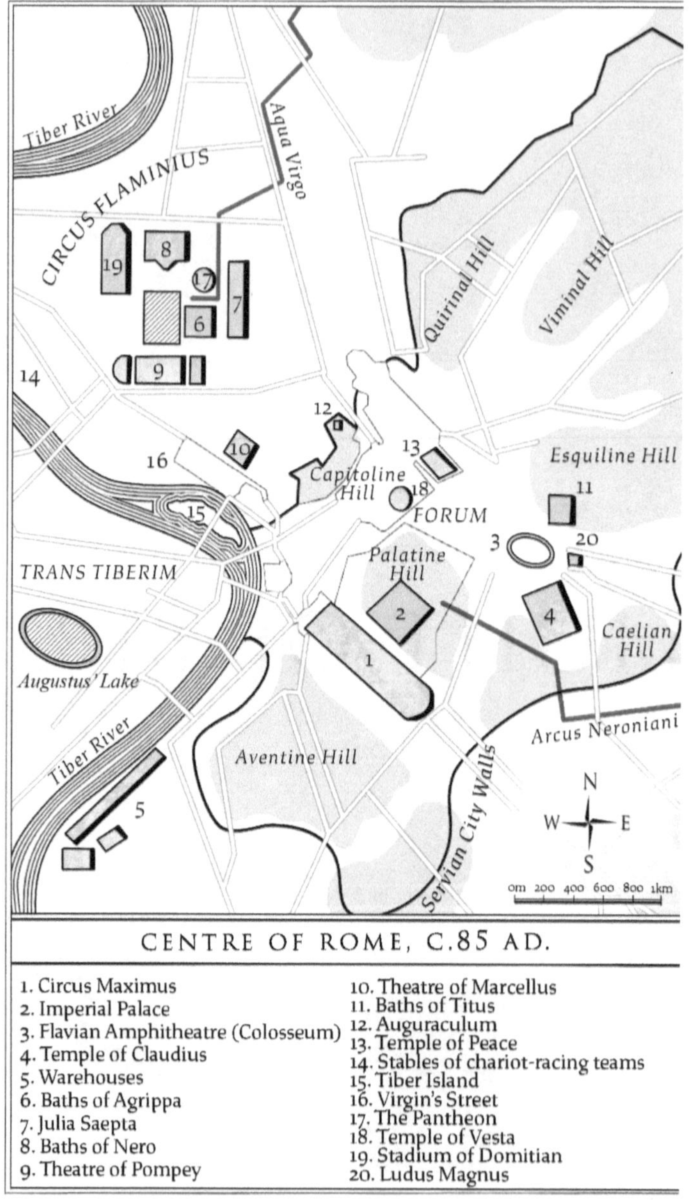

CENTRE OF ROME, C.85 AD.

1. Circus Maximus
2. Imperial Palace
3. Flavian Amphitheatre (Colosseum)
4. Temple of Claudius
5. Warehouses
6. Baths of Agrippa
7. Julia Saepta
8. Baths of Nero
9. Theatre of Pompey
10. Theatre of Marcellus
11. Baths of Titus
12. Auguraculum
13. Temple of Peace
14. Stables of chariot-racing teams
15. Tiber Island
16. Virgin's Street
17. The Pantheon
18. Temple of Vesta
19. Stadium of Domitian
20. Ludus Magnus

*This map shows the locations of some of the places Domitian began building at this time, such as the Imperial Palace and the Stadium of Domitian, as well as the Ludus Magnus. The Ludus Matutinus would have been close to the Ludus Magnus.

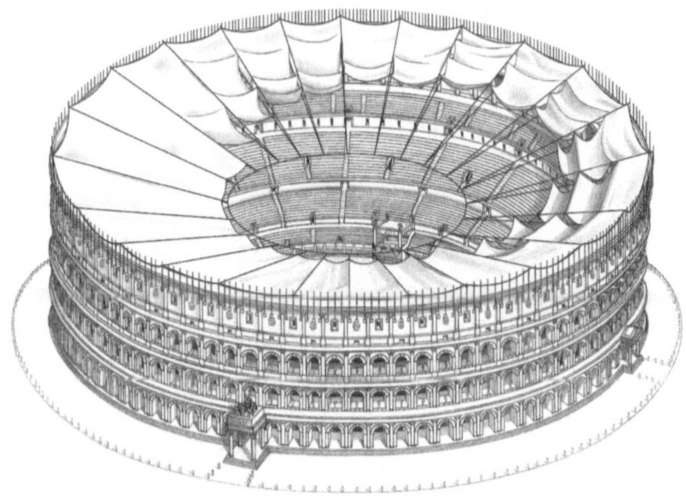

The Flavian Amphitheatre

Rome, October 82AD

The Flight of Birds

"Come on, then," says Marcus. "Let's get it over with."

"Will he be angry, do you think?" I ask. I try to rearrange Marcus' toga, which is sitting poorly on his shoulder, the heavy fabric in a scruffy bunch instead of neat folds. He makes an irritable face. He hates wearing a toga, but it's appropriate for a meeting with Domitian. I'm dressed well too, my best headwrap and tunic, my shoes shined.

"Probably," he says with a weary sigh. "He thinks we're fixtures, that we'll never leave. He won't be pleased. But the contract's up, we're free to go."

"What if he refuses?"

"We'll have to try and persuade him. Otherwise we'll be stuck in Rome managing the Games forever and neither of us wants that."

I try to cheer him up. "Maybe he'll be glad to see the back of us and we can leave as soon as we like."

Marcus smiles at the thought, pulls me close to him for a kiss. "Yes," he says. "Let's hope so. We can spend the winter getting ourselves ready, then head to the farm in the springtime. I can't wait to reclaim it."

We set off, making our way down the wooden staircase into the courtyard below, then pause at Cassia's for breakfast. Marcus has his usual bread and cheese, while I ask for pancakes with date syrup. We're joined by sleepy-eyed Karbo, our adopted son, who wolfs three pancakes in the time it takes me to eat one.

"Stables?" asks Marcus.

"New horse," he mumbles through a mouthful of pancake.

"You helping to train him?"

He nods and swallows, his eyes opening wider. "He's so beautiful. But you can hardly get a harness on him before he's off and running."

"Sounds suited to the races," comments Cassia's husband Quintus, who is helping out at the counter, serving wine and platters of fresh bread and fruit rolls, still warm from the bakery next door.

Karbo shakes his head, earnest. "You can't just let him run. He's got to be more aware of the drivers, or he'll miss their cues."

The racing drivers wrap the long reins round their waists, then steer with their bodies, which means the horses have to be responsive to small movements, not just run wildly down the long track of the Circus Maximus.

Marcus pats him on the back. "Spoken like a true racing expert," he says. "I'm sure you'll be an excellent trainer as you grow to manhood."

"The best trainers were drivers in their youth," says Karbo in a hopeful tone.

"And most of the drivers never made old age," says Marcus. "Come on, Althea."

I gulp the last piece of my pancake and drink some fresh grape juice, hug Karbo and follow Marcus, waving to Cassia.

"Good luck," she calls. "May Janus be with you!"

I wave again and trot after Marcus. "You walk too fast," I say. "You have to slow down when you have a bride-to-be walking with you."

"You managed to keep up when you were my humble scribe."

"A humble scribe is not allowed to question the length of her master's stride."

He slows, grinning. "I'm not sure you were ever humble. But I will do anything for your happiness. Even taking tiny steps."

All too soon the imperial palace looms over us, white and forbidding. The guards make an uninterested gesture to usher us in and we wait on the cold marble benches in the atrium to be summoned.

"Marcus Aquillius Scaurus."

"That'll be us then," whispers Marcus. "Janus, watch over us."

Domitian is seated at a small elegant wooden desk with two scribes in attendance, as well as three guards stationed around the room. He seems engrossed in reading a scroll. The Aedile, the senator supposedly in charge of the Games, is also present, already looking more anxious than usual. My eyes dart to the corner of the room where, as expected, is Gaius Petronius Stephanus, still and quiet in the shadows, as ever. I have never been informed as to what exactly his role is, but he seems to be one of the only people who can manage Domitian's sometimes odd behaviour. His head gives a tiny inclination when my gaze meets his. The other person in the room is an augur, one of the priests who can read the flights of birds and divine from them whether the gods are pleased or displeased with the plans of mere mortals. The augur is dressed in a white senatorial tunic, over which is the vivid toga of his office, in saffron yellow with purple stripes. In one hand he holds an augural wand, a carved piece of wood which starts straight but then curls in a spiral at the end. He has pulled the toga up so it covers his head, which, combined with his self-satisfied air, is making him look somewhat like a male bird about to engage in a mating dance. I look away from him in case I get a fit of the giggles.

"Yes?" says Domitian to Marcus without looking up from the scroll. He is not one for niceties, rarely bothering with even basic greetings.

Marcus is on his best behaviour. "Imperator, as the Aedile will have already informed you, I am to be married and wish to return to my family's farm in the countryside outside Puteoli. My contract as Manager of the Games at the Flavian Amphitheatre has expired. I have been honoured by the opportunity to create Games for the imperial amphitheatre and your illustrious family, but I humbly beg leave to hand in my notice and pass on the role to a worthy replacement of your choosing."

"No," says Domitian.

"Imperator?"

Domitian finally looks up and raises his voice as though Marcus is deaf. "No. I am happy with you as the Manager and your –" he glances at me "– wife-to-be as your assistant. I have been pleased with your work. I do not wish you to leave. You will remain."

Marcus looks towards the Aedile for help, but the Aedile only twists his hands and avoids making eye contact. "Imperator, my contract is complete and I –"

"NO!" screams Domitian.

The guards, startled, pull out their swords, ready to attack, then realise Domitian is only angry and put them back in their scabbards, looking confused.

The Aedile takes a tiny step forwards, his body tight with fear. "Imperator, I can assure you that I will procure the services of another, equally excellent Manager for the Games and that –"

But Domitian is on his feet, his usually ruddy face scarlet with rage. He grabs at the desk and hurls it to one side with enormous force, so that it skids across the polished marble floor and smashes into a wall, one leg breaking off in splinters. "THERE WILL BE NO CHANGE TO THE STAFF OF THE AMPHITHEATRE!" he screams, his voice echoing around the room. He comes closer to Marcus, stands a hand's breadth from his face and speaks so fast it is hard to understand him. "The augurs have spoken and they are certain, there must be no change of management of the amphitheatre or the gods will be displeased, furthermore I do not wish any such changes to be made and as your emperor and master, there is nothing further to be said. You will sign this document." He grabs a scroll from one of the scribes, crumpling it as he does so and thrusts it into Marcus' face. "And you will continue to serve as Manager of the Games." He strides across the room, pulls a sword from the scabbard of the nearest guard and points it at Marcus' throat. "If you refuse to do this, make no mistake, you will find yourself *and* your wife in the arena and you will not leave it alive. I will have you both crucified for treason against Rome. I do not wish you to leave, so you WILL. NOT. LEAVE."

"Ahem." Stephanus has left his post in the corner and is standing to one side of Domitian, calm despite Domitian's scarlet face and heaving chest, the shaking tip of the sword resting in the hollow of Marcus' neck.

I wonder for a terrible moment if the Emperor of Rome is about to cry. Domitian is like a small child who does not get their way and has a tantrum. Marcus is keeping perfectly still, giving no cause for Domitian to be angrier than he already is.

"I feel that it would be best if we were to adjourn this meeting," says Stephanus smoothly. "There is a great deal to discuss, many minor administrative details to be covered and we do not want the meeting to grow over-long and tiring for all concerned. Would you all please excuse us, so that the Emperor may collect his thoughts? I will send someone to fetch you from the atrium as soon as we are ready to continue."

"Of-of course," stammers the Aedile, scurrying out of the room as fast as he can, swiftly followed by the scribes and the augur, who all look petrified.

I put my hand on Marcus' arm. "We will await your command, Imperator," I say, trying to keep my voice from shaking. Marcus steps slowly back, the wavering tip of the sword a hand's breadth from his throat, then another step, his eyes lowered so as not to meet Domitian's gaze. Domitian remains in the same position, sword outstretched, his eyes glittering with unshed tears, face flushed.

"You may also leave," says Stephanus to the guards. "Please take your weapon with you," he adds to the guard whose sword Domitian is holding, as though the guard had somehow chosen to leave it in the Emperor's hand as a useful resting place.

Marcus and I continue edging backwards to the door behind us as the terrified guard eases the sword from Domitian, who lets it go without a struggle. The guard replaces it in his scabbard, salutes and backs away, reaching us as we get to the door. My last glimpse of Domitian is of him standing very still in the room, one hand at his mouth as though biting his fist, Stephanus standing by him as though faintly interested in something they are both looking at in companionable silence.

We close the door and I lean against Marcus, shaking. He wraps his arms around me, speaks over my head to the Aedile in a furious whisper.

"What in Hades was that about? I thought you warned him!"

"I did." The Aedile grovels, wringing his hands. "He was calm when I mentioned it. Nodded and sent me on my way."

The scribes and guards are huddled in a corner, all of them pale. The augur, however, is all but preening.

"It is as the birds foretold," he says. "A highly inauspicious moment."

"Fuck off," says Marcus. "You and your stupid birds. He nearly killed me!" Pressed up against his body, I can feel he, too, is shaking.

The augur looks put out but is not getting any support from the rest of us. "The birds show the will of the gods," he mutters.

"They show whatever you want them to show according to who briefed you," spits Marcus. I've rarely seen him this angry and I put my hand on his chest.

"Let's walk in the Forum."

"What if he calls for you?" asks the Aedile.

"He's not going to calm himself that fast," I point out. "Come," I add to Marcus.

I get water from a fountain, walk us around the busy Forum until Marcus has calmed down.

"He's never going to let us go, is he?" he says.

"Stephanus will do something," I say.

"Do you trust him?"

"I have to hope I can. No-one else has a chance of getting through to Domitian."

"What if we're stuck running the Games forever?"

"We'll find a way," I say. "And even if we are, we have each other and that matters more than anything."

He squeezes my hand. "It does. But I want to get out of here."

We spend more time in the sunshine to steady our nerves, then return to the atrium to wait. The scribes, guards and augur have all gone, only the Aedile remains, seated alone on a bench, his expression forlorn.

"How did he ever get the role of Aedile for the Games?" I whisper to Marcus as we rejoin him.

We wait. And wait. More than three hours pass. My stomach begins to rumble for food, made worse part way through by two slave girls passing us, one with a platter of fresh bread with olives and a dipping sauce, the other with delicately cut fruits laid out on an elegant silver tray and a jug of wine. They both head into the room where we saw Domitian.

At last the door opens and Stephanus appears. "Would you join us, please?"

There's a new table in the room; the smashed desk has been removed. On this new table is a large model of the Flavian Amphitheatre, the width of a man's outstretched arms. But this amphitheatre has a very different appearance to the one I am accustomed to. Around the top tier, vertical wooden poles are set at regular intervals, from which an intricate rigging system of thin cords spans out, holding in place a red awning made of strips of linen, covering the whole of the amphitheatre apart from an open circle in the centre which is held in place by a ring of metal, the size of a man's fist.

Domitian is leaning over the model, closely inspecting it.

"Marcus Aquilius Scaurus and Althea Aquilius," announces Stephanus, as though the whole meeting is beginning again. "And the Aedile of the Games."

"Imperator," we chorus together.

Domitian looks up. His face has returned to its usual complexion and he nods as though he has very little idea of who we are.

"I have suggested a solution to the Emperor which he has found acceptable," says Stephanus. "Marcus Aquillius Scaurus will complete one more season of the Games, during which time we will find someone to continue the role for the foreseeable future, thus avoiding any further changes in staff and releasing Scaurus from his service to the imperial amphitheatre at the end of the season."

Marcus' eyes don't even flicker. "As you command, Imperator," he says, looking at Domitian.

Domitian looks away, as though interested in a marble column on the far side of the room. "I have three additional tasks," he says. "You must carry them out also."

"Imperator?"

"I want a velarium to protect spectators from the sun and an extra tier of seating adding to the amphitheatre. I want you to manage a private event at my villa in the Alban Hills. And I want a naumachia." He pauses, then, like a child forced to apologise, adds in a rush, "And then you will be dismissed from imperial service and be free to go."

"I am honoured to be of service," says Marcus.

Domitian glances at him, then points to the striped awning on the model. "The first task will be to install the additional seating and the velarium in the Flavian Amphitheatre," he says.

We approach the table and look at the model. The strips of red cloth are stretched out across the cord structure, like sails laid horizontally rather than vertically, secured in the centre by the metal circlet, and held in place at the outer edges by the poles.

"Pull those." Domitian points at the ends of the cords. He grasps two himself and Marcus and I each copy his movements. Six sections of the cloth awning move back from the centre circle towards the poles, as though we were lowering sails, each section of cloth folding in on itself until half of the amphitheatre's roof awning is left, the other half open to the sky.

"You can pull back all of it or parts of it, depending where the sun is coming from," says Domitian. "And when the whole thing is fully open, it creates a pool of light in the centre of the arena which draws the crowd's attention to whatever you want them to look at."

Marcus nods, but he looks troubled. "And those are...?" he asks, pointing at the now-revealed interior of the top tier of the building. This is where the women and slaves sit but above the current stone terraces of seating, there is an additional wooden structure.

"Additional seating," says Domitian. "The amphitheatre is proving very popular, even among women. Tickets to the Games are also a good way of rewarding slaves for diligent work. The slaves can be packed in tightly in the new wooden seats allowing more space for women on the stone terraces. They're very steeply raked."

Marcus draws a deep breath. I can see he's holding back but I know what he's thinking.

"Is there a timescale for the works, Imperator?" I ask.

"The tiers and awning to be ready for the start of the season," says Domitian.

"Our current team are not accustomed to that kind of rigging," says Marcus, choosing his words with care. "It may take time to –"

"You'll use sailors," says Domitian. "The amphitheatre will be assigned two hundred sailors from the barracks at Misenum. They will travel here just before the start of each season in March or April, stay in their own barracks at the docks and be dismissed back to Misenum at the end of the season in October or November. The carpenters for the poles and wooden seating tiers have already been commissioned. They start work next week. The rigging and awning will be delivered in mid-March, which gives you two weeks to put it in place and practise using it with the sailors. They are accustomed to putting up and taking down sails. It's the same principle. Any other questions?"

We both know better than to question him.

"No, Imperator," we chorus.

"Excellent," says Domitian. "Now I wish to talk about the private spectacle at my villa in the Alban Hills."

"What kind of spectacle, Imperator?" Marcus asks.

"Gladiatorial Games. I have a five-hundred-seater amphitheatre being built there by my architect Rabirius. It will be completed by June and I'd like it inaugurated in style."

"Absolutely," says Marcus. "We will devise something spectacular."

"So that being all in hand, let's discuss the naumachia," says Domitian, giving one of his odd smiles, teeth bared.

I can actually hear Marcus swallow. "The amphitheatre can no longer be flooded, Imperator, the new underfloor hypogeum does not allow for –"

"Not at the amphitheatre. In Augustus' lake."

"In what?"

Domitian waves us over to another table set at the back of the room, on top of which is the model of Rome we saw last year. He points to a large circle painted blue and surrounded by a low wall, situated just over the river from our own insula. "Augustus' lake. He held a naumachia there to celebrate the victory of Actium. It will need digging out again, of course. Silt and earth will have built up. It will need a wall to surround it and seating. I want a naumachia held there this summer. Bigger and better." He flashes his odd smile again, teeth bared, eyes glinting.

For a moment I think Marcus is going to refuse, but no doubt he is thinking of how it felt to be held at sword point by an apoplectic Emperor of Rome. "As you command, Imperator," he manages. "Perhaps July would be a suitable month? For the best weather?"

"Yes," says Domitian. He looks at the circle. "I believe there are drainage systems and an aqueduct that supplies it. You'll need to bring ships in."

"We will look into everything, Imperator."

I can tell Marcus just wants to get out of here, before Domitian comes up with any other odd requests which will require months of planning to pull off. Perhaps Stephanus is thinking the same thing, because he intervenes.

"You will need to start planning at once," he says. "The Emperor will permit you to leave. It is excellent to have come to an understanding."

Marcus bows his head. "Imperator."

We get as far as the door when Domitian speaks again. "I will visit your animals soon."

"Certainly," says Marcus, hovering on the threshold, his expression growing ever more fixed. "Did you have any particular animal in mind?"

Domitian considers. "Zebras," he says at last.

Marcus takes a couple of steps backwards, desperate to leave. "We look forward to your visit, Imperator."

Domitian nods, losing interest in us. He turns back towards his model and we leave the room, then walk fast away from the palace until we reach a quietish street where we can talk. Our pace finally slows.

"Thank Jupiter we got out of there alive," I say.

"So much for Janus watching over us," mutters Marcus.

"Shh," I say. "Don't anger him."

"I'd have liked a better start to our plans to leave Rome than to be forced to stay another year. And three additional tasks? What does he think this is, some old legend where we have to set out on a quest to please the gods by proving our heroism?"

I can't help but giggle, the fear of the past few hours and the relief of no harm coming to Marcus bursting out. I squat down, face in my hands, and laugh until I'm spent.

"I'm glad you're taking it so well," says Marcus when I finally stop.

"I was terrified," I say. "He's so unpredictable."

"He's losing his mind," says Marcus. "Let's hope he keeps it for one more year so we can get out of here safely."

"He assumes we have animals all year round," I say as we begin walking again.

Marcus shakes his head. "Zebras," he sighs. "At this time of year. Couldn't wait till we're in full Games season and have most things ready to hand?"

I don't think emperors care about that sort of thing," I say. "They want things when they want them. They don't wait, like the rest of us. What will it be like putting on private Games at his villa?"

"I'm less worried about that. Games are Games. We do them all the time. We just find a good theme, pack up everyone who has to perform and take them all to the Alban Hills. It's a day's travel out of Rome."

I nod. "At least one of the tasks is straightforward."

Marcus stops by a fountain to drink and sits on the edge of it. "And another naumachia. Have we offended Poseidon, that we're cursed to put on a water show again?"

"How big does the lake have to be?"

"Big," says Marcus grimacing. "We'll be using real boats, not show boats. Full size."

"We will have two hundred sailors at our command," I say.

"Unless they're busy messing with the velarium's rigging. And what will their commander say when he loses two hundred of his men to the Games for a whole spring and summer?"

"Not our problem."

Marcus laughs and puts an arm about my shoulders. "You're right," he says. "I have you and that's all that matters. Just promise me we're not doing Hero and Leander again for the naumachia. Also, no crocodiles."

"No crocodiles," I say. "A safe, sunny naumachia. Big boats, lots of sailors, impressive fight scenes and we can all go home happy."

"That sounds perfect. I've had enough for one day. Let's go to the baths."

SAFELY BACK AT THE INSULA, we find our landlady Julia passing the time of day with Maria and Adah, the three older women sitting in the autumn sunshine together.

"You're back soon," says Maria. "Good news? Are you free?"

"I'm afraid not," I say.

"Sit," says Julia, pouring us each a cup of wine and pushing it towards us.

Marcus regales them with a description of Domitian losing his mind over our possible departure.

"And afterwards he was all calm? Just like that? After threatening to kill you?" asks Julia.

"Yes, but it took Stephanus a few hours and some food and drink," I say.

"That family are all monsters underneath," says Adah darkly. She hated Domitian's brother Titus for destroying the Temple of Jerusalem, and is quite ready to believe that Domitian is not to be trusted either.

"Time to rest," says Marcus. "Come."

We take our bed mats out onto the rooftop and lie in the sun. The shakiness of the morning is still in my limbs. "He said he would crucify us in the arena," I say, shuddering.

"Crucifixion is dull," says Marcus. "It isn't suitable for spectacle in the Games. They faint from the pain and just hang there. Doesn't work in the arena."

He's right. Crucifixion is mostly used as a deterrent along the roads in and out of Rome, where the hanging half-dead bodies remind Rome's slaves, pirates and state enemies of the kind of death they will endure, should they challenge the empire's laws and might. It is one of the most humiliating and painful deaths imaginable but it's mainly used for treasonous offences against the empire. "It's hardly treason to want to resign."

"I do wonder about his sanity." Marcus shakes his head. "He was so angry he could have killed me, I could see it in his eyes. And a few hours later, completely calm, as though nothing had happened."

"You really think he consulted the augur about who should run the amphitheatre?" I turn onto my side to look at him. "I didn't think he'd consult them for things like that. Weddings and wars and appointing important officials, yes, but can't he just decide for himself when it comes to people like us?"

Marcus rolls his eyes.

"You don't believe the augur?" I ask. Marcus sacrifices at temples on appropriate occasions and has to my knowledge attended at least two augury sessions to bear witness that the omens were right for a wedding.

He shrugs. "In the army there's a pullarius, who looks after the sacred chickens. Before a battle, he'll open their cage and throw bread at them. If they refuse to eat, the omens are unfavourable."

"And?"

Marcus grins. "You can't have an unfavourable omen just before you send men into battle, it takes the spirit out of them. When I served in the army our pullarius once told me if he needed a favourable omen, he'd starve the chickens for a couple of days before the battle. They'd come rushing out, eager to eat everything in sight. They'd get a big cheer from the men. Made them feel invincible."

"And if the battle didn't go well?"

He raises his eyebrows. "Imagine how much worse it would have been, if the sacred chickens had decided it was unfavourable."

"Surely the priests of Rome are better augurs than some drunken soldier on a tour of duty? They can't control the flight of wild birds in the way your pullarius controlled chickens."

Marcus grimaces. "Wouldn't put it past them. They'll do anything to give the answer that's desired."

"But it depends on high or low the birds fly, which direction they come from, all sorts of things."

"You put on a show at the amphitheatre every day," says Marcus. "Are you telling me you couldn't arrange for birds to behave how you wanted them to, if you had to? Remember the coloured doves?"

I think back to the opening ceremony of the amphitheatre years ago, when we dyed five hundred white doves every possible bright colour and set them free just as the ceremony completed, the crowd murmuring approval at what they saw as a good omen. "I suppose you're right," I say.

"And how did we get them to fly high?"

"Released them low," I say.

"Exactly. Release them low with nowhere to go but up if they want to leave the amphitheatre. And if I'd wanted it to look unfavourable, I'd have trained them beforehand, released them high and had their feeding spot and nests down low."

"Don't let a priest hear you or we'll get hired to run the augury instead of the amphitheatre," I say.

"Oh, I'm sure they already have a team like ours, doing just that." He sighs. "We have no choice. One more season and Domitian's three ridiculous tasks. I'm sorry, my love, I know you are tired of the amphitheatre. Shall I run it alone this year? You can stay clear of it."

"What would I do all day?"

"Spend time with Cassia. Plan for the farm. Enjoy some freedom. I've worked you hard all these years. Now that you're about to be my wife I'd like you to enjoy yourself.

You'll be working hard enough when we finally do get back to the farm. At least with the amphitheatre there's an off season and you come home at night. On a farm there is no off season and all sorts happen at night."

"Such as?"

"Animals being born. Storms so you have to rush out and clear ditches to avoid floods, lost livestock you have to go searching for before the wolves get to them..."

I nod. "It would be nice to rest, I suppose, but..."

"But?"

"I'd miss you," I say. "I'm used to seeing you every day and the times when – when things have not been well between us and we didn't see or speak much to one another I hated being distant from you."

He pulls me close to him. "I wish you'd told me sooner. The time we've wasted."

I rest my head on his chest, wrap my arms around him. "The gods chose their moment."

He tightens his hold. "Thanks be to Venus and Juno for bringing you to me."

SONGBIRDS

I WAKE EARLY BUT MARCUS HAS already gone somewhere. He doesn't appear until well after breakfast, carrying something by a metal loop. The package is covered in a large cloth, swaying gently from his hand. Karbo and I follow him across the rooftop.

"What is it?"

"Open it," he says, setting it on the ground. "A gift for my bride-to-be."

I pull away the cloth, unveiling a large birdcage which is divided into two halves. On one side are two nightingales. In the other part, crushed together, are six doves.

"Doves for Venus that she may bless our marriage," says Marcus. "Nightingales so they can sing to you. I'll build larger cages for them, now I've got them home."

Karbo pokes his finger through the slats, touching the doves' delicate feathers. They huddle together, resisting his curiosity.

"They're lovely. Thank you." I wrap my arms around his neck.

"Not more *kissing*," groans Karbo.

I laugh and come to coo at the doves, while Marcus goes to get his tools. He builds a large cage for the nightingales, so that they can hop about and sing, and a pen for the doves. They submit to having their wings clipped, which does not hurt them.

"When they're tame enough you can set them free and they'll always come home," says Marcus. "We'll need to clip their wings for a few months until they are certain of where to come back to. Then they can grow back their feathers and fly again."

The doves flutter but cannot take off. Karbo and I feed them grain, which they are greedy for.

"I'm sorry their wings must be clipped," I say.

"It is only for a while," says Marcus.

"The doves and I are both held here for a while," I say.

"And one day soon you will all be free to fly wherever you wish," he promises me.

The nightingales do not sing at once. They chirp and hop about but keep their songs to themselves, timid of their new home. I will cover their cage at night to keep their little bodies warm in the cooler nights of winter.

MARCUS PLANS TO TRAVEL SOUTH to Puteoli before the cold days of November arrive.

"Domitian may insist on us staying in Rome for one more year," he says, "but I can't wait any longer to secure our farm. I have the money. It would be foolish to risk losing it at the last moment if someone else buys it before us."

"How long will you be gone?"

"Perhaps ten days. Plenty of time for you to fuss about with wedding plans," he adds grinning.

"*I* don't want to hear about wedding plans for ten days." Karbo grimaces. "Can I come to Puteoli too?"

"You're staying here to look after Althea," says Marcus. "You are the man of the house while I'm gone. Can I rely on you?"

Karbo grows a hand's breadth as he stands at his full height. "Of course," he says with pride.

"Good lad. Look at the height of you. You'll be a man soon." Marcus shakes his head and strokes Karbo's soft locks.

It's odd to see Marcus riding away down Sand Street; we have not been apart for ten days since we first met three years ago, that strange day when I was gifted to him as a slave. So much has changed. I wave him off, then, determined to keep busy in his absence, talk to Cassia about food for the wedding.

"Cream pudding," says Karbo more than once.

"I heard you first time," I say. "What else?"

"Cream pudding."

"For every course?"

"Yes, please."

I poke his belly. "Never mind your height, you'll be round like an amphora if you eat as much cream pudding as you're planning to."

"What else are weddings good for?"

"The blessings of the gods?"

"Not as good as cream pudding," says Karbo in a stage whisper.

"Be careful or they'll hear you."

The food left in Cassia's capable hands, I spend the first day sewing my white wedding tunic by Maria's side at her established watching spot on the balcony overlooking the courtyard. We observe the usual comings and goings below us, pass the time of day with our neighbours and by the end of the day my tunic is ready. There is another task I need to complete before the wedding, but I'm uncertain of how to proceed. I make my way to Julia's apartment and she welcomes me.

"Excited about the wedding?"

"Yes," I say, "but before that I have to complete the ceremony of childhood toys and I don't have any toys from my childhood."

"Quintus could carve you something," suggests Julia.

"But it won't really be mine."

She smiles. "It's symbolic," she says. "It is about your intention to leave behind your childhood and become a grown woman, not about what you take to the temple."

I'm reassured. If even a Vestal can see no harm in it, then it must be satisfactory. "Thank you, Julia. I'll ask him."

I get as far as the doorway when she calls me back. "Althea."

"Yes?"

"I will dress you on your wedding day."

I'm touched and a little honoured. "Thank you, I'm grateful."

She waves me away. "Go and find Quintus."

I make my way to Cassia's popina for breakfast and find Fabia amongst the other customers. Standing at the counter like most people do would mean her head would barely be level with her food, so she's sitting at one of the few inside tables, a better fit for her tiny frame. I greet Quintus, who is looking after Emilia. He's carving a small wooden horse, and she is imitating him, holding a little stick as a knife, pretending to whittle away at another piece of wood. I praise her imaginary creation and sit next to Fabia.

"Will you come with me to the temple before the wedding?" I ask her. "I have to give up my childhood toys."

She nods, busy munching on a fruit roll.

"You're always hungry," I say.

"Never get to eat when I'm working," she says her mouth full. "Too much going on."

"You're the head physician," I say. "Don't you get to make the rules about the work?"

"There's always something," she says. "If it isn't a gladiator getting hurt it's one of their women giving birth or Paternus wanting to borrow me for one of his gladiators."

"He'll poach you from Labeo if you're not careful," I say.

She grins and sips from her wine cup. "That might not be a bad thing. A step up in the world. Though I owe Labeo a lot and also, I'm happy to be treating women and dwarfs like myself, I understand them better than most physicians. No-one else cares much about them, they see them as second-class gladiators. You should see the kind of care Paternus' top gladiators get. They're practically nobility. Their own villas and slaves and daily massages, special training regimes developed just for them, making sure they're in tip-top condition for the big fights. I wouldn't want Labeo's gladiators to be forgotten if a new physician took my place."

"At least their status has been elevated by being part of Rome's second biggest school," I say.

Fabia takes another bite of her fruit roll. "So, the ceremony of childhood toys?"

"Yes. Quintus, I came to ask you if you could make me something. I don't have any toys from my childhood. Julia said it would be acceptable."

He looks up from his carving. "What toys did you have as a child, before you were taken as a slave? Can you remember any?"

I try to think. So little of my childhood stays in my memory. I remember hardly anything from before I was taken. "My father gave me quills to write with," I say. "But they weren't toys, he wanted me to be a scribe, knowing that would give me the chance of a better life."

Quintus nods. "I'll make something," he promises me. "When are you going?"

"I wanted to go the day after tomorrow," I say. "Is that too soon?"

He shakes his head. "I'll have something ready."

I'M CURIOUS AS TO WHAT Quintus will come up with. He is already doing well in his apprenticeship for Balbus, carving beautiful toys and learning new skills in toymaking from Balbus and his wife Floriana, who is skilled at weaving and sewing and makes hair and clothes for dolls, manes for horses and tiny colourful woollen trims for everything from soft balls for babies to play with to elaborate feathered strings to amuse the pampered cats of the rich. Quintus already runs the shop by himself one day a week, giving the older couple a much-needed rest, and has even been on visits to the fancy villas on the hill to display the wares to the rich children of senators.

When I come down two days later, Quintus is waiting for me.

"I made you this for the offering," he says. He holds out a wooden doll which looks like a small child, dressed in the Greek fashion with strands of brown wool for hair. In her clasped-together hands she holds a bundle of quills nearly as long as her body.

"Thank you," I say. "She's so lovely. I don't want to give her up."

He laughs. "Then she is a good offering."

Fabia and I walk together to the Temple of Juno, both of us washed and dressed in our best tunics and embroidered headwraps, with colourful woven belts. The temple looms over us, vast columns making us feel small, wafting incense perfuming the air as we enter through the great doors behind many other women come to pray to the goddess of wives. I carry the little doll with me and when it is our turn to reach the altar, I place her there along with a basket of gilded pomegranates and dates, with laurel leaves for decoration. If I had been a summer bride I could have left flowers, but the fruits and foliage will have to do. I hold my hands out, palms up and begin my prayer of offering.

"Lady Juno, hear me. In this place, at this time, in preparation for my wedding day, I lay before you the toys of my childhood and leave behind my childish ways, to become a married woman. Accept my offering of fruits and leaves, that my marriage hearth may be bountiful under your care. I will strive to be a good wife in your image, Lady Juno, and ask for your blessings. Watch over me as I change from girl to woman, from bride to wife, from daughter to mother."

I bow my head and Fabia bows hers alongside me.

"Another wedding," she says, as we leave the temple. "First Cassia, now you, married off."

"Your turn next," I say. "That handsome assistant of yours, Sadiki, is he going to propose to you one of these days?"

Fabia's cheeks go pink. "What nonsense you talk," she mutters.

"Why not? He worships you."

"He respects me," she corrects. "I'm his master."

"Bet he'd like you to be something e-else," I sing-song to her.

"Never mind about that," she says, her cheeks going a deeper shade of pink. "Have you got your veil?"

"I'm wearing Cassia's, as you know full well. Stop changing the subject."

Fabia shakes her head. "I want to marry and have children," she admits. "But I don't want to stop being a physician. I love what I do and a husband would want me to be a wife, to look after our children."

"If he were a physician too he might understand," I say.

"Perhaps," she says. "But I fear not many men would allow such a thing, for their wife to be a physician after the marriage. And until I am sure, I will not risk it. I would have to be a physician in a greater role than I am now to command such respect and not have to give it up after marriage."

"Isn't physician to Labeo's gladiatorial school an important enough role?"

She shrugs. "It's good, but we're the second school. If I were physician to Paternus' school it would be grander."

"Or physician to the Flavian Amphitheatre?" I ask, smiling.

"Father's nabbed that one," she says. "But I'm standing by to inherit it when he retires. Which will be never," she adds. "Father loves his work too much. He'll still be stitching up gladiators years from now. Anyway," she adds, "enough of all this. I have a gift for you. It's a wedding gift but you should have it before the wedding. You will be in need of it right away once you are married."

Back at the insula, she brings me a carefully folded blue cloth. I shake it out to find that it is a beautifully woven and trimmed palla, the wrap that married women wear. I stroke the soft wool, admiring the rich dark blue, the green braid trim. "It's so pretty. Thank you."

"Can't have a married woman going about without a palla," says Fabia, satisfied. "It's a good one for winter, though you'll also need something lighter or you'll burn up in the summer."

I make my way up the stairs, passing Adah on her way to market.

"Almost time," she says.

I grin. "I'm glad you will be giving me away on my wedding day."

She pats my arm and makes her way carefully down the stairs, one tremulous hand clinging to the bannisters.

I'm on the rooftop cooing to the doves and trying to coax the nightingales to sing when I hear the clattering of hooves in the courtyard below and look over the bannisters to see Marcus dismounting, a full day earlier than expected. I run down the steps and fling myself into his arms.

"You're back early!"

"I missed you too much to dawdle," he says.

"Ah, young lovers," says Maria from her usual balcony perch above us. "Welcome home, Marcus."

"It will not be our home for much longer," says Marcus, grinning up at her.

"Did you secure the farm?" I ask. I've fretted over the past nine days that another buyer would have snapped it up from under our noses. Although there are plenty of other places we could find to buy, Marcus has his heart set on reclaiming his family's property, gambled away by his grandfather, thereby restoring their family honour.

"I've made a down payment with the agreement that the rest of the money will follow when they've undertaken some basic repairs to the roof, the courtyard walls and gate. That way, the winter won't cause any more damage to the interior from leaks. When we get there we'll still have to clean the place up and repaint it inside, but at least it'll be dry and wild animals won't be able to get into the courtyard."

"The farm is ours?"

He beams, tightens his arms about me. "It's ours," he says. "I hardly dared to believe it would still be there waiting for me. I didn't even dare say it out loud till just now. It's ours!"

"It rightly belongs to your family," I say. "The gods kept it for you."

"Bona Dea bless you both," says Maria.

Marcus nods, serious again. "I will give thanks at the temple," he says.

Celer appears from his room, nods towards the horse. "Welcome back. You must be tired from the ride, Marcus, shall I take him up to the stables for you?"

"I'd be grateful, thank you," says Marcus, giving Celer a quick embrace. The two of them go outside for a moment, then Marcus returns carrying his saddlebags slung over one shoulder.

"It will be a new start," I say. "We will have everything the way it used to be when you were a boy."

Marcus smiles, his eyes dreamy. "It was such a busy place. Always something happening. We'll have pigs and sheep, horses, chickens and doves. Bees. The old vineyard and the olive and fruit trees will need pruning to bring them back to fruitfulness, but we will have our own wine, our own oil. You can plant vegetables." He starts to lead the way up the stairs.

I laugh, following him. "I'll try. I know nothing about farming."

"You'll learn," he says. "You and Karbo managed to grow beans and salad on a rooftop in Rome. You'll be fine."

We wave to Maria as we pass her and climb to the rooftop, where we settle ourselves to enjoy the pale sunshine, resting our backs on the hut's wall.

"We need a proper pergola with a table and chairs up here," says Marcus. "There was one at the farm with the strawberry grape vine climbing all over it, but it'll need rebuilding."

"I wish everyone could come with us," I say, a wave of sadness rising up. "I'm going to miss them."

"We'll have Karbo." He thinks, his head on one side. "I might ask Strabo. He's a good man, he's been loyal and a hard worker at the amphitheatre but he was brought up on a farm. You could ask Adah if she wants to come and live there with us, look after the bees, enjoy the countryside."

I smile at the thought. "She'll say no," I predict. "She doesn't like change. But I'll ask her. I'll ask everyone."

"Anyone who wants to come from our insula is welcome," he says. "But we will have to say some goodbyes."

"I just want there to be as few as possible."

"It's only a few days' travel. You can come back to visit."

"I won't miss all of it. I'll be glad to leave the Games behind."

"Me too," he says. "I've seen enough of them to last me a lifetime. All I want is a quiet happy life on the farm with you at my side."

"I've been thinking while you were away," I say. "I don't want to sit idle while you run the Games and carry out Domitian's tasks. We've always run the Games together. It's only one more year and we should do it side by side, like always. The velarium and the seating will be done before the Games season opens anyway, so that's one task complete. We've done a naumachia before and it can't be as bad as the one in the amphitheatre. And like you said, Games in his villa can't be as difficult as the ones we put on every day in the season." I hug him tighter to me. "This time next year we'll be on our farm."

A GOLDEN VEIL

THE WEATHER IN DECEMBER IS not looking promising for a wedding. Most days there is a fine drizzle. Once or twice there have been thunderstorms, rain running through the courtyard as though our fountain had leaked, creating little brooks that make their way out into Virgin's Street and join larger rivers out in Sand Street. They all go down to join the Tiber as it swells to its winter height. The nightgales sit silent, unwilling to sing while the doves huddle together for warmth. Our wedding will take place a week before the official Saturnalia period begins and each day we wake to gloomy skies while Cassia speaks confidently of decorations and the feast she will be preparing for our celebrations.

"What if it rains?" asks Karbo.

"It won't," says Marcus with supreme confidence.

"It's been raining for weeks," says Karbo.

"Tomorrow is too important," says Marcus.

"We can set up tables in the storage rooms," says Cassia, ever practical.

IT'S HARD TO GET TO sleep that night. I try to lie in silence, but after a while Marcus speaks.

"Are you still awake?"

"Yes."

"Nervous?"

I take his hand. "Not about marrying you. But the ceremony…"

He squeezes my hand, rolls onto his side so that he can kiss me. "It will be fun. Weddings are fun."

"You haven't gone to sleep either," I point out.

He chuckles. "You've caught me out. I knew I'd chosen a clever woman."

I nestle closer to him, wondering whether Livia has been on his mind. He must remember his first wedding. Livia's family did not much approve of her marrying a penniless wounded ex-centurion, a man descended from a grandfather who had lost everything, even the family farm, to a gambling addiction. But they were happy together. I remember his tenderness with her and I'm glad we are in the dark, because my eyes fill with sudden tears. I don't doubt that Marcus loves me. I don't feel second best to Livia, but the thought of Marcus' grief in losing the woman he loved as well as his baby son to the searing wrath of Vesuvius, now that I know what it is to love someone, is painful.

Perhaps he feels what I am thinking. "You have brought happiness back to my life," he says softly. "I thought I was content, with friends about me. But having you by my side is different. I feel whole again and I did not even know I was still broken."

My nervous excitement about tomorrow drifts away at his words. I inhale the warm scent of him, feel his skin against mine and sleep comes while I am safe in his arms and heart.

WHEN I WAKE MARCUS HAS already gone to the augurs to get the blessings of the gods from the bird omens, as required for a wedding, whatever his own views on their accuracy. Anxious, I check the sky, but we have already been blessed. Although the air is cold, the sky is pale blue with the promise of a bright day of sunlight. I pull on my tunic, leaving it unbelted, for Julia will be dressing me soon in my bridal clothes, already prepared and taken to her own apartment. But first there is something I want to do alone.

I take out two beeswax candles I have been saving for today, place them carefully on the Lararium in my hut and light them in front of the two tiny dolls who symbolise my mother and father. I touch the hair of my mother's doll, dressed in the Greek style by Floriana, Balbus the toymaker's wife, stroke the little wax tablet of my father's doll. I clear my throat, raise my palms.

"Father and Mother, I am to be married today. I wish you were by my side, Father, to give me your blessing. Mother, I wish you were here to place my hands in Marcus' and see my happiness." I have to take a deep breath before continuing, tears falling down my face. "I have been blessed by Venus and Juno to have found Marcus as my husband, but I have been blessed in so many other ways. I have found so many friends here in Rome and even had a child, Karbo, come to me by the grace of Juno that I might adopt him as my own. I pray that your shades walk in peace, hand in hand through the flowery fields of Elysium, that one day I will see you again. I ask for your blessings to make my day complete and my marriage a happy one." I wipe one hand across my face so that I can see more clearly, touch the little dolls one more time, bow my head to them and step away, gather my comb and the ribbons that will be woven into my hair and step outside the roof hut. The nightingales are singing and I pause by their cage to listen to them, a happy omen on my wedding day. The doves potter around the rooftop, unable yet to fly but growing used to my presence after many days of being fed. I go downstairs to Julia.

It's an odd feeling to be dressed by someone who used to be a priestess. I might not notice it so much were she not treating it like a sacred duty. When I helped to dress Cassia for her wedding we chattered together, but Julia has me strip off, then washes me herself with a cloth and warm water, head to toe. She keeps an unnerving silence throughout, only coughing once or twice.

"Are you well?" I ask at last, hoping to break the silence.

"Just a cough," she says. "Maria has given me a syrup for it made with Adah's honey."

I try to think of something else to say, but her silence is forbidding, although I doubt she means it that way. I wonder whether this is something all Vestals learn, not to fill up a silent space while they go about their divine work.

Julia lifts up the white tunic and I lift my arms, am dressed like a small child. She spends time getting the Knot of Hercules just right with my belt and indicates a stool on which I can sit while she prepares my hair. The *seni crines* hairstyle is an ancient style that the first Roman women wore, now worn by Vestals and brides, so Julia of all people would be able to arrange it. It's made up of six braids and I can feel her sectioning my hair with a spear point.

"This is the spear of a gladiator who fought in the Flavian Amphitheatre itself, sent as a gift from Paternus," she says, fingers tugging as she begins plaiting the six plaits that will create the base of the hairstyle. "You can't ask for better luck on your marriage day. You will bring forth brave sons."

I don't much like the idea of a bloodied spear running through my hair, even if the blood did dry a long while back, but it's tradition and weddings are full of superstitions that must be adhered to. Besides, a spear is sacred to Juno and every bride wants Juno to watch over her. I follow Julia's instructions when it comes time to weave in the red ribbon which will bind the plaits together, placing my fingers on my forehead and just above my ears to keep the ribbon in place while Julia plaits it into my hair, so that there will be little flashes of red between my plaits.

It takes a while to braid my long hair, twist it at the nape of my neck followed by a final wrapping of the plaits around my head and a tiny bun to complete the wrapping on to the top of my head. Julia uses so many bone pins to hold everything in place that I wonder if I will look like a hedgehog rather than a bride, but finally she places a wreath of rosemary on my head and adds a few more pins to secure it.

"Your veil," she says at last, lifting up the flame-yellow fabric that Cassia has lent me. She drapes it with care over my elaborate hair and wreath, then indicates my saffron-yellow shoes, made by the cobbler of the insula for me. Not only will they be good omens, but when I wear them in public everyone will know that I am a newlywed. Some women keep the yellow upper leather when the soles wear out and have it turned into their first child's first pair of shoes. I step into them, hampered by the veil, which hangs down the sides of my face and over my forehead, obscuring my view.

"Perfect," announces Julia. "Are you ready for Adah?"

I nod very carefully, in case the whole elaborate headdress falls.

"That's what all the hairpins are for," Julia says. "You can dance as joyously as you wish, no harm will come to the hairstyle."

She holds her hands above my head for a moment. "The blessings of all the gods on you today and always, Althea," she says in her Vestal voice. "Be happy." She coughs as she lowers her hands.

"You need to take more of the syrup," I say.

"I will," she says. "Here is Adah."

Adah is hovering in the doorway, her wrinkled face anxious.

"I'm glad you are taking me to be wed," I say.

She gives a small smile. "Because you asked, child," she says. "Only because you asked. I hope my Lord will forgive that you worship elsewhere." Her own people are Jews and she was anxious about this point when I asked her to give me away.

"Your god will know you care about me," I say and Julia nods.

"Come," Adah says, holding out a hand.

I turn to Julia for an embrace, and she leaves the room ahead of us, making her way into the courtyard where the wedding party will be waiting.

I take Adah's hand and follow her out onto the landing.

"The bride! The bride!" come shouts from below.

I stop walking when I see the courtyard. Not only is it full of red ribbons and fruits laid over greenery, but it is packed with people. Everyone from our insula is here, as well as many from our team at the amphitheatre and others we work with. Strabo our stage manager, of course, but also Paternus, Labeo and his assistant, Fabia and Fabius, with Fabia's apprentice Sadiki and assistant Decima, and even some of the gladiators, such as Alyssa. Carpophorous has arrived, I'm touched to see, even though he is retired from his time as a gladiator. The whole of the baker's family. Maria. Julia. Celer. My eyes sting as tears well up. To see everyone who cares about me gathered together in one small space, their faces tilted up to me in the sunshine, fills me with happiness.

And at the centre of the crowd stands Marcus, with Karbo by his side, Cassia holding Emilia with Quintus and Cassius next to her. Marcus' eyes, full of love, hold my own and my smile is the widest it has ever been. I think of my mother, lost so long ago, and my father, who tried to save me from a life of slavery. I hope that their shades will see my happiness today, that I am a free woman marrying a man I love, with a ready-grown child who has become my own and a whole community of people who care about me. I blink back my tears and walk, following Adah along the landing and onto the stairs. She is murmuring something in her own tongue as we walk.

"What are you saying?" I whisper, bending my head closer to her.

Adah finishes her murmur and peers up at me. She speaks quietly, translating as she goes, so that the words come slowly. "Blessed art thou, O Lord, King of the universe, who hath created joy and gladness, bridegroom and bride, mirth and exultation, pleasure and delight, love and brotherhood, peace and friendship." She gives a little shrug, as though to excuse her words. "A blessing for a wedding among my own people, child," she explains. "You needn't believe in my Lord," she adds, as though I am about to object to her foreign prayers and deity. "But I would have His blessing on you today, child."

Tears prick my eyes and I let go of her hand, wrapping my arms around her fragile, hunched frame. "Thank you, Adah."

"Mustn't keep your groom waiting," she says, lightly pushing me away as I let go of her. But her eyes are wet too and our hands grip each other as we step down the last stairs and into the courtyard, through the beaming crowd and come to stand close to Marcus. I gaze up into his warm brown eyes, his joyful smile lighting up my heart.

The priest begins his declarations but I don't hear him. It is his task to assure the witnesses here that all the bird signs were good for this marriage, that the gods have given their consent and blessing for this union. I am barely aware of wine being poured for the gods, my eyes still fixed on Marcus and his on mine.

"Who gives this woman to be wed?"

Adah repeats her name and mine as she lifts my hands and places them in Marcus'. I smile at her as she lets go, her own eyes brimming with tears, but Marcus pulls me to him at once, holds me in a tight embrace that leaves me breathless, in part at his strong hold on me, in part at sharing his emotion in this moment, the deep breath he takes, his face buried in my neck.

"You must swear your oaths," says the priest, irritated at Marcus ignoring him and the formalities that must be completed.

Marcus loosens his grip, though instead of holding my hands as he should, he puts one arm about me, his remaining hand holding both mine, so that I am held tightly within his embrace. The priest looks as if he is about to intervene, so I begin my vows before he can tell Marcus to let me go.

"When and where you are Gaius, everyman, I then and there am Gaia, everywoman," I say, leaning my head on Marcus' chest.

"When and where you are Gaia, everywoman, I then and there am Gaius, everyman," says Marcus, his cheek pressed to mine. We should be gazing at each other as we repeat our oaths, but this embrace feels more intimate, our skin touching, breathing together as one.

He lets go of my waist only to slip the iron ring onto the third finger of my left hand, takes an unleavened loaf from Fabius and breaks it over my head.

The priest, only mollified by us both remembering our vows unprompted, takes a chunk of the bread and places it on the altar, then looks back at me.

I twist to look up at Marcus. "I am part of your family," I say and he tightens his embrace.

These words, usually an acknowledgement of a bride joining a large family and the connections that will be required of her, today have greater meaning, for Marcus has no family left, a rarity. From today we can rebuild a family together, with me as his new wife and Karbo already adopted by both of us.

Cheers break out as Marcus and I are guided to stools by the altar and given pieces of the loaf with which to feed one another. Being unleavened, the bread is hard to chew, and Marcus shakes his head after the first piece.

"No more bread," he says, reaching out to push back my veil. "I am hungry for a kiss!"

We lean forward from our perches and kiss, the courtyard full of applause and laughter, before Marcus reaches out a hand and pulls me to my feet and back into his arms, where he proceeds to cover my whole face in kisses.

"Enough, enough!" calls Fabius. "We haven't yet feasted and already you're in need of the marriage chamber?"

We break apart for a moment, laughing, and at once we're swept into the crowd in different directions, moving from person to person as we're embraced and kissed by everyone. By the time I can see clearly again Cassia and Julia, Maria and Adah have made a vast long table appear and women are coming from every direction with platters and bowls of food. Fabia is helping the children with the table decorations, green laurel leaves and pine branches entwined with bright red ribbons, pomegranates and pinecones, one of which Cassia's toddler daughter Emilia is trying to eat.

"On the table," encourages Fabia and finding the pinecone too hard to bite into, Emilia adds hers to the centrepieces.

Cassia has outdone herself. There is the traditional wedding cake sweetened with grape juice, but it can barely be seen amongst the dozens of dishes heaped high with good foods. Endless platters of olives and pickles, roasted chickpeas, mushrooms fried with garlic and herbs. A whole deer is the centrepiece, surrounded by chunks of roasted pumpkin, turnips, carrots and parsnips. There are big pots of Cassia's barley grits, known for their aromatic flavouring of cumin, onions and dill and, of course, her saltfish fritters, without which no feast from her hands is complete. Fresh walnut rolls from the bakers are piled high, as well as oil-rich flatbreads studded with olives. We drink warm wine flavoured with spices and sweetened with honey, suitable for the time of year, although the bright winter sun has done its best to warm the sheltered courtyard and most people have discarded their cloaks.

"More people should get married in winter," says Fabia, who is sitting by me. "I thought a winter wedding feast would be odd, but look at all this, it's delicious."

"Here's to the cook!" calls out Marcus, raising his cup to Cassia and everyone applauds.

We eat till we are more than full and then realise we should have saved space for the sweet treats Cassia and the bakery have come up with, all of them irresistible. Tiny hard almond biscuits to be dipped into a strong sweet raisin wine, damson-topped pastries served with a cinnamon custard, as well as nut tarts with a layer of quince preserves.

"And cream pudding!" says Karbo enthusiastically, holding his bowl aloft to secure the largest possible portion of his favourite dish.

"I did promise," I say. I spoon a triple helping into his bowl and embrace him.

"Your veil is in my cream pudding," he remonstrates, but he gives me something approximating a hug back, then hurries to immerse himself in indulgent sweetness.

"Happy?" asks Cassia, pausing at my side as she circles the table, making sure everyone is stuffed to bursting and beyond.

"So happy," I say. I wave my hand at the table, the dozens of friends enjoying the feast and the occasion, laughing and joking with one another, "I never dreamt this could be possible when I was a motherless slave girl."

Cassia leans to hug me, her black curls soft against my cheek. "We've done alright, we motherless ones, haven't we? I think our mothers would be proud of us."

Fabia smiles at the two of us, reaches out to place her hand over ours. "Our mothers are smiling today," she says and although her voice cracks, her smile is wide.

"You're next," says Cassia pointing at her. "Can't have two of us married and not the third. Got your eye on anyone?"

"Her assistant has his eye on her," I say, tilting my head towards where Sadiki is sitting near Fabius, Fabia's father.

"Oh, got ideas above his station, has he? Making friends with your father, I see."

Fabia laughs, but her cheeks have gone pink. "I want to achieve other things before I get married," she says.

"So it's you that's the ambitious one, as if we hadn't noticed," says Cassia. "Imperial physician? Fancy looking after Domitian, perhaps? Cushy job if you can get it."

"No thanks," says Fabia. "Emperors are not always healthy and who gets blamed?"

"Their enemies," says Cassia, refilling Marcus' cup of wine and offering Emilia a spoon of cream pudding, which the child opens her mouth very wide for. "Look at the size of this one, she's grown so fast."

"More," says Emilia through a mouthful of cream.

"Walking and talking," says Fabia, stroking Emilia's hair. "Running soon."

"And climbing everywhere," says Cassia. "And taking all my best pots to play with. Can't find a thing in the popina these days with her on the loose." She bends to kiss Emilia and offers her another spoonful of pudding.

"Sit," says Fabia, moving up the bench. "You've done all the cooking, no need to serve everyone as well, they can help themselves."

"I prefer wandering," says Cassia. "Can't help it. After all the years in the popina, it's a habit. And I like to be sure everyone's been well fed."

Fabia looks over her shoulder. "Time to kidnap the bride," she says to Quintus, who has appeared behind her.

"What?" I say but Quintus, Celer and Fabius have already laid hands on me and lifted me out of my seat.

"We're kidnapping you, Althea!" they say, pulling me away from Marcus, who is laughing and beseechingly holding out his hands to me.

"Kidnapping!" yells everyone, jumping to their feet.

Marcus reaches out and takes my hand. "A bride needs kidnapping," he says, "even if she does live in the same insula as her groom. And besides, I want everyone to see you on your wedding day and know how lucky I am."

He heads towards the courtyard gate with Quintus, Celer and Fabius pushing and pulling at me as though I am being forced to go and everyone follows us out of the gate and into Virgin's Street.

"Oh no!" I call out. "I'm being kidnapped. Help, help!" I can't help laughing though, and Marcus shakes his head at me.

"You're an awful actor," he says. "You have to try harder than that."

"HELP!" I scream and heads appear from all the neighbouring doors and windows of insulas and shops nearby. "I'm being kidnapped!" I shriek.

Marcus pretends to cover his ears as everyone shouts obscenities to drive away any lurking evil spirits while I try to shield myself from handfuls of nuts which are being thrown everywhere.

We wind our way round the block, down the tiny streets, accompanied by ribaldry and applause from all the neighbouring homes, till we come back round the insula, past the cobbler's and Balbus' toy shop and finally Cassia's popina which today has its shutters closed. Outside the courtyard gate we pause. The men let go of me and Marcus turns me to face the crowd.

"When and where you are everyman, Gaius, I then and there am everywoman, Gaia," I say, looking up at Marcus. "I am part of your family."

Everyone cheers and Marcus lifts me into his arms and carries me into the courtyard as they stream in behind us. I cling on to him, giggling, then stroke his face, a tiny moment of intimacy in all the noise and rush around us.

He puts me gently down in front of Julia, who is holding a bowl of water in one hand, a burning brazier in the other, welcoming me back into the insula as a bride into her new home. Smiling, she sets both items aside and takes my hand, leading me up the stairs with Marcus following us, all the way to the rooftop where we turn to wave at everyone gathered in the courtyard below us. Julia leads the way to our roof hut and opens the door. Someone has been busy here. New lamps have been lit, a bright new golden-yellow blanket which echoes my bridal veil has been laid on the bed and bunches of leaves bound with red ribbons have been nailed to the walls.

"It's beautiful," I say. "Thank you, Julia."

Julia turns to us and reaches out, places one hand on each of our heads in a silent blessing, then leaves us alone together.

Marcus takes a deep breath and pulls me towards him. "You have lain in my arms already," he says. "But now you are my bride, I feel nervous."

I lean my head against his chest. "I don't," I say. "I have never felt so safe and loved."

"In that case," says Marcus, "you are about to be loved a great deal more." He sweeps me back up into his arms and I wrap my arms about his neck as he carries me across our threshold and into bed.

I'M WOKEN THE NEXT MORNING by hammering.

"Come in," I mumble, but the hammering keeps going. I roll to my side and put out a hand to Marcus, but he isn't there. "Come in," I say, a little louder. The hammering doesn't stop. I reluctantly climb out of bed, pulling my green tunic over my head.

I open the door and squint in the sunlight. It's later than I thought, I'm used to rising at dawn, when the light is still a pale imitation of daylight. The sky is already blue and the hammering is not stopping.

"The gods," I mutter to myself. I step further out onto the rooftop, grimacing at the brightness, see the source of the noise and smile.

Marcus is surrounded by wooden posts and the hammering stops for a moment as he, Celer and Karbo lift up a long wooden plank and place it across two others. Marcus bends to pick up his hammer again and notices me. He tries to smile, which is hard with nails in his mouth, but his eyes are warm. He pulls first one nail and then the other two out and hammers them in, the plank held neatly in place.

"Morning, my love," he says. "We are making you a pergola for the heat of the summer days. You might as well enjoy your last year in Rome."

I smile and nod, go back into the roof hut where I pull a comb through my hair before pinning it up into a bun, tying a blue and green braided belt round my tunic and putting on my shoes. I don't really need the palla Fabia gave me if it's going to be a sunny day, but it is a novelty to me to wear a married woman's item of clothing, so I wrap it about my head and shoulders.

"Very matronly," says Marcus when I come back out again, a mischievous smirk on his face at the sight of my palla. "Very much the married lady, isn't she?" he adds to Celer.

"Very," agrees Celer with a smile. "Good morning, Althea." He passes Marcus some more nails and picks up another post, ready to hold it in place while Marcus fastens it to the growing structure. "Sorry about the noise," Celer adds. "I said Marcus should let you sleep in."

"Why would she want to sleep late on a glorious day like today?" says Marcus, sorting through a pot of nails to find the ones he wants. "Go have breakfast, we've already eaten," he adds to me.

"I want another breakfast," says Karbo. "The first one was *hours* ago."

"It was an hour, if that," says Marcus laughing.

"It was dark."

"Go with her, you poor famished boy."

I make soothing noises to the doves and nightingales, who are cowering in corners, scared by all the noise. "Come on, Karbo."

I start towards the stairs, Karbo at my heels.

"You're forgetting something," says Marcus.

"What?"

"A kiss," he says. "You don't get to go anywhere without a kiss. I'm your husband now, you have to do whatever I say. No arguing."

"I'm a very obedient wife," I say. I walk to him and place my head on his chest, wrap my arms about him. He puts one arm about me, hugs me to him, then kisses me.

"*Breakfast*," moans Karbo. "Honestly, you two have been cursed by Venus. You can't do anything without kissing first."

I giggle and hug Marcus one last time before following Karbo down the stairs, singing an old dancing song under my breath.

"Morning, Maria," I sing out when I spot her on the walkway.

"Ah, a cheerful bride," she says with a lascivious wink. "Not so sad to stay in Rome after all?"

I shrug. "I have Marcus and Karbo," I say. "And all my friends. It's only one more year, it can't be that bad."

"The gods willing," says Maria.

"The gods willing," I echo. "Would you like me to bring you something up from Cassia's?"

She shakes her head. "Already eaten. But if you spot grapes in the market any time, bring me some back. I've a hankering for them and they should be ripe any day. And if you're a good boy," she says to Karbo, "I'll press you some and you can drink your fill of grape juice."

"That's a rash promise," I say. "Filling Karbo is a difficult thing to accomplish."

Maria smiles, indulgent. "He's a growing boy," she says with fondness. "Got to feed him up so he'll grow up tall and strong."

I watch him clatter down the stairs ahead of me. "He's already grown so much," I say. "He might even be ready for the Liberalia next March."

"Do you think so?"

"We're not sure of his age," I say. "But he's so tall. He might well be."

When we first found Karbo we thought he must be about nine or ten, but perhaps he was older; he could have been an undernourished twelve-year-old. He has grown a good deal since being fed properly, perhaps we misjudged his age. Boys between fourteen and seventeen take part in March's Liberalia festival, when boys become men. I watch Karbo as he crosses the courtyard, wondering if he is already fourteen. He might be. He has the height for it and he is filling out more now, no longer all legs and arms. His shoulders are broader, he feels more solid when I hug him or when he barrels into me at the end of the day, pleased to see me like an enthusiastic puppy that does not understand it is now a large dog and can knock you over with one bound. I think of his local friends and their ages; most of them are over thirteen and some will be heading for the Liberalia in the spring. I decide to speak to Marcus about it. It would be fun to celebrate Karbo's coming of age in Rome, surrounded by all the inhabitants of the insula, for country life will be quieter. And if he is a year younger than he should be, that is no great matter, most families choose when to celebrate the coming of age of their young men and Karbo has been through more than most boys his age. Fausta comes to my mind, how proud she would be if she could see him, so different from the small, frightened boy who curled up in a corner of her room, adopting her as his mother, not caring about her dubious background, only needing the certainty and comfort her fierce demeanour gave him.

In the market I find grapes for Maria and buy some to leave at a local temple to

Venus in Fausta's memory. I wish she could have seen what became of Marcus and me, how we have ended up as husband and wife. I grin at the thought of what kind of pre-wedding night advice an old she-wolf like her might have delivered to me, though knowing her she'd have left me to find out such things for myself and made a few choice comments the next morning to watch me blush.

Back at Cassia's I find Marcus drinking wine.

"You're stuck with the Games again?" says Quintus with sympathy. "Still, we'll be glad to have you here for another year, Cassia will miss you when you're gone, Althea. You're like a sister to her."

"We haven't even got a theme for a new season of the Games," I say, sighing. "I didn't think we'd need one, thought we'd have escaped already."

Cassia nods, one hand pouring batter for pancakes, the other gently pushing Emilia away from the hot fire. She turns to speak to a customer and I pass Marcus some grapes, which he accepts, picking morosely at the bunch. He offers a couple of grapes to Emilia, who reaches up with her chubby little hand to take them and chews, dribbling juice down her chin.

"We could have done without the augur poking his nose in. Cursed birds," says Marcus.

"Your theme is birds?" says Cassia, turning back to hear the last word. "Like what? Leda and the Swan leading to the Trojan war? Or the Dwarfs and the Cranes? I always liked that story when I was little. Father says I used to get two bits of cloth and tie them to my arms and swoop about the place pretending to be a crane, attacking all my friends who were supposed to be the Dwarfs."

Marcus frowns at her while popping more grapes into Emilia's waiting mouth. "What? No, I was saying the augury birds were the cause of us having to do another season, I wasn't –"

"Or," says Cassia, warming to her theme and ignoring a customer who is waving his cup at her for more wine, "Prometheus being punished by an eagle eating his liver, didn't they do that one time in the Games?"

"Yes," I say, grimacing.

Marcus pauses with a grape halfway to Emilia, who glares at him and points to her mouth. "There are a lot of myths about birds," he says. "We could use the velarium to create illusions of light and air. We can have gods and goddesses and people turning into birds or heroes battling them. We can have some lighter touches, the actors can do comedy. And Cassia's right, the battle between the Dwarfs and the Cranes is a good story. We can do elements of it throughout the season and the big battle as the finale."

"Labeo will love you," I say. "You'll clear out his whole gladiatorial school of dwarfs."

Marcus' eyes light up. "Better and better," he says. "We'll dress the gladiatrices up as the Cranes, white tunics and big white wings. Labeo can take care of the whole thing for us, he'll be delighted and it'll be a job off our hands. I'm liking it already."

"You're welcome," says Cassia grinning at our growing enthusiasm and giving a mock bow. "Just remember I want a proper Crane costume in payment for my excellent ideas after all those years making do with strips of cloth."

Marcus lifts Emilia onto his knee and offers her more grapes but now that she is at the right height, she lunges for his fresh bread roll, stuffing it into her mouth with a gleeful smile.

"Your daughter is eating up all my food," says Marcus to Quintus in mock outrage. "Cassia, I'm going to need more bread."

"What do you mean by illusions of light and air?" I ask, trying to work out what will be involved.

"We can use coloured awnings so the arena floor changes colours or use fire if we do a night show. I have some ideas but I need to find the right person to help us. Let me make some plans and I'll show you what I mean."

THE VELARIUM

S ATURNALIA SEEMS TO RUSH PAST after the wedding. A flurry of cold winds and, "Io, Saturnalia!" greetings in the streets, gifts to and from our loved ones and acquaintances. We hold a meal for the amphitheatre slaves, where we wait on them for once, and there is plenty of teasing of Marcus and me for being newlyweds. And somehow it is January and we have three months to get the new season of Games planned, as well as Domitian's first task: the additional seating and the velarium.

"Oh good," says Marcus. "I look forward to installing a velarium in the wind and rain of winter. Lots of wet flapping canvas."

"Let's get the seating underway," I suggest.

Marcus agrees. The first crew to start work will be the carpenters and orders are made for the wood they will need for the seating tiers. The weather is not on our side though. Almost a month of rain and high winds goes by, which makes our plans difficult, the work postponed several times, leaving us hanging around the insula with nothing to do.

"I'm sure it will all come good in the end," smiles Julia when she hears me complaining. "Come and sit with us."

Julia, Maria and Adah have taken to sitting together on rainy and cold days, sometimes sewing or spinning, sometimes telling stories or preparing food, Julia's apartment being one of the few in our insula with cooking facilities.

"You're still coughing," I say to Julia. "Was the syrup no good?"

She shrugs my concern away. "It's fading," she says. "When the sun comes back and the days warm it'll clear up."

While we're stuck waiting, Domitian takes to visiting us most weeks, wanting to see animals. Marcus grinds his teeth each time a message is delivered listing what kind of animal Domitian would like to see next.

"This is a total waste of everyone's time and money, having a beast hunter provide animals out of season so they can be a petting zoo for one man. You deal with this, I don't even want to see him."

Our new beast hunter, brought in to replace Funis after his tragic death, is a taciturn man who does what we tell him to and doesn't ask questions. When I ask for the first two zebras, followed by a lion, and later on a crocodile, he is happy to oblige.

"I'm sorry about it being out of season," I say.

"You pays for it, you gets it whenever you want it," he says.

"The imperial purse is bountiful," I say, grimacing.

"Then you gets whatever you asks for."

I have to stand by while Domitian feeds various animals, from the zebras, who it turns out are like horses and are fond of stored apples, to a tiger which turns up its nose at the ready-prepared meat offered until Domitian demands a live goat be brought in, at which point the tiger suddenly comes to life, ripping the poor beast's throat open in a matter of moments, while Domitian watches the bloody spectacle with calm interest.

"It must have been bored," he says.

"Yes, Imperator," I say.

"Next time I would like to see a bear."

I suppress a sigh. "Of course, Imperator."

I watch him leave, still unsure how I should feel about him. He has undertaken a vast building programme to benefit Rome, he has stamped down on bribery and corruption within the administrative and legal system, he ought to be an exemplary model of a good emperor and yet I cannot erase my memory of his shaking hand holding Marcus at sword point, about to weep with rage at the very idea of his amphitheatre team being changed. Such inconsistent behaviour is unsettling.

FINALLY IN FEBRUARY WE GET a few dry days, allowing us to start. I stand with Marcus in the arena, squinting up at the very top of the amphitheatre.

Above us, behind the top tier of stone seating, a space which until now was empty will have a tightly raked set of wooden seating built into it, as per Domitian's orders. It will allow for more women and slaves to attend. The Games have proved very popular amongst women and tokens to attend have been a way to reward slaves for good service, as well as having them conveniently to hand if their masters wish to be served in any way. I suspect the ladies of Rome will be taking the stone seating tier originally designed for this purpose and sending the slaves to the wooden rows, because the stone pillars at the very top will obscure the view of the arena from certain angles, but a seat at the Games is still a seat at the Games.

"Back to hammering," says Marcus, noticing my pained expression as the team of carpenters get to work.

We've been here since dawn, as cartloads of planks were unloaded and carried, with much sweating and muttered oaths, up the steep stairs to the very top of the building. It's taken a few hours to start assembling the pieces, even though they were all sawn to size before they got here. But now that the right elements are in place, the hammering is going to be continuous for days.

"It never stops," I say. "Every year there's something else being built." I crane my neck to look up at the carpenters. "The materials they've got will barely cover an eighth of the way round so far."

"We have daily deliveries planned for eight days," says Marcus. "The carpenters have to keep up with them. We just need the weather to hold. And that's the easy part of this task. Wait till we try to install the velarium. I'm glad I wasn't in charge of getting that quantity of fabric dyed red."

The sections of the velarium canvas must be cut to an exact set of measurements, wider at the top, narrower at the base, to fit the oval shape of the amphitheatre. They will be sent to us numbered so that we will be able to put them in the right places.

"The extra seating is going to slow the exits at the top," says Marcus. "Wasn't designed to have a few extra thousand people leaving from the top tier."

"That's not something Domitian would worry about though, is it?"

"Exactly."

The hammering continues for the eight days, then, much to my despair, an additional two as the works slip behind due to a few wet days which slow deliveries. But finally the wooden tiers of seating are in place and the hammering stops.

Now the awning poles can be put into the two-hundred-and-forty post brackets that have been waiting for this moment. Made of stone, the brackets were built into the amphitheatre during its construction, since the awning was planned from the start. They sit on the outside of the building at its very top, adding strength to the structure. Most amphitheatres and theatres have retractable awnings, often in bright colours such as red, yellow and purple, sometimes just in the plain cream canvas used for sails on ships. I've seen very elaborate ones, where the cloth has been painted with scenes from mythology or with impressive animals, such as dolphins or elephants, but one colour is sufficient decoration for an audience who is not looking up, but rather down at the arena.

The posts are vast and have to be winched into place from the ground as it would be impossible to carry them up the tight stairs. A team on the ground lines up each pole, fastens ropes to it which are pulled by another team to the top of the amphitheatre and mounted into each bracket. I feel ill watching them, the men who must guide each pole into place standing one step away from a certain death should they fall to the ground far below.

My fear is not shared by the crowd of small children who come to inspect the works every day, fascinated to see the awning progress. They are sent on errands by the builders, to buy food at the local markets or popinas, sometimes sent to another site or home to fetch and carry messages. It's worth coming every day, for the quick and willing can earn food or even a small coin if they make themselves useful. They perch like little sparrows around the site, chattering to each other, enjoying the constant stream of interesting cursing from the builders and the chance to volunteer for a task, before fluttering away to wherever they come from as twilight falls.

On a wet day I visit Labeo's gladiatorial school.

"Dwarfs? My dear, I have all the dwarfs Rome's empire can bring me! And the best gladiatrices. The Battle of the Dwarfs and the Cranes will be glorious. You are too good to me, what will I do without you?"

"I'm sure the Games will continue without us," I say.

"Ah, but you and Marcus understand *spectacle*. Most Games managers just put on round after round of gladiators. They don't mix it up enough. Gets boring. You have to have *variety*, that's what makes for the best Games."

"I'm leaving the Cranes and Dwarfs in your hands," I tell him. "Costumes can be stored in the amphitheatre. I'll send the dancing girls over to teach the gladiatrices some moves. We'll need to have a dance sequence that turns into a battle, so we'll have to mix them together. Your gladiatrices can start the fights and the dancing girls can make themselves scarce."

"It'll be perfect," enthuses Labeo.

"I need to speak with Fabia," I say.

"Busy in her medical rooms," says Labeo.

I go to the physician's bay, where I find Fabia surrounded by scrolls and tablets.

"Fabia, will you visit Julia? She keeps coughing and she just shrugs me away when I mention it. She's taken a few remedies, but nothing seems to be working."

Fabia looks up from her scrolls and frowns. "Bad coughing?"

"Not terrible. But often."

"I'll ask to look her over, see what I can offer."

"Thank you. What's all the scribing for?"

She sighs. "Training and feeding plans for each gladiator. It takes up so much time, making sure they're all accounted for and records are kept. My assistant Decima can't write, though I'm teaching her. Sadiki can, but it takes up hours of both our time. So boring. Father never has to do this nonsense," she adds. "He just patches up gladiators at the amphitheatre and sends them back to their own schools to the physicians there. Too much writing and record-keeping for my liking."

"You just like wounds, don't you?" I say, "Which is what you used to say about your father."

She grins. "Wounds don't require all this nonsense. You stitch them up and move on."

"I don't even believe you," I say. "I never met a woman who liked reading as much as you. All that research you did to find out about that bronze hand you made for Alyssa."

"Reading's one thing," she says. "Who am I doing all this writing for? The cooks know what to feed the gladiators, their trainers know what each one needs in the way of training. It's all for show. Labeo wants to be taken more seriously now that he's one of Rome's two largest gladiatorial schools, so he's insisted everything be recorded."

I pat her on the back. "Get a scribe," I say. "You're wasted in here."

THE NEXT DAY MARCUS AND I set off early, as the sailors from Misenum are due to arrive, ready to install the velarium. We feed the birds and set free the doves for the day. Most of their feathers have now grown back, they take little flights to test their strength, perching on the rooftop wall or going as far as another rooftop before returning.

"They're getting confident," says Marcus with satisfaction. "But they know this is their home now."

Early though we are, when we arrive there are two hundred men in blue-grey tunics standing on the arena floor in military formation, with one commander at the front, who salutes Marcus. He is very young and tall, with a nose dotted with freckles and green eyes, something of a rarity.

"Servius Gratius Celsus, sir. At your command."

Marcus nods. "You're in command of these men?"

"Yes, sir."

"You don't need to 'sir' me. Marcus will do."

"They are good men. Hardworking."

"Ever done awnings like this before?"

"No. Only sails."

Marcus sighs. "We'll go to a theatre later today and try out their awnings. They're a lot smaller but it's the same concept. It's the size of the things that's the problem. There's a light metal ring in the centre, two hundred and forty poles around the amphitheatre, with ropes that connect the poles to the circle. Forty-eight strips of cloth, a heavy canvas. Five poles per strip. The cloth itself is only attached to two of the ropes, and has additional finer ropes which control letting it out to open up the velarium, covering the audience, or pulling it in to close it when it's not needed or not safe. We can leave it open for some days when the weather settles but if we get a lot of rain, it'll be too heavy and the whole thing could collapse. The poles might break and if one of those falls into the audience it could kill someone. And if there's too much wind, the whole thing will rip right off and we'll have to start all over again."

"Yes, sir."

I bite back a smile. The young commander Servius is not going to call Marcus by his name, no matter how much he's encouraged to.

Marcus continues. "So there's two parts to opening the velarium. One is to pull on all the ropes together. This will lift the metal circle off the arena floor and, as the ropes tighten, it will be lifted high over the audience's heads, just below the top of the whole amphitheatre's height. Then we lock those ropes in place unless we wish to lower the whole structure again for repairs, change the cloth strips, or if it's too windy to risk keeping it elevated."

"Yes, sir."

"Once the whole structure is elevated, there are the additional finer ropes which control the canvas strips, and those allow us to open and close the awning at will. They will need to be opened every morning and closed every night, for fear of wind or rain. The canvas needs to be opened and closed with care, especially in regard to balance. It will not be safe to open just one half, for instance, because there will be far greater weight on the other side and it will put too great a strain on the structure as a whole.

So if we wish to open part of the strips only, according to where the sun is, we need to be mindful of that."

"Yes, sir."

Marcus finishes his lecture and leaves Servius to pass on the information to his men.

"He keeps calling me sir," he says to me, rolling his eyes.

"He's very young," I say. "It's his first command and he's not used to working with people like us. He's trained to speak to his superior officers."

"I feel like I'm back in the army. Or old."

"If you're back in the army you must be young," I say.

At the theatre we go to that afternoon, the sailors swarm all over the building watching the awnings being opened and closed by the regular team of stagehands, who are used to the process.

I wince at the sailors walking on the very top of the high walls, without any kind of safety measures.

"I don't want any of them to fall," I say.

Servius, standing next to me, looks surprised. "That will not happen. They are accustomed to keeping their balance on a moving ship. The walls will feel stable by comparison."

I smile at his earnestness, he looks very young to be in charge of such a large team of men. "Is this your first command?"

"Yes," he says, his chest expanding. "My commander said that it was a chance to prove myself, to show that I could be called on for more than sailing, that I could be relied upon to serve the Emperor in a different capacity."

"We're grateful to have you," I say. "It's not an easy task, I would not have liked to have trained our slaves to carry it out."

He looks affronted at the very idea. "No," he agrees. "It is a very skilled task."

"You're stationed at Misenum, is that where you're from?"

He nods. "My father was a sailor too, I follow in the family tradition."

"He must be proud of you."

"He was killed by pirates," he says. "But my mother is very proud that I have been given this posting."

I imagine his mother is grateful that he is safe in Rome's Flavian Amphitheatre opening and closing our awning on demand, rather than chasing pirates round the seas, risking his life as his father did before him.

"My mother was also killed by pirates," I say. "My father and I were taken as slaves."

"I am sorry Rome's navy failed you," he says, his young face fierce.

"I am sure you have dispatched many of them," I say. "It's good that our seas are being patrolled."

THE NEXT DAY SEES THE arrival of the giant metal ring, which again is far too large to enter through any of the arches and has to be winched over the top of the amphitheatre and then brought from the top tier to the arena floor. Thankfully the sailors see this as their job and wrestle the awkward burden to the wooden arena floor. It's fitted with two hundred and forty metal rings, each of which has to be threaded with a rope and tied securely, then the ropes need to be taken up to their equivalent post and secured in place with additional knots and a wooden locking mechanism. There's a lot of swearing, as well as confusion with ropes getting mixed up here and there, but as the hours pass the task begins to near completion, although it takes all day. Marcus, less afraid of heights than I am, goes up at the end with Servius to inspect the work, checking that each rope is locked in place on its post and that it runs smoothly down to the metal circle with no mistaken crossed ropes. I look away from the sight of him, as he makes his way round the top of the amphitheatre on the narrow walkway where the sailors will stand to manage the ropes.

The next day comes the moment of truth: will the structure, the largest ever made, hold up? Or is it too heavy? Marcus wants us to try it without the canvas first. One hundred and twenty men pull their rope on Servius' command and slowly, slowly, the ropes grow taut and the metal circle begins to rise up. When it is dangling half-way up, the men lock the ropes in position and pull in the other hundred and twenty. Once those are locked, they pull the first ones again, bringing the circle to its final place, level with the top of the amphitheatre. Once all the ropes have been tightened and locked, we stand to admire it.

"I keep thinking it will come crashing down," I say.

Marcus and Servius shake their heads. "The circle is heavy but there's a lot of good ropes holding it there and the poles are robust," says Marcus. "What we do need to do is mark the ropes, blue and red alternating, so that we can always be sure we're pulling the right ones. You can't have it all lopsided."

"And the awning fabric?" I say.

"It's coming up from the docks tomorrow morning," says Marcus. "I need a bath after all that."

IN THE MORNING FOUR LARGE cartloads of fabric arrive. Forty-eight strips of red canvas, broader at one end, narrower at the point where they will meet the metal circle. Each one has been ready prepared with metal loops sewn along the sides where they will be attached to thin cords. The strips are unloaded into our corridor and the metal circle slowly lowered back to the arena floor.

"Not looking forward to today," mutters Marcus.

He's right. Attaching the vast strips onto the correct ropes using additional cords takes hours. By the end of the day we've only managed ten, although the work is beginning to speed up as we learn from our mistakes. My eyes hurt from squinting upwards all day and everyone has blisters from running ropes and cords through our hands. The rest of the heavy fabric has to be stored downstairs overnight for fear that it will be stolen if we leave it in the corridors.

It takes three more days till every strip of canvas is correctly in place.

"Baths," says Marcus when we reach the last one and the men cheer. There's still a couple of hours of daylight. We could have tested it's all working, but everyone's patience and energy is running low and even Servius, keen as he is, nods gratefully and leads the men off to the Baths of Titus over the road for a well-earned soak.

"Aquilo, Favonius, Auster and Vulturnus, look on us with kindness and rest your strength," says Marcus the next morning, calling on the four winds as he stands on the arena floor.

"They've heard you," I say. It's a sunny day with hardly a breeze, unusual for March.

Each strip requires two cords to be pulled in order to open or close, so ninety-six men are required for this part.

The men start singing a sea shanty, bellowing out the words to try and keep a steady rhythm.

"Sailors who race over deep waves,

along Triton's salty swells,

Nile-runners who make their sweet way,

sailing over the waters' smile,

friends, tell us your judgment

between the sea and the fertile Nile."

"I'm surprised they have breath enough for singing as well as hauling," I say.

"Helps them keep in time," says Servius, watching them and grimacing. "It doesn't look very smooth. It's getting caught up there on the left." He sighs. "We'll have to start again."

"At least the shanty's clean," grins Marcus. "I've heard a lot worse from sailors. We'll leave you for a while. Althea and I have someone to visit."

"Who are we visiting?" I ask as we leave the amphitheatre, the chorus behind us sounding much bawdier, with reference to sailors having to choose between mermaids and Egyptian beauties.

"A maker of flames," says Marcus. "You'll see."

We thread our way through a confusing jumble of small streets south of the amphitheatre, until we turn into a crumbling insula which reminds me of Julia's before it was repaired. The courtyard is very odd, there is a strong smell in the air and there are patches of pitch and soot everywhere, as though fires have been lit at random points across the cobbles. A little girl stares at us from a balcony.

"I'm looking for Appius Vibius Corda," calls up Marcus.

The little girl stares.

"The flame-maker?"

The little girl disappears but we can hear her calling. "Ignis! Ignis!"

"Looks like he's known by another name," I tell Marcus.

The man who appears from the doorway below the balcony is short, with black curls and dark eyes. His skin would be pale, except that a lot of what's visible is smeared with soot. He comes towards us, then stands, waiting, silent.

"I sent a messenger," says Marcus. "I am Marcus Aquillius Scaurus, manager of the Flavian Amphitheatre. This is my wife Althea, who serves as my scribe and right hand. I need to talk to you about a fire spectacle for the closing night of this Games season. You sent me word back that you could demonstrate what is possible."

The man nods and points towards a decrepit wooden bench nearby, onto which we lower ourselves with care, anxious it will collapse if either of us moves too much. The man goes into a storeroom door at the end of the courtyard.

"Not very talkative, is he?" I murmur to Marcus.

"His tongue was cut out," Marcus says.

I look at him in horror. "By whom?"

He shrugs. "Perhaps someone who didn't want him to reveal his secrets. Or perhaps he revealed the secrets of his trade and was punished for it. He can create sea fire, like the Greeks did. It can be used in battles and not many know how it is done."

I'm about to ask more questions but Ignis emerges with a long reed and two torches, ready prepared with pitch to be lit. He sets the torches up in heavy stone stands made for the purpose, setting the reed aside on another rickety bench.

He goes indoors and returns with a burning lamp, which he uses to ignite the two torches. When they are burning strongly he returns to his storerooms and returns with a series of little metal containers with spouts, which he sets on the bench.

Taking the hollow reed he uses the first little spouted container to pour a grey powder into it. Directing the reed at the first torch, he puts it to his lips and blows quickly. The grey powder hits the torch and the pale flame turns a bright orange.

He repeats the demonstration several times, the flames turning red, green, violet and blue as the different powders hit them.

Marcus is beaming. "Magnificent," he says. "What are the powders?"

Ignis' dark eyes crease into an amused smile and he shakes his head.

"Fair enough," says Marcus. "Have you seen the amphitheatre's new velarium?"

He nods.

"I want to set fire to it."

Ignis' eyes widen.

Marcus smiles. "The ropes will need to be replaced yearly. They will get wet, frayed, weakened by the sun and rain. So at the end of the season, I wish to set fire to the whole structure. I will need it to burn in a myriad of colours and for the fire to spread slowly, so that as the crowds leave with it burning above them none of it falls into the audience."

Ignis considers for a moment. He points to my tablet and I hold it out to him along with my stylus. He scratches onto it, hands it over to me. I read it out.

"Risky."

"No risk, no reward."

He writes again. "Reward?"

"The imperial purse is ample," says Marcus. He looks about the soot-stained courtyard. "Enough for a new workshop away from your own home. I am sure your wife and neighbours would appreciate not having flammable materials so close to home."

Ignis nods and hands back my tablet without further communication.

"You'll test what is possible," says Marcus.

Ignis nods again.

"I'll bid you farewell," says Marcus. "I look forward to seeing what is possible."

THE NEXT DAY IS RAINY, there can be no more practice with the velarium. The canopy cannot hold wet cloth, it would be far too heavy, so the velarium will be left entirely pulled back today and the sailors will have to spend a day in barracks.

But there is always work to do. It's a late start, as there is no rush, but I make my way round the whole of the hypogeum, noting on my tablet the works needed before we re-open. There is always cleaning and mending to be done. When I come to the room where we usually keep the dancers' clothing, I pause on the threshold. The last time I was here I was cradling Funis' dead body, my hands covered in his blood. I have a sudden memory of pressing my bloody palms against the senator's white toga and his look of horror and anger, his bodyguards stepping forwards. It would have gone badly with me if it hadn't been for Stephanus' silent appearance and intervention.

The room is empty, the bright dancing tunics put away over winter and the floor washed; there is no trace of blood. I say a silent thank you to Strabo and our cleaning crew, who never asked what to do. They have erased the violence of that moment from the room, if not from my memories.

Still on the threshold, I write a note about the carpenters needing to build a longer hanging rack so that the clothes can be better organised when fast changes are required. Having fifty-odd dancers rapidly changing in a small space is bad enough without items of clothing being scattered across the floor. I try to be practical, think only of the work to be done, but sadness is pulling at me, along with a welling-up of the terror of that moment.

"Althea."

I nearly scream, whirl about to find Stephanus standing behind me in the gloom, as though I have conjured him up from my memories.

"Apologies, I did not mean to startle you." He speaks calmly as ever, his toga's folds immaculate. I wonder for a moment whether he ever loses his temper or shows any emotion, or whether all his calm is needed to deal with Domitian's sudden outbursts.

"I was…" I wave my hand at the room beyond me.

"Perhaps you would walk with me through the hallways?"

I follow him through the dim hypogeum and up the stairs to the ground floor, wondering whether he's here with some other obscure task that Domitian wants completing. I can't imagine Marcus being willing to accept any more requests, although with Domitian, we don't have any choice.

The vast curved hallway which runs round the amphitheatre allows us to stay dry while the grey drizzle falls outside, as well as letting us see out of each of the great arches we pass to the Forum beyond. The unpleasant weather means that the corridor is fairly quiet. We meet the odd person scurrying along, using the amphitheatre as a break from the rain, but on a day like this much of Rome stays at home or enjoys the comfort of hot baths.

We've walked halfway round the amphitheatre. I stay silent. Whatever he wants, he will reveal it when he's ready.

At last he speaks. "You came from a Greek island? Kefalonia?"

I nod. Barely anyone has ever heard of my home island, tiny as it is, but I'm sure he knows everything about all of us.

"And were enslaved along with your father?"

"Yes."

"How did you end up at the amphitheatre?"

I'm sure he knows this too, but I continue the pretence. "I was slave to a merchant who spent time in Pompeii. He was tasked with finding a manager for the Flavian Amphitheatre. When he found Marcus, he gifted me to him as a scribe, to sweeten the deal."

"Scaurus lost family during the disaster, I believe?"

"His wife and baby son," I say. I try not to think of the endless grey of Pompeii, how Marcus dug through the ashes for hours while I prayed for him, knowing there was no possibility that his loved ones were alive.

Stephanus nods, grave. "I had family in Herculaneum who were fortunate enough to move to Britannia two years before Vesuvius erupted. At the time they left, they felt the loss of their homeland keenly but it seems the gods knew best after all."

"Are they still in Britannia?"

"Yes."

"Not homesick after all these years?"

"For the sunshine, no doubt," he says. "It does not sound like a kind climate."

"I hear it rains a lot," I say. "Like today."

"So it seems."

I'm beginning to wonder where this conversation is headed. Stephanus has never struck me as a person who enjoys small talk, he barely bothers with greetings, and now we are conversing on the weather and everyone's family histories. It's very odd.

"The Emperor is pleased with the progress of the velarium," he says.

"I'm glad to hear it," I say. "It's difficult but we can see signs of progress. The crowds will be delighted. The ladies of Rome don't care for being sunburnt."

"And after this is complete," says Stephanus, "I believe your second task for Domitian was to put on a private spectacle at his villa in the Alban Hills."

"Yes," I say. "We haven't yet planned the themes, but I can assure you it will be spectacular."

"I don't doubt that," he says. "The place is very beautiful and the amphitheatre has been well-designed, I am sure you will find everything you need."

"Is he there often?" I ask.

"He goes whenever possible in the hotter months. Rome's summers can be taxing and the Emperor feels the heat."

This chitchat about weather is beginning to strike me as ridiculous. "Did you want something particular from me today?" I ask, trying to sound polite.

He is silent for the space of three arches. "Can you include a lion in the spectacle?"

"A lion?"

"Yes."

I look at him but he seems to be looking through the arches, to the golden legs of the Colossoss statue which we can see from where we've reached.

"Is there a reason why you want a lion?"

"Yes."

I wait for further information but he doesn't say anything else. "May I know why?"

"No."

I open my mouth again but Stephanus stops and turns to me. His face is serious, and it strikes me that he is sad. "I have not forgotten your friend's untimely death," he says.

"Funis."

"Yes."

"Has the lion something to do with Funis?"

He gazes at me for a moment. "I would like the Games held in the Alban Hills to include a lion," he says. "Can you arrange that?"

"Yes," I say.

"Excellent. I must leave you."

And he's gone, disappearing into the busy Forum and leaving me wondering what is going on. Why would he want a lion? Is he going to throw some poor criminal to it? What would that have to do with Funis' death? I hope that he will not have the man who killed him put to death: much as I despise him, whoever held the knife was only a blade for hire, the real murderer was Funis' own father, who ordered his death, ashamed of having a gladiator and beast hunter for a bastard son by a slave woman, his own strange fixation with being high status leading him to obsessively hunt down and kill his own son, when any other senator or man of high rank would have shrugged and ignored him. I spit at the thought of him, hope that the gods will see what he did and punish him for it, one way or another. In my rage at Funis' death I had even thought of curse tablets, of finding a curse-maker and having my curse engraved in a lead sheet, calling on the gods to find the man and have him die as he had his own son die. Half of Rome has used curse tablets at one time or another, from the most absurd reasons such as their favourite pair of sandals being stolen at the baths to those seeking vengeance for greater misdeeds, but I have never done so myself. They frighten me, for what if they were to turn against the person laying the curse? Instead I have mourned Funis, taken fruits and flowers to temples in his memory, visited his friends in the gladiatorial barracks. I am not sure revenge or retribution could ever be brought down on a senator by plebians.

LATER THAT DAY, I TELL Marcus what has been asked of us.

"Why a lion?"

"He didn't say."

He frowns, turning it over in his mind. "I don't like requests I don't know the reason for," he says.

"I don't think Stephanus is going to share any further information with us."

Marcus shrugs. "Domitian likes wild beasts. If he wants a lion, we'll include a lion. I'm not looking forward to transporting one, mind. It'll be angry after hours of rattling along roads to the Alban Hills in a cart." He thinks. "We'll send it ahead, so that it has a day or so to become calm. Else it may not perform. It can eat before it leaves, so that a few days later it feels frisky again."

"We don't know what he wants it to do."

Marcus laughs. "Sing and dance? It'll be nothing. He'll have taken a fancy to having a lion as part of his Games. Our job is to keep him happy."

I nod as though I agree, but Stephanus' careful request for a lion comes back to me from time to time and I wonder what it may lead to.

ADAH MAKES HER WAY UP to the rooftop to check on her bees. Now that spring has come, they are busy again, coming and going at a steady pace, setting out on their quests to find flowers across Rome, from the gardens of the wealthy up on the Palatine to the smallest patch of scrubby ground with early dandelions showing their bright flowers. The doves cluster around her feet, hopeful for corn.

"Thankfully they don't much care for eating bees," I say, throwing a few handfuls of corn away from her so the doves will get out from under her feet.

She nods. "They make good companions."

"I could have both at the farm. You could teach me how to care for the bees."

She nods but doesn't answer, she has begun a song she sings to them which she claims calms them, a song in her own Jewish tongue.

THE TIME HAS COME FOR the opening Games of the season. We reach the amphitheatre, where the usual ropes have been put up and our staff are manning the entrances to avoid people sneaking in without tokens. We show our own red tokens and make our usual checks of the hypogeum and seating areas. The velarium is folded up.

"You don't want it opened?"

Marcus shakes his head. "We need to open it when everyone's here. It'll get a round of applause which will please Domitian."

Servius is pacing back and forth in one of the corridors.

"What are you doing?" I ask.

"What if it doesn't open smoothly?" he asks. "In front of the Emperor, no less? Will he be very angry?"

I think of Domitian, scarlet with rage, eyes filled with furious tears, a sword in one shaking hand pointed at Marcus' throat. "I'm sure it'll be fine," I say. "Your men have practised a lot. It all seemed to be working well, didn't it? You've fixed any small niggles?"

He nods, miserable. "Could we try it one more time?"

"No," I say. "It takes at least half an hour to open and close it without any problems. I'm not risking it. If we hurry, something will go wrong. The crowds will start to gather in the next hour, I don't want last minute worries."

His shoulders slump.

It's like having a disappointed Karbo in front of me. I pat his arm. "You've done all you can. Now we have to focus on the show."

All too soon the crowds are allowed entrance. The wooden tiers fill up with slaves, as expected, leaving more room for the fine ladies of Rome to see and be seen on this, the opening day, when the most prestigious tickets are issued. They put up their parasols, which have always caused us trouble, since they block the view of those behind them, but I can see some of them peering upwards at the folded up velarium and the rope and metal structures towering over them. They are sitting close to where the velarium will be operated from, I notice quite a few of them casting admiring glances at the young sailors, smart in their blue-grey tunics which show off plenty of arm and thigh muscles ready to be used, unlike the portly toga-clad husbands of the ladies, who may be rich and high status but are perhaps no longer well-endowed with youth and strength.

I go to the corridor where Domitian and the imperial party will soon be arriving. There I meet Marcus and the Aedile, the three of us converging just as trumpets sound, followed by the tramp of heavy feet as his Praetorian bodyguards appear, all dressed in their crisp white togas. Despite their superficial appearance as ordinary citizens, their military haircuts, soldiers' boots and the menacing presence of sword hilts sticking out from their waistbands makes their purpose clear. They surround a small group made up of Domitian and Domitia with a few friends and relatives, invited to the opening day as a special sign of favour. We bow our heads as they swish past us and into the silken enclosure of the imperial box. Domitia's perfume trailing behind her, a heady mix of roses and sweet spices, no doubt the expensive work of Cosmus, Rome's most accomplished perfumier.

Domitian installed, Marcus gives the signal and, to the sound of rippling music, the velarium begins to open. The endless practice has paid off: it opens smoothly, gently, without noise or impediments and the audience breaks into applause as a deep and satisfying rosy-tinged shade covers them, leaving the arena itself shining in the bright sunlight. Servius sighs with relief next to me and I catch Marcus' pleased nod as a flock of white doves is released and heads straight through the open circle above us, a perfectly timed omen of good luck for the season ahead.

The venatores begin the day with a display of hunting ostriches and flamingos, which get the crowd's attention. We have never shown off such large birds and the ostriches are not only fast but violent, turning on their attackers, striking out with their clawed feet and large beaks.

We have a display of what appear to be painted statues of gods and heroes, which come to life and carry out some of the great myths beloved of the people; Zeus transforming into a swan and seducing Leda, who gives birth to a golden egg which becomes Helen, later stolen by Paris and starting the great war of Troy, which allows us to stage a range of battle scenes with our gladiators.

We have our rippling blue cloth sea across which sails Odysseus, who must close his ears to the song of the sirens, who are half-bird, half-woman. They should just be singing but these are the Games, after all, so the chorus provides the singing and a band of gladiatrices attacks a ship full of gladiators for a satisfying battle.

We re-enact Perseus and the Gorgon Medusa, where the gladiatrix playing Medusa first kills five criminals due for execution that day and then battles with Perseus. When she is overcome, from her blood springs forth Pegasus, a white horse whom we have provided with magnificent white wings, which are extended as it gallops around the arena.

Using tightrope walkers, Icarus spreads his wide wings and flies with his father, but comes too close to the sun, melting the wax holding his feathers in place and plummets to the ground, dying as his father grieves over him.

There are a few intervals during the day, where we continue our theme. Peacocks are brought into the arena and coaxed to put on a display for the peahens we have provided, the crowd murmuring at the beauty of their astonishing blue and green feathers trembling in the sunlight. A comedic routine is provided by a man and his wilful geese, who peck at his behind and attack him when he brings out a bucket of grain, having been kept hungry for a few days, leaving him lying flat on his back, disappearing under a pile of feathers. The crowd enjoys these lighter sections, they laugh and jeer while buying and eating snacks purchased from vendors who walk between the tiers with trays of food and drink. Chickpeas that have been salted and spiced, then roasted so that they are crunchy, cups of wine, warm bread and garum sauce to dip it in, fritters including those made with broad beans.

It is time to conclude the day with something special. The audience leaps to their feet, especially those in the cheaper stands, when instead of wooden balls with the names of gifts inscribed on them, we release hundreds of birds with ribbons tied to their feet, which flutter above the crowd, who grab at them and catch many, from the common doves to expensive parrots who have the gift of speech and many songbirds. The amphitheatre is a riot of colours and squawks, shouts and flapping birds. Some make their way to freedom, others think they have found freedom before they are suddenly caught and returned to captivity, either to be eaten or kept as pets.

"An excellent first day," says Domitian as he passes us in the corridor. He pauses and his entourage come to an abrupt halt. "The opening of the velarium was very smooth. How are the sailors doing?"

"They have been most professional," says Marcus. He pushes Servius forward. "This is Servius Gratius Celsus, Imperator, he is on his first command and has been a credit to the navy."

Servius gives a smart salute, standing to attention.

Domitian gives one of his rare smiles. "Excellent," he says. "Keep up the good work, you may make a name for yourself." He sweeps along the corridor, his entourage hurrying to keep up.

Servius is still standing to attention.

"You can relax," I say, laughing. "He's gone and he's happy with you."

He turns to Marcus, eyes wide, cheeks flushed. "You presented me to him."

Marcus grins. "I wanted you to have some credit too. You and your men have done a good job."

"Yes, sir. Thank you, sir. It was a great honour to meet the Emperor himself. My mother will be…" He takes a deep breath and for a brief moment his eyes shine as though he is about to cry. "She will be very proud, sir," he finishes.

Marcus pats his shoulder. "As she should be. Are you ever going to stop calling me sir?"

"No, sir."

"Perhaps a few drinks will loosen your tongue and you'll start calling me Marcus. Let's go. We all deserve a celebration."

Marcus has arranged for cakes and wine to be served when the crowds have gone and we gather in the swept arena, over a thousand of us, slaves, sailors, our staff, a few of the gladiators and Paternus and Labeo. There is a happy atmosphere, toasts are made and drunk to, a few people dance when the musicians strike up. I cannot remember such a celebration since we started. Marcus is full of cheer. The Games are underway, Domitian's first task has been accomplished in style, there are only two more to go and we will be free. The long winter is gone and our spirits are high.

IMPERIAL COLOURS

WE SETTLE INTO OUR ROUTINES, with Games every few days, allowing us the odd rest day when there is little to do, as well as time to prepare for the more elaborate shows. Some elements are repeated, others are one-off spectacles, but the theme of birds is popular. Girls who follow the Games wear feather trims on their best tunics and graffiti appears with various bird mythologies, in particular the battle of the Dwarfs and the Cranes, which we have as a running story. There are fewer arguments in the ladies' stands now that they no longer need their parasols. With things running smoothly we can turn our attention to Karbo's Liberalia festival, when he will become a man.

Two days before, Quintus arrives on the rooftop where I'm listening to the nightingales, who have grown bolder and now sing often. He has a parcel which he hands to me with excessive care. "I had mother put her best slave on the job," he says.

When he's gone I open the parcel and find inside Fausta's toga, which I kept all these years in my chest. The fullery have cleaned it perfectly. I walk down into the courtyard where I find Julia caring for her plants.

"I wanted to put scent on Karbo's adult toga," I tell her.

She helps me pick rosemary, sage and mint from her collection of herbs.

"You have a whole garden in a courtyard," I say.

She straightens, puts a hand to her back. "I started with a tiny rosemary plant, I barely thought it would survive. Now look at it."

It's a huge bush, the children sometimes hide behind it when they play their games. "I'll have to take a cutting with me to the farm," I say.

She smiles. "I would like to think your plants on the farm were kin to mine here in Rome."

I rub the herbs across the creamy folds of the toga to give the scent Fausta always had about her, fold it with care and put it out of sight. At the ceremony, Karbo will give up the purple-bordered toga praetexta of childhood, not that he has ever worn it much, for the plain white toga which will mark him as an adult. I've decided to give him Fausta's to wear. It might seem odd to give him a she-wolf's toga, but she was like a mother to him. This way, he will have a lasting memory of her; Fausta will be wrapped about him every time he goes out into the world as a well-dressed man.

Some of Karbo's friends and their parents are making preparations as well, the fathers booking barbers for their son's first ritual shave, the mothers sewing new tunics and ordering togas. We exchange congratulations and also worries: is it too soon? Should we have waited another year? This fear is in part allayed when we see the boys together, almost the height of men, seriously discussing the merits of one racing team or another, but their excitement gets the better of them and they end up playing their old games of catch, rushing about the courtyard and up and down the stairs, making a huge amount of noise and laughing till they almost cry. On these occasions they look like little children again and we feel like fools for believing they are grown up enough to have a coming-of-age ceremony. But we are committed, the seventeenth day of March is only a few days away and with it will come Liberalia, the festival celebrating Liber Pata, an ancient god of fertility similar to Bacchus for his love of wine and merriment, as well as his consort Libera. Masks are hung in trees all over Rome the day before in preparation and Marcus takes Karbo to the baths, where he will be shaved, so that a little stubble can be placed in his protective bulla necklace.

"Stubble? What stubble?" teases Marcus as they go down the stairs, to applause. Everyone in our insula is leaning from their balconies, doors and windows. "I think we will put it off till next year after all."

"I do have stubble," protests Karbo, rubbing his hand over his chin.

"Ah well, I suppose you are a man." Marcus sighs dramatically. "A man already, in my own household. Who would have thought it, when you first came to us? A pup, that's all you were. And now look at you, you vast hound!" He winks at me as they stride off together down Sand Street.

"He's so grown up," I say to the baker's wife. "A man already."

"Ah, they stay your child for many years to come," she tells me. "Come to think of it, I'm not sure they ever really grow up. You'll see him come running back to you with his worries even when you thought you had him safely married off. Your mother is always your mother."

Karbo returns, glowing from being rubbed down with oil and bathed, as well as from receiving his first shave. He shows me the tiny dots of stubble they have collected and we carefully place them inside his bulla, ready to be offered up at our Lararium, the shrine of our household gods. I take his purple-bordered toga praetexta and lay it on the ground below the shrine.

As head of our household, it falls to Marcus to present Karbo to the household gods. We stand in front of the Lararium, where two candles have been lit, and Marcus raises his palms, speaking with formality.

"Gods of this household and of the world beyond our doors, it is I, Marcus Aquillius Scaurus, master of this home, who asks for your blessings today for the Liberalia ceremony. I present to you my son Karbo, grown to be a man. Accept the toga of his childhood, the bulla which protected him as a boy and the stubble of his first shave. Watch over him now that he is no longer a child. Let him be a good man, honourable and brave, and let him always come home safe to his family. May he live a long and peaceful life, may he find love one day and may he sire many sons."

He lifts the bulla away from Karbo's neck and places it on the small ledge in front of the shrine. I pass him the folded adult toga and he shakes it out, the vast folds of cream cloth taking up most of the room.

"It was Fausta's," I whisper to Karbo and his eyes shine with tears for a moment at the thought of her, but he is beaming as Marcus dresses him with care. The endless quantity of heavy fabric swamps even Karbo's long frame, but I can see that he is delighted and that Marcus, for all his teasing, is bursting with pride.

Dressed in our best clothes, we reach the Forum, where a huge procession has developed. At the centre is the wooden and painted structure of a large phallus, set onto a bier and carried by a multitude of young men celebrating their coming of age. As it moves unsteadily through the crowd, different boys step forward to shoulder the heavy statue and then step back into the crowd, beaming. Karbo wriggles to the front of the crowd and takes his turn, returning to us further down the street.

"It's really heavy!"

Marcus laughs. "The burden of being a good man is a heavy load," he says. "Better learn that quickly. Come, we must sacrifice."

We find one of many roadside altars surrounded by the Sacerdos Liberi, the older women who serve as priestesses to Liber. Today they are crowned with ivy and have baked cakes made with honey and oil. These we place on the altar and pray for Karbo to be granted a long and happy life. There is dancing and the singing of increasingly ribald songs, cakes and wine to eat and drink. As the day comes to a close a respected matron is chosen to place a wreath of foliage and flowers over the phallus and we return home, tired and happy. We both embrace Karbo before he goes off to sleep.

"A good day," says Marcus with satisfaction.

"It was," I agree. I take the little bulla from the altar and tuck it away in my chest of clothes.

"Superstitious?" asks Marcus watching me with a smile.

I shrug. "Everyone does it," I say. If a son should ever receive a public triumph or be otherwise successful, the bulla of his childhood, if kept by his mother, is said to protect him against envy.

"He's going to be a farmer," says Marcus.

"People can be envious for many reasons," I say.

"I envy people who are asleep," says Marcus, holding out his arms to me. "Come here."

FORMAL ANNOUNCEMENTS ARE MADE, BUT they're not needed; word has already spread all over Rome that Domitian is going to introduce two new racing teams to the existing four. The Whites, Reds, Greens and Blues will be joined by the imperial Purple and Gold teams. There's excitement about what this will mean for race days: more teams competing, more combinations of different teams to race each other. There will be opportunities for promising young drivers to be considered for new roles as older, more experienced, drivers receive promotions or leave one team to join another.

The team owners and trainers will have more chances of poaching the best and bravest, luring those who are free away from their existing teams with promises of greater riches and glory, those who are enslaved with their freedom.

The fans are unsure what this will mean. Each fan has been loyal to their own team for years, perhaps even generations, father to son passing down a deep and abiding love for the Reds, or the Blues, sneering at the Greens or the Whites, jeering at their drivers, scornfully assessing their lack of prowess, even to the point of ending up in a scuffle. It would be unthinkable for them to support another team. But what if a favourite driver is poached? Should they follow him to the new colours, or deride him for leaving the team behind? If the new teams have been chosen by Domitian, will they have the very best of everything, making them more likely to win? Will they even, the gods forbid, be given privileges on the track, a tiny headstart? The officials looking the other way when teams or drivers misbehave, try to rig the races? It's all anyone talks about while the drivers preen and pose, hoping for their biggest chance yet to make a name for themselves.

"They'll be recruiting soon," says Celer as I pass him in the courtyard on the way back from the bakery. Karbo is sitting next to him, the two of them engrossed in conversation.

I pause by them, pass each of them a fruit roll. "Who?"

"The Purple and Gold racing teams," says Celer, his shrug making it clear this is the only possible topic he could have been referring to.

"The stables must be in a frenzy," I say.

"They are. They're being expanded to accommodate the two new teams. Building works everywhere. The horses don't like all the noise, it's making them skittish."

"Be careful when you're working, Karbo," I say.

He nods without answering, mouth full of bun.

"They need everything from stable cleaners to drivers," says Celer.

"You sticking with the Blues or hoping to switch to a new team?" I ask Karbo, a teasing smile on my face. I expect an outraged answer complete with all the reasons why it would be unthinkable to leave the Blues, his favourite team.

But he looks thoughtful. "Might be better opportunities on a new team," he says.

"Opportunities? Are the Purple and Gold horses more likely to need their stables cleaning?" I smile, pat his arm and am halfway up the stairs before a sudden thought strikes me and I lean over the bannister. "As long as you have no intentions of going for a driving position, Karbo, you know how I feel about that."

"I know," he says.

"You know as well, Celer," I say, pointing at him. "Don't go putting ideas in his head, if you please. Or you'll have me to answer to."

He raises his hands in a placatory gesture. "Never said a word. Just discussing what they're doing. How things may change. Who's tipped for new drivers, all of that. Only gossip, Althea."

"It had better be all you're discussing," I say. "I want Karbo with me on the farm, where I know he is safe."

Adah is passing and she nods at my warning. "That place is cursed," she says, referring to the Flavian Amphitheatre. "The sooner you leave the better. A farm is a good place for a growing boy."

"See?" I tell Karbo. "Adah agrees with me too."

THE GAMES KEEP US BUSY. Most mornings I head to the amphitheatre to ensure everything is prepared for each show and on the days when the Games are on I am always in attendance.

The criminal in today's Games is going to fight blind. He's been given a real sword, but the helmet that has been forced onto his head, which he cannot remove, only leaves space for his mouth, so he can breathe. Where a face should be, where the eyeholes should be, there is nothing, just smooth metal, making him faceless, blind. He will fight in terrifying darkness, flailing about him with the sword, hoping for death to come quickly, not to suffer too long. I lower my eyes as he is loaded into the lift, shaking and begging for mercy. It's not a kind fate and I hope the professional gladiator he'll be fighting will finish him off as soon as possible.

The fight begins. A young gladiator has been chosen to engage with the blind criminal. He's a promising fighter and may have a good career ahead of him, so it's a good opportunity for him to get attention but not be in much danger; the criminal cannot fight well, being neither a fighter by trade nor even able to see. When the criminal staggers out of the lift he turns this way and that, unsure of where his opponent is, until a fast cut on the arm draws immediate blood. In terrified desperation, the criminal slashes all around him, wielding the heavy sword poorly, at one moment almost dropping it. The gladiator, light on his feet, dances around him, his sword quick and sharp, the criminal crying out when he is cut on his torso and again on one thigh. Frantic, he lunges forwards and by some stroke of luck manages to slice into the gladiator's leg, who steps back in shock, then, angered, rushes forwards and stabs the criminal in the neck, so that a sudden gush of blood spills out. But as the criminal falls, he manages to grab at his opponent's tunic hem and in his dying moments, gives one last swing of his sword and cuts the gladiator's arm open. The referee steps forwards to intervene but it's too late anyway, the criminal sinks to the sand and takes his last breath, while the young gladiator, shocked and wounded, is hurried away to our physician Fabius.

In the medical bay, Fabius is irritable as he patches him up. "Bloody fool, getting your arm cut by a blinded criminal, what will happen to you when you're in a real gladiatorial bout?" he snaps to the crestfallen young man, then gestures for his assistant. "Clean up the leg wound so I can stitch it. Not there, *there*, have you learnt nothing at all in your time with me? Idiot."

It's unlike calm Fabius to be so grumpy, but the young gladiator could do with a telling off for taking stupid chances. A blind man with a sword still has a sword, he should not have risked being injured. If the cuts had been deeper, he could have been limping for the rest of his life and that would have put an end to his career in the arena.

"Are you alright, Fabius?" I ask.

"Yes, yes," he snaps, then sighs. "Sorry, Althea. Can't be doing with this nonsense anymore. Stupid boy. Put your leg there so I can see what I'm doing."

I nod to the beleaguered assistant and slumped gladiator and go home for the day. Fabius does not lose his temper when he's working. Perhaps he, too, is tiring of the Games, or is sorry to be losing Marcus as the manager of the amphitheatre, not knowing who they will choose as a replacement. I should ask Marcus to persuade Fabius to retire to the countryside near the farm so that he can have a peaceful life and Marcus will have his old friend nearby.

THERE ARE A FEW UPDATES from the racing stables over the next few weeks. The head trainer from the Blues has been poached for the Purples, three skilled drivers have shifted from one team to another for the chance of being one of their top drivers. It's all promotions and poaching for a while, along with endless gossip and speculation. I get bored of it soon enough and stop listening. So when Karbo comes home one afternoon and sits slumped in the courtyard while I am washing our tunics, unusually silent, I think of things any mother thinks of.

"Are you well? You're very quiet," I say.

"I'm fine."

"None of your friends here to play today?"

"We don't *play*," he says, huffing. "We talk and things. We're men now," he reminds me.

I think of the yelling and running games that still appeal, Liberalia or no Liberalia. "Of course. But they're not here today? Did you fall out?"

"No."

"Is there anything you need to talk about?"

"No."

I carry on washing my two linen tunics, which have spent the winter in storage and are in need of fresh water and air. My woollen clothes are beginning to get too hot as the days grow ever warmer. I dunk the tunics in the cold fountain water, then immerse them a few more times. They're clean enough but hanging in the fresh warm spring air, followed by a light rubbing of fresh herbs, will make them fragrant again. Karbo's summer tunics, I realise when I hold them up, will barely reach his knees.

"Looks like you need some new clothes," I say, hoping to raise a smile, for Karbo is fond of looking smart, excited by the prospect of a new belt or shoes and always by new tunics.

There's no reply. I glance at him again and see him sitting with his chin on his knees, staring at me.

"Thought of something you want to say to me after all?"

"The Purple team held try outs today."

"Held what?"

"Try outs."

"Which are what?"

"Boys who want to be drivers get a chance to take a chariot and two horses round the arena. Three laps. They start in the morning and the slowest driver in each round gets eliminated. The fastest one at the end of the day gets hired as a driver in the lowest tier, but they can work their way up to be top drivers one day."

Perhaps he has seen one of the horrible accidents that happen on the track involving young drivers or those desperate to prove themselves and it has upset him. "Was there an accident?"

"What? No. Well, yes, but nothing bad. The boy was one of the early ones in the morning, he couldn't control the horses well enough and they crashed into a wall. The left horse was hurt but it can be saved. He was just embarrassed."

"Lucky to only be embarrassed," I say.

Karbo mumbles something but I can't hear him as I pull out a dripping tunic and start squeezing the water out of it.

"What?"

"I tried out."

I drop the tunic into the water. "You tried out as a driver?"

"Yes." He won't meet my eyes.

I sigh, try to manage my emotions. "And it didn't go well? Karbo, I didn't want you to try out. But perhaps it's just as well you did and realised it's harder than it looks. Stick with what you do. You could be a trainer one day, it's a lot safer."

"I won."

"What?"

He lifts his chin, defiant, though his eyes flicker away under my aghast gaze. "I was the fastest. All day. I finished half a lap ahead of the second fastest. They made me race one more time against their top driver. I was one chariot length behind him and he's won everything, he has the finest horses in the stable. They said I'm the best they've ever seen at try outs." He swallows and his newly deep voice wavers with resentment and frustration; I can hear the child he was until not very long ago. "I'm the best they've seen – and you and Marcus won't let me race."

It's my turn to swallow. "Karbo, I –"

He's up and running up the stairs, face screwed up in a crying grimace, a little boy again. I start after him, before sinking back down in despair. I've known this day was coming, I tell myself, it was always coming even though I tried to ward it off. Karbo is truly gifted with horses. They listen to him, they calm at his approach. He begged to work for the Blues, was ecstatic when told he could clean stables and polish leather tack for them. He has watched races with a gleam in his eye which told me there was trouble ahead. And yes, there are racing drivers who are the toast of Rome, who have screaming fans and lavish lifestyles, earning more than most people can dream of making; even the best gladiators struggle to match their money. But the cold hard truth is that the drivers are young, there are no old drivers. It's a young man's game, because the older drivers lose their nerve when they have wives and children and because far too many promising young drivers meet horrible ends, losing limbs and lives to the dizzying speed and lethal corners of the Circus. I've seen such accidents for myself. Celer, who escaped with his life, has terrifying scars down his body and a drinking habit that left him all alone before Julia took him in and kept him more or less in this world. My shoulders sag. It's not what I want for Karbo, nor what Marcus wants. Marcus, as his father, can forbid it of course, can oblige him to come to the farm, to the safe life we have planned in the country, but is that cruel to Karbo, to drag him away from what he so desperately wants, from what he seems born for? I don't know what to do.

I find Marcus and the same conversation plays out between us, this time out loud instead of in my head. It makes it less lonely I suppose, but both of us sigh often, grimace at either option available to us, shake our heads, then start the circular logic all over again. Karbo stays out of sight until Marcus goes to talk to him, but the talk does not last long and Marcus returns looking defeated.

"I feel I'm taking his dreams away," he says. "But I can't bear to think of losing him when I've already…" He trails off, but I complete the thought in my mind. Marcus has already lost one child, his baby son Amantius, only just walking when Vesuvius erupted and crushed Pompeii, taking Marcus' wife and child. To find another child and adopt him, to open up his wounded heart only to have it broken again…

We lie in our bed in gloomy silence. There is nothing we have not already said and when we meet for breakfast Karbo's eyes are red-rimmed and he is silent, poking at his food at Cassia's counter before morosely heading to the stables, where no doubt the team are waiting to praise him and yet he cannot revel in it because he does not have our consent.

"We need to go to the stables," says Marcus at last. "I can't think about anything else with this hanging over us. We have to make a decision."

We trail down the streets hand in hand, neither of us saying anything, until the stables come into view. There's building work everywhere, as Celer told us; making room for two whole new teams is a substantial undertaking and everyone seems to be in a hurry.

"Scaurus!"

Marcus nods at the trainer for the Blues. "Good to see you, my friend."

"Ah but you've raised a star, Marcus! Never seen anything like it. The boy's going to be crowned with golden laurels, I swear it. We should have spotted him sooner and kept him for ourselves. There's no chance now the Purples have seen him, they've got the imperial purse on their side and they know a hero when they see one. Half a lap ahead! And he was one chariot length, perhaps not even that, behind our top driver and that didn't half humiliate him, I can tell you. Neck and neck with a nobody? He'll not hear the end of that soon, I tell you, everyone was calling him 'new boy' and referring to Karbo as 'champion.'"

Marcus nods. "I need a word, though."

"Don't say you won't allow it, Scaurus, the boy is under Neptune's protection, anyone can see it."

"Will Neptune be protecting him when someone comes up too close and there's an accident? They happen all the time, you can't tell me they don't. I can't stand by and let him take the risk."

"We all walk into danger every day that we wake up and get out of bed, Scaurus. The boy has a gift. And he's well liked here, the little boys look up to him and the older ones hang about with him. The trainers always have time for his questions."

"None of that will help on the racetrack."

"It helps if you know what you're doing. I have drivers who have nothing but wool for brains. They're young. They like the speed, they like the thrill. They like the applause and the women afterwards. They take stupid risks and get themselves hurt or killed."

"That's what we're afraid of," says Marcus.

"But Karbo, he's different. He spent weeks with the wheelwrights, learning everything about their trade that he could, he spends hours checking how the tack fits, whether adjustments can be made to better suit each horse, he pays attention to each beast's temperament, whether it would be better suited to the left or the right in training. Everything. Every little detail. He didn't keep pace with the top driver because he whipped on the horses, he kept pace because he chose the right beasts and spent over an hour readying them before he took them out. Every round we put them through he was adjusting tiny things, things no-one else would even bother with. His own stance, the horse's bit, the condition of the track."

Marcus nods, though he doesn't look comforted at hearing Karbo's skills and attention extolled. The trainer is still gushing.

"He walked the track before every single round, did you know that? And when the time came to race Museus, he asked for an extra half hour so the horses could rest, he made sure they had warm water to drink, not cold and he walked the track again even though the other lads were laughing at him and asking how much could it have changed in half an hour? But he was right to do it. Scorpus of the Greens was watching and he said that's a boy he'd like to race in a few years' time. Scorpus said that!"

"I'd like to see him on the track," says Marcus. "Can that be arranged?"

"Of course. The Purples are training today and they'll let him take a chariot out for you to see. He has to have your permission or they'll not be able to have him."

We follow him in silence to the training track, a less ostentatious version of the Circus Maximus. It's shorter on the lengths, but the ends are a similar size, so that the charioteers can grow used to the cornering. Twelve chariots are ready for use, with teams varying from one horse for the beginners to the most used twos and fours, as well as one team of six and one of twelve, used for the impressive effect they give when driven, a test of the driver's skills, not for true racing.

"Karbo is preparing them, as you can see."

Karbo is inspecting a horse's hooves, running one hand down each leg and gently lifting it. The horse is allowing this, although as soon as he has finished it snorts and tosses its head, eager to be let loose on the track. These horses have been born and bred for speed; the racetrack is their home and the place where they are eager to perform. They are restless, stamping feet and sniffing the air, waiting for the moment when they will take flight, their hooves pounding down the track, the screams of the crowd, their driver's voice urging them on.

I tighten my grip on Marcus' hand as the trainer walks down to Karbo and speaks with him. Karbo's head turns quickly in our direction, a guilty look on his face as though we have caught him doing something wrong, even though he is only doing what is expected of a senior stableboy. Marcus raises his hand in salutation and after a moment's hesitation Karbo waves back. The trainer speaks with him again and Karbo's face changes, he frowns and shakes his head.

"He doesn't want to race in front of us," I say.

"We need to see him," says Marcus. "I can't make a decision without seeing him for myself."

"Are you thinking of allowing it? It would mean him not coming to the farm. He would live all alone in Rome."

Marcus looks down at me. "I don't know," he says honestly. "I'm afraid for him, just as you are, that's the truth. But I can't trample on his dreams without being fair to him and the only fair thing I can think of is to see him race for myself. I've seen him with horses before and what they say is true, he does have a gift for them. Is it right for me to take away what he is good at? It would mean him staying here when we go, but our insula would take every care of him."

"He could be a trainer," I mutter, but I have a horrible feeling I am about to lose my case.

"He could," agrees Marcus. "But most of the trainers were once drivers."

"They're the ones who survived," I say.

"Yes," agrees Marcus. He lets go of my hand, puts his arm about me and pulls me closer. "I'm not going against you, Althea. I would not worry you for nothing. But Karbo has a right to be successful, if he has talent."

"I don't care about him being successful," I say. "I'm scared for him."

"Let's see him drive," says Marcus.

It seems Karbo has been persuaded. He is walking the track, looking on the ground as well as all around him as he progresses round the elongated oval.

"What is he looking for?" I ask the trainer, who has made his way back to us.

"Any bumps, dips. The track's kept smooth but even a pebble can throw your chariot off course if you put a wheel on it the wrong way. And he's feeling it, thinking about what he can do at each part, what happens if another driver forces him to take a different part of the track."

"Is he going to drive against someone now?" I ask, anxiety rising.

"Yes, but that proves what I was telling you," says the trainer. "It's just an informal trial and he's still doing all the work."

"Don't the other drivers do this?" I protest.

"They don't," says the trainer with a grimace. "They rely on their trainer, or they do it once in the morning and call it done. They don't do it before every time trial or practice, that's for sure. They don't even bother doing it more than once on race day. They're told it will make them better drivers, but they don't listen. Young men think they're gods, that it's all about talent, no hard work required. They think they're immortal."

"That's what I'm afraid of," I say.

"But that's not Karbo," insists the trainer. "Look at him, he's walked half the track and when he gets back, he won't leap in the chariot and be off. He'll check the harness and the wheels, he'll talk to the horses, he'll check his reins and he'll check his knife."

I shudder at the thought of the knife that every charioteer keeps on their person, the knife that will cut them free of the reins wrapped round their waist, should the worst happen and the chariot be turned over. A driver can be dragged behind the horses, ripping their flesh open, even killing them, if they cannot get free of the reins. Marcus' tightening arm reminds me of the moment when Karbo took Celer's knife and slipped into the dark waters of the flooded amphitheatre to save Marcus' life, while I sat next to the Emperor Titus and believed I was watching them both die. I swallow.

At last Karbo steps into the chariot, which is drawn by two horses. The more senior drivers use four, but two, with a light chariot, can get to astonishing speeds. A stablehand helps to wrap the reins round Karbo's waist, allowing him to steer with his body as well as his hands. Meanwhile a second chariot is being prepared, with a tall young man having reins wrapped about him. He has an arrogant look to him, smirking over his shoulder at Karbo.

"That's Museus," says the trainer. "He's still a slave, but he's going to be rich one day, no doubt about it. He's been the best driver for the Whites since that accident last year when two of their team died. Now he's transferred to the Purples there'll be no stopping him. Except your boy, of course."

I shudder and the trainer catches it. "I know. But did you see Museus walk the track? No, you didn't, because he's an arrogant young pup. He's got his eye on girls and money. Karbo's got his eye on the horses because he cares. He loves being with them. Museus sees them as the means to an end. There's a difference and it shows in their results."

The two chariots are lined up, the horses tossing their heads and sidestepping, the stable hands holding them back so that they won't suddenly take off.

"Three laps," says the trainer. "Enough to see how they do against each other. Museus isn't best pleased about this," he adds. "He thought he'd be the shining star on this team, but Karbo made him look a fool. A stable hand who cleans the tack and shovels the shit, almost beating him? And a freedman, of course, that will rile him too. Museus wants to earn his freedom, but no stables will grant that too soon. It's what makes him a good driver, the need to do well so that he might be free."

I'm sorry for Museus. Still a slave, earning his masters large amounts of money and desperate for his freedom, desperate enough to go that little bit faster, to take the corner that little more recklessly… I give a silent prayer of gratitude that Karbo is already free. If he must race, he can race because he loves it, not out of desperation.

"They're ready," says the trainer. I grip Marcus' hand.

The white handkerchief falls and the horses leap forward, the chariots in full motion where they were stationary only a breath ago. They head away from us, speeding down the track, dust rising under the hooves and wheels. Museus is using his whip, lashing the backs of the horses, while Karbo is swaying in his chariot.

"He's moving them round every little imperfection of the track," murmurs the trainer. "I told you."

Karbo's chariot edges ahead, but it is not enough, Museus manages to take the inside track on the first corner, Karbo just behind, but as they come down the track towards us, he begins to gain.

"Not enough for the corner," says the trainer.

He's right. Again, Museus takes the corner and Karbo is forced to go wider.

"But he's catching up every time," says the trainer in admiration. "Can you see? Even though he's had to go wide twice, he's catching up. If he was in the Circus Maximus, he'd be winning, no contest."

The third corner and the fourth, Karbo is edged out but as he heads out for the final lap he leans forwards more and, incredibly, the horses go faster, even though the reins are looser.

"Letting them feel freedom," says the trainer. "It's risky, because some horses lose focus when you do that. You have to know the team, you have to let them feel the excitement and let them loose at the right moment."

They come down the final straight neck and neck and then Karbo edges ahead, his chariot in line with Museus' horses and Museus' face contorts in a grimace of rage as they finish with Karbo the winner. The stable hands run out to hold the sweating horses, a junior trainer unwinds the reins. Museus turns and stamps away without a word, face dark with anger and humiliation. Karbo watches him go, awaiting his own assistance with patience. At last the reins are unwound and he steps out of the chariot and walks round to the horses, nuzzles each of them, patting their necks, speaks to a stable hand, giving instructions, before heading up towards us.

He stands in front of us, face flushed, eyes pleading.

"Well raced, Karbo," says the trainer.

"Thank you, Dominus," says Karbo respectfully. He looks at Marcus. "You saw me?" he says, knowing full well we have both seen the race.

Marcus nods, his face serious. "We saw you."

"I'm not saying it because you're his parents," says the trainer. "He's the best I've ever seen and I've seen boys and men come and go in the racing game. Poor ones, good one, even the greats. I spotted Scorpus when he was a boy and I knew he had talent. But Karbo, he's even better than Scorpus was at his age. He feels the horses. And they feel him, you can see how they respond and he's a new driver. Wait till he has a team of horses who've raced with him a hundred times."

Marcus is looking at the ground. "I will give my permission," he starts, "but his mother must have her say. I cannot break her heart and I know she is fearful for him. Althea?"

I look down at Karbo's feet, now the size of Marcus', the twitching movement of his toes inside the leather as he waits, anxious, for my reply. I think of how he was the first time I saw him, a struggling scrawny boy held fast in Maria's grip, who told me his name under duress. A street rat, she called him, a runaway slave scraping a living on the street who had to be coaxed with the promise of food and a safe place to sleep at night to become our messenger boy. He had attached himself to Fausta and lost her to the fever, then slowly came to see me as his mother. I wonder where his real mother is, if she would let him become a driver because he wants it so much or whether she would allow her own fears for him to take hold of her and refuse, keep him safe but unhappy at her side. I wish it could be her choosing, but it falls to me.

Swallowing, I bow my head in assent and am almost knocked over by Karbo flinging his arms around me.

"Thank you! Thank you! I'll be safe, I'll be careful, I promise, I promise. Thank you!"

I put my arms around him and try to smile at Marcus, although it's more of a grimace. He pats Karbo's shoulder and nods at me.

"Do your best to keep that promise, Karbo, Althea would be heartbroken should any harm come to you. As would I."

I let Karbo chatter and show us round the half-built Purple stables, look in at the Blues, whom he is still fond of, accepting the praises and well wishes of everyone who knows him. I can see for myself that he is well liked and trusted, that he has built his own community here and that gives me some comfort.

"We should be going," says Marcus at last. "We will see you back at the insula, Karbo."

We walk back together in silence until we reach the rooftop and sit down under the pergola.

"Was I right?" asks Marcus at last.

"Yes," I say. "But I am so afraid." And my tears come. I held them back all this time and now they pour out of me, the fear and worry released. Marcus holds me, allows me to cry without trying to falsely comfort me.

"I want him to be happy and safe," I say at last when the tears have slowed, trying to wipe my face.

"I fear for him as you do," says Marcus. "But I cannot bring myself to forbid him."

I nod, shaky. "I never thought we'd have to make such choices."

"I hoped he'd want to be safe in the countryside with us. But there are few paths in life without some danger attached to them."

"I suppose."

"If Neptune has smiled on him thus far, he will keep him safe."

I allow myself to be comforted, but when Marcus has fallen asleep I take out Karbo's bulla from my chest and say another small prayer to the gods, above all Neptune, to protect the boy they have set on this path. Then I hide it away again, for a driver touted to be as great as Scorpus will one day need protection from envy.

ILL OMENS

THE LONGER DAYS OF MAY have fooled me into leaving the baths late, and twilight is coming. I walk faster, anxious to be back inside the safety of the insula before darkness falls. The streets of Rome are not safe for anyone when night comes. I join Sand Street, relieved to be just a few moments from home, but ahead of me a figure steps out, stands motionless, blocking my way to the welcoming lanterns inside Cassia's popina. I gasp before I realise it is a woman. A dark green palla covers her head and drapes down to her long brown tunic. Her face is hard to see. I could correct my course, move to the left or right of her and keep walking, but there is something about her that makes me think she is here for me, that she wants to address me.

"Can I help you?" I call out, still twenty paces from her, my steps slowing, growing anxious again because of her stillness in the darkening twilight.

"Althea," she says.

"Yes?" I say. "Do I know you?"

She pulls back her palla so I can see her face. The sorceress. The one who lives close to Quintus' family fullery, a few streets away. I have not seen her since the day Cassia's wedding to Rullus failed, when the sorceress threw strange words at us and I grew angry with her. Only afterwards did Cassia and I look back and think that her words had been wise, that she had changed our actions on that doomed day and set the Fates to weave a better story for Cassia – or perhaps she knew all along the story they were weaving and pushed us to take the right steps. Either way, that day her words and actions had saved Cassia from a terrible marriage and so I bow my head with respect, then look up with a smile.

"I never thanked you for what you did, what you said," I say. "Cassia brought you a thank you gift for herself, but I was grateful too." I give a laugh. "And really, I owe you a gift myself. You said that when I knew what my desire was, I should say it out loud. And I did and it took some time, but you were right, my desire did come to me." I gesture at my own palla, wrapped about my head and shoulders against the evening chill. "I am a married woman now."

The sorceress does not smile. She does not act as though she has ever seen me before, only stares into my eyes, her face devoid of expression. "There is a darkness coming," she says.

"What?"

"There is a darkness coming," she repeats. Her voice sounds cold and hard, echoing in the empty street. "A creeping black, seeping into your life. You must leave Rome."

I stare at her. The hairs across the back of my neck rise and a cold shiver ripples across me. "A creeping black? What do you mean? When is it coming? What is it?" My voice is too high, I sound like a child. I swallow and try to speak more normally. "Have you had a vision?" I ask. "Did you see something bad come into my life?" The decision we have made about Karbo's future, have we made a mistake, set something bad in motion?

"Leave Rome," she says again, and her voice has not changed, it is still too loud and cold and without feeling, as if a stone statue is speaking.

She pulls up her palla, so that her face is thrown back into deep shadow and turns away, walks down Sand Street, turns into Virgin's Street and onwards, disappearing into the growing gloom.

The words of the sorceress linger, I cannot dismiss them with ease. I wonder if perhaps she is angry. Her advice to me led, in a way, to knowing my true feelings for Marcus and telling him so, yet I have not offered her payment. Fabia and Cassia both made payments to her and so, the next day, I take some of my savings and go to a jeweller, where I ask for a little dove made in silver, a sign of love and marriage. He works a pretty thing, tiny and yet beautiful. It sits in my palm as I turn it to admire the dainty workmanship. I pay him and make my way towards home, but go further down Virgin's Street, past the welcoming insula gate and the bakery, onwards down a warren of little streets, the acrid stench of the fullery hitting my nostrils. I wave at one of Quintus' brothers as I pass. We know all of his family now, a friendly, noisy group, always cheerful and full of stories and songs to while away time when work is busy.

I turn down another little street. I have reached my destination, the house of the sorceress set in a tiny courtyard. The same silent slave girl I saw before appears and when she sees me she nods, as though I had made an appointment, and gestures to me to follow. I do so and she leaves me in the room I visited with Cassia and Fabia over two years ago. It is full of the smell of incense and dimly lit, tinted red from the scarlet cloth hanging over the single window. I sit down on the low bench that faces the sorceress' carved chair, wishing for the comfort of Cassia and Fabia on either side of me, huddled together for courage.

"I did not expect you."

I jump, even though I knew she would appear like this, all of a sudden from behind the high red screen. I half-rise, then sit again. "When I saw you – when you spoke to me in the street – I said I owed you a gift, and I do," I say.

She stays standing, looking down on me. "A gift?"

I take out the little package of cloth and pass it to her. She takes it, opens it with care, nods her head in acceptance at the silver dove.

"Did you think I was angry because you had not given me a gift in recognition of what I told you about finding your desires?" she asks.

"Yes," I confess.

She shakes her head. "I do not care if those I help acknowledge it or not," she says.

"I thank you for this and am glad you are now a married woman. But I saw a darkness in your future and I needed to tell you of it."

"But what did you see?" I ask. "What exactly?"

"Black," she says.

"Black what?" I ask.

She shakes her head. "I don't know. Everything was black. You were dressed in black, all around you was black. Everything."

I swallow. When we first came to see the sorceress, on a whim of Cassia's, it seemed no more than something to laugh over between friends, for who could know if she really had any powers or was just a fraud? But her words came true for Fabia, followed by her much-needed intervention in Cassia's first doomed wedding plans, and more recently my own union with Marcus has been guided by her and so her words hold more sway with me. I struggle to think what she might mean. "You couldn't see anything around me but black?" I try again.

"Everything around you was black," she corrects me. "A black room, with black walls, black furniture. The light..." she hesitates, as though unwilling to add this detail. "The only light came from a funerary lamp."

I pull back from her, gesturing against evil. I think for a moment with horror at the fate of Cornelia last year, the Vestal Virgin entombed alive for violating her sacred duty by lying with a man. Darkness was all around her as she waited for death to come, buried under the earth while Rome watched in silent horror at what the law required. I am no Vestal, such a fate could not befall me no matter how much I might enrage Domitian, but why would the sorceress see such a thing when she looks at me?

"I do not mean to frighten you but to warn you," she says. She finally takes her own seat, though she leans forward towards me, eager to impart her knowledge. "I saw you in this vision and I came to tell you because I know who you are, it was not a vision of an unnamed woman, it was you I saw."

"And there was danger?" I ask, though how could there not be, with such a vision?

She nods. "It was all around you, but I did not see where you were. Can you think of such a place?"

"No."

She leans back in her seat, looking weary. "I cannot see more than that, I have tried," she says. "I can only warn you that the place is dangerous and that you should avoid it."

"How can I avoid it if I don't know where or what it is?"

"Be wary of anything that may come to resemble it."

I try to think of dark places in my life. Pompeii, lost under unending grey ash. The under-arena. It has already claimed its share of unexpected and unfair deaths, with Funis last year and those who were mistaken for him. The Vestal Virgin's last resting place, but that is sealed up. The Tullianum, the prison I once visited when we needed a condemned man to play the part of Leander and swim across the flooded amphitheatre, braving the dangerous creatures of the dark waters below him. But the Tullianum is reserved for important enemies of Rome, I cannot imagine why I should find myself there again. I shiver at the thought of it, its darkness and stone-cold damp air even at the height of summer.

"Did you think of a place?" she asks, watching my arms grow goosefleshed.

"The Tullianum," I say. "But I am not a threat to Rome."

She sighs. "Visions seldom come to me," she says. "Sometimes they are too strange to understand, other times they are clear. Often they contain symbols. Rarely do I have a vision where I know the person. That is why I came to you, I remembered who you were."

"Thank you for warning me," I say.

She frowns. "Be careful how you tread," she says. "For a common woman, your job takes you close to power, and power is always dangerous."

I shrug. "I – we intend to leave Rome anyway, all being well," I say. "My new husband and I, we will move to the countryside, to a farm, and live there."

"Soon?"

"As soon as we can," I say. "Dom – the Emperor wishes us to complete one more year of the Games."

"Leave as soon as you can," she says. "And should you recognise the place I saw, leave it immediately, no matter the risk."

I wait for her to say something more, but she only sits in silence staring down at the little silver dove. I get to my feet and still she does not stir.

"Thank you," I say.

She nods without looking up. I edge past her back out into the courtyard, where her slave girl escorts me to the entryway.

I return to the insula lost in thought. What can the sorceress have seen? I cannot imagine a place such as the one she has described. I wonder if I should tell Marcus what she said but decide not to, it is all too vague and may come to nothing. He frets enough already about not being able to go to the farm right away. If I start making him worry that we are in danger it will only be worse. I will tell him if I see something that I recognise from her description. No need for him to worry when there is nothing yet to worry about.

THE SEASON IS GOING WELL. Our themes of birds, the illusions and changes, magic and gods that we have drawn on, is proving popular. This morning we have already had a demonstration of the flying skills of two eagles and an archery demonstration by the venatores, who have shot doves out of the air. Now we move on to some light relief before the execution later on of some criminals; the gladiatorial combats will come after lunch.

Fabius is displeased with his assistant, who is setting up the medical area for the day. "More lamps! I can't be expected to see what I'm doing in the dark."

As far as I can recall, the number of lamps has always been the same in Fabius' medical bay, but I suppose it depends on how complex the wounds brought to him are and what details he needs to take care of. Stitching wounds requires precision if the wound is to heal well. I nod to the beleaguered assistant and smile at Fabius, who half-waves a hand at me.

It's a hot day and the awning is fully open, meaning that only a circle of sunlight penetrates, illuminating the man standing at the centre of the arena. He has two assistants, dressed exotically in the Egyptian fashion. Each boy holds a collection of white doves on their outstretched arms, while the man talks about how doves, so white and delicate, are wonderful temple offerings to the gods.

"I sacrifice to the goddess Venus, bringer of love, that she may bring me a bride, a beautiful woman with whom I may share my life."

He takes one dove and puts his hand around its head, in one quick movement twists and pulls the head away, releasing a burst of scarlet blood and showing with his other hand the now-headless corpse of the dove. "Poor creature," he adds. "But its life is over and so it will fly to Venus and ask for her blessing in this matter." He moves his hand and the bird suddenly comes back to life, its head reappearing before it flutters up and through the centre of the velarium, white against the blue sky. The crowd gasps.

"Perhaps you did not see it clearly enough," says the man. "And if Venus is to send me a woman, one dove will not be enough. I do not want an ugly bride!"

The audience laughs.

The man dispatches the remaining birds one after another, each time with a crack of their necks and a spurt of blood, and yet each time, the bird miraculously comes back to life and flies away.

"I have faith that Venus will send me a beautiful bride," says the man. "I even have a palla ready for her, so that she will be clad as befits a virtuous matron of Rome."

He pulls out a delicate palla in fine woven dark red wool, drapes it over the head of one of the young male assistants, then swiftly removes it to reveal, in his place, a young Egyptian woman, with long hair and a shapely body. "Venus! You have outdone yourself. Here is my bride to be!"

The crowd applauds, impressed with the illusions. Standing inside the arena door to the hypogeum, I can hear the hum of voices as they chatter amongst themselves about how to create such an illusion. The illusionist and his assistants walk past me as they leave the arena. Close up, the beautiful and divinely sent bride is of course a boy, albeit now wearing a well-padded white dress, jewellery and a flattering wig. I am still impressed by how fast the assistant can change his costume underneath a palla without wriggling too much, which would give the trick away.

THE GAMES ARE GOING WELL and the first task is completed, but we cannot yet rest on our laurels. I keep reminding Marcus that we need to begin planning both the naumachia and the event at Domitian's villa, neither of which will happen without careful preparation.

"Tomorrow we'll need to go and see the lake," Marcus says with a sigh one afternoon while we're sat in the courtyard. "I need some sense of the size of it."

"You can see the grove of trees surrounding it from the temple of Aesculapius on the Tiber Island," says Julia. She's busy tending to her flowers, but she sits down to rest beside us. "I've never seen the space within the grove, it must be quite wild by now."

THE NEXT DAY, WE GO down Sand Street to the river, cross it partway, onto the Tiber Island, passing the temple of Aesculapius, god of healing, being mindful of the sacred snakes which are plentiful here in his honour. Then up onto the next bridge, which takes us closer to the smell of the tanneries on this far side of the river. The road here is busy with carts trundling back and forth with raw skins for the tanneries. I wrinkle my nose at the stench. Marcus guides me towards a wide grove of trees beyond the busy road.

"Augustus wanted the lake to be surrounded by this grove," says Marcus. "As though it were set in the countryside."

"Wouldn't smell this bad in the countryside," I say.

"True."

The trees must have been saplings when they were planted, but more than fifty years have passed and their trunks are sturdy. The saplings were planted too close together so the grove would seem well-grown right away, so they stand tight-packed, reaching for sunlight amidst their too-close fellows. We walk through the dappled spaces left to us.

"We may have to cull some of these," mutters Marcus. "How are thousands of people supposed to get here quickly?"

The sunlight grows stronger and we come out of the trees and into a wide-open space, with a broken-down wall ahead of us.

"Here," says Marcus, offering his hand to me. I climb after him, stepping through the broken section of travertine wall and down onto the wide cobbled pavement.

We stand at the edge of the basin. Domitian was right. What was once a lake is now a large area of scrubby ground with a dip in it, a marshy look to the very centre of it. The pavement is in need of weeding and the wall surrounding the space is less of a proper structure and more of a suggestion that there ought to be a wall.

"It's big," says Marcus, stating the obvious. He sounds worried. "Too big to control well, not like the amphitheatre when we held the naumachia there."

"Though that was big enough," I say.

"It was." He lifts one hand to shade his eyes, squints at the other side.

"How big is it?"

"Over one-thousand-eight-hundred feet in length, one thousand two hundred feet in width. Digging it out again will be a huge task."

"And filling it?"

"That's less of a problem, we have the aqueduct to help us and this time we don't need to fill it and empty it so fast. It can be done over a few days and we'll keep the stream going to keep it topped up. And that wall needs rebuilding."

"No seating," I say.

"The carpenters who did the seating in the amphitheatre will be spending their next two months down here. As will hundreds of other people if this is to be made ready in time."

"Augustus had more than thirty full-sized ships taking part, with over three thousand men," I say, having read up on the event.

Marcus sighs. "I wish someone hadn't made a note of how many ships and how many men. Domitian will want more."

"Will he?"

"You think he wants to have a lesser show than Augustus?"

I shake my head.

The original basin was the work of Augustus, built to commemorate and celebrate the victory of Actium. Its walls used to be twice the height of a man, although most of them are wobbly and large stretches have collapsed altogether, no doubt encouraged along by local people scavenging building materials. There are eight gates, or gaps for them at least. Within the walls and close to the lapping waters is a wide pavement. Plants are growing through cracks in the mortar and cobbles.

The pavement and walls will allow for five tiers all around the lake, offering seating for about thirty thousand spectators.

"How do we empty it?

Marcus turns back to me. "The Aqua Alsietina aqueduct fills it, the water comes from Lake Alsietinus. To empty it there's a drainage channel that allows it to empty out into the Tiber. It's a bit silted up but we can clear it out. The good thing is that when it's full you can bring boats in via the aqueduct if you're careful."

I SPEND MOST OF THE rest of that day and the next drawing up the plans. We have two months to create a lake, as well as collect enough ships and men. The Games are progressing smoothly, so we decide to shift three hundred of our slaves to work on the basin. We plan to have a man-made island in the centre, which will mean less removal of earth and the creation of an elite viewing platform for Domitian and high-ranking guests. Shovels in huge numbers are the first item to appear on my list.

Within a week, work begins on the basin, with four separate teams attached to it full time. Our slaves will dig out the basin and create the central island. Builders from all over Rome are recruited to rebuild or fix the stone wall which surrounds the oval space. The carpenters plan a five-tier stand of wooden seating which will go all the way around the soon-to-be lake, as well as a wooden bridge which will take Domitian and his guests from the shoreline to the central island. They will also build eight sturdy wooden gates, so that we can lock up the site in the days before the event, to avoid anyone sneaking in without a token. Finally, we pay anyone who wants to earn a few coins, including children, to weed the cobbled pavement to return it to its previous neat appearance. Notifications are sent that we will require prisoners of war and criminals to take part. We will undertake only a few executions in the arena for the next two months, so as to have enough criminals at the naumachia. We send timings for sailors, soldiers and ships to join us one week beforehand for practice sessions.

One trireme ship, so named because they have three rows of oars, making them faster than the biremes which have but two rows of oars, takes one-hundred-and-eighty men to row, so over six thousand rowers will be required to move the ships. We will also have some quadriremes, which have shallow draughts making them suitable for the lake. They are very manoeuvrable, which will be important in the limited space we have available.

A normal ship would have fifty to sixty armed fighters on board, but Domitian will want to see more action, so each ship will have one hundred men, meaning we will need three-thousand-five-hundred men to fight. Of these, we decide that five hundred will be killed, so they must be made up of criminals and prisoners of war, along with any gladiators whom our gladiatorial schools are happy to be rid of. They will be marked on the forehead with a red dot, an indicator to everyone else taking part that they can be killed. Everyone else will fight, but not to kill.

I COME HOME ONE DAY to find Adah and Julia sitting together among the flowers, heads close together, murmuring, but they stop as soon as I enter the courtyard.

"Keeping secrets?" I ask, laughing, as I pass by. "Here, I brought back new plums from the market."

They thank me but as I climb higher up the stairs and leave some plums with Maria I can hear them murmuring again.

"They really must have secrets," I say to Maria.

"They are old friends," she says, looking down at the two of them. "Thank you for the plums, the new season's fruits are always welcome."

A FEW WEEKS INTO OUR preparations, a scroll arrives at the amphitheatre from the imperial palace, which Marcus smiles over.

"Domitian says you are to be the commander of one of the ships in the naumachia," he tells Servius. "Your ship will lead the parade. We will have fifteen ships do an initial parade around the lake to music, then two bouts of fighting between pairs of twenty-six ships, then we'll bring in all thirty-five for a free for all: no-one will be able to manoeuvre of course, but it'll be spectacular."

"The Emperor remembered my name?" asks Servius, awestruck.

"He did. You will be in charge of the lead ship."

"I'm grateful to you, sir, for presenting me to him," says Servius earnestly.

Marcus tries to explain the concept of a naumachia to Servius. He knows what one is, of course, but due to the vast resources required, they are hardly ever put on and he has never witnessed one.

"It's not a real battle, not like you've been trained for. It's not play-fighting either, but only some people will get hurt or killed and they'll be criminals and prisoners of war. What's needed is spectacle. So the movements for fighting need to be bigger, broader, there needs to be lots of shouting and screaming. I'll put all your men on the same ship as you, so you'll all need to fight in the right style for the event. I'll probably send you and your men down to the gladiator barracks for some training."

Servius looks affronted. "Train with gladiators?"

"You need to know how to put on a show. You've been trained for real combat, it's not as interesting to watch, believe me."

Servius and his men acquiesce with reluctance, mostly because they want to take part in the biggest naumachia Rome has seen in decades, but when they arrive in the gladiator barracks at the Ludus Magnus they're stiff, holding themselves apart from the gladiators. The sailors are freeborn men who belong to the Roman army, they consider themselves a cut above gladiators, even though gladiators are known for being irresistible to the ladies. The start of the training does not go well. The men fight as they've been trained and drilled to do by the Roman army; efficient, focused moves. Paternus, who is doing us a favour by training them for a couple of days, looks weary beyond his advancing years.

"Give me a slave any day," he sighs. "Army recruits are the worst. They think they're superior to everyone else, think there's the army way to fight and the wrong way to fight. No flexibility."

But the men start to bond; sharing meals and round after round of training softens the distance between them. The gladiators, used as they are to suggesting ideas to create a more spectacular show, are open with their praise when they see a change in the sailors' fighting style, while the sailors enjoy getting to rub shoulders with some of Rome's top gladiatorial names. By the time the three days are up, they are putting on a better show, shouting with the best of them, their sword arcs wider, their responses more dramatic to everything from a thrust to a near miss.

"Thank you, Paternus," I say.

"Where are you getting three thousand fighters from?"

I shake my head. "Don't ask. The ships come with their own rowing teams. For the fighting crews we've emptied every gladiatorial school in Rome, the Misenum sailors, plus we've borrowed more sailors from Ostia and Misenum and more soldiers from the Praetorian Guards' barracks. We've got our slaves from the amphitheatre to bulk out the numbers, not that they're trained to fight."

"That'll be fun," comments Paternus. "Someone will get killed just because they're waving a sword about with too much vigour."

"I doubt you'll be able to tell with the numbers we've got," I say. "When all thirty-five ships are out there'll be hardly any space between one ship and the next, you could cross the whole lake stepping from ship to ship and never get wet."

"Rather you than me."

I sigh. "I'd willingly trade," I say. "But I'm stuck with it."

THE LAKE IS RAPIDLY TAKING shape. The ground, having already been dug out and replaced but not much used since, is soft and easier to remove than hard compacted earth. The island is in place and I arrange for it to be planted with flowers and grass, making it seem natural. A wooden platform is added with seating for Domitian and his guests. The bridge is swiftly erected, the task made easier because the water has not yet been added, so supporting posts can be sunk into the ground. The cobbled pavement is looking neat again, many hands having removed the weeds and moss in a matter of weeks. The builders have reached the halfway point of the wall and the eight wooden gates are in their proper places.

"How fast will the water drain away?" I ask Marcus, looking over the vast expanse of bare earth, now reaching its full depth, at least the height of two men.

"It's a marshy area anyway, that's why the trees grow so well," he says with confidence. "We'll fill it up and keep the water flowing. The aqueduct is well-sourced and will keep pace with any drainage."

I look round at the scene. "It's shaping up well," I say. "Don't forget the other task, though."

"Domitian's villa," says Marcus with a sigh. "No chance of forgetting that."

THE VILLA OF DOMITIAN

THE WARMER DAYS OF JUNE mean the amphitheatre is full for every show, especially now that we have the velarium to keep the hot sun off the audience. The daily shows are proceeding well; our team are experienced after a few years of this life. Now Marcus and I have to put our heads together to develop a show worthy of Domitian's private villa and amphitheatre.

Based on a well-received show last season to inaugurate Paternus's Ludus Magnus, and partly because it allows us to incorporate a lion as requested by Stephanus, we have decided to reprise the story of Hercules and his twelve labours. This will involve several animals, including a lion, a boar, horses, a deer and a bull, as well as multiple gladiators dressed as animals. In short, we will be in need of a bestiarius, accustomed to fighting wild animals.

"Carpophorus would love it," I say. "How is he these days? Enjoying his retirement?"

"Bored," says Marcus. "He never really wanted to stop. I've heard he hangs around the barracks at the Ludus Magnus half the time, chatting to old friends and even taking part in the training though he doesn't need to. He could be at home in his villa enjoying the attention of his wife and any handy slave girls, eating fine dishes, but instead he's eating barley porridge and swinging a wooden sword at a pole."

"He does private events, doesn't he? Could we use him again?"

Marcus looks interested. "It's a good idea. No one takes down an animal like Carpophorus and since he's kept himself in trim, perhaps we can use him. Have a word."

I find Carpophorus, as promised, in the Ludus Magnus. He's showing a group of new young bestiarii exactly how to approach killing a bull, with a rickety wooden model which looks pathetically puny next to Carpophorus' rippling bulk.

"Don't let it keep its head up,' he explains. "You drop your left arm, see, nice big movement so it lowers its head to charge at you." He nods to an assistant who pushes the model's head downwards. "Now you can get at its shoulders, you need to drive your sword between the shoulder blades, see, and that kills it nice and quick. You step right and to the side, else it'll fall on top of you, and you'll be dead as well as the bull."

The new recruits look appalled at how casually Carpophorus is demonstrating a move which puts his life at risk and needs to be completed in the time it takes to breathe in, yet he acts as though he has all the time in the world.

"Carpophorus," I say. "How are you?"

"Althea! Move, you lot, that's the right-hand woman and wife of the manager of the Flavian Amphitheatre, that is. Mind your manners, she's a good friend of mine."

He embraces me and pats me on the back, which would knock me over, were he not holding me in place with his other arm. Winded, I emerge smiling.

"Drink?" he asks and when I nod he waves a slave over. "Wine," he instructs them and escorts me to a wooden bench.

"How's married life going?" he says.

"Very well."

"Marcus treating you right, I hope."

"He is."

"Ah, he's a good man, Marcus, honest. Honourable." His smile fades. "I still think of Funis," he says. "Haven't forgotten him."

I pat his hand. "We none of us will forget him."

"He was one of us," he says, his face solemn.

I nod. "He thought well of you," I say. "Said he'd never seen a finer bestiarius." Carpophorus glows.

"Are you enjoying retirement?" I ask.

"Of course," he says heartily. "All those years I fought, got my fair share of scars but retired safe and sound, got my wooden sword from the Emperor himself, got a nice villa over in the smart area, good wife. I'm a lucky man."

"I'm speaking out of turn," I say. "I was going to ask if I could coax you out of retirement for one very special event, but I don't want to spoil your comfortable life, you've earnt it."

He narrows his eyes. "What sort of special event?"

I shrug. "At Domitian's villa. He has a five-hundred-seat amphitheatre in the Alban Hills, wants a spectacle putting on. Marcus and I, we thought of Hercules and his twelve labours, something showy. But we need a top bestiarius for that and we couldn't think of anyone good enough since you've retired. Perhaps you can point me to some young man who might do at a pinch? We can make it easier for him, there are ways..."

But as I hoped, Carpophorus' eyes have lit up. "You can't have some second-rate show for Domitian," he says, leaning towards me. "It wouldn't be right. I mean you got to kill the lion and the boar and the bull at the very least and I'm not sure who I'd recommend for that. I know a good lad who's handy with a boar, but he'll get worn out after that. Won't be able to carry off all three in one evening and you can't have Hercules being eaten by a lion, can you? Ruin the whole show."

"I'm a bit worried," I say. "We can't have something that isn't truly spectacular for the Emperor. I wish you'd consider coming out of retirement for me, but you've earnt the rest."

"I'd do it for you and Marcus," he says, "as a favour, I mean I wouldn't do it for anyone, but... Domitian's private villa..." His eyes are shining with enthusiasm.

"Would you?" I ask, one hand on his bulky arm. "We'd be so thrilled. Domitian would be delighted. Everyone would be. And you could take on all the animals and keep going."

He rolls his shoulders. "Might have to get back to my training," he says, looking down at his bulging biceps as though they are embarrassingly puny. "Lost a bit of my full physique. How long till the event?"

"End of the month," I say.

"I'll be in shape by then," he promises me.

"You're making Marcus and me very happy," I say and smile to myself as I watch him strut over to the training area with a new-found swagger in his step.

Our star secured, we hurry along with the rest of the preparations.

"So that's the main part of the show," says Marcus. "And what are we doing for the opening act, something lighter?"

"Acrobats? A tightrope walker?"

Marcus nods. "What's the story?"

"Arachne and Minerva?"

"Good. Have a structure built for them, something we can assemble and take apart easily."

When they do a simple tightrope walk from one place to another, acrobats use a structure of two triangular posts at each side, a rope between them, but having seen the velarium I talk to our carpenters and the acrobat who will perform and we create something more complex, a five-sided structure with a web of ropes passing between the poles, so that the acrobat can go not just back and forth but across to multiple points. Our costumiers create a costume for her according to my instructions and we are ready; the structure and costume are packed up ready for our departure.

Twenty carts set off three days before Marcus and I will follow. Their task is to settle in, calm the animals and prepare things like the acrobat's structure. We will arrive to put the finishing touches on the event and manage it as it plays out in front of Domitian and his guests.

We wave off the procession. The carts contain the acrobat and her structure, a giant from Labeo's school, a lion, musicians and singers, Carpophorus and a whole crew of gladiators and gladiatrices, piles of costumes and armour, as well as a comedian and various slaves who will take care of everyone while we are away. There are additional animals as well, a bull, a deer, snakes, horses and cattle who can walk by themselves which helps, over a hundred white ibis birds and a wild boar with ferocious tusks.

Marcus nods with satisfaction. "They'll take two days to get there, so they'll have a day to settle in before we arrive. Then the performance. We'll travel home the same way, but with fewer animals to transport."

Marcus and I plan to leave the insula well before dawn. When the day comes, Karbo has made ready the cart and horses. We remind him to keep the birds fed and wave to Maria, already in her watching spot. Julia and Adah as well as the rest of the inhabitants are not yet awake, though Cassia is lighting her fire and offers us a bowl of barley porridge if we want it, but we have packed food for the journey so as not to slow our progress. The Alban Hills are to the southeast of Rome, set high above the sea and will take most of the day to reach.

"Sleep," says Marcus, gesturing towards the back of the cart where he has laid out sleeping mats and blankets. I huddle under them, glad of the warmth. At first the jolting of the cart keeps me awake, but after a while tiredness overtakes me and when I open my eyes again it is broad daylight and we are in the countryside, Rome's walls well behind us.

"We can cover a lot of ground this morning," says Marcus when I join him to sit up front. "Once we get to the hills we'll have to go more slowly."

"I've never been there," I say.

"Seen them once," he says. "Lots of important rich people have villas up there, it's cooler in the summers to be in the green hills with a lake nearby and a sea breeze than being stuck in Rome when the heat and smell is unbearable."

"How close is it to the sea?"

"Not close enough to visit every day, but you can see it in the distance. Lake Alban is better for swimming. Much cooler."

It takes another few hours of slow travel but at last we spot the villa on the hilltop and come to a stop nearby. The location is extraordinary. Vibrant green surrounds us, thick woods and lush mountain pastures. Used to Rome's bustling streets, I find the green in every direction almost too much to take in. Marcus is right, even on a hot day, there is a refreshing breeze.

"Welcome to Albanum Domitiani," a voice calls out.

We turn to see Domitian's architect Rabirius standing among a small grove of trees, his large owl-like eyes observing us with interest. His ruffled hair is even more scruffy than the last time I saw him although on this occasion he is not holding armfuls of scrolls, just a tablet like my own.

"Good to see you again," says Marcus, jumping down from the cart and holding up his hand to help me down.

"I am not sure you were pleased to see me when we were building the hypogeum at the amphitheatre," says Rabirius.

Marcus shrugs. "It was not something we wanted while we tried to put on the Games," he says. "But it's done now."

"I hear congratulations are in order," says Rabirius, nodding at me. "May Juno bless your marriage."

"Thank you," I say. "Did you design the villa here?"

"Indeed. It is a very large project and still ongoing. Would you like to see the grounds?"

"Thank you," says Marcus, handing the reins to a slave boy who has appeared at his side.

"So there is the villa, built around three central courtyards, set on the second of three terraces, commanding views of both the sea and the lake. A bathing complex to one side. The lake has its own docks, for ease of use, as you can see." He points.

"They're having a boating party by the looks of it," says Marcus.

I look to where he is pointing and there are a dozen pleasure boats being rowed around the lake, even from here I can see the bright parasols of the ladies in the party.

"The Emperor is fond of taking his guests boating. There is also an archery grove close to the lakeshore, he is very intent on practising his skills with a bow. If you follow me I will show you the stadium and the theatre."

"Stadium?" asks Marcus.

"Indeed," says Rabirius, as though the erection of a racing stadium were a common part of building a villa. "The Emperor is very fond of chariot races and now that we have undertaken so many construction projects related to the Games he is turning his attention to the races. We will be creating a stadium in Rome in the Ninth Region, as well as the one here for his own private entertainment."

"We live in the Ninth," I say.

He nods. "He is adding two new teams to the stables, Purple and Gold."

"Our son Karbo will be racing for the Purple team," I say, unable to stop a bubble of pride at being able to say this, even though the thought of him racing still frightens me.

"The path to the theatre," says Rabirius, waving ahead.

There is a vast avenue ahead, lined with still-young trees on one side, on the other with a high wall set into the hillside in which domed niches house statues of the gods painted in bright colours. I spot Minerva in a prominent position and nod to myself; we made a good choice by including her in the show.

"I'm surprised all of this has been done so fast," I say.

Rabirius nods. "The Emperor was keen to have his own residence made ready as soon as possible. He does not like the heat of the summers in Rome and is sensitive to extremes of temperature. The cooler air here suits him better, he says he can think better."

I wonder whether it helps him keep a cooler temper, but say nothing.

"The racing stadium is there." Rabirius indicates the site ahead.

It is still being built, but the shape of it has been marked out already. Seating is being constructed on one side, using the hillside to make the views evenly raked, looking down onto the elongated oval of the track, with three obelisks down the middle. The ground is still freshly cleared. Though it has not yet been compacted and made smooth for the chariots, it is close to completion.

"We think it may be usable this autumn, before the winter comes," says Rabirius.

The amphitheatre, when we come to it, is beautiful. It is set into the hillside, with five hundred marble-lined seats and the glittering lake and green hills as a natural backdrop. There is a frieze rising above the seating area at the back, depicting tributes to the Flavian dynasty's achievements, including references to Titus' generosity in aiding refugees from Pompeii and Herculaneum and theatrical images of gladiators, dancers, venatores and animals. Marcus' eyes rest briefly on the image of Pompeii before he looks away. Down the balustrades are decorative sculptures of actors' masks and dolphins and there is a space for the musicians and singers to stand so that their music and songs or speech can be heard well across the space. The velarium here is dyed imperial purple and has been beautifully painted with black silhouettes of animals; elephants, lions, giraffes, their unusual shapes lending themselves well to the silhouette-work.

"Very nice," says Marcus, looking around the arena space, which is ample for our planned performances.

"You would like to see the performance barracks, of course," Rabirius says.

Hidden behind a grove of trees close by, so as not to spoil the views, are two long low buildings, one for the animals, locked safely into their cages and pens, one for humans, which includes sleeping and cooking and eating quarters, simple but functional. Rabirius leaves us there, wandering back towards the stadium. Our crew is waiting, everything has been set up in our absence, ready for tomorrow's spectacle.

We have decided that the show should take place at night, complete with shining stars in the dark sky, since we have a location where it will be safe for the audience to return to their beds without risking Rome's dangerous streets.

"Only regular wolves round here at night, eh," says the comedian. "No she-wolves looking for their next customer."

We eat a simple meal of barley porridge, the standard food cooked for gladiators. It's a boring diet compared to Cassia's food, she knows how to turn the simplest ingredients into something delicious. Then it is time to sleep, rows of us laid out on sleeping mats. There is little need for blankets at this time of year, even if the hills are cooler than the city, we sleep in our clothes.

When the day breaks we start to prepare. Some people swim in the lake, I use a bowl of water to wash myself and comb my hair. I hang up my best tunic and headwrap to make them less wrinkled for the evening and wear the tunic I wore yesterday to do my rounds.

The animals look well. Most are being kept hungry, so they are keener to do battle, others like the horses and cattle are well fed to ensure they are docile. I check them off my sheet, watch the acrobat doing her exercises for the day and the gladiators likewise.

We send ten of the slaves off to erect the acrobatic structure at the amphitheatre and dispatch more slaves to scatter sand on the arena floor. The costumes are shaken out and hung up, the armour given a final polish. We eat a hasty lunch of bread and cheese, then erect a large screen of woven branches decorated with grass and flowers. This will be our hypogeum, the space from where we can direct the Games.

The darkness will be our friend, we will fade into the night unless we come close to the edge of the arena.

The light is fading and torches are being lit all around the arena. I check that the floor is well-sanded, then that the ropes for the acrobat's structure have been hidden below the sand, to be revealed when we give the signal.

Slaves are laying out cushions so that Domitian and his guests need not chill their behinds. Aromatic incense is burning, to scent the air and keep away biting insects.

Marcus and I return to the barracks to dress and the animals are brought over in their wheeled cages.

We gather the team, everyone dressed in their costumes or armour. The animal handlers stand by the cages and soon we hear the murmur of many people and see flickering torches heading our way.

"Our audience," says Marcus. "May Jupiter watch over us and bless these Games."

Along the avenue comes a procession of a few hundred people, at their head Domitian and Domitia, flanked by guards and torch bearers, behind them their guests, more guards and torch bearers. They start to take their places. I spot several consuls, senators, and other important men, along with their wives, whose clothes make my best clothes look like those of a slave girl. Their jewellery glitters. Tonight is a chance to show off, to prove they are the elite of Rome, invited specially here to Domitian's own villa. Many of them have or are building their own villas in the area, keen to be seen as neighbours, as people who have the same taste and style as the Emperor. They will mention this evening when they return to Rome, of course, will drop it into conversations that are entirely unrelated and then raise an eyebrow when their friends have to confess they were not there, hurry to reassure them that of course, it does not mean *anything* not to have been invited, it means nothing at all… it was just an event between friends, nothing special at all. Oh yes, of course, there was *some* entertainment, the team from the Flavian Amphitheatre put on a little something, Carpophorus came out of retirement… and they will bask in their elevated status.

Amongst the crowd, I spot Stephanus, seated slightly behind and to the right of Domitian. As always he is well-blended into the background, drawing no attention to himself. But my stomach rolls over at the sight of the man sitting three seats away. Funis' father, the man who had his own son murdered because he was ashamed of him.

"What is that man's name?" I whisper to the comedian. It's the job of comedians to know all the famous faces of Rome, so that they can satirise them or outright mock them.

"Manius Acilius Glabrio. Consul."

My teeth grit together. This man is a consul? A man with no honour, no decency? Next to him is a richly dressed woman, who is adjusting her necklace and brooches, preening to ensure she appears at her very best.

"His wife Priscilla," says the comedian. "They had one son, but no other children."

I look away. Only one legitimate son, perhaps, but there was another and now he is gone.

Our musicians are playing a well-known tune, the singers sing as the audience gradually settles themselves under Marcus' watchful eye. At last he nods and the chorus steps forwards, the music softens so that they can be heard, the audience grows quiet.

"There was once a mortal woman named Arachne," they begin. "She was a most excellent spinner and weaver, but alas, she was also boastful and in her arrogance she claimed that she could out-weave the goddess of weaving herself, Minerva."

The acrobat portraying Arachne dances about the stage, while all around her spin whirling dancers draped with embroidered and woven cloths in bright colours, supposedly her creations.

I glance at Domitian, who is happily nodding to himself. Minerva being the goddess to whom he is most devoted, he will know this story well and appreciate the importance of respecting the deity which the story emphasises.

"So often and so loudly did she boast that Minerva herself heard her, and she was angered. She appeared before Arachne and challenged her to a weaving contest. Rather than fall to her knees and beg for forgiveness, as would have been wise, foolish Arachne agreed and the date was set for one month hence."

Minerva descends into the arena, clad in a white tunic and golden diadem and shoes to indicate her status. She points towards Arachne and her dancers, who shift across to the other side of the stage.

The story continues with each woman undertaking an intricate dance, showing that Minerva wove the images of each Olympian in all their glory and the outcome of Minerva fighting Neptune for control of Athens. But when she is done and it is the mortal's turn, Arachne takes each Olympian and shows them lust-ridden rather than glorious, each transforming into an animal in order to satiate their desires.

Minerva, furious, holds out her arms and from the arena's sand, pulled by many hands, appears a tight-woven spider's web that dwarfs the spectators and performers alike, rising high above us all, hidden hands winching it and securing the ropes into place across the five platforms.

"So enraged was Minerva with Arachne's arrogance and disrespect for the gods that she cursed her, transforming her human shape into that of a spider: forever able to weave exquisite webs, forever despised and silenced."

Shedding her bright dress, Arachne displays a tightly shaped and multi-legged black costume, climbs up through the webbing, dangling above our heads from first one foot and then the other before pulling herself up and walking across the ropes in an acrobatic display while Minerva, arms crossed, watches her with satisfaction as the chorus completes the story.

Domitian dismisses the Arachne-spider with a smiling gesture and she swings from rope to rope until she disappears from view through one of the seating areas. He crowns the Minerva dancer with golden laurels, bowing his head to her as though in tribute to the real goddess.

"That went well," says Marcus with satisfaction. "He seems in a good mood. On with Hercules."

In order to end on the spectacular scene of Carpophorous battling with a lion, we have reversed the order of the labours. The slaves extinguish all the torches so that the audience is plunged into darkness and the chorus speaks, first laying out the birth of Hercules and his angering of Juno, before he begins his tasks, in penance to the goddess.

"Hercules was called upon to visit Hades, the land of the dead, and to fight Cerberus, a deadly three-headed dog."

Carpophorus enters and is greeted with a huge round of applause and much cheering. Holding a burning torch, he peers into the darkness, from which a baying comes, before three gladiators creep towards him, all dressed in black, only their shining metal, dog-head shaped helmets visible to us. The effect is frightening, some of the ladies in the audience squeal, though whether at the mythical beast or Carpophorus' rippling muscles and bare chest, it's hard to tell.

The fight is savage, fast, the chorus bays and howls as Carpophorus dispatches the beast, each gladiator throwing down his helmet as Hercules slices off each head, fading back into the darkness.

Labeo's giant stands in for Atlas in the next task, Hercules taking the weight of the world from his shoulders while Atlas brings back the golden apples of Zeus, then tricking the giant into taking back the heavy burden. Carpophorus takes his time distributing the basket of gilded apples to various ladies in the crowd, leaving the last and best for Domitian's wife Domitia, who accepts, smiling.

He battles monsters for a herd of cattle, before a tribe of Amazons attack him, their Queen Hippolyta offering up her magic belt after succumbing to his sword and charms, a scene watched with interest by men and women alike, for our Amazons are bare-breasted and the clinch between Carpophorus-Hercules and the gladiatrix-Hippolyta is passionate.

Hercules' journey continues, taming four glorious horses and fixing them to his chariot for a victory parade round the arena, before we release a vast black bull, enough to terrify any bestiarius, but a bull is nothing to Carpophorus, who leaps from the chariot and kills the beast with only his sword, all alone in the arena, to deafening applause.

We release over one hundred ibis for the Stymphalian birds, and our Hercules, with the aid of additional hidden archers, shoots them down in droves, their white bodies falling out of the darkness.

This leaves us with an arena full of birds and bloodied sand, so it is the turn of a mock-Hercules to take the stage, our comedian, who pretends to be Carpophorus being Hercules cleaning the stables of Augeas, with a lot of showing off his muscles, admiring his reflection in a well-polished shovel and winking at the ladies, which has the audience in fits of laughter.

"It's going well," says Marcus. The tension is leaving him, he has put on a good spectacle and we are one task closer to leaving Domitian's employ and Rome. I nod, although I can't rest easy until the lion scene has come and gone without event.

The arena clean and fresh sand strewn, it's time for the Erymanthian boar. A huge wild boar is released and despatched with aplomb by Carpophorus. I have to admire his bravery, it's harrowing to watch a single man face such large and aggressive creatures all alone.

Now Hercules must kill a deer sacred to Diana. The deer, its hooves and horns painted gold, bounds into the arena and Carpophorus pretends to kill it with the aid of some of the illusionist's tricks and fake blood, before falling to his knees as Diana descends. Learning of his quest, she forgives him and brings the "dead" deer back to life, allowing Carpophorus-Hercules to carry it over his shoulders in triumph at completing another task.

The eleventh task sees Hercules seeking to defeat the nine-headed water snake, the Hydra. Here Carpophorus battles nine gladiators dressed as snakes, but with the addition of nine real snakes, cobras we have had brought from Egypt to kill as well. For each gladiator he battles he must also kill a snake and the cobras are truly frightening, raising up their hooded heads to hiss at Carpophorus as he approaches each one, striking at him as he strikes at them, the audience screaming and cheering him on. We have kept the largest and most aggressive one for last and I clutch at Marcus' arm when it strikes at Carpophorus while he has half-turned away. But he catches the movement in time, whirls to protect himself and the cobra's head lies in the sand, tongue still flickering in its death throes. Domitian is on his feet, Domitia is screaming, the whole audience rises with them and Carpophorus takes a bow.

"He can't top that," yells someone.

But the audience is aware of what is missing from the twelve famous tasks, they know that we have yet to show them a lion, Hercules' most famous task. They chant Carpophorus' name and stamp their feet, excited to watch the final task take place.

The musicians start a low soft melody while the chorus tells of the Nemean Lion, a savage beast whom Hercules met in battle armed just with a club. And back into the arena strides Carpophorus, naked to the waist, carrying only a heavy club. He spends time posturing around the arena so that the audience can admire his muscles and powerful physique, while the musicians build the tension.

Marcus is about to lift his hand to release the lion from its cage, when Domitian stands and holds up his own hand.

The chorus and musicians come to an uncertain, stuttering stop, trying to look at both Marcus and Domitian at the same time, a difficult task. The audience is silent, craning their necks to get a good view of Domitian, wondering what is going on.

"I salute Carpophorus, a mighty bestiarius and one who has pleased us greatly this evening," says Domitian, throwing a laurel wreath towards Carpophorus. There's a ready round of applause. Carpophorus, confused, picks up the wreath and bows his head in gratitude but glances over his shoulder to get further instructions from Marcus, who gives a small shrug and shake of his head, awaiting clarity from Domitian. The audience is also looking towards the emperor, wondering what is going on. The benevolent gesture is expected, but not before the big moment of the show. Why would it not be given after the fight with the lion?

"However, I think he should leave the arena and allow another man to take his place and complete the story of Hercules."

The crowd murmurs, uncertain of where this is going. Marcus shakes his head, a deep frown on his face. For one terrifying moment I think Domitian will ask Marcus to step into the arena, as punishment for daring to want to leave imperial service. I clutch at his arm and he looks at me, confused.

"Step forward, Manius Acilius Glabrio," says Domitian.

There's utter silence. I can hear Marcus breathing, my own heart pounding. The Consul – Funis' father – does not move.

"Come, come," says Domitian. "Don't be shy, Glabrio. You are a strong man. A lion can be nothing to you, surely?"

The lion we have brought here is a magnificent beast that would stand above any man's waist, its teeth and claws are hungry for the food it has been denied for days, I can hear it behind me, pacing in its cage, ready to fight anyone, given a chance.

"Glabrio!" Domitian is no longer smiling, no longer coaxing. It is a command. The consul's face changes as he realises this is no joke, that he is about to be thrown into the arena in front of his peers, his wife, his emperor. He will have to fight a real lion. He has seen our animals, they have all been strong and powerful beasts, not weak or sick to make life easy for our Hercules. Only an experienced bestiarius like Carpophorus could have taken them on. An ordinary man has no chance against a lion.

Glabrio stands and his wife Priscilla gives a low moan, clutches at his hand, but he pulls away from her. I watch as he makes his way down the amphitheatre, step by slow step, each person whom he brushes against leaning to one side in fear of being tainted by his very touch. His arms seem well muscled, he is not portly like many of the senators. But as he reaches Carpophorus the comparison between them is absurd.

Glabrio holds out his hand, which is shaking, and Carpophorus puts his club into it, eyes flicking to Domitian for permission. Domitian inclines his head, then takes his seat again, crossing his legs and leaning back as though about to do nothing more serious than command a dancer to perform.

"May I know why I am thus called on, Imperator?" asks Glabrio. His voice remains steady, and for a brief moment I admire his courage.

"For conspiring against the empire," says Domitian pleasantly.

"May I refute the accusation?"

"No," says Domitian, still calm. "I call on our Manager of the Games to release the lion of Nemea. Carpophorus, you are dismissed."

Carpophorus, now without a weapon, steps backwards until he reaches us.

"I didn't know what else to do," he hisses to Marcus.

"You did the right thing," whispers back Marcus. "Now keep out of the way. No, wait. Get a sword and get the other men to stand by. This could go very wrong."

Behind me, Carpophorus and the other gladiators gather, their swords unsheathed. Having a lion in the arena is perilous in such a small amphitheatre, it takes an experienced bestiarius to keep its attention on himself and not let it charge towards the audience. This arena has fewer safety features than the Flavian Amphitheatre, where it is very hard for a dangerous animal to get into the audience.

Priscilla has hurried down the steps after her husband, now she throws herself on the arena floor in front of Domitian. "I beg for your mercy, Imperator," she cries out.

"I *am* merciful," points out Domitian as though she is unreasonable in accusing him of any lack of feeling. "I'm allowing your husband to fight for his life. I could just have had him executed for treason."

She stares up at him aghast, tears running down her face, but he waves her away.

"You're blocking my view," he says. "And I think you are in a position of danger, being in the arena when they're about to let loose a lion. I would return to your seat."

She looks over her shoulder at her husband, who nods, face tight with tension. She staggers to her feet and stumbles back to her seat, face white and shocked in the torchlight.

Glabrio removes his toga, gathers the heavy parcel of fabric in his left hand and flings it away from him, keeping the club in his right hand. The last time I saw him I pressed my bloodied hands against his toga, staining it with the blood of his murdered son Funis, wanting to proclaim his guilt. He deserves what is coming. He does deserve it. But still I feel sick at the idea of what we are about to witness. Behind me, there is a growl from the caged lion.

I step out from behind the screen, to the side, where I stand in the darkness and look towards Stephanus. He should not be able to see me in the dark, but perhaps he catches the movement, because his eyes turn towards me. His face does not change expression, but he gives a slow nod and I know, as though he had spoken the words aloud, that this is the justice I requested for Funis' death; a terrible revenge that has now been set in motion, which I cannot stop even if I wanted to.

Domitian nods approval at Glabrio's removal of his toga. He stands in his tunic, club in hand, expression fixed.

"Our hero is ready," Domitian announces. He waves a hand at the chorus. "Continue with the story."

The musicians begin the music prepared for this moment, a dramatic piece which will build to a crescendo as the fight goes on.

The chorus begin to speak, their voices hesitant at first. "The Lion of Nemea was covered in a golden fur, which could not be penetrated by any arrow, no, nor by any sword. And so Hercules took with him only a club and the local villagers prayed for him, believing that he would soon be killed, as so many brave men had been before him."

I turn to the side, where I can see Marcus. He hesitates, but in this moment he has no choice. He gives an abrupt nod and the handler pulls back the bolt of the lion's cage. Two slaves pull on ropes and the cage door flies open.

There is a moment's pause. Glabrio has turned towards the sound of the bolt and all of us hold our breath – and then the lion charges out of the cage and onto the arena floor, where it crouches down, its eyes focused on Glabrio. Its growl shakes the floor and Priscilla screams, but the lion is not distracted by her, all its attention is on Glabrio, who is standing his ground, the club held out to one side.

The lion leaps. It extends to its full length, claws outstretched, jaws open, its pointed teeth exposed. Glabrio brings his club swinging round and up above him, hitting it squarely on the side of the head even as one of its paws slashes across his chest, the tunic ripped away, blood trickling down towards his legs as the lion, furious with pain at the unexpected blow, whirls round and attacks again, slashing at Glabrio's legs as it roars. But the club falls twice more in quick succession and now the lion is hurt, one eye bleeding, its jaw thrown out of alignment. It roars again and swipes but Glabrio closes in on it, the club hitting the wounded animal again and again, crushing its skull until it lies, broken and bleeding on the sand, legs twitching. Glabrio is covered in blood and panting, he falls to his knees, dropping the club by his side, crumpling into a heap on the sand.

The night is silent, broken only by Priscilla's sobs, still in her seat, too afraid to go to her bleeding husband.

Domitian uncrosses his legs and leans forwards, staring at Glabrio. Behind him, Stephanus leans forwards and whispers something to which Domitian nods, then stands.

"Who knew our consul was a bestiarius, after all?"

Silence.

"Rise, Glabrio."

Glabrio stumbles to his feet. He's bleeding and his legs shake under him.

"Bravely done, I suppose," says Domitian. "Although, and this may seem unkind, given your display of courage, but I believe a consul should not also be a bestiarius. It brings Rome's empire into disrepute, and we can't be having that. So, you will resign your post and go into exile. I assume you have some place in the country in which you can go and live a quiet life?"

Glabrio, swaying on his feet, drops his head to his chest.

"Excellent," says Domitian. "Then I think we fully understand one another and it is time for all of us to withdraw for the night. A warm nightcap will be served back at the villa before we retire to the bedrooms. And of course, I was forgetting:

a round of applause for a wonderful evening of Games. We thank the team of the Flavian Amphitheatre and all their performers." He begins clapping his hands and the audience, stunned and terrified at what they have witnessed, hurry to copy him. Glabrio, alone in the arena, the dead lion at his feet, stands still and silent as Domitian graciously offers his hand to Domitia and leads her away, the audience filing out after them in abject silence, the arena growing darker as many of the torch-bearers depart with them. Only Priscilla remains, she stumbles down the steps and throws her arms about Glabrio, who slumps against her, his blood staining her silks. They set off in the dark, he staggering, she trying to support him, following far behind the distant bobbing torches. The amphitheatre is empty, the lion lies in a pool of its own blood and Glabrio's.

Marcus pushes aside the screen and steps into the arena, followed by the lion handler, who kneels to check the beast is dead, then nods. The gladiators and gladiatrices, swords in hand, step forwards, slowly put away their weapons as Marcus checks there is no-one else left, only our own team.

"I'd advise everyone who witnessed this to keep quiet and not gossip about it," he says at last and there are silent nods. "Whatever went on to lead up to that moment, we cannot be sure if Domitian will do more of the same or if he may regret his actions. Either way, it would be best if gossip did not spread from us about this affair. We cannot know whether Glabrio will be recalled from exile and continue to be a powerful man in Rome or not." He takes a deep breath and blows it out again. "Enough. We are all tired, it has been a long evening. We will sleep, and tomorrow we will pack up and leave as soon as it is dawn. With any luck most of us will be back in Rome by nightfall. We can use the horses to speed up our progress and the cattle can be loaded into some of the pens of the animals who are dead, it will be faster than walking them all back. I want all of you out of here as soon as possible."

There is no further talk, everyone finds their beds and sleeps and the next morning all our items and the animals are rapidly packed up, our carts leaving the villa's grounds before the first birds sing, the sun not yet risen. None of us look back.

We say very little on the way home. The hours trundle by as we leave countryside behind us and return to the outskirts of Rome, Marcus and I eat some bread and cheese as we travel, without stopping to rest. Behind us the other carts are also quiet, I cannot hear chatter. Late in the afternoon we finally come back to Rome's walls, allowing the different carts to go their own ways once we are through the gate; most back to our warehouses by the docks, others to their own gladiatorial schools. When we get home Karbo takes the horses and cart for us. We wave away excited questions with promises to tell all about the villa and performing for Domitian tomorrow, and escape upstairs to bed.

Lying in the dark, Marcus lets out a shuddering breath. "I'm afraid," he confesses, voice low. "Losing his temper over us trying to leave his service, throwing people who speak ill of him to the lions, how is Rome to survive if he gets worse?"

I clasp his hand. "Glabrio might have been Stephanus' idea."

"What? Why?"

I tell him about Glabrio being Funis' father, how Stephanus seemed to have a plan for him, that I didn't know what it was until it was underway. Marcus is quiet for a while.

"It's possible that's what happened," he says at last. "Domitian was already pointing the finger at people whom he suspected of not being loyal enough to him and it sounds as though Stephanus just added Glabrio to the list. But Domitian is still acting strangely."

I am still shaken by what happened when we wake in the morning. We give a brief account of the villa, amphitheatre and show to those who ask, but we do not go into detail about what happened at the end. We leave it to others to gossip about the Emperor of Rome and his mental state, we do not wish to find ourselves in trouble because of people hearing what happened and the tale being traced back to us.

I am unsure how I feel about Stephanus. Is he trustworthy, or as strange as the Emperor? What he did, and I have no doubt that it was he who at least suggested it to Domitian, was an act of madness, yet there is a tiny part of me that feels justice was done as he promised me, and cannot help but be glad that Funis was avenged, that his father, so scathing of his son being a beast hunter for the Flavian Amphitheatre, should know what it is to fight with the beasts of the arena, no better than a bestiarius, no better than his son in the end.

Marcus no longer trusts Domitian to take care of our crew when we are gone. He arranges pay rises for as many people as he can manage within the team, he orders further repairs and comforts to be added to the slave barracks, so that their living quarters will be better quality, he arranges for the oldest slaves to be freed and asks for new ones to be brought in, the public purse can stand it.

"We need a meal for guests," he tells me. "Something special?"

He has never asked for such a thing.

"Who are the guests?" I ask.

"Julia, Fabius and Fabia."

I laugh. "They're our friends," I say. "We eat bread and cheese with them. Is there a special occasion?"

"Yes. But it's a secret."

"You can't have secrets from me, I'm your wife," I protest.

"It is a happy secret," he says. "Make a special meal? We'll eat on the rooftop under the pergola."

I cheat by using both Cassia, who fries a batch of her saltfish fritters, and the bakery, where I get oil-rich bread strewn with herbs and olives. To this I add a large salad flavoured with mint and thyme with cubes of fresh cheese, a basket of plums and cherries and little cakes made with soft cheese, honey and poppyseeds. I enlist Karbo to help me carry up a table and some chairs, as well as wine and jugs of water. We set everything up under the pergola, so that we are shaded from the rays of the sun but can enjoy the long warm evening.

"There," I say, putting down a vase of flowers. "A table fit for a feast."

"Why is it a special occasion?" asks Karbo.

"We'll have to wait till Marcus deigns to tell us."

Julia comes upstairs and spends some time with the nightingales, then takes a seat at the table. She looks pale for the height of summer.

"Are you well, Julia?"

"Oh, a little tired," she says. "The delivery carts coming into Rome wake me far too early most days, I sleep lightly."

Fabius arrives. "A beautiful table, Althea," he says. "And I smell good food."

"What is this special occasion?" I ask. "Or are you sworn to secrecy?"

He smiles and puts a finger to his lips. "All in good time."

"Your eyes are twinkling," I say. "I am beginning to think there is mischief afoot."

"Let us say it is a happy occasion," he says.

"That's what Marcus said," I say.

"Here I am," says Fabia, appearing round the corner of our roof hut. She is wearing a blue tunic with slashed shoulders held in place with little brooches and a green woven belt.

"You're so elegant," I tell her, stooping to embrace her little frame.

"Father said it was an important day," she says, then lowers her voice so only I can hear her. "Are we about to get good news?" she asks, nodding in the direction of my belly.

I giggle. "No!"

"I don't know what all this is about then," she says. "But I am hungry, tell me you have lots of food. I only grabbed a bread roll this morning and never got round to lunch."

"Lots," I assure her. "Come and sit down. You should get your assistant to ensure you get proper meals."

She laughs. "She follows me about telling me I need food, then I wave her off to go and eat her own meal while I make notes on my patients."

We settle around the table and begin the meal. I pour wine for everyone and pass dishes back and forth, keeping an eye on Marcus, waiting for him to reveal the purpose of the event.

"I have an announcement," says Fabius.

We all wait.

"I am retiring as physician to the amphitheatre."

I gape at him. "You can't!" I say. "The Games are in full season! And why would you, I thought you liked the work?"

"I do," he says smiling. "But my hands work against me."

"Your hands?"

He lifts them and I see what I have not before, that his long fingers are shaking slightly, a tiny tremor. "Not steady enough for surgery," he says.

"I'm sorry," I say.

"So was I," he admits. "It was a hard truth to accept. I have seen it before in other men, and though it begins gently enough, the shakiness grows over time and most tasks become hard in the end."

"That's why you were grumpy," I say.

"It is," he says. "I confided in Julia and she advised me to tell Marcus, I did not want to lose a good gladiator from some slip of the fingers because of my pride."

Marcus pours more wine for everyone. "I told him it was still early days. That he was more than able to finish this season and whoever comes after us can have the task of finding themselves a new physician. But I had a better idea."

Next to me, Fabia slowly lowers her cup of wine. I can feel her little body tense up, her eyes are downcast, fixed on the food in front of her, which she has stopped eating.

"You've chosen a new physician?" I ask, my heart beating faster. I hope that Marcus means Fabia, but he may have in mind some other person. If he does, Fabia, ambitious to be a great physician, will be crushed. I hardly dare look Marcus in the eyes, but when I do he winks at me, a smile twitching in the corner of his mouth. I hold my breath.

"Yes," he says. "I have found an excellent replacement. A physician of great stature here in Rome, with experience in the field and excellent skills. Fabius agrees with me, he has examined their work personally and recommended them for the role." He pauses, though my eyes are pleading with him to hurry and say the name I am hoping for.

"The only trouble is that of course, being so well qualified, they are already taken," says Marcus and Fabia takes in a little gasp of air, a half-sob.

I shake my head at him. "Don't."

He laughs out loud, a big warm laugh, and reaches out his hand across the table to Fabia. "Fabia Papirius, will you take on the role of physician to the Flavian Amphitheatre?"

Fabia raises her face to reveal both a wide smile and trickling tears, which she wipes away with one hand while taking Marcus' hand with the other and nodding fervently.

"Ah, Fabia," says her father, his own eyes glistening. "You could not have thought I would have recommended anyone else."

Marcus lets go of Fabia's hand and comes round to the other side of the table, his tall frame stooping over to embrace her. "You're the best there is," he says. "If I can't have your father there for old times' sake, you're the only physician I'd pick for the amphitheatre. And I wanted to choose you and have you established before some idiot comes along to take my place who doesn't know anything and picks someone useless."

Fabia finally finds her voice. "I won't let you down," she gulps.

"You'll show us all up, more like," says Marcus. "Embrace your father, he's been desperate to tell you these past few months but I told him we had to get everything in place and that I wanted to celebrate with you when we told you. We've already settled everything with Labeo, he wasn't pleased to be losing you but there's a young physician showing some promise and your father will mentor him for the rest of the season to get him up to scratch, so we can take you right away. Your apprentice and assistant will also join you, of course."

We all take turns hugging Fabia and toast her repeatedly through the afternoon until we are all quite tipsy and need an early night.

"Blessings on you, Fabia," says Julia before she leaves, placing her hand on Fabia's curls. "You are a credit to your profession. May Aesculapius and Minerva give you skill and wisdom." She coughs as she leaves.

"You said your cough would be better by the warmer months," I say.

She waves her hand, already starting down the stairs. "It faded. This one is different. It will be gone soon, I have a tonic from Fabius."

"Meet me tomorrow at the imperial palace," Marcus tells Fabia. "You'll have to sign a contract."

"What if Domitian doesn't want me?" asks Fabia, suddenly sober at the thought.

"He's caused me enough trouble this past year," says Marcus. "It's my turn to make decisions that suit me and that includes having a female physician for the Flavian Amphitheatre."

The next morning, while Marcus takes Fabia to sign legal contracts, I send word for all her equipment and supplies to be brought from Labeo's to the amphitheatre and we re-arrange the medical bay to suit her height, one of our carpenters creating a wooden platform which runs the length of the bay so that she can reach everything she needs to, changing the shelving so that her supplies are lower down and she does not have to rely on anyone else to get what she needs. As physician to the amphitheatre, not only will she have her existing apprentice and assistant but three more assistants as well, but Fabia likes to be independent and when she arrives in the late morning and sees our work her smile is warm. She is glowing with pride at having realised her long-held ambition.

"Thank you for choosing Fabia," I say to Marcus, slipping an arm about his waist as we leave her to settle in. "Some men wouldn't have chosen her, wouldn't have wanted a woman. Or a dwarf."

He shrugs. "She's her father's equal," he says. "I wasn't being polite. What she did for Alyssa…"

I lean my head against him. "Thank you anyway," I say.

"We must care for our own amongst all this madness," he says.

THERE ARE TWO WEEKS TO go till the naumachia and it is time to fill the lake. We open up the aqueduct and water begins to flow. At first it appears somewhat pathetic, mostly draining away again.

"What if it doesn't work?" I ask Marcus, nervous. "What if we end up with a puddle and some mud?"

"Leave it a few days," he says, unflustered. "Then we'll see."

I want to visit daily, but Marcus shakes his head and keeps us away from the basin for four days. When we return, to my surprise the basin is two-thirds full. It is a murky muddy colour, however, not very attractive.

"The mud will settle," says Marcus. "You'll see. You always get mud after heavy rains and this is no different."

By the end of the week the basin is full and the water is beginning to clear. Marcus has a trireme and a quadrireme come through the canal and test rowing around the lake. It goes well, the canal is tight but not impossible and once on the lake they show remarkable speed and manoeuvrability.

"I didn't know they'd be so fast," I say.

"They won't be when there's lots of them," says Marcus. "That's why we'll do the parade first, it'll allow for some speed when we just have fifteen of them."

The water flow is carefully adjusted to allow the basin to stay topped up and the waters continue to clear. The naumachia is upon us.

THE STORM

ON THE EVE OF THE naumachia, I stand with Marcus on the edge of the newly made lake. No matter how annoying Domitian's extra tasks have been for us, nor how strange his behaviour, I can't help feeling pride at the sight before us. The deep blue July sky is reflected in the sparkling blue waters of the vast lake we have created from a patch of scruffy land, now surrounded by a smart high wall interspersed with sturdy gates enclosing neat wooden stands of seating. The pavement beneath our feet is pristine. A wooden bridge reaches out across the water to the central island, which is covered in grass and a multitude of flowers. There are even dragonflies skimming by, having scented the water and come to visit this new body of water. A crane stands on the northern shore, disappointed that the promising waters do not, after all, contain fish.

"Very impressive," I admit. "Do you think it will go well tomorrow?" I check the list on my tablet.

Marcus closes it and pushes my hand away. "Stop fretting," he says, smiling. "You've done everything that needed doing. The physicians and undertakers will be here first thing tomorrow to set up. The audience will arrive late morning, Domitian in the middle of the day. It'll be sunny. The biggest problem we'll have is people complaining there isn't a velarium and I don't care if they do. It's our last task. After this, there's only one month to go and we'll be closing the Games."

I WAKE AT DAWN, BUT Marcus has already gone. I hurry to pull on my tunic and shoes, then step out onto the roof terrace, shivering. Most mornings are warm enough, even in the dark, as there isn't time for the city to cool down before the sun's rays hit it again. But this morning there is a cold breeze, the sky is darker than it should be at this time. It's usually pale grey before the sun rises; this is a heavier colour, as though I have woken an hour earlier than usual. I shake my head and rub my arms, return to the roof hut to fetch my palla and wrap it about me. No doubt I will have to set it aside later, as the day's heat builds. I feed the birds, but the doves do not want to leave their shelter today, they huddle together and peck desultorily at the corn I offer. As I walk down the stairs I catch sight of Maria through her open door.

"It's going to rain," she calls to me, without any kind of greeting.

I walk to her door, where she's still fastening her belt.

"Rain?" I say, doubtful. "In July?"

She shakes her head. "I can feel it," she says, pointing downwards. "In my bones. My legs especially."

"But we never get rain in July," I say.

"I can feel it," says Maria, picking up her basket and following me down the stairs.

"I could do without it," I say. "It's the naumachia today."

"Be careful no-one capsizes," says Maria, about to turn right towards the bakery as I turn left to Cassia's popina.

"It won't be that bad," I say. "These are big ships. Mostly triremes and quadriremes. They're sea-going ships, not some little rowing boat for pleasure. They can take up to two hundred men on board. If anything, they're underloaded."

"Good luck," she calls over her shoulder. "May Jupiter be kind to you."

Cassia has a plate of sliced fruits ready for my breakfast and a cup of well-watered wine. Most days, the fruit is a refreshing start to a hot day, but today I find myself wishing I was eating pancakes or a freshly baked, still-warm fruit bun from the bakery.

"What's with the weather?" I ask.

Cassia shrugs, busy pouring wine with one hand, waving a rattle vaguely in Emilia's direction. "No doubt it'll warm up once the sun rises."

I amuse myself making faces for Emilia for a few moments, say goodbye to them both and head over the river towards the lake. The grove of trees rustle in the breeze, a loud swishing noise as I walk through them.

Marcus is already there. The sky has lightened as the dawn breaks, but is still a sullen grey, not the pale blue it ought to be.

"Are we going to have rain?" I ask Marcus when I reach him.

He puts an arm about my shoulders, pulls me into his chest for a quick kiss. "Hope not," he says. "It should warm up. Are you cold?" He wraps my palla more tightly about me. "There. Aren't you glad you're a married woman? Else you'd have to run home for a cloak. Here come the undertakers."

Given the number of fatalities we are expecting, the undertakers are necessary, there will need to be careful sorting, as the criminals and prisoners of war can be buried in a mass grave, but should there be any deaths of freeborn Romans or any gladiators belonging to specific schools, they must be returned to their families or schools for proper burial. The audience will mostly approach from the east, so the undertakers have located their carts and teams to the west, discreetly hidden behind the high stone wall close to one of the gates, which will enable them easy access once the crowds have left.

The undertakers ready, we welcome the physicians: Fabius and Fabia with their assistants, as well as Fabia's replacement at Labeo's, an experienced man. It is very probable there will be multiple injuries today, three thousand five hundred people fighting with real weapons are unlikely to escape unscathed, even if most of their efforts will be focused on the unlucky five hundred who will die today. We set up medical bays inside the northern gate, in a space we left in the seating, surrounded by screens.

"What happened to the sunshine?" Fabia asks, shivering. "Yesterday I was sweating all day and now..."

I shrug. "I know. We have to hope the wind moves the clouds along and the sun breaks through. Or at least that it doesn't rain."

I GO WITH MARCUS TO check on the ships, which are lined up in the canal with more anchored behind in the Tiber, waiting for their signal to enter the lake. The lead ship is commanded by Servius, his men distributed as fighters between five ships.

"Looking forward to leading out the fleet?" Marcus asks, leaping on board.

Servius is shifting from foot to foot, nervous. "Yes, sir."

"You don't have to reassure us," I say, from the canal path. "It's natural to feel anxious."

"It is a great honour," he says, swallowing.

"You'll do just fine," says Marcus, patting his shoulder. "The music will start, I'll give the signal, three times round the lake with the other ships following you. It gives everyone a chance to admire the speed and the ships and get excited about the fighting to come when they see you all on deck in armour. May Neptune watch over you all today," he adds, jumping down from the deck back onto the canal path.

"Yes, sir," says Servius, straightening his shoulders and I smile at his nervous pride.

It will soon be time for the gathering crowds to be allowed in. We have numbered the gates one to eight, starting on the north gate and going round towards the east and south. Five of the gates are for the crowds, three to the west for the undertakers. People's tokens include the gate number they should come to. Each gate has four soldiers on it, to manage any rowdiness and to ensure everyone has tokens. Compared to the amphitheatre, which is a smaller space but has far more tiers of seating, we have fewer numbers here, but thirty thousand people still require a lot of managing.

"Is that rain?" I ask, feeling a few spits of wetness on my face.

"Better not be," says Marcus. "Here come the musicians and singers."

The musicians and singers are a larger team than we normally have, as they need to be evenly distributed around the lake's edge. Some are also located on Domitian's island, to ensure the Emperor can hear everything perfectly.

AT LAST THE GATES ARE opened and the crowds file in, joking and excited, though there are plenty of passing comments about the weather. After the hot and sunny month we've had, why does today have to be cold and grey?

The stands fill up and already there are vendors of everything, from merchandise including toy ships for children to food and drink, wandering from stand to stand, calling out their wares.

We get advance warning that Domitian is on his way. I walk round the lake, making final checks with physicians, undertakers, guards, nodding one more time to Servius as I pass the canal. Everything is in place, everything seems promising. If only the weather were better.

The wind is getting stronger. It's changed from a boisterous breeze to a real wind, tree branches waving, the surface of the water choppy and dark, reflecting the sky overhead which is a grim grey. The audience moves too, married women wrapping their pallas tight about them or draping them over babies and their smallest children, who huddle close to their parents, men and slaves shifting in their seats, wishing they had brought cloaks, but who brings cloaks anywhere in July?

"Domitian's here," says Marcus, as trumpets sound out from the east gate.

We watch as Domitian, accompanied by guests and guards, makes his way across the bridge to his own special island where he takes up his seat on the wooden platform. From his body language, he seems happy, nodding left and right to his guests when they speak to him and waving graciously to the crowd applauding him.

But there's wetness on my face again, it is beginning to rain, tiny droplets falling from the grey skies. The wind is cold and growing stronger. People shiver and as the gates begin to close, signalling that the show is about to start soon, one family gets up and leaves, having obviously decided that even a naumachia is not worth staying for in this weather. The gate closes behind them and overhead there's a rumble of thunder.

"We can't go ahead like this," I say to Marcus, fear rising up in me. "There's going to be a storm."

He's staring out over the lake, his jaw tight. "Are you going to tell Domitian he can't have his naumachia?"

"Someone has to. He might listen to a woman, take pity."

Marcus shakes his head. "He's not Titus. He's stubborn. When he wants something, he doesn't listen to anyone saying it can't be done and he can't have his own way. You saw him when he lost his temper. I thought he might kill me that day."

"But we can postpone it," I say. "It doesn't mean it's not going to happen at all, we just move it to another day."

"Just?"

"It's a lot of work," I say. "But if the storm breaks over us, we could lose ships. We could lose men. The audience will be soaked for hours. If it rains hard, the visibility will be awful anyway. It won't be a celebratory event, it'll be miserable."

"I should speak to him."

"Let me try," I say. "If a man talks to him he might feel he must be bold. If a woman asks, perhaps he will show kindness."

"Try. But don't get on the wrong side of him. If he's going to be stubborn, just agree and come back here."

I push through the crowds on the busy pavement and get to the bridge, guarded by the Praetorian Guards. The red token I show them indicates that I am a member of the team organising the event and I receive a reluctant nod, hurry across the wooden bridge and onto the island, glancing up at the darkening sky. Is this the blackness that the sorceress foretold? When I'm at Domitian's seating platform I spot the Aedile, who is theoretically in charge of all imperial Games.

"Ah," he says, recognising me. "Um, err... Althea?"

"Yes," I say. I lower my voice. "Aedile, if the storm breaks overhead, there could be dangerous consequences for the performers, the props, even the audience. The Emperor himself could be at risk. Can you convince him to change the date of the performance?"

He is horrified. "Um… the Emperor is not likely to…"

"I know he won't like it. But it would be better for everyone if we move the date."

The Aedile shifts from one foot to the other, his eyes flickering as though searching for an escape route. My patience runs out at his timidity.

"Never mind," I say. "I'll approach him myself."

The Aedile is vastly relieved. "Certainly," he says. "Certainly, if you think it…"

But I don't hear whatever else he was about to say, I'm already moving closer to the imperial seating area, a few steps away from Domitian, whose focus is on the lake. The nearest guard inspects me and lifts his chin in a gesture to approach.

"Imperator?"

Domitian snaps his head round as though startled. "What?"

"I am Althea Sc –"

"I know who you are."

"The weather is getting worse. The storm may break overhead."

"And?"

"We wonder if it might be… wise to reschedule the naumachia, Imperator."

"Reschedule?"

"We can set it all up for another day," I say, grabbing at my palla which is threatening to blow away in the rising wind. "It would be no trouble at all," I lie, with an attempt at a smile, as though re-organising thousands of men and dozens of ships, a vast audience and Domitian's own diary are all of no consequence. "You have only to name the day, we will take care of everything."

"I *have* named the day," says Domitian, and his voice is cold. "I named today."

"But Imperator –"

"You have a palla, do you not?" he says, gesturing at it.

"Yes, Imperator."

He makes an impatient gesture and a slave rushes forwards with a thick woollen cloak, which Domitian wraps about himself. "There," he says.

"Imperator?"

"We are both warm and protected," he says. "So proceed."

"The audience –"

"Can wear their cloaks and pallas. They will be fine."

"They may not all have brought…" I begin, but I am losing this battle, clutching at straws.

"Then they are foolish."

"The storm may endanger the performers," I try one last time.

He gives a snort of laughter. "Hardened gladiators, sailors and soldiers? I think not. They've seen far worse. Continue."

There is nothing I can say. I bow my head and step backwards.

"Wait."

Is he going to reconsider?

"No one is to go."

"Imperator?"

"Members of the audience are forbidden to leave."

"There are children –"

"Then they will be entertained. Inform the guards at the exits to bolt the gates. The guards may use force if necessary to keep people here. No-one is to depart until I do."

This is unheard of. The audience at the amphitheatre is always free to come and go at will. When it rains many audience members leave, which is why most of the Games are held in the spring and summer to avoid poor weather. To force people to stay when a storm is about to break right over their heads is the act of a tyrant.

"Imperator," I murmur, stepping away as quickly as I can, hurrying down the steps from his box. I do not want him to think of anything else to demand. I thought I might make the situation better, even if it meant more work for us, but it is now worse. Much worse.

I return to Marcus and relay the conversation.

He stares, shocked. "Guards on the exits? The gates bolted?"

"Yes."

"There are children here."

"I said that."

Marcus closes his eyes for a moment. Then he opens them again, looks up at the sky. "The storm is going to break over us," he says. "How many children do you think are here?"

I peer around, trying to guess. "One thousand five hundred? Two thousand?" The seating areas are all horribly exposed to the elements.

"There's one small area there," he says, pointing to the other side of the lake. "The trees might break the wind a bit. Can you move the youngest children there, and anyone who is infirm? I will instruct the guards to bolt the gates. Tell people in the crowd that the Emperor has insisted we go ahead and no-one is to leave, to protect themselves as best they can if they have cloaks, pallas, whatever. We will be cold and wet for several hours." He turns his head both ways, absorbing the vast area of seating. "Take as many of our team as you can get hold of to help you spread the word quickly," he adds. "The parade needs to start."

He raises his hand as I move away and the musicians strike up a military theme. I can see Servius' ship move forwards.

I spend the next hour making my way from section to section, trying to explain without sounding critical of Domitian and moving those who are willing. Karbo and thirty other members of our team are doing the same. Behind us, as we face the audience, the fifteen chosen ships circle the lake accompanied by music and singing, interspersed with rumbling thunder which is getting closer. By the time we are finished, the rain is falling steadily and the audience are sullen-faced, huddling as best they can from the rain and wind.

I go back to where Marcus is standing, passing bolted gates with guards standing in front of them, hands on the hilts of their swords. Marcus' face is grim.

"I've done what I can," I say, cringing as a crack of lightning cuts the grey sky to the north of us and the thunder comes almost immediately after it.

"We have to start the battle sequence," he says. "Five sets of two boats. Boarding and fighting."

My shoulders slump as he raises his arm, signalling for five additional ships to join the others and group into pairs. I watch as the ships change directions. They are all commanded by experienced sailors and rowed by professional oarsmen, but still, they are struggling, the wind is against them and the water is choppy, splashing onto the pavements, wetting the feet of those in the bottom audience tier. The ships lower their sails so that their commanders can better control their movement using only the rowers, even though this looks less interesting, less parade-like.

"Should we turn off the aqueduct?" I ask.

Marcus shakes his head. "We need the depth for the ships," he says. "Can't risk them running aground."

The first battle begins, the men and women of each boat trying to force a boarding, bringing their ships close together and attacking those close at hand. I can't see Domitian's face, he is too far and the rain is heavy, but he is leaning forward as though interested. The crowd is not, they sit huddled together, even stranger to stranger, their faces showing nothing but mute misery. There ought to be cheering and booing as the audience takes sides, lending a festive and exciting air to the event, but there is no sound from them. The musicians and singers keep going, the rain falls and the lightning flashes overhead, the thunder rolls above us.

"Can we cut it short?" I shout to Marcus, trying to be heard above the shouts and clashes of fighting.

He shakes his head. "Domitian is aware there's another round to come," he yells back.

I swallow. The final melee consists of thirty-five ships in an all-out battle. Even in calm weather it would have been a squeeze. With a storm breaking overhead, I am not sure how they will manoeuvre at all.

"It's too dangerous," I protest.

"I'll try to cut this part short so we can get on to the final part," he says and I nod. There's little else we can do at this stage.

Fabia arrives at my side. "They're going to be sick." Her face is serious. "This will lead to fevers. There are children and the infirm here. And even those who are healthy…" She shakes her head, angry. "What is he thinking? *Does* he think?"

I shrug, keep my voice low, bend down close to her. "When he wants something, he wants it. And he allows nothing to get in his way. He becomes deaf and blind."

Fabia tightens her lips. "I wonder if he'll open his eyes and ears when people start falling ill."

I am fairly sure about two hundred criminals and prisoners of war have been killed and fallen overboard when Marcus gives the signal, earlier than planned, for the final melee to begin. The ships already on the lake move so there is enough space and the final fifteen ships emerge onto the water.

Marcus is right, with all the vessels in place they can barely move, the whole of the lake is effectively one large ship. None of their sails are up, so they look more like a series of wooden rafts with thousands of oars sticking out everywhere, most of which have to be retracted as there isn't room for them between the ships. A few dozen are smashed to splinters before their commanders decide that there is no point having the oars out as no-one is going anywhere.

The storm has been raging for at least half an hour and I keep hoping it will lose its power, but if anything it is getting worse. The wind and thunder drown out the musicians and singers. It looks as though they are only pretending to sing and play, mouths open and hands moving, no sound emerging. Perhaps Domitian, provided with his own musical ensemble, can still hear them, no-one else can. What I can hear are children crying with cold and fear at the lightning and thunder.

There are groups of men and women at various gates arguing with the guards, demanding that the gates be opened so that they can leave, gesturing towards weeping children. One guard after another draws their sword and the defeated people return to their seats, heads lowered.

I run down to the bridge and stumble back to the island, the wind all but forcing me off the wooden planks. The guards do not even try to stop me, perhaps they hope Domitian will finally give in.

I kneel before him. "Imperator," I call out, raising my voice to be heard. "I beg you on my knees to stop this naumachia. It is too dangerous. Please. In the name of Minerva, goddess of wisdom, I beg for your wisdom in calling a halt to the melee."

Domitian gazes down at me, his face blank. "Minerva is also the goddess of war," he says. "A goddess of war would not call a halt to a battle. Continue."

There is a crack of lighting overhead and an immediate boom of thunder, then another sound, a whoosh, a thud. A woman near me screams and I turn to see one of the ships has burst into flames, hit by the lightning. The ships around it, wary of the flames, try to move away, but this is not possible. The crew on the stricken ship are trying to get off, the men and women on the deck desperate to find a nearby ship they can leap onto. The rowing team on the burning ship are below deck and they are struggling to get out, one hundred and eighty men pushing and jostling in panic.

I turn back to Domitian. Surely, he will change his mind, but he only gazes down at me, making no effort to wipe away the rain falling down his face. "I said, continue," he says. "Did you not hear me?"

I get up and run back across the bridge, which takes me closer to the burning ship. Marcus is on the shoreline nearby, climbing on board one of the ships so that he can give orders, direct the vessels to the canal so that some of them can leave and clear space to safely rescue the crew of the damaged ship. But the ships cannot move.

The burning ship rocks and tilts precariously, then goes too far. The battering ram on its prow, no longer carefully guided away from the ships alongside, slams into one, water immediately rushing in through the gaping hole.

"It's going to sink!" shouts Marcus.

He moves from the first ship to a second, trying to get closer to the two stricken ships, one in flames, the other one sinking fast, so that he can shout orders. The occupants of both are leaping off, onto other ships if they can, into the water if they cannot. But the wind is against them, two ships without commanders, their battering rams threatening to cause more damage to the ships wedged too close to them and worse, the ships round them unable to get out of the way to enable the desperate swimmers space to reach the shore. People in the water try to swim but are crushed between ships or pulled under as they move, their screams reaching me even where I stand.

Commanders and their officers shout orders, but there is too much going on. Marcus manages to get one ship out of the lake and into the canal, moves onto another, trying to achieve the same thing. But this makes some of the ships try to get closer to the canal and a second ship is ploughed into and there are more screams as water rushes in.

The audience are shouting and screaming too, some men rush forwards to try and help, but there is nothing they can do. The three ships in trouble are wedged into the eastern part of the lake, with ships all around them. The second ship to take on water is worse than the first, arms desperately wave from the lower deck where the rowers sit as water gushes into the splintered side. They are trapped by water and jagged broken wood with no way to escape.

Someone grabs my arm and I swing round to find Karbo, panting next to me. "He's leaving!"

I turn towards the bridge and there is Domitian, striding away from the island, hurriedly followed by his entourage and guests, all of them trying to keep their balance in the tearing wind.

"Unlock the gates!" I yell.

Karbo nods and darts away, heading south while I run north.

I run to each gate, telling the guards to unbolt them at once, that Domitian is leaving. The gates swing open and immediately fill with people trying to leave, cramming through the spaces as quickly as they can, while I fight against the oncoming throng to reach the next gate. Now that the Emperor is gone, the crowd might turn angry, but they are too exhausted and cold to do so, too afraid of what is happening behind them on the lake. They swarm out of the now-open exits, shivering and silent except for the children who are crying. The men's faces are rigid with unspoken anger, the women stare as they pass as though seeking explanation for what has happened. I cannot meet their eyes. It's not my fault, but I feel as though it is. If I had pleaded more successfully with Domitian, if I had managed to sway him... the thousands of soaked bodies who pass my post are a silent reproach. They make their way back through the grove of trees, many of which have crashed to the ground, bringing their too-close fellows down with them. I watch Marcus manage to get a further five ships out and into the canal, finally freeing up some space on the lake. But the two mauled ships have gone under, only their masts stick out of the black water. The burning ship still floats, blackened and smoking.

The last people have gone, only our team and the performers are left. I stand at the water's edge as the rain pours down, scanning the scene before me. The musicians and singers trail along the island bridge back to the shoreline, shoulders slumped. On the ships, men and women lean perilously over the decks, trying to reach into the water to pull up injured comrades, pushing and pulling to get sections of ships that have rammed together unstuck so that they will be able to steer back out to the canal and away from this horror. All along the shoreline I can see dead bodies. And Marcus.

I run to him.

He is kneeling on the shore, legs in the water, Servius' dead body in his arms. When I reach him he looks up and his face is stricken, tears trickling down. I kneel next to him in the mud, take Servius' body into my own arms. Marcus sits back on his heels.

"It's my fault," he sobs.

"It's Domitian's fault and no one else's," I say.

"I should have overridden him."

"Then you'd be dead." I look down at Servius' white face, all life drained from his skin, stroke his eyes shut.

"I presented him to Domitian. I made him known to him. He would never have commanded one of the ships if I hadn't done that."

I shake my head. "We needed thousands of men. We would have used everyone we could lay our hands on. Two hundred idle sailors, you think we wouldn't have used them?"

He won't be comforted. "What will his mother say? He kept saying she would be so proud of him. He was a boy and I put him in harm's way, I wanted him to rise and instead I have killed him. I will have to send word to his mother that her son is dead. At sea? By the hand of vicious pirates? No, in a lake we dug in the middle of Rome, for the pleasure of an emperor who has lost his mind."

I wave over two of the surviving sailors from Servius' crew, staggering along the shore, their faces shocked. They come to me and I tell them to carry Servius to the undertakers by the west gate and ensure they know his name. They lift him away. I take Marcus' muddy hands in mine and wipe away his tears, leaving his cheek streaked with dirt.

"We would have been killed if we'd stood against him," I tell him.

"We might have saved hundreds of good men."

I hold him in my arms, the two of us kneeling on the cold shore.

THE RAIN CONTINUES TO FALL, an endless grey misery in which we are trapped for what feels like eternity. We work until it is too dark to see, Marcus first guiding the ships out of the lake and back to the canal which will allow them to escape this cursed place and return, via the Tiber river, to their ports. They must reach safe harbour before darkness comes and their presence in the lake makes all other work impossible. Some ships still have their own commander, a few have lost theirs and their second-in-command officers step up to take their place, anxious at taking a promotion they never wanted to happen in this way. I send Karbo home against his will, telling him to let the rest of the insula know what happened, to get into dry clothes and go to Cassia's to be fed, then to bed. Meanwhile we gather up each lifeless body along the shoreline, log their name if known and deliver them to the waiting undertakers, all the while knowing the murky waters hide more of their fallen comrades. Those whose faces we do not recognise are laid out on the pavement to wait till tomorrow. At one point Fabia sits down and her assistant Sadiki kneels by her, takes her little body in his arms. I would go to her but I have no energy left to comfort anyone, it is all I can do not to sink down and weep myself.

"It's too dark to do more," says Marcus. His voice is hoarse from shouting instructions over the water. "I'm going to open the drainage system so the water will drain out overnight. Tomorrow we can come back for the bodies that have sunk to the bottom."

The rain has slowed to a fine drizzle. We round everyone up and send them back to their homes and barracks, the slaves down to the warehouse with a message to give them extra rations. Marcus and I are the last to leave. We walk hand in hand, though our hands have no heat left in them. Back at the insula, Maria has greeted each returning member of our community with dry clothes and hot water to wash with, and Cassia has a pot of stew ready. Adah has made hot honeyed wine more suited to the winter months, but we are grateful for it. Fabia, Fabius, Marcus and I eat in abject silence, then wish one another good night in low voices, while Quintus hurries away with all our wet muddy clothes to his family's fullery. The rain has finally stopped, the wind has dropped, now the evening is just cold.

I can barely climb the stairs, my legs tremble with each step and when I reach the hut I fall onto the bed, where Maria has laid out the winter blankets we have not used for months. I huddle gratefully under them and move close to Marcus when he joins me, the two of us clinging to one another. Tears trickle down my face until at last, exhausted, I slide into sleep.

I wake again and again in the night, images of Domitian's angry face before me, Servius' body in Marcus' arms, Marcus weeping, the silent miserable crowd. Every time I jolt awake thinking I am waking from a nightmare and then realise that it is true, that tomorrow I will have to face even worse.

THE NEXT MORNING DAWNS CRUELLY bright, sunny and still, with no sign at all of the previous day's storm except for broken branches and fallen trees across Rome. I send word to Strabo that he must manage the Games by himself for two weeks and we head back to the lake where the three hundred slaves of our team designated to the naumachia have gathered for the day's work. They are silent, their faces stricken at the events of yesterday and what is still to come. Also in attendance are Labeo, Paternus and the commanding officers of various ships and regiments, come to identify the dead.

Marcus unlocks the gate and we stand in silence, surveying the scene. The pavement around the bodies we laid out yesterday is covered in mud and leaves, the glittering water has drained away leaving a vast expanse of mud, littered with the wreckage of the two ships and hundreds more bodies. Only Domitian's island sits prettily atop the carnage, green and pleasant, still populated by the hardier flowers. I stare at it for a few moments, then direct the team. The undertakers will be returning soon.

The work is back-breaking and heart-breaking in equal measure. We must wade into the thick mud and drag back bodies, wash their faces and try to identify them, I keep a tally of their names if we can identify them, otherwise of their uniforms and any features that may help us name them later, so that their families will know they fell. The undertakers return hour after hour with carts ready for us to load the dead.

When the bodies have finally been removed, we start work on the broken ships, more carts arriving at the gates to be filled with shattered wood, taken away as the basin slowly empties.

It takes us four days of work to fully clear the site. When it is done, we usher everyone out and Marcus bolts the last gate shut behind us, his face pale, eyes red-rimmed. We spend another five days attending every funeral we can manage between us, from gladiators to sailors, choking in plumes of smoke as they rise upwards. Marcus writes a letter to Servius' mother, praising her son's bravery and respectfulness, his willingness to learn new skills, how the Emperor knew him by name and requested that he lead the parade. He tells her that she should be proud.

FOR THREE WEEKS AFTER THE naumachia people all over Rome are ill. From colds and coughs to fevers, the storm and Domitian's stubborn power can be felt across the city. A few people, already weak, die and there are mutterings against an Emperor so despotic that he insists on going ahead with an event for his own amusement, no matter the cost to his people.

Marcus, exhausted by his grief and guilt over what happened, gets a high fever. I sit by his side for many hours, taking turns with Karbo to hold cool cloths to his head. He recovers but is pale and sad. An imperial scroll is delivered.

"We're summoned to Domitian," I tell Marcus.

"I never want to see him again."

"I'll go alone," I say.

"I don't want you near him, either. He's a madman with no heart."

"We don't have a choice," I say.

"I'll go."

"No," I say. "You're not fit to go. "I'll go."

"If he… if he does anything, Althea, you leave."

Leaving may not be an option if Domitian is in one of his moods but at least I am sure that Stephanus will be with him, who seems able to manage at least some of his strange moods and I'm not about to worry Marcus any more than I have to.

For once I am shown in with no delay. Domitian is looking out of a window. I'm glad to see Stephanus is in his usual place in a discreet corner of the room.

"It is most regrettable that the storm during the naumachia led to many people being taken ill," Domitian says, turning as soon as I am inside the door. His face is sad. "I wish to offer a public banquet to let the populace know that I care for their wellbeing."

I stare at him, trying to change my expression to look less surprised. "Imperator?"

"There will be a private event for the senators and their families and suchlike," he says airily. "You need not concern yourself with that. But there should also be a public banquet, for the plebians. People can come and be fed, you will arrange for that. Set up long tables in the Forum, with shifts so that all who wish to be fed can come. Good warming food, meat from the amphitheatre, to be used in stews. Bread, barley porridge, cheese. Wine, of course. The imperial purse will take care of whatever is necessary." He nods, satisfied at his generosity.

I can't believe what I'm hearing. "And this banquet is your initiative following…"

"Following the storm at the naumachia," says Domitian. "It is given by myself to let the people know that their Emperor feels sad for them for having had such a terrible experience."

I don't dare speak, nor show any emotion. "As you command, Imperator," I say.

"I will escort you out," offers Stephanus.

He walks with me beyond the atrium, out into the busy Forum, where I stop and turn to him. I keep my voice low, but it shakes with the feelings rising up in me, I cannot help myself.

"What happened back there? Has he forgotten how the disaster came to happen? He speaks as though it wasn't his decision to keep us all there!"

Stephanus nods. "The Emperor has his passions and he finds it difficult, in the moment, to see beyond them. But when he has achieved what he wishes to achieve he sometimes reflects on what has occurred and feels…"

"Remorse?"

Stephanus gives a small shake of his head. "It is as though he cannot comprehend that his previous actions were the cause of the damage. He sees only the damage and feels that he can mend it, without perhaps making the link between his previous actions and those he is making now."

"He doesn't *remember* that he forced everyone to stay while a thunderstorm broke over us and hundreds of people died? That thousands were taken ill?"

"The passion of that moment has faded and so he sees the damage without perhaps seeing entirely what led to it, how he could have behaved differently. As though it were not possible for him to have behaved differently, in that moment."

I sigh. "I don't pretend to understand," I say. "It was like talking to someone who couldn't hear me and now it's like talking to someone who doesn't remember what they did."

"Perhaps a good way of thinking of it," says Stephanus. "I must leave you."

"Wait," I say.

He turns back politely. "Yes?"

"Glabrio and the lion…"

"Yes?"

"Did you arrange that?"

"The Emperor had a number of names of those whose behaviour was considered treasonous. The consul's was one of them."

"Did you add him to the list because of what happened last year?"

"The list was the Emperor's."

"And after he defeated the lion and was exiled?"

"It is my understanding that he died soon afterwards."

I raise my eyebrows. "Did you arrange that?"

Stephanus blinks. "His being alive was not in Rome's best interests."

"Really?"

Stephanus steps closer to me, his face calm. "I will repeat to you what I said when Funis died, Althea Aquillius," he says. "I believe in justice."

I gaze into his eyes and reluctantly bow my head in acknowledgement. "I would have liked the world to know what he did. That he had his own son murdered."

"That, I am afraid, is not always possible."

"Did *he* know why he was dispatched?"

"He knew."

And he's gone, walking briskly away, swallowed into the crowd, just one toga amongst many, yet with the power to change destinies.

At home, I open my chest of possessions and pull out a tiny cloth bag, tip the bronze bracelet it holds out into my hand. A bull's head at one end, opposite it the mid-vault body of a bull-leaper, the gift Funis gave me before his untimely death. I look it over, touch the flying body. However it happened, his death has been avenged. Perhaps now his shade will be at peace.

WITH EVERYTHING THAT HAS GONE on it is more than a week before I realise that I haven't seen Julia in the last few days.

"She's taken to her bed," says Maria, when I ask.

"Why?"

"Her cough got worse. She said she was in pain at night, that her back hurt and she couldn't breathe well, even coming up the stairs."

I could kick myself for not having noticed her deterioration. There's been too much going on, but I should have seen that her cough was still bad. When I visit her I'm shocked. She's lost weight in the past month or two, and she was always a slim woman, she had no bulk to spare. Her face appears gaunt, but she tries to wave away my concerns.

"I've had some headaches in the past few weeks, I thought resting would be good," she says, turning her face away to cough.

"I'm sending Fabius and Fabia to you and you're to do whatever they say," I tell her sternly.

But Fabius and Fabia look grave when they've seen her.

"I am not sure she will get well," says Fabius gently.

"What?"

"I've seen this before. We can only keep her comfortable."

"That's not possible," I mutter, shocked.

Fabia puts her hand in mine. "We must be prepared for her to leave us," she says.

A DYING BREATH

IN THE OPPRESSIVE HEAT OF August we take up a vigil in Julia's room, one of us always with her. When it is my turn at night, I keep only one lamp burning so that I can see, the room dim around us. I sleep when I am very tired, but mostly I sit and watch over her, listen to her breathe in and out. Fabius offered opium, burning the sweet-smelling seeds to produce a smoke to be inhaled using a reed, as a way to reduce any pain she might suffer, but she refused. As the days pass, her breathing becomes erratic, several times in a shift I will lean forward, afraid that this is the last moment, that she has taken her last breath, before her chest heaves and she gasps, then continues to breathe, slow in and out, a wheeze at the beginning of each intake, a rattle towards the end of each out breath. I find myself crumpling my tunic with my hands before trying to relax, unclutching the fabric, deliberately placing my hands in my lap, where my fingers intertwine again, pulling, rubbing, as though my thoughts were made flesh.

I cannot imagine the insula without Julia. She has always been here, this insula is built around her presence, even when she is absent. The very street it sits on, Virgin's Street, is named for her, bestowed by an awed local community who found themselves with a retired Vestal in their midst, the daughter of a great family living here in the Ninth Region, a nothing-place, apparently intending to live out her life here. Owner of a crumbling insula, she made it welcoming to all, the rooms taken by those who could only afford a low rent, those in need of care and companionship. She took in Marcus, when he was wounded and didn't know what to do with his life, Cassius and his wife when they were poor and trying to scratch a living by setting up a little popina, then Cassius alone when his wife died and left him with little Cassia to take care of. Maria, widowed young. Adah, old and without a family. Celer, battling drink and no longer able to drive chariots in the races. Balbus and Floriana, childless owners of the toy shop.

And others who came and went over the years. I had not realised how many there had been, but word has gone out across Rome and beyond that Julia is dying, and every day strangers arrive at the insula, hesitating in the gateway to the courtyard, looking about for her. It is usually Maria or Karbo who spots them and asks if they are here for Julia. They are directed up to her apartment, where whoever is on shift will invite them inside. They always come with gifts. Fragrant roses, sweet peaches and soft ripe figs, beeswax candles that fill her room with the smell of honey, fans to keep her cool. When they enter they stand helpless at the sight of her still body, fear that they have come too late to say everything they wanted to say, to give her gifts that are not enough for the gratitude they want to express. They stand or kneel by her, reach out trembling fingers to touch her hand. They speak out loud to her, or whisper. Their eyes fill with tears as they thank her for looking after them at times of hardship in their life.

"When my husband died…"

"My wife…"

"When we lost everything and had nowhere to go…"

"That night in winter when you took us in…"

"Thank you…"

"You helped us…"

"I will never forget…"

"May the gods bless you…"

"Thanks be to Vesta for giving us her handmaiden…"

And her name, whispered over and over again in the dimly lit room, *"Julia, Julia, Julia…"*

They hesitate before leaving, knowing they will not see her again, pause in the doorway, look at her with pleading eyes, desperate for a sign from her, a smile, a word, even for her eyelids to flutter. But she does not move, only breathes in and out, as though it takes everything she has, every last bit of life force, just to do this one thing. They stumble out into the light of day, arms empty of gifts, their faces streaked with tears. Some take time to visit the inhabitants who have been here longest. They chat to the baker's family, they eat a meal at Cassia's, a few of the men spend an evening drinking with Celer before they head home, heavy-hearted at losing a woman who meant so much to them.

"She helped so many people," I say to Maria after a night's shift. My eyes are gritty from lack of sleep and from crying. Hearing all the love and gratitude bestowed upon Julia, as well as the many tales of hardship she helped alleviate, is too much to bear.

"So many owe her a debt of gratitude," says Maria.

I turn at the end of the wooden walkway, conscious suddenly, even in my half-asleep state, that I've never asked Maria how she came to be here. "How did you – ?" I start.

She stares down, into the courtyard, into her past. "My parents died young. I was taken in by an aunt and uncle who were stingy, didn't want me for anything but as a house slave. They married me off as quick as they could to a man who wanted a wife he could control absolutely. He would get jealous over nothing, though Juno knows I never gave him cause. Even going to the market or the bakery to buy food, he'd follow me, ask why I smiled at one of the vendors, why I'd worn such and such a tunic, why I'd left my palla at home, was I trying to pretend I wasn't married? I tried to shop more quickly, closer to home, but nothing would please him."

"Did you at least have friends to visit?"

"I had three friends from my childhood but he discouraged me from going to the baths with them, wouldn't have them visit me and refused to let me visit them. He beat me if he thought I'd disobeyed him, and my uncle and aunt didn't care, they said a man had every right to beat a disobedient wife and that I should try harder to please him and be a good wife. But it didn't matter how hard I tried, it was never good enough. One day he saw some other woman he liked better and divorced me. From one day to another, without warning."

"Good riddance," I say. Her story is sadder than I expected, I had known she was a young widow but had thought she would at least have fond memories of the past.

"That's what I thought. But my uncle and aunt wouldn't have me back in their house. My friends had moved or forgotten me. I had no one and my new freedom was not as I expected. I shook when I had to go to market, I never went to the baths. Leaving the house grew harder and harder. I spent my days huddled at home, eking out food so that I would not have to go out again. His beatings, his jealousies, they were locked inside me, I couldn't let them go." She sighs. "In the end I had no money, I would have had to rent myself out as an indentured servant, little better than a common slave, but who would want a servant that refused to leave the house on errands? The landlord threw me out and I crept from street to street till I saw an open courtyard gate and huddled inside, just to let the trembling still for a few moments. When I heard a voice I tried to run but it was Julia, she caught hold of my arm and asked me what I was doing, what my name was, why I was in her courtyard."

I think of Karbo, how he, too, crept into the courtyard to be safe from the outside world. How Maria saw him and caught him. At the time I thought she objected to street children using the courtyard as their own, now I think she saw in him her own fears and needs, caught him out of kindness, knowing he needed more than a safe space for the night.

She gives a small laugh. "I was afraid of Julia but she took me to the popina and Cassia's mother fed me. When Julia saw how I was afraid of the world outside, yet calm inside the walls of the insula, she told me to stay. I told her I had no money and she shook her head and said it didn't matter. And I have been here ever since. All these years later and still I tremble when I leave the insula."

"I'm sorry," I say. It doesn't seem enough.

"Long time ago," she says, as though speaking of something she has left behind, but there is a tightness in her body that belies her dismissal.

Why have I never noticed before that I hardly ever see Maria leave the insula? Occasionally she will venture as far as our local market, but not even as a regular daily or weekly occurrence, as most people do. She eats at Cassia's or has food sent up to her, shops at the bakery. I often saw Julia bring back two baskets from the market rather than just her own and now I realise why. Maria has fruit delivered to her and makes fine preserves and drinks that Julia or other friends will take to the market and sell for her so she has a little money, but I never thought to ask why she did not run her own market stall. I think of how she sits on the balcony, watching over the insula, knowing everything about everyone, all our comings and goings. I used to find her bright colours, loud voice and nosiness amusing, but now I see her bravado is tinged with sadness. This is a woman who can barely leave the insula without fear, who has made this block and courtyard her whole world. I blink a couple of times, still exhausted from a night spent watching over Julia, then hug her without words. Her solid bulk feels fragile in my arms.

I go back along the walkway, up the stairs and fall into my bed as Marcus awakes, one arm outstretched to receive me into his embrace. He kisses me, slips out of the bed, pulling on his tunic and turning to ensure I am covered up, though the day's heat will soon make his care unnecessary.

JULIA HASN'T SPOKEN FOR MORE than a week, yet still she breathes, in and out. I dribble water into her mouth and her throat moves to receive it, but not enough. Her skin is drawn, her lips dry. I moisten them with oil, wipe her face with a wet cloth, fan her.

When she speaks I jump.

"Cassia." Her voice is so raspy it barely sounds like her.

"Julia?"

"Cassia."

I run to the door. "Karbo!" I call down into the courtyard. "Tell Cassia to come. Right now!"

In a few moments Cassia is hovering in the doorway, out of breath, worried. "Althea?"

"She asked for you," I say, still shocked that Julia has spoken at all.

Cassia walks over to Julia, strokes her sunken cheeks, lightly touches her hand. "Julia?"

She doesn't open her eyes, but she speaks at once, as though she's been waiting only for Cassia, all this time. "Soon you must go to the Temple of Vesta and tell my sisters I am gone."

Cassia looks up at me, startled. "Yes, Julia," she murmurs.

"My will is lodged with them."

Cassia nods. Anyone with an important will leaves it in the care of the Vestal Virgins.

"You are named owner of this insula after my death."

Cassia stares. It takes her a moment to find her tongue. "Julia – I –"

"You have done what I have tried to do. Kept a hearth for the people of Rome. You have done it without being told, it came from your own heart."

"My mother –"

"You did not have to follow her example. Nor mine. You did it because you wanted to."

Cassia stands very still. Her bottom lip is trembling, I can see her try to form words, but they will not come out of her mouth.

"I hope you will continue to offer a refuge to those who have no home, as I have tried to do."

"Yes Julia." It comes out a whisper. "I don't know how to thank –"

Julia's head moves to one side and then the other. "I have seen your good heart from when you were a little girl. May the gods bless you, Cassia."

She falls silent again, exhausted, and though we hover over her, she says nothing more.

"Her time is coming," says Cassia.

We gather in her rooms, Marcus and I, Karbo, Cassia and Quintus with Emilia, Cassius, Celer, Maria, Adah, Fabia and Fabius when they can be spared from work, Balbus and Floriana, other people from the insula and the bakery. Her rooms are full, but very quiet, all of us watching her, unwilling for her to leave us, determined for her not to be alone when she does. We wait all of a day and all of a night and towards the middle of the second day her eyelids flutter.

"Julia?" says Marcus, taking her hand in his. "We are here, Julia. We are all by your side."

"Althea?" she says, her voice tiny in the quietness.

"I'm here," I say, taking her other hand. "I am here, Julia."

"A good man and a good woman," she says, and every word is an effort.

"Rest," says Marcus and she falls silent.

He is right of course, but my shoulders shake in silent sobs. I know, feel certain, this is the last thing she will ever say to me and the idea that Julia should call me a good woman is unbearable, as though a deity has pronounced me worthy and blessed me. Perhaps before, when I sat by her dying bedside for hours on end, I had imagined some grand speech by Julia with her last breaths, that she might say priestess-like blessings over us or speak some sort of prophecy, even though she has never claimed any such ability. But these simple words, the tiny press of her hand, they are worth more than any priestly blessing.

Her breathing goes on and on that afternoon and into night, yet none of us leave her side. We sit in silence, occasionally someone will pour new drinks, watered wine or the plum juice that is Maria's specialty. Quintus and Celer leave and come back with food. The baker's family come and go, one member always with us, the others hurrying to work and then back again as soon as they can. The cobbler closes his shop early and comes to sit with us. The children fall asleep, Karbo's head heavy on my shoulder, Emilia curled up in a ball on a folded blanket. Adah, sitting at my side, occasionally pats my hand or slowly strokes down the length of my back, a comforting silent presence.

And then, in the quiet room, there is silence. Without warning. Without a gasping, a rattle, a struggle. Nothing. Only a breath out, which none of us even noticed among the others, and no breath back in. Nothing. I hear the silence and look up, frown, watch Julia's chest for the gasp that must come. Nothing. I raise my eyes to Cassia, whose own eyes are wide, to Maria, who turns to Fabia, who rises and comes closer, touches Julia's throat, holds her wrist, looks at me and nods. Maria rises to her feet and kisses Julia's lips, to seal her body from her departed spirit. It should be done by Julia's closest relative, but all of us defer to Maria's long friendship with her, in the absence of any relatives.

Sobs break out, lamentations are made, we women scratch at our faces and call out her name. Prayers are whispered. Karbo wakes, sleepy-eyed and when he sees that she is gone he turns his face into my shoulder and cries.

"She was old," I whisper to him, trying to offer some comfort. Really Julia was not that old, she could have lived for many more years, but to Karbo no doubt she seemed so.

"She left the gate open," he says through his tears. My own tears spill at this other, unspoken kindness of Julia's over the many years, that the gate of the insula was never barred shut, even at night, instead left ajar so that homeless children could find somewhere safe to sleep at night, the pile of sleeping mats always stacked in a corner somewhere in our courtyard. I squeeze Karbo to me, grateful that this quiet gesture of hers brought him to me when he was younger and needed a family. I wonder how many people have slept in our courtyard over the years, dragged a clean sleeping mat over the cobbles and found a night of respite, the strength to go on the next day. Julia's quiet kindnesses were multiplied over the years by Cassia, who always has a bowl of soup for anyone who asks, by the baker's family who bring yesterday's bread out each morning and leave it in a basket by the gate of our insula, by Marcus bringing home meat from the arena for Cassia to dole out amongst our inhabitants, a welcome addition to many people's diets of vegetable porridge and bread. I stroke Karbo's wet face and nod to Cassia who gently leads him back to her own apartment to sleep, drowsy Emilia slumped over her shoulder.

Marcus is standing over Julia, his back to me.

"We need to wash her," I say gently.

He turns to me and his face is wet with tears. I put my arms about him and he pulls away from me, wiping his face with the back of his arm.

"I'll fetch the undertakers," he says, voice husky. "Can you manage to lift her?"

I nod. Men should not touch the deceased's body, so it will fall to Maria and I to lift Julia to the ground, Fabia being too short to manage the task.

Marcus leaves, headed for the headquarters of Rome's undertakers on the Esquiline Hill. We see them daily at the amphitheatre, one of them is always on duty at the Games, more when we warn them in advance there are likely to be multiple deaths. Today they are being called for a different task.

"Here," Fabia says, indicating a space on the floor, where she has laid out a blanket. Maria and I move close to Julia and gently scoop our arms under her, Maria by her head and I by her legs. She weighs very little for a tall woman, as though it was her departed spirit that gave her weight. We manage to lower her to the floor without any jolting movements, then the three of us kneel over her and undress her. I'm awkward, removing her clothes without her permission seems wrong. I try to look away but this makes the task harder, so I watch and follow Fabia, who is not awkward but instead both careful and brisk, passing each of us cloths and bowls of warm water that she must have prepared earlier, while we sat through our last drowsy watch. We wipe every part of Julia's body with care and I am grateful to Fabia for warming the water, it would seem unkind to wash her with cold water.

"Oil," says Fabia, pouring some from a little bottle into our hands. "She made it herself. It is right for us to use it," she adds.

I put my hands together and inhale. Jasmine and roses waft over me. Gently I place my hands on Julia's still-warm body and let the fragrance envelop her.

WHEN CASSIA RETURNS FROM THE Temple of Vesta she is in shock. Not only does Julia's will name her owner of the insula but her heir in all matters. There was enough money to upkeep the insula for many years to come as well as for Julia's funerary rites and the instruction that she be cremated.

Most common people would be buried as quickly as possible, dead bodies being offensive to the gods and polluting to those touching them, but Julia's status as a former Vestal Virgin and her origins amongst a great family, however much they have chosen to forget her very existence, means her treatment is closer to that of an elite family's departed. Some of them might lie in their home's atrium for up to a week, but this is a hot month and so Julia will lie for three days in the cool rooms on the ground floor, usually kept for storage but now hastily cleaned out and swept, decorated with cypress branches at the door and over our insula's gate to warn anyone of possible ritual pollution. Her body is placed on a funeral couch, in a reclining position, feet pointed towards the door, a coin placed in her mouth to pay her way to the ferryman Charon to take her across the river Styx and arrive safely in the underworld. But I shake my head at the offer to use cosmetics. I do not want her pale cheeks painted pink, it would look nothing like the woman I knew.

Many people visit over the three days, standing just within the door, whispering prayers and chanting her name. Meanwhile, without even agreeing on this course of action, the whole insula stops its daily routines, as though all of us were her family, bound to cease all normal activities for nine days, only eating and sleeping and watching over Julia, attending her funeral, and recovering afterwards. The shops close their shutters, even Cassia's popina is closed to outsiders, as we are all polluted. We cannot wash ourselves. We turn inwards on ourselves, use Cassia's large popina kitchen to cook meals that will serve all of us, eat in the courtyard in shifts, simple foods that can be quickly made and that are suited to the heat; flat breads and dips, large salads, olives and cheese. Each day outside our gate we find offerings from the local neighbours: bread from another bakery, baskets of fruit and jars of olives. We take them in, grateful for our neighbours' loving care, their tribute to the Vestal Virgin who came to live amongst them, forsaking her own wealthy family and Vesta's temple, choosing this run-down neighbourhood, these small streets and crumbling houses in which to build herself a home. We tell stories about Julia; the first time each of us met her, the times she helped us, the way she would look at you or say something important. We laugh as well, mostly at ourselves for being in awe of her Vestal past before finding her to be warm-hearted and caring. We hug one another.

We have to send messages to Strabo that he should manage the Games, for we have three shows promised during our mourning period and we cannot go to the amphitheatre. We send amended plans which allow for fewer senior staff on site and trust to the gods and Strabo to manage. He sends back messages each day telling us that all is well, setting our minds at rest so that we can focus only on Julia.

We rise well before dawn on the fourth day, the red-dressed undertakers already busy moving Julia's body onto the funeral bier, musicians waiting outside the gate to accompany us to the funeral pyre, to be held on the road outside of Rome. It is not seemly to walk in funerary procession in daylight, so the undertakers hand out torches to several of us, before gesturing the six men forward who will carry the bier. Marcus, Quintus, the baker and two of his grown sons, Celer. Cassius and Karbo, too old and too young, walk behind, as though lending what strength they have to the men carrying her.

We set off in the flickering darkness, through Virgin's Street and down Sand Street, across the slow-moving summer river and beyond, walking through empty streets to the mournful, eerie sounds of flutes and drums. Here and there we come across carts making their deliveries before dawn. The drivers pull aside when they hear us coming and see our burden, bow their heads as we pass but also, by their sides, discreetly gesture against evil spirits, against the pollution of death.

The road outside Rome's gates is lined with graves as far ahead as we can see in the faint light that is beginning to break the sky. Guided by the undertakers we arrive at the designated spot for Julia's funeral pyre, which stands ready for her. The undertakers lift her white-wrapped body from the bier onto the pyre.

A portable altar has been set up, its coals already white-hot, nearby is a tethered pig, softly grunting to itself.

"Her heir?" asks the priest.

Cassia steps forward. Her hands shake as she takes the sacred mola salsa mixture of salt and flour, and sprinkles it over the pig. "An offering to Ceres, warden of the door between the living and the dead," she says. "May you allow our beloved Julia to pass through with ease."

The hammer comes down fast, the pig barely sighs before it is laid on its back and gutted. The priest's assistant hands over an earthenware bowl of the steaming guts to be examined. They are swiftly determined to be acceptable and thrown into the coals to feed the goddess, where they hiss and spit, sending up a thick stink of roast pig and faeces, hard to bear so early in the morning and on an empty stomach. The pig is quickly butchered, most of it will come home with us for the funeral meal, a portion goes to the priest along with their payment, another portion will be burnt with Julia. We will eat later on, it would not do to eat at the same time as Julia's portion is burnt. To share a meal with the dead is an offer to share their world, which none of us are ready for.

It is time to light the flame and we gather around the pyre. Cassia is hesitating to light the fire beneath the white shrouded body. I take her hand and squeeze it and she averts her face from the pyre as is correct, about to lower the torch she is carrying onto the wood. But there is a murmur behind us and we turn to see the crowd parting, heads bowed.

Two large closed litters have appeared, each carried by six slaves. The drapes pull back to reveal a group of women dressed all in white, their hair bound into intricate plaits laced through with red ribbons. The Vestal Virgins. Five of them emerge, one left behind as ever, to guard the sacred flame. The oldest leads the way to the pyre, carrying a burning brazier. The other four follow her in solemn procession, the youngest only a wide-eyed child of seven, chosen to take the place of Cornelia, the Virgo Maxima entombed alive last year. She follows the others, each step particularly careful, anxious to perform correctly in front of all these onlookers.

We step back to let them approach and they slowly circle the pyre, Julia's body making up the sixth white-clad figure, part of a complete set of Vestals for the last time in her life. The new Virgo Maxima kneels and uses her brazier to light the pyre, Rome's most sacred flame brought to this dusty road outside Rome's walls to send a Vestal who served her time on her way to another world, far beyond the city that was her home. The crowd is quiet while the Virgo Maxima lifts her palms and prays, then moves obediently out of the way as the five women turn and return to their litters, the drapes closing behind them as they are carried away, back to Vesta's Temple, the crowd closing behind them as though they had never been here, a vision, born from our imagination.

But the fire has been lit, it stands testimony to their appearance. The first licks of flame here and there give way to a dull roar as the pyre takes hold properly and we stand in silence as the silent figure within slowly disappears, taking Julia away from us and replacing her with nothing but our community, the people standing all around her, touching hands or shoulders, wiping tears or murmuring low comforts.

LATER THAT WEEK THE UNDERTAKER visits us personally, at home, a rare honour. He carries with him an urn, which he holds with reverence. He finds me making cuttings of Julia's herbs, putting them into tiny pots that I can take with me to the farm, where I can grow them in my own garden and think of her when I see them.

"Never done a Vestal," he comments, handing it over. He stares around, curious. "This where she lived?"

"Yes," I say, turning the black urn in my hands, wondering how all of Julia's spirit and presence can possibly be contained in this clay pot, such a small plain receptacle for a woman who tended Rome's most sacred hearth and who caused heads to bow wherever she went, long after she finished serving Vesta. The very first time I saw her, walking down the staircase of the insula, I was struck by how still she was even when she moved, her gaze falling on me and how I would have known without being told that this was a woman who had spent most of her life as a priestess. My eyes prick with tears at the thought that she welcomed me to Rome but will not be able to bless me when I leave.

"What was she like?" asks the undertaker.

"She kept a hearth burning for the people of Rome long after she finished tending Vesta's flame," I say.

"Right," says the man, obviously unable to imagine what I'm talking about.

"Thank you for this," I say, in a voice that suggests he leave. He does so, still looking curiously about him, as though expecting to see something fascinating, not a simple insula like any other in Rome.

I take the urn to Cassia and she, too, turns it in her hands as though bemused by it, by the absence of Julia. Later that day we walk together back to the road outside the walls, to where a waist-high stone-built edifice awaits the urn. Cassia sprinkles wine over the open urn, closes it again and places it carefully on the interior ledge, next to another.

"Back with her husband," I say.

Cassia nods, wipes her tears. "I'm not good enough to do what she did," she says, voice low.

"She didn't ask you to do what she did," I say. "She asked you to do what you already do and gave you the insula so that you could do more of the same."

She gives a watery grimace-smile. "I hope it is good enough."

"It is more than enough," I say. "She saw your good heart, Cassia."

Julia's epitaph has been carved into the stone, under her husband's which praises him for being "a man who gave his protection and love to the handmaiden of Vesta". To which we have added, "who now lies beside him, having cared for Rome's sacred hearth beyond her term of office. May their shades walk together always hand in hand."

THE BATTLE OF CRANES AND DWARFS

I WAKE FAR TOO EARLY BUT I can tell from his breathing that Marcus has done the same.

"WHAT TIME IS IT?" I whisper.

He chuckles. "No idea. I couldn't sleep. I'm too excited. Do you realise that after today we will be free? This is the last day of the Games. Next season will be run by someone else and we will be at our farm."

"We can't even go to Cassia's yet, she won't be open," I say. "And the streets are too dark to go to the amphitheatre. What are we going to do for the next hour or two?"

"Oh, I have ideas for that, don't you worry," says Marcus, drawing me closer.

EVEN AFTER WE HAVE DRESSED and fed the birds we are early, we arrive at Cassia's as she's pulling up the shutters.

"The fire's barely started," she says, laughing at us. "You two are overly keen to get today over and done with, aren't you? You'll have to wait."

Marcus is all jollity, chasing Emilia about the popina and devouring a large breakfast of bread, cheese, wine, fruits and even a fig tart which he shares with Emilia while cracking jokes with our fellow customers.

"I spoke with a neighbouring farmer when I went to the farm last autumn," he says. "There is a stock market in Puteoli in about a month's time, we will attend to buy the animals we need: chickens, doves, pigs, sheep. I gave our neighbour money to buy two oxen this autumn and keep them for the farm, there'll be no time to wait for the market to start the ploughing season. Strabo is a hard worker, but there will need to be slaves, too. There will be a lot to do."

"I can't wait," I say. "Although you will have to be patient with me, I know nothing of farming."

"You knew nothing of the Games," he reminds me. "And you became the domina of the amphitheatre. There was nothing you didn't work out how to manage. Farming will be nothing to you, people will think you were born and bred to it. You will do well."

His cheerfulness is infectious and I giggle at silly puns Marcus and Quintus trade between them and give Emilia a ride on my shoulders, before we walk hand in hand to the amphitheatre. Marcus greets Strabo with a hearty embrace and gathers together our entire team to announce, to cheers, that after today's show there will be wine and cakes for all at the barracks. Strabo is also full of good cheer, giving instructions with a smile. Only Fabia is downcast.

"I'll miss you," she says.

"It's not goodbye today." I sit on her platform so that I'm the right height and wrap my arm around her. "We'll still be here for a few weeks, lots of time to spend together."

"But then you'll be off and what will I do without you?"

I hug her. "I'll miss you. But you'll come and see us? And we'll come back to Rome to see you all."

She nods morosely and carries on setting up for the day. "They're going to start building two more gladiatorial schools. The Ludus Dacius for gladiators who come from Dacian prisoner of war stock and the Ludus Gallicus for Gallic gladiators."

"You'll be so busy you'll forget we're not here," I say.

MARCUS HAS DECIDED THE LAST day of the Games for this season should be an evening show, the better to showcase Ignis' work.

We have spent the past three days preparing the velarium. We removed the canvas awnings and packed them away for next season; they will not be used for the final day. Then we carefully lowered the whole structure back down, so that the metal circle rested on the arena floor. Ignis spent a whole day with our slaves, mixing vile-smelling combinations of pitch and spreading it along the ropes before allowing it to dry. The sailors re-winched it up into position, the circle and its two hundred and forty ropes like a sun with rays hanging above the amphitheatre.

The amphitheatre is packed to bursting for the final show of the season. I'm fairly sure we're stretching our seventy-thousand-seat capacity beyond its maximum capability.

Domitian arrives with the usual fanfare of trumpets and we stand in the corridor to welcome him, eyes lowered. I don't trust him, don't want to interact with him in any way. Today has to go smoothly and then we will be free.

I smell Domitia pass, hear the swish of silks and the thud of marching feet, wait for the second swishing noise, the silk curtains of the imperial box closing behind the imperial party. My head still lowered, I hold out my hand to Marcus and he squeezes it.

"Almost done," he whispers and hurries off to his seat, from where he will give signals for each stage of the show. I go down the steps into the darkness of the hypogeum and to a grid through which I can see into the arena and catch a glimpse of Marcus.

It's already twilight and so we quickly begin with the venatores. We had planned to repeat the story of Hercules and the Stymphalian birds and although Marcus was reluctant to repeat anything linked to that horrific night at Domitian's villa, the theme was appropriate. We release five hundred ibis and a venatore playing Hercules, along with our hidden archers, shoots them down, their fluttering bodies falling in heaps on the arena floor, only a lucky few managing to escape the amphitheatre and disappearing into the night sky.

While we still have some light the jugglers provide light relief accompanied by the musicians, allowing the audience time to purchase food and drink from the wandering vendors, or to visit the toilets.

The stars come out and now we have the criminal executions for the evening, featuring a cruel task: the sixteen criminals we are to dispatch must try to cross from one side of our arena to the other. It seems a simple thing, but perched on a painted rock we have two harpies, the bird-women of myth, personifications of destroying winds. One is played by gladiatrix and trainer for Labeo's school, Alyssa, who despite her bronze hand is still one of the best shots with a bow and arrows that I have ever seen. Beside her is a young gladiatrix whom she has trained up and who has gained a reputation as a fearsome archer. They wear magnificent feather headdresses and feathered armour, their faces boldly painted to accentuate their features.

Our criminals set out across the arena. There are fake rocks here and there, which they try to cower behind, but one after another falls in agony, pierced by arrows. Some die immediately, two have to be dispatched by Charon's deadly hammer, Strabo in his last appearance of the season.

At the end of the sequence Alyssa is chosen by Domitian to approach the imperial box and receive a wooden sword, symbol of her freedom, which she holds aloft in her bronze hand, tears of joy running down her face.

"That's another one who won't actually retire," says Strabo, watching beside me. "She loves the training yard too much. But she'll be safe from the arena and will live to train the other women."

"Thanks to Fabia," I say.

Domitian stands and begins to hurl wooden balls into the audience, aided by our staff across the whole of the amphitheatre. Each ball names a gift for the person who catches it. Today's gifts are all related to birds, from a dozen eggs to birds both alive and dead, fit for eating or singing. Some are even moulded in gold or silver. The balls are snatched up by their lucky winners and exclaimed or gloated over.

It's fully dark. Torches are lit around the edge of the arena so that we can tell the story of the Cranes and the Dwarfs from start to finish. The chorus take their places and the musicians strike up.

"Amongst the Dwarfs there was once born a girl named Oenoe, who was by nature most beautiful but also too proud."

Labeo has found us a dwarf gladiatrix, who has been elegantly attired with jewellery and extra tresses. She enters with the other dwarf gladiators, parading around the arena.

"And when Oenoe married a man and bore her first child named Mopsus, she did not give thanks to Juno for blessing her as a wife and mother, but accepted as her right the many gifts and honours which her people bestowed on her in celebration. And

Juno was angered, and ordained that Oenoe should be made into a crane, and forever lose her child."

A flock of crane dancers enter, their white wings wafting. They surround the unlucky Oenoe and transform her into one of themselves, with a white tunic and wings, her swaddled baby passed back to the dwarf gladiators.

"Lonely for her child, Oenoe the crane flew again and again to the village with her fellow cranes. But the Dwarfs, not knowing her, and fearing that the birds were attacking them, took up their weapons and fought off the birds, killing and wounding many. And from that day to this, the Cranes come yearly to the dwellings of the Dwarfs and attack them, and the Dwarfs live in fear and hatred of them."

The crane-dancers are replaced with crane-gladiatrices and the battle commences in earnest, some bouts focusing on two gladiators against each other, some in groups. The fighters are well matched and the crowd enjoys the rarity of watching dwarfs fighting women in hand-to-hand combat, something we rarely showcase.

Finally the battles are done, the winners garlanded, the losers mortified. The audience is pleased, they whoop and cheer, stamp their feet and Domitian stands to take their applause, his usually expressionless face lit up with pleasure.

"Now," says Marcus and all the torches are extinguished. The crowd murmurs in confusion, surely the show is complete? How are they to find their way out?

But in the darkness Alyssa appears again, standing in the dark arena with only a burning arrow notched to her bow, which she lifts, the audience falling silent, watching.

Like a shooting star, the arrow arcs through the air and touches the metal circle hanging above. It instantly bursts into flames, then splinters outwards, each flame rapidly traversing the ropes, each rope burning a different colour: red, orange, yellow, green, blue, violet, the pattern repeated forty times around the amphitheatre, a glittering sparkling crown which has the crowd gasping in awe as the flames spread outwards, filling the whole of the visible sky with shimmering, flickering colours.

"Magical," I say to Ignis, who is watching by my side. "You have created something wonderful."

He nods, satisfied.

The torches are re-lit, not so many that the crowd cannot still admire the sparkling crown of fire above them, but enough so that they can see to leave. Domitian first, as usual, then the crowds start to leave.

"You are an extraordinary maker of flames," I tell Ignis.

He smiles and walks away, disappearing into our hypogeum's maze-like rooms.

I hurry to our planning area, near the stairs that Marcus will use to join me but I find him already there; he must have all but run back.

"We're done," he says. His shoulders are slumped, but his face is lit up with happiness. "We're done, Althea. Come here." He enfolds me in his arms and I rest my cheek against his chest. We have finished our final task, we are free of this place and its demands on us.

"We're done," I repeat into the folds of his toga. "Thank the gods. We can leave."

"Thank the gods," echoes Marcus. "May Janus watch over us as we start our new life."

There's the tramping of feet and we both turn, Marcus' arm still around my shoulders, to find ourselves face to face with the Aedile. As usual he is surrounded by an entourage, who cram into the limited space, some of them still on the lowest steps.

"Magnificent show," says the Aedile. "Truly spectacular."

"Thank you," says Marcus. "It has been an honour to serve Rome," he adds. "I am grateful for the opportunity I was given and the trust placed in me to serve two emperors in this way. Though I am glad my time has ended now." He smiles. "The honour can go to another man and I will be glad to retire to my farm and live a quiet life."

"Of course," says the Aedile. "And you have more than earned that life. Absolutely." He gestures to his entourage of bodyguards, scribes and hangers-on and they head off through the corridor leading towards the stairs that will take them all out of the amphitheatre, though he remains behind.

Marcus is distracted by Strabo, who is carrying a heavy chest. "It can go in one of the pens, Paternus will send a man to collect it tomorrow," he calls out. "Crane costume helmets," he adds to me by way of explanation. "No doubt they can use them for some other show in the future. Or have them re-fashioned into something else. Expensive pieces."

The Aedile is still hovering.

"Yes?" asks Marcus, over his shoulder. He's less deferential in his manner, he feels free of the service he has performed these past years. The Aedile has no further hold on him.

"The Emperor," begins the Aedile, "has, umm, requested, that you undertake one last task for him."

"No," says Marcus immediately, turning to face the Aedile. "No. I have done everything that was asked of me and more. The season is over and I am free. I will be leaving Rome very soon."

"Ah, yes, ummm…" says the Aedile. He rearranges a fold of his toga, clutching at it for comfort. "He, that is to say…"

"Domitian," says Marcus. "That's his name."

The Aedile swallows, glances over his shoulder. "Yes, of course," he agrees, but still he lowers his voice. "Domitian wishes you to create a private banquet for him. In ten days' time."

Marcus shakes his head. "I already did a private event," he insists. "It was supposed to be a one off. And look how that went," he can't help adding.

"It is a most particular event, and… *he*… would most particularly like you to arrange it."

"Why?"

"He wishes it to be... theatrical. In its... ah... *execution*."

Marcus stiffens. "Execution?"

"An expression."

Marcus stares at him in silence.

The Aedile's shoulders slump. He speaks in a hurried whisper, his words spilling out rather than with his usual endless hesitation. "There is to be a spectacular private banquet in ten days' time. No expense spared. Theatrical. Extraordinary. Invitations will be sent to very high-ranking senators only. He has demanded in no uncertain terms that you must arrange this event for him. That you are not to leave Rome without completing this final task." He finishes, panting, sweat beading on his forehead.

Marcus' voice is so low I can barely hear him. "Are these men going to return home to their families, after this banquet?"

The Aedile's face is pale, his voice a tiny whisper. "I don't know."

"And if I refuse to undertake this... task... will *I* return home to my wife?"

The Aedile's body stays rigidly still, but his head moves side to side, a tiny movement, barely invisible.

Marcus straightens, his shoulders back, chin up, voice clear. "It will be my pleasure to do as the Emperor commands," he says. "I will report to you for my further orders and instructions, Aedile."

The Aedile steps backwards, nodding violently. "I will see you in my office tomorrow, Scaurus," he says, too loudly and then he turns and scurries away. I can hear his shoes on the stairs as he half-trips in his hurry to get out of the darkness.

I look up at Marcus, can only see his profile as he stares after the Aedile, his jaw set hard, his eyes cold.

"Marcus..." I begin, tentatively putting my hand on his arm. I'm not sure what I'm going to say. It's clear he cannot refuse, to do so would bring real danger upon us, but my stomach is heavy with dread at what he's getting himself into. An event that must be theatrical and spectacular, which must be *executed* to perfection? For high-ranking men who may or may not return home safely? How can this end well?

Marcus moves his arm abruptly, dislodging my hand. "I'll do what has to be done," he says. "You, however, will have no part of it."

"But I can –" I begin.

"No," he says and his voice is hard, as though he were talking to a stranger. "You will not be involved in this in any way, Althea. You will continue to plan for our departure from Rome. You will not ask me questions about what I am asked to do, you will not attend any location where I am told to stage this... event. You will pretend you never heard the conversation we have just had. And in ten days' time it will be over and we will ready ourselves to leave for the farm. Do you understand me?"

I nod.

"Good." He turns to face me, his voice softening. "I will not have you caught up in something like this."

"Do you think…?" I begin but he shakes his head.

"You know nothing about this event," he says. "Promise me, Althea."

I hesitate but put my hand in his. "Karbo will be wanting his supper," I say. "We need to get back to the insula."

His hand grips mine more tightly than usual all the way back to the insula, his pace too fast, so that I have to ask him twice to walk more slowly, which he does at once, before speeding up again.

Cassia has put on a good meal for us in the courtyard to mark the last night of the season. Adah is helping her set up a table of food for all to share.

"We'll have a real banquet before you leave," she says. "But tonight should be celebrated."

"May the gods bless you, Cassia," says Marcus, giving her a quick hug. "I could eat a whole sheep."

"Good thing I made plenty," she says. "Here, make yourself useful and carry this platter out to the table."

Most of the insula comes by over the next two hours to sit and eat and drink with us. We toast to Julia's memory and the end of our time at the Games. Cassia keeps the food coming, simple familiar comforts like warm flatbreads to dip in olive oil and garum, salted roast chickpeas, cheese, her tasty barley porridge scented with dill and cumin, platters of new season grapes, pears and apples. Marcus laughs and jokes with our friends, but occasionally his face turns thoughtful, as though his mind is elsewhere, before visibly making an effort to smile at our neighbours or raise his cup for a toast that has been proposed.

When the evening has grown late, we climb the stairs to our hut and in the dark Marcus holds me to him too tightly, as though I might be taken from him.

GOD AND MASTER

WHEN I WAKE LATE THE next morning the sun is fully risen. Marcus is gone and so is his toga, so he must have gone to the Aedile to be briefed on whatever Domitian has ordered for his private dinner in ten days' time. I hope when he returns that I will be able to coax him into telling me what it is all about. Perhaps it really will turn out to be nothing of importance, just more of Domitian's strange stubbornness.

I feed the birds, then make my way to Cassia's for breakfast. It always feels odd when a season has ended and there's no need to rise early, to hurry to the amphitheatre. I will never have to do that again. I am done at last. My shoulders relax, my chin lifts and I arrive at Cassia's with a smile on my face.

"Tay-ah," says Emilia when she sees me, waddling over to me.

"Hello, little one," I say, picking her up. "I see you've eaten your breakfast." I wipe her face, which is smeared with porridge.

"I've got some freshly baked apple rolls," says Cassia, hurrying past with a wine jug.

Emilia wriggles to get down again. "Tay-ah," she repeats, tugging me over to her corner, where she has a half-eaten bowl of barley porridge topped with date syrup.

"Oh, you haven't actually finished," I say. "Big mouth?" I offer her a spoon of the porridge.

She shakes her head vehemently, picking up her small doll, lovingly carved by Quintus, and holding it out to be fed.

"Your porridge is too good for a doll," I say. "I may have to eat it myself." I lift the spoon to my nose and smell it. "Mmm, delicious," I say, but my stomach turns. I drop the spoon and run out into Sand Street, where I vomit copiously across the cobblestones.

"Are you ill?" asks Cassia, her face worried, leaning over the counter towards me.

I shake my head. "I smelt the porridge and it made my stomach turn. It smells horrible, sour."

Cassia starts laughing.

"What?" I ask indignantly. "If there's something wrong with it, Emilia shouldn't be eating it."

"Nothing wrong with the porridge," says Cassia, pouring wine for a customer and winking at another. "What would *you* say was wrong with Althea, Maria?" she adds, spotting her heading to the bakery with a basket over her arm. "Took one smell of my good barley porridge with date syrup and threw up into the street."

"Dea Bona bless you," says Maria. "I knew by your nose."

"Knew what?" I ask.

"A baby on the way," says Maria. "What a blessing. Juno has smiled on your marriage."

I stare after her and turn back to Cassia. "It can't be!"

"Why ever not?"

I stand in the street, one hand pressed to my stomach. "Truly?"

Cassia beams. "I am so happy for you," she says. "Now get out of the street before someone runs you over," she adds. "Come here and flip pancakes for me while I throw a bucket of water to clean up that," she adds, gesturing towards the fetid puddle at my feet.

"I'm sorry," I say.

"You donkey," she says, hugging me as she passes over pancake duties.

"How did Maria know?"

Cassia giggles. "Half the women round here find an excuse to come into our courtyard when they're not sure, noses in the air so Maria can tell them if there's a baby on the way. Doesn't look any different to me," she adds, as I squint at my nose trying to see what's changed. She takes a bucket and disappears into the courtyard to get water from our fountain, returns to sluice the street clean before taking back the pancake-making. "Apple roll?"

I take a small tentative nibble but the soft warm apple smell has me retching.

"Stale bread and water for you, I'm afraid," says Cassia. "Or pickles, if you're that way inclined."

I wrinkle my nose.

"Stale bread it is."

She passes me a piece of yesterday's bread, which I manage to chew and swallow without incident. "Is that all I'm going to be able to eat for months?"

Cassia laughs. "Just a month or so."

"Much use I'll be on the farm if I'm vomiting everywhere."

"It's a hard life being a woman," says Cassia. "Juno and Bona Dea be kindly to you."

WHEN MARCUS RETURNS I WANT to rush to him and share our happy news, but he is grim faced from his meeting and it makes me fearful. He shakes his head at my tentative questions and goes to take off his toga, before eating the food I have ready in silence, ignoring both my troubled face and the nightingales who are singing for all they are worth. That night when we are alone together, I think that if he unburdens himself to me I can comfort him, he will be more cheerful and I can tell him about being with child, there is something forbidding about him being so serious, I do not want to offer up the secret joy I am holding inside.

"I worry about you," I say. "Is there nothing you can tell me that I could help with? It surely can't be any worse than some of the things we've faced over our years together. Worse than Glabrio?"

Marcus' voice is quiet in the darkness. "He's making people call him God and Master," he says.

"*God* and Master?" I repeat.

"Yes."

We're both quiet for a few moments. It's common for an emperor to be declared a god after his death, but not while he's still alive. It echoes the sort of thing Nero did and a shiver goes down my spine. "Is he dangerous, do you think?"

"Possibly," says Marcus and his admitting it frightens me. Before, he has always brushed such questions away, tried to allay my fears. But to declare yourself a god... I tremble and Marcus' arms tighten about me.

"It will be an affectation, that's all," he says quickly returning to his habit of offering comforting words. "Don't worry about it. There are only a few more days left, that's all. It's nothing we need to worry about."

"But this... event he has asked you to arrange..."

"It is nothing for you to worry about," says Marcus. "It will be over soon."

"But –"

"But nothing," says Marcus. "Sleep."

But neither of us sleeps for more than an hour that night, both lying in the silent darkness, unable to stop our fearful thoughts.

I WAKE TO SEE MARCUS tiptoeing from the room.

"Marcus."

"Shh, go back to sleep," he says, bending to kiss me. "I'll be gone all day. Rest."

"I need to tell you something."

"Can it wait?"

"No." When I tell him he will be happy and whatever Domitian has asked of him will pale into insignificance.

He perches on the edge of the bed. "Tell me."

I am suddenly shy. "I... we..." I take a deep breath. "I am pregnant."

He stares at me. "What?"

"We are going to have a baby," I say.

He crushes me to him, so fiercely that I can hardly breathe, his face buried in my neck. When he pulls back his eyes are full of tears but he is not smiling at all, only looking at me with worry.

"I'm well," I say. "Except for not being able to eat Cassia's good food." I grin, hoping he will laugh, but he only strokes my face, his expression still serious.

"Marcus," I say. "Please tell me this... banquet you are arranging for Domitian. You *are* safe?"

He nods at once. "Of course, of course I am safe," he says too quickly. "All is well. You need have no fears, none at all."

"Marcus —"

He lays a finger on my lips and manages a smile at last. "We will be so happy," he says, his voice shaking. "So happy," he repeats, as though to himself, then stands, dropping a final kiss on my head. "I must go."

I sit on the bed when he has gone. Marcus' reaction was not what I was expecting. I had thought there would be laughter and kisses, embraces and chatter between us, names, visions of our future. Happiness. This strange fierce reaction, his tears, they must be connected to what Domitian has asked of him, the joy of a coming child not enough to overcome the task ahead of him. I don't know what form it will take, but I'm convinced that Marcus is in danger and our future — the future of our child — uncertain.

I try to put on a brave face that day. Fabia comes to check on my wellbeing and pronounces herself satisfied.

"I have some news of my own," she confesses when she is done.

"What is it?"

"I will be married next June."

I gape at her. "Sadiki finally asked you?"

She's blushing, I've never seen Fabia so girlish, her usual scholarly demeanour swept away. "Yes. Father is delighted."

"And…" I don't want to crush her happiness, but it matters to her to still be a physician. "Your work?"

She's all smiles. "Sadiki knows I will always want to be a physician and he does not mind. We will work together until he is no longer an apprentice and then he may become a physician in his own right, perhaps for Paternus, as his own physician is getting older. And I told Maria and she is already wanting to care for our children." She giggles and I embrace her.

"I am so happy," I tell her. "You've made me happy enough to be hungry, even. Come to the bakery with me."

At the bakery I discover I can indeed eat without the nausea of the previous day, so I make the most of the reprieve. We fill ourselves with fruit rolls and little cheese breads, laughing at everything and nothing until Fabia says she promised Sadiki they would go to the baths together.

I return to the courtyard from the bakery and find Celer sitting in the pale autumn sunshine. He seems better than when I first met him. In those early days he would have been drunk by breakfast, one cup too many rolling him from one late evening into a befuddled morning. Now, he drinks less frequently of an evening and has a relatively clear head come the morning.

"Can I tempt you with a blackberry pastry?" I say.

He accepts and I sit with him, eating another one. How can one be so hungry one moment and vomiting the next, I wonder.

"I hear there is a baby on the way," says Celer. "Bona Dea bless you."

I smile and touch my belly. "Thank you. It hardly seems real yet."

"It'll be running around in no time," he says. "If you thought Karbo was a handful you've not had a really little one yet. You'll have your hands full."

"I don't want anything bad to happen to Karbo," I tell Celer, anxiety rising up in me.

"I'll be watching out for him, I give you my word by Neptune," says Celer.

"You can't keep him safe on the track, that is in the hands of the gods," I say. "But don't let him…"

"Drink too much? Gamble? Womanise? Get in with the wrong crowd?"

"All those things," I say firmly.

"I understand better than anyone what excessive drinking can do," says Celer. "And I've seen what happens with the rest as well. I care about the boy too much to let him go down those paths, Althea, I'll watch over him like he was my own. I feel as if he is, sometimes," he adds.

"You're an uncle to him," I say. "And you'll have to be a father to him when Marcus is far away. I know you'll do what you can to keep him safe."

He nods. "I drink less when he's around," he says. "He gives me reason to stay sober."

I pat his shoulder. "Thank you, Celer. I'll sleep easier knowing he has you around. And now I need your help."

"Anything."

"We need to buy a second cart and two mules. We have one cart in the storage rooms and we'll take the two horses from the stables, but we'll have a lot to take with us. Strabo will drive one cart and Marcus the other. We'll keep the horses for riding and use the mules for farm work."

"Leave it with me," says Celer, getting to his feet. "I'll get you a good price for the mules and a sturdy cart."

I watch him go, my mouth set in a determined line. I'm not sure what Marcus is doing, but I will not stand by and watch our future be ruined by Domitian's whims. I will not wait for Marcus to have everything ready for our departure to the farm, I will do it myself and as soon as this final task is over, we will leave. I find myself whispering a prayer to Janus, god of new beginnings, to help me. I find myself caught between the past, where Marcus is struggling to satisfy Domitian, and the future, the baby and the farm offering a happier time ahead of us, if we can only escape Rome and reach Puteoli safely.

By the end of the day Celer has already delivered on his word, a second cart has been brought into the courtyard and put in a corner out of the way. It was pulled by two young mules, good-natured and calm. I feed them apples before Celer takes them to be stabled alongside our two horses for the few weeks we will still be here. Adah comes to stand by me, strokes their noses and makes soft sounds to them, before picking up an amphora of water to carry to her room on the roof.

"That's too heavy for you," I say. "You should have called me or Karbo. When I'm gone, promise me you'll ask him for help. He's a strong boy. He'll look after you."

She follows me up the stairs, her feet slow. "Time was I could carry two, all on my own."

"Those days are gone," I tell her. "Ask for help. Promise me."

I turn to look at her and she gives a half nod.

"Can I ask *you* for help?" I say.

"What is it you need, child?"

"Come with us to the farm," I say. "I'm going to be all alone there, Marcus will be out with the animals and the land. I'll be in a new home with a hundred tasks I'm unfamiliar with and a baby on the way. I would like someone with me."

"I know nothing of chickens and farms," she says.

"You know about bees," I say. "There are old beehives there, I saw them years ago, all broken and falling apart. We will have to set up new ones. You could look after the bees and the doves while I learn to care for pigs and chickens and tend a vegetable garden. I'd enjoy the company."

Adah looks away. "I'm too old for change."

"Nonsense," I say. "You don't have any family left here in Rome. We've known each other all these years. Come with Marcus and me. Marcus will have Strabo to be his right-hand man, but I'll be needing a grandmother for this baby. The four of us have hardly any family left to us but between us we can start a new one."

She shakes her head but her eyes are sad.

"Think about it," I say, leaving the amphora by her door, and she shuffles silently back into her room. I watch the door close. Am I promising her something that will never happen? No. I have to believe we are still going to the farm, no matter what Marcus is working on. I have to keep reaching out to the future, making it possible one step at a time, I cannot stand still and allow all our plans to be taken from us.

WHEN I TELL KARBO a baby is on the way he is all smiles, then solicitously asks how I am feeling, which touches me, my once little son now looking after me. We sit together in the pale autumn sunlight and for once I let him talk about his future as a charioteer and keep a smile on my face, do not wince or mutter dire warnings, instead I tell him how brave he is, how gifted with the horses. The decision is made now, and I need him to feel my pride as well as my fears, even if they rush back to me from time to time.

Marcus comes home late but gratefully accepts a bowl of vegetable porridge, a cup of wine and an onion bread. He asks how I am feeling, pats my still flat belly with affection, but does not say anything about his day. I watch him eat, desperate to ask more.

"Are there many people invited to the banquet?" I ask, trying to sound as though I am just passing the time of day.

His shoulders tighten immediately. "We agreed you would not ask questions."

"I was only wondering."

He shakes his head, carries on eating in silence, refuses to meet my gaze until we go upstairs to bed.

"You spoke in your sleep last night," he says in the dark.

"What did I say?"

"'Karbo.'"

"I said his name?"

"And gave a little sob," says Marcus, pulling me close to him. "Are you fretting about our boy?"

"He will be all alone," I say, my voice wavering though I try to control it.

"He absolutely will not be all alone," says Marcus. "I would not allow him to stay if I thought that. He will live here, surrounded by people who are family to him and have been for years. Maria will look after him, Cassia will feed him, he has his own roof hut here and a driving place at the stables. Celer watches over him and his friends seem like good boys."

I let out my breath. Hearing Marcus speak about the future is comforting, even if it is Karbo's racing career. "I know. Just… he is very young. Even if he has done his Liberalia."

"Plenty of people make their way in the world alone at his age," says Marcus. "He will be well cared for. The most dangerous part of his life is the racing and I'm not sure we could have changed that even if we stayed. I could have forbidden him from being a driver, but he would find a way to do it anyway, you know he would."

When I wake the next morning I set to work on Karbo's roof hut. Even though it was only rebuilt recently, I drag everything out of it and clean it thoroughly, patch-painting the odd dirty bit of wall without disturbing the paintings of the chariot drivers.

"You can't touch them," says Karbo in the doorway. "They're my lucky charms. They're the reason I'm going to be a charioteer."

"Never mind them," I say. "Get those cobwebs off the rafters while I take these blankets to be washed and we'll beat your mattress."

"Are you nestbuilding for me?" he asks.

"Yes," I say. "I want to think of you warm and safe in your bed here."

He grins. "You're a fussy mother hen."

"Yes I am," I agree. "It's my right and my duty as your mother."

He drapes one long arm about me and gives me a gentle head-butt with a small sound attached to it which might be a kiss. "You're a kind mother," he mutters.

I hug him but he pulls away too quickly for my liking. "Got cobwebs to clean," he says. "Can't be hanging around cuddling you all day."

I watch him, marvel at his height as he pokes at the cobwebs with a broom, before getting back to my painting. The room smells fresher already, a young man does not always have the most pleasant smell about him after a day's hard work. "You're to wash every morning and go to the baths regularly," I instruct him and get an eyeroll for my trouble.

I bring out the heavy woollen blankets from storage and have them washed at Quintus' family fullers, re-paint the exterior of the hut adding a fresh red trim to the base of the wall, even though it would have done for another few years. The work has already taken me three days. Marcus, coming home early for once, smiles when he sees my project and does not comment. The next day, he drops a bundle of cloth in my lap.

"What is it?"

"Cloth for new tunics for him. And I've ordered him new winter boots at the cobblers and left money for next year too. Maria is stitching him a cloak with a thicker cloth I bought, the height he is now that cloak you made him last year will be too short by spring, might as well sew him a man's size and be done with it."

The cloth is good wool in two colours, a blue and a green, the colours Marcus himself favours. "Thank you."

"We have done all we can to keep him fed and clothed, housed and looked after. He has good friends and this insula is a family to him, even if we are not here."

I nod, trying not to let tears fall. "This lot will keep me busy," I say. "I better get started."

He strokes my hair, drops a kiss on the top of my head and I smile, reassured. It is only when he has gone that I realise that all his comforting words were about Karbo's future, not ours, and feel anxious again.

I SPEND THREE DAYS SEWING for all I am worth, with Adah at my side, who weaves two beautiful belts for Karbo to go with his new tunics. Finally, I stand with Karbo in his refurbished hut, clean and freshly painted, his chest filled with warm clothes and good strong boots for the winter. I lay herbs on top of them to keep a pleasant scent about him and he smiles at the sight of them.

"Fausta used to smell of rosemary and mint. She used to brush her hands along Julia's plants and rub them over her toga."

"She did," I say. The little boy he was, curled up weeping, holding her toga pressed to his face so he could smell her when she had been taken away. It seems a sad recollection, but he is smiling. "She was fierce," he says with admiration. "She made me feel safe, like nothing could get me when she was around."

"I hope you feel the same now," I say.

"I didn't for a while," he admits. "When she died, I thought I was all alone again. But you were there. You and Marcus. And now –" He gestures about himself. "I have a home. I have parents, and even if you are moving away I am a man. I have a job, friends."

"Do you remember anything else from before?"

He shakes his head, but his face is still open. "Nothing worth remembering," he says. "I look to the future."

I can't help welling up. "You're wise for such a young boy," I say. "I'm proud of you."

"Less of the boy," he says lifting his chin and grinning. "But wise, I will admit to."

"I wish you were coming with us," I say. "But I will bring your brother or sister to see you race one day, so you'd better be good at it." *And stay alive*, I add in my head. *To all the gods, keep my boy alive.*

He's already standing taller at the very thought. "Yes," he says. "You can bring them when I am the Purple team's top driver and they can watch me earn a laurel wreath."

"I will do that," I promise. "One of many, I'm sure."

MY EFFORTS AT KEEPING BUSY have used up eight days and the thought of Marcus' mysterious event being in only two days makes me anxious. I find myself searching for more things to do that will help our longed-for future plans come true. I find a seller of seeds and order everything I will need to begin a vegetable garden as well as several sacks of wheat and barley. Marcus and Strabo will need to begin ploughing as soon as we reach the farm in order to plant the crops in good time. I think of the tasks Marcus has mentioned in the past when we have talked about the farm and visit a tool shop to purchase the tools we will soon be in need of, from a plough to shovels, sickles and pruning knives. A farm that has been abandoned for many years will have many trees and vines to prune. No doubt we will need to purchase oxen for the ploughing and slaves to work the farm, but these will be better off being bought locally, city slaves would hardly be accustomed to farm work or have any useful knowledge related to farming. I ask for the heavier items to be delivered to us the next day, carry the smaller pieces back myself. When I come back to the roof I find Adah sitting in the sunshine, having finished tending to the bees. I sit next to her and turn my face to the sun, soaking in its warmth.

"Have you changed your mind, Adah?"

She gives a little smile. "Always persistent."

"Do you remember when we first met? You startled me, appearing out of the darkness, up here on the roof."

She touches my hand. "You asked if I was warm enough. A kind child."

I lean against her. "You always call me that. I'm a grown woman."

"I'm too old for you to be anything but a child to me."

"In that case you should come with me to the farm to care for me. You can't leave a child like me all alone in the world." I make a pitiful face and hear one of her rare chuckles.

"You always were good at persuading people."

I straighten up to look at her. "Is that a yes, Adah?"

She shakes her head. "No. You're right, you're a grown woman, you will find your own way in this new life without help from an old woman like me."

I sigh. "If you change your mind, tell me. Even if our cart is halfway down the street, we would turn back for you. I'll miss you. And your songs. And your honey."

She pats my hand. "I'll pack some for you to take. And candles. You'll need them."

"Won't be the same without you there."

"Marcus will take care of you. He's a good man, a good husband."

"He is the best husband," I say smiling. "Only I'd have liked another woman about the place. I'm leaving behind Cassia and Fabia and Maria. I've already lost Julia. And I have to leave you too. Marcus will have Strabo, but who will be my right hand?"

On the day of Domitian's banquet Marcus does not leave before I wake, as he has the other days. He spends time with me in our hut, gentle and loving, then comes with me to Cassia's for breakfast. Although I have been nauseous on many of the past few days, for once my stomach does not rebel and I wolf three pancakes drenched in date syrup, then gulp fresh grape juice, making up for lost meals.

"Thought you didn't care for sweet things?" I ask Marcus, who has, unusually, ordered the same pancakes as me

"I care for you and what you enjoy," he says, taking another bite. He sips some of the grape juice before grimacing. "That's far too sweet," he decides. "Wine, please, Cassia."

He spends time chatting to Quintus and plays with Emilia, nods when I tell him about the mules and extra cart.

"Most of what we need is ready," I say. "It only needs loading up and the horses and mules bringing for us to leave. When will we go, do you think?"

He turns his face away. "Soon."

I want to keep talking, but Marcus looks up at the sky and frowns. "Time for me to leave."

"Already?" I ask and I can't help holding his arm tighter, wanting him to stay with me.

"There are things to prepare for this evening," he says, and his voice has lost all its happiness.

"Tell me you will be safe tonight, Marcus," I whisper, and my voice shakes.

"You are safe here," he says and touches my belly. "This little one is safe. Karbo is safe. That is what matters."

"That's not what I asked," I say, suddenly cold in the sunshine. "Marcus –"

"I have to go," he says, pulling away from me.

Reluctantly, I let him go, but as soon as I do so, he turns back and hugs me fiercely, crushing me to him. When he lets me go his eyes are serious. "If anything –" he stops and then starts again. "Strabo is a good man, he'll look after you. Trust him."

"Marcus! What do you mean if anything happens – Strabo? – what are you *saying*?"

"Goodbye," he says and he's gone, striding out of the courtyard gate. I stand staring, then run after him but he's already crossed Sand Street and is disappearing into the jumble of tiny streets that will take him towards the Forum and the imperial palace. I want to follow him but a rumbling ox cart is passing in one direction and two smaller mule carts are headed in the opposite direction and by the time they've all moved out of my way I have no chance of catching up with him.

I SPEND THE REST OF the afternoon alone, pacing about the rooftop, uncertain of what to do, if there is even anything I can do. His behaviour, his last words to me, have frightened me more than I can admit to anyone.

I try to comfort myself by thinking of the first time our paths crossed when I was still a slave. The dinner party that Marcus and his team arranged for my rich merchant master could easily have turned into an orgy but Marcus' orders meant that any such notions by the guests were quickly directed elsewhere, protecting us household slaves from being used for their pleasure. I think of his calm and commanding presence over the years I have known him, how he turned difficult and frightening situations around and kept us safe. The sun sinks and I try to imagine what kind of a banquet he has been asked to create for Domitian. A triclinium at the imperial palace, mosaic floors and wall paintings, sculptures and stucco reliefs for decoration, lamps everywhere. Couches with bronze and ivory decorations, gold and silver tableware. The courses: the gustatio of small and tempting treats such as honeyed dormice to whet the appetite, a main course flaunting such extravagances as peacocks served with their feathers re-attached for decoration, sow's udder, giant eels. Sweet items to complete the meal, perhaps cream puddings, honey-soaked cakes, elegant pastries and gilded fruits, elaborately displayed on golden platters. To drink, well-watered fine wines, either heated or iced. Then some form of entertainment: dancing girls, musicians, perhaps gladiators putting on a show. These would all be commonplace at an elaborate meal fit for an emperor and his guests.

But what has Domitian asked for that has kept Marcus busy and fearfully silent for ten days, has made him say goodbye to me as though he might not return, committing me to Strabo's care as though I am about to be widowed?

The guests, who are they? The Aedile only said they were men of importance, senators or the like. Are they about to be punished in some horrific way, as Glabrio was? Poisoning by mushrooms, daggers hidden until it is too late? Something in the wine?

What has Marcus been asked to arrange?

THE DARKEST NIGHT

I CAN'T SLEEP.

I LIE RIGID ON MY back on my bed, staring into the darkness. How long has it been since Marcus left? How many hours? Once again, I imagine the likely event. Some sort of dinner. In the palace. In the old days, the first thought would be some sort of orgy, but Domitian is known for his strict rules against that sort of thing. So what? Games like the ones we held at Domitian's villa, with the aim of punishing someone, as he did with Glabrio? If so, why the secrecy? He hardly bothered to keep the last event a secret, why would he want to do so now? Unless it is even worse? And what would be worse? Attacking multiple people? Torture? I think back to the Aedile's answer when Marcus asked him outright whether the guests would be returning to their families, his fearful uncertainty.

I try to sleep again, roll onto my side and close my eyes. Marcus knows what he is doing. He has created plenty of spectacles in his time, including this kind of overly lavish dinner. If Domitian wishes to harm someone, like he did at the Alban villa, that is his business. Marcus need have nothing to do with it.

Unless.

Unless what he is about to do is so awful that there must be no witnesses.

My eyes fly open again and I stare into the dark as another thought comes to me, a cold weight in my stomach.

Darkness. I am surrounded by darkness, just as the sorceress said. Is this what she saw? Me in the dark, with danger coming closer? If something were to happen to Marcus…

I roll out of bed, stumbling in the darkness to find my shoes and belt. No time to light a lamp. Instead I feel my way out of the hut, where a full moon lights up the rooftop in cold pale shadows. Leaving the door open I reach back to grab my palla and wrap it about me, cross the roof to Karbo's hut, where I knock softly, then pull the door open and lean in.

"Karbo."

"Wha –"

"Wake up."

The shadows move. "What's going on?"

"I need you to get up."

"Why?"

"Just get dressed."

I reach for the lamp he keeps on his shelf, spend a few moments cursing under my breath as I try to light it, the little sparks from the flint and steel striking together failing to ignite the little scraps of linen strands kept for this purpose, before finally a small flame flickers. As the room brightens Karbo squints, half-falls over his shoes and turns to face me. "What's going on?"

"I am afraid for Marcus."

"Why? What's happened?"

"He had to undertake a final task for Domitian tonight at the imperial palace."

"I thought you did all three tasks."

"We did. This is an additional one. A secret event."

"What is it?"

I shake my head. "A dinner for Domitian and his invited guests. Marcus wouldn't tell me the details. But I have a bad feeling about it and I'm worried for his safety."

"I'll go and find him."

"No," I say. "I can't let you do that. I need you to wake Cassia and everyone else who can help and get us ready to leave Rome."

"You're going to leave now?"

"When I find Marcus and bring him back here, yes."

"But things won't be ready."

"They will if you get them ready for us," I say. "Most things are packed, but the two carts need loading. We'll need the horses and mules fetching from the stables and we need food to take with us. Cassia can take care of food and Celer can get the horses. Can I leave you in charge?"

"I don't think you should go alone," he says, his face worried. In the poor light he is a child again and I place my hand on his shoulder.

"I have to go alone," I say. "I can't draw attention to myself. I just want to find Marcus. I don't care what Domitian wants. If Marcus is in danger I need to get him out of there."

"But what if the event isn't finished, or Domitian –"

I pull him towards the door. "There's no time for guessing what's happening," I say. "It's time to act. I have waited too long on the whims of emperors. I won't lose my happiness because of one. I won't lose my husband and your father if he's in danger because of some scheming plan of Domitian's. We have given enough to this life. It's time to claim our own lives back."

"I'm scared," says Karbo, his voice a whisper.

"Don't be scared," I say. "Just do as I say. Get everything ready for Marcus and me to leave while I find him and bring him back here. I'll find a way to get Strabo to join us." I squeeze his hand, hurry down the stairs and across the courtyard as he makes his way to Cassia's apartment to wake her and Quintus.

The courtyard gate is ajar, as Julia always had it. I slip out and jump back, terrified, at the sight of a dark figure standing in the moonlight.

"The darkness has come," she says and I recognise the sorceress.

"I felt it."

"Leave now," she says.

"I will, but I have to find Marcus. He's undertaking a task for Domitian."

"Do you want me to come with you?"

"No."

"What can I do?"

"Pray. Or cast a spell. Or whatever you can do. Keep Marcus safe. Keep this insula safe so that no-one can find us till we leave."

"Run," she says, and walks back down Virgin's Street, into the darkness of the night.

I RUN. THROUGH THE DARK streets, heart pounding from fear, legs shaking under me as shadows move or sounds come from behind me or to one side. Rome's streets are dangerous at night, I am risking my own safety and that of my baby. But I have to find Marcus.

The tangle of small streets leading to the Forum, so well-known to me, seem strange and different at night. I'm grateful there is a full moon, there would be no light at all to guide me otherwise. At last I reach the Forum.

But these vast open spaces are even more menacing. The giant temples and public buildings loom over me and yet contain their own shadows, perfect places for thieves or other evildoers to hide and watch a woman, all alone, making her way towards the imperial palace. I am panting, ragged breaths that sound too loud even to me, that I fear will draw attention to me from unseen eyes.

The burning torches and Praetorian Guard in full uniform outside the palace are a welcome sight as I draw closer. At least there is more light and if I were to scream now someone would come to my aid. Outside the front are more than a dozen dark litters, waiting for their wealthy owners to emerge and be carried home in style. Beside each one, a black-hooded figure with a blazing torch, presumably their servants, although they are standing oddly still, not milling about taking the opportunity to talk to one another and pass the time.

"Althea?"

I jump, but it's Strabo. I could cry with relief. I lean against him and he tentatively puts one awkward arm around me. "Is – is everything alright?"

"I need to get Marcus away from here," I say, still gasping from my run. "I'm afraid for him, Strabo."

He doesn't argue with me. "Me too. Have you seen?"

"Seen what?"

He doesn't answer, only takes me by the hand and leads me to one side of the palace's frontage, where a small gap leads to a narrow alleyway, probably a service entrance which slaves and servants would use, away from the grand palace frontage.

"Look," he says, under his breath.

From this angle, the hooded figures are even more unsettling, their skin seems to be black, but not like Karbo's deep brown, rather an odd glistening black. I squint, tilt my head.

"Painted," says Strabo.

"What?"

"Their skin's been painted."

Everything was black.

"Who are they?"

"The guests arrived and once they'd gone in, Marcus came out and dismissed their own servants and litters. Then these arrived."

Everything was black. You were dressed in black, all around you was black. Everything. The words of the sorceress. I glance at my palla, a rich blue in the flickering light, a darker colour in the night, my pale green tunic under it. *They're not black*, I think, as though this makes any difference to the fear gripping me. But these hooded men, their skin painted black… the odd sheen to their faces, their eyes showing white against the unnatural darkness, some of them now turning to look at us.

"Where is Marcus?" I ask under my breath.

Strabo points down the alleyway. "There's a door there," he says. "I saw him go in there. He told me to stay here, not to move until he emerged."

A safety measure. Marcus has seen fit to have burly Strabo waiting for him to accompany him back to the insula through Rome's treacherous streets. This only serves to unsettle me further. Marcus is not given to unnecessary fuss over his own personal safety.

"I need to find him," I tell Strabo.

He shakes his head. "He said not to go in there."

"I don't care what he said. When did the guests arrive?"

"Not long ago."

"It's very late to be starting a dinner. Strabo, I'm going in. Stay here as Marcus told you to."

He grabs my hand, his face anxious, but I pull away and he lets me go. I stop at the start of the alleyway, staring again at the strange glistening faces turned my way, before walking down the dark alley. It's a tight space, if I were to fully reach out my arms I could touch both walls. Below are neat cobbles, but there are no torches here to light my way. Halfway along, I find a door on my left, a plain wooden thing, nothing like the grand doors at the front of the palace.

I put my hand out, feeling for a handle, but the door begins to move. I take a deep breath and push.

The room I step into is a kind of backstage to an event, familiar from my years under the arena. There are burning lamps for light, additional ones unlit in case anyone should require them. Black cloaks hanging up in a corner, little pots on a shelf with paintbrushes beside them. Scrolls, half unrolled on a table. A pile of plates, as though a meal is about to be served. A knife. A discarded flute and pipes. A giant hammer such as the one Charon carries.

I move further into the room. Opposite the door by which I came in is another door, which must lead further into the palace, to wherever Marcus is. I put my hand on the door, hesitate, but the door moves under my hand, swings open and I gasp, staring up into the black mask of Charon worn under a hood, the figure looming over me.

I scream and the black-clad figure swoops on me, puts a hand over my mouth, holds me so tightly I can't move.

"Be quiet," and even in my terror I recognise Marcus' voice, slump against him in relief and he lets me go. He reaches up and lifts away the black mask, revealing his face underneath. His skin is painted black around his eyes and mouth.

"What are you doing here?" His voice is very low, his skin, where it is not painted black, is pale. I've never seen Marcus this scared and it terrifies me.

I take a step backwards. "I wanted to make sure you were safe."

"I told you to have no part in this! You need to leave."

"But –"

"But nothing. Leave. Leave *now*, Althea." His voice is cold. He is angry, as men often are when they are scared.

"Will you be safe?" I ask, stubborn.

"I don't know," he admits.

He is not even certain enough of his safety to blithely lie to me, pretend that yes of course, all is well, run along, he will be home soon. "I'm not leaving."

"You have to. I can't guarantee your safety."

"That's why I'm staying. Because you can't guarantee yours."

"Please don't make me drag you out of here by force, Althea," he says.

"I'm not making you do anything," I say. "But I'm not leaving."

We stand staring at each other. My heart is beating fast, I think of my baby within me, its mother leading it into danger. But what would my life be without Marcus?

"Tell me what's going on," I say.

"There isn't time."

"I need to know. It's a dinner?"

"Yes."

"Who's attending?"

"Important men. Those who have spoken behind his back. Those who are known to dislike him. Enemies. They've been kept waiting for more than two hours. They have no idea what's going on."

"How many?"

"Seventeen. Plus him, of course. Two tables of nine."

"Is he – is he planning to poison them?"

Marcus swallows, there is fear in his eyes. "I don't know."

"What did he ask you to plan?"

"I'm running out of time, Althea. They're about to arrive."

I clutch at Marcus' arm. "Don't go in there. Whatever's been arranged. Don't go."

"I have to."

"Come with me. We can leave."

He shakes his head. "The doors have all been closed. There's only one way out now."

"But we could use the side door –"

He's fumbling with his mask, fastening it back onto his face with thin leather straps, pulling up his cloak again to cover his hair. "Stay in this room. I may be able to slip away. But not now. If I leave before it is over Domitian will notice."

"I want to be with you. I'm not letting you out of my sight."

"You have to."

I shake my head, still gripping his arm, looking at his eyes through the black mask.

He breathes out in a rush. "You're the most stubborn woman I've ever met. You can't go in there without a costume or you'll be found out." He pulls away, picks up a pile of black cloth and throws it at me.

"Put it on. And come here." He picks up one of the little pots and a brush as I pull on the cloak. "Head up."

He dips the brush into the pot, holds my chin and paints something wet and cold across my face.

"Open your mouth and close your eyes."

The cold wet paint is daubed onto my eyelids, my lips, even my ears, down my neck. When he's done he pulls the cloak tighter about me, uses brooches to pin it so that my clothing underneath is hidden. I try to imagine what I must look like, think of the glistening black faces in torchlight of the hooded figures by the entrance but there's no time, Marcus is kneeling at my feet. He removes my shoes and paints my feet black too.

"What have you arranged in there?" I ask, but he doesn't reply.

"You're done," he says at last. "Follow me. Don't speak. If I give you something to carry, carry it. Otherwise, stand still and be quiet."

"Marcus –"

"There's one moment when we could leave. When Domitian orders a final drink, a nightcap. We can't leave before then or he'll notice. Once that drink has been ordered, slaves will bring the drinks and the evening is over. We can leave at that moment, but we cannot leave before, we cannot draw attention to our absence. You must trust me."

"I trust you," I say, but my voice shakes.

"Follow," he says. "And remember, don't speak."

He's already striding across the room and I follow him. Before he opens the double doors he picks up the large hammer, turns his head and blows out the two lamps, plunging the room into darkness. He pulls at the door and we emerge into the triclinium.

The whole room is black. I almost stop walking, but self-preservation keeps my feet moving, following Marcus' billowing cloak as he enters the room. The ceiling is black.

The walls.

The floor.

Everything is black.

Flickering lamps around the room give light, but even the lamps are disconcerting, they are funerary lamps, like the one the sorceress saw in her vision, like those hung up in roadside tombs, lit by the descendants of the departed.

We are not alone. All around the room, standing against the black walls, are young boys of perhaps Karbo's age. Stripped entirely naked, they have been painted all over with thick black paint. Even their hair has been covered in it and slicked back. They stand in silence, like statues, only their eyes watch Marcus and me as we enter the room.

There are two black tables in the middle of the room, each furnished with three black couches, so that two groups of nine men can eat in comfort.

If it can be called comfort. The couches are plain wood, painted black, bereft of furnishings: no cushions, no drapes. They look like funeral biers. Any Roman would feel deeply uncomfortable at the idea of lying on one.

My stomach lurches. This is the blackness the sorceress saw. Me dressed in black, the black all around me. This was her vision and it is coming true. I had thought the blackness referred to the storm, thought the danger had passed, but I was wrong and now there is no escape. My hand shapes into the gesture against evil spirits. Domitian's guests are doomed. How can he have anything but death in mind for them?

Marcus gestures to me, directing me to a space of wall not taken up by the boys. I stand against it, wrapped in my black cloak, afraid. I have begged to be here, but I will surely be noticed, since I do not look like the others. And if I am not found out, I will be standing here, watching while a dinner takes place, during which, no doubt, the guests will be poisoned or have their throats cut. Why did I insist on coming in here? Why did I not do as Marcus told me and stay out of this altogether? I hesitate and Marcus' eyes are on me at once, a quick shake of the head. It is too late anyway. I can hear footsteps in the corridor and the doors are flung open as the sorceress' warning echoes in my head: *should you recognise the place I saw, leave it immediately, no matter the risk.*

"Welcome, honoured guests," Marcus says, his voice low and deep. "Welcome to this most distinguished gathering."

The guests in the doorway have stopped at the sight of the room. They are older men, balding or with grey or white hair. Usually they would wear togas, as befitting their senatorial or knightly status, but this is a banquet, and so they have arrived in their dining clothes, brightly coloured, loosely-belted synthesis: dining robes, which allow for comfort while lounging on couches eating. At a formal dinner, surrounded by elegant furnishings, they add to a bright and engaging scene, suited to a party. Here, standing in a black abyss, they look like a strange joke, like a gaggle of vain women inappropriately parading their finery at a funeral.

"Enter," says Marcus, to the still frozen group. "Take up your places."

If they could turn and run, they would, but there are guards behind them, blocking the door through which they came. These men were invited to a dinner with an emperor they dislike. Nevertheless, they expected to be safe, have not thought to be fearful, have arrived in their finest clothes. Stripped of their own slaves, who might have protected them, they have realised their mistake. Have remembered that the man they have reviled behind his back has the power of life and death over them, every day, and today he has decided to exert that power.

"Enter," says Marcus again and it is a command, they have no choice but to step into the black room and face their imminent death. Their eyes flicker round and meet the eyes of the silent, black-painted boys. My attire draws a few extra glances, but they return their gaze quickly to Marcus, his height and mask dreadful to them. They have all been to the Games, they have all sat and applauded as Charon has made his entrance, summoned by the chorus calling his name. Striding across the sand, his deadly hammer raised and then the sickening sound of a skull being crushed, another gladiator or criminal dispatched to the underworld. Now they wish they had not enjoyed that spectacle so much, they wonder if Domitian will applaud as their skulls are crushed in this black room, whether their families will ever know what happened to them.

"Take your places," says Marcus.

A dining couch should be relaxing to lie on. Guests at grand dinners hosted by my former masters all but threw themselves onto the couches, with a grunt of pleasure and a call of, "You there, bring me wine," to the nearest slave. These guests shuffle to their places, half-kneel, then lie, stiff as corpses, on the funeral biers. It takes a few slow moments. The men on the table where Domitian will take his place leave a vast gap for their host, while they crush together on the couches. Those on the second table are no doubt grateful to be further away from their host – or is that a bad thing? Are those close to the host there to watch the other table die? Their faces are full of barely suppressed panic as they take their places, stiff and awkward at the bare table in front of them. Usually the tables would already be lavishly laid with dishes of olives, dates, tasty snacks to munch on before the main courses arrive. These tables have only black olives in small black dishes, which no-one seems inclined to touch.

Marcus turns to me and holds out his hammer. I step forward, reach out one hand, take it, return to my place by the wall. The hammer is heavy, I lower it to my side, but the weight of it pulls on my arm.

Marcus claps his hands and the guests wince at the loud sound. Something is about to happen.

The door opens again. The guests are unsure of what to do. They are already lying down but in the doorway stands Domitian, their emperor, whom they should greet with some kind of obeisance, a dignified bow or even embrace, if they know him well. Some half-kneel in an attempt to get up but think better of it. All of them try to bow their heads which results in dipping their heads over the edge of the couches, baring their necks as though waiting for the slice of a sword. They jerk their heads back up, crane to watch Domitian take his place.

He is dressed in a finely woven synthesis robe, as is correct for a dinner, but in an unheard-of black, with a black woven belt, worn loose as though in anticipation of a good meal. His eyes are bright and all can see he is excited by what is to come. He glances approvingly round the room, nodding at Marcus' dark-clad Charon as at a good friend, giving his quick odd smile, teeth bared.

"Time for dinner, I think," he says, and takes his place. The men closest to him pull back so far that they are in danger of falling off the couch.

Marcus gives a tiny nod and the boys around the room come to life. They move away from the walls, whirling to the centre of the room, where they begin a dance without music, an eerie slow spinning about, arms undulating, as though shades of the dead have drifted here from the underworld and are celebrating something we know nothing of, perhaps an imminent increase in their number. The men watch, their faces full of fear. Only Domitian seems calm, entertained.

The dance is over but instead of returning to their places by the walls, the boys pass by the doorway, where an unseen person gives each of them a funerary lamp. The boys reverently place one lamp by each guest, before circling the room again and this time returning with black painted slabs shaped like miniature gravestones engraved with each diner's name. The slabs are placed on the table in front of the diners, as though they were dinner plates. The men recoil from the slabs, though Domitian strokes his engraved name as though admiring the craftsmanship. The boys take up places, one behind each diner. The guests look over their shoulders, searching the boys' hands to see if they are holding a weapon.

"I'm hungry," announces Domitian. "Serve the gustatio."

The doors swing open. The guests, rather than lounging peacefully, indolently waiting to be fed, twist to see what is coming, are not soothed by the entrance of yet more black-painted naked slaves carrying jugs of wine and black cups, one of which is set by each man, the wine mixed, water and ice added. Most diners at such a meal would direct the slave as to their liking: a little more ice, a little more wine. These cowed men remain silent as each slave prepares their drink, except Domitian, of course.

"Not so much ice," he instructs the slave. "Start again. It's a warm night for the time of year but it doesn't agree with my digestion to have too much ice. Don't you agree?" he adds, speaking to the man on his left, a ruddy-faced senator who has turned very pale.

"Absolutely, Imper – our Master and God," stutters the man.

Domitian nods, serious. "I prefer the winter, when we warm the wine," he says, as though speaking of something of great importance. "Poor digestion is not a thing to be taken lightly. I have suffered with it often and my physicians tell me we must be mindful of small matters of health if we do not wish to die before our time."

There are a few awkward nods.

The slaves retreat and then return, laying out spoons and forks carved from black onyx. They hoist up large black platters heaped up with something I cannot see until they lower them to serve the guests.

"The entrails of birds," announces Domitian. "From the Auguraculum. I had them brought here this very day."

The guests are served with heaps of carbonised remains of entrails that have been burnt, such as those offered to the dead at a funeral.

"Eat, eat," says Domitian, using his spoon to scoop up the blackened mess and chewing it with every appearance of enjoyment.

The guests pick up their spoons, poke at the stinking charred piles, tentatively scoop up minute amounts, put it in their mouth, try not to gag, struggle to swallow. To eat the food reserved for the gods or for the dead is a blasphemy and a danger. A blasphemy if it were stolen from the mouths of the gods. A danger from the mouths of the dead, who may feel you are one of them, summon you to the underworld to continue dining with them. These guests might scoff in daylight at the idea of the gods punishing them for some misdemeanour, but not now. Not in the dark night they find themselves in, in this black room they cannot escape, with an emperor run mad.

"You must eat it all," says Domitian. "Else how can I serve the next course?"

They choke it down, the foul-tasting combination of faeces and soot, drink more wine than they should to manage to swallow, even though every sip they take might be poisoned. Somehow, the food is eaten.

"You may bring the next course," says Domitian graciously to the slaves.

The doors are opened, more black platters brought out, this time laden with towering piles of seafood. At the base, shining heaps of black-shelled mussels, atop of which vast black eels are coiled together, mouths propped open to show their razor-sharp teeth. Served alongside is a black bread. I am not sure how the cooks have achieved this, perhaps using squid ink. The diners' faces grow ever more distressed as they are served. Not so Domitian, who has begun to chat with great animation about gladiatorial combat and its origins.

"Of course today it is only for spectacle," he says. "The Flavian Amphitheatre has been my family's great legacy to Rome. The entertainment is magnificently orchestrated, wouldn't you say?"

The diners hurry to assent, mumbling about how wonderful the shows are, such generosity from the imperial purse, the vision of the Flavian dynasty in providing a wonder of the world, nothing like it anywhere in the empire.

"But they did not *begin* as spectacle," says Domitian. "The gladiatorial Games have a distinguished tradition of being performed as part of funeral rituals."

The diners fall silent. Domitian's continued references to death are adding to the horror of the room. They try to continue eating, even though every mouthful of the black food must be an effort.

"What we now call *munera*, the Games," Domitian says. "From *munus*. A gift. A gift for the dead. A tribute to those fallen. Livy talks about their origin in his writing and of course they are well documented during the Punic Wars. Some people suppose they come from burial rites of the Etruscans, but no-one is quite sure, only that they have been linked with funerals from the very beginning. Deaths to honour death." He gives his bared-teeth smile and takes a large portion of eel onto his fork.

"Delicious," he pronounces, when he's finished chewing in the silent room. "Yes," he continues, "the Games have always been a tribute to the shades of those gone before us. A way to honour and remember them. I find the Games most exhilarating, the ceremony and rituals, the rules of combat. I am very particular that referees for the Games should be well-trained and uncorruptible. Rules must be adhered to. Otherwise you have nothing but chaos. People need to understand the rules and what happens if you break them." He gives a bark of laughter which makes several men jump. "Death, of course, if you're a gladiator!" He adjusts his position on the hard wooden bier. "Excellent food," he says. "More eel here."

A slave hurries to fill his plate. Domitian nods benevolently and proceeds to eat more of the eel, occasionally switching to the mussels, dropping the empty shells onto a plate next to him, the clatter of each shell keeping everyone's nerves at breaking point. At last he lifts a finger. "I will need to clean my hands after those excellent mussels."

Black finger bowls and napkins are distributed. Watching, I realise that this dinner is also a conspicuous show of wealth. True deep black is a hard colour to achieve through dyes, Domitian's event is not just frightening in its chosen theme, it is also a demonstration of the riches he can call on to implement whatever undertaking he wishes, the vast power at his fingertips.

"I have made a study of the Games over the years, they are a special interest of mine," says Domitian. "The number of gladiators who actually die during the Games these days is much lower than people think. Of course the promoters like to boast that there will be 'fights to the death' and suchlike, but really there are not that many. Most of the deaths in the arena, as you all know, are criminals, those who have committed misdeeds such as murder or treason."

Two of the senators put down their forks. Everyone seems to be having trouble chewing and swallowing.

"Their deaths provide a warning to others, as well as spectacle," continues Domitian. "I can see their purpose. And I do enjoy the spectacle. Some of them are very elaborate. Very well planned. Complex plots and staging, magnificent costumes and props. Wonderfully engaging to observe."

One of the knights has given up. He drains the dregs of his cup and waves for more wine, so drunk he is barely able to focus.

"Our evening here was arranged by none other than the organiser of the Games at the Flavian Amphitheatre," says Domitian. "I thought he would put on a memorable evening. And of course he already works for me, so there was very little added expense for his time and effort. I like to be mindful of the imperial purse." He beams at the guests and one or two try to smile back, lips stretched across teeth in unnatural grimaces.

"A treat, something suitable for the autumnal season," says Domitian.

The slaves bring out tiny dishes, one for each guest, each with whole, perfect mushrooms, cooked but intact, so that their shapes can clearly be seen. There are yellow ones which grow in a cluster with long stalks which are safe to eat, but also some pure white ones, which could either be deadly, as there are two types of fungi which look identical.

"Delicious," says Domitian. "A favourite at imperial tables, I believe. Eat, eat," he adds encouragingly, holding a white mushroom by the stem and popping it into his mouth in one go.

Claudius. It can be the only thought in the room at this moment. Emperor Claudius died from eating poisonous mushrooms barely thirty years ago.

"*Eat,*" says Domitian.

There is no choice. No possible way out of this. The men pick up the yellow mushrooms first, except for the drunk knight who has chosen to hurry his fate along and has already finished all the white mushrooms on his plate, dropping the yellow ones on the floor in his haste. He is lying back and staring at the ceiling, waiting for the cramps in his belly to start.

Slowly, slowly the mushrooms are chewed and swallowed under Domitian's beaming smile, each man wondering who has been given the deadly fungi. Will it be them? Another man? All of them?

"Delightful," says Domitian when everyone has finished. "Dessert," he adds, waving one hand. The slaves clear the tables, taking away the tiny empty mushroom dishes, the sharp-toothed mouths and skeletal bodies of the eels. "I do enjoy something sweet to finish a meal, even though I try to stay trim, for my health. My digestion is not always good. My poor departed brother Titus, now he was *too* fond of dessert." He laughs and the sound echoes horribly around the black room. "Too fond of the good life and it did not do him any good, in the end."

The guests cannot laugh along with him. They can only think of Titus' plump cheeks, his portly belly and the rumours – were they only rumours? – that his sudden death had something to do with his brother. All that talk of a fever and dying, just like that, with no warning? At the time the rumours faded as quickly as they rose but now, trapped in this room with Domitian and no way out but at his command, they arise again in the minds of all who are here tonight. The room stays quiet, no-one can manage even a small laugh.

"I like the rituals gladiators live by," continues Domitian. "When they are condemned to die, they are given whatever good food they ask for and often, so I hear, even a woman." He thinks about this for a moment. "I am afraid there are no women here tonight for such services." He tuts. "I do not condone such dissolute behaviour, so you will have to do without those delights of life. But food, that I *can* provide and here it is, dessert!"

Of course dessert is black, of course it is. The diners are resigned to their fate, the food is no longer a surprise. Heaps of black-skinned figs, blackberries and black grapes are served in beautifully arranged, intricate patterns on flat black platters, along with a black custard served in black cups with onyx-carved spoons to eat it with. The figs have been split open to reveal their twisting scarlet insides, a shocking burst of colour in this setting but the colour brings no relief. They look like blood, like entrails, which all of them are expecting to see at any moment.

Perhaps the colour is a signal to an unseen hand that holds a knife? Perhaps it will come now?

Or now?

Or now?

It is the waiting that is taking its toll. Some of the men must wish it were all over, they have given up all hope of getting out of here alive and can only hope their end will not be too painful. Poisoning would be worse than a quick knife, perhaps. Most of the men's faces show nothing except a stoic acceptance of the inevitable. They are certain of death. They await the stabbing pain of poison in their guts or the sharp slice of a blade, can only hope there is nothing worse planned after Domitian's endless talk of the Games. Several are sweating copiously, mopping at their faces as discreetly as they dare. Two or three down cup after cup of wine, perhaps hoping to slide painlessly into oblivion when their time comes. One, the furthest away from Domitian, has tears sliding down his face, which he does not dare to wipe away, for fear of drawing attention to himself. There's the sharp tang of urine in the air and I'm fairly sure one of the senators has wet themselves, his fine clothing soaked in fear. After a few moments I can hear the drip-drip-drip of the urine onto the floor, the elegant evening robe unable to absorb it.

"No women," repeats Domitian. "But some entertainment, that we should certainly have."

A group of musicians, dressed all in black, skins blackened, come into the room. They take up a stance and proceed to play the music that would accompany a funeral procession through the streets.

"Wonderful," says Domitian. "Such talent. And now for something in keeping with our earlier conversation."

Two black-painted gladiators enter the room and begin to circle one another, waiting for the opportunity to strike. They wear black leather and black-painted armour, reminding me of our Minotaur last season, a mythical horror made real. Usually, the guests would be cheering and jeering, throwing coins or calling out suggestions, laying bets with each other. The silence is eerie, the only sound the dripping of urine and the shuffle of the gladiators' feet as they circle round each other, then the sudden lunge of one and the hiss-whisper of the blade. The guests' eyes are fixed on the weapons the gladiators are holding. The moment of death has come. The room contains what the men have been expecting for all of this long terrible evening; two men trained to kill, bearing weapons. They may be putting on a spectacle but it would only take a few moments for them to kill everyone in this room, a quick whirling change of direction and focus, the blades falling on scrambling terrified bodies, necks exposed as the guests try to rise from the awkwardly-placed wooden biers, the emperor watching as his plan comes to fruition, the black room filling with blood splattered everywhere, the silence of the night rent with the screams of the dying.

The gladiators finish in a dramatic flourish, one man standing over the other with his sword at the other man's throat, who holds his hands up in submission. Domitian claps loudly, the guests closest to him jerking back in startled fear, one letting out a yelp of terror.

"Very good, very good," says Domitian. He tosses a laurel wreath towards the victor. "A fight well fought, we will not be shedding any innocent blood today, though. You may rise," he says to the defeated gladiator, who rises and then bows his head, before both men leave the room. "A wonderful display. So engaging, when one is so very close to the action, do you not think?" he adds to his nearest companion, a senator. "When there are deaths in the arena, you can actually smell the blood in the air, hear the dying breath of a man. The Games are an emotional experience."

"Yes, Imperator," manages the man in a half-whisper.

"Time for a nightcap," says Domitian.

It's the words I've been waiting for all evening, praying for. I don't even think, just step forward, nodding my head to Marcus as though this was all pre-arranged. I walk briskly from the room and into the service room. The relief I feel when the door behind me closes and I turn to find Marcus has followed me is so great I almost collapse. I rip off the cloak and grab my shoes.

"We're leaving. Now."

He doesn't argue. He drops his cloak on the floor and his mask on the table. I push against the small door, afraid it will creak, that at any moment we will hear a summons from Domitian in the room behind us. We slip out into the passageway and Marcus gently presses the door closed before we all but run back to the front of the palace. We slow as we reach the open space outside the palace, emerging at an overly-casual pace, as though it is perfectly normal to emerge from a side passage of the imperial palace, faces painted black, in the dead of night.

Marcus looks down the street, away from the waiting black-draped litters and the hooded figures, thankfully turned away from us, towards a growing flicker of light. "Here he is."

I can see Strabo's worried face illuminated by the torch he's carrying.

"Marcus," he says with relief. "I thought – never mind. The gods have kept you safe."

"Let's go," says Marcus, touching Strabo's shoulder. We move into deeper shadows, hidden behind a column where our torch's light will be diminished.

I look back over my shoulder at the litters and the hooded figures standing by them.

"Will they get home safely?"

"I don't know."

"Did you arrange… something?"

"No." He breathes out. "That doesn't mean something hasn't been arranged though. Someone else might have been in charge of that part."

"As they go home?"

He shrugs. "Each of them in a litter, travelling across Rome in the dead of night with four unknown male slaves carrying them and a torch-bearer? With none of their own household servants or slaves to accompany them? No bodyguards? Anything could have been arranged."

"Shouldn't we tell –" starts Strabo.

"Who would you like to tell? Someone who ranks higher than Domitian? Who would step in to change something he has arranged, against his will?" He takes a tighter grip on my hand.

"We need to leave Rome," I tell them both.

"Now?"

"Now."

"But –"

I lower my voice. "If Domitian has arranged for all these men to die, do you think he will leave a witness? Do you think he wants the man who arranged this event to tell people what happened?"

"I didn't arrange for them to be killed!"

"You arranged for them to be here."

Rome's streets are truly dark at night. Strabo's torch is barely enough to see by and I stumble more than once on uneven paving. I keep a tight grip on Marcus' hand and it does not comfort me to see that both men have one hand on their belts, where knives are concealed in a fold of their tunics. Their fear echoes in me and more than once I glance over my shoulder for shadows turning into silhouettes.

"What did you plan for the end?" I ask at last, my voice low. I'm not sure I want to hear the answer.

"After the nightcap they're supposed to be taken home by the servants waiting outside."

This in itself may not sound like a frightening prospect after the evening they've just been through, but to a man of distinction, travelling Rome's dark streets at night with servants who are not his own, people who have no loyalty to him, is tantamount to expecting to be killed at any moment by enemies, thieves or any other horrors the night may hold. Their relief in being allowed to leave and their horror when they see they must leave in litters carried by Domitian's own people, not their own.

"And?"

Marcus shakes his head. "When they get home they will receive a visitor 'from the Augustus.' Gifts from Domitian."

My skin goes cold. "A visitor?" A summons, a knock at the door of their home just when they thought they were safe, the calling out to know who is there and to be told that the Augustus, the Emperor, has sent them a gift. They cannot refuse to open the door, they cannot turn away someone under Domitian's protection. Perhaps they will ask if the visitor can return in the morning, in the comforting light of day, and be told no, it must be now and they will open the door and...

"And?"

"It will be the boys who served them. Each one washed and dressed finely, a new slave for their household. Bearing gifts: the silverware they ate from."

"Silver? Everything was black."

"Painted black. The tombstones, the cups, the platters they were served from: all of it was silver painted black. The onyx forks and spoons will stay black, but they will receive those as well."

"And?"

"I don't know," Marcus confesses. "That is what I was told to arrange. Nothing more."

"No harm will come to them?"

"Not that I arranged."

That does not mean anything of course, Marcus was to arrange a spectacle, someone else could have been told to arrange other things.

"You think it was only for show? To frighten them?"

"Perhaps. A joke."

"A *joke*?"

"He's odd. He might have thought it funny to frighten them, a warning without harming them."

"Those men in there are terrified."

"But not dead. So far."

I hardly think a night of terror has done the men no harm, but I can only hope Marcus is right: that the night has indeed been Domitian's strange idea of a joke, a warning without physical harm done to the men who have spoken about him behind his back, whom he may suspect of plotting to undermine or overthrow him. If so, there could be no warning so frightening as this, a night of staring into the eyes of death, of lying on a funeral bier and eating the food of the dead, knowing that at any moment your host need only say the word to end your life.

I am not reassured. Just as Marcus has thought ahead and had Strabo come to protect him on his dangerous journey back to the insula, has Domitian not planned ahead to what Marcus may do? I think again of the Emperor's face, the narrow shape of it, the way his eyes flicker away from direct gaze and yet his utter focus on something of interest to him. His patience with our animals when he wants to approach them and his furious rages when something displeases him. He is not stupid, I'm sure of that. His mind seems full of ideas and visions for Rome that only he can see clearly. It frightens me that Marcus may have misjudged the timing of our escape, that Domitian may have a man or maybe even several in the shadows even now, following us and waiting for their moment, a quick sharp knife to the ribs. Or perhaps ahead of us, not behind us, waiting on a street corner close to Virgin's Street, knowing we must pass that way to get to the safety of the insula. Or has he gone one step further and sent his men to wait inside the insula, perhaps to harm those we have left there? My stomach turns and I walk faster, pulling on Marcus' hand, Strabo lengthening his stride to match our increased pace.

"What is it?" Marcus asks in a low voice.

"Nothing," I say. "Walk faster."

Dawn Flight

T HE GATE OF THE INSULA is closed. We stop and stare at each other. What can this mean? Julia always kept it ajar, even at night, so that anyone wandering the streets in need of safety could slip in and sleep safely in a corner of our courtyard. Marcus pushes it open and we jump back at the sight before us.

Lamps and people are everywhere, but everyone is working fast and silently, gathered around the two carts, one harnessed to our two horses, the other to the two mules. There is no chatter, only the odd whisper. When the gate squeaks everyone turns and there is a collective sigh of relief when they see us.

"You're safe," says Karbo, submitting to a tight embrace from Marcus.

"You did a wonderful job."

"Is there still danger?"

I can't lie to him but I don't want him to be afraid. "I hope not. But we think it's best to be gone by dawn."

"I harnessed the horses and mules."

"Thank you," I say. I'm trying to keep my voice steady, trying not to cry because I do not want to upset and frighten him. "You're so good with them."

Quintus approaches us. "How did it go?"

"We didn't stay to find out," says Marcus. "It seemed safer to leave."

"The dinner or Rome?"

"Rome," says Marcus. "Bar the gate," he adds. "I don't want anyone coming after us without warning." The muscles of his jaw are tight, there is still fear in his eyes.

We've never locked the gate before. At first we can't find the bar that would fit into the brackets, we find it in a corner, forgotten except as a children's toy. We push the gate shut, then drop the bar into the brackets, push it down as far as it will go.

I start checking the carts with Marcus. A lot has already been packed. Everything I had already bought for us, but also amphorae of wine and oil, sacks of grain, jars of preserves.

"This is most of your food stores," says Marcus to Cassia.

"You don't have time to shop right now," she says.

He nods and reaches for his money bag.

Cassia shakes her head. "A gift from Julia," she says firmly and Marcus gives her a quick hug, goes to help Strabo lift up the heavier tools waiting to be packed.

"Do you have to leave now?" asks Cassia.

I'm shivering even though the night air is warm enough. "Marcus is scared and he's not often scared. We were going to leave in a week or so anyway."

Cassia wraps her arms around herself as though she's cold too, then gives herself a shake and nods. "Right," she says. "You'll need food."

"We have enough," I say, but she's already heading to the popina's entrance, determined to do things her way.

I climb the stairs to the roof hut. I thought there wasn't a lot to do, I've always kept it tidy and we don't have many possessions. I've done most of our packing, Marcus will only need to carry our bed, wooden chest and blankets. But I have to pack our cloaks and my sandals, wrap the Lararium in a blanket to keep it safe on the journey. I pause when I lift it from the shelf, take out the little doll with the curly black hair that represents Fausta, set her aside.

Karbo has followed me up; he is hovering in the doorway. "Why did you take Fausta out?" he asks.

I pick her up, hold her out to him with both hands, a sacred object. "I want you to have her. She was like a mother to you."

"You're my mother,' he says and the way his voice trembles stings tears into my eyes.

"I am," I say, pulling him to me. "I always will be. But she was fierce, I want her watching over you on the racetrack when I'm on the farm."

He clings to me, face buried in my shoulder. "I'll stay alive," he says at last.

"That's all I ask," I say. "That and that you be happy."

We smile shakily at each other. He darts away to his own roof hut with the little doll, comes back to help me drag the heavy wooden chest to the top of the stairs to await Marcus and Quintus. We carry the bed rolls first, then return for the lamps and Lararium. The whole insula is awake, people everywhere dashing back and forth with items we may need, piling them up in the carts.

Everyone is trying to feed us. The baker's family load baskets of still scalding bread and pastries into the cart as though feeding a whole army. Quintus is wrapping a large pot of stew in a blanket to keep it warm and wedging it into the back of the cart so it will not spill. He goes back to the popina and returns with wine, water, a basket of late figs and grapes, a bowl of nuts and a platter of Cassia's famous saltfish fritters. Maria is putting little pots of her plum conserve and dried spiced figs into every available gap between our belongings, ignoring Marcus' efforts to load weightier items. Celer lifts in another amphora of wine. Karbo is following Marcus everywhere as he packs the cart, like the early days when he joined us and hero-worshipped him. I want to ask him again to come with us but asking now is unfair, he might say yes in the emotion of the moment and I know it is not what he really wants. But I still have to stop myself, have to swallow the words.

"You must eat something," says Cassia.

"I can't," I say. "My stomach's rolling badly enough as it is, I'll throw up."

"We'll keep Karbo safe," she reassures me, seeing me glance at him.

"What if Domitian –?"

"He'll be safe," she repeats. "I promise."

Emilia sets up a wail, clinging to Quintus' leg and holding out her other hand to Cassia and me.

"What will I do without you?" I say.

"You'll have to learn to cook, for starters," she says. I make a face at her and she laughs, although it sounds like a sob.

"Marcus is going to starve."

"Maybe *he'll* have to learn to cook."

"Will you visit us one day?"

She nods, black curls bouncing like the first time I saw her, smile stretched wide. "We will. About time I had a rest from the popina."

We stand silent for a moment, staring at each other, our eyes filling. "Be happy," I say at last.

She nods, the tears spilling down her face. "You too."

We embrace, crushing Emilia between us, who wriggles and grabs a fistful of my hair and cries when we separate again. I kiss the child's round cheeks and stroke her ruffled hair and she buries her face in Cassia's shoulder, looking at me with reproachful eyes.

"She knows something's up," I say.

"She'll miss you," says Cassia.

I nod. "I'll miss all of you. The insula. Rome. Even the amphitheatre. I can't imagine life on a farm."

"Your hands will get dirty," says Cassia.

"Oh no, really? I hadn't thought of that. I may have to stay here after all."

Fabius is putting a selection of medical supplies in the cart and reminding Marcus about the dangers of ploughs, scythes and stubborn oxen.

Fabia hugs me. "Get in the cart. You're just putting it off."

"I have one thing left to do."

I STAND ON THE ROOFTOP and open the cages of the nightingales and doves. They are sleepy, befuddled. The dawn has not yet fully broken, the dim light makes the doves afraid of too much movement. I reach in and take each one in my hands, lift them out of the cages, place them here and there on the outer wall of the rooftop or on top of the cages. One or two peck at me, thinking me a predator come to grab them in their sleep. They refuse to fly, huddling together, feathers ruffled and uncertain, taking small steps to one side or the other, shuffling to and fro, peering at me. They feel the breeze on their wings, enticing them to fly, but they are still unsure. The nightingales have never known freedom, are unsure of what it might hold or what to do with it.

I watch them, waiting for the moment when they realise they are free, for them to take flight in a glorious moment of release as they search out their new lives, but they do no such thing, only make small uncertain sounds and peer doubtfully over the ledge to the city below.

"I was expecting a more impressive spectacle," I say, half-laughing. My voice sounds too loud in the cold air and the empty space around me. "I'm not sure you're a very good omen for my new life if you won't fly at all."

They stare at me, turning one eye and then the other, as though I am the spectacle.

"I'll leave you to it," I say, disappointed. I had hoped for them to take flight at once, to revel in their freedom, to fully experience the munificence of my actions, but it seems as though they cannot be persuaded. "Goodbye," I call as I hurry back down the stairs. I pause on the second floor, where Julia's apartment used to be, now the home of a new family who have just moved in. The father injured his leg and cannot work, the mother came to Cassia and asked if there was a cheap room they could rent. Julia would have been glad that her rooms were already being used by those in need.

A tug on my sleeve. I turn to find Adah standing by my side. Her wizened face is tilted up to me, her dark brown eyes wary. I wait for her to speak but she hesitates and when I glance further down I see that she is clutching two objects in her left hand; a small bag, bulging as though it has been crammed too full, and her silver candelabra, the one with many arms, her most precious possession.

"Are you – are you coming with us after all, Adah?" I ask.

She gives a shrug. "I will not be a burden to you," she mutters, failing to meet my eyes. "I can work. I can care for the bees. A farm should have bees," she adds as though I have argued against her on this point.

I crush her tiny, hunched body against me in a fierce hug. "I am glad," I say. "So glad, Adah."

She pulls away, shrugs again as though I am making a fuss over nothing. "I will come because you asked it, child," she says. "Only because you asked." But there's a smile on her face, a tentative happiness that fills up my heart.

I grin back at her, a huge, happy grin. "Marcus," I call over the side of the stairs. "Adah is coming with us."

He looks up over his shoulder from where he is packing the cart that Strabo will drive. "I have a warm blanket here for you to wrap yourself in, Adah," he calls back, as though her presence had never been in doubt. "And a sleeping mat for you to rest on. Come here so I can make you comfortable."

She shuffles down the stairs to him and I follow behind. He picks her up as though she were a child and settles her in the cart, the promised blanket wrapped about her as though it were a palla, her meagre possessions lying safely at her side.

"We need to go," he says. Celer and Quintus unbar the gate, look cautiously out, nod. The street is empty, our path is clear.

There is a flurry of hugs and promises, a moment when Marcus, Karbo and I hold tightly together and suddenly I am sitting at Marcus' side at the front of the cart, my palla in disarray about me, the wheels already rumbling out of the courtyard while the crowd follow us to the gateway and stand in a cluster, arms lifted, softly calling blessings. Jupiter for great ventures and Janus for new beginnings, Bona Dea for mothers and children, Juno for wives and hearths, Ceres and Saturn for farming and crops and our own names mixed in amongst them, spoken by those who love us.

I look back, past Strabo's cart following us along the broad length of Sand Street, to the dim flickering lanterns hanging outside Cassia's popina, and the insula above it, the shadowy group of people I can only just make out at the entrance to Virgin's Street, their arms still lifted to wave us farewell. I shape my mouth into an ugly hard grimace as tears fall down my cheeks, the welling up of grief at leaving so many people behind that I love and who love me, fear gripping my stomach at the unknown future ahead.

Marcus sees my tears falling, he takes my cold hand in his warm one and squeezes it, puts one arm about me and pulls me close.

"They will still be there when you need them," he says gently. "And they will all take care of each other, while we build a new life."

I nod and swallow back some of my tears.

"One last look," says Marcus.

I look back. A faint light is rising on the eastern horizon, illuminating the insula. From its rooftop, in the pale dawn sky, a flock of birds take flight across Rome.

I HOPE YOU HAVE ENJOYED the final book in the Colosseum series. If you have, I would really appreciate it if you would leave a rating or brief review, so that new readers can find *The Flight of Birds*. I read all reviews and am always grateful for your time in writing them and touched by your kind words.

As EVER, I AM SAD when I write the last book in a series and have to say goodbye to the characters I have grown to care about, but I hope you will come with me as I journey on to another place and another time, in search of more stories to share with you.

Author's Note on History

This is the fourth and final book in a series that started as a simple question I asked myself: who were the people who made up the backstage team for the Colosseum? There is hardly any mention whatsoever of them and yet Games on such an immense scale could not possibly have been put on without a very large and permanent team in place. The Flight of Birds takes air as its theme, including the fitting of the velarium and the new top tier of seating in the amphitheatre, the Cranes vs Dwarfs battle mythology and the Roman use of birds as omens, which I then used to play with illusions and prophecies, not to mention the final flight of our lead characters from Rome. The other three books in this series focus on the same team through the themes of fire (*From the Ashes*), water (*Beneath the Waves*) and earth *(On Bloodied Ground)*.

One of the ideas I have continued with in this book is that Emperor Domitian might have been on the autistic spectrum. This was first suggested to me by my historical consultant Steven Cockings, who is himself autistic, and is based on the preliminary work of Jen Cresswell, *Domitian and Asperger's Syndrome – a retrospective diagnosis*, which draws attention to Domitian exhibiting certain characteristics linked to autism, including a preference for solitude, some difficulty engaging with people, obsessions (including a huge building programme and the gladiatorial Games/chariot racing), and a love of routine. As my son is autistic, and I found the historical evidence interesting and compelling, I have built in this concept and used examples of behaviour from people I know who are on the spectrum. Domitian seems to have been judged overly harshly by historians in comparison to other emperors and I thought perhaps he lacked some of the social skills required to endear himself to people generally or to explain and promote his actions and choices. I also thought that the more positive aspects of his reign (such as the vast public building programme he undertook and his cleaning up of the administrative system, wiping out excessive taxes, bribery and corruption) might have made people nervous because of Nero's similar building interests. Nero's madness would still have been very much in living memory and I thought that any odd behaviour, coupled to a similar building programme, would have made people around Domitian wary of history repeating itself and therefore quick to judge him. Whereas in *On Bloodied Ground* Domitian stays calm in his behaviour, if a little odd, in this book I allowed him to have a real meltdown moment in response to the idea that there would be key staff changes at the amphitheatre which might derail his building plans and other ideas for events, as change (especially in relation to their areas of special interest) can be very unsettling and upsetting for autistic people.

Domitian had an architect named Rabirius, who undertook most of the emperor's many building works. Very little is known about him, although he is mentioned with praise by the poet Martial. It is likely that he would also have designed Domitian's villa and its surrounding buildings like the amphitheatre.

The velarium was an extraordinary feat of engineering when you see the size of the Colosseum and imagine trying to fit an awning to it. It follows exactly the same principles as the 'Roman blinds' we have today on windows but laid horizontally. There are lots of interesting videos on YouTube with CGI reconstructions if you'd like to see it in action.

I have brought forward the event at Domitian's villa where Domitian had Manius Acilius Glabrio, a consul, thrown to a lion, which he somehow managed to kill before being exiled (and killed while in exile). This happened in 95AD and there is not much clarity about why he was executed. A few high-ranking people were executed around the same time on charges of conspiring against the empire, but we have no further details. I have borrowed the event to have Manius be Funis' father.

The naumachia happened as described: you can see its location at Augustus' Lake on the map at the start of this book. The Roman historian Suetonius says in *The Twelve Caesars*, *"Domitian had a volatile temper and could be quite arbitrary. In AD84 Domitian held a naumachia on the reservoir built by Augustus for his naval games. As the battle raged a sudden storm swept down on Rome. Two of the ships capsized, drowning their crews, while bitterly cold winds and heavy rain lashed the audience. Finally the storm passed, but the audience were drenched to the skin. It was said that for some weeks afterward all Rome was ill, and many people died from the fevers they had caught. Suddenly remorseful, Domitian laid on a free banquet."* This erratic behaviour would have made those around him worry about his state of mind.

I assumed I would need to invent some kind of spectacle for the Colosseum involving birds for my 'air' themed book with birds in the title, but then found a description of the Cranes vs Dwarfs battle put on in the amphitheatre, complete with birds being set loose and even a spectacular light show in the sky. Once again, the history of the Colosseum is more extraordinary than anything a fiction writer could come up with!

The terrifying black dinner really did happen, although probably later than 82AD. Suetonius describes it and it sounded to me like the sort of event Marcus might have been asked to stage manage, given his arranging of private lavish parties back in the very first book of the series. *"On another occasion (Domitian) entertained the foremost men among the senators and knights in the following fashion. He prepared a room that was pitch black on every side, ceiling, walls and floor, and had made ready bare couches of the same colour resting on the uncovered floor; then he invited in his guests alone at night without their attendants. And first he set beside each of them a slab shaped like a gravestone, bearing the guest's name and also a small lamp, such as hang in tombs. Next comely naked boys, likewise painted black, entered like phantoms, and after encircling the guests in an awe-inspiring dance took up their stations at their feet. After this all the things that are commonly offered at the sacrifices to departed spirits were likewise set before the guests, all of them black and in dishes of a similar colour. Consequently, every single one of the guests feared and trembled and was kept in constant expectation of having his throat cut the next moment, the more so as on the part of everybody but Domitian there was dead silence, as if they were already in the realms of the dead, and the emperor himself conversed only upon topics relating to death and slaughter. Finally he dismissed them; but he had first removed their slaves, who had stood in the vestibule, and now gave his guests in charge of other slaves, whom they did not know, to be conveyed either in carriages or litters, and by this procedure he filled them with far greater fear. And scarcely had each guest reached his home and was beginning to get his breath again, as one might say, when word was brought him that a messenger from the Augustus (Domitian) had come. While they were accordingly expecting to perish this time in any case, one person brought in the slab, which was of silver, and then others in turn brought in various articles, including the dishes that had been set before them at the dinner, which were constructed of very costly material; and last of all came that particular boy who had been each guest's familiar spirit, now washed and adorned. Thus, after having passed the entire night in terror, they received the gifts."*

As the guests all got home safely and were given lavish gifts, the event seems to have been a warning or perhaps even a practical joke on the part of Domitian, but it would have been truly terrifying for the men involved, who would have expected to die at any moment.

When I was about four years old, my mother moved house, taking us from a block of flats on Sand Street (Via Arenula – arena means sand because of the sand thrown on the arena floor) in Rome to a farm in the Italian countryside with a grape vine that grew strawberry grapes.

WORLD-WEAVING WITH INVISIBLE STRANDS

As an author of historical fiction, I have always been pleased that many of my best reviews mention my ability to world-build. Writing in this genre, after all, requires a whole world to be rebuilt from nothing but bits of paper and crumbling ruins, from an odd mixture of official records which often forget or deliberately omit whole groups of people and events, to hearsay and quasi-legends passed down orally which you sense hold certain truths but often get questioned if you use them. For my PhD in Creative Writing, I wrote about looking beyond the inevitable 'is it true?' question. I suggested that as well as that question, another question to ask of authors would be: 'What fictional elements did you add to your historical setting and why was it important to your vision of the past?' And one obvious answer, of course, is that when you set out to build your world, you are very likely to find parts missing, strange holes in the tapestry you are weaving which you must fill in, one way or another.

This happened to me when I decided I would like to write a series set in Ancient Rome, following the backstage team of the Colosseum. I spent the first three years of my life in Rome, my mother worked in an office just over the road from the Colosseum, perhaps it had been bubbling away in my brain, waiting for a chance to be included in my writing. I began in my usual fashion, gathering up the first strands with which to string my loom: children's reference books for the basics of daily life in that era, several large tomes entirely dedicated to the Colosseum and its spectacles. These, I reasoned, would give me a good overview of the shape and size of my eventual world, which I could then follow up on with more detailed research.

And then I found the hole. In an extremely well documented time and place in history, right in the centre of one of the most famous buildings left to us from ancient times and featured in countless books and films was... a huge, gaping hole. Because there is no mention of a backstage team. We do not even know the name of the architect who designed the Colosseum, let alone the people who must have run it on a day-to-day basis. Oddly, no academics or authors of substantial works on the Colosseum seem to even mention the existence of this gap in our knowledge, to such an extent that I spent a lot of extra time doubting my research abilities, certain that somewhere, known to all but myself, was a neat list of the team and their roles. But no such list exists. And yet: I could *feel* the invisible strands out there, waiting to be woven. There were 100 to 200 days of Games put on per year, each of which took up most of a day: beast-hunting in the morning, criminal executions at lunchtime, gladiatorial bouts in the afternoon, with a few lighter elements added here and there such as comedic pieces or dancing girls. The Emirates Stadium (a similar sized 50,000-seater arena) today employs 3,000 people. The invisible backstage team *must* have existed. But I would have to create them.

In the end, creating the invisible team required three main strands:

What did they make?

THE HISTORICAL RECORD DOES NOT mention the backstage team. But it does describe what they created. We have mentions of animals, both wild and tamed, which means there were people placing orders for them, catching them, transporting and storing them, as well as taking many months of hard work to train those that were made to perform in specific ways, such as horses who would willingly run through water when the Colosseum was flooded for naval battles and an elephant who would bow of its own accord upon seeing the Emperor (bit of subtle signalling there, do we think?). The gladiators, of course, had to be trained, appropriately kitted out in both battle and theatrical parade armour and patched up by physicians. There were synchronised swimmers, whom the poet Martial admired, asking whether a sea-nymph had taught them, or whether the performing swimmers had been the ones to teach sea-nymphs their moves. As for the criminal executions, many were turned into re-enactments of bloody myths, requiring costumes, scenery and rehearsals. The list of staff quickly grows long when you look at what they created. Even something as tiny as a mention of using coloured sand in the arena leads to the question, where do you get that from? Was there a known supplier of coloured sand in first-century Rome, with a colour chart to pick from and a regular agreed delivery day? Would the manager frown when taking delivery and say that this wasn't the shade they'd agreed on? And why do you need different colours of sand? Are you making patterns? Illusions of water or grass? Vast sand 'paintings' across the arena floor? Even modern-day recreations of, for example, the lifts that brought beasts and fighters up into the arena, only briefly mention that each one requires four to six people to operate, which means easily 150 people just for the lifts during a show, and that's leaving aside the question of, who is giving the signal to release a beast or gladiator from a specific lift to a given schedule? World-building in such circumstances relies on endless questions of this kind, each question making one thread at a time become visible. My novel began to take on a shape: the endless day-to-day logistical challenges of running such a vast amphitheatre, mixed with the vast and terrifying events of 79-80AD, from Vesuvius erupting to a 'pestilence' that killed ten thousand people in Rome, a three-day fire and the knowledge that *not* delivering a spectacular inaugural Games would result in certain death in the very arena the team worked in.

What kind of people were the backstage team, given the era in which they worked?

GLADIATORS, ACTORS, DANCING GIRLS, CRIMINALS, beast-hunters, women who fought... all of these performers at the Colosseum formed part of an underclass that was both despised for not conforming to the norms of society, but that also held a certain allure. We know that actors were considered sexy and that gladiators had enthusiastic fans who followed their careers with interest, much as boxing fans might have their favourites today, often gambling on the outcomes of a bout. If these were the performers, the backstage team would have associated with them and been associated with them, their own status determined by the work they did. There would have been slaves to work the lifts and keep the Colosseum clean, there were up to 200 sailors who rigged the awnings that kept the sun off the audience's heads. There would have been a man whose job it was to play Charon, to kill with one blow of a hammer any gladiator or criminal who would not make it but had not yet died. I spent time talking with modern-day boxing promoter Steve Goodwin, who talked about the ethics of the job, which resulted in the creation of two very different fictional gladiator trainers in the final novel: Paternus and Labeo. Throughout, I had to find a way to make my characters likeable, even though they were engaged in putting on Games that we would find brutal in the extreme. The more I explored the team, the more I saw them as a motley crew of misfits and outlaws: tough, sexy, rude and dangerous.

What is required of any backstage team, regardless of the era?

TWO QUALITIES. SHOWMANSHIP AND ORGANISATION. Like it or not, the Games were a magnificent spectacle, capable of drawing crowds of 50,000 and more, up to 200 days a year. When you read about what they could do, from flooding and draining the arena in half an hour each way to raining down perfumed water to cool the crowds, you can't help but be impressed. Meanwhile, from an organisational point of view, to manage what must have been thousands of staff and performers but without any modern technology, must have been quite a feat. My two main characters came to embody these two qualities: a manager with a gift for showmanship and his female scribe who keeps the team on track, day by day, through tragedy, loss and danger. And the slow-burn romance I have included, developing across four books, comes from the growing intertwining of these two characters and their qualities.

And so back to that question I dislike because of its too-narrow gaze. 'Is it true?' No, it isn't. There is absolutely no record of the team I have created, so it is purely a fiction, albeit set into what I have strived to ensure is an accurate historical setting. But why did I create that fiction and why was it important to my vision of the past? Because I looked into the past and saw a gaping hole at the very centre of one of the most famous historical buildings of all time, and I saw the invisible threads that I could weave together to create a world that must once have existed. The greatest compliment I received on the series was from my lovely historical consultant, Steven Cockings, an expert re-enactor of the era. He told me that the next time he visited Rome and the Colosseum after reading the books, he felt that my team, headed up by Marcus and Althea, must be somewhere nearby on site, making the Games happen for their vast audience and the Emperor.

GLOSSARY

Aedile	A senator in charge of commissioning the gladiatorial games.
Bestiarius	Gladiator specialising in fighting animals (plural bestiarii).
Bulla	Protective amulet worn by boys. Girls wore an equivalent pendant in the form of a crescent moon.
Cithara	Roman precursor to the guitar.
Cosmetes	Beautician (plural cosmetae).
Domina	Mistress.
Dominus	Master.
Fullery	A laundry which washed, dried and also dyed garments. Human urine (collected on street corners) was used as a cleaning and bleaching aid.
Garum	Fish sauce, a very popular condiment.
Gustatio	Hors d'ouvres (starters in a meal)
Imperial Palace	The place indicated on the map is an approximate location of Nero's Golden House (which Titus might have continued to use for official receptions) and also, later, the building started by Domitian at the beginning of his reign and completed in 92AD. There were additional locations, both official and residential, where the emperors would have been located in Rome.
Insula	Block of apartments/individual rooms, often built around a central courtyard.
Lararium	Household shrine.
Liberalia	Festival in which Roman boys became men.
Naumachia	Water-based spectacle often featuring re-enactments of sea-battles, held on lakes or in flooded man-made structures such as the Colosseum.

Nereids   Sea-nymphs (goddesses of the sea).

Ornatrix   Hairdresser.

Palantine   One of the hills of Rome, used by many as an expression to suggest the Emperor's residence.

Palla   A large rectangular outer garment of wool or linen, worn predominantly by married women, draped around the whole body, a fold of which could be placed over the head for protection and as a sign of propriety.

Popina   Streetside café (most poor Romans did not have cooking facilities, so street food outlets were very common and popular).

Tablet   A wooden 'book' of two or three 'pages', filled with wax, on which notes could be made using a metal pen called a stylus, then erased when no longer required. More formal, permanent writing could be done with ink and a reed/quill pen onto scrolls of papyrus.

Triclinium   Dining room.

Tullianum   One of the very few prisons in Rome, used for high status prisoners or those to be made an example of, as prison sentences were not used as punishment, only as brief holding places.

Velarium   Awning at a theatre or amphitheatre.

Venator   Performer who hunted animals for the morning hunt (technically not gladiators or bestiarii as it was hunting, not combat).

THANKS

Thank you to superb cover designer Jessica Bell and to Glendon at Streetlight Graphics who gives me so much more time to write! To editor Debi Alper for your chameleon-like ability to shape your excellent editing skills to my style, it is mightily impressive. Thank you to my beta readers for this series: Helen, Etain, Martin. I am always grateful for your insights.

Thank you to my children Seth and Isabelle, who studied the Romans alongside me. Between them they made a shield, toga, honey biscuits, ate 'dormice', played Gladiators & Beasts in the ruined Roman theatres of Ostia and Gubbio and won their laurel wreaths (and ice-cream, of course) at the Colosseum itself. You made great research assistants.

Many scholars and historians were very helpful during my research period. My thanks for all their fascinating work and especially to:

Steven Cockings for your extraordinary dedication to Roman times and enormous kindness in agreeing to read this manuscript and act as my historical consultant for the series. I am so grateful for your expertise and hospitality.

The Legio Secunda Augusta re-enactment group, including the great gladiators Alisa Vanlint (Alyssa in my books) and James Reah, as well as lucky pecker seller Simon (the real Secundus: the twins story is true!) for a warm welcome and sharing their huge enthusiasm for, and knowledge of, the era. You've no idea how wonderful it is for a writer to see living breathing Romans up close, not just in books or behind glass! Also to expert in Roman clothing, Ratna Drost, for explaining the changes in fashion over time which were causing me confusion.

Professor Kathleen Coleman of Harvard University for her fascinating research on gladiators and naval shows and great kindness in helping me access her articles.

Martina Santangelo was my guide when visiting the hypogeum (the area under the arena floor where the backstage team would have worked) of the Colosseum and also gave me lots of documents on the work that went on there. Professor Kyle Harper at the University of Oklahoma who suggested that the 'pestilence' of 80AD could have been malaria, amongst other options. Professor Donald G Kyle's considerable body of work on Roman spectacles and especially on the disposal of bodies (human and animal) from the arena, was invaluable. Professor Christopher Ellett very helpfully provided me with his work on beast-hunts and executions. Fik Meijer has written a wonderfully vivid book on chariot racing. Richard Bale at the Colchester Archaeological Trust for a very enjoyable series of talks on aspects of Roman life and his kindness in answering my specific questions in great detail. David Corfield at 422 South for the

CGI reconstruction clip of the lifts/slides used to bring scenery up into the Colosseum and to Professor Michael Scott, his assistant Claire and Will at ScanLab for helping me track it down so I could watch it in slow motion! *Birds in the Ancient World* by Jeremy Mynott was very useful to me in writing the final novel, with its theme of air and birds.

Boxing manager Steve Goodwin who very generously spent time talking to me about the boxing industry when I was thinking about gladiators.

My respect and thanks to Caroline Lawrence, who writes wonderful books for children set in the same time period and locations. I learnt a lot from her talks, research and ideas, loved the stories and am grateful for her kind help along the way.

All errors and fictional choices are of course mine.

Current and Forthcoming Books Include:

Historical Fiction

China

The Consorts (novella, free on Amazon)
The Fragrant Concubine
The Garden of Perfect Brightness
The Cold Palace

Morocco

The Cup (novella, free on my website)
A String of Silver Beads
None Such as She
Do Not Awaken Love

Rome

From the Ashes
Beneath the Waves
On Bloodied Ground
The Flight of Birds

Regency

Lady for a Season

Picture Books for Children

Kameko and the Monkey-King

Non-Fiction

The Storytelling Entrepreneur
Merchandise for Authors
The Happy Commuter
100 Things to Do while Breastfeeding

BIOGRAPHY

I WRITE HISTORICAL FICTION SERIES SET in different eras. So far, I've written about 1ˢᵗ century Rome following the backstage team of the Colosseum, 11ᵗʰ century Morocco as a Muslim empire arose across North Africa and Spain, and 18ᵗʰ century China in the Forbidden City. I'm now moving into the Regency era in England, so coming a little closer to home. I have a PhD in Creative Writing from the University of Surrey which looked at the 'play' between fact and fiction in historical fiction and I enjoy speaking at literary festivals. I campaign with the Alliance of Independent Authors for ethics and excellence in self-publishing. I live in London with my husband and two children.

For more information on me and my books, as well as a free
novella, visit my website www.MelissaAddey.com